4/03

CONQUEROR

CONQUEROR

S.M. STIRLING
DAVID DRAKE

CONQUEROR

This is a work of fiction. All the characters and events portrayed in this book are fictional, and any resemblance to real people or incidents is purely coincidental.

A Baen Books Original

Baen Publishing Enterprises
P.O. Box 1403
Riverdale, NY 10471
www.baen.com

ISBN: 0-7434-3594-X

Cover art by David Mattingly

First omnibus printing, March 2003

Library of Congress Cataloging-in-Publication Data

Stirling, S. M.
  Conqueror / by S.M. Stirling & David Drake.
    p. cm.
  "The General series was originally published as five separate novels: The Forge, The Hammer, The Anvil, The Steel, and The Sword. Conqueror is the second and concluding part of the Raj Whitehall saga, which began in the first compendium volume, Warlord."
  Contents: The anvil — The steel — The sword.
  ISBN 0-7434-3594-X
    1. Whitehall, Raj (Fictitious character)—Fiction. 2. Life on other planets—Fiction. 3. Science fiction, American. 4. Space warfare—Fiction. 5. War stories, American. 6. Generals—Fiction. I. Drake, David. II. Title.

PS3569.T543 C63 2003
813'.54—dc21

                                                                    2002038394

Distributed by Simon & Schuster
1230 Avenue of the Americas
New York, NY 10020

Production by Windhaven Press, Auburn, NH
Printed in the United States of America

10   9   8   7   6   5   4   3   2   1

Contents

The Anvil

-1-

The Steel

-209-

The Sword

-417-

III
THE ANVIL

CITY & HARBOR WAGER BAY

NORTH GATE

PARK

CATHEDRON

CIVIC PLAZA

FOUNTAIN GATE

SLUMS

COMMANDANT'S RESIDENCE

EXPEDITIONARY FORCE

COURTET SURRENDERS

CLEARED GLACIS

STADIUM

HARBOR

SULFUR WORKS

GATE

CITY WALL

WEST (SALA) GATE

STEAM RAMS ON STATION

CLIFF

PIER

PIER

CLIFF

FORTRESS

CLIFF WITH OVERHANG

REEFS

SHIPS BEACHED REEFS

REEFS

"SPIRIT OF MAN" SUNK

COURSE OF CHAKRA AND LOTTILA

LION CITY & BAY

CIVIL GOVERNMENT STEAM RAMS

SEAWALL

COLONIST QUARTERS

MOSQUE

BREAKWATERS

WAREHOUSES

TIMBER YARDS

SHIPBUILDING

GUILD HALLS

HARBOR

LIGHTHOUSE

DOCKS & FACTORIES

CENTRAL PLAZA

BARRACKS

CATHEDRON

MAYOR'S PALACE

MAIN GATE

SEAWALL

CIVIL GOVERNMENT CAMP

CHAPTER ONE

"Raj!" Thom Poplanich blurted.

Raj Whitehall's mouth quirked. "You sound more shocked this time," he said.

The way you look, I am *more shocked,* Thom thought, blinking and stretching a little. There was no physical need; his muscles didn't stiffen while Center held him in stasis. But the psychological satisfaction of movement was real enough, in its own way.

The silvered globe in which they stood didn't look different, and the reflection showed Thom himself unchanged—down to the shaving nick in his chin and the tear in his tweed trousers. A slight, olive-skinned young man in gentleman's hunting clothes, looking a little younger than his twenty-five years. He'd cut his chin before they set out to explore the vast tunnel-catacombs beneath the Governor's Palace in East Residence. The trousers had been torn by a ricocheting pistol-bullet, when the globe closed around them and Raj tried to shoot his way out. Everything was just as it had been when Raj and he first stumbled into the centrum of the being that called itself Sector Command and Control Unit AZ12-bl4-cOOO Mk. XIV.

That had been years ago, now.

Raj was the one who'd changed, living in the outer—the real—world. That had been obvious on the first visit, two years after their parting. It was much more noticeable this time. They were of an age, but someone meeting them together for the first time would have thought Raj a decade older.

"How long?" Thom said. He was half-afraid of the answer.

"Another year and a half."

Thom's surprise was visible. *He's aged that much in so little time?* he thought. His friend was a tall man, 190 centimeters, broad-shouldered and narrow-hipped, with a swordsman's thick wrists. There were a few silver hairs in the bowl-cut black curls now, and his gray eyes held no youth at all.

"Well, I've seen the titanosauroid, since," Raj went on.

"Governor Barholm did send you to the Southern Territories?"

Raj nodded; they'd discussed that on the first visit. After Raj's victories against the Colony in the east, he was the natural choice.

"A hard campaign, from the way you look."

"No," Raj said, moistening his lips. "A little nerve-racking sometimes, but I wouldn't call it *hard*, exactly."

observe, the computer said. The walls around them shivered. The perfect reflection dissolved in smoke, which scudded away—

—and returned as a ragged white pall spurting from the muzzles of volleying rifles. From behind a courtyard wall, Raj Whitehall and troopers wearing the red and orange neckscarves of the 5th Descott shot down an alleyway toward the docks of Port Murchison. Each pair of hands worked rhythmically on the lever, *ting,* and the spent brass shot backward, *click,* as they thumbed a new round into the breech and brought the lever back up, *crack* as they fired.

There were already windrows of bodies on the pavement: Squadron warriors killed before they knew they were at risk. Survivors crouched behind the corpses of their fellows and fired back desperately. Their clumsy flintlocks were slow to load, inaccurate even at this range; they had to expose themselves to reload, fumbling with powder horns and ramrods, falling back dead more often than not as the Descotter marksmen fired. A few threw the firearms aside with screams of frustrated rage, charging with their long single-edged swords whirling. By some freak one got as far as the wall, and a bayonet punched through his belly. The man fell backward off the steel, his mouth and eyes perfect O's of surprise.

A ball ricocheted from one of the pillars and grazed Raj's buttock before slapping into the small of the back of the officer beside him in the firing line. The stricken man dropped his revolver and pawed blindly at his wound, legs giving their final twitch. Raj shot carefully, standing in the regulation pistol-range position with one hand behind the back and letting the muzzle fall back before putting another round through the center of mass.

"*Marcy!*" the barbarians called in their Namerique dialect. *Mercy!* They threw down their weapons and began raising their hands. "*Marcy, migo!*" *Mercy, friend!*

Both men blinked as the vision faded—Raj to force memory away, Thom in surprise.

"You brought the Southern Territories back?" Thom said, slight awe in his voice. The *Squadrones*—the Squadron, under its Admiral—had ruled the Territories ever since they came roaring down out of the Base Area a century and a half ago and cut a swath across the Midworld Sea. The only previous Civil Government attempt to reconquer them had been a spectacular disaster.

Raj shrugged, then nodded: "I was in command of the Expeditionary Force, yes. But I couldn't have achieved anything without good troops— and the Spirit."

"Center isn't the Spirit of Man of the Stars, Raj. It's a Central Command and Control Unit from before the Collapse—the Fall, we call it now."

Neither of them needed another set of Center's holographic scenarios to remember what they had been shown. Earth—Bellevue, the computer always insisted—from the holy realm of Orbit, swinging like a blue-and-white shield against the stars. Points of thermonuclear fire expanding across cities . . . and the descent into savagery that followed. Which must have followed everywhere in the vast stellar realm the Federation once ruled, or men from the stars would have returned.

Raj shivered involuntarily. He had been terrified as a child, when the household priest told of the Fall. It was even more unnerving to see it played out before the mind's eye. Worse yet was the knowledge that Center had given him. The Fall was *still* happening. If Center's plan failed, it would go on until there was nothing left on Bellevue—anywhere in the human universe—but flint-knapping cannibal savages. Fifteen thousand years would pass before civilization rose again.

Thom went on: "Center's just a computer."

Raj nodded. Computers were holy, the agents of the Spirit, but Thom's stress on the word meant something different now. Different since he'd been locked in stasis down here, being shown everything Center knew. Nearly four years of continuous education.

"You know what you know, Thom," Raj said gently. "But I know what I know." He shook his head. "We slaughtered the whole Squadron," he went on. *Literally.* "Made them attack us, then shot the shit out of them."

"And how did Governor Barholm react?" Thom asked dryly. By rights, Thom Poplanich should have been Seated on the Chair; his grandfather had been. Barholm Clerett's uncle had been Commander of Residence Area Forces when the last Governor died, however, which had turned out to be much more important.

"Well, he was certainly pleased to get the Southern Territories back," Raj said, looking aside. That was hard to do inside the perfectly reflective sphere. "The expedition more than paid for itself, too—and that's not counting the tax revenues."

observe, Center said.

—and men in the black uniforms of the Gubernatorial Guard were marching Raj away, while the leveled rifles of more kept Suzette Whitehall and Raj's men stock-still—

—and Raj stood in a prisoner's breechclout and chains before a tribunal of three judges in ceremonial jumpsuits and bubble helmets—

—and he sat bound to an iron chair, as the glowing rods came closer and closer to his eyes—

✧   ✧   ✧

Raj sighed. "That *might* have happened, yes. According to Center, and I don't doubt it myself. I *was* a little . . . apprehensive . . . about something like that. I'm not any more; the Army grapevine has been pretty conclusive. In fact, when the Levee is held this afternoon, I'm confident of getting another major command."

"The Western Territories?"

"How did you guess?"

"Even Barholm isn't crazy enough to try conquering the Colony. Yet."

"Yes." Raj nodded and ran a hand through his hair. "The problem is, he's probably too suspicious to give me enough men to actually do it."

Thom blinked again. *Raj has changed,* he thought. The young man he had known had been ambitious—dreaming of beating back a major raid from the Colony, say, out on the eastern frontier. This weathered young-old commander was casually confident of overrunning the second most powerful realm on the Middle Sea, given adequate backing. The Brigade had held the Western Territories for nearly six hundred years. They were almost civilized . . . for barbarians. Odd to think that they were descendants of Federation troops stranded in the Base Area after the Fall.

"Barholm," Raj went on with clinical detachment—sounding almost like Center, for a moment—"thinks that either I'll fail—"

observe, Center said.

Dead men gaped around a smashed cannon. The Starburst banner of the Civil Government of Holy Federation draped over some of the bodies, mercifully. Raj crawled forward, the stump of his left arm tattered and red, still dribbling blood despite the improvised tourniquet. His right just touched the grip of his revolver as the Brigade warrior reined in his riding dog and stood in the stirrups to jam the lance downward into his back. Again, and again . . .

"—or I'll succeed, and he can deal with me then."

observe, Center said.

Raj Whitehall stood by the punchbowl at a reception; Thom Poplanich recognized the Upper Promenade of the palace by the tall windows and the checkerboard pavement of the terrace beyond. Brilliant gaslight shone on couples swirling below the chandeliers in the formal patters of court dance; on bright uniforms and decorations, on the ladies' gowns and jewelry. He could almost smell the scents of perfume and pomade and sweat. Off to one side the orchestra played, the soft rhythm of the steel drums cutting through the mellow brass of trumpets and the rattle of *marachaz.* Silence spread like a ripple through the crowd as the Gubernatorial Guard troopers clanked into the room. Their black-and-silver uniforms and nickel-plated breastplates shone, but the rifles in their hands were very functional. The officer leading them bowed stiffly before Raj.

"General Whitehall—" he began, holding up a letter sealed with the purple-and-gold of a Governor's Warrant.

"Barholm doesn't *deserve* to have a man like you serving him," Thom burst out.

"Oh, I agree," Raj said. For a moment his rueful grin made him seem boyish again, all but the eyes.

"Then stay here," Thom urged. "Center could hold you in stasis, like me, until long after Barholm is dust. And while we wait, we can be learning *everything*. All the knowledge in the human universe. Center's been teaching me things . . . things you couldn't imagine."

"The problem is, Thom, I'm serving the Spirit of Man of the Stars. Whose Viceregent on Earth—"

bellevue, Center said.

"—Viceregent on Bellevue happens to be Barholm Clerett. Besides the fact that my wife and friends are waiting for me; and frankly, I wouldn't want my troops in anyone else's hands right now, either." He sighed. "Most of all . . . well, you always were a scholar, Thom. I'm a soldier; and the Spirit has called me to serve as a soldier. If I die, that goes with the profession. And all men die, in the end."

essentially correct, Center noted, its machine-voice more somber than usual. **restoring interstellar civilization on bellevue and to humanity in general is an aim worth more than any single life.** A pause, **more than any million lives.**

Raj nodded. "And besides . . . in a year, I may die. Or Barholm may die. Or the dog may learn how to sing."

They made the *embrhazo* of close friends, touching each cheek. Thom froze again; Raj swallowed and looked away. He had seen many men die. Too many to count, over the last few years, and he saw them again in his dreams far more often than he wished. This frozen un-death disturbed him in a way the windrows of corpses after a battle did not. No breath, no heartbeat, the chill of a corpse— yet Thom lived. Lived, and did not age.

He stepped out of the doorway that appeared silently in the mirrored sphere, into the tunnel with its carpet of bones—the bones of those Center had rejected over the years as it waited for the man who would be its sword in the world.

Then again, he thought, *stasis isn't so bad, when you consider the alternatives.*

"Bloody hell," Major Ehwardo Poplanich said, sotto voce. "How long is this going to take? If I'd wanted to sit on my butt and be bored, I would have stayed home on the estate." He ran a hand over his thinning brown hair.

He was part of the reason that Raj Whitehall and his dozen Companions had plenty of space to themselves on the padded sofa-bench that ran down the side of the anteroom. Nobody at Court wanted to stand *too* close to a close relation of the last Poplanich Governor. Quite a few wondered why Poplanich was with Raj; Thom Poplanich had disappeared in Raj's company years before, and Thom's brother Des had died when Raj put down a bungled coup attempt against Governor Barholm.

Another part of the reason the courtiers avoided them was doubt about exactly how Raj stood with the Chair, of course.

The rest of it was the other Companions, the dozen or so close followers Raj had collected in his first campaign on the eastern frontier or in the Southern Territories. Many of the courtiers had spent their adult lives in the Palace, waiting in corridors like this. The Companions seemed part of the scene at first, in dress or walking-out uniforms like many of the men not in Court robes or religious vestments. Until you came closer and saw the scars, and the eyes.

"We'll wait as long as His Supremacy wants us to, Ehwardo," Colonel Gerrin Staenbridge said, swinging one elegantly booted foot over his knee. He looked to be exactly what he was: a stylish, handsome professional soldier from a noble family of moderate wealth, a man of wit and learning, and a merciless killer. "Consider yourself lucky to have an estate in a county that's boring; back home in Descott County—"

"—bandits come down the chimney once a week on Starday," Ehwardo finished. "Isn't that right, M'lewis?"

"I wouldna know, ser," the rat-faced little man said virtuously.

The Companions were unarmed, despite their dress uniforms— the Life Guard troopers at the doors and intervals along the corridor were fully equipped—but Raj suspected that the captain of the 5th Descott's Scout Troop had something up his sleeve.

Probably a wire garrote, he thought. M'lewis had enlisted one step ahead of the noose, having made Bufford Parish—the most lawless part of not-very-lawful Descott County—too hot for comfort. Raj had found his talents useful enough to warrant promotion to commissioned rank, after nearly flogging the man himself at their first meeting—a matter of a farmer's pig lifted as the troops went past. The Scout Troop was full of M'lewis's friends, relatives and neighbors; it was also known to the rest of the 5th as the Forty Thieves, not without reason.

Captain Bartin Foley looked up from sharpening the inner curve of the hook that had replaced his left hand. His face had been boyishly pretty when Raj first saw him, four years before. Officially he'd been an aide to Gerrin Staenbridge, unofficially a boyfriend-in-residence. He'd had both hands, then, too.

"Why don't you?" he asked M'lewis. "Know about bandits coming down the chimney, that is."

Snaggled yellow teeth showed in a grin. "Ain't no sheep nor yet any cattle inna chimbley, ser," M'lewis answered in the rasping nasal accent of Descott. "An' ridin' dogs, mostly they're inna stable. No use comin' down t'chimbly then, is there?"

The other Companions chuckled, then rose in a body. The crowd surged away from them, and split as Suzette Whitehall swept through.

Messa Suzette Emmenalle Forstin Hogor Wenqui Whitehall, Raj thought. *Lady of Hillchapel. My wife.*

Even now that thought brought a slight lurch of incredulous happiness below his breastbone. She was a small woman, barely up to his shoulder, but the force of the personality behind the slanted hazel-green eyes was like a jump into cool water on a hot day. Seventeen generations of East Residence nobility gave her slim body a greyhound grace, the tilt of her fine-featured olive face an unconscious arrogance. Over her own short black hair she was wearing a long blond court wig covered in a net of platinum and diamonds. More jewels sparkled on her bodice, on her fingers, on the gold-chain belt. Leggings of embroidered torofib silk made from the cocoons of burrowing insects in far-off Azania flashed enticingly through a fashionable split skirt of Kelden lace.

Raj took her hand and raised it to his lips; they stood for a moment looking at each other.

A metal-shod staff thumped the floor, and the tall bronze panels of the Audience Hall swung open. The gorgeously robed figure of the Janitor—the Court Usher—bowed and held out his staff, topped by the star symbol of the Civil Government.

Suzette took Raj's arm. The Companions fell in behind him, unconsciously forming a column of twos. The functionary's voice boomed out with trained precision through the gold-and-niello speaking trumpet:

"General the Honorable Messer Raj Ammenda Halgern da Luis Whitehall, Whitehall of Hillchapel, Hereditary Supervisor of Smythe Parish, Descott County! His Lady, Suzette Emmenalle—"

Raj ignored the noise, ignored the brilliantly-decked crowds who waited on either side of the carpeted central aisle, the smells of polished metal, sweet incense and sweat. As always, he felt a trace of annoyance at the constriction of the formal-dress uniform, the skin-tight crimson pants and gilt codpiece, the floor-length indigo tails of the coat and high epaulets and plumed silvered helmet. . . .

The Audience Hall was two hundred meters long and fifty high, its arched ceiling a mosaic showing the wheeling galaxy with the Spirit of Man rising head and shoulders behind it. The huge dark eyes were full of stars themselves, staring down into your soul.

Along the walls were automatons, dressed in the tight uniforms worn by Terran Federation soldiers twelve hundred years before. They whirred and clanked to attention, powered by hidden compressed-air conduits, bringing their archaic and quite nonfunctional battle lasers to salute. The Guard troopers along the aisle brought their entirely functional rifles up in the same gesture. They ignored the automatons, but some of the crowd who hadn't been long at Court flinched from the awesome technology and started uneasily when the arclights popped into blue-white radiance above each pointed stained-glass window.

The far end of the audience chamber was a hemisphere plated with burnished gold, lit via mirrors from hidden arcs. It glowed with a blinding aura, strobing slightly. The Chair itself stood four meters in the air on a pillar of fretted silver, the focus of light and mirrors and every eye in the giant room. The man enchaired upon it sat with hieratic stiffness, light breaking in metallized splendor from his robes, the bejeweled Keyboard and Stylus in his hands. From somewhere out of sight a chorus of voices chanted a hymn, inhumanly high and sweet, *castrati* belling out the chorus and young girls on the descant:

> "He intercedes for us—
> Viceregent of the Spirit of Man of the Stars!
> By Him are we boosted to the Orbit of Fulfillment—
> Supreme! Most Mighty Sovereign, Lord!
> In His hands is the power of Holy Federation Church—
> Ruler without equal! Sole rightful Autocrat!
> He wields the Sword of Law and the Flail of Justice—
> Most excellent of Excellencies! Father of the State!
> Download His words and execute the Program, ye People—
> Endfile! Endfile! Ennd . . . fiiille."

On either side of the arch framing the Chair were golden trees ten times taller than a man, with leaves so faithfully wrought that their edges curled and quivered in the slight breeze. Wisps of white-colored incense drifted through them from the censers swinging in the hands of attendant priests in stark white jumpsuit vestments, their shaven heads glittering with circuit diagrams. The branches of the trees glittered also, as birds carved from tourmaline and amethyst and lapis lazuli piped and sang. Their song rose to a high trilling as the pillar that supported the Chair sank toward the white marble steps; at the rear of the enclosure two full-scale statues of gorgosauroids rose to their three-meter height and roared as the seat of the Governor of the Civil Government sank home with a slight sigh of hydraulics. The semicircle of high ministers came out from behind their desks—each had a ceremonial viewscreen of strictly graded size—and sank down in the full prostration, linking their hands behind their heads. So did everyone in the Hall, except for the armed guards.

The Companions had stopped a few meters back. Now Raj felt Suzette's hand leave his; she sank down with a courtier's elegance, making the gesture of reverence seem a dance. He walked three more steps to the edge of the carpet and went to one knee, bowing his head deeply and putting a hand to his breast—the privilege of his rank, as a general and as one of Barholm's chosen Guards. It *might* have done him some good to have made the three prostrations of a supplicant; on the other hand, that could be taken as an admission of guilt.

You never know, with Barholm, Raj thought. *You never know. Center?*

effect too uncertain to usefully calculate, the passionless inner voice said. After a pause: **with barholm even chaos theory is becoming of limited predictive ability.**

Raj blinked. There were times he *thought* Center was developing a sense of humor. That was obscurely disturbing in its own right. Dark take it, he'd never been much good at pleading anyway. Flickers of holographic projection crossed his vision; Barholm calling the curse of the Spirit down on his head, Barholm pinning a high decoration to Raj's chest—

Cloth-of-gold robes sewn with emeralds and sapphires swirled into Raj's view. The toes of equally lavish slippers showed from under them. A tense silence filled the Hall; Raj could feel the eyes on his back, hundreds of them. *Like a pack of carnosauroids waiting for a cow to stumble,* he thought. Then:

"Rise, Raj Whitehall!"

Barholm's voice was a precision instrument, deep and mellow. With the superb acoustics of the hall behind it, the words rolled out more clearly than the Janitor's had through the megaphone. Behind them a long rustling sigh marked the release of tension.

Raj came to his feet, bending slightly for the ceremonial embrace and touch of cheeks. He was several centimeters taller than the Governor, although they were both Descotters. Barholm had the brick build and dark heavy features common there, but Raj's father had married a noblewoman from the far northwest, Kelden County. Folk there were nearly as tall and fair as the Namerique-speaking barbarians of the Military Governments.

The two men turned, the tall soldier and the stocky autocrat. Barholm's hand rested on his general's shoulder, a mark of high favor. Behind them the bidden chorus sang a high wordless note.

"Nobles and clerics of the Civil Government—behold the man who We call *Savior of the State!* Behold the *Sword of the Spirit of Man!*" The orator's voice rolled out again. The chorus came crashing in on the heels of it:

"Praise him! Praise him! Praise him!"

Raj watched the throng come to their feet, putting one palm to their ears and raising the other hand to the sky—invoking the Spirit of Man of the Stars as they shouted, "Glory, glory!" and "You conquer, Barholm!"

Every one of them would have cheered his summary execution with equal enthusiasm—or greater.

Suzette's shining eyes met his.

not quite all, Center reminded him. Behind Suzette the Companions were grinning as they cheered, **far less than all.**

The cheering died as Barholm raised a hand. "On Starday next shall be held a great day of rejoicing in the Temple and throughout the city. For three days thereafter East Residence shall hold festival in honor of General Whitehall and the brave men he led to victory over the barbarians of the Squadron; wine barrels shall stand at every crossroads, and the government storehouses will dispense to the people. On the third day, the spoils and prisoners will be exhibited in the Canidrome, to be followed by races and games in honor of the Savior of the State."

This time the cheers were deafening; if there was one thing everyone in East Residence loved, it was a spectacle. The chorus was barely audible, and the sound rose to a new peak as Barholm embraced Raj once more.

"There'll be a staff meeting right after all this play-acting," he said into Raj's ear, his voice flat. "There's the campaign in the Western Territories to plan."

He turned, and everyone bowed low as he withdrew through the private entrance behind the Chair.

So passes the glory of this world, Raj thought. *Death or victory, and if victory—*

observe, Center said. Holographic vision shimmered before his eyes, invisible to any but himself:

It took a moment for Raj to recognize the naked man: it was himself, his face contorted and slick with the burnt fluid of his own eyeballs, after the irons had had their way with them. Thick leather straps held his wrists and ankles splayed out in an X.

The hooded executioners were just fastening each limb to the pull-chain of a yoke of oxen. The crowd beyond murmured, held back by a line of leveled bayonets.

CHAPTER TWO

Governor Barholm stood while the servants stripped off his heavy robes. The Negrin Room dated to the reign of Negrin III, three centuries before; the walls were pale stone, traced over with delicate murals of reeds and flying dactosauroids and waterfowl; there was only one small Star, a token obeisance to religion as had been common in that impious age. The heads of the Ministries were there, and Mihwel Berg as Administrator of the newly-conquered Southern Territories and representative of the Administrative Service; Chancellor Tzetzas, of course; General Klostermann, Master of Soldiers, Bernardinho Rivadavia, the Minister of Barbarians, and Lady Anne Clerett as well, the Governor's wife. She gave Raj a sincere smile as they waited for the Governor to finish disrobing.

There's one real friend at court, he thought. Suzette's friend, actually.

Barholm sat, and the others bowed and joined him.

"Well, messers," he said abruptly, opening the file an aide placed before him. "It's time to deal with the Western Territories and the barbarians of the Brigade who impiously hold the Old Residence, original seat of the Civil Government of Holy Federation—since we've reduced the Southern Territories quite satisfactorily, thanks to the aid of the Spirit of Man of the Stars, and Its Sword, General Whitehall."

There was a murmur of applause, and Raj looked down at his hands. "I had good troops and officers," he said.

"Your Supremacy," Tzetzas said. "We all give praise to the Spirit"—there was a mass touching of amulets, most of them genuine ancient computer components, in this assembly—"and to our General Whitehall, and to your wise policy, that the barbarian heretics were defeated so easily. Yet I would be remiss in my duties if I failed to point out that the Civil Government is still reeling from the expense of the southern campaign—completed less

15

than a year ago. Which has, in fact, so far served to enrich only the officers involved in the operation."

observe, Center said:

Muzzaf Kerpatik was on the docks in Port Murchison, capital of the reconquered Southern Territories. He was a small dark man from Komar, near the Colonial border; once a merchant and agent of Chancellor Tzetzas, until the latter's schemes had grown too much for even his elastic conscience. Since then he'd proven himself useful to Raj in a number of ways . . . although Raj hadn't known about this one, precisely. He was overseeing the loading of a ship, a medium-sized three-masted merchantman. Bolts of silk were going aboard, and burlap sacks filled with crystals of raw saltpeter, bales of rosauroid hides, and slatted wooden boxes stuffed with what looked like gold and silver tableware. A coffle of women chained neck-and-neck waited to board later: all young and good-looking, some stunningly so, and in the remnants of rich clothing in the gaudy style of the Squadron nobility— families of those barbarian nobles who'd refused to yield to the Spirit of Man of the Stars or missed the amnesty after the surrender, headed for Civil Government slave markets.

Raj thought he could place the time: about a month after the final battle on the docks. It had taken that long, and repeated scrubbings, before the rotting blood stopped drawing crawling mats of flies. *I'd heard about streets running with blood,* he reminded himself. *Never seen it until then.* Vice-Admiral Curtis Auburn had landed ten thousand Squadron warriors on those docks, unaware that the main Squadron host was defeated and Raj in control of the city. Curtis had been lucky enough to be captured almost immediately, but less than one in ten of his men had survived the day.

The vision couldn't be much more than a month after that, because Suzette was riding up and leaning down to examine the checklist in Kerpatik's hand, and both Whitehalls had sailed home when Raj was recalled in quasi-disgrace.

"Should we not pause and recoup our resources?" the Chancellor concluded. "Especially when our internal situation is so delicate."

Due in no small measure to Your Most Blatant Corruptibility, Raj thought ironically. There was a popular East Residence legend that a poisonous fangmouth had once bitten Tzetzas at a garden party, the unfortunate reptile was believed to have died in horrible convulsions within minutes. The Chancellor had raised enormous sums for Barholm's wars and public works projects, and a good deal of it had stuck to his own beautifully manicured fingers.

Raj's expression was blandly respectful and attentive. On the expedition to the Southern Territories, Tzetzas had seen that Raj sailed with weevily hardtack and bunker coal that was half shale; Raj had returned the favor in his last stop in Civil Government territory by exchanging the goods for replacements from Tzetzas's own estates and mines, at full book price.

observe, Center said.

Sesar Chayvez stood before his patron. The plump little man was sweating as Tzetzas sat leafing through the documents in the file before him.

"And here, my dear Sesar, we come to your signature, right next to that of then-Brigadier Whitehall and Mihwel Berg of the Administrative Service, on the bottom of this requisition order. Authorizing the exchange of worthless trash for goods from my estates in Kolobassa District."

His voice was light, even slightly amused. "An exchange which, since the hardtack in question was useful only for pig feed and the coal unsalable in an exporting center like Hayapalco, cost me approximately fourteen thousand gold FedCreds. Not to mention the expenses for repairing estates ruined when Whitehall quartered Skinner mercenaries on them to . . . shall we say, motivate the staff to cooperation."

"Your Most Excellent Honorability," Chayvez said, twining his fingers together.

His eyes flicked around the room, on the cabinets of well-thumbed books, the curios, the restrained elegance of the mosaic floor. Oddly, that was mostly covered with a square of waxed canvas on this visit. He swallowed and forced himself to continue:

"The . . . the hill-bandit of a Descotter occupied my headquarters with troops loyal only to him!" he burst out. "One of his thugs started to *strangle* me with a wire noose until I signed. What could I do?"

"Oh, I can understand your fears," Tzetzas said, waving a deprecatory hand. Chayvez began to relax. "In fact, it isn't the first time that Whitehall and those ruffian Companions of his have caused me substantial trouble. They brutalized a number of my placemen and employees in Komar, when stationed there. Brutalized them so thoroughly—I believe they began to *skin* one of them—that they revealed far, far too much, and I was forced to turn over all my investments in the province to the Chair to avoid serious disfavor."

Barholm had been quite annoyed. The scheme had involved holding up the landgrants usually given to infantry garrison troops, and then pocketing the revenues from the State farms. It might have gone unnoticed if Raj Whitehall hadn't been sent to bolster that particular frontier against the Colony.

Chayvez nodded enthusiastically. "The man is a menace to peace and orderly government, Your Most Excellent Honorability," he said.

"True. You will understand, then."

"Ah . . ." The plump provincial governor hesitated. "Understand, Your—"

"Yes, yes. That I *cannot* have my servants more afraid of Whitehall than of me. I believe his tame thug *began* to strangle you?"

A shadow moved from a corner of the darkened room. It grew into a man, a black man in a long dark robe. Not from one of the highly civilized city-states of Zanj; his tribal scars showed him to be from much farther south and west, from the savannahs of Majinga. The slave was nearly two meters tall, with shoulders like a bull moving beneath the cloth of his *kanzu*. His tongueless mouth gobbled in thick joy as he closed his fingers around the little man's neck and lifted him clear of the floor. Chayvez's arms and legs thrashed for a moment, beating at the boulder-solid form of the black and then twitching helplessly. The massive hands clamped tighter and tighter, closing by increments. When the neck snapped at last the bureaucrat had been still for several minutes. Urine and other fluids dripped to the waxed canvas on the floor.

"Wrap the body, and drop it in an alley," Tzetzas said, in a language quite unlike the Sponglish of civilization. The mute bowed silently and bent to his task as the Chancellor turned up the coal-oil lamp and took another file from the sauroid-ivory holder on his desk.

Raj met Tzetzas's eyes and inclined his head. The Chancellor matched the gesture with one almost as imperceptible and far more graceful.

Barholm explained to Raj: "There's been another outbreak of the anti-hardcopyist heresy down in Cerest. It's nothing serious; just a boil. When you've got a boil on your bum, you lance it and ignore it."

There were shocked murmurs; Raj touched his own amulet, a gold-chased chipboard fragment blessed by Saint Wu herself. "Wasn't that heresy anathematized two centuries ago?" he said.

"Yes, but it's like black plague, always breaking out again," the Governor said. "This time they're taking a new tack; calling circuit diagrams themselves 'false schematics' and corrupted data, not just denouncing allegorical representations. We can't afford trouble in Cerest—"

Raj nodded; a good deal of the capital's grain was shipped from there, and the Tarr Valley was the trade route to the rich tropical lands of the Zanj city-states. Or at least the only route that didn't run through the hostile Colony.

"—so I'm sending a brigade and a Viral Cleanser Sysup to purge their subroutines of heresy for good and all." He shook his square-jawed head; there was more silver in the black hair than Raj remembered. Being Governor was a high-stress occupation too.

observe, Center said.

Blinding sunlight in the main square of Cerest, a prosperous-looking provincial capital. A domed Star Temple, with the many-rayed symbol atop it; the square bulk of a regional Prefect's palace across from it, fountains and arcades all about. A crowd filled most of the open paved space. It moaned as men—and a few women—were led out to a long row of iron posts set deep in the pavement. They shook their heads and refused the offered Headsets, symbolic connection to the Terminals of confession; two spat at the officiating priests. The soldiers hustled them on, supporting as much as forcing. Most of the prisoners' bare feet showed oozing sores where their toenails should have been.

The iron posts were joined in a complete loop by thick copper cables; the ends of the cables disappeared into a wagon-mounted box with an external flywheel belt—driven by the power take-off of a steam haulage engine. As the steel chains bound them to the posts, the prisoners began to sing, a hymn in some thick local dialect Raj couldn't follow. Out in the crowd others took it up, men in the rough brown robes of desert monks, women in the archaic jumpsuits and tunics of Renunciate Sisters, then the ragged *dezpohblado* crowd of town laborers. An officer barked an order and the troops blocking off the execution ground formed, the first rank dropping to one knee, both leveling their rifles.

The belt drive to the generator whined, and a hooded executioner put his hand on a scissor-switch. The Sysup in his gold-embroidered overrobe stood in the attitude of prayer—one hand over his ear, the other stretched up with its fingers making keying motions—and then swept it down. The man in the leather hood matched his gesture with a showman's timing, and blue sparks popped from the dangling cables. The prisoners stopped singing, but they could not scream with the DC current running through their bodies, only convulse against the iron poles.

A rock arched through the air and took one of the soldiers in the mouth. He collapsed backward limply; there was no motion from the others besides a ripple of movement as they closed ranks. They were Regulars, dragoons. . . .

More rocks flew. Raj could see the officer's lips move silently, in a prayer or curse. Then he shouted an order:

"Volley fire!" An endless line of white puffs, and the crowd recoiled, all but those smashed off their feet by the heavy bullets. The soldiers worked the levers of their rifles, reloaded. Another order, and they began to advance in a serried line, bayonets advanced.

Raj blinked. As always, the holographic vision lasted far less time than it seemed. Chancellor Tzetzas was steepling his fingers:

". . . necessary measures, true. Cerest Province is far too valuable to risk."

Especially with what our dear Chancellor makes from the chocolate, torofib and kave monopolies, Raj thought ironically. *And I'll bet he fiddles on the share the fisc is supposed to get.*

probability 97% ±2%, Center said. **however, total receipts to the fisc have increased while he holds the monopolies, due to volume growth.**

"Still, undertaking another campaign at this time—when, as I mentioned, we have yet to recoup the expenses of the last, well . . ." There was a spare gesture of the long hand.

Mihwel Berg, now Administrator of the Southern Territories, sniffed; he was a mousy little man, and watching him defy Tzetzas was like seeing a sheep turn on a carnosauroid. "Your Excellency, I might point out that all out-of-pocket expenses for the Expeditionary Force have already been recouped, with plunder, sale of prisoners, and other cash receipts alone leaving a surplus of no less than seven hundred fifty-four thousand FedCreds to the fisc. Gold."

Barholm sat straighter, casting a sidelong glance at his Chancellor. That was a considerable sum even by the Civil Government's standards. The Governor might be obsessed with reclaiming the territories lost to the Military Governments centuries ago, but he was keenly aware of financial matters.

"Furthermore, and even without the *invaluable* services which Your Excellency's tax-farming syndicates provide to the fisc, the first six months' revenues from the Southern Territories under Administrative Services control, annualized, are tenth out of the twenty-two Counties and Territories currently under effective Civil Government control.

"And," Berg went on, warming to his topic, "that does *not* include the revenues from estates confiscated from deceased or captured members of the Squadron—which amount to nearly half of the arable land in the district, if we include the one-third confiscation of Squadron nobles who surrendered before the collapse and, of course, the Admiral's own lands. Ex-Admiral, that is. That revenue alone will double the overall receipts from the Territories, and this is after we deduct lands to be deeded to peasant militia, infantry garrison plots, and estates to support the Church. Furthermore, the Territories have much untapped potential neglected under the Admirals. If our Sovereign Mighty Lord will examine the proposals—"

He slid a package of documents across the table; Barholm untied the ribbon and began riffling through them with interest. Tzetzas's fingers crooked like talons. The Chancellor usually had a say in what reached the Governor's desk, and he valued that power. Governor Barholm was a hard-working administrator, and an enthusiast for useful public works.

"—a railway to the saltpeter mines alone would increase the total yield of the Territories by fifteen percent"—saltpeter was a Chair monopoly, and the deposits south of Port Murchison were the richest in the known world—"besides making economical the copper and zinc deposits there, closed for three generations. There are also irrigation works to be brought back into operation, road repairs . . . Your

Supremacy, launching the Expeditionary Force was the most lucrative stroke of policy any Governor has made in two hundred years."

Klosterman pulled at his muttonchop whiskers. "Still, even if the Colony is quiet, I'd not like to take too many troops away from the border," he said. The Master of Soldiers' last regional field command had been of Eastern Forces. "Ali's no fool, but he's vain, and he's vicious as a starving carnosauroid to boot."

Barholm shrugged. "He may have killed his brother Akbar, but they'll take a while to recover from their civil war."

Good fortune had given the Civil Government four strong Governors in a row, with no usurpations or civil conflicts—the primary reason for its current strength and unprecedented prosperity—but disputed successions were a problem both the Civil Government and the Colony were thoroughly familiar with.

observe, Center said.

A one-eyed man stood among burned-out ruins. Raj recognized him instantly: Tewfik bin-Jamal, son of the late Settler of the Colony, and commander of all his armies. Raj had lost one minor battle to him, and won a major one by a thin margin; and every day in his prayers the general thanked the Spirit of Man for the Colonist superstition that made Tewfik ineligible for the Settler's throne because he lacked an eye.

The stocky, muscular body filled the regulation crimson djellaba with a solid authority, and the Seal of Solomon marked his eyepatch. Officers of the Colonial regulars and black-robed personal mamelukes followed the Muslim general as he stalked through the shattered building. He kicked at a frame of cindered boards; they slid away in ash that drifted ghostly under the bright sun, revealing the warped brass and iron shape of a lathe. Other machines stood amid the ruins, as did the cast-iron poles that had carried the drive shaft from a steam engine.

Tewfik's face was impassive beneath his spired spike-topped helmet, but the grip of his left hand on the plain wired brass hilt of his scimitar was white-knuckled with the effort of controlling his rage. The Colony armed its forces with lever-operated repeating carbines, and the machine shops that turned them out were a rare and precious asset. Now there was one less.

He turned; the viewpoint turned with him, staying behind his left shoulder. Beyond the fallen door-arch of the factory were more ruins, then intact buildings, and a long slope down to a great river. Flat roofs and minarets, smokestacks, towers glinting with colored tile, narrow twisting streets and irregular plazas around splashing fountains: Al Kebir, the capital of the Colony and the oldest city on Bellevue. Half a dozen huge bridges crossed the river, and the water was thronged with lateen-sailed dhows and sambuks, with barges and rafts and steamboats. Across the river was a burst of greenery, palms and jacaranda trees, and a great interlinked pile of low, ornately carved marble buildings taking up scores of hectares before the sprawl of the city resumed. An endless low rumble carried through the air, the sound of a million human beings and their doings, pierced through with the high wailing call of a muezzin.

The robed men sank to their knees in prayer; Tewfik waited an instant as his attendants spread a prayer rug before he bent his head towards the distant holy city of Sinnar, where the first ships to reach Bellevue had carried a fragment of the Kaaba from burning Mecca.

When he rose he turned to the man in a civilian outfit of baggy pantaloons, sash, turban and curl-toed slippers. At his finger's motion two of the mameluke slave-soldiers—one blond, one black, both huge men moving as lightly as cats—stood behind the civilian. The heavy curved swords in their hands rested lightly on his shoulders.

"Sa'id—" the man began.

Prince. That much Raj would have known, but as always Center somehow provided the knowledge that made the Arabic as understandable as his native Sponglish.

"Prince," the man went on, "what could we do? Your brother Akbar's followers came and demanded the finished arms; then the household troops of your brother Ali attacked them. We are not fighting men here."

Tewfik nodded, his hand stroking his beard. "*Kismet,*" he said: fate. "When the *kaphar,* the infidels of the Civil Government, slew our father, it was Akbar's fate to reach for power and fail"—and leave his head on a pole before the Grand Mosque—"and yours to repair the damage as quickly as may be. If I thought you truly responsible, I would not threaten."

The manager nodded unconsciously; if Tewfik thought that the staff were dragging their feet, there would have been another set of heads on a pole some time ago.

"How long?" Tewfik asked, his voice like millstones of patience that would grind results out of time and fate by sheer force of will.

"If the Settler Ali, upon whom may Allah shower His blessings, advances the necessary funds, we will be turning out carbines again in six months," he said.

Tewfik's right hand rested on the butt of his revolver. One index finger gestured, and the mamelukes pressed the factory manager to his knees with the blunt back edges of their scimitars. The blades crossed before his neck, ready to scissor through it like a gardener's shears through the stem of a tulip.

"Six months!" the man cried; he ripped open his jacket to bare his breast in token of his willingness to die. "Prince Tewfik, we are adepts of the mechanic arts here, not dervishes or magicians! Machine tools cannot be flogged into obedience—six months and no more, but no less. May I be boiled alive and my children's flesh eaten by wild dogs if I lie!"

"That can be arranged . . . if you lie," Tewfik said somberly. The man met his eyes, ignoring the blades so near his flesh. The Colonist general sighed and signed the swordsmen back. "There is no God but God, and all things are accomplished according to the will of God. In the name of the Merciful, the Lovingkind, I shall not make you bear the weight of an anger earned elsewhere. Come, my friend; rise, and we will speak of details over sherbert with my staff. Soon the Dar 'as-Salaam will need the weapons. There is a great stirring in the House of War."

Raj nodded. "Ali will wait; a year, maybe two if he has enough sense to listen to Tewfik.

"Still," he went on, "the Brigade's a more serious proposition than the Squadron was. They've been in contact with civilization longer, and they do have a standing army of sorts; plus they've some recent combat experience."

Mostly against the Stalwarts in the north; those were savages, but numerous, vicious and treacherous to a fault.

"Also the Western Territories are bigger—not just in raw area, the population. Not so much desert. I'd say for a really thorough pacification . . . forty thousand troops. Fifteen thousand cavalry."

There were outraged screams around the table. "Out of the question!" Tzetzas barked, startled out of his usual suavity, and Barholm was looking narrow-eyed.

"That *would* be a little large," he said carefully. "Particularly as we're hoping that General Forker won't fight."

"Sovereign Mighty Lord, Forker may not fight but I doubt the Brigade will roll over that easily," Raj said.

"Fifteen thousand is about as much as we could spare," Barholm said, tapping a knuckle against the table to show that the question was closed. "That proved ample for the Squadron. Another battalion or two of cavalry, perhaps more guns."

The ruler leaned back. "Besides that," he went on, "General Forker—" the Brigades ruler kept the ancient title, although in the Western Territories it had come to mean *king* rather than a military rank "—is by no means necessarily hostile to the Civil Government. He spent better than a year negotiating for help while he was maneuvering to replace the late General Welf."

"He managed to do that *without* our aid, though, didn't he, Sovereign Mighty Lord?"

The Minister of Barbarians shuffled through his notes. "Yes, General Whitehall. In fact, he showed an almost, well, almost *civilized* subtlety during the negotiations. Then he married Charlotte Welf, the late General's widow. That made his election to the General's position inevitable. We were, I confess, surprised."

"Not as surprised as she was when he murdered her as soon as he was firmly in power," Barholm said, grinning; there was a polite chuckle.

observe, Center said. A brief flicker this time; a woman in her bath. Handsome in a big-boned way, with grey in her long blond hair. She looked up angrily when the maidservant scrubbing her back fled, then tried to stand herself as she saw the big bearded men who had forced their way through the door. They wore bandanas over their lower faces, but the short fringed leather jackets marked them as Brigade nobles. Water fountained over the marble tiles of the bathroom as they gripped her head and held it under the surface. Her feet kicked free, thrashing at the water for a moment until the body slumped. Then there were only the warriors' arms, rigid bars down through the floating soapsuds. . . .

Chancellor Tzetzas raised an index finger in stylized horror. "Quite a gothic tale," he said. "Barbarians."

Raj nodded. "We can certainly spare seventeen or eighteen thousand men," he went on. "The Southern Territories are fairly quiet, all they need is garrison forces to keep the desert nomads in order. The military captives sent here will more than replace any drawdown. We could ship a substantial force into Stern Island—" that was directly north of the reconquered Southern Territories, and the easternmost Brigade possession "—and . . . hmm. Don't we have some claim to it, being heirs to the Admirals? It would make a first-rate base for an advance to the west."

The Minister of Barbarians leaned forward. "Indeed," he said, pushing up his glasses. "The former Admiral of the Squadron— ex-Admiral Auburn's predecessor's father—married Mindy-Sue Grakker, a daughter of the then General of the Brigade, and acquired extensive estates on Stern Island as her dower. The Brigade commander there has refused to turn over their administration to the envoys I sent."

"Excellent," Barholm said, leaning back and steepling his fingers. He might be of Descotter descent, but his fine-honed love of a good, legally sound swindle was that of a native-born East Residencer. "From there, we can exploit opportunity as it offers."

"Your Supremacy," Raj said in agreement. "We could move most of the troops up from the Southern Territories? They're surplus to requirements, closer, and I know what they can do. It's going on for summer already, so there's a time factor here."

"Ah," Barholm said, giving him a long, considering look. "Well, General, I'll certainly withdraw some of those forces . . . but it wouldn't be wise to make it appear that you have some sort of private army of your own. People might misunderstand. . . ."

Raj smiled politely. "Quite true, Your Supremacy," he said.

Everyone understands that it's the Army that disposes of the Chair, in the end. Three generations without a *coup* would be something of a record—if you didn't count Barholm's own uncle Vernier Clerett. He hadn't shot his way onto the Chair, strictly speaking, but he *had* been Commander of East Residence Forces when the last Poplanich Governor died of natural causes.

Probably natural causes.

"We certainly don't want people to think *that*," Raj went on. "Half the cavalry battalions from the Southern Territories, then?" Barholm nodded.

"And the infantry?"

"By all means," the Governor said, slightly surprised Raj would mention the subject. Infantry were second-line troops, and Barholm saw little difference between one battalion of them and another.

You haven't seen what Jorg Menyez and I can do with them, Raj thought. "I'll draw the other cavalry battalions and artillery from the Residence Area Forces Group, then?"

Barholm signed assent. "I'll be sending along my nephew Cabot Clerett, as well," the Governor said. "He's been promoted to Major, in command of the 1st Residence Battalion." A Life Guards unit; they rarely left East Residence, but many of the men were veterans from other outfits. Of late, most had been from the Clerett family's estates. "It's time Cabot got some military experience."

Raj spread his hands. "At your command, Your Supremacy. I've met him; he seems an intelligent young officer, and doubtless brave as well." A subtle reminder: *don't blame me if he stops a bullet somewhere.*

"Indeed. Although I hope he won't be seeing *too* much action." An equally subtle hint: *he's my heir.* Barholm was nearly forty, and he and Lady Anne hadn't produced a child in fifteen years of marriage. The Governor smiled like a shark at the exchange. It was worth the risk, since he had other nephews. A Governor didn't *have* to be a general, but he did need enough field experience for fighting men to respect him. He continued:

"In fact—this doesn't go beyond these walls—we are, in fact, negotiating with General Forker right now. The, ah, death of Charlotte Welf . . . Charlotte Forker . . . aroused considerable animosity among some of the Brigade nobles. Particularly since Forker's main claim to membership in the Amalson family was through her. General Forker has expressed interest in our offer of a substantial annuity and an estate near East Residence in return for his abdication in favor of the Civil Government."

"He may abdicate, Sovereign Mighty Lord, but I doubt his nobles would all go along with it. The Brigade monarchy is elective within the House of Theodore Amalson. The Military Council includes all the adult males, and they can depose him and put someone else in his place."

"That," Barholm said dryly, "is why we're sending an army."

Raj nodded. "I'll get right on to it, then, Your Supremacy, as soon as the Gubernatorial Receipt—" a general-purpose authorizing order "—comes through. It'll take a month or so to coordinate . . . by your leave, Sovereign Mighty Lord?"

CHAPTER THREE

How utterly foolish of him, Suzette Whitehall thought, looking at the petitioner.

Lady Anne leaned her head on one hand, her elbow on the satinwood arm of her chair. Her levees were much simpler than the Governor's, as befitted a Consort. Apart from the Life Guard troopers by the door, only a few of her ladies-in-waiting were present, and the room was lavish but not very large. A pleasant scent of flowers came through the open windows, and the sound of a *gitar* being strummed. The cool spring breeze fluttered the dappled silk hangings.

Despite that, the Illustrious Deyago Rihvera was sweating. He was a plump little man whose stomach strained at the limits of his embroidered vest and high-collared tailcoat, and his hand kept coming up to fiddle with the emerald stickpin in his lace cravat.

Suzette reflected that he probably just did not connect the glorious Lady Anne Clerett with Supple Annie, the child-acrobat, actress and courtesan. He'd only been a client of hers once or twice, from what Suzette had heard—even then, Anne had been choosey when she could. But since then Rihvera had been an associate of Tzetzas, and *everyone* knew how much the Consort hated the Chancellor. To be sure, the men who owed Rihvera the money he needed so desperately—to pay for his artistic pretensions—were under Anne's patronage. Not much use pursuing the claims in ordinary court while she protected them.

". . . and so you see, most glorious Lady, I petition only for simple justice," he concluded, mopping his face.

"Illustrious Rihvera—" Anne began.

A chorus broke in from behind the silk curtains. They were softer-voiced, but otherwise an eerie reproduction of the Audience Hall singers, castrati and young girls:

"Thou art flatulent, Oh Illustrious Deyago
   Pot-bellied, too:
Oh incessantly farting, pot-bellied one!"

Silver hand-bells rang a sweet counterpoint. Anne sat up straighter and looked around.

"Did you hear anything?" she murmured.

Suzette cleared her throat "Not a thing, glorious Lady. There's an unpleasant smell, though."

"Send for incense," the Consort said. Turning back to Rihvera, her expression serious. "Now, Illustrious—"

"You have a toad's mouth, Oh Illustrious Deyago—
   Bug eyes, too:
Oh toad-mouthed, bug-eyed one!"

This time the silver bells were accompanied by several realistic croaking sounds.

I wonder how long he can take it? Suzette thought, slowly waving her fan.

His hands were trembling as he began again.

"Are you well, my dear?" Suzette asked anxiously, when the petitioners and attendants were gone.

"It's nothing," Anne Clerett said briskly. "A bit of a grippe."

The Governor's lady looked a little thinner than usual, and worn now that the amusement had died away from her face. She was a tall woman, who wore her own long dark-red hair wound with pearls in defiance of Court fashion and protocol. For the rest she wore the tiara and jewelled bodice, flounced silk split skirt, leggings and slippers as if she had been born to them. Instead of working her way up from acrobat and child-whore down by the Camidrome and the Circus . . .

Suzette took off her own blond wig and let the spring breeze through the tall doors riffle her sweat-dampened black hair. It carried scents of greenery and flowers from the courtyard and the Palace gardens, with an undertaste of smoke from the city beyond.

"Thank you," she said to Anne. There was no need to specify, between them.

Anne Clerett shrugged. "It's nothing," she said. "I advise Barholm for his own good—and putting Raj in charge *is* the best move." She hesitated: "I realize my husband can be . . . difficult, at times."

He can be hysterical, Suzette thought coldly as she smiled and patted Anne's hand. In a raving funk back during the Victory Riots, when the city factions tried to throw out the Cleretts, Anne had told him to run if he wanted to, that she'd stay and burn the Palace around her rather than go back to the docks. That had put some backbone into him, that and Raj taking command of the Guards and putting down the riots with volley-fire and grapeshot and bayonet charges to clear the barricades.

He can also be a paranoid menace. Barholm was the finest administrator to sit the Chair in generations, and a demon for work—but he suspected everyone except Anne. Nor had he ever been much of a fighting man, and his jealousy of Raj was poisoning what was left of his good sense on the subject. A Governor was theoretically quasi-divine, with power of life and death over his subjects. In practice he held that power until he used it too often on too many influential subjects, enough to frighten the rest into killing him despite the dangerous uncertainty that always followed a coup. Barholm hadn't come anywhere near that.

Yet.

"Besides," Anne went on, "I stand by my friends."

Which was true. When Anne was merely the tart old Governor Vernier Clerett's nephew had unaccountably married, the other Messas of the Palace had barely noticed her. Except in the way they might have scraped something nasty off their shoes. Suzette had had better sense than those more conventional gentlewomen. *Or perhaps just less snobbery,* she thought. Her family was as ancient as any in the City; they had been nobles when the Cleretts and Whitehalls were minor bandit chiefs in the Descott hills. They had also been quite thoroughly poor by the time she came of age, years before she met Raj. The last few farms had been mortgaged to buy the gowns and jewels she needed to appear at Court.

"You'll be accompanying Raj again?" Anne asked.

"Always," Suzette replied.

Anne nodded. "We both," she said, "have able husbands. But even the most able of men—"

"—needs help," Suzette replied. The Governor's Lady raised a fingertip and servants appeared with cigarettes in holders of carved sauroid ivory.

"I may need help with young Cabot," Suzette said. "He hasn't been much at Court?"

"Mostly back in Descott," Anne said "Keeping the Barholm name warm on the ancestral estates."

Which were meagre things in themselves. Descott was remote, a month's journey on dogback east and north of the capital, a poor upland County of volcanic plateaus and badlands. Mostly grazing country, with few products beyond wool, riding dogs and ornamental stone. Its other export was fighting men, proud poor backland squires and their followings of tough *vakaros* and yeoman-tenant ranchers, men born to the rifle and saddle, to the hunt and the blood feud. Utterly unlike the tax-broken peons of the central provinces. Only a fraction of the Civil Government's people lived there, but one in five of the elite mounted dragoons were Descotters. Most of the rest came from similar frontier areas, or were mercenaries from the *barbaricum.*

It was no accident that Descotters had held the Chair so often of late, nor that the Cleretts were anxious to keep first-hand ties with the clannish County gentry.

"Seriously, my dear," Anne went on, "you should look after young Clerett. He's . . . well, he's been champing at the bridle of late. Twenty, and a head full of romantic yeast and old stories. Quite likely to get himself killed—which would be a *disaster*. Barholm, ah, is quite attached to him."

The two women exchanged a look; both childless, both without illusion. It said a great deal for Anne that Barholm had not put her aside for not giving him an heir of his body, which was sufficient cause for divorce under Civil Government law.

"I'll try to see he comes back, Anne," Suzette said. *If possible,* she added to herself with clinical detachment. Romantic, ambitious young noblemen were not difficult to control; she had found that out long before her marriage. They could also be trouble when serious business was in question, such as the welfare of one's husband.

"I'm sure you can handle Cabot," Anne said. That sort of manipulation was skill they shared, in their somewhat different contexts.

"Poplanich needn't come back," Anne went on.

She smiled; Suzette looked away with a well-concealed shudder. A strayed ox might have noticed an expression like that on the last carnosauroid it ever saw.

Anne clapped her hands. "Thom Poplanich, Des Poplanich—Ehwardo would make a beautiful matched set, don't you think?" And it would leave the Poplanich *gens* without an adult male of note. Thom's grandsire had been a well-loved Governor.

"Des was a rebel," Suzette said carefully. "I've never known what happened to Thom. Ehwardo is a loyal officer."

"Of course, of course," Anne said, chuckling and giving Suzette's hand a squeeze.

Raj's wife chuckled herself. *There's irony for you,* she thought: *I really don't know what happened to Thom.*

Raj simply refused to discuss it, and he had been *different* ever since he came back from the tunnels they'd gone exploring in; the ground under East Residence was honeycombed with them. Suzette might have advised quietly braining Thom Poplanich and leaving him in the catacombs, as a career move and personal insurance—except that she knew that Raj would never have considered it. He had changed, but not like that.

You are too good for this Fallen world, my angel, she thought toward the absent Raj. *It is not made for so honorable a knight.*

Then Lady Clerett's mouth twisted; she covered it with her palms and coughed rackingly.

"*Anne!*" Suzette cried, rising.

"It's nothing," she said, biting her lip. "Go on; you'll have a lot to do. Just a cough, it'll pass off with the spring. I'll deal with it."

There was blood on her fingers, hidden imperfectly by their fierce clench. Suzette made the minimal bow and withdrew.

"*At the narrow passage there is no brother, no friend,*" she quoted softly to herself. And no allies against some enemies.

"So, what do we get?" Colonel Grammeck Dinnalsyn said; the artillery specialist had seen to his beloved 75mm field-guns, and was ready to take an interest in the less technical side of the next Expeditionary Force.

Raj and the other officers were riding side-by-side down the Main Street of the training base, in the peninsula foothills west of East Residence.

"5th Descott Guards, 7th Descott Rangers, 1st Rogor Slashers, 18th Komar Borderers, 21st Novy Haifa Dragoons, and Poplanich's Own from the cavalry in the Southern Territories. And all the infantry and guns."

"Jorg will be glad to get out of the Territories. Spirit knows I went and Entered my thanks when I got the movement orders for home. Not much happening there now, except that idiot they sent to replace you giving damn-fool orders."

"*I'm* glad we're getting Jorg. Nobody else I know can handle infantry like Menyez."

Most commanders didn't even try; infantry were used mainly for line-of-communication and garrison work in the Civil Government's army. Jorg had had his own 17th Kelden Foot and the 24th Valencia under his eye since Sandoral, nearly four years ago. Raj and he had done a fair bit with the other infantry battalions during the Southern Territories campaign, and Menyez had been working them hard in the year since.

"Then for the rest of the cavalry, the 1st and 2nd Residence Battalions, the Maximilliano Dragoons, and the the 1st and 2nd Mounted Cruisers from here." The artillery specialist raised an eyebrow at the last two units.

"Yes, they're *Squadrones*—but coming along nicely. Full of fight, too—for some reason they don't seem to resent our beating the *scramento* out of them. Quite the contrary, if anything. Eager to learn from us."

observe, Center said:

"Right, ye horrible buggers," the sergeant said. "Who's next?"

He spun the rifle in his hands into a blurring circle; the bayonet was fixed, but with the sheath wired on to the blade. The three big men lying wheezing or moaning on the ground before the stocky Descotter had been holding similar weapons. The company behind them were standing at ease in double line with their rifles sloped. None of them looked very enthusiastic about serving as an object lesson. . . .

"Ten-'hut!" the sergeant said. The men were stripped to their baggy maroon pants, web-belts and boots; he was wearing in addition the blue sash, sleeveless grey cotton shirt and the orange-black checked neckerchief of the 5th Descott. "Now, we'uns will *learn* how to *use* the fukkin' baynit, *won't we?*"

"YES SERGEANT!" they screamed.

"Right. Now, yer feints to the eyes loik *this*, then gits 'em in t'belly loik *this*. Baynit forrard! An' *one* an' *two*—"

"Eager to learn from *you*, sir, actually," the artilleryman said. He was a slim man of medium height, with cropped black hair and black eyes and pale skin, and a clipped East Residence accent.

"It soothes their pride," he went on. "They call you an Avatar of the Spirit. And what man needs to be ashamed of yielding to the Spirit Incarnate? Not that I'd dispute you the title myself."

Raj frowned, touching his amulet. Dinnalsyn's casual blasphemy was natural enough for a man born in the City, but Raj had been raised in the old style back home on Hillchapel. A soldier of the Civil Government was also a warrior of the Spirit.

the ex-squadron personnel are undergoing transference, Center said, **a common psychological phenomenon, and technically, you are an avatar.**

"Speak of the Starless," Dinnalsyn noted.

He and Raj turned their dogs aside as a battalion came down the camp street toward them. First the standard-bearer, the long pole socketed to a ring in his right stirrup; the colors were furled in a tubular leather casing. Then the trumpeters and drummers, four of them. The battalion commander and his aides in a clump with the Senior Sergeant of the unit; then the six hundred and fifty men in column-of-fours, each man an exact three meters from the stirrups of his squadmates on either side, half a length from the dog before and behind. Triple gaps between companies, the company pennant, signaler and commander in each. An Armory rifle in a scabbard before each right knee, and a long slightly-curved saber strapped to the saddle on the other side.

The men wore round bowl-helmets with neckguards of chainmail-covered leather, dark-blue swallowtail coats, baggy maroon pants tucked into knee boots. Their mounts were farmbreds, Alsatians and Ridgebacks for the most part, running to a thousand pounds weight and fifteen hands at the shoulder. Everything regulation and by the handbooks, all the more startling because the men wearing the Civil Government uniforms were *not* the usual sort. The predominant physical type near East Residence was short, slight, olive to light-brown of skin, with dark hair and eyes. There were regional variations; Descotters tended to be darker than the norm, square-faced and built with barrel-chested solidity, while men from Kelden County were taller and fairer. The troops riding toward Raj and his companion were something else again. Big men, most near Raj's own

190 centimeters, and bearded in contrast to local custom; fair-skinned despite their weathered tans, many with blond or light-brown hair.

The massed thudding of paws and the occasional whine or growl was the only sound until a sharp order rang out:

"2nd Mounted Cruisers—eyes *right*. General salute!"

A long rippling snap followed, each man's head turning sharply and fist coming to breast as they passed Raj. Raj returned the gesture. It was still something of a shock to see the barbarian faces in Army uniform. Even more shocking to remember the Squadron host as it tumbled toward the line of Civil Government troops; individual champions running out ahead to roar defiance, shapeless clots around the standards of the nobles, dust and movement and a vast, shambling chaos . . .

The ones who couldn't learn mostly died, he thought.

The battalion commander fell out and reined in beside them as the column passed in a pounding of pads on gravel and a jingle of harness.

"Bwenya dai, seyhor!" Ludwig Bellamy said.

He's changed too, Raj thought, offering his hand after the salute. Karl Bellamy had surrendered early to the Expeditionary Force, to preserve his estates and because he hated the Auburns who'd usurped rule of the Squadron. His eldest son had gone considerably further; the chin was bare, and his yellow hair was cut bowl-fashion in the manner of Descotter officers. His Sponglish had always been good in a classical East Residence way—tutors in childhood—but now it had caught just a hint of County rasp, the way a man of the Messer class from Descott would speak. Much like Raj's own, in fact. The lower part of the Squadron noble's face was still untanned, making him look a little younger than his twenty-three years.

"Movement orders?" he said eagerly. "I'm taking them out—" he tossed his head in the direction of his troops "—on a field problem, but we could—"

"*No es so hurai,*" Raj said, fighting back a grin: *not so fast.* He had been a young, eager battalion commander himself, once. "But yes, we're moving. Stern Isle, first. You'll get a chance to show your men can remember their lessons in action."

"They will," Bellamy said flatly. Some of the animation died out of his face. "They remember—they know courage alone isn't enough."

They should, Raj thought.

Their families had been settled by military tenure on State lands as well, which meant their homes were here too.

"And they're eager to prove themselves."

Raj nodded; they would be. Back in the Southern Territories, they'd been members of the ruling classes, the descendants of conquerors. Proud men, anxious to earn back their pride as warriors.

I just hope they remember they're soldiers, *now,* Raj thought. Putting a *Squadrone* noble in command had been something of a risk; he'd transferred a Companion named Tejan M'Brust from the 5th Descott to command the 1st Cruisers. So far the gamble with the 2nd seemed to be paying off.

Aloud: "Speaking of education, Ludwig, I've got a little job for you, to occupy the munificent spare time a battalion commander enjoys. We'll be having a young man by the name of Cabot along."

The fair brows rose in silent enquiry.

"Cabot Clerett. I'd like—"

CHAPTER FOUR

The longboat's keel grounded on the beach, grating through the coarse sand. Sailors leaped overside into water waist-deep, heaving their shoulders against the planks of its hull. Raj vaulted to the sand, ignoring the water that seethed around his ankles, and swept his wife up in his arms to carry her beyond the high-tide mark. Miniluna and Maxiluna were both up, leaving a ghostly gloaming almost bright enough to read by even as the sun slipped below the horizon.

Offshore on a sea colored dark purple with sunset the fleet raised spars and sails tinted crimson by the dying light. Three-masted merchantmen for the most part, with a squadron of six paddle-wheel steam warships patrolling offshore like low-slung wolves. Not that there was much to fear; unlike the Squadron, who had been notable pirates, the Brigade didn't have much of a navy. Some of the smaller transports had been beached to unload their cargo; the rest were offloading into skiffs and rowboats. Except for the dogs. The half-ton animals were simply being pushed off the sides, usually with a muzzle on and fifteen or twenty men doing the pushing. Mournful howls rang across the water; once they were in, the intelligent beasts followed their masters' boats to shore. A few who'd been on the expedition against the Squadron jumped in on their own.

As Horace did; the big black hound shook himself, spattering Raj and Suzette equally, flopped down on the sand, put his head on his paws and went to sleep. Raj laughed; so did Suzette, close to his ear. He jumped when she ran her tongue into it briefly.

"When you start ignoring *me* even when I'm in your arms, my sweet . . ." she said playfully.

He walked a few steps further and set her down. In linen riding clothes, with a Colonial-made repeating carbine across her back, Suzette Whitehall did not look much like a Court lady of East Residence. But she looked very good to Raj, very good indeed.

"To work," he said.

The camp was already fully set up, a square half a kilometer on a side and ringed with ditch and earth embankment, and a palisaded firing-step on top. Within was a regular network of dirt lanes, flanked by the leather tents of the eight-man squads which were the basic unit of the Civil Government's armies. Broader lanes separated battalions, each with its Officers Row and shrine-tent for the unit standards. The two main north-south and east-west roadways met in the center at a broad open plaza, and in the center of *that* was a local landowners house that would be the commander's quarters. Dog-lines to the east, thunderous with barking as the evening mash was served; artillery park to the west; stores piled up mountainously under tarpaulins . . .

"Nicely done," he said. *And exactly where we camped the last time*, he thought, with a complex of emotions.

A tall rangy man with a moustache pulled up—on a riding steer, an unusual choice of mount. Especially for a man with a Colonel's eighteen-rayed gold and silver star on his helmet and shoulder-patches. The inflamed rims around his eyes told why; he was violently allergic to dogs. A misfortune for a nobleman, disastrous for a nobleman set on a military career. Unless one was willing to settle for the despised infantry, of course. Probably a source of anguish to the man, but extremely convenient to Raj Whitehall. Usually the infantry got the dregs of the officer corps, men without either the connections or the ability to make a career in the mounted units.

"Nicely done, Jorg," Raj repeated, as the man swung down.

Jorg Menyez shrugged. "We've had three days, and I haven't wasted the time we spent stuck down there around Port Murchison," he said. They saluted and exchanged the *embhrazo*. "Spirit of *Man* but I'm glad to be out of the Territories! Nineteen battalions of infantry, five of cavalry, thirty guns, reporting as ordered, *seyhor!* And campgrounds, food, fodder and firewood for five more battalions of mounted troops." He bowed over Suzette's hand. "Enchanted, Messa."

"Excellent," Raj said again. It was *damned* good to have subordinates you could rely on to get their job done without hand-holding. That had taken years.

indeed, Center said.

"All the old *kompaydres* together again, eh?" Jorg went on, as Gerrin Staenbridge came up. His eyes widened slightly as Ludwig Bellamy joined them, dripping.

"Sinkhole," the ex-member of the Squadron said, and sneezed.

"Make that sixty field guns, now," Grammek Dinnalsyn noted. "We brought another thirty, and some mortars. They may be useful."

"Staff meeting at dinner," Raj said. He toed Horace in the flank. "Up, you son of a bitch."

The hound sighed, yawned and stretched before rising.

❖   ❖   ❖

"To fallen comrades," Bartin Foley said, rising and offering the toast as junior officer present. The remainder were battalion commanders and up, two dozen men who would form the core of the Western Territories Expeditionary Force from this day on. Plus the Honored Messer Fidal Historiomo, the head of the Administrative Department team who would handle civil control, but he had been notably quiet.

"Fallen comrades," the others replied, raising their wineglasses as the servants cleared away the desserts which had followed the roast suckling pig and vegetables.

Raj rose in his turn. "Messers, the Governor!"

"The Governor!" Then they all stood. "To victory!" At that the wineglasses went cascading out the tall glass doors which stood open around three sides of the commandeered villa's dining room. A mild curse from one of the sentries followed the tinkle and crash of shattering crystal. A louder one followed, from his NCO.

The ladies withdrew in a flutter of fans and lace-draped head-dresses; ladies by courtesy, for the most part, of course. Except Suzette, and she stayed. Nobody looked surprised at that, except possibly Cabot Clerett, and *he* had been looking at her with a sandbagged expression all evening as she teased him gently out of shyness. The servants set out liqueurs and kave, and withdrew.

Raj rose and walked to a map-board on an easel that had probably served the local squire's daughter when she dabbled in watercolors, before the Civil Government armada landed. Now it held a tacked map of Stern Isle, a blunt wedge shape of about thirty thousand square kilometers. The bottom of the wedge pointed south, and the Expeditionary Force was encamped on the northern coast. It was an excellent map; the Civil Governments cartographic service was one of its major advantages over its barbarian opponents. Center could give him more data, in any form it pleased . . . although some of it was a thousand years old, the time-lag since Bellevue's surveillance satellites had died.

Silence fell as he took up a pointer. "All right, messers," he said quietly. "Most of you have campaigned with me before; those who haven't, know my reputation."

Which was why there had been a flurry of resignations and shifts of posting among the commands of units assigned to him. The first time he'd led an army in the field he'd broken one in six officers out of the service before the campaign even started. This time there had been plenty of officers volunteering for the slots opened; in fact, there had been duels and massive bribery to get *into* the Expeditionary Force. That had not happened the first time, out on the eastern frontier. The type who *wanted* to join a field force under Raj Whitehall's command presented their own problems, of course.

Better to be forced to restrain the fiery war-dog than prod the reluctant ox, he thought, and went on:

"Let me sketch out the general situation. We have eleven thousand

Regular infantry, about seven thousand Regular cavalry, since some of the battalions are overstrength, and about a thousand tribal auxiliaries. Mostly mounted. Including six hundred Skinners, who will be useful while there's fighting and a *cursed* nuisance the rest of the time." There were a few chuckles at that. "The Skinners will join us when and if we move to the mainland—leaving them on this island for any length of time would wreck it.

"The Brigade territories have a total population of about thirty million." Less than a third what the Civil Government did, but still a vast number for thirty-one battalions to attack. "Of those, the overwhelming majority are civilians."

Worshippers of the Spirit of Man of the Stars, and closely related to the population of the Civil Government proper. In theory, they— more importantly, the landowners, priests and merchants among them—would be on the invaders' side.

"One and a half million are *Brigaderos*. Unlike the late unlamented Squadron, the Brigade has a regular army, besides the private retainers of noblemen—some of whom have whole regiments, by the way. Fifty thousand of the General's troops are under arms at any one time; they have a system of compulsory service. Another two hundred thousand can be called out at need, not counting mercenaries—and all of them will have *some* military experience. The Brigade has strong enemy tribes on its northern frontiers, and most of their standing army has seen action.

"Furthermore," he went on, "also unlike the Squadron, the Brigade troops are *not* armed with flintlock smoothbores." Raj nodded to the orderlies standing in the back of the room. The men laid half-a-dozen long muskets on the table among the kave-cups.

"An external percussion cap fits under the hammer," he said, as the officers examined the enemy weapons. "It's loaded with a paper cartridge and a hollow-base pointed bullet, from the muzzle. Two rounds a minute, but the extreme range is up to a thousand meters. Note the adjustable sights. At anything under six hundred meters, it's man-killing accurate against individual targets. The *Brigaderos* are landed men, mostly, even those who aren't full-time soldiers. They like to hunt, and most of them are crack shots."

Which was more than could be said of the Civil Government force, especially the infantry, even after more than a year under Jorg Menyez' training.

Cabot Clerett stirred. Like his uncle, he was a square-faced, barrel-chested man. Unlike him he had the weathered look of an outdoorsman despite being in his twenties.

"The Armory rifle fires at better than six rounds a minute," he said. "Twelve, in an emergency."

"I'm aware of that, Major Clerett," Raj replied dryly. A flush spread under the natural olive brown of the younger man's skin. Suzette leaned close to whisper in his ear, and he relaxed again.

"However, it means we're not going to be able to stand in full sight and shoot them down outside the effective range of their weapons, the way we did with the *Squadrones*. Nor can we count on them simply rushing at us head-on, like a bull at a gate. They're barbarians and will fight like barbarians—"

They'd better, he added to himself, *or Center or not we're fucking doomed.*

"—but they won't be *that* stupid."

observe, Center said.

Rat-tat-tat beat the drum. The line of blue-coated Civil Government infantry stretched across the fields, wading through the waist-high wheat and leaving trampled desolation behind them. The battalion colors waved proudly ahead of the serried double rank of bayonets; officers strode before their units, sabers sloped over their shoulders. Sun glinted on edged steel, hot and bright. Shells went by overhead with a tearing-canvas sound, to burst in puffs of dirty-white smoke and plumes of black earth at the edge of the treeline ahead. Apart from the shelling and the crunching, rustling sound of the riflemen's passage, the battlefield was silent.

Then malignant red fireflies winked in the shadow of the trees. Thousands of them, through the offwhite smoke of black powder rifles. Men staggered and fell down the Civil Government line, silent or screaming and twisting. The Armory rifles jerked up in unison in response to shouted orders and volley-fire crashed out; then the bayonets leveled and the men charged forward with the colors slanting down ahead of them. More muzzle flashes from the treeline and the snake-rail fence that edged it, again and again, winking through the growing cloud of powder smoke and tearing gaps in the advancing line. It wavered, hesitated—trapping itself in the killing zone, caught between courage and fear.

Raj blinked. The audience was still attentive; it had only been a few seconds, and men were used to Raj Whitehall's peculiar moments of introspection. Night had fallen, and glittering six-winged insects flew in through the opened windows to batter themselves against the coal-oil lanterns along the pilastered wall.

"—so we have two problems, tactical and operational." *I get the strategic worries.*

"Tactically, we're going to have to make use of our strong points. Artillery, and we've twice the guns a force this size usually does. The Armory rifle's higher rate of fire and, even more important, the fact that it can be loaded lying down. Field entrenchments wherever possible; you'll note the number of shovels which have been issued. You'll also note that the cavalry have been ordered to hang their sabers from the saddle, not their belts. The cult of cold steel is strictly for the barbs, messers—I want nobody to forget that.

"Our true advantage is our discipline and maneuverability, and that applies to tactics *and* operations. I intend to move fast, keep the enemy off balance, and never fight except at a time *and* place of my own choosing. I need to know—*must* know that my orders will be obeyed with speed and precision *and* common sense, at all times. Against an enemy with respectable weapons and reasonable organization who outnumbers us eight or more to one, we cannot afford to lose a battle, we cannot afford to lose even a major *skirmish . . .* and since we can't possibly win a war of attrition, we can't be excessively cautious, either. Is that clear?"

Nods, and a few uncomfortably thoughtful faces. "Good." *Because it's all right if the* men *think I'm invincible, but the* Spirit *help us if you do.*

With Center whispering in his mind's ear, he was unlikely to fall victim to that illusion himself. Occasional doubts about his own sanity were another matter. Night sweats when he thought about the Spirit having a direct link to his own grimy soul were part of it, too—although come to think of it, *everyone* had a Personal Computer, according to orthodox doctrine.

"Which brings us," he went on, balancing the pointer with an end in each palm, "to Stern Isle. I regard this as in the nature of a training exercise—assuming that the negotiations with the Brigade leaders fail and we have to conquer the mainland. Because, gentlemen, if we can't take this island from the Brigade with dispatch, then we'd cursed well better blow our own brains out and send the troops home before we do *real* damage to the Civil Government.

"According to the Ministry of Barbarians' files and Colonel Menyez' scouting reports"—collated and interpreted by Center—"there are about twelve thousand *Brigaderos* males of military age on the island. No more than three thousand are actual professional fighting men, including those in the service of individual nobles. We'll snap the rural nobles and their retainers up with mobile columns. I want you messers to pay particular attention to perfecting movement from battalion to company columns and from column into line-of-battle in any particular direction. The enemy are fairly slow at that, and we'll need any advantage we can get.

"We'll then move the main body of the army south"—he traced the route across the center of the island—"to the provincial capital at Wager Bay. The city itself shouldn't be much of a problem; the enemy doesn't have enough men to hold the walls."

He flipped the map, revealing another of Wager Bay itself. Over it Center painted a holographic diagram, rotating it to show different angles. Raj blinked back to the flat paper his officers would see. The city was a C with the open end pointing south at the ocean, around a harbor that was three-quarters of a circle.

"Wager Bay; most of the island's trade goes through here. About

forty thousand people, virtually none of them *Brigaderos.* So, no
problem . . . except for the fortress."

His pointer tapped the irregular polygon which topped the hill
closing the east flank of the harbor. Raj had memorized schematic
drawings of all the major fortresses within the Civil Government,
and quite a few without. Center amplified that knowledge with
three-dimensional precision. Deep stone-lined moats all around and
a steep drop to the shingled beaches on the water side where an
arc of cliffs fronted the sea. Low-set modern walls of thick stone
and earthwork behind the moats, built to withstand siege guns.
They mounted scores of heavy built-up smoothbore guns, able to
sweep the bay. Bastions and ravelins, outworks giving murderous
crossfire all along the landward side, a smooth sloping approach
with neither cover nor dead ground.

"We're certainly not going to take *that* with a rush. But take it
we must, and soon."

observe, Center said.

—and ships sailed into Wager Bay, their blunt wooden bows casting
back plumes of white spray from blue ocean; whitecaps glittered
across the broad reach of the harbor. There was a stiff breeze, enough
to belly out the brown canvas of the sails and snap the double lightning flash flag of the Brigade from every masthead. The decks were
black with troops, dozens of ships, thousands of men.

A Civil Government steam ram came butting through the waves,
water flinging back in wings from the steel beak just below the
surface at its bows, frothing away from the midships paddle-boxes.
Black coal smoke streamed from its funnel, and five more rams
followed behind. Behind them the city rose from the waterside in
whitewashed and pastel-colored tiers, its tile roofs glowing in the
sun. The fortress on its headland was built of dun-colored rock,
squatting like a coiled dragon on the heights. No cannon fired
from the water could reach that high, and the walls were broad
and squat and sunken behind their ditch, built to resist fire from
guns far heavier than the converted fieldpieces the rams carried
on their decks.

Guns as heavy as the ones mounted in the fort's casements. The
first of them boomed like distant thunder, a long rolling sound that
echoed from the cliffs and the facing buildings across the bay. The
sound of the shell passing was like thick sailcloth ripping, tearing
the sky. A long plume of smoke with a red spark at its heart blossomed from the bay-side wall of the fortification. The forty-kilogram
cast-iron cannonball was a trace of blur in the air, and then a fountain
of spray near one of the rams. The ships ignored the shot—the ranging shot, it must be—and kept on toward the Brigade transports a
kilometer away. Their formation began to open out, as each steamship
picked a target and fell out of line behind the leading vessel. A

whistle screeched a signal, and the flat huff*chuff* of their engines blatted louder as they went to ramming speed.

Staccato thunder rolled across Wager Bay. *BOOM-BOOM-BOOM-BOOM* as the cannon fired one after another at two-second intervals, then *bambambambambambambmmmm*—as the echoes slapped back and forth across the water. The whistling shriek of the projectiles was a diminuendo under the coarser sounds of the discharge. Suddenly the warships were moving amid a forest of waterspouts, dozens of them . . . except for the two ships that were struck.

The heavy cannonballs had been fired from mounts over a hundred meters above sea level. They were plunging almost vertically downward when they struck the plank decks of the ships. They went through the inch-thick decking without slowing perceptibly, sending lethal foot-long splinters of wood spinning like shrapnel across both flush decks.

One ship was struck near the stern. Some of the splinters flicked through the vision slit of the sheet-iron binnacle that was raised and bolted about the wheel and slashed the face off the steersman there. His convulsing body spun the wheel, but the ship was already turning so rapidly that it heeled one paddle almost out of the water; the cannonball had snapped and jammed the underdeck chains that connected wheel to rudder. The captain clinging to the bridge that crossed the hull between the paddle boxes could only watch in horrified fascination as the vessel's ram drove at full speed into the hull of the warship next to it—aimed with an accuracy no deliberate skill could have equaled. He was flung high by the impact, an instant before the steel tip of the ram gashed open the steamer's boiler. Beams, bodies and pieces of machinery fountained skyward.

The other ship hit by plunging fire had been struck amidships; its paddles froze in their boxes as the boiler rang and flexed and cracked along a rivet-line. Superheated steam flooded the tween-decks spaces, scalding men like lobsters in a pot. Water from the boiler shell cascaded down onto the glowing-hot coal fires in the brick furnaces beneath. It exploded into steam. That and the sudden flexing as ceramic shed heat into the water ripped the iron frames of the firebrick ovens apart like the bursting charge of a howitzer shell, sending them into the backs of the screaming black gang as they ran for the ladders. It also ripped ten meters of hull planking loose from the composite teak-and-iron frame of the warship; the vessel stopped dead in the water, heeled, and began to sink level as seawater gurgled into the engine room.

The cannon began to fire again, more slowly this time, and a little raggedly with the different reloading speeds of their crews. Another ship was struck, this time twice by rounds that crashed straight through the decking and deflected off major timbers to punch out through the hull below the waterline.

One of the warships turned back; the captain reversed one paddle-wheel and kept the other at full ahead, and the vessel spun about in almost its own length. The lead ram plunged forward into the midst of the Brigade ships. They were backing their sails to try and steer clear of it, but the Civil Government warship pirouetted with the same swift-turning grace that its sister had shown in fleeing. Cannon spoke from the bow as it lunged for the flank of a trans-port, and canister chopped the *Brigaderos* warriors along the near rail into a thrashing chaos. Then the whole transport surged away as the steel beak slammed home below the waterline.

Just before it struck, the Civil Government ram had backed its paddles, trying to pull the beak free. This time the heavy sailing transport rocked back down too quickly, and its weight gripped the steel of the underwater ram, pushing the warship's bow down until water swirled across its decks. Brigade marksmen picked themselves up and crowded to the rail, or swarmed into the rigging to sweep the steamer's decks.

Beyond, the rest of the relief force sailed forward to anchor under the fort's walls, protected by its guns, and men and supplies began to swarm ashore.

observe, Center said, and the scene changed:

—to night. Dark, with both moons down and only the stars lighting the advancing men. They moved silently up the long slope toward the landward defences of Fort Wager, carrying dozens of long scaling ladders and knotted ropes with iron grapnel hooks. Silent save for the click of equipment and breathing, and the crunch of hob-nailed boots on the coarse gravel soil beneath them.

Arc lights lit along the parapet with a popping crackle and showers of sparks. Mirrors behind them reflected the light into stabbing blue-white beams that paralyzed the thousands of advancing troops as thoroughly as the carbide lanterns hunters might use to jacklight a hadrosauroid. Less than a second later, nearly a hundred cannon fired at once, from the main fort wall, from the bastions at the angles and from the triangular ravelins flung out before the works. Many of the guns were of eight-inch bore, and they were firing case-shot, thin tin sheets full of lead musket balls. Multiple overlapping bursts covered every centimeter of the approaches, and most of the Civil Government troops vanished like hay struck by a scythe-blade. . . .

"We'll deal with the fortress when we come to it," Raj concluded. Acid churned in his stomach. "In the meantime, it's an early day tomorrow. Gerrin, you'll take half the 5th Descott and the 2nd Cruisers—"

"You think too much, my darling," Suzette whispered in the dark. "Well, Starless Dark take it, *somebody* has to," he mumbled, with an arm thrown over his eyes. The bedroom was dark anyway, and the arm could not block out the visions Center sent; nor the images his own mind manufactured.

They've got artesian water and supplies for a year in there, he thought. *How—*

"I can't tell you how to take the fort," Suzette said. "But you'll think of a way, my heart. Right now you need your sleep, and you can't sleep until you stop thinking for a while," Suzette's voice said, her voice warm and husky in the darkness, her fingers cool and unbearably delicate, like lascivious butterflies. "That I *can* do."

And for a while, thought ceased.

CHAPTER FIVE

"*Surely 'tis brave to be a king, And ride in triumph through Persepolis,*" Bartin Foley quoted to himself.

"Ser?" his Master Sergeant said.

"Nothing," the young officer replied; it was unlikely that the NCO would be interested in classical Old Namerique drama.

He bowed left and right and waved to the cheering citizens of Perino. Sprays of orange-blossom and roses flew through the air, making the dogs of the 5th Descott troopers behind him bridle and curvette; two hundred men and a pair of field-guns followed at his heels, less those fanning out to secure the gates and the warehouses. Perino was a pleasant little town of flat-roofed pastel-colored houses sloping down to a small but snug harbor behind a breakwater, and backed by lush vineyards and sulphur-mines in the hills. The walls were old-fashioned, high narrow stone curtains, but the inhabitants hadn't shown any particular desire to hold them against the Civil Government anyway—even the few resident *Brigaderos* had mostly been incoherent with joy when they realized the terms allowed them to retain their lives, personal liberty, and some of their property.

The town councilors had been waiting at the open gates, barefoot and with ceremonial rope nooses around their necks in symbol of surrender. The clergy had been out in force, too, spraying holy water and incense—orthodox clergy, of course, not the Spirit of Man of This Earth priests of the heretical Brigade cult, who were staying prudently out of sight—and a chorus of children of prominent families singing a hymn of welcome. One of them was riding on his saddlebow at the moment, in point of fact, held by the crook of his left arm. She was about eight, flushed with joy and waving energetically to friends and relatives; the wreath of flowers in her hair had come awry.

"Stop wriggling," he mock-growled under his breath. "That's an order, soldier."

The girl giggled, then looked at his hook. "Can I touch it?" she said.

"Careful, it's sharp," he warned. Children weren't so bad, after all. For that matter, he was the father of two himself, or at least had a fifty-fifty chance of being their father. It wasn't something he had expected so soon, not being a man much given to women. He grinned to himself; you couldn't exactly say he'd saved Fatima from a bunch of troopers bent on gang-rape and revenge for a foot in the testicles and an eye nearly gouged out, back at the sack of El Djem. More in the nature of the Arab girl insisting on being rescued, when she came running out ahead of the soldiers and swung him around bodily by the equipment-belt. It had been Gerrin who talked the blood-mad trooper with the bayonet in his hand into going elsewhere, with the aid of a couple of bottles of *slyowtz;* he'd wanted Bartin to get used to women, since he'd have to marry and beget for the family honor, someday.

Somehow the girl had kept up with them during the nightmare retreat from El Djem after Tewfik mousetrapped the 5th Descott and wiped out the other battalion with them; and she helped him nurse the wounded Staenbridge back to health in winter-quarters outside Sandoral. She'd been pregnant, and Gerrin—whose wife back home in Descott was still childless, despite twice-yearly duty-inspired visits— had freed her and adopted the child. Both children, now.

"Did you kill him with your sword?" the awestruck child went on with bloodthirsty enthusiasm, after touching the hook with one finger. They were nearly to the town plaza. "The one who cut off your hand."

"Possibly," Bartin said severely.

Actually, it had been a pom-pom shell, one of the last the enemy fired in the battle outside Sandoral. That had been right after he led the counterattack out of the command bunker, past the burning Colonist armored cars. Probably the enemy gun-crew had been slaughtered as they tried to get back to the pontoon bridge across the Drangosh.

Who can tell? he thought. There had been so many bodies that day; dead ragheads, all sizes and shapes, all dead; dead Civil Government soldiers too, piled in the trenches. Bartin Foley had been on a stretcher travelling back to the aid station in town.

"Right, we'll—" he began to the NCO beside him.

Crack. The bullet went overhead, far too close. *Crack. Crack. Crack.* More shots from the building to his left—the heretic Brigaderos church, it must be fanatics, holdouts.

Someone was screaming; a lot of people were, as the crowd scattered back into the arcades. The child whimpered and grabbed at him. Foley kicked his left leg over the saddle and vaulted to the ground.

"Take cover!" he shouted. "Return fire! Lieutenant Torridez, around and take them from the rear."

Armory rifles crackled, their sounds crisper than the Brigaderos' muskets. Foley dashed to the arcade opposite, his dog following in well-trained obedience; the officer shoved the girl into the arms of a matron with a lace mantilla who was standing quietly behind a pillar—unlike most of the civilians, who were running and shrieking and exposing themselves to the ricochets that whined off the cobblestones and the stucco of the buildings around the square. Without pausing he ran around the other side of the pillar and back into the square, pulling free the cut-down shotgun he wore in a holster over his right shoulder.

"Stay!" he ordered the animal. Then: "Follow me, dog-brothers!" A fat lead slug from an enemy musket plucked at the sleeve of his jacket as he ran, opening it as neatly as a tailor's scissors, and then he was in the shadow of the church portico.

A dozen troopers and an NCO were close behind him; the rest of the detachment were circling 'round behind the building, or returning fire on the roof and upper story from behind watering-troughs, treetrunks, overturned carts or their own crouching dogs. Bullets spanged and sparked off the stone overhead, and sulfur-smelling gunsmoke drifted down the street past the trampled flowers and discarded hats that the crowds had been waving a moment before.

Idiots, he thought. Sniping from a bell-tower; downward shots were difficult at best, and stood no chance of hitting another man *behind* your target.

"One, two, *three!*" he said.

Two of the troopers blasted the lock; metal whined across the colored tile of the portico, and someone shouted with pain. Foley ignored him, ignored everything but the tight focus that pulled everything into crystalline clarity in a tunnel ahead of him. They smashed through the tall olivewood doors of the barbarian church. He'd closed his eyes for just a second, and the gloom inside didn't blind him. A long room with wooden benches and a central aisle, leading up to an altar with the blue-and-white globe that the heretics substituted for the rayed Star of the true faith. Reliquaries along the walls under small high windows, holding the bones of saints or holy computer equipment from before the Fall.

And men coming down the stairs at either far corner of the room; evidently somebody had had a rush of intelligence to the head, a few minutes too late. Ten men, the leader in the blue jumpsuit and ear-to-ear tonsure of the Earth Spiritist clergy.

Foley took stance with his left arm tucked into the small of his back and the coach gun leveled like a huge pistol. *Whump,* and the hate-filled face of the Brigadero priest disappeared backward in a blur of red that spattered over the whitewashed walls. Buckshot shattered glass and peened off silver and gold around the altar; the Earth-Sphere tumbled in fragments to the floor. The massive recoil jarred at his leather-strapped wrist, and he let it carry the weapon high before gravity dropped it back on target. Two of the enemy returned the fire, the only ones with loaded muskets; one had been reloading, and his shot sent the iron ramrod he'd forgotten to remove spearing across the church to lance into a bench like a giant arrow. Neither hit anything, not surprising since they were snapshooting in a darkened room. The bullet thudded into wood.

Another man leaping over the dead priest, charging down the aisle with clubbed musket. *Careful*, a corner of Foley's mind thought. *Long musket, big man. Three-meter swing.* He waited, you were never too close to miss, and fired the left barrel of the coach gun into his belly. *Whump* again, and the man folded backward a meter, sprawling in a puddle of thrashing limbs and blood and intestines that spilled out through the hole the buckshot ripped. A swordsman leaped forward with his long single-edged broadsword raised; Foley threw the coach gun between his feet, and the man tripped—as much on the body fluids that coated the slick marble floor as the weapon. His blade clanged off the young officer's hook; then he spasmed and died as he tried to rise, the point of the hook going *thock* into the back of his skull.

Muzzle flashes strobed from around Foley, the troopers with him firing aimed rounds toward the stairwells. The last Brigadero tumbled, the revolvers falling from his hands before he could shoot.

Foley put a boot on the shoulder of the dead man before him and freed his hook with a grunt of effort. Overhead, on the second floor, came another crash of Armory rifles; screams, a spatter of individual rounds, then Torridez' shout:

"Second story and tower clear, sir!"

Foley took a long breath, and another; a band seemed to be locked around his chest. His throat was raw, but he knew from experience that taking a drink from his canteen would make him nauseous if he did it before his muscles stopped their subliminal quivering. The air stank of violent death, shit and the seaweed smell of blood and wet chopped meat, all underlain by decades of incense and beeswax from the church. It was a peculiarly repulsive variation on the usual battlefield stench.

Join the Army and see the world; then burn it down and blow it up, he thought with weary disgust. His aide picked up the coach gun and wiped it clean with his bandana.

"Cease fire!" Foley called out the door as he flicked the weapon open and reloaded from the shells in his jacket pocket; that was a knack, but you learned knacks for doing things if you lost a hand. "Cease fire!"

Soldiering wasn't a safe profession, but he didn't intend to die from a Civil Government bullet fired by accident. The plaza had the empty, tumbled look of a place abandoned in a hurry—although, incredibly, some civilians were drifting back already, even with the last whiffs of powder smoke still rising from the gun muzzles.

"Torridez?"

"Sir," the voice called down from overhead. "I've got men on the roofs, the whole area's under observation. Looks like it was only these barbs . . . their families are in the back rooms up here. Couple of men prisoner."

"Keep them under guard, Lieutenant," Foley called back. "Post lookouts at vantage points from here to the town wall. Sergeant, get me the *halcalde* and town councilors back here, and—"

A man came running down the arcade before the town hall, with several others chasing him. He was a Brigadero by the beard and short jacket; the pursuers looked like prosperous townsmen, in sashes and ruffled shirts and knee-breeches with buckled shoes. All of them had probably been standing side by side to greet him fifteen minutes ago.

"You! You there!" he called sharply, and signed to a squad seeing to their dogs.

The would-be lynch mob skidded to a halt on the slick brown tiles of the covered sidewalk as crossed rifles swung down in their path and the dogs growled like millstones deep in their chests; the Brigadero halted panting behind them. He blanched a little as Foley came up, and the young man holstered his coach gun over his shoulder and began dabbing at his blood-speckled face with his handkerchief.

"You've nothing to fear," he said, cutting off the man's terrified gabble. "Corporal," he went on, "my compliments to Senior Lieutenant Morrsyn at the gate, and I want redoubled guards on all Brigadero houses; they're to fire warning shots if mobs approach, and to kill if they persist."

He glanced around; the woman he'd handed off the child to was still pressed tightly into the reverse of her pillar, standing with the girl between her and the stone to protect the child from both sides.

Sensible, Foley thought. "You know her family?" he said.

"My cousins," the woman said quietly.

Foley followed her well enough, the Spanjol of the western provinces was closely related to his native Sponglish, unlike the Namerique of the barbarians . . . although he spoke that as well, and Old Namerique and fair Arabic.

"Take her home. You, trooper—escort these Messas." He stepped over the back of his crouching dog, and the animal rose beneath him. "Now, where the *Dark* are those—"

The *halcalde*—Mayor, the word was *alcalle* in Spanjol—and the councilors came walking gingerly back into the plaza a few minutes later, as if it were unfamiliar territory. They shied from the bodies laid out before the Brigade church, and the huddle of prisoners.

As they watched, troopers of the 5th were shaking loose the lariats most of them carried at their saddlebows and tossing them over limbs of the trees that fringed the plaza. Others pushed the adult males among the prisoners under the nooses; most of them were silent, one or two weeping. One youngster in his mid-teens began to scream as the braided leather touched his neck. Foley chopped his hand downward. The troopers snubbed their lariats to their saddlehorns and backed their dogs; the men rose into the air jerking and kicking. Nobody had bothered to tie their hands. One managed to get a grip on the rawhide rope that was strangling him, until two of the soldiers grabbed his ankles and pulled. Others tied off the ropes to hitching-posts.

Foley waited until the bodies had twitched into stillness before turning his eyes on the town notables. His dog bared its teeth, nervous from the smell of blood and taking its cue from its rider's scent; he ran a soothing hand down its neck. An irritable snap from a beast with half-meter jaws was no joke, and war-dogs were bred for aggression.

"Messers," he said. "You realize that by the laws of war I'd be justified in turning this town over to my troops to sack? I have a man dead and four badly wounded, after you yielded on terms."

The *halcalde* was still wearing the noose around his neck; he touched it, a brave man's act when a dozen men swung with bulging eyes and protruding tongues not a dozen meters from where he stood.

"The responsibility is mine, *seynor*," he said, in the lisping western tongue. "I did not think even Karl Makermine would be so foolish . . . but let my life alone answer for it."

Foley nodded with chill respect. "My prisoners—" he began; a long scream echoed from the church, as if on cue. "My prisoners tell me this was the work of the heretic priest and his closest followers. Accordingly, I'm inclined to be merciful. Their property is forfeit, of course, along with their lives, and their families will be sold. The rest of you, civilian and Brigaderos, will have the same terms as before—*except* that I now require hostages from every one of the fifty most prominent families, *and* the Brigaderos of Perino are to pay a fine of one thousand gold FedCreds within twenty-four hours. On pain of forfeiture of all landed property."

Some of the heretics winced, but the swinging bodies were a powerful argument; so were the Descotter troopers sitting their dogs with their rifles in the crook of their arms, or standing on the rooftops around the square.

"Furthermore, I'm in a hurry, messers. The supplies I specified—" to be paid for with chits drawn on the Civil Government, and you could decide for yourself how much they were really worth "—had better be loaded and ready to go in six hours, or I won't answer for the consequences. *Is that clear?*"

He watched them walk away before he rinsed out his mouth and then drank, the water tart with the vinegar he'd added. Another old soldier's trick.

"I should have gone into the theatre," he muttered.

❖   ❖   ❖

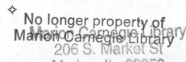

"Tum-ta-*dum*," Antin M'lewis hummed to himself, raising the binoculars again. The air was hot and smelled of dust and rock, coating his mouth. He spat brownly and squinted; with the wind in their favor, there wasn't much chance of being scented by the enemy's dogs.

There wasn't much ground cover here, in the center of the island. The orchards and vineyards that clothed the narrow coastal plain to the north, the olive groves further inland, had given way to a high rolling plateau. In the distant past it had probably been thinly forested with native trees; a few Terran cork-oaks were scattered here and there, each an event for the eyes in the endless bleakness. Most of it was benchlands where thin crops of barley and wheat were already heading out, interspersed with erosion-gullies. There were no permanent watercourses, and the riverbeds were strings of pools now that the winter rains were over.

The manor houses which dotted the coastlands were absent too; nobody lived here except the peon serfs huddled into big villages around the infrequent springs and wells. Like the grain, the profits would be hauled out down the roads to the port towns, to support pleasant lives in pleasant places far away from here. Flowing downhill, like the water and topsoil and hope.

Pleasant places like Wager Bay, which was where the long column ahead of him was heading, southeast down the road and spilling over onto the fields on either side in milling confusion. Dust smoked up from it, from the hooves of oxen and the feet of dogs and servants, and from the wheels of wagons and carriages.

"There goes t' barb gentry," M'lewis muttered to himself, adjusting the focusing screw.

Images sprang out at him; the heraldic crest on the door of a carriage drawn by six pedigree wolfhounds, household goods heaped high on an ox-wagon. Armed men on good dogs, in liveries that were variations on a basic gray-green jacket and black trousers; some were armored lancers, others with no protection save lobster-tail helmets, and all were armed to the teeth. He saw one with rifle-musket, sword, mace, lance and two cap-and-ball revolvers on his belt, two more thrust into his high boots, and another pair on the saddle. He made an estimate, scribbled notes—he had been a literate watchstander even before he met Raj Whitehall and managed to hitch his fortunes to that ascending star.

Behind him, a man whispered. One of the Forty Thieves, a new recruit from back home.

"D'ye think we'll git a chanst at t'women?"

A soft chuckle answered him. "Chanst at t'gold an' siller, loik."

M'lewis leopard-crawled backward, careful not to let the morning sun catch the lenses of his binoculars. The metalwork on the rifle slung across his elbows had been browned long ago and kept that way.

"Ye'll git me boot upside yer head iff'n ye spook's 'em," he said with quiet menace.

"Ser," the man whispered, and shut up.

M'lewis' snaggled, tobacco-stained teeth showed; he might not be messer-born, but by the *Spirit* he could make this collection of gallows-bait obey. Not least because the veterans had spent the voyage vividly describing all the booze, cooze and plunder they'd gotten in the last campaign to the recruits. He looked along the northeast-trending ridge that hid most of his command. The dogs hidden in the gully behind him were difficult to spot amid the tangled scrub, even knowing where to look. Most of the men were invisible even to him, spread out with nearly a hundred meters between each pair. He slid down to the brown dusty pebbles of the gully bottom; a little water glinted as his feet touched.

"Cut-nose, Talker," he called, very softly. There was a trick to pitching your voice so it carried just so far and no further. One of the many skills his father had lessoned him in, with a heavy belt for encouragement.

Two other men crawled backward out of a thicket, then stepped down from rock to rock, raising no dust. Cut-nose had lost most of his to a knife when he tried to sell a saddle-dog back to the man he stole it from, which was an example of the unwisdom of drinking in bad company; he was a second cousin of M'lewis, and looked enough like him to be a brother. Talker was huge, taller than a *Squadrone* and broad with it. A bit touched, perhaps— he'd pass up lifting a skirt or a purse to kill—but he knew his business.

And he was devoted to Raj, in his way. Where Messer Raj led, death followed.

"Here. Git thisshere t' the Messer, an' tell him. Quiet an' fast."

"Is this report completely reliable, sir?" Ludwig Bellamy asked.

Raj and Gerrin Staenbridge looked at him, blinking with almost identical expressions of surprise. Raj held out a hand to stop Gerrin from speaking, asking himself:

"Why would you doubt it?"

"Ahh—" Bellamy cleared his throat. "Well, this man M'lewis, he *was* a bandit. A man like that—how can we be sure he didn't take the easy way out and go nowhere near the enemy? Men steal because it's easier than working, after all."

Both the older men grinned, not unkindly. Raj gripped him companionably on the shoulder for an instant; Gerrin forbore, since he'd noticed his touch made the ex-*Squadrone* nervous.

"Oh, M'lewis was a bandit, all right—it's virtually hereditary, where he comes from," Raj explained. "It's just . . . well, he was a bandit in my home County."

Gerrin chuckled. "And if you think stealing sheep from Descotters is an easy living, Major . . . let's put it this way, I don't know any better preparation for hostile-country reconnaissance."

Bellamy smiled back. "If you say so, sir." He turned his attention to the map. "What are your plans, General?"

Raj looked up. Four companies of the 5th Descott, only half the unit since it was at nearly double strength, the whole of the 2nd Cruisers, and four guns; the dogs were crouched resting, and the men mostly squatting beside them. A few were watering their animals, drinking from their own canteens, or enjoying a cigarette. There was little shelter on this scorched plain, none at the dusty crossroads where they had halted. Nearly a thousand men, more than enough . . .

"Let me hear your plan, Major Bellamy," he said formally.

The younger man halted in mid-swallow, lowering the canteen and looking up sharply. Raj met his gaze with bland impassiveness, and Ludwig nodded once.

"Sir." He traced the line of the road with his finger. "Two thousand fighting men, according to the report. Say six thousand people in all, proceeding at foot pace. Hmmm . . . we don't summon them to surrender?"

Raj shook his head. Most of these were from the western end of the island, around the towns of Perino and Sala. He'd sent out flying columns to round up those willing to give in without a fight, promising to spare the lives, personal liberty and one-third of the landed wealth of anyone on the Brigade rolls who'd swear allegiance to the Civil Government. These Brigaderos ahead had heard the terms and decided to make for Wager Bay and the illusory security of its walls instead. Showing too much mercy was as bad as too little; he didn't need Center to show him the endless revolts he would face behind his lines, if men thought they could defy him and get amnesty for it. He had seventeen thousand troops to conquer a country of half a million square kilometers, full of fortified cities and warlike men. Best to begin as he meant to go on.

"They've had their chance," he said.

"Well, then," Bellamy nodded. "We don't want any of the men to get away even as scattered individuals; they might make it to Wager Bay. That column has to go *here*. They're not going to get wheeled vehicles across this ravine without using the bridge. We could—"

Henrik Carstens looked back over his shoulder. The dust-clouds were growing larger, three of them—one to either side of the road, one on it. *About four, maybe five clicks*, he decided, and a couple of hundred mounted men each at least. Distances were deceptive in these bare uplands, what with the dry air and heat-shimmer. Coming up fast, too; they were going to reach the column of refugees well before they crossed the bridge. Nothing it could be but enemy cavalry. He cursed tiredly and blinked against the grit in his bloodshot blue eyes, fanning himself with his floppy leather hat.

Sweat cooled for a second in the thinning reddish hair of his scalp, then the sun burned at his skin and he put it back on. The helmet could wait for a moment, he needed his brains functioning and not in a stewpot.

It was a pity. The bridge would have made a perfect spot for a rearguard to hold them off while the families and transport reached Wager Bay, or at least got within supporting distance of the patrols operating out of the city.

Of course, Captain of Dragoons Henrik Carstens would have ended up holding that rearguard anyway. He hawked and spat dust into the roadway. A man lived as long as he lived, and not a day more. Forty-five was old for someone who'd been in harm's way as often as he had, anyway. His battered pug-nosed face set, jaw jutting out under a clipped beard that was mostly gray.

The problem was that now he couldn't just hold a defensive line. The open wheatfields were no barrier to men on dogback, or even to field guns, not anywhere short of the bridge over the Trabawat. He'd have to maneuver to hold the enemy off the refugees long enough for them to get over the bridge.

And damn-all to maneuver with, he thought.

A hundred of the fan Morton family retainers, whom he'd managed to lick into some sort of shape since he signed on here. He'd expected a Stern Isle noble's household to be a good place for a nice quiet retirement, Stardemons eat his soul for a *fool.* The rest were fairly numerous, but they were odds-and-sods, household troopers more like guards and overseers than soldiers. Pinchpenny garrisons from here and there thrown in. *None* of them were worth the powder to blow them away! Carstens was from the northwest part of the Brigade territories, where many of the folk were pure-bred Brigade and only serfs spoke Spanjol. Hereabouts, some so-called unit brothers barely knew enough Namerique for formal occasions. To his way of thinking, even the Brigade members on the Isle were little better than natives.

His employer included. Fortunately Jeric fan Morton was in Wager Bay on business when the alert came, and his wife was worth two of him for guts and brains. Between them, she and Carstens had gotten most of the household out before the *grisuh* cavalry arrived, and the neighbors too.

"Gee-up, Jo," he said; the brindled Airedale bitch he rode took her cues from balance and voice, spinning and loping back down the column of fleeing Brigade members. The gait was easy, but the small of his back still hurt and the sun had turned his breastplate into a bake-oven, parboiling his torso in his own sweat.

Grisuh, he thought. Civvies, natives. Nobody in the Military Governments had taken them very seriously; hadn't their ancestors overrun the whole western half of the Civil Government without much trouble? Natives were fit only for farming, trading and paying taxes to their betters. The Civil Government made fine weapons, but they'd as soon pay tribute as fight. Heretic bastards besides. Carstens had fought the Squadron—not too difficult, they had more balls than brains—and the Guard, who had started out as a fragment of the Brigade who stayed in the north instead of migrating into the Midworld Sea lands generations ago. And the Stalwarts, who'd moved south from the Base Area in his grandfather's time; so primitive they were still heathen and fought on foot with shotguns and throwing axes, but terrifyingly numerous, fierce and treacherous. This would be the first time he'd walked the walk with civvie troops.

From what the bewildered Squadron refugees had been saying over the past year, counting out the *grisuh* was a thing of the past. Especially under their new war-leader, Raj Whitehall. Come to think of it, Whitehall had a Namerique sound to it . . .

He pulled up beside the fan Morton carriage. Lady fan Morton was in there with her teenage daughter and the other children. She shielded her eyes against the sun with her fan and leaned out to him, still dressed in the filmy morning gown she had worn when the courier had come into the manor on a dog collapsing from exhaustion.

"Captain?" she said.

"They're coming up on us fast, ma'am. We've got to get moving, and I'd appreciate it kindly if you'd talk to the other *brazaz*—" officer-class families "—because I need some men to slow them up."

Sylvie fan Morton's nostrils flared; she was still a fine-looking woman at thirty-eight, and Carstens had thought wistfully more than once that it would be nice if her husband fell off his dog and broke his neck. Which wasn't unlikely, as often as he went hunting drunk. She would make a very marriageable widow.

"I don't like the thought of running from *natives*, Captain," she said.

"Neither do I, ma'am," Carstens said sincerely. "But believe me, we don't have much time."

In the event, it took nearly half an hour to muster a thousand men, all mounted and armed—more or less armed, since some of the landowners skimped by equipping their hired fighters with shotguns instead of decent rifles. Good enough for keeping peons in order, but now they were going to pay in spades for their economizing. Or rather their men would pay, which was usually the way of it. That left a thousand or so to shepherd the convoy on.

"Spread out, spread out!" he screamed, waving his sword. The fan Morton men did, lancers to the rear and dragoons forward. For the others it was a matter of yelling, pushing and occasionally whacking men and dogs into position with the flat of his sword and the fists of his under-officers. Only the manifest presence of the enemy saved him from a dozen death-duels, and that barely. Two young noblemen *did* promise to call him out, when he had to pistol their dogs after the beasts lost their heads and started fighting. In the end, the Brigade men were deployed north-south. That gave him more than a kilometer of front at right-angles to the road, but it was thin, men stretched like a string of dark or steel-shining beads across the rolling cropland. He had no confidence in their ability to change front, and the worrisome clouds of dust to his right and left could still curl in behind him and strike for the refugees.

For the moment he had only the dust-cloud coming straight up the road. They ought to reach him first; if he could see them off for a while, he might be able to turn and counterpunch one of the side-columns before they could coordinate.

A man had to hope.

"Here they come," his second-in-command grunted beside him, pulling at his grizzled beard. "Still say we should have signed on for another go at the Stalwarts, boss."

"Shut up." Carstens raised his brass telescope, squinting through the bubbled, imperfect lenses. "Damn, they've got a cannon." Rolling along behind a six-dog hitch, with men riding several of the draught-dogs, on the carriage, and beside it. The rest of them in their odd-looking round helmets with the neck-flaps, riding in a column of fours. "No more'n a hundred. Must be their vanguard."

He licked his lips, tasting salty sweat and dust; Jo was panting like a bellows between his knees, and the day was hot. A brief vivid flash of nostalgia for the rolling green hills and oakwoods and apple-orchards of his youth seized him; he pushed it away with an effort of will and swung his own helmet on. The felt-and-cork lining settled around his head, the forehead band slipping into the groove it had worn over the years, and he pulled the V-shaped wire visor down and fastened the cheek-flaps. Those and the lobster-tail neckguard muffled sound and sight, but he was used to that. It would come to handstrokes before the day was over. He took a moment to check his pistols and carbine and glance back. With men prodding the oxen with sword-points, the convoy had gotten up some speed at the cost of shedding bits of load and stragglers.

An enemy trumpet-call, faint and brassy, answered by the whirring roar of his own kettledrums. Ahead the Civil Government column split; a moment later there were four smaller units coming at him, holding to a slow canter. Another movement, and the platoon columns swung open like the back of a fan. Less than two minutes, and he was facing a long line. Another trumpet, and the enemy stopped stock-still, the dogs crouched beneath the riders, and the men stepped forward with their rifles at the port. Muffled with distance, the actions went click*clack* as the troopers worked the levers and reached to their bandoliers for a round. *Clack* in unison as they thumbed a round home and loaded, marching without breaking stride.

Tiny as dolls with distance, like toy soldiers arranged with impossible neatness.

"Shit," Carstens mumbled into his beard. That was as smooth as the General's Life Guards on the parade-ground in Carson Barracks. Faster, too—Brigade troops would have stopped and countermarched to get into position. Aloud, he shouted:

"Dragoons, dismount to firing line!" The fan Morton men did, swinging out of the saddle and forming up two deep, one rank kneeling and one standing. Few of the others did anything but watch.

"Martyred Avatars bleeding *wounds!*" he screamed, riding out in front of the straggling line. "Everyone with a fucking rifle, get ready to shoot!"

He sheathed his sword and pulled out his own carbine, thumbing back the hammer. He also heeled his dog behind the firing line; no way was he going to have his ass out in front of *this* lot when they pulled their triggers.

"Wait for the word of command. Set your sights, set your sights!"

A rifle could kill at a thousand meters, but only if you estimated the range right—the natural trajectory of the bullet was above head-height past about three hundred, so you had to elevate the muzzle and *drop* the bullet down on your target. That was why some commanders preferred to wait until two-fifty meters or less; Carstens did himself, unless he were facing one of the huge densely-packed Stalwart columns where a bullet that missed one man would hit another. Here—

Shots banged out along the line. "Hold your fucking *fire,*" he screamed again. At nine hundred meters distance the Civil Government line was utterly undamaged. A shouted order, and the enemy all went to ground, first to one knee and then prone. Carstens felt his testicles drawing up. He'd been in this position before from the other side, facing Stalwart warbands with greater numbers but no distance weapons. The enemy rifles could be loaded while a man was flat on his belly, while his rifle-muskets had to have the shot rammed down their muzzles.

As if to punctuate his thought, a volley crashed out from the enemy, *BAM-BAM-BAM-BAM* as the platoons fired in unison. Greasy off-white smoke curled up from their positions, then drifted away in the scudding breeze. Something went whirrr-*brack* past his ear. Dogs and men screamed in pain and shock, mostly among those still mounted, but a few in the firing-line as well.

"Fire!"

An unnecessary order, and a ragged stutter sent demon-scented fog back into his face. His men had barely grounded their muskets and reached for a paper cartridge when the next enemy volley came. Another after they'd bitten open the cartridges and poured powder and minié bullet down the barrels; a third as they pulled out their ramrods. Just then a dull *POUMPF* came from the enemy field-gun, fifteen hundred meters back and well out of small-arms range. A tearing whistle and a *crack* of dirty smoke in mid-air, not twenty meters ahead of his riflemen; half a dozen were scythed down by the shrapnel. Then the Brigade warriors were capping their weapons and firing again—he ground his teeth as he saw a few ramrods go flying out toward the enemy—and beginning the cumbersome task of loading once more. Three more enemy volleys cut into his makeshift command; he could see men looking nervously backward out of the corners of his eyes.

He wasn't particularly worried about that, though. Raw courage was not the quality in short supply here today, and he'd also loudly ordered his lancers to ride down any man who fled without permission.

"Remember it's your families we protect," he called, keeping his voice calm. "One more volley and we'll—"

POUMPF. This time the tearing-canvas sound went right overhead, and the shell went *crack* sixty meters behind him. Dogs reared, then whimpered as their riders sawed on reins that connected to levers on the bridles, pressing steel bars against the animals' heads.

One under, one over, and I know *what comes next,* Carstens thought. His head whipped from side to side; the dust-columns weren't closing in as fast as he'd feared, and neither was the one behind the enemy vanguard. That heartened him, since it was the first mistake the civvies had made.

"—one more volley and we'll give them the steel."

He touched toes to Jo's forelegs, signaling her to stock-stillness, and fired his own rifled carbine. More as a gesture than anything else, but it made him feel better. A little.

"Everybody mount up," he called, riding out in front again. Enemy bullets pocked the earth around him.

POUMPF-*crack.* This time the shell burst right over the position he'd been in a few minutes before. Shrapnel skeened off body armor and tore into flesh; pistol-shots followed as injured dogs were put down. The wounded men probably wished they rated the same mercy, but needs must. Jo hunched her back slightly and laid her ears down at the sounds of pain.

"Easy, girl, easy," he said. He drew a revolver in one hand and his basket-hiked broadsword in the other. No sense in getting too subtle, just get out in front and wave them forward. *"Charge!"* he shouted, and the ancient Brigade warcry: *"Upyarz!"*

His legs clamped on the barrel of his dog. Jo howled and leaped forward off her hindquarters, building to a flexing gallop. From the chorus of shrieks behind him, human and canine, most of the scratch force were following. The *grisuh* dragoons rose and fired a volley standing; then half of them turned and trotted back to their dogs. Another volley, and they were all mounted and wheeling away. Behind them the gunners were adjusting their weapon, and a shell raced by to throw up a poplar-tall column of black dirt with a spark at the center. Men and dogs and parts of both pinwheeled away from it. The gun crew fired a final round of canister that cut a wedge out of the Brigade line as cleanly as a knife. The Civil Government troops were trotting to the rear now, heeling their mounts into a canter and then a gallop with the same fluid unison that had disturbed him before. The gunners snatched up the trail of their fieldpiece as it recoiled, running it back onto the caisson and jumping aboard as the team-master switched his mount into motion.

"Shit," Carstens said again. Lanceheads were bristling down on either side of him, but the enemy had had plenty of warning, and their dogs were fresher and less heavily burdened. The distance closed to a hundred meters, still beyond mounted pistol shot— and several of the blue-coated, dark-faced troopers turned in their saddles to pump fists at the Brigade troops with an unmistakable single finger raised. Then the gap began to grow again, with increasing speed. The fieldgun was a little slower, but it had had an extra half-kilometer of distance to start with.

He looked left and right, standing in the stirrups. Yes. Those tell-tale dust-clouds *were* closing in, moving fast past him on either side. He could catch the first winks of sunlight on metal from both directions. Plus the men he was chasing were retreating toward a force of unknown size.

"Halt, *halt!*" he shouted. The fan Morton house-troopers halted as the family pennant did, beside Carstens . . . but big chunks of the motley host kept right on pursuing.

"Tommins, Smut, Villard," Carstens snapped to his under-officers. "Stop 'em, *and fast.*"

He spurred his dog out ahead of the closest pack, curving in front of them and waving his sword in their faces. That made some of them pull up, at least.

"*Ni, ni!*" a Squadron refugee-mercenary shouted in their thick guttural dialect of Namerique. "No! The cowards flee!"

The man was literally frothing into his beard; Carstens wasted no time. The point of his broadsword punched into the man's stomach through the stiff leather and doubled him over with an *ooff* of surprise. His dog started to snap in defense of its master, but Jo already had her jaws around its muzzle; it whined and licked hers in surrender as the *Squadrone* fell to the ground vomiting blood.

Carstens felt no regret; you had to stop a rout before it got started, and a rout forward was just as bad as one going to the rear. *No wonder they lost,* he thought of the Squadron. Although the mindset was not unknown among the Brigade, either. He'd just had too much experience to keep up that sort of illusion.

"How many have we?" he asked his second-in-command, when they had the band mostly turned around and trotting to the rear.

"Seven hundred, maybe fifty more," the man said. "Fifty dead 'r down, and two hundred kept after the civvies."

Carstens grunted, grunted again when rifle fire broke out anew over the rise a kilometer to their rear where the pursuit had gone. What the incurably reckless had thought was a pursuit, at least. More rifle fire than before, much more, twice as many guns. "We won't be seeing them again," he said.

"Nohow," the other man agreed. "But the civvies will be up our ass again in half an hour."

Carsten pushed back his visor and looked northeast and southwest. Then he blinked dust out of his eyes and unlimbered the telescope again, on one flanking force and then the other.

"Suckered, by the Spirit!" he said.

At a soundless question, he went on: "Fucking *grisuh* were dragging bush to make more dust—look, there's troops there, but not anything like what they seemed. *Eh bi gawdammit!* Now they've dropped it and they're making speed, see the difference in the dust-plume? I *thought* they were co-ordinating too slow."

The Civil Government company had been dangled out like a chunk of meat in front of a carnosauroid, and now a much bigger set of jaws were closing on the outstretched head. On his whole force, if he hadn't pulled back.

"We still delayed them," his second said.

Faint thunder rolled from a dear sky. Coming from the southeast, down the road toward the bridge. Field guns; Carstens' trained ear counted the tubes, separating the sound from the echoes.

"Four guns," he said hollowly. Men were shouting and calling questions to each other all along the rough column. The alarm turned to panic as a burbling joined the deeper sound of the cannon. Massed rifles volleying.

"Bastards are ahead of us," the second-in-command said. His voice was calm, the information had sunk in but not the impact. "At the bridge, waiting at the bridge."

"Hang on, Sylvie!"

The Brigade warriors rocked into a gallop behind him.

"Well done, Major Bellamy," Raj Whitehall said, clapping him on the back. He raised his voice slightly. "Very well done, you and your men."

The headquarters company of the 2nd Cruisers raised a roaring shout at that, Bellamy's name and Raj's own, crying them hail.

"And you too, Gerrin," Raj went on, as the three senior officers and their bannermen turned to ride down the length of the refugee column.

One or two of the wagons were burning—that always seemed to happen, somehow—but most were in place, looking slightly forlorn with their former owners sitting beside them with their hands clasped behind their necks under guard. Or off digging hasty mass graves for the tumbled bodies, stacking captured weapons, the usual after-battle chores. The smoke smelled of things that should not burn, singed hair and cloth.

"It was young Bellamy's plan," Gerrin said. "And a damned sound one, too." He nodded to where a priest-doctor and his assistants were setting up, with a row of stretchers beside them. As they watched, the first trooper was lifted to the folding operating table. "Not many for the butcher's block, this time."

Ludwig flushed with pleasure and grinned. "The 5th carried off the difficult part, drawing away their rearguard," he said. "My boys just had to stand in the gully and shoot over the edge when they tried to rush the bridge."

A dispatch rider pulled up in a spray of gravel, his dog's tongue hanging loose. He wore the checkered neckcloth of the 5th Descott over his mouth as a shield against the dust. When he pulled it down the lower part of his face was light-brown to the caked yellow-brown of his forehead.

"Ser!" he saluted.

Staenbridge took the papers, opened them at Raj's nod. "Ah, good" he said. "From Bartin. Perino and Sala are secured. A few minor skirmishes; terms of surrender, hostages, supplies on the way—the usual."

He flipped to the other papers. "And the same from Ehwardo, Peydro and Hadolfo," he said, listing the other flying-column commanders. "The cities of Ronauk and Fontein opened their gates and tried to throw a party for the troops. Jorg back at base reports civilian and Brigaderos landowners coming in by the dozens to offer submission."

They were coming up to the head of the refugee column; the smell of powdersmoke still hung here, and of death. Flies swarmed in black mats, drawn by the rotting blood and meat already giving the hot day a sickly odor; hissing packs of waist-high bipedal scavenger sauroids waited at the edge of sight for living men to depart, their motions darting and impatient. Leathery wings soared overhead, spiraling up the thermals, and the ravens were perched on wagons. An occasional *crack* came as riflemen finished off wounded dogs, or Brigade warriors too badly hurt to be worth the slave-traders' while. Nearly to the front of the column was a huge tangle of dead men and mounts, with lances and broken weapons jutting up from the pile. Near the center was a man in three-quarter armor, lying with his sword in hand and his drying eyes peering up at the noonday sun. Lead had splashed across his breastplate, and blood from the three ragged holes that finally punched through the steel.

That armor really did seem to offer some protection, at extreme range and against glancing shots. Raj reflected it was just as well he'd ordered brass-tipped hardpoint rounds for this campaign as well as the usual hollowpoint expanding bullets. Generally those were sauroid-hunting ammunition, but they'd serve very well.

"They died fairly hard, here," he said. "What's your appraisal, messers?"

Bellamy shrugged. "Up at the bridge they charged us and we shot them," he said. "When they ran away, we chased them and shot them." He waved a hand at the scattered clumps of Brigaderos dead out over the fields. The ones away from the convoy were already seething with winged and scaled feasters.

Gerrin ran a thoughtful finger over his lips. "Rather better at my end," he said. "Those rifle-muskets of theirs do carry. And their unit articulation was much better than the *Squadrones*— particularly considering this was a thrown-together job lot of landowners' household troops. Some of the individual units worked quite well; they all stood fire, and *some* of them even managed a retreat when it seemed called for. Which is why I didn't get the whole of their rearguard."

He paused. "That was this fellow, I think," he said, nodding at the armored corpse and the banner that lay across his legs. "From the way they acted, I'd say their usual tactic was to push their dragoons forward to pin you with fire and hit you in the flank with the cuirassiers. I wouldn't like to take a charge of those lancers while I was in the saddle, my oath, no. The damned things are three meters long. And that heavy cavalry would be a nasty piece of work in a melee. They didn't have enough drilled troops to do it here, but I doubt we'll have as easy a time in the west."

Raj nodded. "That's about what I thought," he said. "Remember the old saying: *a charging Brigadero would knock down the walls of Al Kebir.*" A little of the animation died out of Bellamy's face.

"Still, a good day's work," Raj said judiciously. "Ludwig, I'm leaving you this sector; push some patrols down the road, and find out how much of a perimeter whoever-it-is in Port Wager is trying to hold. I doubt he'll even try to hold the city. We've taken the island in less than four days; these here were the only ones we'd have had to worry about, and they make a good negative example to contrast with those who surrendered in time."

Some of the Scout Troop were living up to their informal name; the loot in the bulk of the column was being tallied for later distribution, but several of the Forty Thieves were slitting pouches and pulling rings off fingers—or cutting off the fingers, and ears with rings in them—as they moved among the enemy dead. Men riding to what they think is sanctuary will take all their ready cash with them. One big Scout was ignoring the dead. Every time he came to a man still breathing he took him by the chin and the back of the head and twisted sharply. The sound was a tooth-grating crunch.

Several other troopers surrounded a carriage at the very front of the column; beyond it was only the drift of enemy dead where they'd charged for the stone-built bridge, and gunners policing up their shell casings. Those around the coach were a mixed group from the 5th Descott and the 2nd Cruisers. Dead wolfhounds lay in the traces, and a cavalryman was sitting at some distance having a gunshot wound in one shoulder bandaged. Another jumped up to the running board and ripped open the door, then tumbled backward with a yell as the pointed ferrule of a parasol nearly gouged out his eye.

"*Scramento,*" the man yelled, clapping a hand to the bleeding trough in his face.

His comrades laughed and hooted. "*Hole* for the pihkador, Halfonz!" one of them cried, slapping his thigh. "Lucky fer ye t'hoor didn't hev anither derringer."

A huge 2nd Cruiser trooper batted the parasol aside with one hand and reached in with the other to pitch the wielder out; she was a tall buxom woman in her thirties, richly dressed in layers of filmy silk. A teenager followed her, shrieking like a rabbit as the big soldier's strength tore loose her frantic grip on the carriage and set it rocking.

He looked inside, holding the girl three-quarters off the ground despite her thrashing. "*Ni mor cunne,*" he grunted in Namerique. "*Kinner iz.*"

"*Ci,* just kids," a Descotter said, and slammed the door shut again.

The older woman was hammering at the Cruiser with two-handed strokes of her umbrella. The man she had nearly blinded came up behind her and ripped her gown down to the waist, pinning her arms and exposing her breasts, then kicked her feet from under her.

"Hold 'er legs, ye dickheads," he said irritably. Two did, spreading them wide and back as he tossed up her skirts and ripped off the linen underdrawers. Blood from his face wound spattered her breasts as he knelt, but she did not begin to scream until her daughter was thrown down beside her.

Raj heeled Horace to one side with a slight grimace of distaste. War was war, and soldiers soldiers. He'd had men hung for murder and rape in friendly territory, or towards enemies who'd surrendered on terms—crucified men for plundering a farm on Civil Government territory, once. Very bad for discipline to let anything like that go by. The sullen resentment he'd meet if he tried to deprive men of their customary privileges towards those who *hadn't* surrendered on terms would be even worse for order and morale. Besides which, of course, all the prisoners in this convoy were going to the slave markets—to domestic service or a textile mill if they were very lucky, more probably to die in the mines or building Governor Barholm's grandiose new temples, dams, railroads and irrigation canals.

"Shall I send everything back to base, then?" Staenbridge said, waving a hand toward the convoy.

"No," Raj said. "We'll be moving to someplace with a harbor soon. Just take them back a village or two, somewhere with good water; we'll pass you by and pick you up with the baggage train. And it'll be a good object lesson for the district."

"*Ci*," Ludwig Bellamy said. "When Messer Raj offers you terms, you take them. Or get your lungs ripped out your nose. Sure as fate; sure as death." Gerrin nodded somberly.

Raj looked up. *Perfect sincerity,* he thought. Center confirmed it wordlessly with a scan of face-temperature, bloodflow, voice-tension and pupil dilation.

It bewildered him sometimes, that such men would move so willingly into his orbit and live for his purposes. He could understand why someone like M'lewis followed him, more-or-less. But Ludwig Bellamy could have gone home to the Territories and lived like a minor king on his estates, and Staenbridge had more than enough in the way of charm and connections to get a posting in East Residence, not too far from the bullfights, the opera and the better restaurants. Raj knew why he did what he did; he would always do what he thought of as his duty to the Civil Government of Holy Federation and the civilization it protected. He also knew that that degree of obsession was rare.

i know the reason, raj whitehall, Center said. **but although you know what you do, you will never understand all the effect it has on others, and while i can analyze it, i cannot duplicate it. for this, as much as any other factor, i chose you and trained you to be what you are.**

Raj neck-reined Horace about. The escort platoon fell in behind him. The day was getting on for half-done, with a mountain of work yet to do, he should look in on the wounded, they liked that, poor bastards—and Suzette was waiting for him back at base-camp.

"Ah, general," Bellamy said. Raj leaned back in the saddle and Horace halted with a resentful wuffle. He tried to sit, too, until Raj gave him a warning heel. The blond officer's voice dropped, even though nobody else was within normal hearing.

"You remember you told me to strike up an acquaintance with young Cabot?"

Who is fully three years your junior, Raj thought "Yes?" he said.

"I did. A very . . . energetic young man. Intelligent, I'd say. Brave, certainly."

"And?"

"And . . . we were drinking one night on the voyage. He commiserated with me, saying he knew how it was, to be forced to serve an enemy of one's family."

"Ah," Raj said. "Thank you again, Ludwig."

"I'll probably hoist a few with him again, sometime, Messer." A shrug. "He knows some remarkably good filthy drinking songs, too."

CHAPTER SIX

"Thank you, thank you," Suzette said. Her servants bore out the glittering heap of gifts. "You have nothing to fear, messas, nothing at all. The proclaimed terms are open for *everybody*."

The crowd of women looked at her desperately, willing themselves to believe. Most of them were civilian landowners' wives, with a fair sprinkling of *Brigaderos* magnates' spouses; they came in a clump, for mutual protection. She smiled at them, willing gracious reassurance. They seemed to take some comfort that the fearsome Raj Whitehall had brought an actual wedded wife along with him; it made him seem less of the ogre who had slashed the neighboring Squadron into oblivion in one summer's campaign.

"But," she went on, "your husbands really will have to come in themselves. Or I can't answer for what will happen to you and your families. And that is the final word."

Suzette sighed and sank back on her chair as the whispering clump left the room; it was an upper chamber of the little manor house. She fanned herself against the mingled odor of perfume and fear, until the sea-breeze dispelled it and left only a hint of camp-stink in its place. This was the second time the Whitehalls had stayed here. The jumping-off camp for the Southern Territories campaign had been on this spot, although the Brigade had been neutral in that war. Those memories were far from uniformly happy.

At her feet, Fatima cor Staenbridge strummed her *sitar*. The *cor* meant that she had been legally freed from chattel-slave status; it was followed by her patron's name, because that relationship carried a number of obligations.

"Strange," she said, in Sponglish that now carried only a trace of throaty Arabic accent "They come to plead for their men, yes?"

"Yes," Suzette said. "It's a tradition, rather out of date, but the customs here on Stern Isle are like the clothes, a generation behind

East Residence. I take it they wouldn't have done so back in the Colony?"

Fatima laughed. She was dressed in the long pleated skirt, embroidered jacket and lace mantilla of an East Residence matron of the middle classes, but she had the oval face and plump prettiness of Border Arab stock from the desert oases south of Komar. After two children, only her consistent practice of her people's dancing—what outlanders called belly-dancing—kept her opulence within bounds.

"Muslim general throw them to his men as abandoned women," she said. "Muslim man cut off his wife's nose rather than take life from her hands after she see enemy with face uncovered."

"Interesting," Suzette said.

And rather appalling. Our own men are bad enough, most of them, sometimes.

One of the few men she knew who had little or no false pride of that sort was Gerrin Staenbridge—which was understandable, all things considered. It made him disconcertingly hard to fool, more so even than Raj, and Raj had grown disturbingly, delightfully insightful over the past four years. She glanced down at Fatima; the Arab girl had had an interesting life so far as well. The rather bizarre menage a trois she'd fallen into seemed to suit all parties, though. Gerrin got the children he'd wanted, and which a nobleman needed; he and Bartin both got a willing woman at the very, very occasional times they desired one—Bartin more often than Gerrin, but then he was much younger; and Fatima acquired the legal status of an acknowledged mistress and mother of acknowledged heirs to a wealthy nobleman.

Certainly better than what the other women of El Djem were undergoing now; most of them were probably dead. If Fatima ever desired something more passionate than the avuncular/brotherly relationship she had with Gerrin and Bartin, she never showed it. *Of course, she was harem-raised.* And the despised daughter of a minor concubine at that.

"I have a problem," she said. "With young Cabot."

Fatima sat erect, bright-eyed. Suzette and Raj had stood Starparents to her children, a close bond, and had sponsored her into the Church. "Anything I can do, my lady. I poison his food?"

"No, no," Suzette laughed. *Actually, my dear, when I need poisons I have Ndella or Abdullah.* "I need *advice* about him. He grovels at my feet, but he talks to you, occasionally; you're more nearly his age, and you aren't born Messa."

"He want you, and he hate Raj," Fatima said. "His uncle would send Raj the bowstring—" she fell back into Arabic for that phrase "—if he did not need him so much."

Suzette nodded. The Arab girl continued more slowly: "His uncle hate and fear Raj. Cabot, he hate and envy Raj. Envy his victory in war, envy that the soldiers love and fear Raj as he were All—, ah, as he were the Spirit of Man." She frowned. "He would not be bad young man, if he not an enemy."

The East Residence patrician chuckled: "My dear girl, you've lived among us of the Civil Government for years and not noticed that the *definition* of a bad man is someone who belongs to the other faction?"

"Oh," Fatima said, with her urchin grin, "Arab think that way too." More seriously, she continued: "The *Sultan al'Residance*, he would kill Raj for spite. Young Cabot, he would *be* Raj if he could. Want his fame, want his glory, his followers. Want his woman— not just open her legs, but have her love. He want all. That why he must think bad of Raj, but can't be away from him either; he think to learn from him, then take all that is his. But maybe in deepest heart, he love Raj like other soldiers do, and hate himself for love."

"You," Suzette said, chucking Fatima under the chin, "are a remarkably perceptive young lady."

"I learn from you, Lady Whitehall. Gerrin talk to me a lot too, and I learn," she replied. Her head tilted to one side. "Why is it, lady, that man who want bed woman all the time, very much, what's the word?"

"*Muymach.*"

"Ah. Muymach man, often not want to *talk* to woman? Like, oh, Kaltin?"

"Kaltin Gruder's a loyal Companion," Suzette said. *Who hates my guts, but that's neither here nor there.* Kaltin Gruder had lost a brother and acquired scars external and mental in Raj's service, but he remained very . . . straightforward. Intelligent, but not subtle.

"Yes, a man-of-men. I friend with his concubine; they say he like bull in bed, but they lonely—he never *talk* to them. Back home," she went on, "man never talk to woman, not even father to daughter."

"And I have the best of both worlds," Suzette said with a fond smile for an absent man. "Do keep talking to Cabot," she went on. "You've been very helpful."

She touched a handbell. The door opened and a man looked through; for effect with the locals, he was dressed in his native costume of jellabah and ha'aik, with a long curved dagger and sheath of chased silver thrust through his belt. The Star amulet around his neck was protective camouflage; Abdullah al'Azziz had been born a Druze, and was authorized by the tenants of his own faith to feign the religion of any region in which he lived. Suzette had seen him imitate an Arab sheik of Al Kebir, a Sufi dervish, a fiercely orthodox Star Spirit-worshipping Borderer from the southeastern marchlands of the Civil Government, an East Residence shopkeeper, and a wandering scholar from Lion City in the Western Territories. No, not imitate, *be* those things. Though she had saved him and his family from slavery, she suspected that the man served her as much for the opportunity to use his talents as from gratitude.

"Who's next, Abdullah?" She switched to Arabic; hers was far better than Fatima's Sponglish, and the tongue was little known this far west outside enclaves of Colonial merchants.

"A lord of the Brigade, *saaidya*," he said. "And the merchant Reggiri of Wager Bay."

"Ah," Suzette said, frowning. "The *Brigadero*, my Abdullah; does he give his name?"

"No, lady. He is of middle years, with more grey than black in his beard, and wears a bandana, thus." The Druze covered his lower face. "He seeks to show humility but walks like a man of power; also a man who rides much. The guards hold him in an outer room."

"I'll bet they do," Suzette murmured.

Reggiri has the information we need, she thought. He'd been most generous with information before the invasion of the Southern Territories, information he'd gotten through his trading contacts. Crucial information about Squadron movements. *Of course,* she thought coldly, *he was paid in full, one way or another, after that little supper-party of his I attended. Doubtless he'd like another installment.*

Decision crystallized. "Bring the Brigadero. Send refreshment and entertainment to Messer Reggiri and tell him . . . ah, tell him my chaplain and I are Entering my sins at the Terminal." *He would laugh at that. Let him.* He would be far from the first man she'd had the final and most satisfying laugh on.

The Brigadero entered between three of the 5th Descott troopers assigned as her personal bodyguards. He was a stocky man, not tall for one of the barbarians, and wrapped in a long cloak. Together with the bandana and broad-brimmed leather hat, it was almost comically sinister. Conspicuous, but effective concealment for all that.

"Thank you, Corporal Saynchez," she said. "You searched him for weapons, of course."

"Yis, m'lady," the noncom said in thick County brogue. "Says ye'll know him an' wouldna thank ussn fer barin' his face."

"You can leave, now. Wait outside."

"No, m'lady," the man said. He stood three paces to the rear of the stranger, with drawn pistol trained. The other two rested their bayoneted rifles about a handspan from his kidneys.

A dozen generations of East Residence patricians freighted her words with ice:

"Did you hear me, corporal?"

"Yis, m'lady."

"Then *wait out in the hall.*"

"No, m'lady. Might be 'n daggerman, er sommat loik that. Messer Raj, he said t' see ye safe."

The stolid yeoman face under the round helmet didn't alter an iota in the searchlight of her glare. Suzette sighed inwardly; she was part of the 5th's mythology now, the Messer's beautiful lady who went everywhere with him, bound up troopers' wounds . . . *flattering as hell and extremely confining.* This bunch would obey any order except one that put her in danger.

"Very well, corporal . . . Billi Saynchez, isn't it? Of Moggersford, transferred from the 7th Descott Rangers last year?" She smiled, and the young trooper swallowed as if his collar was too tight as he nodded. "Now, if you would stand off to one side, in the corner there? And you, messer, whoever you are, pull up that stool."

She rang the handbell again; her servants came and placed kave, biscuits and brandy. Fatima looked up at her for a moment with shining eyes; she'd told her patroness once that the cruelest thing about harem life was that nothing ever happened.

Softly, she began to sing to the sitar, a murmur of noise that would drown out the conversation to anyone more than a few paces away. It was a reiver's ballad from the debatable lands below the Oxhead mountains, the long border between the sea and the Drangosh where Borderer and Bedouin fought a duel of raid and counter-raid nearly as old as man on Bellevue. Suzette had heard a version sung in south-country Sponglish with the names and identities reversed. The Colonial's started:

> *O woe is me for the merry life*
> *I led beyond the Bar*
> *And trebble woe for my winsome wife*
> *That weeps at Shalimar.*

"The girl speaks no Namerique," she said in that language. "And I don't speak to men with masked faces."

"Lady Whitehall," the man said. He lowered the bandana; the hat would hide him from view from the rear. "A pleasure to see you once again."

"And the same for me, Colonel Boyce," she said softly. The square-cut beard was greyer than she remembered, but the little blue eyes were still cool and shrewd.

"No names . . . and the circumstances are less fortunate than our last meeting." Boyce had been rather more than a friendly neutral as commander of the Brigade forces on Stern Isle when Raj passed through to the Southern Territories.

"I've been relieved of command, as of last week. Colonel Courtet is now in charge of Stern Isle, or at least of Wager Bay, since that's all the idiot has been able to keep."

"Would you have been able to hold more, against my husband?"

"No, I would have surrendered on demand," Boyce said. "Which is why the local command council deposed me, the fools. The Stern

Isle garrison was here to keep the natives down and guard against Squadron pirates. With the Southern Territories in Civil Government hands, we're indefensible against a determined attack. Outer Dark, we're an island with no naval protection!"

> They have taken away my long jezail,
>   My shield and saber fine,
> I am sold for a slave to the Central Bail
>   For lifting of the kine.

"Do have some kave," Suzette said, pouring for them both. "That's very intelligent of you, I'm sure," she went on. "I expect you'll be taking the amnesty, then?"

"Only if nothing better offers," he said. "Two sugar, thank you. The terms of the amnesty specify that those who surrender don't have to take active part in operations against the Brigade."

"I take it you also object to the provision for the surrender of two-thirds of landed property?" she murmured, taking a brandy snifter in her other hand.

"By the Spirit of Man of . . . the Spirit, I do, Messa! So will my sons, some day; they'll find that real estate wears better than patriotism."

"Let me see if I understand you, Messer Boyce," Suzette said. "Your main properties lie on the mainland, don't they?" He nodded. "If the Brigade wins this war, you stand to recover the mainland properties at least—even if you take the amnesty, and even if we retain this island. On the other hand, if you aid us openly, those lands will be forfeit to the General. Unless we win. You're telling me you *expect* us to win? And want to be on the winning side, of course."

"Of course." Boyce sat silent for a moment, and the throaty Arabic music rang louder.

> The steer may low within the byre
>   The serf may tend his grain,
> For there'll be neither loot nor fire
>   Till I escape again.

"Messa," he went on slowly, "I know you call my people barbarians. The Squadron are—were, rather. The Guards are, since they haven't had our contact with the Midworld Sea; the Stalwarts most *assuredly* are. We of the Brigade have ruled the Western Territories for a long, long time, though. Give us credit for learning something. Give me credit, at least.

"Yes," he continued, "*I* think your Messer Raj—" he used the troops' nickname "—may win this war. *May.* It seems unlikely from the numbers, but I've visited the Civil Government. I know its potential strength when there's a strong Governor with an able commander. That's happened now, and we, well, I wouldn't trust

General Forker to lead a sailor into a whorehouse, to be blunt. Most of the possible replacements are worse, we've managed to turn Carson Barracks into a stew of intrigue as bad as East Residence, only with less sense of long-term interests. Most of all, I've seen Raj Whitehall. I've studied his campaigns in the east, and I had a ringside seat for the destruction of the Squadron.

"You *may* win. Even if you don't, the war will be long and bloody. If we kick you out, we'll still be so weakened the Stalwarts will roll over us like a rug. We're having more and more trouble holding the border against them anyway."

He leaned forward, the blunt swordsman's fingers incongruous on the delicate china.

"And win or lose, the worst thing that could happen to us is a long war. If we win, the Stalwarts will pick our bones. If we lose, the Western Territories may be so weakened that you can't hold them against the northern savages either. And in any case, if we lose after a long struggle we may just . . . vanish as a people, the way it's happening to the Squadron. Ordinary nations can lose their nobles and soldiers and priests—" he snapped his fingers "—and they'll produce a new set of 'em in a few generations, even if they have to throw off a foreign yoke first. We of the Brigade, we haven't had a peasant class of our own since we left the Base Area. If we lose our lands and positions, we lose *everything*."

> *And God have mercy on the serf*
> *When once my fetters fall*
> *And Heaven defend the noble's garth*
> *When I am loosed from thrall.*

Suzette looked at him with new respect "So since you *know* that General Whitehall can't be beaten easily, you think a swift Civil Government victory is the best thing for your people?"

"Exactly, my lady. You'll *need* us. Need our fighting men, not least. In a generation or two, who knows?" He hesitated. "I wouldn't describe myself as an idealist, Lady Whitehall. Let's say I value civilization, if nothing else because it's so much more comfortable than sitting in a drafty log hall eating bad food and listening to worse poetry. The more thoughtful members of the Brigade have always considered themselves guardians of the culture we took over. General Whitehall claims to be defending civilization by uniting it. The Stalwarts have taken a third of our mainland possessions since my grandfather's time—they're like ants. As I said, I'm interested in preserving my sons' heritage."

"And your lands," Suzette said.

> *It's woe to bend the stubborn back*
> *In a coal-mine's inky bourne*

> *It's woe to hear the leg-bar clack*
> *And jingle when I turn!*

"And my lands. All of them, not one-third. The information I have is worth it."

"Why come to me?"

"Too many eyes on your husband, my lady. Too many patriotic fools ready to kill a middle-aged traitor; my excessively honorable sons, for starters. I don't want to see them buried in a ditch and my grandchildren sold as slaves; on the other hand, I don't want them to kill *me*, either. They'll quiet down when it's over."

Suzette sat in silence, setting down the empty kave cup and sipping at her brandy. Beads of sweat ran down from the Brigade noble's hairline, but his features were very steady.

> *But for the sorrow and the shame,*
> *The brand on me and mine,*
> *I'll pay you back in the leaping flame*
> *And loss of the butchered kine.*

"Corporal!" she called. The Descotter gunmen came over at the trot, weapons poised.

"M'lady," Saynchez said, bracing to attention.

"This man is to be put under arrest . . . there's a vacant room with an iron door in the cellars here, isn't there?"

"Yis, m'lady."

> *For every sheep I spared before—*
> *In charity set free—*
> *If I may reach my hold once more*
> *I'll reive an honest three.*

"Take him there. Let nobody see his face. He's to have food, water and bedding, but nobody, and I mean *nobody*, is to enter his cell or have conversation with him until I or General Whitehall authorize it. You will see that he's guarded by men who know how to keep their mouths shut. Do you understand?"

"Yis, m'lady." Corporal Saynchez quivered with eagerness, like a war-dog just before the charge is sounded "T'barb 'ull vanish offn t'earth."

> *For every time I raised the lowe*
> *That scarred the dusty plain,*
> *By sword and cord, by torch and tow*
> *I'll light the land with twain!*

"Abdullah," she called, when the soldiers had gone. Not quite at a run, and their hobnails grinding on the pavement.

"Saaidya."

"Messer Whitehall should be back in—" she looked out the window; Miniluna was three-quarters, and a hand's breadth above the horizon "—five hours. Please set a table for three in the lower alcove in time for him. Serve us yourself, please." That room had a stair to the cellars. "And take this to Messer Reggiri."

She pulled a ring from her finger; it was in the shape of a serpent biting its own tail, ruby-studded. "Tell him," she went on, after a pause for thought, "that I will give him a better gift than this, and a sweeter. But not here, in Wager Bay; and that I trust his discretion absolutely."

The dog runs better if you dangle the bone, she thought coolly. Her mind felt sharp as crystal, completely alive. The puzzle in her brain was not solved, but the pieces were there, and she could feel her consciousness turning and considering them. She had no genius for war; that was Raj's domain, and no human living could match him. At plot and counterplot and the ways of devious treachery, she was his third arm. She would give him what he needed to know, and he would wring victory out of it.

> *Spur hard your dog to Abazai,*
> *Young lord of face so fair—*
> *Lie close, lie close as Borderers lie,*
> *Fat herds below Bonair!*

"And Cabot?" she said, in answer to an unasked question. "I don't know. There's a great many things I don't know."

> *The one I'll shoot at the twilight-tide,*
> *At dawn I'll drive the other;*
> *The serf shall mourn for hoof and hide*
> *The March-lord for his brother.*

"But I do know what my Raj can do, if he has the tools he needs to work with. What he needs. And I'll bring him what he needs, whether he knows it or not."

> *'Tis war, red war, I'll give you then,*
> *War till my sinews fail;*
> *For the wrong you have done to a chief of men,*
> *And a thief of the Bani Kahil.*
> *And if I fall to your hand afresh*
> *I give you leave for the sin,*
> *That you cram my throat with the foul pigs flesh*
> *And hang me in the skin!*

CHAPTER SEVEN

"Not as enthusiastic as they were in Port Murchison," Raj said.

The capital of the Southern Territories had greeted his army with flowers and free wine; the men still talked about it with wistful exaggeration. Here the streets were mostly empty, save for a few knots of men standing on streetcorners watching the Civil Government's army roll by. The ironshod wheels of guns on the cobbles and the thunder-belling of nervous dogs rattled oddly through the unpeopled streets, a night-time sound on a bright summer's morning. Hobnailed boots slammed in earthquake unison as the infantry marched; he was keeping most of his cavalry bivouacked outside, in villages and manors in the rich coastal countryside. Less chance of disease breaking out, and better for the dogs.

"They're not as sure we're going to win as they were in Port Murchison," Kaltin Gruder pointed out.

They all snapped off a salute as the banner of the 24th Valencia Foot went by, and the standard dipped in response. The Companion considered them with a professional eye.

"Their marching's certainly sharp," he said dryly; cavalry in general and Descotters in particular didn't spend much time on it.

Raj shrugged. "It helps convince them they're soldiers," he said.

The foot-soldiers were mostly conscripted peons from the central provinces, several cuts below the average cavalry recruit socially. *You just have to know how to treat them,* he thought. Tell a man he's worthless often enough, and he'd act like it. For initiative and quick response, the infantry were never going to match a mounted unit like the 5th or Kaltin's 7th Descott Rangers. But they could be solid enough, if you handled them properly.

His eyes went back to the fort. "Well, the good citizens certainly got some evidence for doubting our chances," he pointed out.

The main north gate of Wager Bay gave them a good view downslope and to the east, where Fort Wager sat atop its headland.

Every ten minutes or so a cannon would boom out, and a few seconds later a heavy roundshot would crash through a roof in the town below. Mostly they were falling in the tenement-and-workshop district of the town, narrow streets flanked by four-storey limestone apartment blocks, soap works, olive-oil plants and sulfur-refineries. Columns of black smoke marked where fires had started.

"Kaltin, see to getting those out, would you? There's a working aqueduct here, so it shouldn't be so difficult. Coordinate with the infantry commanders if you need more manpower."

The Companion nodded. "At least we know that they're not short of powder," he went on.

"That and a good deal else," Raj said absently.

He trained his binoculars on the harbor, studying the narrow shelf below the bluff and the fort. There were piers at the cliff-face nearest the harbor, but the ground rose steeply, no access except by covered staircases in the rock. Impossible to force; the defenses were built with that in mind. The main guns of the fort couldn't bear on the beach, but anyone trying to climb the cliff would face streams of burning olive oil out of force-pumps, at the very least. Further on, the cliffs bent sharply to the east; even steeper there, and waves frothed in complicated patterns on rock and reef further out.

following changes since last data update, Center said.

I hate it when you suddenly drop into Church jargon, Raj grumbled. He counted himself a pious man, but he'd never understood why the priests had to call commonplace facts "data." It wasn't as if they were speaking of something from the Canonical Handbooks, for the Spirit's sake. Center had the same unfortunate habit at times. One had to make allowances for an angel, of course. . . .

thank you. The water vanished from his sight, leaving the pattern of underlying rocks clear; then schematics snowed the flow of currents.

"Hand me that map, would you?" he asked A clipboard braced against his saddlebow, and he sketched without looking down. "There."

"Also the Brigade's not as unpopular with its subjects as the Squadron was," Muzzaf Kerpatik said as he reclaimed the papers.

"Details?" Raj said.

"I have used my contacts," the little man said; he seemed to have an infinity of them, from Al Kebir and the Upper Drangosh to all the major ports of the Midworld Sea. As usual, he was dressed in dazzling white linen, a long-skirted coat after the fashion of Komar and the southern border Counties; he was one of the new class of monetary risk-takers growing up there in recent years. The white cloth and snow-white fur of the borzoi he rode contrasted with the carefully curled blue-black hair and goatee and the teak-brown skin.

The pepperpot revolver tucked into his sash had seen use, however.

"The Brigade commanders here have followed general policy; no persecution of Spirit of Man of the Stars clergy unless they meddle in politics."

Raj nodded; the Brigade depended on the old civilian power structure to maintain administration, and the civilian magnates stubbornly refused to abandon the orthodox faith for the heretical This Earth cult. Down in the Southern Territories the Squadron had run a purely feudal state; they had dispossessed the native aristocracy completely, and didn't much care if urban services went to wrack and ruin. They'd had a nasty habit of burning Star Spirit churches with their clergy in them, too. The piratical heritage of old Admiral Geyser Ricks, and one which had simplified Raj's task.

"In fact, there are large colonies of Colonial Muslim merchants, and even Christos and Jews, here and in most Brigade-held port cities. Merchant guilds are in charge of collecting the customs dues and urban land-tax, since the Brigade commanders care little as long as the money comes in. This arrangement is less, ah, *rigorous* than that common in the Civil Government."

Raj nodded again. The Civil Government's bureaucracy was corrupt, but that was like caterpillars in a fruit tree, tolerable if kept under reasonable control. What was important was that it *worked*, which gave the State a potentially unbeatable advantage. The laxness of the Military Governments was a compound of sloth and incompetence, not policy—they couldn't tighten up much no matter what the emergency.

"Speaking of religion, Messer . . . a delegation of priests in East Residence has presented a petition to the Chair and the Reverend Hierarch Arch-Sysup Metropolitan of East Residence, protesting your policy of toleration towards This Earth cultists in the Southern Territories."

"*Damn!*" Raj bit out. Barholm took his ecclesiastical duties as head of Holy Federation Church quite seriously. Theology was a perennial hobby of Governors, Church and State being as closely linked as they were. He didn't need Center to tell him what the consequences would be if the Chair tried to reunite the faiths by force and overnight—

revolt in former military government territory, probability 72% ±5, Center said. **mutiny among ex-squadron personnel with expeditionary force, probability 38% ±4. mutiny among ex-squadron troops elsewhere in civil government area, probability 81% ±2.**

And there were six battalions of former *Squadrones* on the eastern frontier, keeping watch on the Colonists. Wouldn't *that* be a lovely gift to Ali, hungry for vengeance for his dead father! The Fall seemed to continue by mere inertia. There were times when he felt like a man condemned to spend eternity trying to push an anvil up a slope of smooth greased brass.

indeed, i have done so for a thousand years.

"Tzetzas," he said aloud.

"The Chancellor may have been involved in gathering the petition," Muzzaf said, and grinned whitely.

Back when he'd been the Chancellor's flunky and accomplice he had lived in terror, and in the certain knowledge that Tzetzas would throw him aside like a used bathhouse sponge whenever he ceased to be useful. Now he was one of the Companions of Raj Whitehall, and he knew with equal certainty that Tzetzas would have to come through Raj and every one of the Companions to get him—and had better make sure that none of them survived to avenge him, either. That didn't make him feel immortal; the casualty rate among the Companions was far too obvious. It did make him feel just as dangerous as Chancellor Tzetzas, which was *better* than feeling safe. If he'd wanted to be safe, he would have stuck to running a date-processing business like his father.

"However," he went on, "Governor Barholm has stated that any reversal of policy is premature." Raj relaxed.

"Not until we've got the Brigaderos safely under his thumb," Kaltin said with cold cynicism. "Then he'll send in the Viral Cleansers."

probability 96% ±2 within five years of successful pacification, Center said, **consequences—**

I can imagine. "We'll take the problems one at a time," Raj said.

Muzzaf turned pages. "The soldier's market will be held in the main square," he went on. Troopers were generally expected to buy their own rations out of their pay when the army wasn't on the march, and an efficient market was important to morale and health. More armies had died from bad food and runny guts than all the bullets and sabers ever made. The markets Muzzaf supervised were generally very efficient. "Bulk supplies are coming in with acceptable speed, since we pointed out that the Government receipts used to pay for them are exchangeable against taxes. In fact, a secondary market in receipts has arisen."

Raj blinked in bewilderment, then waved aside the explanation. He'd abandoned attempts to understand that sort of thing when Kerpatik tried to tell him how you could make money by buying tobacco that hadn't been planted yet on land you didn't own and then selling it before it was harvested. Every word he'd said had been in Sponglish, but it might as well have been an Azanian witch doctor explaining the esoterica of his craft. *The cobbler should stick to his last, and I to the sword,* he thought.

"And I have coordinated the six-month receipts for your personal accounts with Lady Whitehall and your clerks."

Raj accepted the paper, raised his brows at the total, and handed it back. For himself he'd as soon have just bought land with his share of the plunder; it was the traditional safe investment, even successful merchants always tried to buy an estate. Kerpatik had convinced him—convinced Suzette, actually—that it would be better to spread it out in part-shares of the new combined capital ventures all over the Civil Government. It certainly seemed to work, and was less trouble even than collecting rents. For that matter, he'd be content to live from his pay and the income from Hillchapel, the Whitehall estate in Descott. Wealth was a tool, occasionally useful but not central to his work.

"And the special equipment will arrive from Hayapalco within the month."

"Good work, Muzzaf. My thanks."

"Oh, and Kaltin," Raj said.

They heeled their dogs out to follow the last infantry unit; the 7th Descott Rangers were bringing up the rear, and the troopers raised a baying cheer to see their Major and Raj fall in below their banner, a running war-hound over the numeral seven and the unit motto: *Fwego Erst*—Shoot First. The dogs joined in, a discordant but somehow musical belling.

"Suzette and I are having a small get-together tonight," Raj went on. "Provided we can get those imbeciles—" he nodded toward the fortress "—to stop showing how brave they are by shelling the slums. The usual thing, reassure the local grandees; we need them cooperative. I know you're busy, but why don't you drop by?"

Gruder looked over at him; the left side of the Companion's face was lined with parallel white scars, legacy of the Colonial pompom shell that had also scattered his younger brother's brains across his torso.

"I, ah, have—"

"A billet that just happens to contain a pretty young widow?" Kaltin Gruder was not nicknamed "The Rooster" by his men for nothing.

Kaltin coughed into one hand. "Grass widow, actually."

"Leave her or bring her," Raj said offhand. The Companion eyed him narrowly. "Everyone will be there. Old friends, like Messer Reggiri."

They were passing a lone Star Spirit priest, come out to bless the representatives of Holy Federation Church. Kaltin's sudden clamp of legs around the barrel of his dog made the animal skitter sideways in an arc that nearly smashed the unfortunate cleric against the wrought-iron grillwork of a courtyard door.

"Sorry, Reverend Father," the Descotter cast over his shoulder, as his usual skills reasserted themselves and the mount went dancing back in a sidling arc to Raj's side.

"I don't need a new dog, or a slavegirl," Gruder said. Kaltin had led the escort party that took Suzette to Reggiri's manor for a dinner-party Raj was *too busy* to attend. The officers in that escort had all been sent off with lavish gifts; it was notable that Kaltin Gruder had sold the dog immediately. Although he'd kept the girl, a redhead of Stalwart background named Mitchi.

"Oh, I somehow suspect Messer Reggiri will be giving us *all* gifts," Raj said quietly.

The two Descotters met each other's eyes. After a moment, they began to smile.

"Why thank you, Cabot," Suzette said, fanning herself and taking the glass of punch.

The ballroom was bright with oil lanterns and hot, despite the tall glass doors that stood open to the early summer night Couples swirled across the marble, bright gowns and jewels and uniforms glittering under the chandeliers. A band of steel drums, sitars and flutes filled the room with soft music; few of the revellers bothered to look up at the fortress on the bluffs, silhouetted against the great arc of Maxiluna. Suzette sang softly to the slow sweep of the music:

> *"If every man does all he can—*
> *If every man be true*
> *Then we shall paint the sky above*
> *In Federation blue . . ."*

"Are those the words to that tune?" Cabot asked.

They were leaning on the railing just outside the windows, looking down over the city. There were fewer lights than usual, except the reddish glow of the fires that persisted long after the shelling had ceased in accordance with the twenty-four hour truce. The flames gave a brimstone tinge to the air, under the breeze coming in from the sea and the gardens of the Commander's palace.

"Very old words, but old songs are a hobby of mine," Suzette said, leaning a little closer.

"Very true, too," Cabot replied. He looked up at the fortress, and his strong young swordsman's hands closed on the fretted bronze and iron of the rail. "If we'd all just work at it, that barb wouldn't be up there laughing at us."

Suzette put a hand on his forearm. "I rather think Colonel Courtet is feeling more inclined to gnash his teeth, at the moment, Cabot. Since this is his residence we're dancing in."

The young man shook off his mood. "Another dance?" he said.

She shook her head, laughing and tapping him on the shoulder with her fan. "Do you want the other ladies to scratch my eyes out? Four quadrilles in a row with the Governor's nephew! Poor things, it's not often they get the chance to whirl in the arms of a handsome gallant from the capital, and here I'm monopolizing you."

"Provincial frumps," Cabot said, bowing over her hand "Let them suffer—and make me happy."

"Later, you scamp. Let an old woman have a chance to catch her breath."

"Old!" he said breathlessly, tightening his grip on her hand "You—you're as ageless and as beautiful as the Stars themselves."

"Now you'll get me in trouble with the Church."

Not to mention that at several years short of thirty it was early days to be calling her *ageless.*

"Nonsense; I'll proclaim a new dispensation from the Chair."

Don't let your uncle hear you talking like that, she thought. *He doesn't have much of a sense of humor.*

"Later, Cabot. I really do need some rest and it's a sin for a dancer like you to be wasted even for an hour. I'll meet you later by the fountain."

She watched him go, tapping her chin thoughtfully with the fan. "Hello, Hadolfo," she said, as Reggiri leaned against the railing in turn.

The black and silver of his jacket and breeches made a contrast with her white-on-white torofib silk and the platinum-and-diamond hairnet that drifted in veils of mesh around her bare shoulders. He had a weathered seaman's tan, and there were calluses on the hand that held hers as he made his bow.

"You seem to be seeing a lot of that young spark," he said.

"Well, he *is* the Governor's nephew, Hadolfo. I can scarcely throw a drink in his face."

"My dear, you not only could, you could make him—or any man—thank you for it."

She laughed, a low musical chuckle, and tucked her arm through his. "Maybe I should work my witchery on Colonel Courtet," she said, nodding toward the fort.

"You might," he said. "I've had considerable dealings with the good Colonel, and in my experience he's extremely susceptible to feminine charm; unfortunately, also to Sala brandy and to whoever talked to him last."

"You know a great deal about affairs here," she said.

"I try to keep informed . . . as you may remember, dear Suzette."

"Then why don't we go somewhere a little more private for conversation, Hadolfo?"

He looked at her sharply, flushing. "*Here?*" he said.

"Well, not *exactly* here," Suzette replied, steering him around the couples sitting out the dance and crowding to the punchbowls and buffets. "But it is a fairly large mansion, and one learns the way of things at Court; there's far less privacy in the Governor's Palace, believe me."

She snapped open her fan, and flicked a breeze across his neck. "You're glowing, Hadolfo. Now stroll along with me, and tell me *all* the gossip, and we'll find a sofa somewhere for a cosy chat."

Hadolfo Reggiri felt himself flushing and fought not to stammer as they pushed open the doors to the lower room; it was a storey down from the ballroom and across a courtyard, close enough to hear the music, but shadowed with the black velvet curtains. His tongue felt thick, far more so than a few glasses of wine would account for, caught between memory and desire.

Get a grip on yourself, man! he thought. *You're not Spirit-damned sixteen any' more!*

He could see how the witch kept the great General Whitehall dangling at her skirts. He could almost feel sorry for the man.

The glow of two cigarettes in the far corner of the darkened room was like running into a wall of cold salt water. He stopped dead, his hand tightening unconsciously on Suzette's where her fingers rested on his right arm. She rapped him sharply across the knuckles with her fan, and walked to the waiting men with the same slender swaying grace, her gown luminescent against the dark woodwork and furniture. Reggiri kept walking numbly forward, because there simply didn't seem to be much else to do. His mind was like a ship he had once seen, whose cargo shifted during a storm. Staggering, everything out of alignment suddenly.

He recognized the men as he approached; Raj Whitehall, and one of his officers, Kaltin Gruder. The scar-faced one he'd been convinced for a moment was going to shoot him last year, until Suzette's voice whipped him into obedience like a lash of ice. The self-appointed guardian of his master's honor.

Both the officers were wearing long dark military-issue greatcloaks, probably to disguise the fact that they were also wearing saber and pistol—real weapons, not the fancy dress cutlery appropriate at a ball. Behind them were four cavalry troopers; they'd been washed up and their uniforms were new, but they carried rifles in their crossed arms. Bull-necked, bow-legged Descotters, as out of place at a party in the mansion as a pack of trolls at an elf convention. Their eyes stayed fixed on the merchant, more feral than any barbarian of the Brigade he'd ever seen.

Hadolfo Reggiri was a good man of his hands; nobody could trade so long in the wilder parts of the Midworld Sea and survive unless he was. He also had no illusions about his own chances with Raj Whitehall or one of his picked fighting comrades; the troopers were a message, not a precaution. They paced out behind him now, hobnails grating on the parquet, looming presences at his back.

"*Bwenyatar, heneralissimo,*" he said, sweeping a bow. "Good evening, Most Valiant General. I've been hoping you'd have the time to speak to me for several days; as a loyal man, I've information on the enemy—"

"I don't doubt you do," Raj said. He flicked at his cigarette and considered the ember. "Eighteen hundred men in the fort, half regular gunners, about four thousand refugees . . ."

It was considerably more complete than the file Reggiri had been compiling.

"Then, if I can't be of assistance, and since you're undoubtedly very busy," he began.

Raj drew another puff. "Actually, messer, there is something you could help the war effort with. My aide Muzzaf Kerpatik tells me you have four ships currently at Sala."

"Preparing to load sulphur, ornamental stone and fortified wine for East Residence," he confirmed.

"They're needed for the war effort. I'd appreciate it if you'd send orders to their captains. They're to report to my base on the north coast and place themselves under the orders of Colonel Dinnalsyn of the Artillery Corps."

"Artillery," Reggiri whispered. "You're going to waste my ships against that bloody fort!"

"That's *Messer General*, t'yer," one of the troopers growled. Raj waved him to silence.

"What," Kaltin said, "would be the penalty, sir, for denying aid to officers of the Civil Government in time of war?"

"Oh, crucifixion," Raj said pleasantly, "for treason. But that doesn't arise, I'm sure. Not waste, Messer Reggiri. *Use.* But I do think they'll be used up. War does that; ships, ammunition, men."

"My ships," Reggiri said. They didn't carry insurance against war losses or acts of government; losing them would wreck him. "You can't steal my ships! Messer General," he added hastily as the soldiers stirred behind him. "I have friends at court."

"I wouldn't dream of stealing them," Raj said. Beside him Suzette pulled a document from her reticule and handed it to her husband. He extended it to the merchant.

Reggiri strained to read it; one of the troopers helpfully lit a match against his thumbnail and held it over his shoulder. The hand stank of dog and gun-oil.

Three thousand gold FedCreds, he read. Not quite robbery, but not replacement value for the ships either. And—

"This is drawn on Chancellor Tzetzas!" he blurted. "I've a better chance of getting the money out of Ali of Al Kebir!"

"Not satisfactory?" Raj said.

He plucked it back out of the other man's fingers and tore it in half. Suzette produced another sheet of parchment, and handed it to Raj. Reggiri took it with trembling fingers. It was identical to the first, except that the amount had been reduced to twenty-five hundred.

Reggiri looked up at Suzette; she stood beside her husband, one delicate hand touching fingertips to his massive wrist. Her eyes had seemed like green flame earlier; now they reminded him of a glacier he had seen once, in the mountains of the Base Area in the far north.

"Bitch," he said, very softly. Then: "*Unnhh!*" as a rifle-butt thudded over his kidneys. White fire turned his knees liquid for a moment, and ungentle hands beneath his arms steadied him.

"Watch yer arsemouth!" the trooper barked "Beggin' yer pardon, messer, messa."

"Kaltin," Raj went on, his expression flat. "Messer Reggiri seems to have had a bit too much to drink, since he's forgotten how one addresses a messa. I think he needs an escort home."

Gruder nodded: "Well, he is a slave-trader," he said in a pleasant tone. "Probably learned his manners pimping his sisters as a boy."

Reggiri's hand came up of its own volition. Gruder's face thrust forward for the slap that never came, the scars that disfigured half of it flushing red.

"Please," he said, his voice husky and earnest. His lips came back from his teeth. "Oh, *please*. One of my men will lend you a sword."

Raj touched his elbow. "Major," he said, and Gruder's hand dropped from the hilt of his saber. "I really do think Messer Reggiri needs that escort. And a guard for the next week or so, because he seems to be remarkably reckless in his cups."

"I gave you Connor Auburn on a platter!" Reggiri burst out. The troopers fell in around him, as irresistible as four walking boulders.

"And you're not dying on a cross right now," Raj said in the same expressionless tone. Only his eyes moved, and the hand bringing the cigarette to his lips. "Now leave."

Suzette's fingers unfastened the buckle of Raj's military cloak and tossed it on the chaise-lounge behind them. She backed a step and curtsied deeply; Raj replied with an equally deep bow, making a courtiers leg. Music drifted through the open windows behind the black-velvet curtains, and the fading tramp of boots through the door.

"Messa Whitehall, might I have the honor of this dance?" he said.

"Enchanted, Messer Whitehall."

Their right hands clasped, and she guided his left to her waist before they swirled away, alone on the dim-lit floor.

CHAPTER EIGHT

"I told you these'd come in useful," Grammek Dinnalsyn said.

The weapon in the revetment of sandbags, timber and sheet-iron on the forecastle of the *Chakra* was a stubby cast-steel tube nearly as tall as a man, joined to a massive circular disk-plate of welded wrought iron and steel by a ball-and-socket joint. It was supported and aimed by a metal tripod, long threaded bars and handwheels to turn for elevation and traverse. The bore was twenty centimeters, more than twice that of a normal field-gun, and rifled. Beside the weapon was a stack of shells, cylinders with stubby conical caps and a driving band of soft gunmetal around their middle; at the rear of each was a perforated tube. The crews would wrap silk bags of gunpowder around the tubes before they dropped them down the barrel, a precise number for a given range at a given elevation. The base charge was a shotgun shell; when it hit the fixed firing pin at the bottom of the barrel, it would flash off the ring charges around the tube.

One thing Boyce had told them was that the casements of Fort Wager had no overhead protection. None was needed with normal artillery, given the placement of the fort.

"I know they're useful, Grammeck," Raj said. "Their little brothers were extremely handy in the Port Murchison fighting." It had been more like a massacre, but never mind. "They're also extremely *heavy.* Get me one that can move like a field gun, and I'll take dozens of them with me wherever I go."

He walked down the deck of the *Chakra,* striding easily; it had been two days from the north coast to Port Wager, more than time enough to get his sea legs back. Many of the platoon of 5th Descott troopers aboard were still looking greenly miserable, landsmen to the core. They'd do their jobs, though, puking or not, and he intended to give them a stable firing platform. The huge sails of the three-master tilted above him; she was barque-rigged, fore-and-aft sails

on the rear mast and square on the other two. Water, wind and
cordage creaked and spoke; he squinted against the dazzle and made
out the tall headland of Fort Wager to the north. There was a brisk
onshore breeze, common in the early afternoon. Center had predicted
it would hold long enough today—

probability 78% ±3, Center corrected him. **i am not a prophet.
i merely estimate.**

—and at worst, they could kedge in the last little way, hauling
on anchors dropped out in front by men in longboats.

He leaned on the emplacement. The crew looked up from giving their weapon a final check and braced; most of them were
stripped to boots and the blue pants with red-laced seams of their
service.

"Rest easy, boys," he said, returning their salute.

Artillerymen were mostly from the towns, and their officers from
the urban middle classes; both unlike any other Army units in the
Civil Government's forces. Many cavalry commanders barely acknowledged their existence. *Pure snobbery,* he thought, *they're invaluable
if you use them right.* Their engineering skills, for example, and general
technical knowledge. Far too many rural nobles weren't interested in
anything moving that they couldn't ride, hunt or fuck, like so many
Brigaderos except for basic literacy.

"This one's all up to you," he went on to the gunners. "Infantry
can't do it, cavalry can't do it. You're the only ones with a chance."

"We'll whup 'em for you, Messer Raj!" the sergeant growled.

"So you will, by the Spirit," he replied. "See you in the fort."

Inwardly, he was a little uneasy at the way that verbal habit had
caught on; *Master Raj* was the way a personal retainer back on the
estate would have addressed him. His old nurse, for example, or
the armsmaster who'd taught him marksmanship and how to handle
a sword. *Curse it, these men are soldiers of the Civil Government,
not some barb chief's warband!* he thought.

you are right to be concerned, Center said. **however, the phenomenon is useful at present.**

He took a slightly different tack with the cavalry troopers waiting belowdecks. The ship's gunwales had been built up and pierced
with loopholes, but there was no sense in exposing the men or
hindering the sailors before there was need.

"Day to you, dog-brothers," he said with a grin, slapping fists
with the lieutenant in command. "Done with your puking yet?"

"Puked out ever-fukkin'-thin' but me guts, ser," one man said.

"It'll be tax-day in Descott when you lose your guts, Robbi
M'Teglez," Raj said. He'd always had a knack for remembering names
and faces; Center amplified it to perfection. The trooper flushed and
grinned. "You're the one brought me that wog banner at Sandoral,
aren't you?"

"Yisser, Messer Raj," the man said. "Me Da got it, an' the carbine 'n dog ye sent. 'N the priest back home read t' letter from the Colonel on Starday 'n all."

The troopers comrades were looking at him with raw envy. Raj went on: "We'll be sailing in through the barb cannonade; oughtn't to be more than twenty minutes or so. Not much for those of you who saw off the wogboys at Sandoral. For those who weren't there—well, you get to learn a new prayer."

"Prayer, ser?" one asked.

He had the raw look of a youth not long off the farm, barely shaving, but the big hands that gripped his rifle were competent enough. Most yeomen-tenants in Descott sent one male per generation to the Army in lieu of land-taxes. There were no peons in Descott, and relatively few slaves. Widows, however, were plentiful enough.

A squadmate answered him. *"Per whut weuns about t'receive, may t'Spirit make us truly thankful,"* he said. "Don't git yer balls drawed up, Tinneran. Ain't no barbs got guns loik t'ragheads."

That brought a round of smiles, half tension and half anticipation. Those who'd waited all day in the bunkers while the Colonist guns pounded them, waiting for the waves of troops in red jellabas to charge through rifle-fire with their repeating carbines . . . they'd know. Those who hadn't been there couldn't be told. They could only be shown.

"Once we're through, the gunners have their jobs to do. It's our job to make sure the barbs don't come down the rocks, wade out and take 'em the way the wild dog took the miller's wife, from behind. You boys ready to do a man's work today?"

Their mounts were back at the base-camp, but the noise the men made would have done credit to the half-ton carnivores they usually rode.

"So commend your souls to the Spirit, wait for the orders, and pick your targets, lads," he finished. "To Hell or plunder, dog-brothers."

"I thought they were about to mutiny, from the sound," Dinnalsyn said as Raj came blinking back into the sunlight on the quarterdeck.

"Not likely," Raj said.

The headland was coming up with shocking speed and the four ships were angling in on the course he'd set, the one that would expose them to the least possible number of guns as they cut in toward the cliffs. *Spirit of* Man, *but I feel good,* he thought. Frightened, yes. Harbors attracted downdraggers, and he still had bad dreams about the tentacles and gnashing beaks and intelligent, waiting eyes crowding around the wharfs when they tipped the Squadron dead into the water after Port Murchison. Eight thousand men dead in an afternoon; the sea-beasts had been glutted, dragging corpses away to their underwater nests when their stomachs wouldn't take any more flesh.

So he wasn't easy about the chance of going into the water here, no. But after the grinding anxiety of high command, the prospect of action on this scale made him feel . . . young.

Starless Dark, he told himself. *I'm not thirty yet!*

"You shouldn't be here, sir," Dinnalsyn said, lowering his voice.

"You aren't exactly the first one to tell me that, Colonel," Raj said. His exuberance showed in the light punch he landed on the East Residencer officer's shoulder. "But I *have* to take it when my wife says it. Let's get on with the job, shall we?"

The *Chakra* was commanded from the stern, where the quarter-deck held the tall two-man wheel that controlled the rudder and the captain could direct the first mate. Nothing could be done about the vulnerability of the deck crew, who trimmed the lines and climbed into the rigging to wrestle with canvas in response to orders bellowed through a megaphone. Dinnalsyn had seen to putting a C-shaped iron stand around the helm itself, though, with overhead protection and vision-slits, boiler-plate mounted on heavy timbers.

The captain turned to Raj. "Rocks 're bad here," he said. In Spanjol, with a nasal accent; he was a tall ropey-muscled man with flax-pale hair shaven from the back of his head and long mustaches. The tunic he wore was striped horizontally with black and white, heavy canvas with iron rings the size of bracelets sewn to it. With fighting possible, he had shoved the handles of short curve-bladed throwing axes through the rings, and had two long knives in his belt.

A Stalwart wandered down from the north, one of the latest tribe of barbarians to move south out of the Base Area. Possibly the fiercest of all; they would have been much more dangerous if fratricide and patricide hadn't been the national sport of their kings. The day one of them managed to kill off all his rivals and unite the tribe would be a dangerous one for the world.

Raj was not particularly worried about treachery from Captain Lodoviko; offshore, the black plumes showed where the Civil Governments steam rams waited. They were too deep-draught to do this job themselves, but he'd given instructions that any ship which turned back without orders was to be sunk and everyone knew it. He'd also promised every man on board a bonus equivalent to a year's pay, with new berths and commands for the mates and captains and enough to buy a share in their ship. Plus, of course, he had forty of his own troops on each ship, ready to shoot down any man who abandoned his station. Everyone knew that, too.

"Steer this course," Raj said. A colored grid dropped down before his eyes, and he swung his arm to align with the pointer Center provided. "*Precisely* that course, Captain Lodoviko, and change *precisely* when I tell you. Understood?"

Lodoviko squinted at him, and murmured something in his dialect of Namerique; probably an invocation to one of the dozens of heathen gods the Stalwarts followed. Glim of the Waves, perhaps, or Baffire of the Thunder. Then he grunted orders to the helm and his first mate. The wheel swung, and feet rushed across the deck. Men swarmed into the ratlines, agile as cliff-climbing rogosauroids.

The ship's bow swung and its motion altered as it took the waves at a different angle. The three ships behind swung into line, following as nearly as they could in line astern.

"We're going too fast," Raj said again, his tone remote. "Reduce by . . . two knots, please. Make ready to turn the boat to the left."

"Ship to port. This ain't steered from the same end as a dog, General." Another set of orders from the megaphone, and canvas was snatched up and lashed to spars.

"Whatever. That's right. Now turn to this angle." His arm swung.

Ahead, they were close enough to see the tall cream-colored limestone cliffs, scarred and irregular but nearly vertical; the stone of the fort was the same color, only the smoothness and block-lines marking where it began and the native rock left off. Surf beat on the shingle beach below, and more white water thrashed over rocks and reefs further out. Any one of them could rip the timber bottom of the *Chakra* open the way a bayonet did a man's belly.

I don't envy Gerrin trying to make them think he's going to do a mass attack in broad daylight, Raj thought, at some level not occupied with his passionless translation of Center's instructions.

Dinnalsyn and his aide had quietly drawn their revolvers, standing behind the binnacle that held the wheel. "Spirit, it's really working," the gunner whispered, in the abstracted tones of a man speaking to himself. "Spirit, maybe he is a bleeding Avatar."

"This heading. Keep this heading."

They were slanting in towards the cliffs at a sixty-degree angle, still more than a kilometer out. The breeze freshened. A cannon boomed, and everyone except Raj jumped. He was too fixed in the strait world of lines and markers Center had clamped over his vision.

"Colonel Staenbridge is demonstrating against the fort, and they're warning him off," he said calmly. "They don't have enough men to crew all their guns. They'll see we're coming in soon enough."

The path to the little pier around the harbor-side angle of the cliffs was much easier sailing, but the last thing he wanted was to be right at the foot of the covered staircase up to the fort. For one thing, small-arms fire from the ramparts could reach a ship there; for another, he was fairly sure the garrison wasn't going to let him sit and shell them without trying to pay a visit.

His back was to the stern rail; he drew his own pistol and thumbed back the hammer. Lodoviko scratched his ribs; he *might* not have been toying with the haft of one of his axes.

BOOM. Smoke vomited from an embrasure on the seaward side of the fort.

"Think they've seen us," Dinnalsyn said. The air ripped, and water fountained white two hundred meters off the *Chakra's* bow.

BOOM. It went overhead this time, and the ball struck rock barely submerged a few hundred meters to their left, with a sound like an enormous ball-peen hammer on granite. It bounced back into the air and wobbled another hundred meters to splash in deeper waves.

"Yep, they've seen us all right," the gunner went on dispassionately. "Undershot and overshot. Tricky, with a moving target like this."

"Turn right. This far."

"Y'heard the lubber, port ten!" Lodoviko snapped. Sweat was running down his boiled-lobster face and soaking his tunic, but his directions were precise.

BOOM. BOOM. BOOM. BOOM. BOOM. BOOM.

A wall of smoke along the gunports of the fort where the wall faced them.

Inside, the gunners would be leaping through their intricately choreographed dance. Swabbers to push sponge-tipped poles down the barrels to quench the sparks. Gunner standing by with his leather-sheathed thumb over the touch-hole to keep air out. Linen bags of gunpowder rammed down the muzzle next. The gunner lifting his thumb and jabbing the wire pricker down the hole to split the fabric. A wad going in, a heavy circle of woven hemp rope. Then the ball—four men with a scissor-grip clamp, on guns this heavy. Ram another wad on the ball, as the gunner pushed home the friction fuse and clipped his lanyard to it. Men heaving at ropes and the block-and-tackle squealing as the long black pebbled surface of the cast-iron barrel came back to bear, and the gunner standing on the platform at the rear to aim as the officer called the bearing and men spun the screws.

Fire, as the crew sprang back from the path of recoil, mouths open and hands over their ears. Noise and choking smoke, and the whole thing to do again and again. . . .

BOOM. BOOM. BOOM. BOOM. BOOM. BOOM. BOOM. BOOM.

"Turn right. Hard right, for the beach," Raj said.

He shook his head as the visions faded, and had to grab the captain and scream the directions into his ear; the man turned eyes gone almost black as the pupil swallowed the iris, but he shouted in his turn—then cuffed the helmsman aside and spun the wheel himself, ropy muscle bulging on his bare arms. This time the ripping-cloth noise was much louder, almost shrill, and water splashed across the deck as spouts half as high as the masts collapsed onto them. Instinct made him cover his revolver with his hand as the salt water drenched him.

Dinnalsyn was looking aft. "Damnation to the Starless Dark," he said. "They got the *Ispirto dil Hom.*"

The next ship in line was turning around the pivot of the toppled mainmast, a tangled mass of wood and canvas leaning over the side into the waves. As he watched two more balls struck. One into the deck, but the next was a very lucky accident. It hit the mortar tube square-on, and the piled ammunition went up in a ball of orange fire. When it cleared the whole front of the ship was missing; the stern slid forward on the same course. Men climbed frantically as the rudder flapped into view; then the merchantman slid out of sight. The water was scattered with flotsam, some of which screamed for help to the next vessel through.

Smooth flukes tossed water upward as the downdraggers came, the only help those men would receive today. Tentacles lashed around a floating spar and the men clinging to it. Their shrieks carried a long way over the water.

Raj turned, stomach knotting. Lodoviko was screaming to the sailors in the rigging to drop sail; the bow rose and fell in a choppy motion as the spars came down in a controlled disaster of crashing weight.

"We have to get in," Raj said, grabbing the man by the shoulder.

"We *will*, you lubber of a soldier! Double-moon tide and an onshore breeze: if we come in too fast, the masts'll come down on your precious popgun when she grounds her belly."

Lodoviko seemed to be an intelligent savage. If that mortar didn't work, they would all be joining the crew of the *Spirit of Man* very soon.

BOOM. BOOM. BOOM. BOOM. BOOM. BOOM. BOOM. BOOM.

"Over," Dinnalsyn said, tracing the trajectories. "Over, over, over . . . over . . . over, *over*! Overshot, by the Spirit! Their guns can't depress this far."

Raj cast a look back. The next ship, the *Rover's Bane*, was coming through the gauntlet of waterspouts. *Crack.* Not undamaged; the top of the middle mast—mainmast, he reminded himself—went over the side, and broken staylines snapped across the deck like the whips of a malignant god. They were turning, now, turning straight in for the beach. *City of Wager* right behind.

BOOM. BOOM. BOOM. BOOM. BOOM. BOOM. BOOM. BOOM.

"Hit, she's hit," Raj said, peering through distance and spray.

"Took out her wheel and the second one smashed her rudder," Dinnalsyn said grimly. Then: "She's still steering, Spirit bugger me blind!"

Lodoviko showed teeth like an ox's, yellow and strong. "Florez. That he-whore is a seaman, by Glim. He takes her in with the sails alone—onshore wind, it can be done. He has balls, that one."

The Stalwart drew two of his axes and turned, clashing them together over his head at the fortress. He brayed out a long war-cry, the overhanging yellow fuzz of his mustache standing out from his lip in food-stained glory with the volume.

"Come out and fight, you Brigade heroes! You pussy-whipped suckers of priest's cocks! Come out of that stone barn and fight— *everyone grab a line.*"

The final rush to the cliff was shocking; a pitching glide, and the rough stone rising to blot out the sky above. The keel caught and grated, then caught again in a chorus of groans and snaps and rending noises. Rigging gave way with sounds like gigantic lute-strings, but none of the masts went over. The impact seemed slow and gentle, but Raj felt his feet jerked out from under him by inertia, and only the iron grip of his sword-hand on the tarred cordage by his side kept him from falling forward. One seaman still in the rigging screamed as he described a long arc shorewards, ending in abrupt silence as he impacted on the cliff and fell limply to the narrow strip of stony beach.

Silence fell for an instant, and then the ship quivered as it settled. The hulls of all four—all three—were U-shaped in section with edge-keels rather than a single deep keelson-mounted fin. The *Chakra* ground her way down into the loose rocks of the shore and settled almost level. The comparative absence of noise seemed unnatural, like a ringing in the ears. Off to the left the other two ships were grounded rather further out; there was twenty meters of water between the *Chakra* and dry land, twice that for each of the others.

Dinnalysn picked himself up. "We made it," he said. "They can't touch us now."

"Professional tunnel-vision, Grammeck," Raj said with a grim smile. He checked the loads in his pistol and wiped the surfaces dry with the tail of his uniform jacket. "You mean their *artillery* can't touch us," he went on, and pointed to their left. The rock bulged out and then curved away; most of Port Wager was hidden by it.

"Nothing to prevent them coming down the stairways around that corner of the cliff and trying their best to beat us to death. Nothing at all."

"No, up two more turns with the same charge," Raj said.

The mortarman looked at him with awe and spun the elevating screw. The four loaders lifted the heavy shell with its sausage-rings of gunpowder at the base and eased it into the muzzle. Everyone else in the sandbagged emplacement on the forecastle bent away, closing their eyes and opening their mouths, jamming thumbs against their ears.

"Fire in the hole!"

Fffumph. The 20-cm tube belched a blade of fire taller than a man; everyone was coughing and waving to clear the dense cloud of smoke. The projectile was visible as a dark blur through the air, then a dot that hesitated high above, and then a blur again.

crump. Muted, because it was exploding within the walls of Fort Wager, but still loud. The shells had a ten-kilogram bursting charge, and their target—the land-facing guns of the fort—had no overhead protection. Only thin partitions between each of the guns on the firing deck, as well. The seaward-facing guns might as well be in Carson Barracks for all the good they were doing the Brigade now.

The problem was that there was no way to observe the fall of shot from the ships; the target was not only half a kilometer north, it was three hundred meters higher up and behind a thick stone wall. The main Civil Government force, massed just out of cannon-shot of the fort walls on the other side, *could* observe roughly where the shells landed. The signals were rough as well, color-coded rockets; green for "too far," red for "short," white and black for "left" and "right." Even with Center to help with the calculations it was taking time to walk the shells of each gun onto the target. Time they might not have.

"Ser! Here t'barbs come agin!"

Raj vaulted over the sandbags, pivoting on his left hand, and landed in a crouch on the deck. That put him below the level of the built-up railings, which were turning out to be a very good idea. The cluster of boulders at the bulge of the cliff was four hundred meters away. The Brigaderos had gotten set up in there, and proved to be deadly accurate. Not very fast, but there were a lot of them, and they tended to hit what they aimed at. Tinneran, the recruit with the big hands, had found out the hard way when he stood up to get a better shot; he was lying wrapped in canvas and out of the way, with a round blue hole in his forehead and the back blown out of his head. The lieutenant was dead, too. Exactly according to the odds. The two most dangerous positions in a cavalry platoon were junior officer and raw recruit.

Two other fatals, and two too badly hurt to shoot even kneeling and through a loophole. That left him thirty rifles. The loopholes had saved their *butts*. It was a good thing there was no way to hide coming down the cliff directly overhead, and a man rapelling down on a rope had proved to be a very good target.

He duckwalked to the side of the ship and squinted through a narrow slit in the wooden barricade. Bullets made their flat *crack* overhead, or thocked into the ship's timbers, or peened as they struck metal. Puffs of smoke rose from the rocks as the marksmen increased their covering fire; at a guess, each was a picked man with two or three others passing him loaded rifle-muskets. The 5th troopers kept hunched down behind the bulletproof sheath of planking that Center had added to Raj's plan. It wasn't worth the risk to stick their rifles out the firing slits until they had better targets.

Which would be shortly. None of the bodies from the last attack was floating; the downdraggers had gotten them all. They'd even gone for the ones on the narrow strip of beach, until both sides shot half a dozen of the repulsive beasts while they dragged themselves half out of the water to seize their prey.

"Here t' bastids come," called the NCO.

"Pick your targets," Raj said, loud but calm. "Fire low."

A first wave came pelting up the beach beneath the cliffs. They wore green-gray jackets and black pants, lobster-tail steel helmets with nasals and cheek-flaps. General's Dragoons, part of the Brigade's regular army. Their rifles were slung, and they carried short ladders.

"Now!"

The Armory rifles began to speak, a steady beat. Men fell, others picked up their ladders and came forward again. Another hundred and another, and the third had no ladders but waded out into the water directly towards the *Chakra*. The bow was thigh-deep, but there was another four meters or so of sheer hull to climb if they made it that far. The midships railing was half a deck lower than the forecastle, but the water there was waist to chest deep.

Damn, but those are brave men, he thought.

The downdraggers were out there; the men had to come in a dense phalanx and prod with their bayonets. Even so some went down in the tentacles at the edge or rear of the formation, and more stayed to stab and hack at the smooth grey flesh of the predators. For a moment, because the water was being whipped to froth by fire from the *Chakra* and the other two ships. They were too far out to be attacked, but they could support their sister.

A slapping sound and a grunt. Just down from him a trooper slumped backwards twitching and coughing out sheets of blood from a soft-lead slug through the upper chest. Bullets were cracking into the planking like hail, and if enough came your way one was going to get through the loophole. He switched positions. The hundred men in the first wave were more like thirty now; one turned and tried to run back the way he'd come, and an officer shot him at point-blank range with his pistol. Now they were level with the *Chakra*'s bow and curving out into the water with their ladders, knees coming up high as if in unconscious reluctance to let their feet touch the surface.

"First squad, *follow me!*" he called, and led them to the bows.

Past the mortar, where another shot came, and another—they were firing for effect, how had he missed the signal they were on target? Up to the bows, and the rough pole ends of an improvised ladder slapping against the boards. He stuck his revolver over the edge and squeezed off three shots; somebody screamed, and a dozen bullets hammered the edge of the planking as he snatched the hand back. *Good. Decoyed, by the Spirit.* There might be something in the world more futile than trying to reload a musket while standing in a meter of monster-haunted water, but he couldn't think of it offhand.

A Brigadero head came over the rail. He shot, and the bullet keened off the lobster-tail helmet; the man's head jerked around as if he'd been kicked by a riding dog, and he vanished to splash below. One more shot; it missed, but the trooper beside him didn't. The Brigade warrior folded around his belly and jackknifed, flopping across the rail. Raj holstered his revolver and swept out his saber.

"Come on!" he said, and set the point against the ladder.

The trooper did likewise, putting the tip of his long bayonet against the other upright. They pushed—sideways, not straight back. The ladder slid out of sight, and the timbre of the screams below changed from fury to terror. Raj risked a look; something like a mass of animated worms around a serrated beak the length of an arm had the man who'd held the ladder at the base. It was pulling him seaward and biting chunks out of him at the same time; three of his comrades were hacking at it with their swords although the victim was obviously dead; even *following* it. Which he wouldn't have believed, if he hadn't seen some of the things men would do in combat . . . The squad with him fired point-blank at the next set of men with a ladder.

"*Ser.*"

He whipped around. A Brigadero had gotten to the deck, twenty feet away where the sailors were holding a section with cutlass and boarding axe. Down in the waist of the ship, the ones who'd come without ladders must be climbing over each other's shoulders to get on board. The first man on jerked two revolvers from crossdraw holsters. Raj and the trooper beside him ran back toward him. The Brigade warrior took a careful stance and shot the trooper. The man went over with a yell, clutching his thigh as if to squeeze out the pain and rolling into a tangle of sailcloth and rope hanging to the deck. Raj dove forward over the edge of the forecastle half-deck, kept hold of his saber but landed with his ribs on something *hard,* and came up wheezing.

Not ten feet from the Brigadero. The man was grinning, or snarling, impossible to say. He aimed with care, as much outside the range of Raj's saber as if he'd been on Maxiluna or lost Earth itself—

Something bright flashed by, rotating into a blur. It stopped at the pistoleer, turning into one of Lodoviko's axes. The bit took the Brigadero at a flat angle between neck and shoulder. Blood jutted through the cut cloth and flesh, spurting; shock convulsed both the mans hands, and the pistols fired. By luck, good or bad, one barked into the deck-planking by Raj's foot, turning a thumb-sized patch into a miniature crater.

He hurdled the dying man's body and turned the next stride into a full-sweep kick at the next man coming over the low rail. The steel-reinforced toe of Raj's riding boot thudded into his chest with an impact that brought a twinge of pain to Raj's lower back. The Brigadero toppled backward and splashed into the water. He came up bent over and gasping with his mouth barely above the surface, wading back towards shore with empty hands. Raj leaned over the rail.

He met the eyes of the man there, the one who had been standing chest deep so his comrades could climb up him and onto the ship. The bearded snarling face showed only an intense concentration;

his right hand went back for the sword slung over his shoulder. Raj could see something else; a smooth upwelling in the water, a track heading straight for the enemy soldier's back. He leaned and thrust; the point punched into the standing man's neck. His eyes were turning up as he slid off the point.

A *mercy*, Raj thought.

Fdump. Much louder than the previous mortar-shells. A column of black smoke atop a dome of fire rose over the edge of the cliff, over the barely-visible wall of the fort beyond. Red dots trailing smoke and sparks shot skyward, and heavier debris tumbled briefly into sight.

secondary explosion, Center said. **gun bay three, frontal sector to the right of the main gates.**

Then something much heavier went off. Shards of rock as big as dogs quivered loose from the cliff, and the noise thumped at his face.

Raj nodded, wheezing back his breath. A fragment of red-hot iron slicing into a bagged charge . . . ripple effect. Massive guns flipping out into the air, and pieces of the crews with them. Chunks of rock and concrete blasting in all directions.

A yell went up from the sandbagged mortar enclosure. Nobody noticed along the sides of the ship for an instant. There was a final snarling fury of shots fired with the muzzles touching flesh and bayonet clashing on swords. The enemy fell back, realizing by instinct that there were too few of them to push home their attack. They saw the pillar of fire as they retreated, and ran.

Then the crew and soldiers were cheering too; another trio of mortar shells puffed upwards, and the sound of their firing slapped back from the cliffs like the applause of giants.

"Cease fire, riflemen," Raj croaked, keeping well down—the marksmen among the tumbled boulders could shoot again now, with their own men dead or out of the way. Lodoviko looked up from bandaging a gash in his hairy thigh and hooted laughter; Raj nodded.

"Ser?" the platoon sergeant said. "We could git sommat more of 'em—"

"No," Raj said. He remembered the man standing in the water, waiting while others climbed to safety over him. Or at least out of reach of the tentacles. "I need men like that. All I can get."

as do i, raj whitehall, Center said. **as do i.**

Colonel Courtet had probably been a fine figure of a man, back before twenty years of inactivity and Sala brandy took their toll; the vast bush of beard that hid his face was probably a mercy. He hadn't been drinking recently, but that probably only worsened the trembling of his liver-spotted hands. His body was large and soft, straining against the silvered armor he wore, and his dog shifted as if sensing its rider's unease.

"Colonel Gerrin Staenbridge," the Civil Government officer said, saluting crisply.

The other man's reply was a vague wave followed by silence. Gerrin was in no particular hurry, within reason. The two parties were meeting under a white flag in the cleared no-man's-land in front of the fort, which gave a wonderful view of the tumbled ruin of the main defensive bastion beside the gate. Eroded-looking stumps stood up above rubble that had filled in the moat and made a perfect ramp up into Fort Wager. In fact, it even looked accessible on dogback. Every minute that Courtet had to watch it from this angle was a blow struck at his morale, which looked none too steady to begin with. According to the intelligence, he'd been pushed forward by the local military council because he was the only officer of sufficient birth and rank who wasn't as defeatist as Colonel Boyce.

As completely defeatist as Boyce. Senior officers with military ability or ambition didn't come to Stern Isle.

Besides, Courtet's aide was worth a little attention: he looked the way a noble Military Government warrior was supposed to in the legends and so rarely did in practice. Twenty, broad in the shoulders and narrow in the hips, regular bronzed features and tourmaline eyes, long blond hair flowing to his shoulders and close-trimmed barley-colored beard. Uniform of beautiful materials, elegantly understated, but the breastplate commendably hacked, battered and lead-splashed.

Gerrin fought down a friendly smile; besides, Bartin was acting as *his* aide. The senior officer, a junior, and a bannerman, as was traditional.

"There's no point in wasting time," Staenbridge went on, when it was plain Courtet would not speak. Possibly could not. "You're getting the third and last chance to surrender."

"Ah . . ." Courtet coughed rackingly. "Same terms?" He wet his lips, visibly thirsty. Out of the corner of his eye, Gerrin could see the fine-drawn lip of the Brigadero aide curl.

"Of course not," Staenbridge snapped. "You know the laws of war concerning fortified places, colonel. We summoned you first when we invested the fort, and again before we commenced firing. Terms become more strict with each refusal."

He pointed with a gauntleted hand. "Now we've put a workable breach in your defenses. If you refuse and we storm the position, your lives are forfeit. And believe me, if you force us to take unnecessary casualties, we'll throw any survivors over the cliffs and their families will be turned over to the men. Who will *not* be in a gentle mood."

Courtet looked from one Civil Government officer to the other, from the dark suave face of a killer to the cheerful, handsome young man with the razor-edged steel hook for a left hand. The flower tucked behind his ear made the sight worse, not better.

"What terms, gentlemen?" he said hoarsely.

"Personal liberty for your families. All able-bodied males and their households to be sent to East Residence, men to be enrolled in our forces under the usual provisions—no service against the Brigade. The remainder to be released after giving their parole never to bear arms against the Civil Government. Personal property except arms to be retained by the owners, and officers' sidearms and dogs for those discharged. Forfeiture of real property beyond one house and forty hectares. And if that seems harsh, messers, consider the alternatives."

"Can I, ah, consult with my officers?"

"With this gentleman and no others." *Although I wouldn't mind consulting with him myself, under other circumstances.* "Are you in command, Colonel Courtet or not?"

Probably not but he could lead his men in the obvious direction. There was nothing more demoralizing than being shelled without a chance to reply, except possibly knowing your family was there with you. The blond aide drew Courtet aside and whispered urgently in his ear.

When he turned back, the Brigade commander's face was like gelid fat. His aide dismounted and helped him to the ground; they both drew their swords and offered them hilt-first across their forearms.

A huge roaring cheer rose from the Civil Government troops downslope, in their hasty fieldworks. Even with the mortars in support, taking the fortress would enact a big enough butcher's bill to daunt anyone. The fort's ramparts were black with watchers as well, and the sound that came up from them was a long hollow groan, the sort of noise you hear on a battlefield after dark when the wounded lie out. Calling for water, or their mothers, or in wordless pain.

The Civil Government officers each took his counterpart's blade, flourished it overhead, and returned it. Then Staenbridge pulled out his watch.

"My felicitations on an honorable but difficult decision," *which you should have made yesterday, you butchering moron.* "Colonel Courtet. Your men will march out within twenty minutes and stack arms," he said, "or you'll be in violation of the truce. Colonel, you'll remain with me until that's done. Sooner begun, the sooner we can get the wounded attended to and your women and children settled."

Courtet nodded heavily, resting one hand on the saddle of the dog beside him.

"Where's Whitehall?" he burst out.

The two Descotters looked at him expressionlessly. He blinked, and amended: "Where's Messer General Whitehall? They say," the Brigadero went on, "the demons fight for him. I could believe that."

"General Whitehall is where he thinks best," Staenbridge said. *And I violently disagree; he should be here, and I on that boat.* "And the holy Avatars fight for him, Colonel. He is the Sword of the Spirit of Man—hadn't you heard?"

Courtet was silent but his aide bowed courteously. "I had heard that, sir," he said, in fair if slow Sponglish. "We yield our swords to the might of the Spirit, then, to take them up again against Its enemies, heathen and Muslim." He turned and spurred for the gates.

They opened, and remained that way. A squad came forward to put Courtet under guard; Bartin Foley murmured to the lieutenant in charge, and a table, chair and tumbler of brandy appeared. The fat old man in too-tight armor looked at them and then put his face in his hands, his shoulders heaving.

Staenbridge heeled his dog off to one side. Bartin leaned toward him.

"You said that as if you meant it," the younger man said. "About Messer Raj being the Sword of the Spirit; and here I thought you were a sceptic."

"I find myself growing less sceptical, comrade of my heart. Less sceptical than I would wish."

"Envious?" Bartin grinned.

Gerrin Staenbridge shuddered elaborately and began stripping off his gloves. "Merciful Avatars—if there are any—no! Plenty of fame in being one of the selfless, faithful Companions, as I don't doubt the lying histories will call us all, forgetting we're each the central characters of our own stories." He thought for a moment, watching the screeching gulls and cawing dactosauroids over the harbor.

"Bad enough to be a hero, and carry the burdens of human expectations. To shoulder those of Something Else . . . even a soul like Raj's will crack under the burden in the end. No matter that all of us do what we can to help."

He looked at the younger officer and smiled. "The flower's charming, by the way. And since it's on the left today . . . ?"

CHAPTER NINE

Raj Whitehall looked past his booted feet where they rested on the table, down the long conference chamber and out the french doors and balcony at the other end. From here you could just see the blue-and-silver Starburst banner of the Civil Government floating over Fort Wager against the violet morning sky and the pale translucent globe of Maxiluna. Soon to be renamed Fort Tinneran, for all the good it would do. There *was* something satisfying in the sight. Also in getting some honest work done. This meeting was informal, the Companions and one or two others, but there were things that needed doing.

Grammeck Dinnalsyn ruffled a stack of papers. "Just mason's work for now, general," he said. "The fort's sound."

"Not until it gets overhead protection for the guns, and something that can drop plunging fire on the beach," Raj said crisply. "Cursed if I'll see it taken back by the same tricks *I* used, Grammeck."

Although that would be a lot more difficult without Center. It had been close enough even with the Spirit lending a direct hand.

i am not god.

No, but you're the closest approximation available within current parameters, Raj thought.

"I do have an idea about that," the gunner said. "It'll be a while before we can get real howitzers or mortars there; they'll have to be ordered from East Residence Armory or the Kolobassian forges. Which requires formal funding from the Master of Ordnance . . ."

Half a dozen people groaned. "Exactly. You can steal money for yourself, but Star Spirit help you if you spend money irregularly for the State. What we *can* do, is take some of the surplus smoothbores, cut them down, and mount them in pits. Some sort of turntable, but that's blacksmith level work. Then timber-and-earth covers, with removable sections. Solid shot, and time-fused shell, of sorts. I wouldn't care to have forty kilograms of either dropped on my head."

Raj nodded. *Spirit, but I like a man who can think for himself.* With Center's matchless ability to store and sort information, he really didn't need all that much of a staff. He had set himself to train one anyway; the Civil Government *needed* something better than ad-hoc organizations whenever a field army was set up. There was a big gap in the table between the administrators who saw to pay and garrison work, and the battalion-level unit organizations.

a deliberate one, Center observed. Field armies made coups easier. *We get the coups anyway,* Raj replied.

"Draw up the plans," he said. "We may not have time for it, but at least our successors will get some help. How are the public works, town water supplies, that sort of thing?"

"In fair-to-good shape, no new work but maintenance is sound. Nothing like the pigsty we found down in Port Murchison; but the roads are pretty bad."

"See if you can get the same organization working on transport, then," Raj said.

"Sir," Ludwig Bellamy cut in, "speaking of Port Murchison—"

Raj nodded, and the ex-*Squadrone* went on, "I've had a letter in from my father."

He smoothed the sheaf of crinkled pages out; they were covered with a thick quasi-literate scrawl. Karl Bellamy had had expensive tutors shipped in from East Residence for his son, as he might have had a concubine or swordsmith. In fact, most *Squadrone* fathers would much rather have spent the money on girls or guns than possibly sissifying *grisuh* learning. The elder Bellamy had seen no need for such polish for himself, and the letter was too confidential for secretaries.

"Colonel Osterville has been removed as Vice-Governor of the Territories," he said.

There was a general murmur of satisfaction around the table. Osterville was one of Barholm's Guards—a semi-official group of troubleshooters-cum-enforcers of good birth, usually men with few prospects save the Governor's favor. Raj had been a Guard, to begin with. Osterville still was, and he'd been sent to relieve Raj at the end of the reconquest under what looked suspiciously like official disfavor.

"The man's got the soul of a pimp," Kaltin Gruder said flatly. "I had to spend six months under his command, and the Spirit spare me any such service again. Who got him, Ludwig?"

"Administrator Berg," Ludwig said, raising his brows. "Malfeasance in office, peculation, suspicion of usurpation of Gubernatorial honors." The last would be the decisive one. Far more dangerous to wear the wrong color shoes than to strip a province bare. "He's being posted as garrison commander to . . . ah, Sandoral."

More satisfied smiles. A hot, dusty town uncomfortably close to the Colony. None of them expected Osterville to shine if it came to serious skirmishing.

observe, Center said. A brief flash; Osterville's face streaked with sweat and dust, bracing himself against the rocking of a railway car. The view out the window was not unlike central Stern Isle, but Raj recognized it as the plateau north of the Oxheads, east of salt-thick Lake Canpech. On Governor Barholm's new Central Railway, heading east away from East Residence and the rich lands of the Hemmar River country.

"*Hingada* Osterville," Hadolfo Zahpata said, in his sing-song southern accent; he was from northwest of Sandoral, and so were most of his 18th Komar Borderers. "I would wish a more able man in the post, though. Ali will be moving sometime. Malash; the Spirit appoints our coming up and our going down."

"Endfile," Raj said, and rapped his knuckles on the table. That was pleasant news, but not strictly germane. "Now, Muzzaf?"

The Komarite cleared his throat. "There is a machine shop which can do the work you requested," he said, setting a Brigade cap-and-ball revolver down on the table. It was a five-shot weapon, loaded with paper cartridges from the front and with nipples for the percussion caps on the back of the cylinder.

"The original design was copied from the Civil Government model," he went on, "so the calibre and pitch of the rifling are the same. Once the cylinder is bored through and tapped, and the hammer modified, it will accept the standard brass cartridge case—and ammunition is available in sufficient quantity if we indent for it now. I, ah," he coughed, "know of certain channels to expedite matters."

"Go for it," Raj said. "Initial order of six thousand, we certainly captured enough. I want every cavalryman to have one by the time we ship out of here; we don't want melee actions, but I'm damned if I'm going to have my lads facing a man with four revolvers and them with nothing but a sword. Messer Historiomo?"

"I see no reason not to authorize the expenditure," the Administrative Service representative said cautiously; but then, he did *everything* cautiously.

"Which brings us," Raj went on, "to the fund. My lady?"

"Every battalion has agreed to contribute in proportion to their losses," she said. "I talked to the officers' wives . . ."

"Good, very good." The Civil Government made little provision for the families of casualties, or for men rendered unfit-for-service. He'd established a tradition of using plunder to set up a pension fund; the men trusted him not to steal it. "Muzzaf, put it in something suitable. Land, I suppose, or town properties. Arrange for trustees, trustworthy ones."

"My love?" Suzette went on.

He nodded. Some people found his conferences a trifle eccentric—Fatima, for example, was acting as secretary to Suzette and had her nine-month-old daughter, named Suzette for her patroness, in a cradle beneath the side table they were using—but they got the work done.

Raj's wife produced a list of her own. "We have about fifty troopers who've got injuries that make them unfit-for-service but not really incapacitated—ones without somewhere to retire to back home, that is. I've looked up about the same number of young Brigaderos widows or orphaned maidens of good reputation and appropriate rank who were covered by the amnesty; there were a fair number of men with medium-sized farms held in fee simple, here. Widows and daughters wouldn't inherit in the absence of male offspring under Brigade law but would under ours; the ones I've talked to are willing and ready to convert to orthodoxy to avoid ending up as spinsters living on their relatives. For that matter, there are a couple of hundred who'll settle for a man on active service; that's a Brigade tradition too. If you know some unmarried troopers you'd like to see get a farm to come back to eventually . . ."

Raj nodded. The same thing had happened spontaneously in the Southern Territories after the conquest, and worked out surprisingly well. Soldiers and their relatives had solid legal status under the Civil Government, and could hold land under low-tax military tenure; desirable qualities in a husband, in uncertain times. Having a farm to retire to after mustering-out was the dream of most troopers who didn't stand to inherit one or a good tenancy. It was a good way to start integrating new territory into the Civil Government as well.

"See to it, then, my sweet. Ah—we could hold a mass ceremony here. The men would like that, and it'll make them remember they're soldiers first and foremost, active or on the invalid list."

Kaltin laughed. "Advise the active-service men to get the brides pregnant before they leave," he said.

"I don't doubt they'll try, Kaltin," Gerrin said. "The dispositions, Raj? We're still scattered to hell-and-gone."

He swung his feet down as servants brought in the breakfast trays. "That is next," he said, accepting a plate and shoveling it in without looking. After a moment he tasted what he was eating and looked over at his wife. "How *do* you manage to dig up a good cook wherever we go?" he asked. Their regular was an East Residence native who refused to leave the walls for whatever reason.

"Hereditary talent, my sweet."

"Well. Now, I'm sure all you gentlemen are having a wonderful time relaxing, but we've got to get Kaltin back into the field before he fades to a sylph and gets worn down to a nub."

"You underestimate me, sir. It's only been a week."

"Nevertheless. Gerrin, you are hereby appointed Purple Commander." He slid a clip of papers down to the other Descotter, who looked through them and began to hand them out to the men who would be his subordinates for the field maneuvers.

"I will be Orange Commander," Raj said, and did likewise.

"Jorg, you'll be in charge of the referees, and I want it as real-istic as we can get without massive casualties. We'll do a thorough briefing this afternoon, but in essence I want to get us better at marching divided—" he held out a hand, fingers splayed "—and fight-ing united." The hand closed into a fist.

"Oh, and we'd better arrange some sort of substantial prize for the best units; the men are starting to think this is going to be a military picnic like the Southern Territories."

"I doubt many who were in those boats with you think that, Raj," Gerrin said soberly.

"Learning by experience can be prohibitively expensive," Raj said. "Next, the *Brigaderos* we sent back to East Residence. They'll need to be retrained, and then they'll need officers. We won't be in charge of that, but between us I think we can have some influence, and it'd be a shame to waste material that good under incompetents. Messers, I'd appreciate it if you'd each prepare me a list of men you think suitable, and we'll see what we can do. Next, promo-tions, demotions, and gold-of-valor awards."

They worked their way through the *huwacheros,* toast and kave, then through a round of kave and cigarettes. He saved the disagree-able signing of death-warrants for last. There was always someone who didn't believe the stories about how hard-ass Messer Raj was about mistreating locals. None from the 5th Descott this time, thank the Spirit . . .

"Does that wrap up the military end of it?" Raj said. He looked out the window; with a little luck, he could get his butt into the saddle this afternoon and do some hands-on work. A chance to avoid Bureaucrat's Bottom a little while longer.

"All but the Star question, oh Savior of the State," Gerrin said. "When do we get on with the rest of the bloody campaign?"

"According to the latest dispatches from East Residence," Raj said judiciously, "negotiations between the Ministry of Barbarians and General Forker are proceeding, mmmm, *in an orderly but discreet fashion* due to *turbulent elements* in Carson Barracks. Interpret that as you will."

"Meaning, Messer," Dinnalsyn said sourly, with the experience of a man brought up in East Residence, "that Forker can't decide whether to crap or get off the pot, because the barb commanders are run-ning around rubbing their heads and wondering what hit them. And the Ministry bureaucrats are sending each other memos consisting of competitively obscure literary allusions and strings of references to precedents back six hundred years. Which is probably what their predecessors were doing six hundred years ago when we lost the Old Residence to the Brigade in the *first* place."

"Pen-pushers," Zahpata said, striking his forehead with his palm.

"I'm assured that the *relevant experts are working earnestly for a peaceful solution to the issues in dispute,*" Raj went on dryly.

"That bad?" Kaltin said. He tore open a roll. "With the relevant experts working for peace, you *know* we're going to have war, Messer—but not until the worst possible time."

"Bite your tongue, major," Raj said. "My estimation is that between them Forker and the Ministry will do exactly that, string things out until the onset of the winter rains and then decide to fight after all. Decide that we should fight."

This time the curses were genuine and heartfelt. With local variations the whole Midworld basin had a climate of warm dry summers and cool-to-cold wet winters. The northerly sectors of the Western Territories got snow, and the whole area had abundant mud. On the unmaintained roads of country under barbarian rule that meant morasses that clogged dogs' feet, sucked the boots off men and mired guns and wagons. Plus foraging would be more difficult, that long after harvest, and even hardy men were more likely to sicken with chest fevers if they had to sleep out in the rains. Disease had destroyed more armies than battle, and they all knew it.

Spring and fall were the best seasons for campaigning; early summer after the wheat harvest was tolerable, although bad water meant cholera unless you were very careful about the Church's sanitation edicts. High summer was bad. Winter was a desperation-only nightmare.

"Nevertheless, if it has to be done, we'll do it," Raj said. He quoted from an ancient Civil Government military handbook: "*Remember that the enemy's bodies too are subject to mortality and fatigue; they are initiated also into the mysteries of death, as are all men.* And even their rank-and-file include a good many landed men, their reservists particularly, who won't be used to living hard. I want us *ready.*

"Ehwardo," he went on. The last living Poplanich looked up. Raj tapped several red-covered ledgers beside him. They had the Ministry of Barbarians seal on their covers, with the odd grain-sheaf subseal of the Foreign Intelligence division.

"Coordinate with Muzzaf and see what you can do about these intelligence reports. I want digests, including what new information you can get from local sources. Chop out the political bumpf and verbiage and the unfounded speculation; give me hard information. Manpower, weapons, road conditions, weather patterns, regional crops and yields and foraging prospects, what railroads the barbs have running, local landowners and Sysups and how they lean."

"General," Ehwardo said, already looking still more abstracted. Raj nodded; Thom's cousin was one of the few noblemen he knew who really appreciated numbers and their uses.

"Messers . . . to work."

The room felt larger after the officers had left, with a clack of the heel-plates of their boots and a jingle as they hitched at their sword-belts. Historiomo cleared his throat and glanced at Suzette and her protege.

"Messa Whitehall has my complete confidence," Raj said.

"Ah. So I was given to understand." A long pause. "I am to understand, then, that the Most Valiant General is pleased with mine and my colleagues' work?"

"Pleasantly surprised," Raj said. "It's important to this war that we have a secure and productive forward base; Stern Isle is the obvious candidate."

He ran his hand over a preliminary report on land tenure on Stern Isle as it had been under the Brigade and would be with the massive transfers of ownership following the conquest. Dry stuff, but crucially important. Cities and trade were the way a few people made their living and the odd merchant grew rich, but land was absolutely crucial to everything. Not just that the overwhelming majority everywhere were peasants, land tenure was the foundation of revenue and political and military power. His own studies, his instincts, and everything Center had taught him agreed that there was nothing more useless than an unconsolidated victory. Conquest without follow-up would crumble away behind him.

The problem was that he was to expert administration what say, Colonel Boyce was to combat command—he could recognize it when he saw it, but lacked inclination and talent himself for anything but the rough-and-ready military equivalent. Which was to the real thing as military music was to music.

"Yes." Historiomo pushed his silver-rimmed glasses up his nose. He was the sort of soft little man you saw by the scores of thousands on the streets of East Residence, with carefully folded cravats and polished pewter buckles on their shoes and drab brown coats. So nondescript it was always a bit of a surprise to see him, as if you'd never met him before.

"Yes, Chief Administrator Berg did tell us that you and your household were not the general run of military nobility, Most Valiant—"

"Messer will do."

"Messer General, then."

"Berg," Raj said with a cold smile, "struck me as being not in the ordinary run of bureaucrat. Once he'd been convinced that I wanted him to cooperate, but intended to get the job done whether he did or not."

"Indeed." Historiomo took the glasses off again and polished them. His voice grew a touch sharper, as if the blurring of vision removed some constraint. "You find us of the Administrative Service, ah, excessively cautious, do you not, Messer Whitehall?"

Raj shrugged. "I have a job of work to do in this world," he said. "To do it, I have to take men as I find them."

"We're used to being despised," Historiomo said with polite bitterness. "The military nobility always have; it's *find us supplies for twenty thousand men,* or *why aren't the roads ready?* But do they listen when we explain? Never. They worship action at the expense of thought, and think that you can overcome any problem with a sword and willpower. They impose solutions that make problems *worse* and we have to work around the wreckage. Or a Governor shoots his way to the Chair and then thinks he can order us to do the impossible. We're the ones who have to tell them no.

"The patricians—" he cast a cautious look at Suzette; the urban nobility was her class, and that of Chancellor Tzetzas "—make an art of intrigue and a god of form at the expense of content. They monopolize the great offices of State and plunder them without shame or thought for long-term consequences, and *we* take the blame. And everybody mocks us, our forms and paperwork, our fussy little precedents. Yet who is it that preserves the institutional memory of the State, who keeps the Civil Government from turning into another feudal hodgepodge of squabbling barons? Who keeps things together and the public services functioning through defeats and civil wars and bad Governors? We do."

"Agreed," Raj said.

Historiomo started, cleared his throat and fiddled with his pen-case.

"Messer, I'm called the Sword of the Spirit of Man. That means I know what you *can't* do with a sword. I'm *not* the pen, the voice, or the conscience of the Spirit. I'm the Sword; I chop obstacles out of the way; I keep the barbarians from burning the cities around the ears of people like you. I do my job; and when I find someone else who can do *his,* then I don't care if they're nobleman, patrician, clerk, merchant. Starless Dark, I don't give a damn if they're Colonists or barbs."

"Most Valiant General," Historiomo said, rising and neatly stacking his document boxes before fastening them together with a leather strap, "I won't say it's a pleasure to work with you. Alarming, in fact. But it is a *relief*, I assure you. Messa Whitehall."

He bowed deeply and walked out with the strap over his shoulder.

"Well, that'll teach us not to judge a scroll by the winding-stick," Suzette said. She bent over the crib beneath her table. "I think this young lady needs to be changed, Fatima."

When they were alone, she smiled at Raj. "And what, my darling, is *my* function with the Sword of the Spirit?"

"You keep him from going completely fucking insane," Raj said, smiling back.

"So far."

"So far."

CHAPTER TEN

"You are all conspiring to drive me *mad*," Filip Forker said, pulling off the light ceremonial helmet and throwing it to the floor with a clang. "Mad, mad!" Shocked murmurs rolled for a moment down the long chamber, until the armored guards along the walls thumped their musket-butts on the floor. Once, twice, three times; when they returned to immobility, the silence was complete.

Attendants closed in around the Brigade monarch; one passed a damp cloth over his face, and another got in a lick with a polishing cloth at the thin silver breastplate the slight little man wore. A minister murmured in his ear; after a while Forker's face set in an expression of petulant resignation, and he sat again.

"Go on, go on."

Even the high arched ceiling and meter-thick walls of the Primary Audience Hall couldn't take any of the muggy heat out of a Carson Barracks summer. The temperature outside was thirty Celsius, and the city was built out of dark basalt blocks and set in the middle of a swamp; in winter the building would be chilly and dank instead, for all the great arched fireplaces at either end of the Hall. The skylights sent shafts of light ten meters down into hot gloom, with the wings of insects glittering as they crossed from shadow into sun. Very little light or air came in through the narrow slit windows.

The men who had built—ordered the building—of the Hall hadn't exactly intended it as a fortress. If anything, it had originally been designed to hold large assemblies for public address, and incidentally to intimidate petitioners. Standing off attackers had not been far from the builders' minds, though, and ordinary comfort just wasn't something to which they had attached much importance.

The Civil Government embassy rose from their stools below the Seat and bowed, hands on chests.

"If Your Mightiness will deign to examine these documents once again," their leader began again, with infinite patience. "Much will be made clear, as clear as the Operating Code of the Spirit."

His Namerique so perfectly adjusted to upper-class Brigade ears that it was more conspicuous than an accent, coming from a dark clean-shaven man in a long embroidered robe. A gesture suggested the age-yellowed papers on a side table below the Seat without the vulgarity of actually pointing.

"You will see that by agreement between your . . . predecessor His Mightiness General Oskar Grakker and the then Admiral of the Squadron Shelvil Ricks, in the time of our Sovereign Lord and Sole Autocrat Laron Poplanich, Governor of the Civil Government of Holy Federation, may the Spirit upload the souls of the worthy dead into Its Nets, the bulk of Stern Isle was granted as dower property to Mindy-Sue Grakker and the heirs of her body and Shelvil Ricks. Which is to say, the Admirals of the Squadron, which is to say—since ex-Admiral Connor Auburn has been persuaded by grace of the Spirit to lay down the unseemly usurped sovereignty which Geyser Ricks unrighteously seized—which is to say, the heir is our Most Sovereign Mighty Lord Barholm Clerett, Viceregent of the Spirit of Man upon Earth. In no way, most Mighty General, could the repossession of Stern Isle therefore be held a usurpation or aggression; for on the contrary righteousness consists of acting rightly—"

The voice droned on for another twenty minutes of rhetorical strophe and antistrophe, spiced out with appeals to truth, justice, reason and comparisons to events that no Brigade member in the Hall besides Forker himself had ever heard of. Unlike most of his nation, General Forker had had a comprehensive classical education; it was one major source of his unpopularity.

At last he broke in peevishly: "Yes, yes, We will read your position paper, Ambassador Minh. At our leisure. These matters cannot be settled in a day, you know."

"Your Mightiness," Minh said, bowing again in profound agreement.

"Who's next?' Forker asked, as the Civil Government ambassadors bowed themselves backward, as neatly choreographed as dancers. Despite the heat and the prickly rash under his ceremonial uniform, the sight mollified him a little.

They know how to serve, he thought.

"Your Mightiness, the inventor and newsletter producer Martini of Pedden, currently dwelling in Old Residence, desires—"

"No!" This time Forker brushed aside the helping hands as he rose. "When will you learn not to waste my time with trivialities?" The minister leaned close again, but the Brigade ruler interrupted him: "I don't care *how* much he paid you. This audience is at an end. We will withdraw. Send the Chief Librarian Kassador to my quarters, *after* I've had a bath."

Stentor-voiced, a Captain of the Life Guards called: "Hear the word;

this audience is at an end. So orders our General, His Mightiness Filip Forker, Lord of Men."

The great hall echoed, cracking as the guards stamped their musket butts again on the floor and then brought the long weapons to port arms. Two platoons along either wall marched up to the Seat and out across the vacant space between the petitioners and the commander's dais, then did a left-wheel to face the crowd. The captain snapped another order, and they began to march forward in slow-pace: with the foot remaining poised for an instant before it came down in a unified hundredfold crash. It was a showy maneuver and perfectly timed. It also let everyone get to the big doors at the rear in an orderly fashion, without allowing any loitering. Nobody who saw the Life Guards' faces doubted that getting in their way would be a bad idea.

Forker and his entourage left by exits in the high arch behind the Seat. The remaining men were officers and nobles too important to be hustled out with the bulk of the petitioners and not close enough to Forker to leave by the VIP entrance within the royal enclosure. They made their own way out the main doors, as the Guards countermarched back to the walls and settled into position again. Footsteps echoed, with most of the sound-muffling human bodies out of the barn-like structure. Banners hung limp above their heads in the still, musky air. The bronze clamps that held ancient energy-weapons to the walls were green with verdigris; the lasers themselves were as bright as the day reverent hands had set them there, down to the stamped *591st Provisional Brigade* on the stocks.

"What do you know, Howyrd," Ingreid Manfrond said, lowering his voice slightly as they walked out past another line of guards onto the portico. "His Maybeness actually made a decision without countermanding it."

"Wrong, Ingreid," Howyrd Carstens replied.

His friend wore the fringed jacket and tweed trousers of an off-duty noble, the leather strips ending in gold beads; there were gold plaques on his sword-belt, rubies on the elaborate basket guard around the hilt, and his spurs were platinum. The sword-hilt and the hand that rested on it had both seen real use. Carstens was in the green-grey-black uniform of the General's Dragoons, with Colonel's insignia.

"He must've settled something with the *grisuh* last night," the officer said. "This was to confirm it publicly. And he chickened out; probably afraid we'd hack him to pieces on the Seat." A rare occurrence but not entirely unknown in Brigade history.

They paused and lit their pipes, two gentlemen with gray in their beards and long clubbed hair talking idly in the shade of the portico on a hot summers day, beneath one of the three-story columns hewn in the shape of a Federation assault landing boat. Ushers came and returned their revolvers: nobody but the Life Guards carried firearms inside the Hall.

The parade square ahead of them was five hundred meters on a side; the black bulk of the Palace behind them, the four-square Cathedron of the Spirit of Man of This Earth to their left, with its facade of glass mosaic, and the Iron House of War to the right. Dead ahead to the north was a gap, where the road ran down off the artificial mound into the main part of the city. Canals were as numerous as roads, and the houses were squat two-story structures with few exterior windows but a good deal of carving and terracotta-work painted in bright colors. Carson Barracks was the only major town in the Western Territories built wholly since the Brigade arrived down from the Base Area two centuries after the Fall.

The low-sunk defenses were a lip in the earth from here; they'd been modernized a century or so ago. Carson Barracks didn't really need walls. It stood at the center of several thousand square kilometers of marsh and bog, hardly a hectare of it capable of bearing a man's weight and much of it quicksand. Melancholy wastes of swamp were visible from where they stood, with only the arrow-straight causeway and canal that led north to the railhead on solid ground near the Padan river to vary the landscape. Waving reddish-green native reeds, the green-green Terran variety, an occasional glint of water through the thick ground-haze. The air stank of vegetable decay and the sewage that drained into the swamp and moved, very slowly, downslope toward the river.

Not many Brigade members lived in Carson Barracks by choice, although duty brought many there for a time. Most of the permanent population were slaves, or administrators drawn from the old native upper classes.

"It's probably a good thing fuckin' Forker waffled again," Ingreid went on. "The only thing he could make up his mind on would be to sell us out to the civvies."

"Yeah. What we *ought* to be doing is mobilizing. You remember my cousin Henrik?"

Ingreid rubbed his bearded chin. Hairs caught in the thick layer of horny callus that ringed the thumb and forefinger of his right hand where it controlled his sword.

"Bit younger than you? Had a captaincy in the regulars, then killed . . . shit, what's-his-name—"

"Danni Wimbler's son Erik."

"—over a woman, had to make tracks. Good man, as I remember." Ingreid snapped his fingers. "I do remember. He's the one cut the head off that Stalwart chief at, oh, up near Monnerei."

"Yeah; good man, but no luck. The *grisuh* killed him on Stern Isle."

"Spirit of Man of This Earth download his core," the other man said.

Howyrd touched a lump of blessed agate he wore around his neck. "Yeah. Thing is, one of his men lived, knocked out by a shell. Got shipped out on a slaver after the *grisuh* caught him, then pirates jumped the ship and sold crew and cargo in Tortug. This guy, Eddi, he killed a guard and stole a sailboat, turned up half-dead . . . anyway, he told me about the fighting. More like what a sicklefoot pack does to a herd of sheep. The Squadron wasn't any accident. Ingreid, we ought to be mobilizing. Right now."

The other noble shook his head. "Damned if I thought we'd ever be running scared of the civvies," he mused.

"More like running scared of this Whitehall."

"Think he's really got the Outer Dark workin' for him?"

They spat and made a gesture with their left hands. "*Ni*, he's just one grenade-on-toast of a fighting man," Howyrd said. "They say when he had some Skinners fighting with him, he hung one for killing a civvie trooper, then rode into their camp alone—and they made him a blood-brother or something."

Ingreid winced. "I fought the Skinners once. In maybe a hundred years, I'll want to do *that* again." He shook his head. "Tell you what I'm going to do, I'm going to hire and outfit another regiment of guards, and start buying powder and lead, and check that all my tenants-in-chief and freeholder-vassals have their rifles ready and their swords sharp. *And* I'll tell everyone I know to do the same, down to the petty-squires and fifty-hectare men. And if Forker doesn't like it, Forker can go suck a dead dog's farts. He's not going to have *me* drowned in my bath like he did Charlotte Welf."

Carstens sighed and knocked the dottle out of his pipe against his heel; the spur jingled sweetly as he did. "Watch out you don't get a native uprising," he cautioned. His friend was wealthy even by the upper nobility's standard, but he would have to squeeze his serfs fairly hard to support an extra twelve hundred men and their dogs and gear.

"Then we get practice whipping peon butt," Ingreid snorted. "Heretic bastards deserve it, anyway. They're all civvie-lovers, from the ploughboys to the so-called gentry—whatever they say to your face. *He's* no better," he went on, jerking a thumb over his shoulder at the Palace. "Books, librarians, it's enough to make a real man puke. Outer Dark, he's got to look at some book before he knows what hole to put it in. If he's got anything to put."

"Yeah, and I've got to waste my time and my regiment's back on the border," Howyrd said.

"They're not coming by land?"

"*Ni*. Nothing but rocks up there, or swamps worsn' this."

As if to counterpoint his words, a distant honking roar came out of the reedbeds. A hadrosauroid herd by the sound; the big grazers had been preserved around Carson Barracks for hunting and as emergency food supplies. Hadrosauroids ranged up to four or five tons each, and they flourished on the reeds. Howyrd flipped a finger at an entirely different sort of sauroid tooth hanging on his amulet chain, a curved cutting dagger serrated on both sides and long as a woman's hand.

"Only there's still a lot of big meat-eaters around there, so you have to build palisaded camps. Not enough cleared land or farmers for major campaigning; most of what the civvies've got there is tribal stuff, mercs. Naw, when they come, they'll come by sea."

Grooms brought up their dogs, big glossy mastiffs standing chest-high to a tall man at the shoulder. A squad of Carsten's dragoon Regulars rode up as escorts for their colonel, armed with rifle, broadsword and revolver; they had the worn look of a weapon that fits a man's hand easily when he reaches. Ingreid's guards were in the buff and gray of his household regiment; half the hundred-man detachment were dragoons, half heavy cavalry on Newfoundlands, with steel back-and-breasts, helmets, arm-guards and thigh-tassets. They carried twelve-foot lances as well as the usual swords and firearms, and the long slender ashwood poles stood like a steel-tipped thicket above the square.

"Off to see Marie?" Howyrd said.

Ingreid gathered his reins. "No such luck. Marie Welf tells me that I'm old enough to be her father—my sons *are* older than her— and I should go looking for a nice widow of forty with tits like pillows if I want to marry again."

They exchanged a look. Whoever married Marie Welf would be technically an Amalson, and eligible for the Brigades elective monarchy. Those elections were settled by weight of shot as often as numbers of votes, but that was one rule always observed. Forker was childless and getting old. Any sons Marie bore . . .

Ingried shook his head. "She's got guts, have to say that for the bitch."

"Not the only thing she's got, by the Spirit," Carstens said with a man-to-man grin. More harshly: "And she'd better get a protector soon. Does she think she can breathe bathwater, just because her momma got the chance to try?"

"*Women,*" Ingreid said. "Hail and farewell, friend. See you on the battlefield."

"And some people think he's a simple soldier," Cabot Clerett said bitterly, beside her on the church steps.

Fatima wiped at her eye with a lace handkerchief, managing a final sniffle. Civil Government convention was for ladies to weep when a guest at other peoples weddings; it seemed bizarre to her, but custom was custom. The ceremony had been beautiful, she had a lovely new dress of light-blue silk, torofib woven in Azania, and Gerrin and Bartin—she smiled to herself—had promised her another present as well, fitting to the occasion. It was *hard* to cry under those circumstances.

The newly married couples were parading two by two out of the high brass-and-steel doors of the Wager Bay Cathedron, newly converted back to the Spirit of Man of the Stars; only fair, since there had been barely enough Earth Spirit cultists in town for a congregation. The newlyweds passed beneath an arch of sabers held by their comrades, on to awnings and trestle tables. Whole oxen and pigs were roasting over portable grills; there was to be a feast for the battalions of the men concerned, courtesy of the commanding officers of the units and Messer Raj.

"They *are* simple soldiers, Messer Cabot," Fatima pointed out ingenuously.

It was just going on for sundown, but the post-siesta crowds of townsfolk were kept out of the square by pickets tonight. Both moons were up, and paper lanterns had been strung from the official buildings which ringed the plaza. A breeze from the sea tempered the days late-summer heat to a languorous softness.

The troops were on their best behavior, with detachments in *guardia* armbands to see that they stayed that way later after the wine had flowed. The wedding songs they were bawling out ranged from the bawdy to the obscene, but that was customary in most places. That the couples had barely met before the ceremony was also common enough; and if the grooms had been among those who slaughtered the brides' fathers or former husbands in the fighting around Fort Wager, that too was not unknown among a warrior people like the Brigade. Nobody knew for sure who had killed who . . . and life would not be easy for Brigade women without protectors among a hostile native populace, in a province newly conquered by aliens of a different faith.

"No, not them," Cabot said. "The men are all right; good soldiers, they deserve a holiday, they've been working hard."

"Too hard, some," Fatima said.

She generally helped out in the 5th's field hospitals, and there had been a full complement of broken bones and heatstroke during the field exercises. Moving thousands of men at speed through rough country was dangerous even without live ammunition. Plus cracked heads and ribs from over-enthusiastic encounters with practice sabers, sheathed bayonets and rifle butts during the melees. Especially between units with a history of bad blood like the 5th Descott and the Roger Slashers.

"Well, if they didn't like to fight they wouldn't be much use, would they?" Cabot said.

His voice was friendly in a patronizing way. Fatima suspected he talked to her only because he was fairly sure she didn't understand him most of the time; doubly sure, since she was both a woman and a Colonist. Also he was lonely in the Expeditionary Force, close only to Ludwig Bellamy and constrained with him. Most of the men of comparable rank were either Companions or professionals deeply respectful of the General's abilities; they were older, too. For all that, he was a nice enough young man, she thought. No problems after her firmly polite refusal of a *pro forma* attempt at seduction, the sort most men felt obliged to make toward another's mistress. Of course, Fatima was often near Lady Whitehall. . . .

"No, it's the *land,*" Cabot Clerett said. "I can't think what Historiomo is thinking of, to let him distribute *land* to men under his command! Cash donatives are bad enough, but if you give a man a farm you've got him for life. *And* it makes all the others hope for the same thing." The faint hope of saving enough for a homestead out of plunder was one major reason so many younger sons of yeoman-tenants and freeholders joined the cavalry.

"Government would give them farms?" Fatima asked, making her eyes go wide. Suzette had shown her how to do that.

"Ah, no." His face lit. "There's Lady Suzette—"

His eyes sought her out. Raj and his wife were strolling between the tables, exchanging a word here and there and toasting the couples. It wouldn't be appropriate or dignified for a man of his rank and birth to actually sit at table with enlisted men in a social gathering, unlike a campfire on a battlefield. The first table started to raise a cheer, then quieted at a single motion of Raj's hand. The singing immediately grew less raucous when Suzette came by; two of her maidservants followed her with sacks, and she was handing gifts to the brides, small things like shawls or brooches. Words of reassurance probably meant more, to young women now alone with men with whom they might not even share a common language beyond a few words of the Spanjol foreign to both.

"I don't understand it," Cabot muttered, half to himself. "One minute he's trying to buy their favor, and then . . . He works them like peons right after they've won a battle; he keeps the strictest discipline I've ever seen, flogs and hangs for minor offenses against peasants—"

"He make them win," Fatima said.

"Yes," Cabot said; again to himself. "He's got guts and he knows his trade, I'll grant him that. And he wins. That's what makes him dangerous."

"General who lose is not dangerous to his *Sultan?*" Fatima asked. Cabot shot her a sharp glance, then relaxed at her palpable innocence.

"Yes, Fatima," he said. "That's the problem, you see. Bad generals may ruin you; good ones may overthrow you. Now, a *Governor* who was a successful general . . ."

"Besides," Fatima went on, frowning, "I think—thought—Lady Whitehall have the idea for the weddings."

"Oh, Lady Suzette," Cabot said, the throttled anger in his voice vanishing. "Suzette. She's an angel. I'm sure she didn't have anything in mind but helping—"

"Excuse me, Messer Clerett," Gerrin Staenbridge said. "I've come to collect my mistress."

"Of course," Cabot said, bowing. "And I complement you on your taste, Messer Staenbridge . . . in this at least."

Gerrin's grin was toothily insincere as he bowed the other man on his way. "No style at all," he murmured to himself after the Governor's nephew had moved out of earshot. "Bottom like a peasant, to boot. Very boot-able, in fact."

Fatima was thinking over Cabot's last remark to her. "Gerrin," she said, "tell me: why smart young man stupid about a woman?" *My lady Suzette is a djinni, not a houri,* she thought in her mother tongue.

"What was that?" Bartin Foley said, coming up on her other side.

"I ask why all young men so stupid," Fatima said, taking his arm as well.

"Imp," he said. She stuck out her tongue at him.

"Are you sure you will not need me more here, saaidya?" Abdullah said.

Suzette looked around her sitting room; while she did, her hands straightened the pile of papers before her. The punkah overhead made a languid attempt to stir the air, and hot white light speared in through the slats of the shutters. A cat on a pile of silk cushions beneath writhed in its slumber, spreading a paw. From the court-yard garden came the sound of splashing water and a rake slowly, very slowly, gathering leaves.

"We won't *be* here much longer, my faithful one," she said. "Now: here is the report from Ndella. Read and destroy it."

"Ah, that one," Abdullah said with professional appreciation.

Ndella cor Whitehall had been born in the Zanj city of Liswali and trained as a physician, before being captured by Tewfik's men and sold north to Al Kebir. As a freedwoman of Suzette Whitehall she plied her old trade and a more discreet one among the servants of the Gubernatorial Palace.

"Men tend to ignore women and servants," Suzette said judiciously.

"Fools do," Abdullah conceded. "But then, most men are fools. Even the wise among us can be led into folly by the organ of generation. Or so my wife claims."

"So I've found," Suzette agreed. "Now, there are some juicy details in there on just how far along Forker went toward surrender at one point. Use them with extreme discretion, but anyone who knows him will probably believe it.

"Here," she went on, "are *ayzed* and *beyam.*" Zanj, an abortificant and poison respectively; brewed from native Bellevue herbs known only in the far south and utterly untraceable in the western Midworld. Suzette sighed: "I only wish there were two of you, Abdullah."

The Druze smiled. "Am I not multitudes, saaidya?"

Right now he was a Spanjol-speaking merchant of Port Murchison; down to the four-cornered hat with modest plume, green linen swallowtail jacket with brass buttons, striped cravat and natty chiseled-steel buckles on the shoes below his knee-breeches. He made a flourish with the hat, bowing and letting his hand rest on the hilt of a plain sword.

"I shall be welcome in Lion City." Particularly bringing a sloop with a cargo of Stern Isle sulfur and Southern Territories saltpeter. Both restricted cargoes in time of war, of course, but a few hundred pounds would make no real difference.

"Less so in Carson Barracks," she said. More briskly:

"Now: unless I miss my woman and your reports are false, Marie Welf is well aware that she's the sheep at the carnosauroid's congress. Forker and half the nobles in the Brigade want to murder her, the other half to marry her and father an heir to the Seat—and once she's had a male child, she's an inconvenience and danger. None of the prospects pleases, and most of the men are vile.

"You will approach her *only* when she's desperate. This isn't a girl who waits for a rescuer, but she's inexperienced. She'll jump at a way out. Forker keeps her isolated, but she has friends, and the Welfs have partisans. Investigate them also."

"Ah, saaidya," Abdullah said, tucking the small case of vials into an inside pocket of his tailcoat. "Were you a man, what a ruler you would be!"

"Were I a man," Suzette said tartly, "I'd have better sense than to want to be a ruler."

"As I said, my lady."

She extended a hand, and Abdullah bent over it in the style of the Civil Government. Suzette dropped back into Arabic:

"Go, thou Slave of God," she said, which was what his name meant. "May my God and thine go with thee."

"May the Beneficent, the Lovingkind, be with thee and thy lord."

Alone, Suzette picked up a packet of letters—they were copies of Cabot's reports to his uncle—and put them down again. Raj was out with most of the Expeditionary Force, on maneuvers again. Cabot and she were to meet at a little cove, where the swimming was safe. Quite respectable, since several of her women would be along; the Civil Government had a nudity taboo but not during bathing.

"Some men," she murmured, stroking the cat, "are governable by the fulfillment of their desires, and some by their frustration." For the present, Cabot Clerett *wanted* to worship from afar; his concubine was probably sitting down rather carefully these days.

How long he could be controlled that way was another matter, of course. A man who knew himself able, but also knew he owed everything to his uncle's preferment. Wild to accomplish something of his own . . . and dangerously reckless in his hate, from the evidence in the letters. Far too dangerous to Raj to be tolerated.

✧   ✧   ✧

"That Bureaucrat's Bottom is slowing you down, Whitehall," Gerrin Staenbridge taunted, and lunged.

Clack. The double-weight wooden practice sabers met, touched. Lunge, parry from the wrist, feint, cut-stamp-cut. They advanced and retreated across the carefully uneven gravel-rock-earth floor of the salle d'armes. The scuff of feet and slamming clatter of oak on oak echoed from the high whitewashed walls. For a moment they went corps-a-corps.

"Save your breath . . . old man," Raj grunted. A convulsive heave sent them to blade's length again.

In fact, neither man was carrying an ounce of spare flesh, something fully apparent since they were stripped to the waist for the exercise, with only face-masks as protection. Staenbridge was a little thicker through the shoulders, Raj slightly longer in the arm; both big men and hugely strong for their size, moving with the carnivore grace of those who had killed often with cold steel and trained since birth. Raj was drilling hard because it was a way to burn out the poisons of frustration that were worse with every passing week. Staenbridge met the fury of his attack with six extra years of experience. Sweat hung heavy on the dry hot air, slicking down torsos marked with the scars of every weapon known on Bellevue.

"Ahem." Then louder: "Ahem!"

They disengaged, leaped back and lowered their blades. Raj ripped the face-mask off and turned, chest pumping like a deep slow bellows. The salle d'armes of the Wager Bay commandants seemed frozen for a moment in time; Ludwig Bellamy practicing forms before a mirror, Kaltin Gruder on a masseurs table; Fatima on a bench keeping a careful grip on young Bartin Staenbridge, the three-year-old was supposed to be getting his first taste of training but showed a disconcerting tendency to run in wherever there was action. Outside in the courtyard Suzette wrote a letter at a table beneath a trellis of bougainvillea. Her pen poised over the paper. The slapping of the masseurs' hands ran down into silence.

Bartin Foley was sweating too, as if he had run some way in the heat.

"Far be it from me, Messers, to disturb this tranquil scene—"

Raj made a warning sound and snatched at the paper that the younger man pulled out of his helmet-lining. Everyone recognized the purple seal. Raj's hands shook very slightly as he broke it.

He looked up and nodded, then tossed the Gubernatorial Rescript back to Foley and accepted the towel from the servant

"The Brigaderos won some skirmish on the frontier," he said. "A regiment of their dragoons whipped on some tribal auxiliaries of ours. Forker is claiming that indicates who the Spirit of Man favors. The Governor has ordered me to reduce the Western

Territories to obedience, commencing immediately. With full pro-consular authority for one year, or the duration of the war."

A sigh ran through the room. "Everything but the men, the dogs and a change of underdrawers is on the ships," Staenbridge said.

Raj nodded again. "Tomorrow with the evening tide," he said softly.

The main municipal stadium of Port Wager had superb acoustics; it was used for public speaking and theatre, as well as bull-fights and baseball games. It was well into the morning when the last unit filed in; since there were so many This Earth cultists in the ranks now, Raj had held religious services by groups of units rather than for the whole force. And dropped in on every one of them personally, and be damned what the priests would say back in East Residence.

He knew what the Spirit of Man, of This Earth *and* the Stars, needed. What his men needed.

Silence fell like a blade as he walked out. The tiers of seats that rose in a semicircle up the hillside were blue with the uniform coats of the troops; the paler faces turned toward him like flowers towards the sun as he walked up the steps of the timber podium. The blue and silver Starburst backed it; beyond that was the harbor and the masts of the waiting ships. In front the unit banners of thirty battalions were planted in the sand.

Raj faced his men, hands clenched behind his back.

"Fellow soldiers," he began. A long surf-wave of noise rose from the packed ranks, like a wave over deep ocean. The impact was stunning in the confined space. So was the response when he raised a hand; suddenly he could hear the blood beating in his own ears.

"Fellow soldiers, those of you who've campaigned with me before, in the desert, at Sandoral where we crushed Jamal's armies, in the Southern Territories where we broke a kingdom in one campaign—you and I, we know each other."

This time the sound was white noise, physically painful. He raised his hand again and felt it cease, like Horace answering to the rein. The raw intoxication of it struck him for a moment; this was true power. Not the ability to compel, but thousands of armed men willing to follow where he led—because he could *lead.*

remember, you are human, Center's voice whispered. They would follow; and many would die. Duty was heavier than mountains.

"You know what's demanded of you now," he went on.

"For those of you who haven't been in the field with me before, only this: obey your orders, stand by your comrades and your salt. Treat the peasants kindly; we're fighting to give them right governance, not to oppress them. Treat captive foes according to the terms of their surrender, for my honor and yours and the sake of good faith between fighting men.

"And never, never be afraid to engage anyone who stands before you. Because nowhere in this world will you meet troops who are your equal. The Spirit of Man marches with us!"

The shouting started with the former *Squadrones*, the 1st and 2nd Cruisers.

"*Hail! Hail! Hail!*"

Their deep-chested bellows crashed into the moment of silence after Raj finished speaking. The 5th Descott and the 7th, the Slashers— one by one they rose to their feet, helmets on the muzzles of their rifles.

"*RAJ! RAJ! RAJ!*"

"By the Spirit, these are good troops," Gerrin Staenbridge said, watching the troopers lead their mounts onto a transport. The big animals walked cautiously onto the gangplanks, testing the footing with each step.

"About the best fighting army the Civil Government's ever fielded," Raj said.

using reasonable equalizing assumptions, that statement is accurate to within 7%, Center observed.

Staenbridge rapped his knuckles on the helmet he carried in the crook of his arm. "My oath, with sixty thousand like them we could sweep the earth."

bellevue, Center corrected in Raj's mind, **so restated, and speaking of the main continental mass, probability of victory for such a force over all civilized opponents would be 76% ±3, under your leadership,** Center said.

"Unfortunately, Gerrin," Raj said, settling his own helmet and buckling the chinstrap.

A groom brought up Horace; was towed up by Horace, rather, when the hound scented its master. He put a hand on the smooth warm curve of the black dog's neck.

"Unfortunately, the question isn't whether we can conquer the world with sixty thousand—it's whether we can conquer two hundred thousand Brigaderos warriors with less than twenty thousand."

probability of successful outcome 50% ±10, with an exceptionally large number of overdetermined individually contingent factors, Center admitted, **in colloquial terms, too close to call.**

Raj took Horace's reins in his hand below the angle of his jaw. Suzette was coaxing her palfrey Harbie towards the gangplank as well; the mounts knew they would be separated from their riders for the voyage, and were whimpering their displeasure. That was why it was best for the owner to settle the dog, if their primary bond was to the rider and not the grooms.

He took a deep breath. "Let's go find out."

CHAPTER ELEVEN

Sixty or so dogs waded out on the beach in a group; they shook themselves in a salt-water thunderstorm and fell to greeting each other after the voyage in an orgy of tail-wagging, behind-sniffing, muzzle-licking, growling and stiff-legged hackle-showing.

"Just like a bunch of East Residence society matrons at a ball," Suzette observed in passing, shouldering her Colonial-made carbine.

The command group gave a harsh collective chuckle and turned back to the map pinned to the stunted pricklebark tree.

"Landing's going well," Jorg Menyez observed.

"Ought to, the practice we've had," Raj said.

The Civil Government fleet lay off a low coastline of sand, scree, heather and reddish native groundrunner; inland it rose to clumps of dark oakwood separated by meadows where the grass was thigh-high and straw yellow. Sandspits a kilometer offshore broke the force of the surf, and a gently shelving sandy bottom made it easier to beach the smaller vessels. Those had been run in at high tide a few hours ago, and a steam ram was already towing an empty one off stern-first to make room for the others. Piles of bales and crates and square-sided, rope-handled ammunition boxes were going up above the high-water mark; there were even a few determined camp-followers, soldiers' women and servants—cavalry troopers were allowed one per eight-man squad—wading ashore already as well.

A 5th master-sergeant and two other troopers came up to the dogs; they each bridled the dominant animal in a platoon-pack and led it off after a few warning nose-thumps with the handles of their dogwhips convinced the beasts that it was time to go back to work.

"Follow t'heel, ye bitches' brood!" the noncom shouted, and set off at a trot upslope to the perimeter the first-in units had established. Cavalry might fight mostly on foot, but they felt extremely uncomfortable without their mounts to hand. The rest of the giant carnivores followed along after, heads up and sniffing the wind

119

blowing from inland. More dogs were swimming for the shore; from the way a few pursuing longboats darted about out by the skerries, the usual scattering of animals determined to try swimming back to their last port of call were being rounded up.

The larger ships, four hundred to eight hundred tons, were anchored offshore. Cargo nets swung stores and equipment down to boats; or a field-gun down to a stout raft of barrels and timbers Dinnalsyn's men had knocked together. Rowboats towed it toward the shore, the brass fittings of its breech glittering in the morning sun, as bright as the droplets of spray cast up by the oars. Company after company of infantry scrambled down nets from the grounded ships, fell in to the shouts and whistles of their officers, and marched upslope. The metal-leather-sweat-dogshit smell of an Army encampment was already overlaying the clean odors of sea and heath.

Twenty thousand humans and ten thousand dogs were coming ashore, and Raj intended to have the whole process completed by nightfall.

"Jorg," he went on. The infantry colonel sneezed and nodded. "I want your infantry to—"

"Make the standard fortified camp, I know," he said. "We also serve who only dig ditches." The ground was fairly flat, so the men would scarcely need the artillery to drive stakes for layout; they could make a standard camp in their sleep, and sometimes did after a forced march. He looked around; there were no large Brigade settlements within a day's march, by the map.

"Since we're only staying a few nights, is that entirely necessary? There's a great deal else for the men to do."

Raj grinned like a carnosauroid. "That's what I thought at Ksar Bourgie," he said. "And nearly got converted to a hareem attendant by Tewfik. Dig in, if you please. The men can set up their tents or not, the weather looks to stay fine, but I want the firing parapet, the pit-latrines and the water supply laid on as if we were going to be here a month."

"Ci, mi heneral."

"The armored cars are coming ashore," Dinnalsyn noted. "Do you want them assembled?"

The artilleryman sounded slightly ambivalent. Raj knew how he felt. The vehicles were boiler-plate boxes on wheels, propelled by the only gas engines in the Civil Government, expensively hand-made. They were temperamental and delicate, required constant maintenance, and had to be hauled by oxen if they moved any distance overland. They were a hell of noise and fumes and heat for the crews in operation. Still, with riflemen or light cannon firing from behind bulletproof cover, they could be decisive at a critical point—and that made up for the endless bother of hauling them around.

Raj nodded. "Just the frames and shells," he said. The engines and armament could be fitted in a day or two and the empty shells were much easier to transport.

"Right," Raj went on, "this is the Crown Peninsula." He tapped the thumb-shaped outline on the map; it stuck out from the main coast of the Western Territories on the eastern fringe. "We're here." On the west coast, a hundred kilometers up from Lion City, the provincial capital, and across five hundred klicks of open water from the coast nearest the Old Residence.

"We'll secure the Crown and Lion City, then advance north"—he traced a line northwestward—"cross the Waladavir River at the bridge here or here where it's fordable, then move southeast toward Old Residence. What exactly we do then depends on opportunity and the enemy, but I intend to have the city before the winter sets hard.

"Our immediate objective is to pacify the Crown outside Lion City. The city has the only real garrison, about four thousand of the General's regulars; for the rest, it's the landowners' household troops we'll be facing. I expect most of them to give up, but don't count on it in any particular case.

"Gerrin, you take two-thirds of the 5th, the 2nd Residence Battalion and two guns, and head northwest up the coast road." His other hand pointed inland. "Hadolfo, your Borderers and the 1st Cruisers, two guns, northeast. Kaltin, you take the 7th Descott and three guns—you've got a couple of crossroads towns and may need them—and head directly east. Ehwardo, you've got Poplanich's Own and the Maximilliano Dragoons and a battery. Go southeast, to the other side of the Crown, down the main spinal road. Ludwig, you take the 2nd Cruisers and the Rogor Slashers and two batteries. Head straight south down to the gates of Lion City, and make sure nobody gets in or out. The city's going to be enough of a problem without too many household units stiffening their defense."

Suzette returned, with a string of HQ servants bearing trays of grilled sausages in split rolls. Everyone grabbed one; Raj used his to gesture between bites.

"You've all seen the sicklefoot and trihorn matches?"

A chorus of nods. Trihorns were browsing sauroids with bone armor on their head and shoulders, up to six tons of vile temper, common in thinly-peopled wilderness. Sicklefeet were smallish carnosauroids, a little more than man-size with a huge curved dewclaw on their hind feet, usually held up against the leg; they hunted in packs, vicious and incredibly agile, leaping in the air to extend their claws and kick-slash their prey to death. The two species rarely interacted in their natural habitats, but they were often matched in large city stadiums in the Civil Government.

"We're the sicklefeet, the Brigaderos are the trihorns. If we let them use their strength, they'll crush us. We slash and move and let them bleed to death."

Raj put his hand on the map, palm on the landing ground and

fingers splayed out across the map. Then he rotated the hand, pulling the fingers together as they approached Lion City.

"You'll move south clockwise, sweeping the countryside repeatedly; Ludwig, you're the anvil for any who filter past. Speed and impact, everyone—don't pee on them, boot their heads. If we give them time to catch their breath, we'll have bands of them hiding in the woods for years, and we do *not* have enough troops to garrison. Stamp on anyone who actively resists; stamp hard, strike terror. Strip those who surrender of every weapon down to their belt-knives and every man who even looks like a soldier and send them back to base; we'll run them to East Residence in the returning transports and commandeered shipping. I don't want an ounce of powder or lead left available, either. Destroy whatever weapons you can't easily cart away; once we've got the area pacified, Administrator Historiomo will be raising a police and militia from the native population, and we can use the captured weapons to arm them.

"Again, messers, the *only* way we can dominate so large an area with so few troops is to roll them up before they realize what's hit them. If we look like winners, the native population will also rally to us, and we *need* their active support against the Brigaderos. What happens in the Crown will be crucial to the whole campaign.

"Jorg, there's going to be plenty for you to do as well. All the flying columns will be sending back prisoners by the hundreds; they'll also be calling on you for temporary infantry garrisons to hold confiscated supplies, weapons, and strategic spots.

"You've all got the intelligence reports," he went on. "I've noted the magnate families I want hostages from. We'll move them back here on a temporary basis until we have something better available, along with the soldiers, but they can't be mixed in. Suzette—"

"I'll see to it," she said.

Keeping the hostages—not happy—but not impossibly demoralized would be difficult, with the stringent limits on resources available. A dead hostage was worse than a dead loss, and a mistreated one could provoke suicidal resistance among the Brigade nobility. Most of them would be women and children, and of noble birth; Lady Whitehall would sooth some of the fears and prickly status-conciousness. Thus keeping them out of his hair, and the families they stood surety for quiet as well. That could be worth more than battalions of troops in garrisons in pacifying the area.

"Muzzaf?" Raj went on. The Komarite had been ashore for a day, operating under cover.

"*Seyor,* I've already contacted some of the local merchants in the farm-towns. We can expect them, and local peasants and native landowners, to be bringing in supplies within a day at any point we designate. I didn't tell them where, of course."

Raj nodded approval. "Do so now. What with prisoners, camp followers and troops we'll have to feed forty thousand or better soon.

Now, you may all have noticed that it's cooler here." They all nodded; the temperature was warm-comfortable, rather than the blazing heat of Stern Isle in late summer. "The rains start earlier here—and it rains more than back home. We're racing against time. Questions?"

"Sir," Cabot Clerett said "My mission?"

Raj looked at him for a moment, then slid his finger up the map. "Major Clerett, I'm giving you a rather different role. You'll take your 1st Residence Life Guards, and the 21st Novy Haifa, and move right up here to the Waladavir River."

Clerett looked crisp and warlike in the bright sun, helmet tucked under one arm and black curls tossing. "I'm to perform a screening function, sir?"

"Rather more than that," Raj said. "I want you to secure the bridge over the Waladavir at Sna Chumbiha and the fords—put in earthworks and your guns—then send appropriately-sized raiding parties from the two cavalry battalions over the river westward to attack the magnates' estates and small garrisons. Colonel Menyez will be moving four battalions of infantry up to occupy the bridge and the fords and relieve your men; they and the 21st Novy Haifa will anchor our line of advance.

"We want to conceal our intentions, and hopefully to panic every Brigadero between the Waladavir and the Padan River into thinking we're on their doorstep. I want them running for Carson Barracks, carrying the family silver and howling about the boogeyman. Don't try to hold territory west of your bridgeheads; kill and burn, but selectively, just the Brigaderos and men only as much as you can. I don't want to have to march across a desert in a couple of weeks. Make the refugees overestimate your numbers by moving quickly so they think you're everywhere at once. With luck the natives will rise on their own."

"Sir!" Cabot was quivering with surprise and suspicious delight. It was an assignment with plenty of opportunities for dash and daring; he'd expected to be kept to something dull and safe.

"Major Clerett," Raj went on. "Pay careful attention." He waited an instant. "I'm confident of your courage and your will to combat; a cavalry officer without aggression is a sorry thing. This mission will also test your skills; I'm familiar with the weaknesses of aggressive young commanders, having been one myself back in the dawn of time."

There were grins at that; Raj Whitehall was the youngest general in five hundred years, and his battalion commanders were nearly a decade below the average age. Only two of the Companions were over forty.

"Remember that the Brigaderos are thicker on the ground the further west you go; some of the great nobles have private armies of battalion size or better. Do *not* get out of touch, do *not* go too far in, and do *not* let your men get out of hand—a raid makes discipline difficult but more essential than ever. Colonel Staenbridge will be in constant communication, and he's your reserve if you run into something bigger than the intelligence reports indicate; do *not* hesitate to call for help if you need it. You're being sent to give an appearance of strength, so if any of your units is mousetrapped we'll have a *real* problem up there. Give them the taste of victory, however small, and they'll be attacking us instead of running away. We can beat any nobleman's following, but that would take *time*. Keep your men moving, and don't let yourself get bogged down."

Which meant, among other things, keeping them from burdening themselves with too much loot; a real test of command skills, when they'd be fanning out on *razziah* across rich countryside.

Suzette spoke softly. "I'm sure Major Clerett won't disappoint us, Raj."

probability clerett will act according to instructions within acceptable parameters, 82% ±4 based on voice-stress and other analysis, Center said.

And Barholm can't complain I'm not giving his nephew an opportunity to shine.

Cabot clicked heels. "Rest assured, Messa."

Raj nodded. "I'm giving you no more than one week of raiding," he went on. "Then I'll need you back at Lion City. Throw out a wide net of scouts west of the river—the native locals will probably give you information enough, especially with some—" he rubbed finger and thumb together "—but you'll have to check. Then turn over command to Major Istban and make tracks for the city, which will be invested.

"This is a complex set of movements, gentlemen, to be carried out at speed, but you're all big boys now. Exercise your initiative."

Gerrin cleared his throat. "What'll you be doing, Raj?"

"Ah, well, our tribal auxiliaries have arrived. Including eight hundred Skinners."

"The gentle, abstentious people," someone muttered.

"A two-edged sword, but a sharp one," Raj admitted. "They, and the two companies of the 5th, will form a central reserve under my direct command. When you run into anything unusual, gentlemen, tell me and I'll bring them up. After that happens once or twice, even the most onerous surrender terms will start looking very good indeed.

"No more questions? Then let's get our men together and be about our business." The Companions and a few of the other battalion commanders stepped closer, and they slapped their raised fists together in a pyramid. The leather of their gauntlets made a hard cracking sound.

"Hell or plunder, dog-brothers."

"Anither seven in t' trees, ser," M'lewis said, without turning his head. "Half a klick, loik."

"Good eyes, Lieutenant," Raj nodded.

Skinners didn't set lookouts, really. It was just that there were always groups of men lying-up around one of their camps, and they saw and heard and probably scented everything. At home on the plains of the far northeast they lived by hunting sauroids. All shapes and sizes, from sicklefoot packs to the big grazers to carnivores ten meters tall. Bellevue's sauroids hadn't had a million years of exposure to hominids to give them an instinct to avoid men. Most inhabited areas had to be kept shot out of all the larger types; the Skinners lived *among* the native life, and throve.

"Trumpeter, sound the canter. Remember the instructions."

The cool brassy notes sounded, and the two hundred men broke into a swift lope, the butts of their rifles resting on their thighs. As they broke through the screen of brush around the big meadow, they raised them and fired them into the sky, then flipped the long weapons down and sheathed them in the scabbards before their knees. A gesture of contempt, not reassurance . . . a statement: *you're not worth carrying a loaded gun to meet.*

There was an etiquette to dealing with Skinners.

Nobody got up as the soldiers approached, unless they happened to be standing at the moment. Those who wanted to stare did; those who were sleeping or drinking kept on doing so. One man did amble out, peering as if in surprise.

"Eh, *mun ami!*" Chief Juluk Paypan said. He turned and shouted in Paytoiz, the Skinner tongue:

"*Iles de Gran' wheetigo! E' sun bruha. L'hum qes' mal com nus!*"

Many of the Skinners looked up at that; a few gave quick yelping barks of greeting, and started drifting toward their chief and the general who was—theoretically—their commander.

"Which means?" Suzette asked. She had ridden into a near-riot in the Skinner camp with him on the last campaign, to face down their chiefs after Raj hung two Skinners for murder. This was her first glimpse of them in a peaceful mood.

Of course, on that occasion they'd had four battalions with leveled rifles and a battery of artillery behind them.

Raj translated: "It's The Big Devil and his witch. The man who's *bad like us.*"

"Is that a compliment?"

Raj grimaced. "To a Skinner."

He had never learned the Skinner tongue, not himself—the knowledge had the ice-edged hardness of something Center had implanted. Thinking about that always gave him a queasy feeling, like a mental image of bad pork.

It was not a good idea to think of smells when you were around Skinners. The bandy-legged little nomads had only been ashore a day, but the stink of their camp was already stunning. One man was standing in his sketchy saddle to urinate as they entered; he waved cheerfully and readjusted his breechclout without embarrassment, then rode off with a whoop. A few of them had put up leather shelters on poles, but most of the nomad mercenaries slept as they ate, defecated and fornicated—as and where the impulse took them. Dung, human and canine, and bits and scraps of things unidentifiable dotted the encampment. A monohorn carcass lay in the center of a ring of fires; those were medium-sized browsers, about twice the weight of a large bull, with columnar legs and a bone shield that extended from the long horn on their nose to the top of their humped shoulders. A single round hole above one eye showed what had killed it; the Skinners had probably camped where it died. The body and the ground for meters around was black with a carpet of flies.

As Raj watched, a Skinner backed out of its stomach cavity with a length of huge glistening purple-grey intestine in his teeth. He sawed it free a foot or so from his mouth, then threw back his head to swallow it without chewing. A visible bulge went down his throat to the already rounded stomach as they watched.

Juluk was grinning from ear to ear. He was fairly typical of his race, shorter than Suzette but twice as broad, a normal man compressed halfway down to dwarf size. Face and body were the color of old oiled leather; it was difficult to tell what his shaven scalplocked head and round button-nosed face would have looked like naturally, because of the mass of scar tissue. About half of it was tribal markings. He wore fringed leggings and breechclout of soft-tanned sauroid leather, with long knives on his thighs; crossed belts on his chest held shells for the two-meter tall rifle he leaned on, and each brass cartridge was longer than a man's hand, each bullet bigger than Raj's thumb. His hound lay at his feet; it cocked an eye up at Horace and went back to sleep.

Only Skinners habitually rode hounds, and entire males at that. Horace was one reason they regarded Raj as a human being. Most of it was the number of bodies his battles had piled up, impressive even to the tribes the Church called the Scourge of the Spirit's Wrath.

Juluk drank and passed him up the leather flask. "Hey, mebbe we kill you now, sojer-man, wait too long anyway. You come to hang more of *mes gars* for killing farmers? That why you bring half-men?"

He jerked his head at the two companies of the 5th sitting their dogs behind Raj and Suzette. Half-men was a compliment; the Skinners had a quasi-respect for Descotters. Their name for themselves translated into Sponglish as Real Men. Or The Only Real Men.

Raj took a long swig of the *arrak,* date gin yellow with distilling byproducts and spiked with cayenne peppers, chile and gunpowder. Then he leaned over and spat half of it on the nose of the Skinner's dog. The big animal leapt to its feet, growling: Raj's boot and stirrup-iron met its nose with a nicely-timed swing, and Horace showed teeth as long as a man's fingers centimeters from the other animal's throat. It reconsidered, turned its back and ambled off, dishcloth-sized ears flapping.

"I only keep you alive to make me laugh, Juluk," Raj said, drinking again. He'd eaten half a loaf of bread soaked in olive oil just before coming to the Skinner camp. "I brought real men here to show your little boys how to fight. Where'd you get this sauroid-vomit? I piss it out on your bitch-mother's grave."

This time he swallowed most of it, forcing himself not to gag. To his surprise, Suzette took the skin next and managed a healthy swallow. Some of the Skinners frowned at her presumption, and one or two shook medicine bags at her, but most of them laughed uproariously, Juluk included. A woman with *baraka,* spirit-power, was an even bigger joke than a non-Skinner with real balls. His neck-lace of finger-long sauroid fangs clattered against his bandoliers.

"Eh, even your woman got balls, sojer-man! Big stone-house chief, he tell me you make war on the long-hairs of the west. Good fighting where you make war."

"Where's your friend Pha-air?" There had been two chiefs with this band on the last campaign.

"Oh, I kill him a season ago," the Skinner chief said with a shrug. "He give me this—good man with knife." A grimy thumb traced a new scar, still shiny, across the chief's belly.

Raj raised his voice: "Are you women ready to go fight, or are you only good for drinking and eating sauroids that die of disease?"

More hoots and trills of laughter; the Skinners looked and smelled like trolls but their voices had the high pitch of excited schoolgirls.

Juluk fired the huge rifle over his shoulder without bothering to move it. The brass-cored 15mm slug cracked by within a meter of Raj's head, but he was as safe as if the weapon had been in East Residence. The Skinner chief would slit his own throat in shame if he ever shot a man without intending to.

Men and dogs boiled out of the camp, and out of thickets round-about. It was chaos, an instant change from sleepy lethargy to whooping, screeching tumult—but in less than five minutes the liquor and ammunition had been thrown on spare dogs, and the warriors were mounted and ready to move.

Center had taught him Paytoiz, but Raj had always been able to get on with the Skinner mercenaries.

"Are they really worth the trouble?" Suzette asked, as her escort fell in around her for the short journey back to the base camp.

"My sweet, you've only seen them twice, and in camp," Raj said. "As soldiers, they're a disaster—they devastate any place you sta-tion them, and you might as well try to discipline sauroids, and when they're drunk, which is usually . . . But if you could see them *fight*—" He shook his head. "Yes, they're worth the trouble."

❖   ❖   ❖

"Why's the road so far inland?" Bartin Foley asked.

"Pirates," Gerrin Staenbridge replied. "More profit in longshore raiding than attacking ships, if you've got a target that doesn't have signal heliographs, a fleet of steam rams and quick-reaction forces the way the Civil Government does."

Company A of the 5th was lead unit on the ride north, next to the battalion banner and the HQ squad. They were staying in column, for speed's sake, with outriders flung out ahead and to either side; they could see them dodging into small woods and jumping fences occasionally, off at the edge of sight.

"*Squadrone* pirates?" Bartin went on.

"Probably not the last generation, but there are plenty of freelancers operating out of islands like Blanchfer and Sabatin, just south of here . . . Ah, that should be our Hereditary Colonel Makman's place, coming up."

The maps said this was a main military highway; in the Civil Government, even in Descott, they'd have called it a track and left it at that. Mostly it was beaten earth, possibly it had been graded with an ox-drawn scraper within the last couple of years, and somebody had scattered gravel on the low points at some time in the past. Snake-rail fences edged it on either side; inland of the belt of forest along the coast the country opened up into rolling fields. Small shaws of oak, hazelnut and some native tree with hexagonal-scaled bark and scarlet leaves topped an occasional hill. The wheatfields were long since reaped, but there were many fields of *mais*—*kawn* in Namerique and *gruno* in Spanjol—full of dry, rustling stocks chest-high to a rider.

A hogback ridge rose ahead and to the right, eastward of the road. The two officers raised their binoculars; the manor was a big four-square building, whitewashed stone, with a squat tower rising from one corner flying the double lightning flash banner of the Brigade and a personal blazon of complicated interwoven loops, white on dark gray. The lower story was pierced only by narrow windows, but the upper had balconies and broad stretches of glazing. A number of long low structures stood nearby; stables undoubtedly, and the barracks.

"Almost homelike," Gerrin said dryly.

Descott architecture had some of the same features and for the same reason, except that things had never been either peaceful or prosperous enough for long enough to widen the second-story windows.

Staenbridge threw up a hand, and the trumpet sounded. "Battalion—"

"Company—"

"Walk-march . . . *halt.*"

"Let's hope Makman sees sense," the commander of the 5th said.

"I hope so too," Foley replied. He turned in the saddle: "Flag of truce, Lieutenant, and follow me if you please." He turned back to Staenbridge. "Probably won't, though. Not the first one we call on."

"You *what?*" the old man roared.

"Summon you to surrender in the name of the Civil Government of Holy Federation," Foley said tightly.

His hand was on his pistol, but he was fully conscious of what a sniper could do. The white pennant snapped from his bannerman's pole. That had been cold comfort to poor Mekkle Thiddo last year, after he'd delivered Connor Auburn's head to his brother the Admiral. His mind tried to replay scenes of the Squadron blunderbusses belching smoke, the white flag falling . . . and instead it insisted on showing him Raj Whitehall's face, as he rode down the row of thirty-one crosses, each bearing the twisting body of one of the men responsible for that violation of the laws of war.

That had probably been cold comfort to Thiddo too.

A bell was tolling in the tower of the estate; frightened faces peered out at him from the second-story window, and dogs were *yowrp*ing in the stables as men rushed to saddle them. Behind him the platoon's mounts shifted and growled softly, conscious of the aggression of intruding on another pack's territory but trained out of instinctive reluctance. The gravel of the driveway crunched under their paws; the smell of their massed breath was rank, overpowering the scents of woodsmoke and garden.

Hereditary Colonel Makman was tall, about a hundred and ninety centimeters, with little spare flesh on his heavy bones, and his red face contrasted violently with the white muttonchop whiskers that framed it. The unexpected visitors had evidently surprised him at lunch, and a napkin was tucked into the collar of his shirt.

He glared at Foley. "*Grisuh,* you've got your nerve, coming on to *my* land with a story like this," he snapped, in the tones of a man who hasn't been contradicted in a very long time.

Foley smiled and raised his hook. "Messer, that term *grisuh* is impolite, not to mention inappropriate. The last man to use it to me was one of Curtis Auburn's house-troops, and he came to a bad end." Sudden doubt washed over Makman's face.

"*Seyor,*" the platoon commander said. *Sir.*

Foley turned his head; a group of men was double-timing up the grassy slope to the right. In bits and pieces of hastily-donned uniform, but all carrying rifles and wearing their swords. They checked at the sight of the mounted men, then came on again at a more measured pace.

The young captain nodded. The lieutenant barked an order, and half the platoon turned their dogs with a touch of the foot. Another, and the animals crouched; the men stepped forward with their rifles at port

"Slope arms! Fix bayonets!" Smooth precision as butts thumped and hands slapped the hilts, not parade-ground stiffness but the natural flow of actions performed as part of a way of living, a trade practiced daily. The bayonets came out, bright and long as a man's forearm, and rattled as they clipped to the ring-and-bar fasteners. "Shoulder arms—front rank, kneel—ready—present—pick your targets—prepare for volley fire. On the word of command!"

Hands slapped iron and the long Armory rifles jerked up to shoulders. Behind the kneeling riflemen the second file drew their sabers and sloped them back, resting on their shoulders. The dogs barred their teeth and growled like boulders churning in a flooded river, long strings of slaver running from their opened half-meter mouths.

Makman surprised Foley; he spoke quietly. "You came under a flag of truce."

Bartin Foley's face had been delicately pretty once; it was still slim-lined and handsome in an ascetic fashion. Black eyes met blue, and the Brigade nobleman's narrowed in memory. From the battered look of his thick-fingered hands he had seen action enough once; enough to recognize the look of a man poised on the edge of killing violence.

"Messer, I also once saw an officer murdered under flag of truce by the barbarians of the Squadron," the young man said.

Makman snatched the handkerchief from his shirt and half-turned. "Siegfrond!" he snapped. "Ground arms, you fool."

The Brigadero troopers had formed a ragged firing line. Now their muzzles came down; there were about thirty of them, with more straggling up from the barracks by ones and twos, like crystals accreting in a solution.

"And somebody stop that damned bell."

A servant from the crowd around the Brigade nobleman scampered away, and the bronze clanging faded away to silence.

A woman came out onto the broad verandah of the fortified manor; she was in her twenties, in a long white dress with a yoke of pearls, and a child of four or five was by her side.

"Grandfather," she began, "what's—oh!" She swept the child behind her and put one hand to her throat.

Makman was studying the soldiers before his house, *seeing* them for the first time, Foley suspected. "*Gubernio Civil,* right enough," he said, and looked up at their officer. "Is this some sort of raid? You've a good deal of brass, young man, coming this far inland with less than forty men."

"This is the vanguard of General Raj Whitehall's army," Foley said, with a coldly beautiful smile. The woman gasped, and Makman's ruddy face paled.

"He's on Stern Isle," he whispered.

"*Was,*" Foley corrected. "The Sword of the Spirit of Man is swift. And in case you doubt that there are more of us here—"

He drew his saber and turned in the saddle, waving the blade slowly overhead. Downslope of the house gardens was an open field, full of black-coated cattle grazing. Beyond that was cultivated land, with a scattering of small half-timbered thatched cottages, and a line of trees. Red light winked from the edge of the forest Half a second later the flat *poumpf* of a 75mm field gun came, and the ripping wail. A tall bottle-shape of dirt fountained out of the pasture; cattle were running and bawling, except for three that lay mangled, blood red and intestines pink against their black hides. Steel twinkled all along the distant field edge as five hundred men stepped into the open and the sun caught their bayonets. A frantic voice called from the tower that more were in sight behind the manor, among the peon village.

2nd Residence, right on time, Foley thought.

"What . . ." Makman rasped. "What are your terms?"

"General Whitehall's terms are these; you are to take oath of obedience to the Civil Government and cooperate fully with all its officers and administrators in furnishing supplies and war levies. All arms and armed men to be surrendered; soldiers to be sent to East Residence for induction into our army. You personally will accompany our troops to encourage surrender among your military vassals and neighbors. In return your life and liberty, and one-third of your real property, are spared."

"One-third!"

"It's a great deal more than you'd enjoy in the grave, Messer. Because my orders are that if you refuse this place will be sacked and any survivors sold as slaves." He looked up at the young woman. "I doubt your granddaughter would find life as a whore in a dockside crib in East Residence very pleasant." He cut off the beginnings of a roar. "I've seen it, Messer. I've *done* it. Believe me."

The old man slumped. Foley's voice went on inexorably; "You will also deliver a hostage of your immediate family as surety for your good behavior."

"Who?" Makman said, scrubbing a hand over his face. "My son is ten years dead, my daughters with their own husbands, and my grandson holds a commission with the Makman Mounted in Carson Barracks—" He halted, frowning.

The young woman turned white and glared at Foley, and Makman's great age-spotted hands clenched. The young man almost laughed, but managed to keep his face grave. Things were not *quite* out of the woods yet; these were barbarians, after all.

"Your granddaughter-in-law and great-grandson will be under the protection of Lady Suzette Whitehall," he soothed. "She may take one maidservant and a suitable chaperone, and since you'll have to come in to swear allegiance with General Whitehall, you may deliver her to Lady Whitehall yourself. And rest assured, on my word as a gentleman and officer, that her honor is safe with me."

If you only knew how very *safe,* he thought.

✧   ✧   ✧

"Upyarz! Upyarz!"

The Brigaderos roared as they fought. Clerett's Life Guards used their sabers with bleak skill; the Governor had carefully picked the men to send to war with his heir. Steel crashed on steel across the fields, pistols banged, dogs howled and men shrieked in sudden agony too great for flesh to bear. The failing light of sundown was blood-red, but the true red of blood was turning to black despite the flames from the burning farmhouse on the north side of it. The wagons the refugees had tried to draw into a circle for defense burned too. Powder-smoke drifted pink-tinged over the heads and thrashing blades of four hundred men. The air smelled of sulphur and feces, the wet-iron stink of blood, and burning thatch.

Cabot Clerett watched narrowly. His hand chopped down, and his heels clapped to his dog's ribs; with a hundred men behind him he swept out of the timber and put his mount at the rail fence. The big mastiff gathered itself and soared as its rider leaned forward in the saddle. The banner of the 1st Residence Life Guards streamed at his side, and all around him the blades of the sabers snapped down in unison to lie along the necks of the dogs, point toward the enemy. They were turning to meet him, a lancepoint flashed by, *trannggg* and a breastplate shed the point of his Kolobassian blade and nearly dragged him out of the saddle. The Civil Government line smashed into the melee.

A dismounted trooper was before him, backing with sword working while a Brigadero lancer probed for his life and another kept the soldier's dog at bay.

Cabot spurred forward again. This time the enemy warrior could not turn in time, the inertia of his lance too much for his arm. The young officer poised his hilt over his head and stabbed, down into the neck past the collarbone to avoid the armor. The resistance was crisp and then heavy-soft; he wrenched the blade free and the barbarian reeled away on a bolting dog, coughing blood in sheets down his breastplate. The loose Life Guard's dog snapped, its neck extending like a snake and closing on the lance-shaft below the steel lappets. Ashwood crunched and the Brigadero was backing and cursing as he drew his sword. Cabot let him escape, dropped his reins, and clamped the bloody saber to his side while he drew his pistol and tossed it to his left hand.

"Thankee, ser!" the trooper yelled, straddling his dog as the animal crouched for him to mount.

Cabot flourished the saber with a grin. *I'm not afraid, I'm not afraid!* he realized exultantly. A sword flickered in the corner of his eye; he blocked the blow with his own near the hilt. The force of it slugged him to one side, leaning far over; he pointed the revolver under his own armpit and fired into the Brigadero's torso. The enemy dog locked jaws with his dog's, both animals slamming at each other's legs with clawed paws the size of plates. Cabot heaved himself back erect and leaned forward to fire again with the muzzle half an inch from the other dog's eye. It collapsed in mid-growl, falling with a thump that made his own mount jump backwards.

The HQ group had caught up with him, stabbing and shooting; the enemy were recoiling under the weight of the flank charge, but they still had numbers and weight of metal on their side. He signaled the trumpeter and the brassy notes rang out over the lessening clamor. Almost as one man the Civil Government troops turned and fled in a rout, pouring across the meadow and into the narrow road that spiked into the forest on the south.

The Brigaderos, household guards and part of a dragoon garrison regiment, scrambled after them four hundred strong. Here the lighter gear of the easterners was their advantage; the big Airedales and Newfoundlands were fast enough, but slower off the mark than the rangy Descotter farmbreds and Colonial-style Banzenjis the invaders rode. Slather flew from the mouths of the dogs as they lunged for the shadowing trees. The narrow wedge of open land at the road's mouth squeezed the larger Brigade force harder than their quarry, and for a moment the whole mass of men and dogs slowed as the warriors on the outside pressed inward.

Four hundred riflemen volley-fired from the edge of the woods into the clumped Brigade troops. In the dusk the muzzle-flashes were long and regular, like spearheads of fire along an endless phalanx. Crisp orders sounded, pitched high to carry. Platoon volleys slammed out like a crackle of very loud single shots, each one a comb of flame licking toward the enemy. Bullets hammered into dogs and men; a few spanged off armor, red sparks flicking up into the gathering night, but the range was close—and for this campaign, half of the standard-issue hollowpoints had been replaced with rounds carrying a pointed brass cap. Four companies of trained men with Armory rifles could put over three thousand rounds in a single minute. None of the Brigaderos was more than a hundred meters from the forest edge when the firing started, and the barricade of burning buildings and wagons was less than six hundred meters away. At that distance a bullet aimed level would strike a mounted man anywhere along its flight path.

The trumpet rang again in darkness, behind the firefly glimmer of the crossfire raking the Brigade men from two sides of a triangle. Panting dogs and cursing men sorted themselves into ranks. Snarls and snaps like wet coffin-lids falling punctuated the jostling, until men soothed their mounts to obedience.

"Damned if it didn't work, sir," the Senior Captain of the 2nd said in Cabot's ear.

He jumped slightly, glad of the darkness; he could feel the glassy stare of his eyes. His hands were steady as he reloaded.

"I rather thought it would, Captain Fikaros," the Governor's nephew said hoarsely. "I rather thought it would."

Both moons were up, enough to see a few survivors scattering across the meadow. Few made it past the burning buildings on the other side, although a number of riderless dogs with jouncing stirrups did.

"Let's collect our wounded and head for the river," Cabot said. "This bunch were a little too numerous for my taste."

"Sir!"

The men cheered as he rode past with the unit banner and the trumpeter.

Wait until Uncle hears about this, he thought. *Wait until Suzette hears.*

Glory!

CHAPTER TWELVE

Major Ehwardo Poplanich looked up at the row of shackles that rattled along the stone wall of the courthouse, below a bricked-in sign reading *runaway* in Spanjol and Namerique. The cuffs hung at about two meters off the ground. A meter and a half below each set the stucco was scored with a half-moon of smooth wear from flailing feet. A man hung by his hands with no support beneath cannot draw air into his lungs if he lets his full weight fall on his wrists; his chest crushes the diaphragm with the weight of his lower body. He must haul himself up at least a little with every breath. Once fatigue sets in, suffocation follows—a slow, gradual suffocation, as each despairing effort brings less oxygen and burns more.

"Well, that's one way to make sure a serf regrets it if he leaves the estate," he said mildly.

The set smile of the Brigadero magistrate did not alter; he bobbed his head in agreement, as he would have to anything Poplanich said at that moment. A big burly man, he was a noble by courtesy under Brigade law because he was on the muster rolls, but most of the native members of the town council had owned more land than he. Town marshall was not a rank true nobles, the *brazaz* officer class of the Brigade, aspired to. Now the councilors owned *much* more, and what had been a substantial farm if not an estate for the magistrate would shrink to a smallholding as soon as the new administration produced a cadastral survey.

With a battalion of Poplanich's Own in town, he wasn't going to object very forcefully. A few had tried, and their bodies hung from the portico of the This Earth church as a warning.

Ehwardo looked at the fetters again. A strong man, or a light wiry one, could probably live quite a few hours hanging there. *I shouldn't be upset,* he told himself. Serfdom—debt-peonage—was close to a universal institution around the Midworld Basin; back home a runaway who couldn't pay his impossible, hereditary debts would be flogged and turned back to his master. That had started long ago to prevent peasants from absconding from their tax obligations; and Spirit knew there didn't seem to be any other way to keep civilization going in the Fallen world. Not that anyone had told him, at least . . . but there was nothing like this on the Poplanich estates. A landlord who was willing to stand between his people and the tax farmers didn't have to flog much to keep order.

And where *was* that damned infantryman? He had better things to do than stand here talking to a gang of provincial boobies. He was supposed to be turning everything over to an infantry battalion so he could move on south, and it was taking a *cursed* long time.

In normal times he supposed Maoachin was a pleasant enough little place, a market town for the farms and estates roundabout. There was a large, gaudily decorated church for the This Earth cultists, and a more modest one for the Star Spirit worshippers; a few fine houses behind walls, a few streets of modest ones mixed with shops and artisan crafts, cottages on the outskirts. No fountain in the plaza, but the streets were cobbled and lined with trees.

Now the streets were jammed solid. With oxcarts full of grain in sacks and flour and cornmeal in barrels, and sides of bacon and dried beef and turnips and beans. Furniture and silverware too, and tools; many, many wagons of swords and rifle-muskets and shotguns and revolvers, ammunition, kegs of powder and ingots of lead. Riding dogs on leading chains, muzzled with steel-wire cages over their jaws and driven frantic by stress, and palfreys for the hostages. Hundreds of prisoners, Brigaderos fighting men going back to be packed into transports and shipped across the Midworld and inducted into the Civil Government's army. They walked with their eyes down, avoiding looking at the smaller groups, battered and bloody and in chains, who'd tried to fight. *They* and their families were headed for slave markets.

The noise and dust, the howls of dogs and sobbing of children, were beyond belief; the harsh noon sun beat down without mercy.

He looked back down at the magistrate standing at his stirrup, and the town councilors. Most of them were natives, Spanjol-speaking followers of the orthodox faith they shared with the Civil Government. More than a few of them were smiling at the magistrate's discomfort They had kept two-thirds of their land, and had pleasure of seeing the bottom rail put on top, as well. When the confiscated Brigade estates came on the market, they would be positioned to expand their holdings in a way that would more than make up for the initial loss.

"But, ah, with respect—" the bearded judge-gendarme said, his Sponglish clumsy and full of misplaced Spanjol endings "—you then leave me at all no armed men, how do I under put native risings?"

A councilor *did* laugh at that. The magistrate whirled on him, frustration breaking through in a scream as he dropped back into Spanjol. Ehwardo could follow that well enough. Out of sheer inertia the Civil Government had maintained it as a second official language all these centuries, and he had been trained to public service.

"*Iytiote!*" he screamed: *fool.* "Do your peons love you because you have the same priest and demand your rent in the same tongue? How many have I scourged back to their plows for you? If they taste a master's blood and he is a Brigade noble, won't they want yours?"

The councilors' smiles disappeared, to be replaced with thoughtful expressions.

"Don't worry, Messers," Ehwardo said. "The Civil Government will keep order."

It had to. Unless the peasants paid their landlords a share of their crop and forced labor, they would eat everything they produced. How could the armies and cities be supported then? Not to mention the fact that landlords were the ruling class at home, as they were everywhere. Still . . .

"Did you know," he went on in the local language, "that my great-uncle was Governor in East Residence?" They hadn't, and breath sucked in; he waved away their bows. "Listen carefully, then, to a story Governor Poplanich told my father, and my father to me.

"Once there was a mighty king, who ruled broad lands. His minister read the king's plans for the coming year, and went to his lord.

"'Lord,' the minister said, 'I see you spend millions on soldiers and forts and weapons, and not one *senthavo* to lighten the sufferings of the poor.'

"'Yes,' said the king. 'When the revolution comes, I will be ready.'"

A color-party of the 17th Kelden Foot was forcing its way through the press toward him; Ehwardo sighed with relief. He smiled down at the councilors, and tapped a finger alongside his nose.

"A wise man, my great-uncle," he said, grinning. "*Vayaadi, a vo, Sehnors.*"

The narrow forest lane was rutted even by Military Government standards, but the ground on either side was mostly open, beneath huge smooth-barked beech trees ten times taller than a man. Green gloom flickered with the breeze sighing through the canopy, but it was quiet and very still on the leaf-mould of the floor. The two companies of the 5th were spread out on either side of the road in platoon columns, moving at a brisk lope; the Skinners trickled along in clumps and clots around them, ambling or galloping. Three field-gun carriages followed the soldiers, with only half the usual six-dog teams; despite that they bounced along at a fair pace. The moving men started up a fair amount of game; sounders of half-wild pigs, mono-horns, a honking gabble of some sort of bipedal greenish things that stopped rooting for beech-nuts and fled with

orange crests flaring from their long sheep-like heads and flat bills
agape.

Luckily, there were no medium-to-large carnosauroids around; those
were mostly too stupid to be afraid, although there was nothing wrong
with their reflexes, bloodlust or ferocious grip on life even when
mangled. Killing one would be noisy.

Sentinels with the shoulder-flashes of the 7th Descott stepped out
from behind trees.

"What've you got for me, Lieutenant?" Raj asked their officer,
pulling up Horace in a rustle of leaves.

"Seyor," the man said, casting an eye at the Skinners who kept
right on moving as if the sentry-line did not exist. "Major Gruder's
got a pig-farmer for you."

"Took a while to get someone who could understand him, General," Kaltin Gruder said. "I *think* he's giving us pretty detailed
directions to those holdouts."

The peasant—swineherd by profession—had an iron thrall-collar
around his neck and a lump of scar tissue where his left ear should
have been. His long knife and iron-shod crook were the tools of a
trade that took him into the woods often, and his ragged smock
and pants and bare calloused feet wouldn't have been out of place
in most villages in the Civil Government.

Raj listened closely to the gap-toothed gabble. The language problem was a little worse than he'd anticipated. Spanjol and Sponglish
were very different in their written forms and grammar, but the most
basic terms, the eight hundred or so words that comprised every-
day speech, were quite similar: *blood* in Sponglish was *singre* and
in Spanjol *sangre,* for instance, quite unlike the Namerique *blud* or
Skinner *zonk.*

The trouble was that neither the local peasants nor most of his
soldiers spoke the standard versions of their respective national languages. When a Descotter trooper tried to talk to a Crown Peninsula
sharecropper, misunderstanding was one of the better alternatives.
Starless Dark, some of his Descotters had trouble in East Residence!

"Yes, that's what he's saying," Raj said after a moment. There was
an icy feeling behind his eyes, more mental than physical, and the
mouthings became coherent speech. "They're about . . . ten klicks that
way. There's a valley . . . no, it sounds like a collapsed sinkhole. 'Many'
of them—at least two thousand guns, I'd say. Possibly twice that; I
doubt he can count past ten even barefoot."

Kaltin ran a hand through his dark bowl-cut hair. "Lucky thing
I didn't go in with only the 7th," he said. "I *thought* I'd been running
into an awful lot of empty manors." He looked up sharply. "If he's
telling the truth, of course."

probability of 92% ±3, Center said.

"He is," Raj replied flatly. "Let's see *exactly* where." That was an exercise in frustration, even when they brought in others from the circle of charcoal-burners and swineherds. They were eager to help, but none of them had even heard of maps; they could describe every creek and rock in their home territories—but only to a man who already knew the area that was their whole world.

"All right" he said at last. "It's about three hours on foot from here; call it ten kilometers. There's a low range of hills; in the middle of it's a big oval area, sounds like fifteen to thirty hectares, of lumpy ground with a rim all around it and a stream running through— it's limestone country, as I said. The axis is east-west. Natural fortress. Only one real way out, about two thousand meters across, on the eastern side of the oval. Evidently some native bandits—or rebels, depending on your point of view—used it until this man's father's time, then the Brigaderos finally hunted them down and hung them."

As he spoke, Raj sketched, tracing over the projection Center laid on the pad; training in perspective drawing was a part of the standard Civil Government military education, and he had set himself to it with unfashionable zeal as a young man.

Kaltin whistled through his teeth as he looked at the details. "Now that's going to be something like hard work, if we want to do it quick," he said. "Plenty of cover, lots of water, getting over the edge just won't do much good, not with all those hummocks. And if they're determined—well."

Which they would be, having refused the call to surrender. The problem with making examples was that it worked both ways; having looked at the alternatives, these Brigaderos had evidently decided that at seventh and last they'd rather die.

In which case they were going to get their wish.

"Then we'd better move quickly, before they have a chance to get set up," he said, with a slight cold smile. "We certainly can't afford to take a week winkling them out, or bringing up a larger force. The garrison in Lion City might sally if we did—four thousand trained men, and far too mobile for my taste if we let them loose."

Kaltin raised an eyebrow. "You think there's enough of us?" Slightly over six hundred in the 7th Descott, two companies of the 5th, and the Skinners. "For storming a strong defensive position, that is."

"Oh, I think so. Provided we're fast enough that they don't realize what's happening."

"Can we get the guns in there?"

"We can try; it's open beech forest for the most part, nearly to the sinkhole area. I'm certainly bringing those. Take a look; the ship missed us in Port Wager and pulled in here a few days ago."

Raj nodded toward three weapons on field-gun carriages, standing beside the rutted laneway. Kaltin looked them over, puzzled. At first glance they were much like the standard 75mm gun. At second, they were something very different.

"Rifle-barrels clamped together?" he said.

"Thirty-five of them, double-length," Raj said. "Demonstrate, Corporal."

The soldier threw a lever at the rear of the weapon, and a block swung back horizontally, like the platen of a letterpress. Another man lifted out a thin iron plate about the size of a book-cover with a loop on the top. The plate was drilled with thirty-five holes, and an equal number of standard 11mm Armory cartridges stood in them.

"Dry run, please," Raj said.

The crew inserted an empty plate; the gunner pushed the lever sharply forward and the mechanism locked with a *dunk* sound. He crouched to look through the rifle-type sights, spun the elevation and traverse screws, and turned a crank on the side of the breech through one complete revolution. A brisk *brttt* of clicks sounded. Then he threw the lever back again; the crew repeated the process another four times in less than thirty seconds.

"Three hundred and twenty-five rounds a minute, with practice," Raj said. "I know it works—that is, it'll shoot. Whether it's as useful as appearances suggest, the Spirit only knows and experience will show. I'm certainly not counting on it this time, not during the field-test, but it can't hurt."

Kaltin whistled again. "Turning engineer, Messer Raj?" he said. That would be beneath the dignity of a landed Messer and cavalry officer, but Raj's eccentricities were legend anyway. "No, a friend suggested it."

provided schematic drawings suitable to current technological levels, Center corrected pedantically. **after correcting certain design faults in the original.**

Thank you, Raj thought.

you are welcome.

"It looks handy," the other officer said appraisingly. "No recoil?" Cannon bounced backward with every shot and had to be manhandled back into battery.

"None to speak of, and it's less than a quarter the weight of a field gun. Muzzaf had some of his innumerable relatives run it up— in Kolobassia district, but out of the way. We're calling it the splat-gun, from the sound."

The other man nodded; that southwestern peninsula was one of the primary mining and metalworking areas in the Civil Government.

"Don't tell me you got the Master of Ordnance to spring for this," he said.

The last major innovation had been the Armory rifle, nearly two hundred years before. The Civil Government quite literally worshipped technology—but technology was what the miraculous powers of the UnFallen could accomplish, flying faster than sunlight from world to world and inspired by the indwelling Spirit of Man. Ironmongery did not qualify.

Raj's grin grew savage. "Tzetzas paid for it," he said. "I used some of the surplus we got from his estates when we sold him back his rotten hardtack and waste-dump bunker coal."

He turned back to the map. "Let's get to work."

Hereditary Major Elfred Stubbins bent to look through the telescope. One of his neighbors was an amateur astronomer, and had imported the thing from East Residence at enormous expense years ago; most thought it mildly disgraceful, even religiously suspect— wasn't the Spirit of Man of This Earth alone? Why look at a heavens which held only the Outer Dark? Stubbins considered himself an up-to-date and broad-minded man, able to both read and write. He had remembered the instrument when his neighbors met in hasty conclave to plan their flight to the Crater, and it was proving very useful. Clumsily, his sword-calloused hands turned the focusing screw.

A man leaped out at him, brought from two thousand meters to arm's length. Round and brown and button-nosed, with a tuft of scalplock on the crown and bracelets of brass wire up the forearms. The rifle he balanced across a bronze-shod shooting stick was a *joke*, longer than the man aiming it. What in the Outer Dark was—

CRACK.

The 15mm bullet drove the narrow final segment of the telescope four inches into Stubbins' brain. He pitched backward onto the gritty surface of the limestone block, limbs thrashing like a pithed frog, beating out a tattoo on the dusty stone. Men exploded from all around him, to stand staring as the body stilled, lying spread-eagled with a four-inch stub of tattered brass protruding from one eye-socket

CRACK. A man's head splashed away from the monstrous sauroid-killing bullet.

The Brigade warriors didn't need a third prompt. Every one of them was down behind cover within a few seconds.

"What the fuck is happening here?" someone cried. "Is it the civvies?" Kettledrums began beating the alarm in the camps below them where the refugee households had set up.

A few muskets crashed, firing blind towards the hills to the north, then fell silent. The small figures moving out of the low scrub there on the karstic hills were plainly visible, but they were scattered, too far for any effective fire from the rifle-muskets that most of the men carried. More and more of the strangers were strolling forward; not looking in any particular hurry, calling to each other in high mild voices, yipping and hooting.

A Brigade officer came panting up the rocky way; there was a faint path worn just enough to be visible through the thirst-tolerant native vegetation that drove tendrils into the rock. Limestone drains freely; down lower where there was soil, trees grew. Many of them were fruit trees run wild, others spiky red-green Bellevue vegetation. Men had lived here before, the native forest-thieves of a generation ago, before that others from time to time, from century to century. The Brigade fugitives had found scraps of PreFall plastic and ancient charcoal beneath a deep overhang. Troops followed the officer, and further back women with their skirts kirted up and loads in their hands.

"Skinners," the officer said, as he stoop-crawled around the block Stubbins had used to set up his telescope. A ripple of curses ran along the waiting riflemen; most of them had heard of the tribe, at least. They were childhood boogies among the more northerly of the Brigade.

Another savage crack, and a man who had raised himself to fire slid backward with the top taken off his head the way a spoon does a hard-boiled egg. Freshly exposed brain oozed pink out of the shattered bone and white lining tissue; the limbs twitched for a second, the body hung in equipose, then began sliding further down the slope. Some of the women screamed as it bounced and rolled by, but they kept coming.

"Nomads from up northeast of the Stalwarts, east of the Base Area," the officer went on, for the benefit of those who *hadn't* heard of the Skinners. Few of their raids had penetrated to the edge of Brigade territory, although their pressure was one factor forcing the Stalwarts south.

"Spread out there, and keep your heads down. Adjust your sights for maximum and don't forget to shorten 'em again when they get closer."

The men obeyed, as they might not have the retainer of another landowner; the officer was a General's Dragoon. There was still a snarl in the voice of one who asked:

"What're they doing *here*? And what are those *gawdammit* women doing?"

"Coming up to load," the man called, raising his voice so everyone on the knoll could hear. "We're going to try and hold these high spots along the crater wall. Three women are going to load for each of you. Remember to check the sights. Shift rocks—they'll be looking for your powder-smoke."

"You can't bring women into a battle zone!" one man protested; a prosperous freeholder by his cowhide jacket.

"Fuckhead!" the officer screamed, frustration suddenly snapping his control. "Fuckhead! D'you think the Skinners will kiss their hands if they get through? They'll cut their throats and rape the dead bodies, you shit-eating civvie-breed. I've *fought* them before. The *grisuh*'ve brought them as mercs, Spirit eat their eyes for it.

"All of you!" he went on. "The only way we're gonna stop them is kill every one of them, because otherwise they'll keep coming till they blow away every swinging dick in this valley. Get ready!"

The Skinners ambled forward, climbing nimbly over the tumbled whitish-grey rock. Some of them were smoking pipes, and now and then one would stop to adjust his breechclout or take a swig of water from a skin bag. Big flop-eared brindled hounds walked behind them, some riding animals, some with wicker panniers of extra ammunition. Those came forward whenever a Skinner whistled, and the man would grab another handful of the carrot-sized shells. They were firing more often now; a nomad would stop, let the shooting stick swing down, aim, fire, reload, and start forward again in ten seconds or less. Most of them were catching their spent brass and tucking it into belt pouches. A Brigade warrior lurched back screaming with his hands to his face as rock-fragments clawed across his eyeballs from one near-miss.

The women had made it to the top of the trail, scurrying along well below the crestline to take positions below each rifleman before they set down their burden of hundred-round ammunition boxes. The men with them were carrying several muskets each; they used their swords to pry open the lids of the boxes and then handed out the weapons. Many of the women's palms were bleeding from the rough hemp of the rope handles, and some were crying silently, but they started loading immediately. More slowly than a trained fighter, but there were many of them. Two older women travelled from one clump of loaders to another, distributing small leather boxes of percussion caps they held in a fold of their skirts.

"Let 'em have it!" the officer shouted, as the Skinners came to about a thousand meters, maximum effective range.

Smoke jetted from hundreds of muzzles. Half a dozen of the Skinners were hit, of the hundreds swarming down the slope; some of those rose again. Some of those too badly wounded to rise—even a Skinner could not force a shattered thighbone to function no matter how indifferent to pain—tied rough bandages or tourniquets and started firing from a prone position. The rest of the Skinner force slowed their advance; not from fear, but because this was the optimum range. Their rifles were more accurate than their enemies', and nearly every Skinner could use his to the limit of the weapon's capacities.

The Brigade men reached behind for new weapons thrust into their hands, fired, fired again. Any man who raised his upper body for a better shot died, and many who showed only an eye and a rifle-barrel through a crack in a boulder did too. The iron-and-shit stink of death began to hang heavy; bodies bled out quickly when fist-sized holes were blasted through their torsos. Blood sank quickly into the porous rock, turning the surface slick and greasy. Screams and moans from men blinded or flayed by rock-fragments were continuous. The women dragged wounded men backward, and fresh riflemen—many of them boys and white-bearded grandfathers, now—climbed the trail to take their places. After a while, some of the women themselves climbed up to take the spots of men who'd been killed and not replaced. Few of them were as accurate as the men, but the Skinners were much closer now. Everyone could hear them hooting and laughing as they walked forward, laughing and killing with every shot.

The officer who had fought Skinners before lay behind a rock; the tourniquet which had saved his life let only a dribble of blood out of the shattered stump of his left forearm. He kept his head well down the rock; his face was mud-grey with shock and covered with fat beads of sweat. His lip bled too, where he had bitten it to make himself stay conscious. Four revolvers lay conveniently near his right hand, and his unsheathed sword.

"Halt," Kaltin Gruder said, as the rise steepened to twenty degrees, fissured water-rotted rock beneath their feet.

No point in taking the dogs forward further. They were sure-footed, much more so than a hoofed animal, but size and the stiff backbone needed to bear the weight of a man exacted its price in agility. A saddle-dog had to watch its step on going like this, and there was worse ahead. Mice can fall hundreds of feet and walk away; a cat may or may not escape with bruises or break a bone; a man dropped from the same height will almost surely die. A twelve-hundred-pound wardog would *splash*.

The officers and noncoms passed it down the line verbally; the Brigaderos would probably realize they were here soon, despite the continuous crackle of firing and thick pall of smoke from the far northern side of the crater, but there was no point in advertising with a trumpet-call designed to carry. The action was about three long rifle-shots from the southern rim, and as many more from his present position. The long slopes were thick with scrub oak, chin-quapin, and witchhazel, too thin-soiled to support the big beeches that predominated further south. Ahead the scrub thinned to occasional patches dominated by reddish-green native climbers and many-stalked bushes. The slope was also littered with boulders from head-size to twice man-height, almost all the way up to the notched rim that stood like a line of decaying teeth a hundred meters high.

The dogs crouched, and men stepped out of the stirrups and loaded their rifles.

"Fix bayonets." Rattle and snap, and a subtle change in attitude. There was nothing like that order to drive home that it was about to hit the winnowing-fan. "Company A in reserve. B, C, and D will advance in extended skirmish order, by squads."

Eight-man squads moved forward cautiously, covered by the next; they took firing positions behind cover and waited alertly while their comrades leapfrogged forward. It was part of the drill, albeit not one used all that often. The dark blue of their jackets and the dull maroon of their pants blended well with the shade and varied colors of vegetation, soil and rock. In a minute or two nothing remained but an occasional glimpse, a stirring of leaves against the wind, or the clink of metal on stone. Back here the lines of dogs waited motionless, the riderless whining softly and staring with fixed attention at the direction their masters had taken.

Kaltin Gruder was nervous. Not about his men's performance. Even if this wasn't the most common form of combat, they'd trained for it . . . and they were all hunters at home, skirmishers when they or their squire had a quarrel with the neighbors. His own first smell of powder had come that way, stalking through a maze of gullies and canyons after a sheep-lifter, and you could die just as dead as in a major battle.

What worried him was the loss of control. He couldn't *see* more than a few of the men. In most situations a battalion commander expected to keep his whole force under observation, or at least ride around to his company-level officers checking on things. In this scrub even the *lieutenants* wouldn't have direct control over their units. Shouldn't be a problem keeping the advance going unless it got real sticky, no—although he pitied an infantry commander with a job like this. Men didn't join or stay in the 7th Descott Rangers unless they could be relied on to keep moving toward the sharp end without someone prodding them up the arse. The troops wouldn't stand for anyone like that, and they had emphatic and very practical ways of making it known.

The other thing that worried him was that his men knew the Skinner attack had got in before theirs. That was fine, keep the barbs' attention pinned one way, they'd still have men on the south fringe but not as many or as alert. But the Spirit of Man with a nuke in Its hand couldn't stop Skinners from lifting everything worth taking if they got into the refugees' stores first. His men wouldn't endanger the mission for loot . . . but since they were supposed to attack in that direction anyway, he knew they'd move faster than they should. Some of them, and the rest would keep up with their friends.

Everything's a tradeoff. Soldiers were useless without the will to fight. But men trained to kill and too proud to show fear in the face of fire were never easy to control.

Starless Dark with this, he thought. He certainly wasn't going to maintain control if they couldn't see him.

"Captain." Company A was always overstrength and commanded by a captain rather than a senior lieutenant. "I'm taking the HQ squad forward. You'll act to prevent a breakthrough if the barbs counterattack, and advance on order or signal"—a red rocket—"or at your discretion after one hour."

"Yes, sir," Captain Falcones said with notable lack of enthusiasm.

"Your turn will come, Huan. You men, follow me!"

The signaler brought his trumpet, but he licked his thumb and wet the foresight of his rifle as they moved forward. A crackle of shots broke out, nearer than the slamming firefight along the north edge of the crater. Echoes slapped back and forth from the rocks.

"This way."

✧   ✧   ✧

Braaaaaaaap.

The splat-gun to Raj's left fired. Thirty-five rounds slapped into the Brigaderos rush, and men went tumbling. Only five or six out of nearly sixty, but the rest stopped to shoot back—exactly the wrong thing to do. Bullets cracked through air, dipped leaves from the bushes, sparked and pinged off stones. Few of them were aimed in his direction anyway, and if his luck was that bad he'd better get it over with.

He looked right and left; the two companies of the 5th were advancing in staggered double line, with five meters between platoons. Thin, but he didn't have very many men with him to cover over a kilometer of front. North and south of that the ground got too rugged for easy movement and the barbs didn't look to be in any mood for fancy flanking maneuvers; clots and dribbles of them were filtering through the narrower neck of the exit and attacking as they came without waiting to mass. Bad tactics, but they were being squeezed forward toward him like a melon-seed between two hard fingers.

"Platoon will advance with volley fire," the lieutenant of the platoon he had with him shouted, pointing with his saber. The front rank went to one knee, dipping in unison. Their rifles steadied.

"Fire!"

BAM. Greasy gray-black smoke spurted. The spent brass went flying backward as they worked the levers, and the bolts retracted and slid down; one man had a jam, the thin wrapped brass cartridge heat-welded to the walls of the chamber and the iron base torn off by the extractor.

"Scramento," the trooper muttered, snatching out his boot-knife and ignoring everything around him as he probed delicately to peel the foil away from the steel.

Braaaaaaaap. Another splatgun fired, chewing into the stationary Brigaderos as they frantically bit open cartridges and dumped the powder down the barrels of their rifles. Ramming, withdrawing the rod, fumbling at their belts for a cap . . .

The second rank of 5th troopers walked through the first, knelt, fired.

BAM.

Click. From the first rank. Rounds pushed down the grooves on top of the bolts and into the chamber with the thumb. *Clack.* Levers pulled back to lie along the stock, the same motion locking the bolts into the lugs at the rear of the chamber and cocking the internal firing pins. They rose, trotted through the reloading second rank, knelt, fired.

BAM.

Braaaaaaaap.

The lieutenant looked up and down the line, where variations on the same scene were happening. Most of the enemy in front of him were still loading.

"Charge!" he shouted.

One of the Brigaderos fired from the hip, his ramrod still in his rifle. By a chance someone who'd never seen a battlefield wouldn't have believed it speared through the chest of the Descotter charging him. Both men wore identical expressions of surprise, until the Civil Government trooper went to his knees and then his face, the iron rod standing out behind his back. The Brigadero was still gaping when the trooper's squadmate fired with his muzzle not two feet away. The barbarian flew backward, punched away as much by gasses that had no chance to dissipate as by the bullet, his leather jacket smouldering in a circle a foot wide over his belly.

The rest clubbed their muskets or drew swords; the Brigaderos carried bayonets but evidently didn't much like to use them. The troopers fired again at point-blank range and then there was a brief flurry of butt and bayonet, the ugly butcher's-cleaver sound of steel parting flesh.

More rifle fire from ahead, from behind a boulder. Two or three men . . .

"Prone!" the lieutenant snapped; he stayed on one knee, as did Raj and his HQ group. "Somebody get—"

Braaaaaaaap. The surface of the boulder sparked and spalled under the impact of another thirty-five rounds. Something hit; a rifle-barrel jerked up over the squarish boulder and stayed there.

"Forward," Raj said, and then to his trumpeter: "Sound maintain advance."

Behind them he could hear the ground crunching as the splatgun's crew manhandled it up at a trot. *That solves that problem,* he thought; he'd been wondering if the new weapon was more like close-range artillery or small arms. They were best deployed well forward, probably in the gaps between units, to shoot men onto their objectives. *Maybe an iron shield on either side of the barrel?*

"*Mi heneral?*" the lieutenant asked, hopping a step to keep up with Raj's longer stride.

The men were moving forward again, the line of bayonets glittering . . . or in some cases, dull. Nothing ahead for the moment, but the burbling echoes of the firefight in the crater were getting closer. So far they'd seen the ones the enemy had stationed here, or the quickest-witted and fastest on their feet. A serious attempt to force the gap could come any moment.

"Yes?" Raj asked, startled out of a world of lines and distances, alternatives and choices.

"Why are we attacking the enemy, sir? Not that I mind—but wouldn't it be tactically sound to make them come to us? We're across their line of retreat."

Raj looked at the painfully earnest young face. He nodded in recognition; he'd always wanted to know how to do his job better too.

"Son, if we had four or five companies, yes. As it is, we can't hold this width of front, even with those little beauties." He gestured back at the splatguns with his revolver. "There are probably still enough of them to pin us down while a lot of the rest get through and scatter into the hills.

"But. We're not really attacking them, we're hustling them, they're bouncing around like bees in a bucket and we're not going to give them *time* to sit down and organize a breakout attack. Defeat takes place in the mind of the enemy." The puppy awe in the young man's face was embarrassing. "We'll hold a bit further forward, where the chokepoint narrows."

"*Watch it!*"

They crouched slightly, instinctively, and ran forward. There had only been one Brigadero behind the boulder, and a girl loading for him. The man lay dead, slumped back against the stone with his brains leaking down the rough surface. The girl was lying curled on her side, a dagger with a gold-braid hilt and gold pommel sunk to the guard under her ribs. Her mouth was a soundless O, her eyes round and dark as her body shuddered.

Missed the kidney, Raj knew. It might take her some time to bleed out, blood leaking into her stomach cavity like water around a badly packed valve.

"Kicked t'rifle outta her hands, but t'cunt cut belly affore I could stop her, ser," the corporal said apologetically.

The girl made a small sound; the lieutenant looked at her and swallowed. The older man knew it was because he'd suddenly seen her as a *person,* not a target, not another barb; perhaps because she'd done pretty much what a Descotter woman would have in her place. Raj moved forward and put his revolver to the back of her neck, squeezing the trigger carefully; even touching was far enough away to miss, if you jerked. The body bucked once, but the sound of the shot was almost lost in the noise of battle.

He looked up. The entrance to the crater was narrowing here, and there was less in the way of large boulders for cover.

"All right," he said to his runners. "My compliments to Captains Fleyez and Morrisyn, and we'll hold here—men to take cover. Get that splatgun up here, this is a good position for it."

The trumpet sounded, and the long line of blue-coated men sank into the ground; hands shifted rocks to give good firing rests and make improvised sangars. The splatgun came bounding up under the hands of its enthusiastic crew, one wheel crunching over the Brigadero woman's legs before the weapon settled into the depression behind the boulder. That put its muzzle at waist height above the ground.

"Ah, good," the artillery corporal in charge of it said. He noticed the gold-chased dagger and pulled it out, wiping the blade on the girl's stockinged leg and checking the metal of the blade by flicking it with a thumbnail before sticking the knife into his boot-top.

Raj moved a few meters to another boulder, sat and uncorked his canteen. "The 7th and the Skinners will drive them to us," he said, half to himself. From the volume of fire, within a few minutes.

"Drive them to us, sir?" the lieutenant said. "The 7th is finally doing the 5th a favor?" His color was returning, a little.

Raj looked over at the boulder, where the gunners were piling head-sized stones in front of their weapon. They'd tossed the bodies out to have more room; the girl's long black hair hid what was left of her face.

"Nobody's doing anybody any favors here today, Lieutenant," he said. "Nobody."

"Here theyuns come, tall's storks n' thick as grass!"

Kaltin Gruder had a girl on the saddlebow before him when he rode up to the command-station at the exit to the crater. That might have been expected—although it was a bit early for an officer as conscientious as Gruder to be looting, with the odd shot still going off behind him. Except that she was about eight years old, a huge-eyed creature with braided tow-colored hair in a bloodied shift.

"Took her away from a Skinner," he said, at Raj's raised eyebrows, his voice slightly defensive.

Embarrassed at impulse of compassion, something as out of place here as a nun in a knockshop, Raj supposed. Feelings were odd things. Antin M'lewis had adopted a three-legged alley cat that spring and lugged it all the way from East Residence.

Gruder shrugged: "Well, Mitchi"—the slave-mistress Reggiri had given him last year—"can use a maidservant, or whatever. There, ah, weren't many prisoners. Most of the Brigaderos civilians killed themselves before we broke through, when they could tell nobody was getting out."

Raj nodded. That simplified things for him . . . and for them, come to that, if they felt like that about it. He could understand that, too.

Gruder was looking around at the number of bodies lying in the five hundred meters before the final stop-line the 5th's two companies had established. A D-shape of corpses, two or three deep in spots, a thick scattering elsewhere.

"Hot work," he said.

"The splatguns," Raj said. "We put them on the flanks and had the Brigaderos in a crossfire; they were worth about another company each, in sheer firepower on the defensive."

Kaltin frowned, stroking the whimpering girl's head absently. She clung to the cloth of his uniform jacket, although the right-hand sleeve was sodden and streaking her bright hair with blood.

"This was certainly more like a battle than most of what we've seen this campaign, Messer," he said. "I've got twenty dead, and as many again badly hurt."

"Ten from the 5th," Raj confirmed. *Spirit dump Barholm's cores into the Starless Dark, I told him to give me forty thousand men. Even thirty thousand—*

He sighed and rose, swinging into Horace's saddle. "Let's see if there's some wheeled transport for our wounded."

Chief Juluk was riding up, seven-foot rifle over his shoulder. He looked as if he'd waded in blood, and quite possibly had; one of the subchiefs behind him had managed to cram his body into a ball-gown covered in ruffled lace and had a bearded head tied to his saddlebow by its long hair. That must have been a brave man, to be worth preserving.

The Skinner looked around at the carnage. "Bad like us!" he giggled. "You one big devil, sojer-man. Bad like us!"

Raj felt his head nodding in involuntary agreement.

no, raj whitehall, you fight for a world in which there will be no men like him at all.

Or like me, he thought. *Or like me.*

"Lion City next," he said aloud. "Spirit of *Man,* I hope they have sense enough to come to terms."

Kaltin had been trying to disengage the girl's hands so that he could turn her over to an aide, but she clung desperately and tried to keep him between her and the Skinners.

"What do we do if they don't accept terms?" he said with professional interest, giving up the attempt. "We've nothing that'll touch their walls."

"Do?" Raj said. He reached out and touched the girl's hair with careful tenderness; she buried her head in Gruder's shoulder. "Anything we have to. Anything at all."

CHAPTER THIRTEEN

"Excellent work, Abdullah," Raj said.

The maps were sketched, but accurate; street-layouts, the location of listed merchants' and landowners' mansions, the waterworks, warehouses, estimates of food-reserves, number of men in the militia and their commanders. A little of it overlapped with the Ministry of Barbarians' reports, somewhat more with Muzzaf Kerpatik's data from his merchant friends, but a good deal was new—particularly the information on the large Colonist community that controlled Lion City's grain trade. He flicked through; faster than he could read, but Center was looking out from his eyes and recording. He'd have to go over it again; Center's knowledge was not accessible to him in really useful form most of the time, not directly. Center could implant it; without the learning process it was there, but not understood.

The man bowed, touching brow and lips and chest; it looked odd, when his appearance was so thoroughly Southern Territories.

"Saayid," he said.

"Your family is still living in that house in the Ox-Crossing, isn't it?" Raj asked.

That was a suburb of East Residence, outside the walls and across the bay. Abdullah nodded.

"It's yours, and the grounds," Raj said, and waved away a pro-forma protest. "Don't deprive me of the pleasure of rewarding good service," he said.

"Thank you, saayid," Abdullah said. "And now . . . I think the merchant Peydaro Blanhko—" he touched his chest "—should vanish from the earth. Too many people will be asking for him."

Raj looked at Suzette as the Druze left the tent. "Someday I'm going to get the whole story of that one out of you," he said.

"Not with wild oxen, my love."

Raj stepped up to the map and began sketching in the extra data. "No, but I suspect that if I tickle you around that tiny mole, you'll tell all. . . . Right, that's the shipyard. Now—"

✧   ✧   ✧

The flap of the command tent had been pinned up, leaving a large three-sided room open to the west. In full dark the camp outside the walls of Lion City was a gridwork of cooking fires and shadowed movement; Raj could hear the tramp of feet in the distance, howling from the dog-lines, and a harsh challenge from a sentry on the rampart.

They can probably see our fires from the walls, Raj thought, standing with his hands behind his back; the center of the camp was slightly higher than the edges, and he could make out the pale color of the city walls. Lantern-lights starred it. Much brighter was the tall lighthouse, even though it was on the other side of the city. The light was a carbide lamp backed by mirrors, but the lighthouse itself was Pre-Fall work, a hundred meters tall.

There were probably plenty of nervous citizens on the ramparts, besides the civic militia. Looking out at the grid of cooking fires in the besieger's camp, and thinking of what might happen in a sack.

Then they'd bloody well better give up, hadn't they? He turned back to the trestle table. "First, gentlemen," he said to the assembled officers, "I'd like to say, well done. We've subdued a province of nearly a million people in less than two weeks, suffered only minor casualties"—every one of them unpleasantly major to the men killed and maimed, but that was part of the cost of doing business—"and your units have performed with efficiency and dispatch.

"Colonel Menyez," he went on, "you may tell your infantry commanders that I'm also pleased with the way they've shaken down. Their men have marched, dug—and shot, on a couple of occasions—in soldierly fashion."

A flush of real pleasure reddened Menyez' fair complexion. "I've had them under arms for a full year and a half or more now," he said. "Sandoral, the Southern Territories and this campaign. I'd back the best of them against any cavalry, in a straight stand-up firefight."

Civil Government infantry usually lived on State farms assigned to them near their garrisons, and were paid cash only when on field service away from their homes, unlike the cavalry. The farms were worked by government peons, but it wasn't uncommon in out-of-the-way units for the enlisted men to be more familiar with agricultural implements than their rifles. Menyez's own 17th Kelden County Foot had been in continuous field service since the Komar operation four years ago, and many of the other infantry battalions since the Sandoral campaign on the eastern frontier. The fisc and Master of Soldiers' office had complained mightily; finding regular hard cash for the mounted units was difficult enough.

Raj went on: "I'd also like to particularly commend Major Clerett for his management of the preemptive attack over the Waladavir; a difficult operation, conducted with initiative and skill."

Cabot Clerett nodded. Suzette leaned to whisper in his ear, and he nodded again, this time letting free the boyish grin that had been twitching at his control.

"And now, Messers, we get the usual reward for doing our work."

"More work, General?" somebody asked.

"Exactly. Lion City, which we certainly can't leave in our rear while we advance. Colonel Dinnalsyn?"

The artillery commander rose and walked to the map board. "As you can see, the city's a rectangle, more or less, facing west to the sea. Here's the harbor." A carrot-shaped indentation in the middle with semicircular breakwaters reaching out into the ocean and leaving a narrow gap for ships.

"The breakwaters, the lighthouse, and the foundations of the sea walls are adamantine." Pre-Fall work; the material looked like concrete but was stronger than good steel, and did not weather. "The walls are about four hundred years old, but well-maintained—blocks up to two tons weight, height five to ten meters, towers every hundred-and-fifty meters or so. The main gate was modernized about a century ago, with two defensive towers and a dog-leg. There are heavy pieces on the sea walls, and four- and eight-kilogram fortress guns on the walls, some of them rifled muzzle-loaders firing shell. They outrange our field guns."

"Appraisal, messer?"

"The sea approaches are invulnerable. Landward, my fieldpieces could peck at those walls for a year, even with solid shot. I could run the wheels up on frames or earth ramps to get elevation and put shells over the walls . . . except that the fortress guns would outrange my boys. That goes double for the mortars. The only cheering word is that there's no moat. If you want to bring the walls down, we'll have to ship in heavy battering pieces—the ones from Fort Wager would do—and put in a full siege."

Everyone winced—that meant cross- and approach-trenches, earthworked bastions to push the guns closer and closer to the walls, artillery duels, then however long it took to knock a suitable breach. Desperate fighting to force their way through into the town.

observe, said Center.

—and powder-smoke nearly hid the tumbled rabble of the shattered wall. Men clawed their way upward, jerking and falling as the storm of bullets swept through their ranks. Another wave drove upward, meeting the Brigaderos troops at the apex of the breach. There was a brief point-blank firefight, and then the Civil Government soldiers were through.

They charged, bayonets levelled and a tattered flag at their head. But beyond the breach was a C of earthworks and barricades taller than a man, thrown up while the heavy guns wrecked the stone wall. Cannon bucked and spewed canister into the advancing ranks—

—and Raj could see Lion City ringed by circumvallation, lines of trenches facing in and another line facing out. Beyond the outer line sprawled the camps of the Brigade's relieving armies, improvised earthworks less neat than the Civil Government's but effective enough, and stunning in their number.

A sentry leaned against the parapet of the outer trench. His face had a bony leanness, and it was tinged with yellow. His rifle slid down and lay at his feet, but the soldier ignored it; instead he hugged himself and shivered, teeth chattering in his head.

"Thank you, Colonel," Raj said, blinking away the vision. Dinnalsyn resumed his seat with the gloomy satisfaction of a man who had told everyone what they were hoping not to hear.

"The garrison," Raj went on, "consists of a civic militia organized by the guilds and cofraternities, and the household guards of merchants and town-dwelling landowners, about five thousand men of very mixed quality, and a force of Brigaderos regulars of four thousand—they were heavily reinforced shortly before we landed. Nine thousand, including gunners, behind strong fortifications. They've ample water in cisterns if we cut the aqueduct, and this city exports foodstuffs—there's probably enough in the warehouses for a year, even feeding ·the Brigaderos' dogs.

"I don't want to lose either time or men; but at this point, forced to chose, I'll save time and spend men. Colonel Menyez, start putting together scaling ladders of appropriate size and numbers for an assault force of six thousand men. As soon as some are ready, start the following battalions training on them—"

He listed them; about half and half cavalry and infantry. Everyone winced slightly. "Yes, I know. We'll try talking them into surrender first."

Filipe de Roors was *alcalle* of Lion City because of a talent for dealing with his peers among the merchant community. Also because he was very rich, with ships, marble quarries outside the city and the largest shipyard within, lands and workshops and sawmills; and because his paternal grandfather had been a member of the Brigade, which the other merchants thought would help when dealing with the local *brazaz* military gentry and the authorities in Carson Barracks. The post of mayor usually combined pleasure, prestige and profit with only a modicum of effort and risk.

Right now, de Roors was silently cursing the day he decided to stand for the office.

After the tunnel gloom of the main gate, even the orange-red light of a sun not yet fully over the horizon was bright, and he blinked at the dark shapes waiting. He added another curse for the easterner general, for insisting on meeting at dawn. The air was a little chill, although the days were still hot.

"Messer de Roors?"

De Roors jerked in the saddle, setting the high-bred Chow he rode to curvetting in a sidle that almost jostled one of the soldiers' dogs. The Civil Government cavalry mounts didn't even bother to growl, but the civilian's dog shrank back and whined submissively.

"Captain Foley, 5th Descott Guards," the young officer said.

Raj Whitehall's name had come west over the last few years, and something of the men who accompanied him. The 5th's, especially, since they had been with him since the beginning; he recognized the blazon fluttering from the bannerman's staff, crossed sabers on a numeral 5, and *Hell o Zpalata* beneath—*Hell or Plunder*, in Sponglish. De Roors looked at the smiling, almost pretty face with the expressionless black eyes and then at the bright-edged hook. The dozen men behind him sat their dogs with bored assurance; they weren't tasked with talking to him, and their glances slid across him and his followers with an utter indifference more intimidating than any hostility.

"This way, if you please, Messer," the officer said.

Watching the invaders build their camp had been a combination of horror and fascination from the walls; like watching ants, but swarming with terrible mechanical precision. Closer up it was worse. The camp was *huge*, there must be twenty thousand people inside, maybe twenty-five, more than half the number in Lion City itself. A road had been laid from the main highway southeast, graded dirt with drainage ditches, better than most highways on the Crown Peninsula. Around the camp was a moat, one and a half meters deep and two across at the top; the bottom was filled with sharpened stakes. Inside the ditch was a steep-sloped earthwork of the reddish-brown soil thrown up by the digging, and it was the height of a tall man. On top of it was a palisade of logs and timbers, probably taken from the woodlots and cottages that had vanished without trace.

At each corner of the camp and at the gates was a pentagonal bastion jutting out from the main wall; the bastions were higher, and their sides were notched. Through the notches jutted the black muzzles of field guns, ready to add their firepower to the wall or take any angle in murderous crossfire. The gate bastion had a solid three-story timber observation tower as well, with the blue and silver Starburst banner flying from the peak.

All of it had been thrown up in a single afternoon.

"Ah . . . are you expecting attack, then?" he asked.

The captain looked at him, smiling slightly. "Attack? Oh, you mean the entrenchments. No, messer, we do that every time we camp. A good habit to get into, you understand."

Spirit.

The escort had shed traffic along the road to the encampment like a plough through thin soil, not even needing to shout for the way. Things were a little more crowded at the gate, although the barricades of spiked timbers were drawn aside; nobody got in or out without challenge and inspection, and the flow was dense and slow-moving. De Roors was riding at the head of the little column, with the officer and banner. A trumpet rang out behind him, loud and brassy. He started slightly in the saddle, humiliatingly conscious of the officer's polite scorn. *Puppy,* he thought. No more than twenty.

Another trumpet answered from the gate parapet; an interplay of calls brought men out at the double to line the road on either side and prompt the other travellers with ungentle haste.

A coffle was halfway through, and the officer threw up his hand to stop the escort while the long file of prisoners got out of the way. There were forty or so men, yoked neck to neck with collars and chains and their hands bound together; many of them were bandaged, and most were in the remnants of Brigade uniform. The more numerous women wore light handcuffs, and the children trudging by their stained and grimy skirts were unbound. None of them looked up as they stumbled by, pushed to haste by armed and mounted men not in uniform but dressed with rough practicality.

"Apologies, Messer Captain," said one, as the captives stumbled into the ditch to let the troopers through. He didn't seem surprised when Foley ignored him as if he were transparent.

"Slave traders," the captain said, when they had ridden through into the camp. "They follow the armies like vultures."

Maybe that was staged for my benefit, de Roors thought. The ancient lesson: this is defeat. Avoid it. *But the Brigaderos were real.*

Inside the camp was nothing of the tumult or confusion he'd expected from experience with Brigade musters. Instead it was like a military city, a regular grid of ditched laneways, flanked by the leather eight-man tents of the soldiers. Most of them were still finishing their morning meal of gruel and lentils and thin flat wheatcakes, cooked on small wrought iron *ybatch* grills. Every occupied tent—he supposed some men were off on fatigues and so forth—had two wigwams of four rifles each before it, leaning together upright with the men's helmets nodding on them like grain in a reaped field. The men were wiry olive-skinned eastern peasants for the most part, with cropped black hair and incurious cleanshaven faces. Individually they didn't look particularly impressive. Together they had shaken the earth and beaten nations into dust.

The Captain drew closer, courteously pointing out features: De Roors was uneasily aware that the hook flashing past his face was sharpened on the inner edge.

"Each battalion has a set place, the same in every camp. There are the officer's tents—" somewhat larger than the men's "—and the shrine for the unit colors. This is the *wia erente,* the east-west road; the *wia sehcond* runs north-south, and they meet in the center of camp, at the *plaza commanante,* with the general's quarters and the Star church tent. Over there's the artillery park, the dog lines—" a thunder of belling and barking announced feeding time "—the area for the camp followers and soldiers' servants, the—"

De Roors' mind knew the Brigade's armies were vastly more numerous. His emotions told him there was no end to this hive of activity. Men marching or riding filled the streets, traffic keeping neatly to the left and directed at each crossroads by soldiers wearing armbands marked *guardia.* Wagon trains, supply convoys, officers riding by with preoccupied expressions, somewhere the sound of hundreds of men hammering wood.

The commander's tent was large but not the vast pavilion he expected; the canvas church across the open space from it was much bigger, and so was the hospital tent on the other side of the square.

His escort split and formed two lines, facing in. The guard at the door of the tent presented arms to Foley's salute, and the young officer dismounted and stood at parade rest beside the opened door flap.

"The *Heneralissimo Supremo;* Sword-Bearing Guard to the Sovereign Mighty Lord and Sole Autocrat Governor Barholm Clerett; possessor of the proconsular authority for the Western Territories; three times hailed Savior of the State, Sword of the Spirit of Man, Raj Ammenda Halgren da Luis Whitehall!" he called formally, in a crisp clear voice. Then:

"The *Alcalle* of Lion City, Messer Filipe De Roors." A murmur from within. "You may enter, Messer."

De Roors was dimly conscious of his entourage being gracefully led away. The tented room within was lit by skylights above; there was a long table and chairs, and a map-board with an overhead view of Lion City. Nothing of the splendor that a high Brigade noble would take on campaign, nothing of what was *surely* available to the conqueror of the Southern Territories. Nothing but a short forged-steel mace inlaid with platinum and electrum, resting on a crimson cushion. Symbol of the rarely granted proconsular authority, the power to act as vice-governor in the *barbaricum.*

The man sitting at the middle of the table opposite him seemed fairly ordinary at first; certainly his uniform was nothing spectacular, despite the eighteen-rayed silver and gold star on either shoulder, orbited by smaller silver stars and enclosed in a gold band. A tall man, broad in the shoulders and narrow-hipped, with a swordsman's thick shoulders and wrists. A hard dark face with startling gray eyes, curly bowl-cut black hair speckled with a few flecks of silver. Looking older than the young hero of legend—and less menacing than the merciless aggressor the Squadron refugees and Colonist merchants had described.

Then he saw the eyes, and the stories about Port Murchison seemed very real.

You've met hard men before, de Roors told himself. *And bargained them into the ground.* He bowed deeply. "Most Excellent General," he said.

This one could sell lice to Skinners, Raj thought a few minutes later. A digest of Lion City's internal organization, constitutional position in the Western Territories, and behavior in previous conflicts rolled on, spiced with fulsome praise, references to common religious faith, and earnest good wishes to the Civil Government of Holy Federation.

"Messer, shut up," he said quietly.

De Roors froze. He was plump, middle-aged and soft-looking and expensively dressed, a five-hundred-FedCred stickpin in his lace cravat. Raj didn't think the man was consciously afraid of death, not after coming in under a flag of truce and guarantee of safe-conduct. He knew the impact his own personality had, however, and that it was magnified in the center of so much obvious power. Yet de Roors was still bargaining hard. There were more types of courage than those required to face physical danger, and they were rather less common.

"Contrary to what you may have heard, messer, not everyone in the *Gubernio Civil* is in love with rhetoric. I'll put it very simply: Lion City must open its gates and cooperate fully with the army of the Civil Government. If you do, I'll not only guarantee the lives and property of the civilian residents; Lion City will be freed from external tax levies for five years—and you'll get a fifty-percent reduction in harbor dues and charges at East Residence."

He leaned forward slightly. "If you *don't* . . . they call me the Sword of the Spirit, messer *alcalle,* but I'm not the Spirit Itself. If my troops have to fight their way in, they're going to get out of hand—soldiers always do, in a town taken by storm." De Roors blanched; a sack was any townsman's worst nightmare. "Furthermore, in that case I'll have to confiscate heavily for the customary donative to the men. Those aren't threats, they're analysis.

"Messer, I *want* Lion City to surrender peacefully, because I'd prefer to have a functioning port under my control in the Crown. I *will* have the city, one way or another."

De Roors mopped his face. There was a moment's silence outside as a gong tolled, and then the chanting of the morning Star Service. Raj touched his amulet but waited impassively.

"*Heneralissimo supremo,* I can't make such a decision on my own initiative." At Raj's blank lack of expression he stiffened slightly. "This isn't the east, Excellency, and I'm not an autocrat—and the General of the Brigade couldn't make a decision like that by himself.

"And there's the garrison to consider. Usually we have a few hundred regular troops here, enough to, ah—"

Raj nodded. *Keep the city from getting ideas.* Free merchant towns were common on some of the islands of the Midworld. A garrison reminded the impetuous that Lion City was on the mainland and accessible to the General's armies.

"After the news of Stern Isle came through, the General sent three regiments from Old Residence, more than thirty-five hundred men of his standing troops under High Colonel Piter Strezman. A famous commander with veteran troops. They won't surrender."

"Quite a few *Brigaderos* around here have," Raj pointed out.

"They weren't behind strong walls with a year's supplies, your Excellency," de Roors said. "Furthermore, their families weren't in Old Residence standing hostage for them."

What a splendid way to build fighting morale, Raj thought. *I'll bet it was Forker came up with that idea; he's had too much contact with us and went straight from barbarism to decadence without passing through civilization.*

"As you say, this isn't the east," he said dryly. De Roors flushed, and Raj continued: "Let's put it this way: you open the gates, and we'll take care of the garrison."

De Roors coughed into his handkerchief. Raj raised a finger; one of the HQ servants slid in, deposited a carafe of water, and departed with the same smooth silence.

"That might be possible, yes," de Roors said. He drank and wiped his mouth again. "The problem with that, Excellency, is, ummm, you understand that we're not encouraged to meddle in military matters, and—might I suggest that Lion City is of no real importance in itself? If you were to pass on, and either defeat the main Brigade armies, or take Old Residence, we'd be delighted to cooperate with you in a most positive way, most positive, you'd have no cause to complain of our loyalty then. Until then, well, it really would be imprudent of us to—"

Raj grinned. De Roors flinched slightly and averted his eyes.

"You mean," Raj said, his words hard and cold as the forged iron of a cannon's barrel, "that if you open the gates and we lose the war later, the Brigade will slaughter you down to the babes in arms. Quite true. Look at me, messer."

Reluctantly, de Roors' eyes dragged around again. Raj went on:

"I and my men can't hedge our bets, messer *alcalle;* neither can the Brigaderos, and neither of us will let *you* hedge, either, and thereby encourage every village with a wall to try and sit this war out in safety. If you try to straddle this fence you'll end up impaled on it. No doubt that strikes you as extremely unfair, and no doubt it is; it's also the way this Fallen world is and will continue to be until Holy Federation is restored. Which, as Sword of the Spirit, it is my duty to accomplish."

"I'll certainly, ah, certainly present your views to my colleagues, Excellency—" de Roors' fear was breaking close to the surface now,

not least from the realization that what might be a religious plati-
tude in another man was deadly serious intent in this.

"Oh, you'll do better than that," Raj said.

"The man is mad!" de Roors said, as his party rode back towards
the city gates. Considerably more slowly, as there was no escort to
part the traffic ahead of them this time.

"What will you do, master?" his chief steward said. The iron collar
had come off his neck many years ago, but some habits remained.

"Prepare to hold a town meeting," de Roors snarled. "Precisely
as the *Heneralissimo supremo* demanded."

"Barholm's nephew . . ." the steward shook his head and leaned
closer, putting the dogs close enough to sniff playfully at each other's
ears. "What a hostage!"

De Roors cuffed the man alongside the head with the handle of
his dogwhip. "Shut up. If we touched one hair on the Clerett's head
after giving safe-conduct to address the meeting, Whitehall would
sow the smoking ruins with *salt.*"

He paused, thoughtful; the other man rubbed the side of his head
where the tough flexible bone had raised a welt.

"And High Colonel Strezman would nail us up on crosses to look
at it; you know how some of these Brigade nobles are about oaths,
and he's worse than most."

"If you say so, master."

"No, our only hope is that he'll march on rather than waste
time with us . . . if we *could* open the gates he'd keep his . . . no,
too risky—and the others would never go along with it, they
haven't met him and they don't, they don't—" de Roors shook
his head. "He really believes it, he thinks he's the Sword of the
Spirit."

The chief steward looked at his patron with concern, the blow
forgotten. His fortunes were too closely linked to the merchant's
in any case; they had been so for many years. He had never seen
him so shaken in all that time. De Roors' hands were trembling
where they fumbled with whip and reins.

"Maybe," he said, trying humor, "he really *is,* master. The Sword
of the Spirit, that is."

De Roors looked at him silently. After a while, the steward began
to shake as well.

"He's cheating me again!" Cabot Clerett broke out. "First he makes
a great noise about rounding up and slaughtering some refugees in
a hole, while I was fighting *real* Brigade soldiers. Now this!"

I wonder if it's hereditary? Suzette thought. Barholm Clerett never
forgot a slight either, real or imagined. Men who'd wronged him
when he was in his teens had discovered that with painful finality
when he was enchaired as Governor thirty years later.

"Your uncle might well feel he's endangering you needlessly," she said in cautious agreement.

"Oh, it's not that!" Clerett said. He smiled. "I'm glad you care for my safety, of course, Suzette. But I can't be too cautious, or . . . It's this mission. He's going along to spoil any chance I have of a real success."

Suzette sank down beside him on the bench and took his hand. "Oh, Clerett," she said. "I thought he was going incognito?"

He took the hand in both of his. "Sometimes you seem so wise, Suzette, and sometimes so innocent, like a girl. Of course it'll come out that he went along. And since he's not covered by name in the safe-conduct, it'll look as if *he* were doing the real, the risky work. He'll be the hero, and I'll be the flunky with the walk-on part."

The young man brooded for a moment. "And that—that fellow Staenbridge."

"Cabot, you will have to learn to work with all sorts of men when you're Governor." She smiled and patted his cheek. "And women, but you'll find that *much* easier, I'm sure."

He flushed, grinned, and raised the hand to his lips. "Thank you. And," he went on, "you're right about working with all types. Although," he said thoughtfully, "the first thing I'll do is kill Tzetzas, if Uncle doesn't do it first. With all he's stolen, it'll fill the fisc nicely."

Suzette nodded. "You'll make a great Governor, Cabot," she said, her voice warm. *Paranoid ruthlessness is an asset in that job, most of the time.*

Cabot half-rose from the bench, and dropped to one knee. "Oh, Suzette," he said, his voice suddenly stumbling over itself. "You're the only one who really *understands*. Could I—could I have something of yours, to carry into battle? A pledge . . ."

A few of the oldest stories, old even before the Fall, told of such things. Suzette reached into a pocket of her campaign overalls and drew out a handkerchief. Cabot Clerett received it as if it were a holy relic, a circuit board or rolldown screen, then tucked it into an inner pocket of his uniform jacket.

"Thank you," he breathed.

I wonder, she thought, as he left, *if he minds that it's used?*

Probably not. In fact, that might make it seem more valuable. She shook her head. *They let that boy read too much old poetry,* she thought. Being so close to the Chair could restrict a child's social contacts. *Far too much.*

The final kilometer or so of the main road into Lion City was paved. The original surface had been stone blocks of uniform size set in mortar from the time the Civil Government ruled this area; that had been long before the development of coal mining made concrete cheap enough to use for surfacing. When one side wore too much under the continual pounding of hooves and paws and wheels, the blocks could be turned over, leveled on a bed of gravel and remortared into place. That had happened often enough for the remaining to be lumpy from having been turned several times. Holes in the paving had been patched, with flagstones and spots of brick and gravel set in cement.

The paws of the detachment's mounts made a thud-*scuff* sound on the hard, slightly uneven surface. Light from the setting sun cast their shadows behind them, and a blackness from the walls and gates loomed ahead. The arch of the gate glowed yellow with the coal-oil lanterns hung within the arch; that light glinted off edged metal within.

"This is extremely foolish of you, Whitehall," Gerrin Staenbridge said.

They were both riding behind the color party, dressed in ordinary troopers' uniforms with the 1st Lifeguards' *Vihtoria O Muwerti* and leaping sicklefoot on the shoulder flashes, and Senior Sergeant chevrons on the sleeves. Suzette's retainer Abdullah had given them a few tricks, a gauze bandage liberally sprinkled with chicken blood for the side of Raj's face, and two rubber pads to alter the shape of Gerrin's. Mostly they relied on the fact that few outside their own force had ever seen them closely, and more important, that few men of importance *looked* at common soldiers. They could both give a fairly convincing imitation of a pair of long-service Descotter NCOs. Which was, Raj reflected, probably what they'd both have been, if they'd been born yeoman-tenants instead of to the squirerarchy.

Raj clicked his tongue. "I need to know exactly what we're up against, and if we can find a deal acceptable to the citizens, or most of them."

From de Roors' description, Lion City was accustomed to a fair degree of autonomy in internal affairs. The ways they had of settling policy sounded odd—more like a prescription for standing in circles shouting and waving their arms and hitting each other—but that was the way most large towns were managed, here in the west.

"We need the active support of the townsmen," he went on, "if we're going to get anything done with inadequate forces. Now, *you* coming along is stupid. You're my right-hand man."

"Exactly." Gerrin's grin was white in the shadows. "Look, you're the one who'd invade Hell and fight the demons of the Starless Dark if Barholm said he needed the ice for his drinks. Damned if *I* am going to be left holding the ball if they shorten you, Whitehall. I know my limitations; we all should. I'm a better than competent commander, but I do best as a number two—when you found me, I was so bored I'd nothing better to do than diddle the battalion accounts, for the Spirit's sake. You might have some chance of pulling this campaign off; I wouldn't, and worse still, I might be expected to try. Jorg or Kaltin could hold the Crown easily enough, with the Expeditionary Force—and nobody would expect them to do more."

Raj nodded tightly. The *real* problem was that Barholm might send someone like Klostermann out to take over if he died . . . but he certainly couldn't win by playing safe, in any event. They fell silent as the embassy approached the gate.

There was an exchange of courtesies at the entrance; then General's Dragoons fell in around the Civil Government party. Raj looked them over, a perfectly natural thing for his persona to do. They were well mounted and well-equipped, with sword, two revolvers and a percussion rifle-musket in a boot on the left side of the saddle; they all wore similar lobster-tail helmets and grey-and-black uniforms. The officers wore breastplates as well, and the unit had maneuvered neatly to shake itself out beside his party. Altogether better-ordered than the *Squadrones* had been, and just as tough; the *Squadrones* had been down from the Base Area only a century and a half, but they'd spent most of that sitting on their plundered estates watching the serfs work with no strong enemies near them. The Brigade had an open frontier to the north, exposed to the interior of the continent. These men all looked as if they'd seen the titanosauroid more than once.

If their leadership were as good as their troops, we'd be fucked, Raj thought.

correct, Center acknowledged, **enemy weakness in that regard was one factor among many in my decision to activate my plan in your time, raj whitehall.**

The main gate of Lion City was a massive affair, four interlinked towers in pairs on either side of the passageway with a squarish platform twenty feet thick joining them at third-story level. The main defenses were old-style curtain walls with round towers, running straight into the ground. Up until a couple of centuries ago cannon had been too feeble to threaten a stout stone wall, so defenses went high, to deter attempts at storming. Since heavy battering guns came into use the preferred solution was to dig a broad deep moat and sink the walls on the other side until they were barely above the outer lip. That way little of the wall was exposed to artillery, it could be backed with heavy earthworks and so support massive guns of its own, and a storming force still had to climb out of the moat and up the protected wall. Someone had done some work on the gate, though: the tower bases were sloped backward at a sharp angle to shed solid shot.

The gateway looked like a compromise, avoiding the horrendous expense of modernizing the whole city wall, which was still perfectly adequate against pirates or raiding savages. Raj looked up with professional interest as they passed in; first heavy timber gates strapped with iron and over half a meter thick, then a portcullis of welded iron bars thick as a man's arm. The arched ceiling overhead held murder-holes—gaps for shooting and dropping unpleasant things on anyone coming through—and there was a dogleg in the middle of the passageway to further hinder invaders.

Eyeballs glittered in the torchlight as the embassy came through at a walk; the gaslights common in the east were unknown here, but there were enough burning pine-knots to compensate tonight. Somebody had been busy, and piles of flimsy lath marked where the reserved area within the walls had been swept clear of sheds and shacks. The citizens crowded it, waiting to see their fates decided; there were more all along the road to the central plaza, which was not far from the gate. The usual buildings stood around it; a cathedron, here with the round planet rather than the rayed Star at its dome, a porticoed city hall, mansions. A speaker's podium had been erected in the center around the sculptured fountain, and several thousand men stood in front of it. Pretty well all men, as opposed to the crowd back along the streets, and many of them armed.

He sized up the group on the dais. A tall thin-featured man in three-quarter armor; that would be High Colonel Strezman. Blade features framed by long white hair streaked with black, penetrating blue eyes, and about a company of his dragoons on the pavement below, apart from a clump of officers. The syndics of the town had as many of their militia with *them,* and they stood on the opposite side of the podium—interesting evidence of a potential split. The heads of the guilds were there as well, each with his entourage behind him and supporters clumped on the cobblestones— merchants, artisans, and big clumps of ragged *dezpohblado* laborers ranged beside the laborers' chiefs. Many of the individual magnates had their guards with them as well, variously equipped; there was a big clump of men in robe and ha'ik, or turbans and long coats and sashes, also armed. The Colonial merchants.

Sure to be against us, Raj thought. The Colony and the Civil Government routinely used economic sanctions and outright attacks on each others' resident citizens as part of their ongoing struggle.

De Roors came to the front of the podium as soon as the greeting rituals were out of the way. He raised his hands to still the low murmurs and spoke:

"Citizens of Lion City! We are here to listen to the embassy of General Whitehall and the Civil Government army camped outside the walls of our city. To do us honor, General Whitehall has sent the noblest of his officers to treat with us; none other than the Most Excellent Cabot Clerett, nephew to the Governor of the Civil Government himself!"

Another long rustle and hum from the crowd. "As courtesy and the ancient customs of our community demand, The Most Excellent Major Clerett will speak first, listing the terms and demands of the Civil Government. The heads of the guilds, and High Colonel

Strezman, will reply and the guilds will express their will to the syndics."

More ceremonies followed; blessings from Star Spirit and This Earth priests—the liturgies differed only in detail, but the Brigade cult was given pride of place—before Cabot Clerett stepped to the speaker's position.

He paused to remove his helmet and tuck it under one arm, then lifted the other palm out, slowly. It was an effective gesture, but he had the benefit of training by the best rhetoricians available in East Residence. He looked down on the sea of upturned faces, face underlit by the torches that brought out highlights in his curly black hair, face stern and sharp-boned.

"People of Lion City!" he called, in a voice pitched slightly higher than usual to carry. Training put the full power of strong young lungs behind it, and kept it from sounding shrill; his Spanjol was accented but fluent. "Hear the terms which are most generously granted to you; for wisdom lies not in rash fury, but in reasoned council and moderation. I offer—"

Gerrin stirred behind him; that was supposed to be *General Whitehall* offers. The young emissary was sticking to the agreed text, but substituting his own name or something like "the Civil Government" or "His Supremacy, my uncle" whenever Raj's name was called for. They were flanking Cabot to the left and right and a step to the rear, leaving the bannerman directly behind him to show the Civil Government's flag. Heavy silk hissed against the polished stanauro wood of the pole; the breeze was from the ocean, carrying scents of tar and stagnant water and a hint of clean seawater beyond. Out beyond the seawall to their left red lights glowed, reflected furnace-light on the smoke from the war-steamers' furnaces.

Raj kept his attention on the crowd and the leaders, checking only that the terms were as he'd specified. Cabot's voice rose in an excellent imitation of passion at the conclusion; Bartin Foley had written it, cribbing from his studies of Old Namerique classical drama. Not much of that had survived the Fall—most of the stored data had died with the computers—but fragments had been written down from memory by the first generation, and fragments of that had survived the eleven hundred years since. He finished the promises; now on to the threats.

"Therefore, you men of Lion City, take pity on your town, and on your own people, while yet my soldiers—" Cabot's voice rolled out.

"*My* soldiers, you little *fastardo?*" Gerrin muttered. His voice was almost inaudible, but Raj was very close. Close enough to nudge the other man with his boot unnoticed.

"—are in my command; avoid deadly murder, spoil and villainy, such as accompany a sack; yield peacefully. For if not, look to see the blood-drenched soldiers with foul hands defile the thighs of your shrill-shrieking daughters; your fathers taken by the silver beards, and their most reverend heads dashed to the walls; your naked infants spitted on bayonets; while the mad mothers with their howls break the clouds in anguish!"

Cabot stopped, clicked heels and stepped back. The sea of faces rippled as men turned to speak to their neighbors. A voice called out from the ranks of the laborers:

"It ain't our war! This General Raj, he's treated peaceful people right well out in the country, from what they say. What have we ever got from the Brigade but taxes and a boot up our bums? Open the gates!"

"Open the gates! Open the gates!" A claque took up the chant.

Out of the corner of his eye Raj could see High Colonel Strezman's tight-held jaw. He murmured an order to an aide, who hopped off the podium; seconds later a squad of Brigade soldiers was heading for the man who'd spoken. There was a moment's commotion as the laborers closed ranks, and then thrust the man scrambling backward between their legs to lose himself in the crowd. Before the rifle-butts could force a way, a squad of civic militia shifted nearer. The Brigadero officer in charge of the squad looked over his shoulder at Strezman, then turned his men around and retired, followed by jeers and catcalls, but not by rocks.

Not yet, Raj thought.

Strezman shifted, and de Roors led him to the speaker's position.

"Silence!" he shouted.

When the murmuring grew, Strezman signed to the aide and a ten-man section of dragoons threw their rifles to their shoulders and fired into the air. And immediately reloaded, Raj noted.

Silence came at last. "Civilians of Lion City," Strezman began. His Spanjol was more heavily accented than Cabot's had been, with a Namerique clang to it.

Not too tactful, Raj thought. Civilian meant "second-class citizen" at best in the Brigade lands. Only slightly more polite than *grisuh,* civvie.

"In his wisdom," Strezman continued, "His Mightiness, General Forker, Lord of Men—" that fell flat, and he ignored scattered jeers.

I imagine Strezman isn't too thrilled about Forker's little hostage play, Raj thought. The man seemed to be something of a soldier, in his way, and the intelligence report indicated he was a Brigade noble of the old school.

"—has sent a strong garrison to defend your city from the butcher Whitehall and his host." More murmurings from the crowds, and a voice called:

"Yeah, he butchered a whole *lot* of you dog-sucker barbarians down in the Southern Territories." Another, from a different section of the crowd:

"And restored Holy Federation Church, you heretic bastard!"

The crowd's growl was ugly. The militia shuffled, looking to the syndics. The armed retainers of the rich and the Colonists closed around their masters. Spots of red burned on Strezman's cheeks; this time there was a flash of armored gauntlet as he gave his orders. The Brigade troops marched out in front of the podium and brought their rifles up to face the crowd in a menacing row. Men surged away from their aiming point.

De Roors walked hastily to the High Colonel's side and waved his arms for silence. Strezman gave him a curt nod and went on, as the soldiers went to port arms.

"We have four thousand men, all veterans of the northern frontier, and plenty of powder and shot for small arms and the cannon on the walls both. Whitehall can't stay here long; the Brigade's armies are mustering, and they outnumber his pitiful force by five or ten to one. Unless he moves, he'll be caught between the relieving armies and the walls of Lion City."

Accurate enough, Raj thought. *If hostile.* He hoped there weren't too many more like Strezman in the Brigade's upper ranks.

"Whitehall will have to march away soon, if we defy him. He doesn't have heavy guns either.

"The Brigade—His Mightiness the General—have allowed you a high degree of self-government within these walls," Strezman went on; from his tone, he thought that a mistake. "In order that the walls and your civic militia could be of help in time of war. That you are even entertaining this madman Whitehall's offer is a sign that policy *may* have been mistaken. If you were so foolish as to accept it, after the war is over and the Civil Government's little force is crushed, *you* will be next. His Mightiness won't leave one stone standing on another, or one citizen alive. Furthermore, I and my command will fight regardless of your decisions, so all that treason would gain you is to transfer the battle from outside the defenses to your own hearths."

Strezman stood for a moment, the firelight breaking off his armor, then stepped back. "Carry on," he said to de Roors; gesture and voice were full of contempt for civilian sloppiness and indecision.

Speaker followed speaker; most seemed to be for holding out, although quite a few hedged so thoroughly that it was impossible to tell which course they favored. A few were so incoherent or drunk that the maundering was inadvertent. At last the representative of the Colonists took the podium; he was a plump man in a dazzling turban of torofib, clasped with a ruby and a spray of iridescent sauroid feathers. A scimitar and pistol were thrust through the sash of his long coat, but the voice that addressed the crowd was practiced and smooth.

"Fellow citizens," the Colonist began. "Let me assure you that the Jamaat-al-Islami—"

League of Islam, Raj translated mentally. That would be the local association of Colonists.

"—will fight by your side. We know this *banchut* Whitehall, our kin have told us of him—bandit, murderer, defiler of holy places! Our warehouses contain enough food to feed the whole city for a year and a day. There is nothing to fear from siege. We must defy the infi—the invader Whitehall. Were his followers within the walls, no man's goods would be safe, nor the honor of his women."

A man walked into the light below the podium; he was dressed in workman's clothes, old but not ragged, and there were bone buckles on his shoes. An artisan, not wealthy but no *dezpohblado* either.

"Your goods will be safe, you mean, Haffiz bin-Daud," he said. "I—" de Roors was making motions. "I'm one of the Sailmaker's Syndics, Filipe de Roors," the man on the pavement snapped. "I've as much right to talk as any *riche hombe.*" His face went back to the Arab. "And as for the honor of our women, how safe was Therhesa Donelli from your man Khaled al'Assad?"

Another of the dignitaries on the dais pushed forward; he was an old man, richly dressed, with a nose like a beak and wattles beneath his chin. He waved his three-cornered hat angrily.

"Mind your place, Placeedo, and stick to the issues," he warned. "That case was settled and compensation awarded."

The sailmaker Placeedo crossed his arms and looked over his shoulder. Voices out of the darkness spoke for him:

"Compensation? Our daughters ain't hoors!"

"You *riche hombes* is in bed with the Spirit-deniers and the barb heretics too!"

"*Riche hombe* bastards squeeze us and use the barb soldiers if we complain; now they expect us to die to keep them in silk."

"Yes, and they bring in slaves and peons to do skilled work against the law, to break our guilds!"

Evidently that was a long-standing sore point; the bellow of the crowd rilled the night, and de Roors had to wave repeatedly to reduce the noise enough that he could be heard.

"Citizens! An army is at our gates, and we must not be divided among ourselves. Syndic Placeedo Anarenz, is there anything more you wish to say?"

"Yes, *alcalle* de Roors. My question is addressed to syndic Haffiz bin-Daud of the *Jamaat-al-Islami.* He says his countrymen have enough in the warehouses. Will he give his word of honor that the grain will be dispensed free during the siege? Or even at the prices of a month ago? Will the city feed the families of men thrown out of work because the gates are closed and the *Gubernio Civil*'s fleet blockades the harbor? There are men here whose women and children go hungry tonight because trade is disturbed. Poor men have no savings, no warehouses of food and cloth and fuel. Winter is coming, and it's hard enough for us in peacetime. Well?"

Haffiz made a magnificent gesture. "Of course we—"

Before he could speak further, a rush of other men in turbans and robes surrounded him, arguing furiously and windmilling their arms. From the snatches of hissed Arabic Raj could tell that whatever politic generosity he'd had in mind was not unanimously favored by his compatriots.

The sailmaker's syndic smiled and turned, gesturing to the crowd. A chant came up:

"Open the gates! Open the gates!" Anarenz grinned broadly; that turned into a frown and frantic waving as other calls came in on the heels of the first.

"Kill the rich! Kill the rich! *Dig up their bones!*"

"Down with the heretics!"

This time a scattering of rocks did fly. Amid the uproar and confusion, Raj saw the old syndic go to the edge of the platform. He gave an order to a man standing there, a Stalwart mercenary in a livery uniform. The man slipped away into the night. A few seconds later, something came whirring in out of the dark and went *thuck* into Anarenz' shoulder-blade: it was a throwing axe, the same type that Captain Lodoviko had used to save his life back on Stern Isle. This one would end the sailmaker's, unless he got to a healer and soon.

Shots rang out, and the voices rose to a surf-roar of noise. Many of the dignitaries on the podium deck dove to the floorboards, and some ran around the other side of the fountain that protruded through the middle, taking shelter behind its carvings of down-draggers and sea sauroids. Cabot Clerett stayed statuesquely erect, his cloak held closed with one hand. As would have been expected of any escort, Raj and Staenbridge closed up around the bannerman and the officer.

"This may be about to come apart," Gerrin said tightly.

Raj shook his head, eyes moving over the tossing sea of motion below. The militia had—mostly—turned about and faced the crowd with their weapons. Bands of house retainers made dashes into the edge of it, arresting or clubbing men down, apparently according to some sort of plan; he saw Anarenz carried off in a cloak by a dozen men who were apparently his friends, and the crowd slowing pursuit enough for him to escape.

"I think they'll get things back under control," Raj said.

"Silence in the ranks," Cabot said distantly, his eyes fixed on something beyond the current danger.

A kettledrum beat, and there was a massed thunder of paws. A column of Brigaderos cavalry burst into the square, with men scattering back ahead of it; they spread out along one edge facing in, their dogs snarling in a long flash of white teeth and their swords bright in their hands.

Silence gradually returned, with the massed growling a distant thunder in the background. De Roors stepped up to the podium. "Let the vote be tallied!" he said.

It went swiftly; votes were by guild, with the rich merchant and manufacturer guilds casting a vote each, as many as the mechanics' organizations with their huge memberships, and the single vote of the laborers. Those whose leaders were absent were voted automatically by de Roors, as *alcalle* of the town.

He turned to Cabot and bowed. "Most Excellent, with profound regret—I must ask you to leave our city. March on, for Lion City holds its walls against all attack."

"Move it up to a trot," Raj said, as soon as they were beyond the gate.

"Sir," Cabot replied stiffly. "Our dignity—"

"—isn't worth our asses," Raj said, grinning. "Trot, and then gallop, if you please, messers."

He touched his heels to Horace. The Civil Government banner flared out above them, the gold and silver of the Starburst glowing beneath the moons.

CHAPTER FOURTEEN

Fatima cor Staenbridge twisted her hands together in the waxed-linen apron that covered the front of her body. The operating tent was silent with a deep tension, a dread that knew what it awaited. Doctors, priests and Renunciate Sisters, waited with their assistants beside the tables; beside them were laid out saws and chisels, scalpels and curiously shaped knives, catgut and curved needles and piles of boiled-linen bandages. Jars of blessed distilled water cut with carbolic acid waited beside the tables, and more in sprayers along with iodine and mold-powder. And bottles of liquid opium, with the measuring-glasses beside them. Most battalions had priest-healers attached. The ones with the Expeditionary Force had served together long enough that General Whitehall had organized them into a corps under a Sysup-Abbot.

"Will it be bad?" Mitchi asked. "Kaltin told me not to worry."

Kaltin Gruder's concubine was about nineteen, with long bright-red hair now bound up on her head; the milk complexion, freckles and bright-green eyes showed it was natural. She and Fatima waited at the head of the other helpers; Civil Government armies had fewer camp followers than most, and those led by Raj Whitehall fewer still— one servant to every eight cavalry troopers, others for officers, and the inevitable spill-over of tolerated non-regulation types. Raj insisted that everyone without assigned military duties do *something* useful, and Suzette had organized the more reliable women for hospital duty in the past two campaigns, with Fatima as her deputy.

"It will be worse than last year," Fatima said. Mitchi had been a gift from the merchant Reggiri just before the Expeditionary Force left Stern Isle for the Squadron lands. The casualties in the Southern Territories had been light. Light for the Civil Government force.

"I hope, not as bad as Sandoral," Fatima went on. Softly: "I pray, not so bad as that." The tubs at the foot of the operating tables had been full that day, full of amputated limbs.

171

She knew the litany now, from experience; bring the wounded in, and sort them. A dog-sized dose of opium for the hopeless, and take them to the terminal section. Bandage the lightly wounded and put them aside for later attention. For the serious ones—probe for bullets, debride all foreign matter out, suture arteries and veins, disinfect and bandage. Sew flaps of muscle back into place and hope they healed straight. Compound fractures were common, bone smashed to splinters by the heavy fat lead slugs most weapons used. For those, amputate and hope that gangrene didn't set in. Dose with opium before surgery, but there was no time to wait and sometimes it didn't work. Then strong hands must hold the body down to the table, and the surgeon cut as fast as possible, racing shock and pain-induced heart failure as well as blood loss.

A hand tugged at Mitchi's sleeve. "Is there going to be shooting?" a small voice asked in Namerique.

They both looked down in surprise. It was the girl Kaltin had brought back. She'd been very quiet and given to shivering fits and nightmares and didn't like to be alone.

"Not near here, Jaine," Fatima said gently. "We safe here."

The child blinked, looking around as if fear had woken her from a daze. "There was a lot of shooting when Mom and Da went away," she said. "We left the farm and went to a place in the woods with a lot of other people. Da said we'd be safe there, but then there was shooting and they went away. They told me to wait and hide under the bundles."

Mitchi met Fatima's eyes over the child's head, then lifted her into her lap. "Shhh, little one," she said, holding her close.

"They're not coming back, are they?" Jaine asked solemnly. Fatima shook her head. The child sighed.

"I didn't think they were, really," she said. Her face twitched. "Then the Skinner came. I thought Skinners only came and got *bad* children, but I wasn't bad. I stayed real quiet like Da said. Honest I did." Tears began to leak out of the corners of the blue eyes.

Allah—Spirit of Man—why now? Fatima thought. Or maybe it was a good time. Gerrin wasn't out of the city yet. Men were watching for the embassy to reach safety, that was the signal. Raj and Gerrin were in there in disguise, among the enemy. Anything was better than waiting with nothing else to think of.

The child went on: "He didn't skin me and eat me the way Skinners are supposed to eat bad children. He tried to get up on top of me as if I were a big grown-up lady." Her voice was still quiet, but a little shrill. "He *hurt* me."

"Nobody can hurt you here, little sparrow," Fatima said, stroking the girl's face.

"I know," Jaine nodded. "Master Gruder came in and shot him." Her face relaxed slightly. "Then he kicked him off and shot him lots more times."

The two adults exchanged another glance; nobody had told them *that.*

The noise of the camp was subdued, but the roar from the city was like distant surf. Fatima shivered again, remembering the sound when the 5th broke into El Djem like water over a crumbling dam. It had been dawn then, just the start of another day like every other. The day when everything changed.

A few minutes passed and then Jaine spoke again, smearing the half-dried tears off her face with the heels of hands: "Are you slaves?" she said, and raised her hand to touch her neck. Mitchi understood the gesture: Brigade law required chattel slaves to wear metal collars.

"Yes, I am—we don't have to wear collars in the *Gubernio Civil,*" she said. "Fatima used to be a slave, but she's a freedwoman now."

The girl frowned. "Am I a slave now too?" she said. "Da—Da used to hit the slaves sometimes."

Mitchi hesitated. Fatima nodded and spoke soothingly. "You belong to Messer Gruder, but don't worry, little one. He's a very kind man. If you're a good girl and do what Mitchi and Messer Gruder tell you, you'll be fine."

Out through the entrance flap of the big tent, she could see a rocket arch into the night. It burst with a loud *pop* and a red spark.

"Mitchi, take Jaine over to the children's area," Fatima said tightly. *It has begun.*

The child began a pout; Fatima forestalled it. "I want you to help look after little Bartin and baby Suzette, all right?" she said.

Jaine nodded, and put her hand in Mitchi's.

From beyond the encampment's trench, man-made thunder boomed. Something in Fatima's stomach clenched as she recognized the sound, but her primary emotion was relief. Gerrin would be safely beyond range; that had been the signal.

"Let's go, men!" Colonel Jorg Menyez called. "Show the dog-boys what you're made of. Forward the 17th!"

The six hundred men of the 17th Kelden County Foot rose from the ground and roared, dashing forward to the bugle's call. They kept their alignment, running in a pounding lockstep; the lines wavered but didn't break up into clots as untrained men might have. The colonel ran with them, under the flapping banner. Ahead, the southside walls of Lion City gleamed pale under the moons. Even in the dark of night, it had been a major accomplishment to get so many men so close to the defenses without attracting attention. Even militiamen, however, weren't going to overlook two battalions of men running full-tilt toward them. Not even with the surf-roar of the assembly-cum-riot still sounding through the night.

A ladder passed him, on the shoulders of the grunting, panting men who bore it. Their boots struck the ground in unison, free hands pumping in rhythm. The stolid peon faces were set in grimaces of effort, the rictus of men who are pacing themselves strictly by the task in hand. The colonel was only a little over thirty and in hard condition, but it was far from easy to keep up with his men.

Spirit, he thought. He'd seen men run less eagerly toward a barrel of free wine.

Major Hadolfo Zahpata swung his saber forward. "*Dehfenzo Lighon!*" he called. *Defend the Faith.* The motto of the 18th Komar Borderers.

"*Aur! Aur!*" his men screamed, as they advanced at the run. "*Despert Staahl!*" It was the ancient war-cry of the southern borders of the Civil Government: *Awake the iron!*

Zahpata grinned as he ran, feeling the chainmail neck-guard of his helmet beat on his shoulders. Jorg's idea had been a good one; he could hear officers and non-coms shouting to the men:

"*Will you let* infantry *reach the wall ahead of you?*"

The ladders they carried were ten meters long and broad enough for two men abreast to climb. Hasty training had taught the men to relieve the squads bearing the burden of the clumsy, heavy things while at full speed. That way they could be carried all the way to the wall at a running pace, despite their weight.

Zahpata grinned again, this time a baring of the teeth that had nothing to do with amusement. Two battalions of grown men were racing toward guns stuffed with grapeshot and exposing their defense-less bodies to enemies protected by a stone wall, for the honor of seeing who would put a cloth flag on top of that wall first.

Faith is a wonderful thing, he thought, legs pumping. *I have faith in you, Dinnalsyn. Do not disappoint me.*

"Now!" Grammeck Dinnalsyn said, and clapped heels to his dog.

Thirty guns sprang forward; they had approached at a slow walk, with muffled wheels and brightwork covered by rags. Now they pounded forward at a lunging gallop, the crews leaning forward in the saddle. At twelve hundred meters from the walls they halted and swung into battery. Teams wheeled, so sharply that they were just short of turning the guns over in a disastrous spin. Sparks shot out into the night as the men on the caissons pulled brake levers. Dogs squatted on their haunches to shed momentum as soon as the muzzles turned; there was a man on the last dog in each team as well as the first, and he pulled the cotter pin linking the chain traces to the caisson. The teams trotted forward another five meters, enough to be out of the way but close enough for a quick getaway, then crouched to the ground in their traces.

The gunners jumped down and flung themselves at their weap-ons; an iron clangor filled the air as they unlocked and pulled the locking rod and lifted each trail off its limber. This time they did not let the ends of the trails thump to the ground. The caissons each carried two iron triangles tonight, with one side curved inward. They hammered them home with stakes, one in front of each wheel, and then hauled the wheels upward and held them to the top of the curve. Others swung hasty picks and shovels behind, digging pits for the end of the pole trails. When the trails dropped into the holes, the guns could not run backward down the iron surfaces. Breachblocks clanged and rang as the loaders shoved home rounds and levers pushed the blocking wedges behind them.

Dinnalsyn winced as he cursed his men to speed. This was one way to get extra range or elevation out of field guns, whose normal job required long flat trajectories. It also subjected the frames to wracking stresses, because they weren't able to recoil backwards in the usual fashion. *We ought to have more howitzers, light ones,* he thought: the stubby high-elevation weapons were officially considered useful mainly for siege work, and built heavy in large calibres.

Other gunners were setting up heavy carbide lamps on tripods, with curved mirrors behind them; signalling equipment in normal times, but modified for tonight. The beams came on with a hiss and sputter and chemical stink, bathing the ramparts in harsh yellow-white light. It shone eerily on the backs of hundreds of Skinners who were loping their dogs past the artillery, then dismounting and ramming their cross-topped shooting sticks into the dirt.

Similar floodlights were opening up on the city walls, amid a chaotic noise of drums and horns and hand-wound sirens. A cannon boomed with a long white puff of smoke, and a solid iron ball ploughed into the ground a few dozen meters in front of the foremost troops. Dinnalsyn swept his saber downward.

"*Fire,*" he shouted.

A huge *POUMPF,* thirty times repeated. Shells ripped out over the heads of the troops—contact fused, nobody was in a mood for accidents tonight. Some sailed over the wall, to raise flickering crashes in the city beyond. Others plowed short, gouting up poplar-shapes of dirt and rock. Most hit the wall; the explosive charges did no more than scar it, but they would shake the men on the firing platforms above. A few struck exactly where aimed, along the row of gunports and the crenellations of the wall itself. One was uncannily lucky, and punched right through a gunport just as the cannon there was about to fire. A giant belch of yellow flame shot out through the port as the piled ammunition beside the gun went up, and chunks of stone flew skyward. Bits and pieces of the crew did as well; the cast-iron barrel probably went out backwards off the wall.

Some of the gunners cheered. "Man your fucking *guns,*" Dinnalsyn screamed, trotting his dog down the gunline. "That was a fucking *miracle.*"

Cottony clouds of brimstone-stinking gunsmoke drifted around the position. The first few ranging shots were critical, because after that you were often firing blind into your own smoke.

"Mark the fall of shot, it's right in front of you. Battery three— you're all *short*. Elevation, elevation, Spirit eat your eyes!"

The crews in question spun the elevating screws beneath their weapons. Their next salvo was high, screeching at head-level over the crenellations and into the city. The guns bucked wildly on the pivot-lever formed by the trail, swinging nearly upright with the muzzles pointing at the sky, then slamming back down with an earsplitting anvil chorus of iron-shod wheels on iron frames. Every time he heard it, Dinnalsyn felt his hand clench involuntarily on the hilt of his saber, waiting for the loud unmusical *twang-crunch* of a trail breaking, a wheel shattering or—Spirit forbid—a trunnion cracking and sending the barrel pinwheeling off the carriage and into the crew. Every one of those rounds was taking more off the service life of the gun than fifty normal firings.

More cannon were firing from the wall. Solid shot, many of them, and aimed at *him*. That was the plan. He had a fair degree of respect for town-militia gunners; they practiced on fixed pieces with a single range of ground before their muzzles, and they could get to know both quite well. They didn't have the wide range of skills and adaptability that the full-time professionals in his crews did, but they didn't need them. Still, they were amateurs and their instinct would be to strike at the weapons that were firing at *them*, not at the far more dangerous infantry. He couldn't possibly win a counter-battery shoot with the guns on the walls: they were protected by stone, and his men were as naked as so many table-dancers in a dockside bar.

He was a sacrificial *goat*, by the Spirit.

Ahead of him the Skinners opened fire; not a volley, but the two-meter rifles were all firing at a steady four or five rounds a minute. The long muzzle flashes of the giant sauroid rifles were crimson and white spears through the night; within seconds, every search-light on the walls and towers ahead had died. Then the nomad mercenaries shifted their aim to the firing-slits and gunports; they began drifting forward to keep out of their own gunsmoke, firing every dozen paces. The stone sparked and spalled around the targets, but not very often. Most of the shots were going through, peening off the metal of cannon, ricocheting on stone, ripping through flesh and shattering bone.

Cannon still boomed from the ramparts. Some of them were firing round shells whose crude fuses traced red lines through the night until they burst and showered the ground with splinters. A roundshot smashed into one of the Civil Government's fieldpieces with a giant *clung* sound; the noise of men screaming came a minute later, as the smashed cannon and the pieces of the roundshot scythed through the crew. Stretcher-parties were running forward . . .

"Come *on*," he whispered to himself. "Move. Damn you, *move*." Another fieldpiece was out of action, canted off the triangular braces with a cracked trail, toppling backward as the crew dove out of the way.

The first ladder went up against the wall.

"Maximum elevation," Dinnalsyn called, loud but calm. The battery commanders repeated it. "Maximum elevation, three-quarter charge." They'd made up the charges for that earlier today. Just enough to lob the shells over the wall and into the cleared space beyond.

"Come on, lads, keep it moving!" Jorg Menyez shouted.

Grapeshot plowed through the ranks near him, near enough to hear the malignant wasp-whine of the lead balls. Men flopped, shredded by dozens of hits. Others staggered at the edge, called out in pain, toppled or kept moving forward. A roundshot hit just short of a file carrying a ladder and skipped forward along the ground, knocking the men over like bowling-pins . . . except that it shattered legs and ripped them off at the knee, ten men down and their comrades on the other side of the ladder untouched except for the torque that slapped the wood out of their hands. An officer raised his sword to wave his men forward; an instant later he was staring in disbelief at the stump of his arm, the ragged humerus showing pink for an instant before the welling blood covered it.

Shit and blood and sulfur, it's always the same, Jorg thought. He stood with the saber sloped over his shoulder and the banner of the 17th beside him, watching up and down the line. There would be a first foothold, and there . . .

"Up with it, up with it!"

They were below the walls now. A ladder started to rise. Hand-thrown bombs fell sputtering, one at the foot of the ladder; it burst and the wood exploded out in splinters. Sickly yellow light mixed with the red glare of cannon to pick out eyeballs, bared teeth, the edges of the long bayonets. The cannon above fired continuously, amid the whirring crash of the Civil Government shells hammering the wall and then lifting over it. The Skinners were firing all along their support line, heedless of anything but their aiming points— heedless of the ricochets that rebounded into the Civil Government soldiers below. Men were shrieking, in pain or raw terror or a perverse exultation.

"*Volley* fire. Fire."

More and more ladders were going up against the wall. The men not lofting them stood and fired upward, aiming for the slits in the parapet where defenders were leaning over to fire rifles and big siege-shotguns down into the storming parties. The ladders rattled on the stone, braced far out at the base. Men in fanciful militia uniforms leaned over with hooked poles to try and push them down, and toppled from the wall as Skinner or infantry bullets struck them.

The carbide searchlights played over their faces, blinding them but lightening the darkness for the attackers. More hand-bombs arched over; one exploded in midair as a Skinner struck it in flight in a miracle of marksmanship. Most landed below. An explosion on the parapet sent a dozen men somersaulting through the air, as a grenadier was brain-shot as he drew his arm back to throw and the missile landed beneath his crumpling body.

"Come on, 17th!" a Captain called, scrambling up a ladder.

His trumpeter stood at its foot, sounding *charge* over and over. A roar, and the burly peons-in-uniform were following him, climbing with both feet and one hand and holding their rifles in the other, a wave of blue coats and bowl helmets and steel points. Up to the top, and the officer was falling backwards, time enough to twist head-over-heels before he struck the ground. The men following him were on the top rungs, shooting and then exchanging bayonet-thrusts with men on the parapet—gunners there too, swinging their rammers like giant clubs. Men in the second rank on the ladders were firing past their comrades, and he hoped to *hell* they were picking their targets. A lieutenant shouldered his way up, emptied his revolver into the press and jumped up . . . over the parapet and down onto the fighting platform, by the Spirit, and the company pennant waving over him!

Not so bad for the bloody infantry, Menyez thought, grinning like a shark.

He looked left and right. Three quarters of the ladders were up, in his sector. About the same to his right, where Zahpata's 18th Komar were making their tooth-gritting yelping screech and climbing up even as bodies fell down past them.

Menyez looked up again. Men were still climbing up the ladder beside him, the pennant was still waving from the ramparts . . . and he could see shoulders and rifle-butts above the crenellations as they struggled to expand their foothold.

He took a deep breath. "We're going to plant the 17th Kelden's banner on the walls," he shouted, and drew his pistol. The bark of the rough pine logs that made up the ladder was rough and sticky under his *hand. "Follow me!"*

"Sir!"

Raj was still in his noncom's tunic, but the staff, signallers and couriers were accreting around him like coral around a shell as he pulled up Horace behind the gun-line that supported the escalade against the city wall. He stood in the stirrups and levelled his binoculars.

"That's a battalion flag on the ramparts, by the Spirit of Man!" he said exultantly. "The 17th . . . Hadolfo's got the 18th Komar up there too!"

"Shall I send in the reserve battalions?" someone asked behind him. One of Jorg's subordinates . . .

"No, of course not," Raj said, controlling his desire to turn and clout the man over the head with the glasses. "There's no room until they get a foothold over the wall." And absolutely no point in cramming men into a killing zone without room to deploy, either.

A dispatch rider reined in. "Ser. Major Gruder says sally-ports're openin' on t'main gate 'n t'north gate both, ser. Sally in battalion force from each, he says, er mebbe more."

Scramento! Raj thought. Close under the protection of the wall and its guns, the Brigaderos dragoons could mass and then try to strike at the flanks of his attack. Not successfully, but . . .

"High Colonel Strezman thinks entirely too fast," he said grimly. "Gerrin. The 5th and the 7th, and see them off."

Now it all depended on what happened on the wall. The flame-shot darkness stretched out ahead of him; there were still enemy cannon firing from the towers and from the wall to the left and right of his salient. The frustration was unbearable, the desire to get out there and *lead* . . . but if he put his banner on that wall nothing could prevent the whole army from following him. A milling mass of flesh for the enemy to shoot into. No.

no, Center agreed. **defeat followed by destruction of the expeditionary force probability of 79% ±3 in that eventuality.**

"Get me a beachhead over the wall, Jorg," Raj said softly. "Give me room."

Jorg Menyez ducked behind the cannon on the fighting platform of the city wall. Bullets went crack-*tinng* off the scorching-hot metal, and it put him right next to the face of the dead militia gunner lying over it. He looked around the breach; another squad was trying to get the satchel charge to the iron-faced door of the tower that dominated this stretch of wall. A man fell, but another hurdled him and snatched it up. Tongues of fire licked out from the loopholes around the door, and infantrymen outside fired back from the cover of the guns or from behind bodies. The ricochets were probably as much danger to the running man as the riflemen within. He jerked, hit once, then again, went to his knees, pitched the bundle of gunpowder sacks the last two meters.

CRUMP. Most of the explosion was outward, in the line of least resistance. Enough of it hit the door to smash the sheet-iron and thick wood behind into a splintered wreck . . . that was still not enough ajar to admit a man. Hand-bombs arched down from the tower summit, and small-arms crackled from the firing slits. Civil Government infantry rushed up to the shattered door, firing through the wreckage—

"*Back!*" Menyez shouted. Too late, or the huge racket of battle overrode his voice.

Above them the stream of burning tallow cascaded down from

the tower-top. It struck and clung like superheated glue; even in the middle of the melee, the screams of men who leaped from the wall burning were loud.

Menyez's head turned to the city. Between the wall and the houses was a clear strip fifty meters wide. Until recently it had been built over in patches, with flimsy hutments and corrals that could be passed off as temporary. Now the area *was* clear, and the rubbish and scrap lumber from the demolished shacks was piled up along the inner edge, a chest-high barricade. Beyond that were the streets; he could see mounted men there, a column of them. Shells were falling and fires burning in the cleared space, in the edge of housing beyond it. The column halted and dismounted, running forward to form up behind the barricade. The firelight shone on their helmets; General's Dragoons, not town militia.

He looked left and right. Men down, men firing at the towers, or at the approaching dragoons. The problem wasn't manpower, it was the towers and the lack of cover on the parapets from the rear— designed in for situations just like this. If he tried to send men down on ropes, they'd be vulnerable to the towers *and* the dragoons; he couldn't feed them in fast enough through this narrow lodgement. Not fast enough to do anything but the piecemeal the way they were doing now.

Tears cut runnels through the powder-smoke on his face. Of grief, and pure rage.

"Sor."

The runner from the 17th Kelden Foot was clutching his left arm with his right, to try to stop the bleeding.

"Sor, Colonel Menyez says, can't get a lodgement past the wall. Brigaderos dragoons behind barricade, too many of 'em. Can't take the towers either, not just from the parapet."

Raj sat silent for a moment, watching the flickering muzzle flashes on the parapet, like fireflies in spring.

"Go get that treated, soldier," he said. Then: "Sound retreat. Colonel Dinnalsyn, prepare to open up on the parapet again; I want their heads down while we pull our people out."

The soldier arched up off the operating table with a cry of pain that drove a spray of blood from scorched lips.

"*Hold* him, damn you," the doctor snapped.

Fatima grabbed the arm and weighed it down through the padding she clutched in both hands. Mitchi refastened the strap, her natural milk-white complexion gone to a grave-pallor that made her freckles stand out as if they were burning. The opium wasn't doing this patient much good at all; the mixture of burning pitch and tallow had caught him across most of his torso, with spatters up and down from there. One had turned his whole forehead into a blister that had burst and shed a glistening sheet of lymph across his face. The doctor was using a scalpel to separate the remains of the tunic from the skin and cooked meat to which it had been melded by the fire— this one had been a marginal, nearly triaged into the terminal section.

The doctor's hands moved with infinite deftness, swift and sure, although sweat ran down his cleric's shaven scalp into the linen of his face mask.

"More carbolic," he said.

Fatima seized the moment and slipped a leather pad into the soldiers mouth to replace the one he'd screamed out. When the antiseptic struck the burned surfaces, the young man on the table went into an arch that left him supported only by heels and the back of his head. Muscles stood out like iron rods in his cheeks, and he might well have splintered teeth or bitten out his tongue without the pad.

He fainted. "Good," the doctor said. "More carbolic. Wet him down here. Now the scissors. *Spirit*. We'll have to cut this tissue, debride down to living flesh."

On the next table, the grating sound of a bone saw hammered at her ears. A pulsing shriek rose further down the big tent, and a sobbing that was harder to bear.

The smell was what made her swallow a rush of sick spit. Fatima had managed to make herself eat roast pork, since she'd converted to the Star faith. She didn't think she could ever do that again.

CHAPTER FIFTEEN

"Damn, *damn,*" Jorg Menyez said. It might have been the pain of his shoulder, dislocated when he went back down the ladder, but Raj doubted it.

"Sit still," Raj replied.

I hate the hospitals, he thought. Visiting the wounded was about the worst chore there was; and it bewildered him a little that the men liked it—seeing the author of their pain. *Perhaps it gives them a focus.* Something to concentrate the will on.

It was a smoky dawn in the command tent; there was still a bit of noise from the hospital pavilion across the *plaza commanante,* but most of the severely wounded had either died or been doped to unconsciousness by now. The burn victims were the very worst, the pain seemed to be so bad that even opium couldn't do much.

"Damn," Menyez said again.

Hadolfo Zahpata was in the hospital tent himself, with two broken legs. Clean fractures of the femur, likely to heal well, but he was in plaster casts and suddenly primary contender for commander of Crown garrison forces when the rest of the Expeditionary Force moved on.

"I lost a hundred, hundred and twenty men—and we were so *close,* if we'd gotten up just a little sooner—"

Raj made a chopping motion with his hand, as he stood at the head of the table looking out the opening.

"*If*'s the most futile word in Sponglish," he said. "There was nothing wrong with the execution of the plan, Jorg—the plan was wrong, and that's *my* responsibility. You pulled out at the right moment; if you hadn't, you and Hadolfo would have lost your battalions."

"A broader attack—"

"—would have repeated the same failure on a larger scale." He sighed wearily. "The fact of the matter is, I was relying too much

182

on the militia being disorganized by the town meeting. Maybe a lot of them wanted to open the gates, but they *didn't* want our men coming over the wall with blood in their eyes, not with their families behind it.

"And Strezman was waiting for us—a force ready to sally and another in central reserve to punch back anyone who got to the top of the walls. High bloody Colonel bloody Strezman is just too good to bamboozle easily—we've been fighting dumb barbs too long. I underestimated him."

He quirked a smile and lit two cigarettes, handing the other to Menyez. "If it's any consolation"—which it wasn't, he knew—"the force that sallied against our flank got cut up pretty badly before they made it back to cover. Good work, by the way, Gerrin."

Staenbridge shrugged; his eyes were red-rimmed by exhaustion as well. "Standard little affray," he said. "Incidentally, I was right back on Stern Isle. Their regular army is a different proposition from the landholders' retainers. A bit slow to deploy, though, too reluctant to get out of the saddle."

"As to what we do next—" Raj began.

observe, Center said.

This time the vision was of Lion City before the Fall. He hadn't known there was a city here back that far. Low colorful buildings, a few towers, streets of greenery with vehicles floating through on air cushions. More such advanced craft at the docks behind the same adamantine breakwaters as today, and others that had sails in bright primary shades and seemed to serve no purpose but pleasure. Yet there were so *many* of them, as if the city held hundreds of nobles wealthy enough to maintain a yacht. People strolling along the tree-shaded avenues, richly dressed in alien fashions, all healthy and well-fed and unconcerned, none bearing arms save a hunter with the head of a carnosauroid floating behind him on a robot platform. People bathing nude in the harbor itself, away from the docks, in water that was crystal clear and free of downdraggers. How could harbor water not stink and attract scavengers?

The view stabilized overhead and then flashed to a schematic of the city's hydraulic system. Water flowed in through pipes from the sea, flashed into vapor in a processing plant, flowed out through distributor pipes to every house, however humble. Even while he focused his attention on the overall view Raj marvelled at that. The lowliest peasant with hot and cold water running in any room he chose, like a great lord! With no need to send his wife to the public fountain for water or with the slops bucket to a sewer inlet—and only wealthy, civilized towns in these Fallen times had even so much. Waste water collected in a giant pipe that struck north to a mysterious factory that seemed to do nothing but sterilize the water, even though the whole ocean was nearby for dumping.

The Fall came. Most of the bright airy structures fell swiftly, to fire or hammered apart as salvage; they were uninhabitable for folk with nothing but fire to heat with, and they had been built of perishable materials. For generations only a small farming and fishing village stood on the site of Lion City. Rich land and a fine self-scouring harbor with a lighthouse brought growth. When men were numerous enough for their wastes to be a problem, a long ditch was built and connected to the storm-drains that flowed at low tide through the adamantine seawall; rainwater flushed it, now and then. A later generation covered the ditch with brick arches and built drains down individual streets connecting to it. The old sewer outlet was forgotten, deep underground. When men built the city wall, they built it over the pipe, to defend a smaller, more densely packed settlement.

A final vision: the outlet pipe ending in a gully north of the town, with a projection of Raj standing next to it.

1.5 meters in diameter, Center said.

For a moment all Raj could feel was incandescent anger. *You let my men die when there was a better way?* he thought. *Not even the Spirit—*

i am not god, Center said. **the pipe may be blocked, is probably blocked where the weight of the wall rests on it. or the inlet may not connect to the surface within lion city. in any case, "supernatural" interventions such as this increase the amount of noise in the system and reduce the reliability of my predictive function. nor did i select you to be the puppet of my tactical direction.**

"Raj?" Suzette said with concern.

He shook back to himself. The Companions were used to his moments of introspection, but not to one accompanied by the expression he could still feel twisting his face.

furthermore the attention of the garrison will now be firmly riveted on the walls.

Shut—up, he thought savagely. Perhaps that was reckless disrespect to an angel, but at the moment he didn't much care.

Raj looked up at the walls of Lion City. "They're really going to regret burning my men," he said softly.

Jorg Menyez was normally a mild and considerate man. At that moment his battered face resembled the surface of an upraised maul—also battered, but poised to smash anything in its path, stone and iron included. It matched his commander's expression quite closely.

"Oh, my oath, yes," Gerrin Staenbridge, almost whispering. A rustle of carnivore alertness went through the circle of commanders.

"Ehwardo," Raj began. "Move the cavalry around outside the walls—make it look as if you're setting up dispersed camps." An essential step in keeping dogs healthy over a long stay in a confined spot. "Jorg, starting at dawn, give the best imitation you can of a man starting massive siege works; parallels, the whole show."

"I gather it's a ruse, Whitehall?" Gerrin Staenbridge said.

"Correct. The rest of you are to prepare for a general assault—if and only if something I . . . have in mind succeeds. Colonel Dinnalsyn, get those damned armored cars ready, too. If you'll excuse me, Messers? And Gerrin," he went on, "send me M'lewis."

Antin M'lewis usually blessed the fate that had thrown him into Raj Whitehall's path. Since then life had never been boring, and it had been lucrative—if not beyond his wildest dreams, then beyond all reasonable expectation. Particularly after he happened to be one of the two men with Raj when he put down the botched coup attempt that used Des Poplanich as its front-man. Governor Barholm had been hysterical when he promised to make the two Companions present the richest lords in the Civil Government if they saved him. He'd remembered enough afterwards to translate one Antin M'lewis, free commoner and soldier of watch-stander rank, into the Messer class and to deed him a thousand hectares of land—and not in stony, desolate Descott County, either. Good fat riverside fields, near the capital. Yes, usually he blessed the day then-Major Raj Whitehall had hauled him up on charges for stealing a shoat.

Then again, there were times when he wished he'd let the peons *keep* their damned pig.

The pipe was tall enough for him to stand in if he stooped a bit. The greasy-smooth material it was made of was like nothing he'd ever seen outside a shrine, and it led downward into the earth—into the Starless Dark, the freezing hell of the orthodox. Where the Spirit of Man of the Stars cast the unregenerate souls not worthy even of lowly rebirth, dumping their core programs into chaos.

Good thing me ma were a witch, he thought. This might be a real problem for a pious respectable yeoman, but everyone in the M'lewis family accounted themselves probably damned anyway and certainly hung if found out. So were the Forty Thieves, but even they looked queasy at the arguably supernatural and definitely menacing passageway into the earth.

They watched him silently as he stripped off his uniform jacket and boots; unlike most enlisted men, who preferred sleeveless vests of unbleached cotton beneath in summertime, he wore a shirt. Unlike most officers, his was dyed rusty black. Through the back of his belt he tucked a sheathed skinning knife, and tested that the wooden toggles of his garotte were ready to his hand for the quick snatch-and-toss. Then he tied a plain brown bandana over his hair and palmed mud over his cheeks.

"Yer nivver goin' t'leave yer gun, ser?" one of the men whispered.

It was the young recruit; M'lewis remembered him from the

action on Stern Isle, where he'd wondered if he'd have a chance at the women in the refugee convoy.

"Son—" M'lewis began. Which was *just* possible; they were certainly cousins, and he'd been friendly with that branch of the family as a lad. "—whin yer sneakin', yer sneaks *quiet*. With t'gun, all I could do 'd be ter bring four thousand barbs down on me head. Jist noise an' temptation, onna sneak loik this."

Spirit. Then again, he'd probably have drunk and fucked himself into an early grave by now if he'd retired to rusticate on the new estate. Certainly the other Messers wouldn't accept him socially there, a stranger of common birth. His sons, probably, when he got around to having them, but not him. And it would be dull.

Raj stepped up and gripped forearms. "Careful and slow, M'lewis," he said. "Don't let them hear you."

The snaggled teeth showed in a grin, and he offered a fist to slap—a trifle familiar perhaps, but then, what could you do to a man on a suicide mission?

"Nao clumpin' barb'll hear this mither's chile, ser," he said.

His bare feet were noiseless on the plastic. The soft cold of it was like nothing he'd ever touched as he walked forward and down, crouching.

Raj Whitehall was motionless beside his dog. Less bound by need than the man, Horace shifted uneasily from foot to foot to foot, whining slightly. His hand soothed the animal automatically, gauntleted fingers scritching in the slight ruff at the back of the neck, just forward of the saddlebow. Other dogs shifted and murfled in the darkness, two kilometers from the main gates of Lion City. Fifteen thousand men waited, gripping their rifles or the ladders, wondering if the next hour would bring a ladle of burning pitch in the face, a limb lost, eyes, genitals, whatever their particular dread might be. The air was full of the smell of rank sweat and dog, men and animals both full of knowledgeable fear and suppressed eagerness.

Everyone thought it was payback time. Everyone, Spirit help them, thought Messer Raj would pull another miracle out of the hat.

It was full dark; neither moon would be up for another hour. Watchlights burned on the walls of Lion City, but experience had taught them that Skinners could shoot out any reflector-backed searchlight from a comfortable range . . . and the men manning it.

It was also long after he should have received word from Gerrin. When the dispatch rider reined in, he forced himself not to whirl.

"Ser," the man said.

Something's wrong.

"Spit it out," Raj said. Nightmares—the 5th destroyed in a trap, burning pitch and tallow pumped down on them in the tunnel while they died helpless—

"Ser," the rider said, his eyes fixed over the general's head.

"Captain Suharez reports . . . beggin' yer pardon, ser . . . Cap'n reports the 5th has retreated from the tunnel."

Raj stalked over to the rider and slapped the muzzle of his dog. *"Down,"* he said. The animal crouched obediently. That put his eyes on a level with the man's.

"From Captain Suharez?" he said, in a calm voice. The man flinched. That was the second-ranked company commander in the unit.

"Yesser. Colonel Staenbridge an', an' some members went beyond the second dip—there was 'n other, ser, ten meters beyond t'one Lieutnant M'lewis found. The rest . . . the rest turned back, ser."

Raj pivoted on his heel, ignoring the dispatch rider. "Major Bellamy," he said. Wide eyes stared at him out of darkness as he stepped over Horace's saddle. "Up, boy . . . Major Bellamy, you will accompany me with the 2nd Cruisers. Major Gruder, you're in charge of the gate. Colonel Menyez, you're in overall command. Await the signal, then proceed as planned."

He kicked heels into his mount. Horace leaped forward, and Ludwig Bellamy and the bannerman of the 2nd fell in beside him. Behind them the massed paws of the 2nd Mounted Cruisers beat a tattoo through the night.

The ravine where the old sewer outlet surfaced was packed with men; the dogs were crouched a few hundred meters further north, together with those of the ex-*Squadrone* soldiers Raj had brought. He could see the 5th only as a shadowy presence, a sullen mass that recoiled slightly as he walked up to them.

"You retreated without orders?" he asked the Captain.

"Yes, sir," the man said. He was braced to attention and staring ahead.

At least he isn't offering excuses, Raj thought. He was moving carefully, very carefully so that he wouldn't shatter the ice surface of control that bound him.

"Ser," a voice from the dark mass said. "Ser . . . 'tis damnation there! 'T road to t'Starless—"

"Silence in the ranks," Raj said. His voice was as clear and precise as water is when it falls over a ledge of stone, before the spray and thunder. "You," he went on to the unit bannerman. "Did you turn back?"

"No ser," the man said.

He was a grizzled veteran, a thirty-year man; carrying the battalion standard was a jealously guarded privilege, open only to men three times awarded the Gold of Valor.

"Colonel Staenbridge, he ordered t'color party to remain here. Seein's t'colors wouldn't fit, ser."

"Then you may carry the colors back to the central Star shrine in camp," Raj said. "Where they will be safe from men unworthy of them."

A low moan broke from the assembled ranks of the 5th, and the bannerman sobbed, tears running down his leathery cheeks as he turned smartly and trotted for his dog. Nor was he the only one weeping.

"Tears are for women," Raj went on in the same glass-smooth tone. "Senior Captain Suharez, take this unit and report to Major Gruder, placing yourself under his orders. For whatever tasks he judges it fit for."

Suharez' face might have been carved from dark wood. "Yes, sir." He saluted and wheeled.

Raj turned toward the tunnel mouth. Behind him there was a forward surge among the ranks of the 5th Descott. He wheeled again, flinging out his hand and pointing silently back towards the main force. An officer broke his saber over his knee, and the men fell into their ranks and trotted forward behind Suharez.

Faint starlight sheened on the eyes and teeth of the 2nd Cruisers. Ludwig Bellamy stepped forward and saluted smartly.

"I'm ready to lead my men through, sir," he said.

"No, Major," Raj said. "You'll bring up the rear. Nobody is to turn back, understood?"

He raised his voice slightly, pitching it to carry in the heavy-breathing hush. "As I have kept faith with you, so you with me. Follow; quietly, and in order."

Raj turned and stooped, entering the tunnel.

The men's hobnailed boots clattered on the surface of the pipe; the sound was dulled, as if they were walking on soft wood, but the iron left no scratches on the plastic of the Ancients. The surface beneath the fingers of his left hand might have been polished marble, except for the slight trace of greasy slickness. There was old dirt and silt in the very bottom of the circular tube, and it stank of decay; floodwater must run down from the gutters of Lion City and through this pipe when the floods were very high.

Behind him the rustle and clank of equipment sounded, panting breath, an occasional low-voiced curse in Namerique. Earth Spirit cultists didn't have the same myth of a plastic-fined tube to Hell; the center of the earth—This Earth—was their paradise. This particular tunnel was intimidating as Hell to *anyone*, though. Particularly to men reared in the open air, there was a touch of the claustrophobe in most dog-and-gun men. There certainly was in *him*, because every breath seemed more difficult than the last, an iron hoop tightening around his chest

this is not an illusion, Center said helpfully. **the oxygen content of the air is dropping because airflow is inadequate in the presence of over six hundred men. this will not be a serious problem unless the force is halted for a prolonged period.**

Oh, thank *you,* Raj thought.

Even then, he felt a grim satisfaction at what Army discipline had made of last year's barbarian horde. *Vicious children,* he thought. Vicious grown-up children whose ancestors had shattered civilization over half a continent—not so much in malice as out of simple inability to imagine doing anything different. Throwing the pretty baubles into the air and clapping their hands to see them smash, heedless of the generations of labor and effort that went into their making. *Thirteen-year-olds with adults' bodies . . . but they can learn. They can learn.*

The roof knocked on the top of his helmet. "*Halto,*" he called quietly. The column rustled to a halt behind him.

A quick flick of the lens-lid on his bullseye lantern showed the first change in the perfect regularity of the tunnel. Ahead of him the roof bent down and the sides out, precisely like a drinking straw pinched between a man's fingers.

you are under the outer edge of the town wall on the north side, Center said. **.63 of a kilometer from the entrance.**

M'lewis had come this far on his scout; he'd checked that the tunnel opened out again beyond this point, and then returned. Raj had agreed with the decision, since maximum priority was to avoid giving the entrance away. And the little Scout had been right, air *was* flowing toward him, he could feel the slightly cooler touch on his sweating face.

Of course, the air might be coming through a hole the size of a man's fist.

"Crawl through," he said to the man behind him, clicking off the light. "Turn on your backs and crawl through. There's another pinch in the tunnel beyond. Pass it down."

He dropped to the slimy mud in the bottom of the tunnel and began working his way further in. The plastic dipped down toward his face, touched the brim of his helmet. Still smooth, still untorn. The weight of the city wall was on it here, had been for five hundred years. Mud squished beneath his shoulderblades, running easily on the low-friction surface of the pipe. The weight of a wall fifteen meters high and ten thick at the base, two courses of three-by-three meter stones on either side, flanking a rubble-concrete core.

Do not *tell me how much it weighs,* he thought/said to Center.

Now he was past the lowest point, and suddenly conscious of his own panting. Something bumped his boots; the head of the man following. One man following, at least. At least two or three more, from the noise behind. No way of telling what was further back, how many were still coming, whether the last five hundred or five hundred and fifty had turned and trampled Ludwig in a terror-filled rush out of this deathtrap, this anteroom to hell. The plastic drank sound, leaving even his breath muffled. Sweat dripped down his forehead, running into his eyes as he came to hands and knees. He clicked the bullseye open for a look when the surface began to twist beneath his feet. Another ten meters of normal pipe, and then—

Spirit, he thought What could have produced *this?*

the pipe crosses under the wall at an angle of forty degrees from the perpendicular, this section is under the edge of a tower, Center said with dispassionate accuracy.

The towers were much heavier than the walls. The sideways thrust of one tower's foundations had shoved the pipe a little sideways . . . and squeezed it down so that only a triangular hole in the lower right-hand corner remained. This time the fabric *had* ruptured, a long narrow split to the upper left. Dirt had come through, hard lumpy yellow clay, and someone recent had dug it out with hands and knife and spread it backwards.

Raj waited until the man following him came up behind. "No problem," he said, while the eyes in the bearded face were still blinking at the *impossible* hole. "Come through one at a time; take off your rifle, helmet and webbing belt, then have the man behind you hand them through. Pass it on."

He kept moving, because if he didn't, he might not start again. One man panicking here and the whole column would be stalled all night.

He took off the helmet and his swordbelt, snapped the strap down over the butt of his revolver and dropped the bundle to the floor.

"Keep the lantern on," he said to the soldier behind him.

Right arm forward. Turn sideways. Down and forward, the sides gripping him like the clamps of a grab used to lift heavy shells. Light vanishing beyond his feet; they kicked without purchase, and then the broad hands of the trooper were under them, giving him something to push against. Bronze jacket buttons digging into his ribs hard enough to leave bruises. Breathe in, *push.* Buried in hell, buried in hell . . .

His right hand came free. It groped about, there was little leverage on the smooth flaring sides of the pipe, but his shoulders came out, and that was the broadest part of him.

For an instant he lay panting, then turned. "Through," he called softly. "Pass my gear, soldier." A fading echo down the pipe, as the man turned and murmured the news to the one behind *him.*

It had only been a little more than his body length. Difficult, but not as difficult as concrete would have been, or cast iron, anything that gripped at skin and clothing. The light cast a glow around the slightly curved path of the narrow passage.

Again he waited until the first man had followed, grabbing his jacket between the shoulderblades and hauling him free.

"Second birth," he said.

The *Squadrone* trooper shook his head. "The first was tighter, lord," he said. His face was corpse-pallid in the faint light, but he managed a grin. Then he turned and called softly down the narrow way:

"Min gonne, Herman."

Not much further, Raj thought, looking ahead. Darkness lay on his eyes like thick velvet.

.21 kilometers.

"I'll have them *decimated,*" Gerrin Staenbridge hissed.

Raj didn't doubt that the other man meant exactly what he said; that he'd line up his battalion and have one man in ten taken out of the ranks and the others forced to beat him to death with rods. It was the traditional penalty for mass cowardice in the face of the enemy.

"I don't think that will be necessary," he said, his voice remote.

Gerrin turned and began a motion that would have slammed his fist into the concrete wall.

"Neither will that," Raj said, catching the thick wrist. "We have a job to do, Major."

"Yes, sir," Staenbridge said, straightening and running a hand under the neck-guard of his helmet. His hand kneaded brutally at the muscles at the base of his skull. "We've improvised, as you can see."

There were a little over a hundred men of the 5th Descott in the huge underground chamber, most of Company A and the twenty men of the Scouts who'd gone in first. It was large enough that they didn't crowd it, even with more and more of the 2nd Cruisers coming out of the pipe, jumping down the two-meter drop to the floor or lowering themselves by their hands. Not quite jet-black, the risk of a covered lantern was worth the lessened noise when men could see what they were doing.

The chamber was nearly twenty meters across and about three high. Originally it had been domed, but the roof had buckled at some unknown time. Bent and twisted rods of metal protruded from the concrete, and the huge writhing shape of a large tree's taproot. Staenbridge had been busy; the men must have made a human pyramid to lift one up, and he had hitched a rope made from buckling rifle slings together to one of the steel rods. Beyond that a darkness gaped.

"That connects to an old storm drain," the Major said, pointing. "Beyond that, an exit onto a street. M'lewis is there with a couple of his scouts, keeping it warm. Fairly deserted."

"It should be, it's past midnight," Raj said.

He walked over to the dangling slings; they were of tough sauroid hide, supple and very strong—the Armory tested them by hanging a hundred-kilo weight to one end and rejecting any that stretched or cracked.

"Send everyone on up, and then follow," he said.

He bent his legs and jumped, his sword-hand clamping down on a buckle hard enough to bend it. Arm over arm, he pulled himself smoothly upward toward the light.

✧   ✧   ✧

The streets of Lion City had been laid out by cows. Quite literally, back in the days when it had been a little farming village where the odd ship called. When stone buildings went up, they stood by the sides of laneways worn by herdsmen driving their beasts back to their paddocks at night, and once the pattern was set it was too difficult to change. Too difficult for the people who'd run Lion City; back in the Civil Government a town this size would have had at least some semblance of a gridwork imposed at one time or another. If nothing else, a spiderweb of narrow streets flanked by three to five-story buildings was simply too easy for rioters to hold against troops, throwing up barricades and dropping roof-tiles down on stalled columns.

I've got something of the same problem, Raj thought. Maxiluna was up, but it was still dark in the alleyway; Lion City didn't run to gaslights, either, and even in East Residence a neighborhood like this wouldn't have been lit. Dark and very quiet, only the squall of an alley-cat breaking the silence. With the militia standing watch-and-watch on the walls and their families laboring to carry them food and water and do whatever else a city under siege needed, most folk would be well and truly asleep when they could find the time. Probably a few eyes were peering at him from behind shuttered windows, but men—and women—see what they expect. It would take a while for anyone to realize that this was not another unit of Brigade troops going out to relieve a section of wall.

He had just that long, and enough more for the damnably alert High Colonel Strezman to receive the report and get his garrison moving. If that happened before he was where he had to be, then he and everyone with him was dead.

Center's street-map of Lion City was eleven hundred years out of date, but the machine intelligence had seen everything he had. With his own eyes, and through reports—Muzzaf's, Abdullah's, the Ministry's. A glowing hologram opened before his private vision, and a green thread showed him the closest route to the gates. Not so good, they had to jink around the easternmost tip of the harbor.

"Gerrin, Ludwig," he said.

The two men were at his side; one dark, one fair, but otherwise much of a size.

"We're going to form up in column of fours—" all that could get through many of these streets, with the sleeves of the outer men brushing the brick and half-timber buildings on either side "—and head straight for the main gates at a run; I'll lead."

The two battalion commanders glanced at each other. How *anyone* could lead through this blacked-out maze was a question, but they'd learned that this man didn't claim what he could not do.

"Gerrin, you take the right-hand tower complex. Ludwig, give me your Company A; I'll take the left. You deploy in the main plaza just inside the gates and keep the reaction force off our backs—because they will hit, soon and hard. Understood?"

Two sharp nods, and they turned away to pass the orders to their subordinates.

Raj raised his voice slightly. "Keep it quiet, men, and keep it fast, and don't stop for anything at all."

Pavement racketed beneath their feet, echoing as they pounded into a run. Raj held his saber-sheath in his left hand to keep it from slapping him as he loped. This wasn't all that subtle a way to manage the movement, but at present subtle mattered a lot less than quick; seven hundred foreign soldiers were a big conspicuous object in any town, much less one under siege. Streets went by, narrowing or widening, cobbles or brick or occasionally hard-pounded dirt underfoot. Now and then a ragged beggar woke in a doorway and fled squalling; the normal Watch would be on the walls with everyone else. Buildings looming on either side, mostly dark, once a yellow blaze as a window was thrown open above. He caught a moment's glimpse of a woman holding a candlestick in one hand, catching her nightgown at the throat with the other, her face a study in shocked surprise.

"Faster!" he called.

He was breathing deeply; it had been a long hard day already, but a run of a klick or so didn't bother a man in good condition. It had *better* not bother any of his troopers, dog-soldiers or no.

"Halt!"

A bit of jostling as some of the rear didn't get the word. The plaza stretched ahead of him, the wooden platform still around the fountain; that was dry, with the city's outside water supply cut. For a moment he wondered what had happened to the Syndic of the Sailmakers, the man who'd wanted to open the gates. Only a single street of houses on the other side before the cleared space that ringed the wall, and a broad street through them from plaza to gates.

"At a quick walk," he said to Staenbridge. "Try out your Namerique, Gerrin. Captain Hortez—" one of the Descotter officers he'd posted to the 2nd Cruisers as company commanders "—tell the men to fix bayonets, load and shoulder arms. Sling their helmets." That would show their barbarian haircuts and coloring. "Follow me."

The towers bulked ahead, squat pairs on either side of the gate joined by a bridge over the arch itself, making the gateway into a huge block of masonry twenty meters high. There were lights there, one above the gate itself, another over each tower door on the rear. Not many lights inside, because the troops would be peering out at the encircling army and wouldn't want to destroy their night vision. The door to each tower was half a story up, with a staircase leading to an arched door wide enough for two men. Those were open, with soldiers lounging on the stairs.

Gerrin's company peeled off to the right. *Ignore them*, Raj told himself. Nothing he could do, and if he couldn't count on Gerrin Staenbridge he didn't have a single competent man with him and might as well die anyway. . . .

Closer. The soldiers were in General's Dragoon uniforms. *Damn.* He'd been hoping for city militia, but High Colonel Strezman had done the sensible thing. Certainly what Raj would have done, were he holding a city whose leaders had publicly considered surrender. He was willing to bet the other three gates were in the hands of Brigaderos regulars as well.

His mouth was dry with the running. He worked it to moisten it, concentrating on marching. Not stiff, just a company of soldiers going where they were told to, with the easy swing of men who'd done the same thing a thousand times before and would again. Really not much light, only a single kerosene lamp over the doorway, far too little to see details. The civic militia wore dozens of different outfits or their street-clothes according to whim and the depth of their pockets, so the distinctive Civil Government uniform might pass, *would* pass until it was too late.

"*Whir dere ko?*" a man challenged in Namerique. *Who goes there?* A young man's voice, probably a noncom. Strezman would be stretched thin, watching his putative allies along kilometers of city wall and keeping a big enough reaction force ready as a reserve.

The men at the gate scooped up their dice and stood, buttoning their jackets. They reached for their weapons, not concerned, just veterans' reflexes.

"Captain of Guards Willi Kirkin," Raj said.

His Namerique had something of a Squadron accent, and he let the harsh syllables roll across his tongue. There were quite a few Squadron refugees serving as mercenaries among the household troops of the magnates of Lion City.

The other man's reply sounded nervous, which was to be expected after the riot of the previous evening.

"What're you doing here, then, southron? Halt. Halt, I said!"

"*Ni futz, greunt,*" Raj went on in a bored voice. *Don't get upset, trooper.* "The Colonel thinks the *grisuh* may try something tonight, and we've been sent to reinforce the gate. Better us than those chicken-hearted civvies."

Raj was at the foot of the stairs. He pulled a piece of folded paper from his pocket. Time slowed as the corporal reached for the note, then got his first good look at Raj's face. His beardless, brown-tanned Descotter face, with the cold gray eyes like slitted ice under the brim of the bowl helmet.

The young Brigadero had only a ginger fuzz on his own cheeks. His eyes were green and very wide. They bulged as Hortenz' pistol bullet took him under the angle of the jaw and snapped him around like the kick of a plow-ox.

"*Go!*" Raj screamed.

His shoulder hit the door to the tower as his hand came clear of the holster with his revolver. Raj was no gunman, no pistol-artist, just a fair to middling shot. The sword had always been his personal weapon of choice, and with that he was very good.

There was a ready room beyond the door, with five men in it— three sitting around a plank table playing cards, another two lying on benches. A grid flashed over Raj's vision, and the outline of one man glowed. The man with the pistols already nearly out of the holsters strapped to his thighs as he surged backward from the table. *The one good enough to fill the doorway with bodies while his comrades rushed to swing the iron-strapped teak closed again.*

A green dot settled on the man's chest as Raj swung the pistol toward him. The weapon bucked and roared, and the gunman's chest blossomed with a red flower exactly where the dot had rested. Dust puffed from the grey-green cloth around the impact point, the man was falling and Raj wheeled. The dot slid across a face. *Crack,* echoing within the stone walls. An eye erupted. On a neck. *Crack.* Arterial blood spouted against the whitewashed wall and ceiling as the brigadero spun. Against ribs. *Crack.* Another man had rolled behind a bench, fumbling with the hammer of his rifle. *Crack* through his pelvis.

The hammer clicked twice more by reflex. Raj staggered for a moment, wheezing in the fetid air through his mouth: he had ample strength and speed for that three-second burst of gunplay, but the skill was as much beyond him as a circus juggler's talents. The first kill's body was still twitching in a great pool of spreading blood. The men on his heels hesitated for a second, awe on their faces.

"Go, *go,*" Raj ordered, over the moaning of a dying Brigadero.

His hands clicked open the revolver, dumped the spent brass, reloaded. Hortenz dashed by, through the ground-level door to secure the first floor of the towers and the exterior gunslits. Another squad of 2nd Cruiser riflemen went past to the staircase in a bristle of bayonets, behind a lieutenant. Raj tossed his revolver into his left hand and drew his sword with his right. One part of his mind was still shuddering with the icy feeling of . . . otherness, of being a weapon, pointed like a rifle by a directing hand. He'd use the trick again if he had to, as he'd use anything that came to hand. That didn't mean he had to like it.

The stairs were a narrow spiral, almost pitch-black. Iron hobnails and heel-plates gritted and clanged on the stone, from the squad ahead and the men following close behind. It would be a great pity if he slipped and toppled back onto their bayonets. The thought twitched at the set grin that rippled his lips back from his teeth. Gunfire crashed ahead of him, red muzzle flashes blinding in the dimness. Men shouted; he kept going past the door, past the tumbled bodies of Brigaderos and a trooper of the 2nd. All the enemy bodies had multiple bayonet wounds; the 2nd had learned to make very sure of things.

"Get those charges up here," he shouted down.

Men came back into the stairs, their rifles slung and their arms full of linen powder-bags for the light swivel guns on the second level of the tower; one of them had a coil of matchcord around his neck. *Remember that face. That's a sergeant, if he lives.* More gunfire slapped at his ears, echoes bouncing through the narrow corridors, screams, shrieks of fury and fear and raw killing-lust.

"GITTEM, GITTEM!" That was his ex-*Squadrones* forgetting themselves, giving the Admiral's war shout.

The stair gave out at the third-story landing. Only a ladder led above to the top of the tower; he snapshot, and a man tumbled down it and halted halfway, his legs tangled in the rungs. Blood spattered across Raj's face. He stepped aside, swearing mildly to himself, and let the next dozen or so behind him take the ladder without pausing, ripping the corpse free and bursting out onto the tower roof. More followed, including an officer; he could hear orders up there, and then a staccato volley.

"Quick," he said to the man with the charges.

The door opening right into the rooms above the arch of the gateway was barred. Raj thrust his pistol into the eyeslot and pulled the trigger; there was a scream, and somebody slammed an iron plate across it. The cloth bundles of gunpowder tumbled at his feet.

"Good man," Raj said "Now, pack them along the foot of the door, in between the stone sill and the door. Cut them with your knife and stick the matchcord—right." He raised his voice; more men were crowding up the stairs, some to take the ladder and others filling the space about him. *"Everyone down the corridor, around the corner here. Now!"*

The quick-witted trooper and he and another lieutenant—Wate Samzon, a *Squadrone* himself—played out the cord and plastered themselves to the wall just around from the door. The matchcord sputtered as it took the flame. Raj put his hand before his eyes. White noise, too loud for sound. He tensed to drive back around to the door—

—and strong arms seized him, body and legs and arms.

"Ni, ni," a deep rumbling voice said in his ear. "You are our lord, by steel and salt. Our blood for yours."

Lieutenant Samzon led the charge. A second later he was flung back, hands clapped to the bleeding ruin of his face, stumbled into the wall and fell flat. The men who followed him fired into the ruins of the door and thrust after the bullets, bayonets against swords, as their comrades reloaded and fired past their bodies close enough for the blasts to scorch their uniforms. When they forced through the shattered planks the men holding Raj released him and followed them, with only their broad backs to hold him behind them.

The only Brigaderos left in the big rectangular room were dead, but the troopers of the 2nd Cruisers were still looking terrified— of the winches and gear-trains that filled the chamber. A year ago, anything more complicated than a windmill had seemed like sorcery to them, and some had screamed with fear at their first sight of a steam engine. They'd gotten over that, but they had to *do* something with these machines, these complex toothed shapes of black iron and brass.

Raj knew fortifications and their ancillary equipment from years of study. "You, you, you," he said crisply. "Take that maul and knock those wedges loose. Pull those lockbars out—those long iron rods through the wheels with the loops on the end. The rest of your squad, grab that crank and get ready to put your backs into it. Those winches too."

The inner gates were not held by a bar across the leaves. Instead, thick iron posts ran down from this chamber through loops on their inner surfaces into deep sockets set in the stone beneath, covered with wooden plugs when the gates were open. Toothed gearwheels raised and lowered the massive posts, driving on notches cut into their sides. Metal clanked and groaned as the troopers heaved at the crank-handles. Winches running iron chains lifted the portcullis into a slot just in from the channels for the bars. The chain clacked over the drums, making a dull ringing as the great iron gridwork rose over the tunnel way.

"Ser!" A panting trooper with the 5th's shoulder flashes. "Colonel says they've got the outer gateway."

Which was controlled from the right-hand towers, as this inner one was from the left. Raj nodded curtly and stepped out of the chamber, calling up the ladder to the top of the tower:

"Two white rockets!"

General assault, all around the circuit of the walls. Back inside the lifting room, gunfire blasted, needles of pain in the ears in such a confined space. A duller explosion followed.

"Shot through the door," the sergeant of the platoon said, as Raj returned. "It started to open."

He nodded to the door at the outer side of the room; that would give to the middle section of the arch over the gate, a series of rooms above the roadway where the murder-holes gave onto the space below. It was wood and iron; there were lead splashes on the planks and frame where the soft hollowpoint bullets had struck—they had terrible wounding power but no penetration. The brass-tipped hardpoints had punched through, and then an explosion from the other side had buckled the whole portal.

"Thought they was goin' to chuck a handbomb through," the sergeant said. A few of his men were down, wounded by ricochets from their own weapons. "Must've gone off in their hands," he went on with satisfaction.

Raj nodded. "Get those prybars and open the door," he said. "Quickly, now."

They'd have to clear out the men there, or the troops coming through the tunnel would get a nasty surprise. Gerrin would be working his way in as the men under Raj's command worked out through the line of rooms over the tunnel.

And it was time he checked on Ludwig. Now that the focus of concentration was relaxing a little, he could hear a slamming firefight going on out in the plaza. No point to the whole thing if the Brigaderos broke through to the towers before his men got here.

"Prepare to receive cavalry!"

The company commander was down with a sucking chest wound, and Ludwig Bellamy was doing his job as well as trying to oversee the battle.

The Brigaderos cavalry were charging again, straight down the street. It was wide, by Lion City standards, which meant they were coming in six abreast and three ranks deep. The front rank of 2nd Cruisers knelt with their rifles braced against the cobbles and the points of their long bayonets at chest height. Two more ranks stood behind them with rifles levelled. It seemed a frail thing to oppose to the big men on tall dogs that raced toward them, the shouting and the long swords gleaming in the pale moonlight—but the pile in front of the position gave the lie to that: dead men and dogs lying across one another in a slithering heap.

Once Ludwig Bellamy had believed that nothing on foot could stand before brave men charging with steel in hand. Messer Raj had disabused him of that notion, him and what was left of the Squadron.

The charge slowed at the last instant. War-dogs were willing to face steel, but their instincts told them to crouch and leap, not impale themselves in a straight gallop.

"Fire!"

The sound crashed out, like one giant shot impossibly long and loud. The muzzle flashes lit the dim street with a light as bright as a red day for an instant. It lit the edges of the Brigaderos swords and the fangs of their dogs like light flickering from hell. A hundred heavy 11mm bullets drove into the leading rank of the charge. All of the first mounts were struck, most of them several times, and the muscular grace of the wardogs turned to flailing chaos in a fraction of an instant. Half-ton bodies cartwheeled into the barricade of flesh, or dove head-first into it if they had been brainshot, as several had. The sounds of impact were loud but muffled. Few of the men had been shot, but they parted from their tumbling animals, arcing to the pavement or disappearing under thousands of pounds of writhing flesh.

Their screams were lost in the sounds of the wounded dogs. One came over the bodies, its hind legs limp and with an empty saddle, dragging itself up to the soldiers. It was still snarling when two bayonets punched through its throat.

"Reload!"

The Brigaderos in rear ranks had managed to halt their dogs in time. They tried to come forward at a walk, levelling their revolvers. Men fell in the front rank of the Cruiser line as the pistols spat. Behind him a shout rose, and rockets soared from the gate towers.

"*Fire!*"

The Brigaderos turned and spurred their dogs, turning aside into alleys as soon as they could. Behind them was a solid block of dismounted dragoons, filling the roadway from side to side and coming on at the quickstep. The 2nd Cruiser lieutenants shouted:

"Prone, kneeling, standing ranks." The first line of men propped their rifles over dead Brigaderos and dead wardogs. "*By* platoon sections, *volley fire, fire.*"

BAM. BAM. BAM. BAM.

The enemy raised a shout and charged, rifles at the port, leaning forward as if against rain. Men from the rear ranks pushed forward to fill the gaps each volley blasted, and they came on. Not pausing to fire until they were close, not when they loaded so much more slowly.

"This is it, boys—they're going to run over us or die trying. Make it count, aim low. *Fire!*"

BAM. BAM. BAM. BAM.

Bellamy skipped back to view the rest of the action. Holding the roadways into the plaza wasn't too much trouble, no—but it tied down too many of his men. Even with all five hundred, minus Company A, he wouldn't have enough to hold the whole perimeter of the plaza, and Strezman was sending in everything he had. More than three thousand men, coming through the houses and mansions around the square, firing from windows and rooftops. Ignoring everything else to retake the main gate before the assault force reached the wall.

Just what Messer Raj told me he'd do.

Any second now he'd have to pull back to prevent his men being overrun in detail. How long a battalion line would last in the open against five times its numbers the Spirit alone knew.

They'd last as long as they lived.

"Damnation to Darkness," Raj swore softly.

Cannon were going off all along the walls of Lion City, shaking the stone beneath his boots. But raggedly, and fewer than he would have thought. A lot of them could see the open gates, and more could see the glare of fire shining from the gate-tower windows, or hear the firing from within the walls.

The room with the winching material was full of smoke; powder-smoke, and from the barricade of burning furniture the holdouts were defending one room in. Wounded men were coming out of the door, and more troopers of the 2nd Cruisers forced their way toward the action. His eyes watered and he coughed as he leaned out the slit window, but the breath of air on his sweat-sodden skin was like a shock of cold. So was what he could see. The bulk of the 2nd Cruisers were withdrawing across the plaza toward him, backing three steps and volley-firing, backing again; the stuttering crash of their rifles carried even over the cannonade from the walls. Their line had bent back into a C-shape as Brigaderos swarmed after them, thrown into confusion by their passage through house and alley, but attacking relentlessly despite gruesome casualties.

The light was bad and his eyes were watering, but he could see the battalion flag of the 2nd Cruisers in the center of the bowing line. The enemy were pressing in, a reckless close-range exchange of slamming volleys that no troops could stand for long. The ex-*Squadrones'* rate of fire was much higher, but there were so *many* of the enemy. Their firepower was diffuse, but it was enormous in relation to the target, and they were swarming around the flanks. In minutes the 2nd would be forced to form square, and hundreds of enemy troops would pour past them to hold the gate. And the gatehouse was *still* not clear.

A solid pulse of noise bounced through the gate towers: men and dogs howling. Raj stiffened, gripping the stone sill and craning to see. He could just make out the opened inner gate. Red flashes came through it, and then a sudden sullen wash of fire—handbombs and burning pitch being poured into the roadway. Not as much as there would have been if the gate towers were fully manned, but too much, too much. Some of the first men through were reeling with wounds, and others rode dogs with burning fur that streaked off across the plaza or rolled whether their riders jumped free in time or not.

Yet the troops were in hand, not panicking. Those hale enough spilled through and then formed on either side of the gate in three-deep lines, then trotted-cantered-galloped into the plaza in response to trumpet calls. Split into two rectangles of men and dogs and bright swords, and charged for the flanks of the 2nd Cruisers, where the Brigaderos lapped around them like waves eroding sand at high tide. The enemy were unformed, focused on the single task of driving toward the gates. They had no chance of forming to receive a mounted charge; and when they saw the line of saber-points and snarling wardogs coming out of the darkness and firelight their will broke. Screaming, they turned and ran back for the shelter of the buildings, running across the hundreds of their dead.

"The 5th, by the Spirit," Raj said softly. His voice was hoarse from the smoke. Mostly from the smoke.

More men were riding through the gate-mouth, in pulses like water pouring through a hole in the hull of a sinking ship. They dismounted, the dogs peeling off as the handlers led them, the men fixing bayonets. Trumpet calls and shouted orders sent them forward at the double, with a long ripple down their line as the files closed around the places of absent men. An armored car followed with a mechanical pig-grunt from its engines that racketed back off the stone; a splatgun jutted from the bow, in place of the usual light cannon. The brass hubs of the tall wire-spoked wheels shone as it rattled off across the uneven pavement in the gap between two companies of the 5th Descott. Seconds later the rolling crash of a full battalion's platoon volley-firing echoed back from the plaza, and the savage *braaaaaaap* of the new weapon. The cannonade from the walls had stopped. A moment later an explosion somewhere deep in the gate towers punished his eardrums and made the stonework shudder under his feet. The flash of handbombs from the murder holes stopped; to either side of the towers, he could see pennants waving as the assault force gained the walls, and some were already sliding down ropes to the inner side. A column of men on foot broke out of the gate below him, and then a pair of guns rumbling along behind their dog-teams.

The firing was dying away, but lights were going on all across the town amid a bee-hum of civilian panic; down by the harbor, ships were casting loose from the docks to try their chances with the steam rams outside the breakwater—they must have been ready and waiting for the signs. With a roar like heavy surf collapsing a breakwater in a storm, the army of the Civil Government broke over the walls and flowed in to the helpless city behind.

"This's as far as it's safe," Gruder said.

All the other towers had surrendered quickly enough, when Civil Government troops came calling at the back entrance with field guns for doorknockers. Some of them were empty even before the soldiers arrived, their militia defenders tearing off their uniforms and running back towards their homes. All except those here on the northeast quadrant, where the men holding them had hauled down the Lion City banner of a rampant cat and left their own flag of white crescent on a green field flying defiantly.

"Hate to waste men on the rag-heads," Gruder said, scratching at a half-formed scab on his neck.

Raj's smile was bleak as the dawn still six hours away. "I don't think that will be necessary," he said quietly. "I've sent—ah."

Juluk rode up, his pipe between his teeth. His men ambled behind him, their dogs wuffing with interest at the smells on the night air.

"Hey, sojer-man, you do *wheetigo* trick, fly over walls, eh?"

"I didn't want to stay home scratching my fleas with you sluggards," Raj replied. Horace and the Skinner chief's dog eyed each other.

He pointed at the towers ahead. "Know who's there?" he said.

Juluk stretched and belched, knocking the dottle out of his pipe

against one bare horn-calloused heel. "Wear-breechclout-on-heads,"
he replied.

The Skinners' home range touched on the Colony's northeast
border. That was their name for the Arabs; they called the people
of the Civil Government the *sneaks,* and the western barbarians
long-hairs. Or they just used their generic term of contempt, farmer.

"They think they're heroes," Raj said. "I say that if any of them
are alive when the sun comes up, your women will laugh you out
of the camps when you go home. They'll offer you skirts and birthing-
stools."

Juluk's giggle broke into a hoot. He turned to his followers: *"L'gran
wheetigo konai nus! Eel doni l'bun mut!"*

The big devil knows us! He's given us the good word!

"And that," Raj said as the nomad mercenaries pounded by,
screeching like powered saws in stone, "takes care of that."

"Further resistance is hopeless," Raj called up toward the second-
story window. "Colonel Strezman, don't sacrifice brave men without need." *Not least because the Civil Government can use them,*
he thought. Whatever happened here in the west, there would be
war with the Colony again within two years.

His skin prickled. He was quiet sure High Colonel Strezman
wouldn't order him shot down under a flag of truce. He wasn't at
all sure that one of his men might not do it anyway.

The last of the Brigaderos regulars had holed up in several mansions not far from the plaza. Like most rich men's homes throughout
the Midworld basin they were courtyard-centered dwellings with few
openings out to the world; their lives were bent inward, away from
noise, dust, thieves and tax-assessors. Their thick stone walls would
turn rifle bullets, and the iron grills over the windows might make
them forts in time of riot. How little they resembled real forts was
shown by the smashed courtyard gate and the rubble beside it, where
a single shell from the field-gun back down the road had landed.
Most of the windows were dark, but there was enough moonlight
for the riflemen crouching there to see the street quite well; also
a building was burning not too far away.

A long silence followed. The street-door of the central house
creaked open, and Strezman walked out surrounded by a knot of
his senior officers.

"My congratulations on a brilliant ruse of war," he called, stopping ten meters away. "Your reputation proceeded you, Messer
Whitehall, and now I see that it is justified."

He spoke loudly, a little more loudly than the distance called for.
There was blood on the armor covering his right arm, and on the
blade of his single-edged broadsword. He wore no helmet, and his
long white hair fluttered around an eagle's face in the hot wind
from the fire. Torchlight painted it red, despite his pallor.

"My congratulations, High Colonel, on a most skillful and resolute defense," Raj said sincerely.

Given the cards he was dealt, Strezman had played them about as well as he could—as well as anyone could without Center whispering in their ear.

"Will you surrender your remaining men?" Raj asked formally. "Your wounded will be cared for, and the troopers and junior officers given honorable terms of enlistment in the Civil Government forces on another front. Senior officers will be detained pending the conclusion of the war, but in a manner fitting to their rank and breeding."

Strezman swallowed, and spoke again. Still louder, as if for a larger audience.

"My orders from His Mightiness are to resist to the last man," he declaimed. "Therefore I must decline your gracious offer, Messer Whitehall, although no further *military* purpose is served by resistance. To honor the truce, I hereby warn you of my intention to attack."

Their eyes met. *The hostages,* Raj knew. The lives of these mens' families were forfeit, if they surrendered . . . or if they were *known* to have surrendered. Even though a stand to the death here accomplished nothing, not even much delay.

The officers with Strezman drew their swords and threw away the scabbards. They raised the blades and began to walk forward, heads up and eyes staring over the massed rifles facing them.

Raj chopped his hand down. Smoke covered the scene for an instant as a hundred rifles barked; when it cleared every man in the Brigaderos party was down, hit half a dozen times. The High Colonel was on his knees; blood pulsed through teeth clenched in a rictus of effort and he collapsed forward. The tip of his sword struck sparks as it left his hand and spun on the cobbles, a red and silver circle on the stones.

Raj flung up his hand to halt the fire. In a voice as loud as the Brigadero colonel's a moment before, he called:

"Let the bodies of High Colonel Strezman and his officers be returned to their households—" the servants who followed their masters to war "—to be delivered to their prince, in recognition of how their men—how *all* their men—died with them in obedience to General Forker's orders."

The vicious little sod, he added silently. He hoped the Brigade didn't depose Forker any time soon; the man was worth five battalions of cavalry to the Civil Government all by himself. If shame didn't keep him from harming the garrison's families, fear of his other commanders probably would, after Strezman's final gesture. Although if there was any justice in this Fallen world, the Brigade would chop him, and soon.

"Gerrin," he went on in a normal voice. The other man's torso was bound with bandages over ribs that *might* only be cracked, but he was still mobile.

"Get the rest of them out; there must be eight hundred or so. Down to the docks before daylight, suitable guards, and onto those two merchantmen Grammeck commandeered. Have someone reliable, Bartin say, handle it. The ships can pick up pilots and a deck officer apiece from the rams, they've come into the harbor. I want them sailing east by dawn, understood?"

No need for a decimation, Raj thought grimly. The 5th Descott had lost more than that, running the gauntlet of the murder-holes of the gatehouse and in the headlong charge that cleared the plaza for the men behind them.

He looked down once more from the podium around the fountain; only a day and a night since the town meeting gathered here . . . now the square was filled with soldiers. The 5th and the 2nd Cruisers still in neat ranks before him; many of the others mixed by the surge over the walls and the brief street-fighting that followed. Many missing, already off among the houses. The only firing came from the sector of wall still held by the Colonial merchants, the burbling of their repeater carbines and jezails as an undertone to the savage hammering of Skinner long rifles. He didn't think that would take long; he could see one of the towers from here, and squat figures made stick-tiny by distance capered and danced on its summit, firing their monstrous weapons into the air.

Every once and a while, a figure in Colonist robes would be launched off the parapet to flutter in a brief arc through the air. Some of the screams were audible this far away.

"Fellow soldiers," Raj said. "Well done." A cheer rippled across the plaza, tired but good-natured. "A donative of six months' pay will be issued." The next cheer had plenty of energy. "I won't keep you, lads; just remember we need this place standing tomorrow, not burnt to the ground. You've done your jobs, now the city—and all in it—is yours until an hour past dawn. All units dismissed!"

Behind them the gate-tower he'd stormed was fully involved, a pillar of flame within the round stone chimney of the building. With luck it wouldn't go beyond that . . .

The 5th Descott still stood in ranks before him, immobile as stone. Certain things had to be done by the forms. He nodded, and spoke again:

"Colonel Staenbridge."

"Sir."

"I have need of trustworthy men to guard key locations and apprehend certain persons tonight."

Thus missing the sack, one of the rare pleasures of a common soldiers' hard, meagre and usually boring life. Most of the troopers would think of it as a far worse punishment than being the lead element through the gate—which Kaltin Gruder had assigned the 5th on the unanimous insistence of officers and men.

"Are the 5th Descott Guards ready to undertake this duty?"

"*Mi heneral*, the 5th is always ready to do its duty." The sound that came from the ranks was not a cheer; more like a short crashing bark.

"Excellent, Colonel." He paused. "I see that the 5th's banner is absent. Please see that it is returned to its proper place immediately."

"*Mi heneral!*"

Mitchi sat and held up the hand-mirror and preened, throwing a hand behind her tousled mass of red hair and arching her back. The necklace of gold and emeralds glittered in the lamplight between her full pink-tipped breasts. The tent was a warm cave in the night, light strong panels of tanned and dyed titanosauroid gut on a framework of skeelwood and bronze. All the furniture was similar, including the bed she and Kaltin Gruder shared, expensive and tough and very portable.

"You're vain as a cat," Gruder said, running a hand up her back. He was lying with one arm beneath his head. She shivered slightly at the calloused, rock-hard touch. "Aren't you ever going to take the damned thing off?" There were red pressure-marks beneath it.

"I may be vain, but you stink of dog and gunpowder, Kaltin," she said tartly. "Mmmmm." He began kneading the base of her slender neck between thumb and forefinger.

"Well," he said reasonably, "I fought a murthering great assault action last night, did some hard looting, then worked my arse off all day keeping the city from burning down and getting the men back in hand. A busy man doesn't smell like a rose."

"Not too busy to find this," she said, turning and lying on his chest. She propped her chin on her elbows, and the jewels swung between them. "Or that little dog you found for Jaine."

"Or a good deal else," he agreed, chuckling. "Professional soldier's instincts. She'll need a riding dog on the march . . . How's she settling?"

"Jaine? Very well; she's got neat hands with my hair and clothes, she's clean and biddable. Sweet little thing, too, everyone likes her." She moved a leg over his hips and giggled. "You're not settled at all. I'd have thought you'd be worn out on the town matrons."

"I like my women smiling and running toward me, not scream-ing and running away," he said, putting his hands around her narrow waist and lifting her astride him. Her breath caught as she sank back on her heels and began to move.

"Besides," he went on, running his hands up and gripping her breasts, "as the wog saying goes: *Stolen goods are never sold at a loss.* Hard loot looked like a better way to spend the time, with fifteen thousand men inside the walls and running loose. Lineups."

Mitchi gave a complex shudder and threw back her head, stroking the hands that caressed her. "What's that sound?" she asked.

"That?" Gruder said.

A roar like angry surf was coming from Lion City. Louder than the town meeting had been, since all the gates were open. "That's a rarity, wench—some people getting what they deserve. Now shut up."

Syndic Placeedo Anarenz looked as if he was going to survive the wound the throwing-axe had put in his back, although the left arm might never be as strong again. Right now it was strapped to his chest by the Army priest-doctor's bandages. He stood as straight as that allowed, meeting Raj's eyes. The general's face might have been a Base Area idol rough-carved out of old wood, his eyes rimmed and red with fatigue.

"Your tame prince certainly predicted our fate accurately, *heneralissimo supremo,*" Anarenz said bitterly.

Raj rubbed his chin; sword-callous rasped on blue-black stubble. "I don't think many infants were tossed on bayonets," he said mildly.

Or that many silver-haired elders got their brains beaten out, he thought. Not unless they were foolish enough to get between a soldier and something he fancied.

Lion City was orderly now, with infantry in *guardia* armbands on every corner seeing that their comrades went nowhere but to authorized taverns and knocking shops. Little remained from the previous night of rape, pillage and slaughter but the occasional gutted building, and not many of those. Guards had kept the major warehouses from damage, and the shipyards and other critical facilities; the rest of the town was missing most of its liquid wealth and small valuables, and several hundred young women smuggled out to the camp. They would probably be sold in a few days, at knock-down prices along with the households of the Colonial merchants and the magnates he'd put under proscription.

"Also," he went on, "I saw how your own guild reacted to my warning."

Placeedo Anarenz started slightly, and stared for a moment. "You," he breathed. "You were one of the guards?"

Raj nodded. "This—" he indicated the podium and the plaza "—is something of a reunion. Even the syndics are here."

They were standing under guard in front of the assembled citizens. It was a larger crowd than the town meeting, most of the adult population of Lion City. Much quieter as well, ringed with troops holding their bayoneted rifles as barricades; battered-looking men, many in remnants of militia uniform. Equally battered-looking women, in ripped and stained clothing hastily repaired or still gaping. Torches on poles lit their upturned faces, staring at him with dread.

Another building-block in the reputation of Raj Whitehall, he thought bitterly.

"I was a syndic," Anarez said. "Why aren't I down there with them?"

"Because you argued for opening the gates," Raj pointed out. "Also you're the next Mayor."

Anarenz grunted in shock, staggering until the two burly sailmakers at his side steadied him. Pain-sweat glistened on his forehead from the jostling that gave his wound.

"Why *me?*" he said. "I thought you'd have some bureaucrat ready . . . or one of our local arse-lickers who'd buy his way into your favor the way he did with the Brigade. De Roors is good at that."

Anarenz was a brave man. He still shivered slightly at Raj's smile.

"You actually care about the welfare of the citizens," the general said. "That makes you more predictable; men like de Roors don't stay bought. I'm going to need stability here. I'll be leaving plenty of the Administrative Service to oversee you, don't worry. Messer Historiomo to begin with, but he'll be taking over all occupied territory, and I've advised him to consult you."

Raj turned to face the wounded man. "There's a saying, Goodman—Messer *Alcalle*—Anarenz, back in the east. That the Governor's Chair rests on four pillars of support: a *standing* army of soldiers, a *sitting* army of bureaucrats, a *kneeling* army of priests, and a *creeping* army of informers. It's a settled way of doing things, and it functions . . . but here I need the active support of the people I'm liberating from the Brigade."

He nodded to the huddle of Syndics below the podium. "After this, I don't think the magnates of other cities will try to sit things out."

Aloud, he went on: "Citizens of Lion City!"

A signal, and the soldiers ripped the rich clothing from the former oligarchs of the town, leaving a group of potbellied or scrawny older men edging away from the bright levelled menace of the bayonets, and a few others trying hard to look brave—a difficult task, naked and helpless. There were a hundred or so of them, all the adult males of the ruling families.

"Here are the men," Raj went on, pointing, "who are the true authors of your misfortunes. Here are the men who refused to open the gates peacefully and exposed your city to storm and sack."

An animal noise rose from the crowd. Oligarchs were not popular anywhere, and right now the commons of Lion City needed a target for their fear and fury, a target that wasn't armed. De Roors turned and knelt toward the podium, bawling a plea for mercy that was lost in the gathering mob-snarl. A rock hit the back of his head and he slumped forward. The old Syndic who'd had his guard try to assassinate Anarenz spat at the mob, lashing out with his fists as work-hardened hands cuffed him into the thick of it. A knot of women closed around him, pried-up cobblestones flailing in two-handed grips. The others disappeared in a surge of bodies and stamping feet, dying and pulping and spreading as greasy stains on the plaza pavement.

"Spirit of *Man*," Anarenz shouted, pushing forward. "Stop this, you butcher! *Hang* them if you want to, that'll terrify the syndics of the other cities."

"No," Raj replied.

His voice cut through the noise much better than the sailmaker's did, and the mob were recoiling now—from themselves, as much as from what remained of the city's former rulers.

"No, doing it this way is better. The magnates elsewhere will know I've a much more terrible weapon to use against them than my army." He nodded to the crowd. "And *they* will know there's no going back; if the Brigade wins, it'll make an example of Lion City."

Anarenz looked at him with an expression more suitable for a man who'd stumbled across a pack of carnosauroids devouring an infant.

"For the *Spirit's* sake, is there *anything* you won't do to win your bloody war?" he shouted. "Anything?"

Raj's head turned like a cannon moving with a hand on its aiming-wheel. "No, Messer *Alcalle*," he said. "There's *nothing* I won't do to unite civilization on Bellevue, and end things like this forever. For the Spirit's sake."

Suzette sank down beside Raj and leaned her head against his shoulder. "You did what you had to do, my love," she said softly.

His hands knotted on the table, and the empty bottle of *slyowtz* rolled away. The spray of plumb-blossom on the label curled about a stylized H; it was the Hillchapel proprietary brand. How long was it since he'd been home?

"Only what you had to do."

Raj's arms groped blindly for his wife. She drew his head down to rest on her bosom, rocking it in her arms.

lady whitehall is correct, Center said. **observe—**

I know! Raj cut in. Lion City rising behind him, other cities closing their gates. Costing him men, costing him time, neither of which he had to spare.

"I know," he said aloud.

"Shhhh, my love." The commandeered room was quiet, only the light hissing of the lantern breaking the silence. "You're with me now. No need to be the General. Peace, my love. Peace."

For a moment the hard brilliance of another image gleamed before Raj: the Old Residence seen in the near distance, its wall towers and walls silent but threatening simply for their enormous extent.

The vision faded, **yes,** said Center. **peace, for now.**

IV
THE STEEL

The Planet
BELLEVUE
In the Age of Raj Whitehall
c. 1104 After the Fall

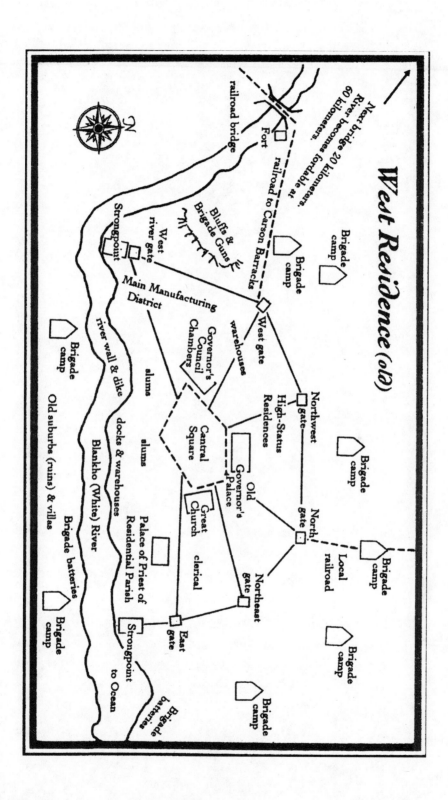

West Residence (old)

N

Next bridge 20 kilometers.
River becomes fordable at
60 kilometers.

railroad bridge

Fort

railroad to Carson Barracks

Brigade camp

Brigade camp

Bluffs & Brigade Guns

Strongpoint

West river gate

Main Manufacturing District

West gate

Governor's Council Chambers

warehouses

slums

Northwest gate

High-Status Residences

Brigade camp

river wall & dike

slums

Central Square

Old Governor's Palace

North gate

Local railroad

Brigade camp

docks & warehouses

Great Church

clerical

Northeast gate

Blankho (White) River

Palace of Priest of Residential Parish

Brigade camp

Old suburbs (ruins) & villas

East gate

Strongpoint

Northeast gate

Brigade camp

Brigade batteries

Brigade batteries

to Ocean

Brigade camp

CHAPTER ONE

Thom Poplanich floated through infinity. The monobloc exploded outward, and he *felt* the twisting of space-time in its birth-squall. . . .

I think I understand that now, he thought.

excellent, Center said. **we will return to socio-historical analysis: subject, fall of the federation of man.**

He had been down here in the sanctum of Sector Command and Control Unit AZ12-b14-c000 Mk. XIV for years, now. His body was in stasis, his mind connected with the ancient battle computer on levels far broader than the speechlike linkage of communication. It was no longer necessary for him to see events sequentially. . . .

Images drifted through his consciousness. Earth. The True Earth of the Canonical Handbooks, not this world of Bellevue. Yet it was not the perfect home of half-angels that the priests talked of, but a world of men. Nations rose and warred with each other, empires grew and fell. Men learned as the cycles swung upward, then forgot, and fur-clad savages dwelt in the ruins of cities, burning their books for winter's warmth. At last one cycle swung further skyward than any before. On a small island northwest of the main continent, engines were built. Ones he recognized at first, clanking steam-engines driving factories to spin cloth, dragging loads across iron rails, powering ships. The machines grew greater, stranger. They took to the air and cities burned beneath them. They spread from one land to the next, springing at last into space.

Earth floated before him, blue and white like the images of Bellevue that Center showed him—blue and white like all worlds that could nourish the seed of Earth. One final war scarred the globe beneath him with flames, pinpoints of fire that consumed whole cities at a blow. Soundless globes of magenta and orange bloomed in airless space.

the last jihad, Center's voice said. **observe.**

A vast construct drifted into view, skeletal and immense beside the tubular ships and dot-tiny suited humans.

the tanaki spatial displacement net. the first model. Energies flowed across it, twisting into dimensions describable only in mathematics that he had not yet mastered. The ships vanished, to reappear far away . . . here, in Bellevue's system. The Colonists, first men to set foot on this world. They landed and raised the green flag of Islam.

even more than the jihad, the net made the federation of man essential, Center said. **the empire that rose this time expanded until it covered all the Earth, and leaped outward to nearby stars. a century later, its representatives landed on distant Bellevue, much to the displeasure of the descendants of the refugees, and the net was its downfall. expansion proceeded faster than integration.** Long strings of formulae followed. **once the tipping point was reached, entropic decay accelerated exponentially.**

The higher they rise, the harder they fall, Thom thought.

true. There was a slight overtone of surprise in Center's dispassionate machine-voice.

More images. War flickering between the stars, mutiny, secession. Bellevue's Net flaring into plasma. The remnants of Federation units turning feral when they were cut off here, bringing civilization down in a welter of thermonuclear fire. Swift decay into barbarism for most areas, a pathetic remnant of ancient knowledge preserved in the Civil Government and the Colony, degenerating into superstition. Now a thousand years and more had passed, and a tentative rebirth stirred.

cycles within cycles, Center said. **the overall trend is still toward maximum entropy, unless my intervention can alter the parameters. fifteen thousand years will pass until the ascendant phase of the next overall historical period.**

An image eerily familiar, for he had seen it with his own eyes as well as through Center's senses. Two young men out exploring the ancient catacombs beneath the Governor's palace in East Residence. Unlikely friends: Thom Poplanich, grandson of the last Poplanich Governor. A slight young man in a patrician's hunting outfit of tweed. Raj Whitehall, tall, with a swordsman's shoulders and wrists. Guard to the reigning Barholm Clerett, and like him from distant Descott County, source of the Civil Government's finest soldiers. Once again he saw them discover the bones outside the centrum, the bones of those Center had considered and rejected as its agents in the world.

Raj will do it, Thom thought. *If any man can reunite the world, he can.*

if any man can, Center agreed. **the probability of success is less than 45% ±3, even with my assistance.**

He's already beaten back the Colony. The battle of Sandoral had been the greatest victory the Civil Government had won in generations. *Destroyed the Squadron.* The Squadron and its Admirals had held the Southern Territories for more than a century, the most recent of the Military Governments to come down out of the barbarous Base Area. *And he's beating the Brigade.* The 591st Provisional Brigade were the strongest of the barbarians, and they held Old Residence, the original seat of the Civil Government at the western end of the Midworld Sea.

to date, Center acknowledged, **he has taken the crown peninsula and lion city. the more difficult battles remain.**

Men follow Raj, Thom said quietly. *Not only that, he makes them do things beyond themselves.* He paused. *What really worries me is Barholm Clerett. He doesn't* deserve *a man like Raj serving him! And that nephew he's sent along on this campaign is worse.*

cabot clerett is more able than his uncle, and less a prisoner of his obsessions, Center noted.

That's what worries me.

CHAPTER TWO

The cavalry were singing as they rode; the sound bawled out over the manifold thump of paws from the riding dogs, the creak of harness and squeal of ungreased wheels from the baggage train:

Oh, we Descoteers have hairy ears—
We goes without our britches
And pops our cocks with jagged rocks,
We're hardy sons of bitches!

"Hope they're as cheerful in a month," Raj Whitehall said, looking down at the map spread over his saddlebow. His hound Horace shifted beneath him from one foot to the other, whining with impatience to be off at a gallop in the crisp fall air. Raj stroked his neck with one gauntleted hand.

The commanders were gathered on a knoll, and it gave a wide view over the broad river valley below. The hoarse male chorus of the cavalry troopers sounded up from the fields. The Expeditionary Force snaked westward through low rolling hills. Wagons and guns on the road, infantry in battalion columns to either side, and five battalions of cavalry off to the flanks. There was very little dust; it had rained yesterday, just enough to lay the ground. The infantry were making good time, rifles over their right shoulders and blanket-rolls looped over the left. In the middle of the convoy the camp-followers spread in a magpie turmoil, one element of chaos in the practiced regularity of the column, but they were keeping up too. It was mild but crisp, perfect weather for outdoor work; the leaves of the oaks and maples that carpeted the higher hills had turned to gold and scarlet hues much like the native vegetation.

The soldiers looked like veterans, now. Even the ones who hadn't fought with him before this campaign; even the former Squadrones, military captives taken into the Civil Government's forces after the conquest of the Southern Territories last year. Their uniforms were dirty and torn, the blue of the tailcoat jackets and the dark maroon of their baggy pants both the color of the soil, but the weapons were clean and the men ready to fight . . . which was all that really mattered.

"Looks like more rain tonight," Ehwardo Poplanich said, shading his eyes and looking north. "Doesn't it *ever* not rain in this bloody country?"

The Companions were veterans now too, his inner circle of commanders. Like a weapon whose hilt is worn with use, shaped to fit the hand that reaches for it in the dark. Ehwardo was much more than a Governor's grandson these days.

"Only in high summer," Jorg Menyez replied. "Rather reminds me of home—there are parts of Kelden County much like this, and the Diva River country up on the northwestern frontier."

He sneezed; the infantry specialist was allergic to dogs, which was why he used a riding steer, and why he'd originally chosen the despised foot-soldiers for his military career, despite high rank and immense wealth. Now he believed in them with a convert's zeal, and they caught his faith and believed in themselves.

"Good-looking farms," Gerrin Staenbridge said, biting into an apple. "My oath, but I wouldn't mind getting my hands on some of this countryside."

And Gerrin's come a long way too. He'd commanded the 5th Descott before Raj made them his own. Back then garrison-duty boredom had left him with nothing to occupy his time but fiddling the battalion accounts and his hobbies, the saber and the opera and good-looking youths.

There were a good many orchards hereabouts; apple and plum and cherry, and vineyards trained high on stakes or to the branches of low mulberry trees. Wheat and corn had been cut and carted, the wheat in thatched ricks in the farmyards, the corn in long rectangular bins still on the cob; dark-brown earth rippled in furrows behind ox-drawn ploughs as the fields were made ready for winter grains. Few laborers fled, even when the army passed close-by; word had spread that the eastern invaders ravaged only where resisted . . . and the earth must be worked, or all would starve next year. Pastures were greener than most of the easterners were used to, grass up to the hocks of the grazing cattle. Half-timbered cottages stood here and there, usually nestled in a grove, with an occasional straggling crossroads village, or a peon settlement next to a blocky stone-built manor house.

Many of the manors were empty; the remaining landlords were mostly civilian, and eager to come in and swear allegiance to the Civil Government. Here and there a mansion stood burnt and empty. Ill-considered resistance, or peasant vengeance on fleeing masters. Some of the peons abandoned their plows to come and gape as the great ordered mass of the Civil Government's army passed, with the Starburst fluttering at its head. It had been more than five hundred years since that holy flag flew in these lands. Raj reflected ironically that the natives probably thought the 7th Descott Rangers' marching-song was a hymn; there was much touching of amulets and kneeling.

> *We fuck the whores right through their drawers*
> *We do not care for trifles—*
> *We hangs our balls upon the walls*
> *And shoots at 'em with rifles.*

"Area's too close to the Stalwarts for my liking," Kaltin Gruder said. His hand stroked the scars on his face, legacy of a Colonial shell-burst that had killed his younger brother. "Speaking of which, any news of the Brigaderos garrisons up there?"

"The Ministry of Barbarians came through on that one," Raj said, still not looking up from the map. "The Stalwarts are raiding the frontier just as we paid them to, and most of the enemy regulars there are staying. The rest are pulling back southwest, toward the Padan River, where they can barge upstream to Carson Barracks."

Bribing one set of barbarians to attack another had been a Civil Government specialty for generations. Cheaper than wars, usually, although there were dangers as well. The Brigade had come south long ago, but the Stalwarts were only down from the Base Area a couple of generations. Fierce, treacherous, numerous, and still heathen—not even following the heretical This Earth cult.

"Right," Raj said, rolling up the map. "We'll continue on this line of advance to the Chubut river—" he used the map to point west "—at Lis Plumhas. M'Brust reports it's opened its gates to the 1st Cruisers. Ehwardo, I want you to link up with him there—push on ahead of the column—with two batteries and take command. Cross the river, and feint toward the Padan at Empirhado. It's a good logical move, and they'll probably believe it. Engage at your discretion, but screen us in any case."

The Padan drained most of the central part of the Western Territories, rising in the southern foothills of the Sangrah Dil Ispirito mountains and running northeast along the range, then west and southwest around its northernmost outliers. Empirhado was an important riverport, and taking it would cut off the north from the Brigadero capital at Carson Barracks.

"Actually," Raj went on, "we'll cut southeast again around Zeronique at the head of the Residential Gulf and come straight down on Old Residence. I want them to come to us, and they'll have to fight for that eventually—it is the ancient capital of the Civil Government. At the same time, it's accessible by sea up the Blankho River, so we've a secure line of communications to Lion City. Strategic offensive, tactical defensive."

Everyone nodded, some making notes. Lion City was a *very* safe base. Its ruling syndics had tried to resist the Civil Government army, fearful of Brigade retaliation and confident in their city walls. Raj had found an ancient Pre-Fall passageway under them and led a party to open the gates from within. After the sack, the syndics who'd counselled resistance had been torn to bits—quite literally—by the enraged common folk of the city. The commoners' only hope now was a Civil Government victory; if the Brigade came back they'd slaughter every man, woman and child for treason to the General . . . and for the murder of their betters.

"Meanwhile, I'm going to keep five battalions of cavalry with the main column and send the rest of you out raiding. Round up supplies, liberate the towns and incidentally, knock down the defenses— we don't want Brigaderos occupying them again in our rear. Be alert, messers, there'll probably be more resistance soon. I've furnished a list of objectives of military significance. Grammeck?"

"I don't like these roads," the artilleryman-cum-engineer said.

Like most of his branch of service, Grammeck Dinnalysn was a cityman, from East Residence. Unlike most of the military nobility, Raj Whitehall had never hesitated to use the technical skills that went with that education.

"They're just graded dirt, and it's clay dirt at that. Much more rain, and it's going to turn into soup."

Raj nodded again. "Nevertheless, I intend to make at least twenty klicks per day, minimum."

Jorg Menyez shrugged. "My boys will march it," he said and sneezed, moving a little aside to get upwind of the dogs. "I'm surprised we haven't seen more resistance already," he added. "We're well beyond the zone Major Clerett raided."

Raj grinned. "A little dactosauroid flew in and whispered in my ear," he said, "in the person of the Esteemed Rehvidaro Boyez— he was one of the Ministry talkmongers at Carson Barracks, bribed his way out—that the Brigade has called a Council of War there."

Harsh laughter from the circle of Companions. The Council of War included all male Brigade adults, and decided the great issues of state in huge conclaves at Carson Barracks, the capital the Brigade had built off in the swamps. Or to be more accurate, debated the issues at enormous length. To men used to the omnipotent quasi-divine autocracy of the Civil Government, it was an endless source of amusement.

"No, no—it's actually a good move. They have to decide on their leadership before they can *do* anything. Filip Forker certainly won't." Forker was a mild-tempered scholar, very untypical of the brawling warrior nobility of the Brigade; he was also a defeatist who'd been in secret communication with the Civil Government.

"So they have to get rid of him and elect a fighting man as General. Of course, they have left it a little late."

The troopers below roared out the last verse of their marching song:

> *Much joy we reap by diddlin' sheep*
> *In divers nooks and ditches*
> *Nor give we a damn if they be rams—*
> *We're hardy sons of bitches!*

"Let's get moving, gentlemen. I expect some warm welcomes on the way to Old Residence."

"Compliments to Captain Suharez, and Company C to face left, on this line," Gerrin Staenbridge said. He sketched quickly on his notepad, and tore off the sheet to hand to the dispatch rider. The man tucked it under his jacket to shelter the drawing from the slow drizzle of rain.

Gerrin raised his binoculars. The lancepoints of the Brigaderos cuirassiers were clearly visible behind the ridge there, four thousand meters out and to the west. From the way the pennants whipped backward, they were moving briskly. Bit of a risk to spread his front, but the fire of the other companies should cover it. Better to stop the flanking movement well out than to simply refuse his flank in place.

"And one gun," he added.

The messenger spurred, and the trumpet sounded. Men moved along the sunken lane to his front, where the main line of the two battalions faced north. A company crawled back and stood, then double-timed west in column of fours. Water spurted up from their boots, and squelched away from the gun that followed them, its dogs panting and skidding on the surface of wet earth and yellow leaves as they trundled out of sight to meet the enemy's flanking attack. The remaining men moved west to occupy the vacant space, spreading themselves in response to barked orders.

The paws of the colonel's dog squelched too as he rode down the lane; it was barely nine meters wide, rutted mud flanked on either side by tall maple and whipstick trees. North beyond that was a broad stretch of reaped wheat stubble with alfalfa showing green between the faded gold of the straw. Beyond that was a line of orchard, and the Brigaderos, those whose bodies weren't scattered across the field between from the first failed rush.

"That's right, lads," Staenbridge called out, as he cantered toward the center of the line, where the standards of the 5th Descott and the 1st Residence Life Guards flew together, beside the main battery. "Keep those delectable buttocks close to the earth and pick your targets."

The men were prone or kneeling behind the meter-high ridge that marked the sunken lane's northern edge. The trees and the remains of a rail fence gave more cover still; there were a scatter of brass cartridge cases and the lingering stink of sulphur under the wet mud and rotting leaf smell. Most of them had gray cloaks spread over their backs; Lion City had had a warehouse full of them, woven of raw wool with the lanolin still in them, nearly waterproof. Staenbridge had thoughtfully posted a guard on that when the city fell, and lifted enough for all his men and a margin extra. Raindrops glistened on the wool, sliding aside as the men adjusted sights and reloaded. The breechblock of a gun clanged open and the crew pushed it forward until its barrel jutted in alignment with the muzzles of the riflemens' weapons.

He drew up beside the banner. "Captain Harritch," he went on, "shift a splatgun to the left end of the line, if you please."

The commander of the two batteries shouted, and the light weapon jounced off down the trail, the crew pulling on ropes; there was no need to hitch the dog team for a short move, but it followed obediently, dragging the caisson with the reserve ammunition.

"We could put a mounted company behind the left and countercharge when those lobster-backs are stalled," Cabot Clerett offered.

It was the textbook answer, but Staenbridge shook his head. "Fighting barbs with swords," he said, "is like fighting a pig by getting down on your hands and knees and biting it. I prefer to keep the rifles on our firing-line. We'll see if they come again."

"These're going to," Bartin Foley said emotionlessly.

He was peeling an apple with the sharpened inner curve of his hook; now he sliced off a chunk and offered it. Staenbridge took it, ignoring Cabot Clerett's throttled impatience. It was crisper and more tart than the fruit he was used to. *Probably the longer winters here,* he thought.

Cabot Clerett probably resented the fact that Bartin Foley had started his military career as a protegee—boyfriend, actually—of Staenbridge's. Although the battles that had taken the young man's left hand, and the commands he'd held since, made him considerably more than that.

"Look to your right, Major Clerett," Gerrin said. "They may try something there as well."

Long lines of helmeted soldiers in gray-and-black uniforms were coming out of the orchard three thousand meters to their front. Serried lines, blocks three deep and fifty men broad all along the front, then a gap of several minutes and another wave, but these in company columns.

"Two thousand in the first wave," he said. "A thousand in column behind. Three thousand all up."

"Plus their reserve," Foley noted, peering at the treeline.

Clerett snorted. "If the barbs are keeping one," he said.

"Oh, these are, I should think . . . this is Hereditary High Colonel Eisaku and . . ."

"Hereditary Major Gutfreed," Foley completed. "Thirty-five to forty-five hundred in all, household troops and military vassals."

To the right a battery commander barked an order. The loader for the guns shoved a two-pronged iron tool into the head of a shell and turned, adjusting the fuse to the distance he was given. Within the explosive head a perforated brass tube turned within a solid one, exposing a precise length of beechwood-enclosed powder train. Another man worked the lever that dropped the blocking wedge and swung the breechblock aside, opening the chamber for the loader to push the shell home. The blocks clattered all along the line, five times repeated. The gunner clipped his lanyard to the release toggle and stood to one side; the rest of the crew skipped out of the path of recoil, already preparing to repeat the cycle, in movements better choreographed than most dances. The battery commander swung his sword down.

POUMPF. POUMPF. POUMPF. POUMPF. POUMPF. Five blasts of powder smoke and red light, and the guns bounced backward across the laneway, splattering muddy water to both sides. Crews heaved at their tall wheels to shove them back into battery, as the loaders pulled new shells out of the racks in the caissons.

The *crack* of the shells bursting over the enemy followed almost at once. Men died, scythed down from above. Staenbridge winced slightly in sympathy; overhead shrapnel was any soldier's nightmare, something to which there was no reply. The Brigaderos came on, picking up the pace but keeping their alignment. The columns following the troops deployed in line were edging toward his left; he nodded, confirmation of the opposing commander's design. It was a meeting of minds, as intimate as a saber-duel or dancing. Closer now, it didn't take long to cover a thousand meters at the trot. A thousand seconds, less than ten minutes. The Brigaderos dragoons had fixed their bayonets, and the wet steel glinted dully under the cloudy sky. Their boots were kicking up clots of dark-brown soil, ripping holes in the thin cover of the stubblefield.

POUMPF. POUMPF. POUMPF. POUMPF. POUMPF. More airbursts, and one defective timer that plowed into the dirt and raised a minor mud-volcano as the backup contact fuse set it off.

Nothing like the Squadrones, Staenbridge thought. The barbarians of the Southern Territories had bunched in a crowded mass, a perfect target. These Brigaderos were much better.

POUMPF. POUMPF. POUMPF. POUMPF. POUMPF. Powder smoke drifted along the firing line, low to the ground and foglike under the drizzle.

At least the Southern Territories were dry, he thought. Descott County got colder than this in midwinter, but it was semi-arid.

"I make it eleven hundred meters," Foley said. Getting on for small-arms range.

"*Ready,*" Staenbridge called. Officers and noncoms went down the firing line, checking that sights were adjusted. "I wonder how the left flank is making out."

✧   ✧   ✧

"Did ye load hardpoint?" Corporal Robbi M'Telgez hissed.

The rifleman he addressed swallowed nervously. "Think so, corp," he said, looking back over his shoulder at the noncom.

Company C were kneeling in a cornfield, just back from the crest of a swell of ground. The corn had never been harvested, but cattle and pigs had been turned loose into it. Most of the stalks were broken rather than uprooted, slick and brown with decay and the rain; they formed a tangle waist-high in wavering rows across the lumpy field. Just ahead of the line of troopers was the company commander, also down on one knee, with his signallers, and a bannerman holding the furled unit pennant horizontal to the ground. The field gun and its crew were slightly to the rear.

"Work yer lever," M'Telgez said.

The luckless trooper shoved his thumb into the loop behind the handgrip of his rifle and pushed the lever sharply downward. The action clacked and ejected the shell directly to the rear as the bolt swung down and slightly back. The noncom snatched it out of the air with his right hand, as quick and certain as a trout rising to a fly. There was a hollow drilled back into the pointed tip of the lead bullet.

"Ye peon-witted dickehead recruity!" the corporal said. "Why ain't ye in t' fukkin' *infantry?* Ye want one a' them pigstickers up yer arse?" Hollowpoint loads often failed to penetrate the body-armor of Brigaderos heavy cavalry.

He clouted the man alongside the head, under his helmet. "Load!"

The younger man nodded and reached back to his bandolier; it was on the broad webbing belt that cinched his swallowtail uniform coat, just behind the point of his right hip. The closing flap was buckled back, exposing the staggered rows of cartridges in canvas loops—the outer frame of the container was rigid sauroid hide boiled in wax, but brass corrodes in contact with leather. This time there was a smooth pointed cap of brass on the lead of the bullet he thumbed home down the grooved ramp on the top of the rifle's bolt. Hunting ammunition for big thick-skinned sauroids, but it did nicely for armor as well.

"Use yer brain, it'll save yer butt," the corporal went on more mildly.

He sank back into his place in the ranks, watching the platoon's lieutenant and the company commander. The lieutenant was new since Stern Isle, but he seemed to know his business. The platoon sergeant thought so, at least. They'd both behaved as well as anybody else in that *ratfuck* in the tunnel. M'Telgez smiled, and the young trooper who'd been looking over to him to ask a question swallowed again and looked front, convinced that nothing he could see there would be more frightening than the section-leader's face. M'Telgez was thinking what he was going to do if—when—he found

out who had started the stampede to the rear in the close darkness of the pipe tunnel. There'd been nothing he could do, nothing
anyone could do, once it started. Except move back or get trampled
into a pulp and suffocated when the pipe blocked solid with a jam
of flesh.

The 2nd Cruisers, jumped-up Squadrone barbs, had gone in
instead of the 5th Descott. With Messer Raj. The stain on the 5th's
honor had been wiped out by their bloodily successful assault on
the gates later that night . . . but M'Telgez intended to find out
who'd put the stain there in the first place. The 5th had been
with Messer Raj since his first campaign and they'd never run from
an enemy.

The gunners were rolling their weapon forward the last few meters
to the crest of the slight rise, two men on either wheel and three
holding up the trail.

"*On* the word of command," the lieutenant said, watching the
captain. A trumpet sounded, five rising notes and a descant.

"Company—"

"Platoon—"

"*Forward!*"

One hundred and twenty men stood and took three paces forward. The lieutenants stopped, their arms and swords outstretched
to the side in a T-bar to give their units the alignment.

To the Brigaderos, they appeared over the crest of the dead ground
with the suddenness of a jack-in-the-box.

Five hundred meters before them about a quarter of the Brigaderos
column was in view, coming over a slight rise. They rode in a column
six men broad; expecting action soon, they'd brought the three-meter
lances out of the buckets and were resting the butt-ends on the toes
of their right boots. The dogs they rode were broad-pawed Newfoundlands, shaggy and massive and black, weighing up to fourteen hundred pounds each. They needed the bulk and bone to carry
men wearing back and breastplate, thigh-guards and arm-guards of
steel, plus sword and lance and firearms and helmet. Their usual
role was to charge home into Stalwart masses already chopped into
fragments by their dragoon comrades' rifle fire. Sometimes the savage
footmen absorbed the charge and ate it, like a swarm of lethal bees
too numerous for the lancers to swat. More often the cavalry scattered the Stalwarts into fugitives who could be hunted down and
slaughtered . . . as long as the lancers went in boot to boot without the slightest hesitation.

It was a style of warfare that had ended in the eastern part of
the Midworld basin two centuries ago, when breechloading firearms
became common. The Brigaderos were about to learn why.

Of course, since there were nearly a thousand of the cuirassiers,
the Civil Government troops might not survive the lesson either.

POUMPF.

The field gun recoiled away from the long plume of smoke. The first shell exploded at head-height a dozen yards from the front of the column; pure serendipity, since the fuses weren't sensitive enough to time that closely. It was canister, a thin-walled head full of lead balls with a small bursting charge at the rear. The charge stripped the casing of the shell off its load and spread the balls out, but the velocity of the shell itself made them lethal. The first three ranks of the lancers went down in kicking, howling confusion. The commander of the cuirassier regiment had been standing in his stirrups and raising the triangular three-bar visor of his helmet to see what had popped up to bar his command's way. Three of the half-ounce balls ripped his head off his torso and threw the body in a backwards somersault over the cantle of his saddle.

Behind him the balls went over the heads of the rear of the column, protected by the dip in the field in which they rode. The projectiles struck the upraised lances instead, the wood of the forward ranks and the foot-long steel heads of those further back and lower down. The sound was like an iron rod being dragged at speed along the largest picket fence in the universe. Lances were smashed out of hands or snapped off like tulips in a hothouse for a dozen ranks back. Men shouted in fear or pain, and dogs barked like muffled thunder.

The cuirassier regiment was divided into ten troops of eighty to ninety men each, commanded by a troop-captain and under-officers. None of them knew what was happening to the head of the column, but they were all Brigade noblemen and anxious to close with the foe. They responded according to their training, the whole mass of lancers halting and each troop turning to right or left to deploy into line. When the Civil Government or Colonial dragoons deployed for a charge under fire they did so at the gallop, but the Brigaderos were used to fighting men equipped with shotguns and throwing-axes. Used to having plenty of time to align their lines neatly.

M'Telgez watched his lieutenant's saber out of the corner of his eye. It swung to the right. He pivoted slightly, taking the general direction from the sword as his squad did from him; a group of lancers opening out around a swallow-tail pennant, borne next to a man whose armor was engraved with silver, wearing a shoulder-cape of lustrous hide from some sauroid that secreted iridescent metal into its scales. The corporal picked a target, a lancer next to the leader—no point in shooting the same man twice, and he *knew* someone wouldn't be able to resist the fancy armor. The rear notch settled behind the bladed foresight, and he lowered his aiming-point another few inches—six hundred meters, the bullet would be coming down from the top of its arch at quite an angle.

"—volley fire—"

He exhaled and let his forefinger curl slightly, taking up the trigger slack. The strap of the rifle was wound round his left hand twice, held taunt with the forestock resting on the knuckles. He might not know who'd fucked up in the tunnel, but at least he was going to get to kill *somebody* today.

"Fire!"

Bullets went overhead with an unpleasant *wrack* sound. Down the line from the command group a trooper slumped backward with his helmet spinning free to land in the mud and the top taken off of his head. He'd been holding two rounds in his lips like cigarettes, with the bases out ready to hand; they followed the helmet, a dull glint of brass through the rain.

Gerrin Staenbridge looked back and forth down the sunken lane. Stretcher-bearers—military servants—were hauling men back, crouching to carry them without exposing themselves over the higher northern lip of the laneway. Other bearers and soldiers were carrying forward ammunition boxes, ripping the loosened tops off and distributing handfuls to the troopers on the firing line. Ahead the Brigaderos were advancing again, one line running forward and taking cover while the second fired and stood to charge their clumsy muzzle-loading rifle muskets. He checked; yes, the company and platoon commanders were dividing their fire, keeping both segments under fire and not letting the men waste bullets on prone targets.

"Hot work," Bartin Foley said beside him. He gave the—literal—lie to his words by shaking his head and casting a scatter of cold rain from his helmet and chainmail neck-flap.

"Bloody hell," Staenbridge replied, raising his voice slightly. "Fight in the desert, and you want rain. Fight in the rain and you want the sun. Some people are never satisfied."

He lit two cigarettes and passed one to the young captain. A lot of the enemy rifle-muskets were misfiring; percussion caps were immune to rain, but paper cartridges were not. Another line of the Brigaderos rose to advance, and a crashing stutter of half-platoon volleys met them. At three hundred meters more shots hit than missed, but the remnants came on and stood to fire a return volley of their own. Wounded men screamed and cursed down the lines of the 5th and the Life Guards; but they were protected, all but their heads and shoulders. The enemy were naked. The Civil Government's rifle was a single shot breechloader; not the least of its blessings was that it could be loaded lying down.

Off to the east the firing line was thinner, where Company C had been detached; the 5th was still overstrength, but not so much so since Lion City. The splatgun there gave its *braaaaak* sound, thirty-five rifle barrels clamped together and fired by a crank. A Brigaderos column was caught six hundred meters out, as it began the ponderous countermarch they used to get from marching column into fighting line. Seconds later two field-gun shells arrived at the same target, contact-fused; they plowed up gouts of mud and toppled men with blast and heavy casing fragments. Staenbridge stepped off his crouching dog and walked down behind the line, the banner by his side. It had a few more bulletholes, but the bannerman kept it aloft in the gathering rain.

"Ser, would ye mind inspirin' ussn where ye won't draw fire?" a sergeant called back to him.

"Inspiration be damned, I'm checking that your leatherwork is polished," Staenbridge said.

A harsh chuckle followed as he strolled back to the center. *Spirit, the things one says under stress,* he thought.

A runner squelched up, a Life Guardsman. "Ser," he said to Cabot Clerett. "Barb movement in t'woods. Mounted loik."

Staenbridge nodded at the Governor's nephew's glance. "We're holding here," he said. "Take a company . . . and the other two splatguns."

"Whitehall's toys," Clerett said.

"Useful toys. Take them, and *use* them."

Clerett nodded and turned, calling out orders. He straddled his dog and the animal rose, dripping; the rain was coming down harder now, a steady drizzle. Water sizzled on the barrels of the splatguns, and the gunners left their breeches locked open as they hitched the trails to the limbers and wheeled. Men on the far right of the 2nd Life Guard's section of the line fired one more volley and fell in behind him, reloading as they jogged. There was a slapping sound, and the 2nds bannerman gave a deep grunt and slumped in the saddle. Cabot reached out and took the staff, resting the butt on his stirrup-iron as the other man toppled.

"See to him," he said. "You men, follow me." He kept the dog to a steady quick walk as they moved in squelching unison behind him.

"Spread it out there," Foley said sharply. The rightmost company of the 5th and the leftmost of the 2nd shifted to fill in the gap, ducking as they moved to keep under cover.

"He's got nerve," Staenbridge murmured. "Still, I'm happier seeing his back than his glowering face."

"I could resent that remark," Foley said, sotto voce. Aloud: "Lieutenant, they're clumping to your left. Direct the fire, if you please."

"Fire!"

M'Telgez straightened from his crouch and fired. The Armory rifle punished his shoulder, the barrel fouled from all the rounds he'd put through it this afternoon. This was the fifth charge, and looked to be the worst yet. A hundred yards to the front dogs went over and men died; they were close enough that he could hear the flat smacking of bullets hitting flesh and the sharper *ptung* of impacts on armor. He worked the lever and snatched a round he was holding between the fingers of his left hand, thumbing it home.

"Here they come!" he snarled.

The Brigaderos were getting smarter; they'd dismounted some of their men behind the ridge over there to use their rifles for a base of fire. The commander of Company C had backed his troopers half a dozen paces, so that they could load crouching and pop up to fire, but they were still losing men. The enemy were also still trying to charge home; expensive, but although they might win a firefight, they couldn't win it in time to affect the main action half a klick away—and the lancers had been supposed to sweep down on the flank of the 5th's position.

Below in the slight swale between the low ridges the lancers came on in clumps and as stragglers. Their dogs' feet were balls of sticky mud, and the cornstalks there had been trampled into a slippery mass that sent some riders skidding in disastrous flailing tumbles even if the bullets missed them. More came on, though, laboring up the slope.

"*Fire!*"

The corporal fired again. A ragged volley crashed out around him, the muzzle-blasts deafening—particularly the one from the man behind, whose muzzle was nearly in his ear.

"Watch yer *dressin'*, ye dickead!" he screamed, jerking at his lever, and the man shuffled a few steps right. At least the rifle wasn't jamming; there was *some* benefit to the cold rain that was hissing down into his eyes.

He could see the dogs snarling, and the men behind their visors. Mud flew chest-high on the dogs as they came closer at a lumbering gallop.

"*Fire!*"

More died and half a dozen turned back, some as their dogs bolted to the rear despite sawing hands on the reins and the pressure of bridle-levers on their cheeks. The rest came on, those who still had lances leveling them. The shafts were tapered and smooth, save for a grapefruit-sized wooden ball just in front of the handgrip; the heads were straight-sided knives a foot long, honed and deadly, with steel lappets another two feet down the shaft on either side. M'Telgez' fingers had to hunt for a second to find a cartridge in his bandolier; the upper rows were empty. He clicked it home just as the straggling charge reached the Civil Government line.

The lieutenant pirouetted aside from a point like a matador in the arena. His saber slashed down on the shaft behind the protective steel splints that ran back from the head, and the razor edges tumbled. He let the motion spin him in place, and shot the rider in the back point-blank with the revolver in his left hand.

M'Telgez had lost interest in any lance but the one pointed at his chest. His lever clicked home when it was only a couple of meters away; the corporal threw himself on his back in blind instinct, falling with a thump as the steel dipped. It passed a hand's breadth over his head and he shot with the butt of his rifle pressed to the earth by his side. The bullet creased the Newfoundland's neck, cutting a red streak through the muddy black fur. The animal reared and then lunged, the huge jaws gaping for his face in a graveyard reek of rotting meat. M'Telgez screamed and flung up his rifle; the dog shrieked too, when its jaws closed on two feet of bayonet. The weapon jerked out of the Descotter's hands and the mud sucked at his back. The Brigadero was standing in his stirrups, shouting as he shortened the lance to stab straight down from his rearing mount.

The young trooper M'Telgez had disciplined for misloading stepped up on the other side and fired with his bayonet touching the Brigadero's armored torso. It didn't matter what he had up the spout at that range. The lancer pitched out of the saddle as the bullet punched in under his short ribs. The armor served only to flatten it before it buzzsawed up through liver, lungs and heart to lodge under his opposite shoulder. Blood shot out of his nose and mouth. He was dead before his corpse hit the ground with a clank of steel.

The dog was very much alive. Its huge paws stamped down on either side of the recumbent Descotter; they were furnished with claws and pads rather than a grazing animal's hoof, but they would still smash his ribs out through his spine if they landed. The great loose-jowled jaws were open as the beast shook its head in agony, splattering rainwater and blood from its cut tongue. The trooper shouted and drove his bayonet toward its neck as the fangs turned toward the man on the ground. The human's attack turned into a stumbling retreat as the dog whirled and snapped, the sound of its jaws like wood slapping on wood.

M'Telgez remembered his pistol. Most of the troopers had strapped the new weapons to holsters at their saddlebows—they were supposed to be for mounted melees. He'd stuffed his down the top of his riding boot when they dismounted, on impulse. Now he snatched it free and blazed away at the furry body above him, into the belly rear of the saddle's girth. The dog hunched up in the middle and ran, its rear paws just missing him as it staggered a dozen paces and fell thrashing.

"*Fastardos!*" he wheezed, picking up a dead man's rifle and loading as he rolled erect.

The Brigaderos were retreating across the swale, many of them on foot—dogs were bigger targets than men.

"Bastards!" M'Telgez fired, reloaded, fired again. "Bastards!"

Shots crackled out all down Company C's line, then the beginnings of volley-fire. It slammed into the retreating men, killing nearly as many as had died in the attack before they made it back to the dead ground behind their starting-point. The field gun elevated and began dropping shells behind the ridge, the gunners and half a dozen troopers as well slipping and sliding in the muck as they ran it back up the slight rise until the muzzle showed.

Return fire was coming in as well; retreat unmasked the Civil

Government line to the Brigaderos across the swale. M'Telgez went back to one knee as the minié bullets crackled overhead and jerked the trooper beside him by the tail of his jacket.

"Git yer head down, ye fool," he growled, looking around.

Not far away a man writhed with a broken-off lance through his gut, whimpering and pulling at the shaft. It jerked, but the steel was lodged in his pelvis far beyond the strength of blood-slippery hands to extract. Another fumbled at his belt for a cord to make a tourniquet; his arm was off above the elbow. The blood jetted more slowly as the man toppled over. M'Telgez knew there was nothing anyone could do for either of the poor bastards. When it was your time, it was time . . . and he was *very* glad it hadn't been his.

"Kid," he went on, as the young man obediently dropped to one knee and looked at him apprehensively. "Kid, yer all right."

"Will theyuns be back then, corp?" he asked.

M'Telgez wiped rain and blood out of his eyes—none of the blood his, thank the *Spirit.*

"Nao," he rasped.

The low ground ahead of him was thick with corpses of armored men and dogs. Particularly in front of the Company pennant; the Brigaderos had clumped there, driving for the center—and also for the gun, meeting point-blank blasts of case shot.

"Nao, they won't be back." He looked up and down the line. "Dressin'!" he barked sharply. What was left of his section moved to maintain their line.

M'Telgez grinned, an expression much like that the lancer's dog had worn when it lunged for his life. "Hoi, barbs!" he shouted at the distant enemy. "Got any messages fer yer wives? We'll be seein' 'em afore ye do!"

Cabot Clerett caught the bayonet on his sword. It was a socket bayonet, offset from a sleeve around the muzzle so that the musket could be loaded and rammed while it was fixed. Metal grated on metal; he fired into the Brigadero's body beneath their linked arms. The man pitched backward as the H-shaped wadcutter bullet put a small hole in his stomach and a much larger one in his back.

"Forward!" the governor's nephew said. "*Vihtoria O Muwerti!*" The motto of the Life Guards. Or victory *and* death, but nothing came free.

Braaaaap. The splatgun fired from not far behind, to his right. Bullets sprayed down the aisles between the trees; this was a planted oakwood, regular as a chessboard. About sixty or seventy years old, from the size of the trees, and regularly thinned as they grew. Water dripped down from the bare branches. Dim figures in gray-and-black uniforms were running back. A few paused to reload behind trees, but they were only protected from directly ahead. Life Guardsmen strung out to either side picked them off, mostly before they could complete the cumbersome process.

Men flanked him as he walked forward, the new bannerman holding the battalion flag. The company commander was out on the right flank with the other splatgun. He could hear it firing, trundled forward like the one with him to support the advance. Men walked on either side of him, reloading as they dodged the trees. They were cheering as they shot; the platoon commanders turned and flung out arms and swords to remind them to keep their line.

"Runner," Cabot said. "To Colonel Staenbridge; enemy were advancing in column on our right flank. I've driven them back and will shortly take them in enfilade all the way back to their original startline."

The splatguns *were* useful. It took less than ten seconds to replace each iron plate with thirty-five rounds in it, better than three hundred rounds a minute. With them and a hundred-odd riflemen, he would shortly be in a position to rake the front of the Brigaderos firing line from the right side and chop up any reserves they still held in the orchard.

Let that *marhicon* see how a Clerett managed a battle, by the Spirit!

"So we moved forward and caught them on the other side of the orchard as they tried to break contact," Staenbridge said. "Cut them up nicely, then pursued mounted, stopping occasionally to shoot them up again. They retreated to a large fortified manor house, which burned quite spectacularly when we shelled it, rain or no. The outbuildings had some very useful supplies, which will be arriving shortly at ox-wagon pace along with the noncombatants.

"Major Clerett," he went on, "led the right wing with skill and dash."

Raj nodded to the younger officer. "The supplies will be useful," he said. "Difficult to get enough in, when we're moving at speed."

He inclined his head downslope. Most of the troops were trudging by with their rifles slung muzzle-down; their boots had churned the fields on either side of the road into glutinous masses. Some of them were wearing local peasant moccasins; the thick mud rotted the thread out of issue boots and sucked off the soles. Further out the cavalry plodded on, stopping occasionally to scrape balls of mud off their mount's feet; the dogs whined and dragged, wanting to stop and groom. On the roadway itself men—infantry and military servants, with gunners acting as foremen—labored in mud even deeper, laying a corduroy surface of logs and beams. As the officers watched a gun-team came up with its draught chain looped around a hitch of fresh-cut logs. They rumbled down the slope to general curses as men dodged the timber.

"I hope," Raj went on, "that you kept me some Brigaderos prisoners of rank. We need more information about what's happening at Carson Barracks."

CHAPTER THREE

A hereditary officer from just west of the Waladavir River was speaking:

". . . a dozen farms and a village burned, my manor looted— only by the grace of the Spirit of Man of This Earth and the intervention of the Merciful Avatars did I and my household escape the devil Whitehall. What does His Mightiness intend to do about it?"

The Hall of Audience was lit by scores of tapers in iron sconces, above the racked battle lasers of antiquity. They cast unrestful shadow across the crowd that packed it, nearly a thousand men. Light glittered restlessly from swordhilts, from the jeweled hairclasp of one lord or the platinum beads on the jacket-fringe of another. The air was cold and dank with the autumn rains that fell outside, but it smelled powerfully of sauroid-fat candles and male sweat. An inarticulate growl rose from the crowd; these were each powerful men in their own right, nobles who commanded broad acres and hundreds of household troops.

Their like crowded Carson Barracks, filling housing blocks that usually echoed emptily at this time of year; the petty-squires and military vassals and freeholders who had come as well camped in the streets. Right now they filled the vast parade square outside the Palace. Crowd-noise came through the stone walls like an angry humm, occasionally breaking into a chant:

"Fight! Fight! Fight!"

General Forker rose from the Seat to reply. The light glittered coldly on the engraved silver of his ceremonial armor, and on the vestments of the Sysups and councilors grouped around his throne.

"We have suffered grievously with the sufferings of our subjects," he began.

A snarl rose from the crowd, and he swallowed nervously as he continued.

"That is why we have summoned you, my lords, to share your

council with Us. Our diplomacy at least delayed this attack, and now the rains are upon us, and winter comes on. We will have ample time to prepare—"

Another lord stalked into the speaker's position, on the floor below the Seat and just outside the line of Life Guards.

"We've *had* time; Stern Isle fell five months ago!" he bit out. "All we *did* was to throw High Colonel Strezman and his men into Lion City—just enough to hurt us if they were lost, and not enough to halt the enemy. Now Strezman and his men are dead!"

"Lord of Men," he went on, his tone cold, "you may not wish to campaign in winter but the enemy don't seem to share your delicate sensibilities. Whitehall is over the Waladavir, and his men have been sighted not three days' ride from Empirhado."

A roar swelled across the hall; the banners hanging from the rafters quivered.

"Rumors!"

"Truth!" the noble shouted back. "This is no raid, no border war for a province or an indemnity. The Civvies mean to grind us into dust the way they did the Squadron, kill us and take our lands, throw down our holy Church and enslave our women and children. They're coming, and the natives have already risen in half a dozen provinces."

A ripple of horror went through the hall. It was six hundred years since the Brigade came down out of the Base Area and conquered the Spanjol-speaking natives of the Civil Government's western territories, but the peoples were still distinct in blood and language and faith, and the natives were overwhelmingly in the majority. Like the Civil Government, they followed the cult of the Spirit of Man of The Stars, rather than of This Earth as the Brigade and its cousins did.

The nobleman turned his back on the Seat, a breach of protocol that stunned the watchers into silence.

"We need a fighting man to lead us. Not this book-reader who's plotting with the enemy behind our backs. I *move for impeachment.*"

Forker's face was working with rage and a trapped-beast fear. He forced his voice, turning it high and shrill.

"You are out of order. Arrest that man!"

The guards started forward, but a score of nobles grouped around the speaker drew their swords. The edges threw the light back as the heavy blades rose warningly.

"I am not out of order," the noble replied. "As Hereditary High Major, I have the right to call for impeachment before this assembly."

"I, Hereditary Brigade-Colonel Ingreid Manfrond, second the impeachment." Another man stepped into the speaker's circle, thickset and muscular and grizzled. "And place my name in nomination for the position of General of the Brigade."

"You!" Forker hissed. "You're not even of the House of Amalson."

"Collateral branch," Ingreid said. "But tomorrow I wed Marie Welf, daughter of General Welf—which makes my claim strong as iron." He turned to the assembly. "And as General, my first act will be to mobilize the host. My second will be to lead it to crush the invaders of our land!"

Forker signed to his guard. There was a pause, one that made the light parade breastplate feel as if it were squeezing his heart up into his mouth. Then they thumped their rifle-butts on the floor. It took a moment for the rumbling to quiet enough for him to speak.

"You lie, Ingreid Manfrond. The hand of Marie *Forker,* my step-daughter, is mine to give or withhold—and she rests content under the guard of *my* household troops."

Another man shouldered forward to stand beside Ingreid. "My name," he shouted in a commander's trained bellow, "is Colonel of Dragoons Howyrd Carstens. Forker lies. My own men guard Marie Welf, and she has agreed to marry our next General, Ingreid Manfrond—worthy heir to the great General Welf. And as bridal gift, she asks for the head of Filip Forker, murderer of her mother. Woman-killer and coward!"

He raised his sword. "Hail General Ingreid!"

"Hail! Hail! Hail!"

"I'd rather rut with a boar and farrow piglets!" Marie Welf shouted through the locked door.

She gripped the pistol more firmly. On either side of the door one of her gentlewomen waited, one with a tall brass candlestick in her grip, the other with a jewel-hilted but perfectly functional stiletto.

"Please, Mistress Fo—ah, Mistress Welf." The house steward's voice quavered, his Spanjol accent stronger than usual. "The soldiers say that you *must* open the door."

"I'll kill the first five men to step through it," Marie said. Nobody listening to her could doubt she would try.

Silence fell. Riding boots clumped on the parquet floors outside, and the strip of light under the door brightened as more lamps were brought.

"Marie, this is Teodore," a man called.

"What are you doing here, cousin?" Marie said.

She was a tall full-figured young woman, with strawberry blond hair in long braids on either side of a face that was beautiful rather than pretty, high cheek-boned and with a straight nose. Spots of anger burned on either cheek now, and she held the pistol with a practiced two-handed grip.

"Talking to you. And I'm not going to do it through a closed door. Watch out."

Shots blasted, and the brass plate of the lock bulged. A man yelled in pain in the corridor outside, and a chilly smile lit Marie's face. The door swung out, and a man stood there; in his mid-twenties, five years older than the woman. His bluntly handsome features were a near-match for hers under the downy blond beard, and he wore a cuirassier officer's armor. The plumed helmet was tucked under one arm, half-hidden by the deinonosauroid cloak that glittered in the lamplight. At the sight of her leveled pistol he spread the other arm away from his body.

"Shoot, cousin, if you want to see one less Welf in the world."

Marie sighed and let the pistol drop to the glowing Kurdish carpet. "Come in, Teodore," she said, and sank down to sit on one corner of the four-poster bed.

The ladies-in-waiting looked at her uncertainly. "Thank you, Dolors, Katrini—but you'd better go to your rooms now."

Teodore set his helmet down on a table and began working off his armored gauntlets. "You wouldn't have any wine, would you?" he asked. "Cursed cold night and wet besides; a coup is hard outdoor work."

She pointed wordlessly to a sideboard, and he smiled as he poured for both.

"You're making a very great deal of fuss about something you'll have to do anyway," he pointed out, handing her the glass and going to sit by the fire.

The velvet of the chair dimpled and stretched under the weight of his rain-streaked armor. The wall beside him held the fireplace, burning with a low coal blaze, and a bookshelf. That carried a respectable two dozen volumes; the Canonical Handbooks in Wulf Philson's Namerique translation, lives of the Avatars, and histories and travelogues in Spanjol and Sponglish.

"You'd fuss too if you'd been kept a prisoner since that beast murdered my mother," Marie said. The wine was Sala, strong and sweet. It seemed to coil around the fire in her chest.

"I was fond of Aunt Charlotte myself. 'That beast' is now off the Seat, and running for his life," Teodore pointed out. "Something which I had my hand in."

"Ingreid is a pig. And he supported Forker. I'm certain he was one of the ones who murdered Mother for that *coward*."

"That was never proven. And Ingreid is a *strong* pig," Teodore said, casting a quick look at the door. They were talking quietly, though, and he had told his men to move everyone down the corridor. "The fact that he supported Forker tells in his favor; the alternative was civil war. The alternative *now* is civil war, unless Ingreid Manfrond has an unassailable claim to the Seat. If you don't think that civil war is possible with invaders at the frontiers, then you've read less of our history than I thought." He waved at the bookcase.

"Can Ingreid read at all?" she said bitterly.

"No, probably," Teodore said frankly. "That'll make him all the more popular with the backwoods nobles, and the petty-squires and freeholders. Civvies will keep the accounts as usual, and he's got advisers like Carstens and—" he rapped his breastplate "—for the more complicated things. He can certainly lead a charge, which is more than you can say for that pseudo-scholar Forker."

He leaned forward, a serious expression on his face. "I'm ready to fight and die for him, as General. All you have to do is marry him."

"You aren't expected to go to *bed* with him, Teodore."

"There is that," the young man admitted. "But you'd have to marry somebody sometime; it's the way things are done at our rank."

"I'm a free woman of the Brigade; the law says I can't be married against my will," Marie said.

Teodore spread his hands. She nodded. "I know . . . but he smells. And *he's fifty.*"

"You'll outlive him, then," Teodore said. "Possibly as Regent for an underage heir. And you *will* marry him tomorrow. If necessary, with a trooper standing behind you twisting your arm. That won't be dignified, but it'll work."

"*You* would make a better General, cousin!"

"So I would, if I had the following," Teodore said. "So would you, if you were a man. But I haven't and you aren't. The enemy won't wait for me to acquire a majority, either."

"And how much will *my* life be worth, once I've produced a healthy heir?" Marie said. "Not to mention the question of his own sons, who'll have Regent ambitions of their own."

Teodore went to the door and checked that his cuirassier troopers were holding the servants at the end of the corridor.

"As to the heir," he said, leaning close to Marie's ear, "time will tell. In a year, the war will be over. Once the *grisuh* are back across the sea . . ."

Marie's eyes were cold as she set down the wineglass. "All right, Teodore," she said. "But listen to me and believe what I say: whatever I promise in the cathedron Ingreid Manfrond will get no love or loyalty from *me.* And he'll regret forcing me to this on the day he dies, and that will be soon. Spirit of Man of This Earth be my witness."

Teodore Welf had broken lances with Guard champions on the northwestern frontier, and fought the Stalwarts further east. He had killed two men in duels back home, as well.

At that moment, he was conscious mainly of a vast thankfulness that it was Ingreid Manfrond and not Teodore Welf who would stand beside Marie in the cathedron tomorrow.

Thunder rippled through the night, and rain streaked the diamond-pane windows of thick bubbled glass. Teodore looked away from his cousin.

"At least," he said, "the enemy won't be making much progress through *this*. We'll have time to get our house in order."

Thunder cracked over the ford. The light stabbed down into a midday darkness, off wet tossing trees and men's faces. Oxen bellowed as they leaned into the traces, trying to budge the gun mired hub-deep in the middle of the rising river; they even ignored the dogs of the regular hitch straining beside them. Dozens of infantrymen heaved at the barrel and wheels, gasping and choking as water broke over them. Others labored at the banks, throwing down loads of brush and gravel to keep the sloping surfaces passable. Wagon-teams bawled protestingly as they were led into the water; men waded through the waist-high brown flood with their rifles and cartridge-boxes held over their heads.

One of the work-crews was relieved, and stumbled upslope to the courtyard of the riverside inn.

"Wat's a name a' dis river?" one asked a noncom.

"Wolturno," the man mumbled, scraping mud off his face. It was a winding stream, meandering back and forth across the flood-plain where the road ran. The Expeditionary Force had already crossed it several times.

"Ever' fukkin' river here is named Wolturno," the soldier said. They slouched into lines before the kettles.

"Thank'ee, miss," the infantryman said, taking his bowl and cup.

He stumbled off a few paces to crouch in the lee of a wagon, spooning up the stew of beans and cubed bacon and taking mouthfuls of the cornbread bannock. More of his squadmates crowded through beneath the awnings to the bubbling cauldrons; like him they were dripping with more than the slashing rain, and so filthy it was hard to see the patches and tears in their uniforms; one was wrapped completely in a shrouding of earth-stained peasant blankets.

Fatima cor Staenbridge—*cor* meant freedwoman, and the name was her former master's—filled the ladle again and swung it out to the outstretched bowl.

"Not much, but it's hot," she said cheerfully. Rain leaked down through the makeshift awning, but most of it ran off the thick wool of the hooded cloak she wore. "Take all you can eat, soldier, eat all you take."

"Bettah dan whut we eaat a' hume," the footsoldier said, in a thick peasant dialect of Sponglish she couldn't place. There were so many. From the looks of his thin young face, the young peon conscript probably hadn't eaten this well before the Army press-gangs swept him up. "Yu an angel, missa."

Mitchi plunked a hunk of cornbread on his bowl, and took his cup to dip it in a vat of hot cider.

"Thank Messa Whitehall, she organized it," she said.

Dozens of the cauldrons were cooking in the courtyard, hauled from the inn kitchens and from houses nearby. Army servants, women—even wives, in a few cases—and miscellaneous clergy carried out fresh loads of ingredients and dumped them in to cook. Rations were issued when there were no markets, but each eight-man squad of soldiers was generally supposed to cook for themselves—that was one of the duties military servants did for the cavalry troopers. Today that would have meant hardtack and cold water for the infantry laboring to keep the ford passable, without Lady Suzette Whitehall rounding up camp-followers and supplies for this. And there would be the usual camp to build at the end of the day's march, with wet firewood and sopping bedding. Exhausted men forgot to take care for themselves and let sickness in.

"Messer Rahj an' his lady, dey sent by de Spirit," the soldier blurted. His face was pinched and stubbled. "Dey treet de commun sojur right, not jus' dog-boys."

The men were too tired for enthusiasm, but they nodded and muttered agreement as they shuffled forward. Fatima swung the ladle until it was scraping the bottom of the cauldron.

"Take all you can eat, eat all you can—Messer Raj!"

"Thank you, Fatima," he said.

The mud was mainly below the swordbelt, his uniform and boots were sound, and he wore one of the warm rainproof cloaks. Apart from that he looked nearly as exhausted as the infantrymen who'd been shoveling stone and hauling brushwood to the ford. The other officers with him looked no better. A low murmur went through the courtyard as he was recognized, but the men kept to their scraps of shelter at a half-gesture from one hand.

Cabot Clerett looked dubiously at the bowl. The others started shovelling theirs down unconcerned. "I hope there's something better at the end of the day," he said.

Fatima stood aside as more helpers staggered up with pails of well-water, sacks of beans and half a keg of the chopped bacon. The Renunciate leading them tossed in a double handful of salt and some dried chilis. The cauldron hissed slightly as the ingredients went in, and one of the servants dumped more coal on the embers beneath.

"Messa Whitehall said," Fatima put in, "that the headquarters cook had found a lamb, and some fresh bread."

"Something to look forward to." That was Major Peydro Belagez of the Rogor Slashers. "By the Spirit, *mi heneral*, before I met you I spent fifteen uneventful years patrolling the Drangosh border and fighting the Colonials once every two months. The sun shone, and between patrols I lay beneath orange trees while girls dropped nougat into my mouth. Now look at me! *Mi mahtre* warned me of the consequences of falling into bad company—Malash, she was right."

The major from the southern borders was a slight man in his late thirties, naturally dark and leathery with years of savage desert suns and windstorms, wearing a pointed goatee and a gold ring in one ear. His grin was easy and friendly; Fatima swallowed as she remembered the same pleasant expression last year after Mekkle Thiddo, the Companion who commanded the Slashers, was killed under flag of truce, and Belagez rounded up the men responsible, even in the chaos of the pursuit after the Squadron host was broken. Raj had ordered them crucified, but Belagez had seen to the details, even to having the victims' feet twisted up under their buttocks before they were spiked to the wood. A man lived much longer that way, before asphyxiation and shock killed him.

She had never felt easy around Borderers; the feuds along the frontier between Colony and Civil Government were too old and bitter. Fatima had hated her father, the Caid of El Djem . . . but she remembered too well how he had died, in a huge pool of blood with a Borderer dancing in glee around him, the jiggling sack of the old man's scrotum impaled on the curved knife which slashed it free.

Belagez' smile was innocent as he glanced at her. She was the woman of a friend, and so he would cheerfully face death to defend her.

"Messa Whitehall says she found some good wine, too," Fatima went on.

For that matter, the 5th Descott would fight for her now—and they were the men who'd burned her home and would have gang-raped her, if she hadn't managed to get Gerrin and Bartin Foley to protect her. *Life is strange.* From despised minor concubine's daughter to slave to a freedwoman and mother of the acknowledged son of a wealthy Civil Government nobleman-officer in a year . . . of course, the child could have been Bartin's, just as likely. But Gerrin had adopted it, and he had no other heir. Messer Raj and his lady had stood Starparents.

"If it does not pucker the mouth to drink it," Belagez said. "Spirit, the wine here is even more sour than that dog-piss you northerners like—which I had not believed possible."

Kaltin Gruder grinned. "You mean it's not syrup like that stuff they make south of the Oxheads," he said. "Too sweet to drink and too thick to piss, no wonder you cut it with water."

Raj finished his mug of cider and sighed, wiping his mouth on the back of his hand. "Well, Messers," he said. "No rest for the wicked. I've an uneasy suspicion that some of the Brigaderos at least realize we're not going to curl up somewhere cozy in front of the fire until the rains stop."

"Those who aren't too busy dealing with each other," Bartin Foley said. He handed his bowl back to Fatima with a smile of thanks.

"Even if most are politicking, that leaves an uncomfortable number otherwise employed," Raj said. "Gerrin, you have the main column for the rest of the day. Major Clerett, you and I will—"

✧   ✧   ✧

Filip Forker, ex-General and no longer Lord of Men, stuck his head out the window of the carriage.

"Faster!" he said, coughing into a handkerchief. *What a time to have a headcold,* he thought.

The road northwest from Carson Barracks had been paved once, very long ago. Even now chunks of ancient concrete made the light travelling coach jounce as it rocked forward through a dense fog. Moisture glittered in the moonlight on the long white fur of the wolfhounds and streaked the carriage windows. There was a spare hitch behind, another carriage with his mistress and the essential baggage, a light two-wheel wagon for the gear, and an escort . . . although the escort was smaller than it had been a few hours ago. Much smaller than it had been when they left the city, although he had promised rich rewards to any who stayed with him until they reached his estates on the Kosta dil Orhenne in the far west.

Some would stay, because they had eaten his salt. There was a bitterness to seeing how few felt bound to him.

"Why aren't you going faster?" he called to the driver.

"It's dark, master, and the road is rough," the man replied.

Even his tone had changed, although he wore an iron collar and Forker had the same power of life and death over him that he'd had before his impeachment. For a moment Forker was tempted to order him shot right now, simply to demonstrate that—but he had few enough servants along. Let a flogging wait until he reached his estates, among the Forker family's military vassals. He would be secure there. . . .

Men rode across the road a hundred meters ahead. They were wrapped in dark cloaks, but most of them held rifles with the butts resting on their thighs. The clump at their head had naked swords, cold starlight on the edged metal.

Forker swallowed vomit. He mopped at his raw nose and looked wildly about. More were riding out behind him, out of the eerie forest of native whipstick trees that covered the land on either side. The officer of his household troopers barked orders to the handful of guards who'd remained, and they closed in around the carriages, pulling the rifle-muskets from their scabbards. Hammers clicked as thumbs pulled them back, the sound loud and metallic in the insect-murmurous night.

"Halt," the leader of the cloaked men said.

"In . . ." Forker began, hacked, spat, spoke again: "Ingreid Manfrond promised me my life!"

"Oh, General Manfrond didn't send me to kill you," the man said, grinning in his beard. "The Lord of Men just told me where I could find you. Killing you was my own idea. Don't you remember me? Hereditary Captain Otto Witton."

He rode close enough so that the riding lanterns on the coach showed the long white scar that ran up the left side of his face until it vanished under his hairline. It was flushed red with emotion. His dog crouched, and he stepped free.

"Just a little matter of wardship of my cousin's daughter Kathe Mattiwson—and her lands—and she was promised to *me,* and she wanted *me,* you bastard. But *you* assumed the wardship and sold her like a pig at a fair, to that son of a bitch Sliker. Get *out* of there."

Forker found himself climbing down to the roadway without conscious decision. Thin mud sucked at the soles of his gold-topped tasseled boots.

"An, ah, an honorable marriage—"

"Shut up, you little shit!" Witton screamed. The scar was white against his red face, and his sword hissed out. "Now you're going to *die."*

The houseguard captain stepped between them. "Over my dead body," he said, calmly enough. The tip of his own sword touched the roadway, but his body was tensed for action the way a cat's does, loose-jointed. There were hammered-out dents in his breastplate, the sort a full-armed sword cut makes.

"If that's how you want it," Witton said.

He looked to the men sitting their dogs around the carriage. "But it'd be a pity, the Brigade needs all the fighting men it can get— this little Civvie-lover will be no loss, though."

"The Brigade doesn't need men who'd let their sworn lord be cut down by thirty enemies on the road," the retainer said. "He may be a cowardly little shit, but we ate his salt."

It said a good deal for the situation that Filip Forker ignored the comment. Instead he squealed: "That's right—my life is your honor! Save me and I'll give you half my lands."

The captain looked over his shoulder at Forker, expressionless. Then he turned back to Witton.

"A man lives as long as he lives, and not a day more," he said. "Sorry to miss the war with the Civvies, though."

"You don't have to," Witton said. This time his grin was sly. "An oath to a man without honor is no oath. We won't overfall your gold-giver with numbers. I'll challenge him here and now; you can be witness to a fair fight."

He stepped closer and spat on Forker's boot. "I call you coward and your father a coward, and your mother a whore," he said. "You've got a sword."

The guard captain stepped back, his face clearing. Both men were wearing blades, neither had armor, and they were close enough in age. If the former monarch was weedy and thin-wristed while Witton looked as if he could bend iron bars between his fingers, that was *Forker's* problem; he should have been in the salle d'armes instead of the library all those years.

Forker looked around; the code said a man could volunteer to fight in his place, but it wasn't an obligation. Some of his men were smiling, others looking away into the night. None of them spoke.

"It's time," Witton said, thick and gloating. He raised the blade. "Draw or die like a steer in a slaughter chute."

"Marcy!" Forker screamed, falling to his knees. There was a sharp ammonia stink as his bladder released. "*Marcy, migo!* Spare me— spare my life and everything I have is yours."

Witton's smile turned into a grimace of hatred. Forker shrieked and threw up his arms. One of them parted at the elbow on the second stroke of Witton's earnest, clumsy butchery. The stump of the arm flailed about, spurting blood that looked black in the silvery light. That jerked the attacker back to consciousness, and his next blow was directed with skill as well as the strength of shoulders as thick as a blacksmith's.

"Book-reader," the warrior said with contempt, standing back and panting. Thick drops of blood ran down his face and into his beard, speckling the front of his fringed leather jacket.

The dead man's servants came forward to wrap the body; it leaked blood and other fluids through the rug they rolled it in. Forker's mistress looked on from the second carriage; she raised the fur muff that concealed her hands to her lips and stared speculatively over it at the guard captain and the heavy-set assassin.

Witton spoke first. "I hope you don't feel obliged to challenge," he said to the guardsman.

The retainer shrugged. "We were contracted, not vassals. He fell on his own deeds." A wintry smile. "I guess there won't be much trouble finding a new berth for me and my guns."

His expression grew colder. "Although if I catch those pussies who bugged out before we got this far, I don't think they'll ever need another gear-and-maintenance contract as long as they live."

The fog had turned to a light drizzle. Witton lofted a gobbet of spit toward the body the servants were pushing into the carriage. The wolfhounds in the traces whined and twitched at the smells of blood and tension, until the driver flicked his whip over their backs.

"Can't blame them for not wanting to fight for Forker," he said.

"*Fuck* Forker," the guard captain said. "My contract was with him, but theirs was with *me.*"

Witton nodded. "You can sign up with my lot," he said. "I'm down twenty rifles on my assigned war-host tally."

The guardsman shook his head. "Wouldn't look good," he said. Witton grunted agreement; a mercenary's reputation was his livelihood. "We'll head back to Carson Barracks, somebody'll sign us on for the duration, maybe the Regulars. Figure the call-up'll come pretty soon anyway, might as well beat the rush."

He turned and called orders. His men eased back the hammers

of their rifles and slid them into the scabbards on the left side of their saddles. There was a moment's pause as one man bent in the saddle and grabbed the bridle of the dogs pulling the baggage wagon, turning it around, and then the fading *plop* of their dogs' paws.

Witton waved the carriage with Forker's body onward. They'd take it back to his ancestral estates for burial, although even in this cool weather it'd be pretty high by then. He had no problem with that, after his second-in-command down the road made a search for the getaway chest with the money and jewels Forker would undoubtedly have been carrying. He looked up at the second carriage. The woman there lowered the fur that hid her face and gave him a long smile. The maid cowering beside her was obviously terrified, but Forker's ex-mistress was a professional too, in her way. Huge violet-colored eyes blinked at him, frosted in the fog-blurred light of the moons.

And quite spectacular. Well, the little bastard *had* been General, no reason he should settle for less than the best. He wiped at his face, smearing the blood, and smiled back while his hands automatically cleaned and sheathed his sword.

"This should be very useful indeed," Raj said.

The estate was well off from the army's line of march, in a district of rolling chalk hills. There was little cultivation, but the ground was mostly covered with dense springy green turf, and grazed by huge herds of sheep and large ones of cattle; pigs fed in the beechwoods on the steeper slopes. Evidently the land hereabouts was held in big ranching estates and yeoman-sized grazing farms rather than let to sharecroppers; the manor they'd just taken was surrounded by outbuildings, great woolsheds and corrals and smokehouses, a water-powered scouring mill for cleaning wool and an odorous tannery off a kilometer or so. The cured bacon and barreled salt beef and mutton would be very welcome. The herds would be even more so, since they could walk back to the main force.

The bolts of woolen cloth woven in the long sheds attached to the peon village would be more welcome still. It wasn't raining right now here, and the soil was free-draining. The air was crisp, though, the breath of men and dogs showing—and a lot of his soldiers were patching their pants with looted bed-curtains. This area would give every man in the army another blanket, which might make the difference between health and pneumonia for many. Enough for jacket-linings too, if there were time and seamstresses.

"I hope everything is satisfactory, sir," Cabot Clerett replied. The *of course it is* and *why are you meddling?* were unspoken.

Cabot Clerett's respect for Raj's abilities as a commander was grudging but real.

"Quite satisfactory," Raj replied. *I'm glad I don't hate anyone that much,* he added to himself.

only partly hatred, Center's pedantic machine-voice said in his mind. **a large element of fear, envy and jealousy as well.**

Tell me, Raj thought.

Cabot envied everything from Raj's military reputation to his wife. Suzette could play him like a violin, of course, and that was probably all that had kept Cabot from goading his uncle into a disastrous recall order for Raj. Not that it would take much goading; Barholm Clerett's paranoia went well beyond the standard Gubernatorial suspicion of a successful commander.

That doesn't mean I have to like it, Raj thought. Then: *back to the work of the day.*

The lord of the estate had surrendered promptly and been given receipts for the supplies the 1st Life Guards were methodically stripping from the barns and storehouses. Clerett's men seemed to be well in hand; they were helping the estate's serfs load the wagons, and keeping the lined-up manor staff under their guns, but nothing more. Undoubtedly a few small valuables would disappear, not to mention chickens, but nothing in the way of rape, arson or murder was going on. Pickets were posted, keeping the surroundings under observation. . . .

Raj's eyes passed over the lord of the manor, a stout Brigadero in late middle age, standing and ignoring the troopers guarding him with a contemptuous expression. It was mirrored on the hatchet-faced, well-dressed matron at his side. Three younger women with children looked only slightly more apprehensive. One twelve-year-old boy with his tow colored hair just now grown to warrior length and caught with a clasp at his neck glared at the Civil Government commander with open hatred. More Brigadero women and children clustered in the windows of the manor, or in medium-sized cottages separate from the peon huts.

"Right, we'll pull out," Raj said.

It took considerable time to get the wagons and bleating, milling, mooing herds moving down to the road that rolled white through the chalk hills. From the look of the grass, and the iron-gray clouds rolling overhead, there had been as much rain here as in the valley where the army toiled south toward Old Residence. The chalk soil didn't vanish into mud the way bottomland clay did, since it was free-draining, but it would be awkward enough. Many of the Life Guard troopers had been *vakaros* back in Descott or the other inland Counties; they swung whips and lariats and yipped around the fringes of the herds.

"What bothers me is where all the men are," Raj said. "Not just here, but the last couple of manors in this area and the bigger farms."

The two officers rode at the head of a company column of the 1st upslope from the road, out of the milling chaos of the drive and the heavy stink of liquid sheep feces. Other columns flanked the convoy as it drove downward.

"Well, they've been mobilized," Clerett said.

Raj nodded; that was the first thing Ingreid had done after he took the Seat. The rally-point named was Carson Barracks, in the circulars they'd captured.

"That might be where the nobles' household troops have gone," he said. "I don't think they need big garrisons here to keep the natives in line."

The peons in the manors had looked notably better fed and more hostile to the Civil Government troops than most they'd seen. Herding is less labor-intensive than staple agriculture, and produces more per hand although much less per hectare.

"The problem is," Raj went on, "that this *is* a grazing district."

Clerett looked at him suspiciously. Raj amplified: "It's too thinly peopled to shoot the carnosauroids out," he said.

The younger man nodded impatiently. "Lots of sign," he said.

Strop-marks on trees, where sicklefeet stood on one leg to hone the dewclaw that gave them their name. There had been a cerato-sauroid skull nailed over a barn door at the last manor, too: a meter long counting the characteristic nose-horn, and the beast would be two meters at the shoulder, when it ran after prey with head and tail stretched out horizontally over the long striding bipedal legs. Shreds of flesh and red-and-gray pebbled hide had clung to the skull.

"Nice string of sicklefoot dewclaws beneath it," Raj went on. "You're a Descotter too, Major." *More of one than Barholm,* he thought.

The Governor had spent almost his whole life in East Residence, while Cabot stayed home in the hills to keep the Cleretts' relations with the Descott gentry warm. It was no accident that the County which provided a quarter of the elite cavalry also supplied the last two Governors.

Clerett's face changed. "Vakaros," he said. *Cowboys.*

Raj nodded. Ranching meant predator control on Bellevue; and giving rifles and riding-dogs to slaves or peons and sending them out to ride herd was a *bad* idea, generally speaking. Most of the bond-labor at the estate they'd just left had been there for processing work, putting up preserved meats, tanning hides, and weaving, plus gardening and general chores. There had been a number of barracks and cottages and empty stables surplus to peon requirements, and a lot of Brigaderos women of the commoner class. The herdsmen were gone.

"That's why all the estate-owners here seem to be Brigaderos." In most of the country they'd passed through the land was fairly evenly divided between Brigade and civilian. "Brigade law forbids arming civilians. I don't think they enforce it all that strictly, but most of the vakaros—whatever they call them here—would be Brigaderos as well."

And there was no better training for light-cavalry work. Keeping something like a ceratosauroid or a sicklefoot pack off the stock tested alertness, teamwork, riding and marksmanship all at once. Not to mention fieldcraft and stalking.

"Shall I spread the scout-net out wider?" Cabot said.

Raj stood in the stirrups and gave the surroundings a glance. None of the canyons and badlands and gully-sided volcanoes that made much of Descott County a bushwacker's paradise, but the bigger patches of beechwood and the occasional steep-sided combe in thick native brush would do as well.

"I think that would be a very good idea, Major Clerett," he said.

Marie Welf—Marie Manfrond now—lay silent and motionless as Ingreid rolled off her. The only movement was the rise and fall of her chest, more rapid now with the weight off; she lay on her back with her hands braced against the headboard of the bed and her legs spread. Blood stained the sheet beneath the junction of her thighs, and some of the scented olive oil discreetly left on the nightstand, which had proven to be necessary. The high coffered ceiling of the General's private quarters was covered with gold leaf and the walls with mosaic; they cast the flame of the single coal-oil lamp over the bed back in yellow lambency.

Naked, Ingreid's paunch and graying body-hair were more obvious, but that simply emphasized the troll strength of his blocky shoulders. His body was seamed with scars, particularly down the left side and on the lower arms and legs. Puckered bullet wounds, long white fissures from swords, a deep gouge on one thigh where a lancepoint had taken out a chunk of meat when it hammered through the tasset. Neck and hip and joints were calloused where his armor rested, and there was a groove across his forehead from the lining of a helmet. Strong teeth showed yellow as he smiled at her and raised a decanter from the bedside table.

"Drink?" he said. Marie remained silent, staring at the ceiling.

"Well, then I will," he said, splashing the brandy into a glass. The ends of his long hair stuck to his glistening shoulders, and his sweat smelled sourly of wine and beer.

He wiped himself on a corner of the satin sheets and got up, moving about restlessly, picking up objects and putting them down. After a moment he turned back to the bed.

"Not so bad, eh? You'll get better when you're used to it."

Marie's head turned and looked at him silently. The eyes were as empty of expression as her face. Ingreid flushed.

"You'd better," he said, gulping down the brandy. "I was supposed to marry a woman, not a corpse."

Marie spoke, her voice remote. "You got what you bargained for. That's all you're getting."

"Is it, girlie?" Ingreid's flush went deeper, turning his face red-purple under the weathering. "We'll see about that."

He threw the glass aside to bounce and roll on the carpets, then jerked her head up by her hair. His hand went *crack* against her face, the palm hard as a board. She jerked and rolled to the edge of the bed, her long blond hair hiding her face. Then her head came up, the green eyes holding the same flat expression despite the red handmark blazing on her cheek.

"I've got better things to do than teach you manners, bitch," Ingreid snarled. "For now. When the war's won, I'll have time."

He threw on a robe. Marie waited until he had slammed out the door until she stood as well, moving carefully against the pain of pulled muscles and the pain between her legs. A servant would come if she pulled one of the cords, but right now even such a faceless nonentity would be more than she could face. She walked into the bathroom and turned up the lamp by the door, looking at herself in the full-length mirror without blinking, then opened the taps to fill the seashell-shaped bath of marble and gold. Hot water steamed; the General's quarters had all the luxuries. It wasn't until the bath was full and foaming with scented bubble soap that she realized it was the same tub that her mother had been drowned in.

She managed to make it to the toilet before she started vomiting. When her stomach was empty she wiped her face and stepped into the bath anyway. She would need all her strength in the days ahead.

"That was too easy," Raj said, resting his helmet on his saddlebow. *And for once, it isn't raining.* The breath of men and dogs showed in frosty clouds, but the sun was bright in a morning sky.

The little town of Pozadas lay at the junction of the chalk downs and the lower clay plain; it had no wall, although the church and a few of the larger houses would have done as refuges against bandits or raiders. So would some of the mills along the river. They were built of soft gold-colored limestone; napping and scutching mills and dye-works for woolen cloth, mostly. The town had many cottages where weavers worked hand-looms and leatherworkers made boots and harness. Wisely, the citizens had offered no resistance, but they were sullen even though the Civil Government had paid in looted gold for most of what it took.

It was a prosperous town for its size; the town hall was new and quite modern, with large glass windows below and an open balcony on the second story, overlooking the roofs of the other buildings.

"Glum-looking bastards," Cabot said, rising in the saddle to look over Raj's shoulder.

Few were on the streets—the troops and the huge herds of livestock they were driving through the main road took up too much room—but there were scowls on the faces peering from windows and doorways.

"Not surprising," Raj said.

He nodded to a vast bleating mat of gray-and-white sheep churning up the chalky flint-studded dirt of the street; it moved like a shaggy blanket, with an occasional individual popping up, struggling for a few steps across its neighbors' backs, and then dropping back into the press. There was a heavy barnyard odor, overwhelming the usual outhouse and chemical reek of a cloth-making town.

"We're taking their livelihood," the general went on. "It'll take years for the herds back there—" he inclined his head back toward the downland they'd just finished sweeping "—to breed back up again. That's assuming that things don't get so disrupted the carnosauroids finish off the breeding stock we left. In the meantime, what'll they do for wool and hides?"

A large army was like a moving suction-machine; his was travelling fast enough that it wouldn't leave famine in its wake, but nobody else would be able to move troops along the same route anytime soon.

"I still wonder where all those men went," Raj said meditatively.

Cabot drew his pistol and pointed it. Raj threw himself flat in the saddle, and the bullet cracked where he had been.

Horace whirled in less than his own length, paws skidding slightly on the sheep-dung coated mud of the street. The Brigadero who'd been behind him pitched backward with a third hole in line with his eyebrows, his floppy-brimmed hat spinning off. There were a dozen more behind him, some still charging out of the opened doors of the town hall courtyard, and more on foot behind them. Still more on balconies and rooftops, rising to fire. Shots crackled through the streets and men screamed, dogs howled, and the bleating of berserk sheep was even louder as the near-witless animals scattered in all directions into alleys and squares and through open doors and windows.

"*Thanks!*" Raj shouted. *Now I know where the herdsmen went.*

The man behind him had a sword raised for a sweeping over-arm cut. Raj dodged under it as Horace bounced forward, his saber up and back along his spine; the swords met with an unmusical crash and skirl, and he uncoiled, slashing a third Brigadero across the face. Then his personal escort had faced about and met the rest, shooting and stabbing in a melee around Raj and Cabot and their bannermen. More Brigaderos were charging out of the mills. Raj scanned the housetops. A couple of hundred enemy, and they'd found the best way to hide the scent of their dogs; in the middle of a textile town, with thousands of livestock jamming through it.

Bloody Starless Dark, he thought disgustedly. Another cock-up because he hadn't enough troops to nail things down.

The problem with relying on speed and intimidation was that some people just didn't intimidate worth a damn.

"Rally south of town," he shouted to Cabot Clerett. "Spread out, don't let them get back into the hills. Pin them against the river as you come in."

"They'll swim the stream and scatter," the younger man replied.

Raj gave a feral grin. "Not for long," he said. "Get moving!"

The major jerked a nod, wheeling his dog and waving his pistol forward. His bannerman fell in beside him, and the trumpeter sounded *retreat-rally* as they pounded south, toward the spot where the Civil Government column had entered the town. Men fought free of the herds and plunder-wagons and joined him in clumps and units. Some fell, but everyone understood the need to break contact until they could rally and unite. If they stood, the prepared enemy would cut them up into penny packets and slaughter them.

"Follow me!" Raj barked.

His escort had taken care of the first Brigaderos to attack, but even as he spoke he saw a man and a dog go down. A bullet cracked by his head with an unpleasant puff of wind against his cheek, which was *entirely* too close. He had a full platoon of the 5th Descott with him, beside messengers and aides. That ought to be enough.

He pointed his saber at the town hall and clapped his heels to Horaces flanks. The hound took off from bunched hindquarters, travelling across the muddy sheep-littered plaza in a series of bounds that put them at chest-height from the ground half a dozen times. As he'd expected, that threw off the marksmen; they'd been expecting the troops they ambushed to mill around, or try to return fire from street level. *Never do what they expect.*

Thirty dogs pounded up the stairs to the arcaded verandah of the hall. A final crackle—too ragged to be a volley—at point-blank range knocked another six down. Smoke puffed into their faces, blinding them for an instant. Then they were scrabbling across the smooth tile of the portico and crashing through tall windows in showers of glass and the yelping of cut dogs. Horace reared and struck the big double doors with his forepaws. A jolt went through Raj's body, and he felt his teeth clack once like castanets; something seemed to snap behind his eyes.

The doors boomed open, crushing bone and tearing men off their feet. Horace's jaws closed over the face of another; the inch-long fangs sank in, and the hound made a rat-killing flip that sent the body pinwheeling back in a spray of blood. There were thirty or forty Brigaderos in the big reception hall that backed the portico; from their looks, he'd found the missing herdsmen. With another twenty-five riding dogs, the place was crowded, too crowded for the enemy to recharge their muzzle-loaders. Some of them clubbed muskets, but most drew swords or fighting-knives. Raj's men emptied their revolvers into the press and swept out their sabers. The dogs stamped on men trying to roll under their bellies and cut, snapped with fangs and hammered with their forepaws.

A Brigadero dodged in and cut at Raj's left thigh, always

vulnerable in a mounted man. Horace spun on one leg, and Raj stabbed down over the saddle. The blow was at an awkward angle, but it sank into the bicep of the man's sword-arm. His weapon flew free as Raj jerked his steel free of the ripped muscle; then a Descotter wardog closed its jaws in his back and threw him over its shoulder with a snap. Raj lashed back to his right with a backhand cut across the neck of a man trying to come in on his bannerman's rear. The man with the flag had a revolver in his right hand; he was keeping his mount stock-still with a toe-to-foreleg signal and picking his targets carefully.

A last shot barked out. Powder-smoke was drifting to the ceiling; a few more men in blue jackets and maroon pants ran in, troopers whose dogs had been hit outside. As always, the melee was over with shocking suddenness. One instant there were shots and screams and the blacksmith chorus of steel on steel, the next only the moans of the wounded and the quick butcher's-cleaver sounds of troopers finishing off the enemy fallen.

"Dismount!" Raj barked. "Dogs on guard."

Horace pricked up his floppy ears at the word. So did the other mounts as the men slid to the ground, drawing their rifles from the saddle scabbards. Anyone trying to get into the ground floor was going to have a very nasty surprise.

"Walking wounded cover the front entrance," Raj went on. They could bandage themselves and the more severely hurt as well. "The rest of you, fix bayonets and follow me."

He switched his saber for an instant, juggled weapons to put his revolver in his left hand, and led the rush up his half of the curving double staircase with the lieutenant of the escort platoon on the other. Marksmen dropped out halfway up to cover the top of the stairs, firing over their comrades' heads. Hobnails and heel-plates clamored and sparked on the limestone. Center's aiming-grid dropped over his sight . . . which was a bad sign, because that only happened in desperate situations. No time for thought, only a quick, fluid feeling of total awareness. Everyone crouched as they neared the top of the stairs; he signed right and left to the men whose bayonet-tips he could see on either side.

"Now!"

The bannerman dropped flat two steps down, jerking the flag erect and waving it back and forth. The Brigaderos waiting in the upper hallway behind an improvised barricade of tables reacted exactly the way Raj had expected. The pole jumped in the bannerman's hands as a bullet took a piece out of the ebony staff and others plucked through the heavy silk of the banner itself. Raj and the leading riflemen crouched below the lip of the stairs as minié bullets and pistol rounds blasted at the top step. Time seemed to slow as he raised his head and left hand.

Green light strobed around a man with a revolver, aiming between

the slats of a chair. Maximum priority. *Crack*. He pitched backward
with a bullet through the neck, his scrabbling spraying body fouling several others. Raj fired as quickly as his wrist could move the
dot of the aimpoint to the next glowing target, emptying the five-
shot cylinder in less time than it took to take a deep breath. Much
more of this and he'd get a reputation as a pistol-expert on top of
everything else. As he dropped back under the topmost step four
men levelled their rifles over it and fired. The heavy 11mm bullets
hammered right through the barricade; the four ducked back
down to reload, and another set a few steps lower down stood
to fire over their heads. The sound echoed back off the close stone
walls, thunder-loud.

Not a maneuver in the drill-book, but these were veterans. He
shook the spent brass out of the revolver and reloaded, judging the
volume of return fire.

"Once more and at 'em," he said. *"Now."*

They stood to charge. A man beside Raj took a bullet through
the belly, folding over with an *oof* and falling backward to tumble
and cartwheel down the stairs. Troopers behind him shouldered
forward; all the Brigaderos behind the improvised barricade were
badly wounded, but that didn't mean none of them could fight. There
was a brief scurry of point-blank shots and bayonet thrusts.

Raj stood thinking as the soldiers searched the rooms on either side
of the corridor, swift but cautious. No more shots . . . except from
outside, where the steady crackle was building up again. His eyes fell
on an unlit lamp. It was one of a series in brackets along the wall.
Much like one back home; a globular glass reservoir below for the
coal-oil, and a coiled flat-woven wick of cotton inside adjusted by a
small brass screw, with a blown-glass chimney above.

"Sergeant," Raj called, stepping over a dead Brigadero.

The blood pooled around the enemy fallen stained his bootsoles,
so that he left tacky footprints on the parquet of the hallway. Light
fell in from rose-shaped windows at either end of the hallway.

"Get those lamps, all of them," he said.

"Ser?" The noncom gaped.

"*All* of them, and there should be more in a storage cupboard
somewhere near. Distribute them to the windows. Quickly!" The
trooper dashed off; the order made no sense, but he'd see it was
obeyed, quickly and efficiently.

"Lieutenant," Raj went on. The young man looked up from tying
off a rough bandage around his calf.

"Mi heneral?"

"A squad to each of the main windows, if you please. Send someone
for extra ammunition from the saddlebags."

"Sir."

"And check how many men able to shoot there are below. Send
some troopers to help them barricade the doors and windows."

"Ci, mi heneral."

He led his own small group of messengers and bannerman through the room opposite the staircase. It looked to be some sort of meeting chamber, with a long table and chairs, and crossed banners on the wall. One was the crimson-and-black double thunderbolt of the Brigade, the other a local blazon.

"Get the table," he said. "Follow me out."

The balcony outside ran the length of the front of the building, wrought-iron work on a stone base. The signallers came out grunting under the weight of the heavy oak table, and dropped it with a crash on its side and up against the railings. They dropped behind it with grateful speed, as riflemen in windows and rooftops across from them opened fire. Luckily, nothing overlooked the town hall except the tower of the church, and it was too open to make a good marksman's stand. Other squads were bringing out furniture of their own, some from the Brigaderos' own barricade at the head of the stairs.

"Keep them busy, lads," Raj said.

A steady crackle of aimed shots broke out; along the balcony, from the windows at either end of the hallway behind, and from the smaller windows on the rear side of the town hall. Raj took out his binoculars. A cold smile bent his lips; the enemy seemed to be coming out into the streets and milling around in surprise, mostly—even a few townspeople joining them.

Amateurs, he thought.

Tough ones, good individual fighters, but whoever was commanding them didn't have the organization to switch plans quickly when the first one went sour. That was the problem with a good plan—and it had been a cunningly conceived ambush—it tended to hypnotize you. If you didn't have anything ready for its miscarriage, you lost time. And time was the most precious thing of all.

South of the town the Life Guards were deploying, just out of rifle range. Dogs to the rear, extended double line, one company in the saddle for quick reaction; right out of the manuals. Also the guns. Four of them, and the first was getting ready to—

POUMPF. The shell went overhead with a whirring moan and crashed into one of the mills. Black smoke and bits of tile and roofing-timber flew up. More smoke followed; there must have been something like tallow or lanolin stored there.

"Sir." It was the lieutenant and his platoon-sergeant.

The latter carried a *dozen* of the coal-oil lamps and led men carrying more, with still others piled high on a janitors wheeled wooden cart.

"Sir," the young officer went on, "there's ten men downstairs fit to fight, if they don't have to move much. We've barred the back entrance; it's strong, and they won't get through without a ram. The front's another story, we've done what we can, but . . ."

Raj nodded and took a package of cigarettes out of his jacket, handing two to the other men.

"Right," he began, and spoke over his shoulder. "Signaller, two red rockets." Turning his attention back to the other men:

"In about five minutes," he said, waving the tip of his saber at the town, "the barbs are going to realize that with us sitting here they can't even defend the town against the Life Guards—we can suppress their rooftop snipers too effectively from here.

"So they'll try rushing us. There's only two ways they can come; in the back, and in the front the same way we did. We don't have enough guns to stop them, not and keep the snipers down too. And once they're close to the walls, we won't be able to rise and fire down from up here without exposing ourselves."

They nodded. Raj took one of the lamps and turned the wick high, lighting it with his cigarette. The flame was pale and wavering in the bright morning sunlight, but it burned steadily.

"They'll have to bunch under the walls—by the doors, for example." Raj tossed the lamp up and down. "I really don't think they'll like it when we chuck these over on them."

The two officers and the noncom smiled at each other. "What about the front?" the sergeant asked. "There's this—" he stamped a heel on the balcony's deck "—over the portico."

"That," Raj went on, "is where you'll take the keg." He nodded at the clay barrel of coal-oil on the cart, with a dozen lamps clinking against it. "And hang it like a *pihnyata* from one of the brackets."

"Roit ye are, ser," the sergeant said, grinning like a shark. "Roit where she'll shower 'em wit coal-juice as they come chargin' up t' steps, loik."

He took the heavy container and heaved it onto his shoulder with a lift-and-jerk. "Ye, Belgez, foller me."

"A hundred thousand men?" Ingreid asked.

Teodore Welf nodded encouragingly. "That's counting all the regular garrisons we've been able to withdraw, Your Mightiness, and the levies of the first class—all organized, and all between eighteen and forty."

Ingreid's lips moved and he looked at his fingers. "How many is that in regiments?"

Howyrd Carstens looked around the council chamber. It was fairly large, but plain; whitewashed walls, and tall narrow windows. The three of them were alone except for servants and civilian accountants—nonentities. Good. He liked Ingreid, and respected him, but there was no denying that large numbers were just not *real* to the older nobleman. For that matter, a hundred thousand men was a difficult number for him to grasp, and he was a modern-minded man who could both read and write and do arithmetic, including long division. He had enough scars, and enough duelling kills, that nobody would call it unmanly.

Teodore spoke first. "Standard regiments?" A thousand to twelve hundred men each. "A hundred, hundred and ten regiments. Not counting followers and so forth, of course."

Ingreid grunted and knocked back the last of his kave, snapping his fingers for more.

"And the enemy?"

Carstens shrugged. "Twenty thousand men—but more than half of those are infantry."

The Military Governments didn't have foot infantry in their armies, and he wondered why the Civil Government bothered.

"Of mounted troops, real fighting men? Seven, perhaps eight regiments. They have a lot of field artillery, though—and from what I've heard, it's effective."

Ingreid shook his head. "Seven regiments against a hundred. Madness! What does Whitehall think he can accomplish?"

"I don't know, Your Mightiness," Teodore Welf said. The older men looked up at the note in his voice. "And that's what worries me."

Burning men scrambled back from the portico of the town hall. A few of them had caught a full splash of the fuel, and they dropped and rolled in the wet dirt of the square. More leaped and howled and beat at the flames that singed their boots and trousers. The bullets that tore at them from the windows were much more deadly— but every man has his fear, and for many that fear is fire. The smell of scorched stone and burning wool and hair billowed up from the portico, up in front of the overhanging balcony in a billow of heat and smoke. From the ground floor the dogs howled and barked, loud enough to make the floor shiver slightly under his feet. The men along the balcony above shot and reloaded and shot, their attention drawn by the helpless targets.

"Watch the bloody *roofs*," Raj snapped, hearing the command echoed by the non-coms.

The Brigaderos began to clump for another rush at the portico, as the flames died down a little . . . although there was an ominous crackle below the balcony floor, from the roof-beams that ran from the arches to the building wall and supported it. Another shower of glass lanterns full of coal-oil set puddles of fire on the ground and broke the rush, sending them running back across the plaza to shelter in the other buildings.

Raj looked left and south. Cabot's Life Guards were advancing, with the battery of field guns firing over their heads. The gunners had the range, and the buildings edging the town there were coming apart under the hammer of their five-kilo shells.

"Messer Raj." The platoon sergeant duckwalked up to Raj's position, keeping the heaped wooden furniture along the balustrade between him and any Brigadero rifleman's sights.

"We singed 'em good, ser," the noncom said. His own eyebrows looked as if they'd taken combat damage as well. "Only t' damned roof is burnin', loik. We'nz gonna have t'move soon."

"The barbs will move before we roast, sergeant," Raj said. I *hope,* he thought. He also hoped the warmth in the floor-tiles under his hand was an illusion.

The enemy *should* run. Pozadas had helped set up the ambush—something its citizens were going to regret—but the Brigaderos were countrymen. Caught between two fires, their instinct would be to head for open ground, out of the buildings that were protection but felt like traps.

He wiped his eyes on the sleeve of his jacket and brought the binoculars up. *Yes.* Groups of men pouring out of the houses, pouring out of the mills—most of those were burning now, from the shellfire. On foot and dogback they streamed north to the river, crowding the single narrow stone bridge or swimming their dogs across. The battery commander was alert; he raised his muzzles immediately. The ripping-sail sound of shells passed overhead. One landed beyond the bridge; the next fell short, pounding a hole in the roadway leading to it—and scattering men and dogs and parts of both up with the gout of whitish-gray dirt. The next one clipped the side of the bridge itself, and the whole battery opened up. Shells airburst over the river, dimpling circles into the water, like dishes pockmarked with the splash-marks of shrapnel.

"Out, everybody out," Raj said.

The Life Guards were charging, cheering as they came. The mounted company rocked into a gallop ahead of them.

"Check every room," he went on. Someone might be wounded in one of them, unable to move. "Move it!"

The lieutenant came in from the back, hobbling on his ripped leg and grinning like a sicklefoot. "Bugged out," he said. "All but the ones we burned or shot while they tried to open the back door with a treetrunk."

"Good work," Raj said.

He threw an arm around the young officer's waist to support his weight and they went down the stairs quickly; the lower story was already emptying out. The dogs wuffled and danced nervously as they crossed the hot tile of the portico. Puddles of flame still burned on the cracked flooring, and the thick beams of the ceiling above were covered in tongues of scarlet.

Guess I didn't imagine the floor was getting hot after all, Raj thought. The coal-oil had been an effective solution to the problem of Brigaderos storming the building . . . but it might have presented some serious long-term problems.

Of course, you had to survive the short term for the long term to be very important.

Horace snuffed him over carefully in the plaza, then sneezed when he was satisfied Raj hadn't been injured. The mounted company of the Life Guards streamed through, already drawing their rifles. Two guns followed them, limbered up and at the trot. Raj looked south: the dismounted companies were fanning out to surround the town and close in from three sides.

Cabot Clerett pulled up before the general, swinging his saber up to salute. Raj returned the gesture fist-to-chest.

The younger man stood in the saddle. *"Damn* it, a lot of them are going to get away," he said. The measured crash of volley-fire was coming from the direction of the bridge, and the slightly dulled sound of cannon firing case-shot at point-blank range.

Beside Raj, his bannerman stiffened slightly at the younger officer's tone. Clerett grew conscious of the stares.

"Sir," he added.

Raj was looking in the same direction. The land on the other side of the river was flat drained fields for a thousand meters or so. Brigaderos were running all across it, those with the fastest dogs who'd been closest to the river. Bodies were floating down with the current, now. Not many who'd still been in the water or on the bridge when the troops arrived would make it over; as he watched a clump toppled back from the far bank.

"Oh, I don't think so, Major Clerett," he said calmly. Horace crouched and he straddled the saddle.

Beyond the cleared fields was a forest of coppiced poplar trees, probably maintained as a fuel-source for the handicrafts and fire-places of Pozadas. The glint of metal was just perceptible as men rode out of the woods, pausing to dress ranks. The trumpets were unheard at this distance, but the way the swords flashed free in unison and the men swept forward was unmistakable.

Clerett looked at him blank-faced. A murmur went through the men nearest, and whispers as they repeated the conversation to those further away.

"You expected the ambush, sir?" he said carefully.

"Not specifically. I thought we could use some help with all that livestock . . . and that everything had been too easy."

"If you'd told me, sir, we might have arranged a more . . . elegant solution without extra troops."

Raj sighed, looking around. The civilians were still indoors, apart from a few who'd tried to follow the Brigaderos over the river, and died with them. The fires were burning sullenly, smoke pillaring straight up in the calm chill air. He reached into a saddle bag and pulled out a walnut, one of a bag Suzette had tucked in for him.

"Major," he said, "*this* is an elegant way to crack a walnut."

He squeezed one carefully between thumb and forefinger of his sword hand. The shells parted, and he extracted the meat and flicked it into his mouth.

"And it can work. However." He put another in the palm of his left hand, raised his right fist and smashed it down. The nut shattered, and he shook the pieces to the ground. "This way *always* works. Very few operations have ever failed because too many troops were used. Use whatever you've got."

Cabot nodded thoughtfully. "What are your orders, sir?" he asked. "Concerning the town, that is."

The wounded were being laid out on the ground before the town hall. Raj nodded toward them.

"We'll bivouac here tonight, your battalion and the Slashers," he said. "Get the fires out or under control—roust out the civilians to help with that. Round up the stock we were driving. Send out scouting parties to see none of the enemy escaped or are lying up around here; no prisoners, by the way."

"The town and the civilians?" Clerett asked.

Raj looked around; Pozadas had yielded on terms and then violated them.

"We'll loot it bare of everything useful, and burn it down when we leave tomorrow. Shoot all the adult males, turn the women over to the troops, then march them and the children back to the column for sale."

Clerett nodded. "Altogether a small but tidy victory, sir," he said.

"Is it, Major?" Raj asked somberly. "We lost what . . . twenty men today?"

The Governor's nephew raised his brows. "We killed hundreds," he said. "And we hold the field."

"Major, the Brigade can *replace* hundreds more easily than I can replace twenty veteran cavalry troopers. If all the barbarians stood in a line for my men to cut their throats, they could slash until their arms fell off with weariness and there would still be Brigaderos. Yes, we hold the field—until we leave. With less than twenty thousand men, I'd be hard-pressed to garrison a single district, much less the Western Territories as a whole. We can only conquer if men obey us *without* a detachment pointing guns every moment."

Raj tapped his knuckles thoughtfully on the pommel of his saddle. "It isn't enough to *defeat* them in battle. I have to *shatter* them— break their will to resist, make them give up. They won't surrender to a few battalions of cavalry. So we have to find something they can surrender to."

He gathered his reins. "I'm heading back to the main column. Follow as quickly as possible."

Abdullah al'-Aziz spread the carpet with a flourish.

"Finest Al Kebir work, my lady," he said, in Spanjol with a careful leavening of Arabic accent—it was his native tongue, but he could speak half a dozen with faultless purity. He was a slight olive-skinned man, like millions around the Midworld Sea, or further east in the

Colonial dominions. Dress and more subtle clues both marked him as a well-to-do Muslim trader of Al Kebir, and he could change the motions of hands and face and body as easily as the long tunic, baggy pantaloons and turban.

This morning room of the General's palace was warm with hangings and the log fire in one hearth, but the everlasting dank chill of a Carson Barracks winter still lingered in the mind, if nowhere else. Abdullah was dispelling a little of it with his goods. Bright carpets of thousand-knot silk and gold thread, velvets and torofib, spices and chocolate and lapis lazuli. Since the Zanj Wars, when Tewfik of Al Kebir broke the monopoly of the southern city-states, a few daring Colonial traders had made the year-long voyage around the Southern Continent to the Brigade-held ports of Tembarton and Rohka. If you survived the sea monsters and storms and the savages it could be very profitable. The Civil Government lay athwart the overland routes from the Colony, and its tariffs quintupled prices.

Marie Manfrond straightened in her chair. "This is beautiful work," she said, running a hand down a length of torofib embroidered with peacocks and prancing Afghan wolfhounds carrying men in turbans to the hunt.

"All of you," she went on, "leave me. Except you, Katrini."

Several of the court matrons sniffed resentfully as they swept out; attendance on the General's Lady was a hereditary right of the spouses of certain high officers of state. Marie's cold gray gaze hurried them past the door. Men in Guard uniforms stood outside, ceremonial guards and real jailers. Abdullah looked aside at Katrini. She went to stand beside the door, in a position to give them a few seconds if someone burst through.

"Katrini's been with me since we were girls," Marie said. "I trust her with my life."

Abdullah shrugged. "Inshallah. You know, then, from whom I come?"

His long silk coat and jewel-clasped turban were perfectly authentic, made in Al Kebir as their appearance suggested.

"Raj Whitehall," Marie said flatly. "The Colonial traders don't come to Tembarton this time of year; the winds are wrong."

"Ah, my lady is observant," Abdullah said. Marie nodded; not one Brigade noble in a thousand would have known that.

"But I do not come from General Whitehall . . . not directly. Rather from his wife, Lady Suzette. If Messer Raj's sword is the Companions who fight for him, she is his dagger, just as deadly."

"What difference does it make?" Marie asked. "Why shouldn't I turn you over to my husband's men immediately?"

Abdullah smiled at the implied threat, that he would be turned over *later* if not now. The subtlety was pleasing. He owed Suzette Whitehall his freedom and life and that of his family, but he served her most of all because it gave him full scope for his talents. He could retire on his savings if he wished, but life would be as savorless as meat without salt.

"Forgive me if I presume, my lady, but my lady Suzette has told me that your interests and those of General Ingreid are not . . . how shall I say . . . not always exactly the same."

"That's no secret even in Carson Barracks," Marie said. Not a month after the wedding, with a fading black eye imperfectly disguised with cosmetics. "But Ingreid Manfrond is General, and my people are at war. Do you think I would betray the 591st Provisional Brigade and its heritage for my own spite?"

"Ah, no, by no means," Abdullah said soothingly, spreading his hands with a charming gesture.

"Lady Suzette is moved by sisterly compassion—and the conviction that General Ingreid will do the Brigade all the harm a traitor could, through his incompetence. Also the Spirit of Man—I would say the Hand of God—is stretched over her lord. He is invincible. Lady Suzette's concern is that you yourself might suffer needlessly from Ingreid's anger."

"And I can believe as much or as little of that as I choose," Marie said.

Silence weighed the warm air of the room for a moment; outside fog and soft raindrops clung to the walls and covered the swamps.

"Is it true," the young woman went on in a neutral voice, "that she rides by his side?"

Abdullah bowed again, a hand pressed to his breast. "She rides with his military household," he said. "And sits in all his councils. At El Djem her carbine brought down a Colonial whose sword was raised above Messer Raj's head."

Marie rested an elbow on the carved arm of her chair and her chin on her fist. "What help can she be to me?"

"Has not General Ingreid said, in public for all to hear, that as soon as you are delivered of an heir he has no use for you?"

The words had been rather more blunt than that. Marie nodded. Once Ingreid had an heir of her undoubted Amalson blood, he would not need their marriage to make his eligibility for the Seat incontestable. She had been throwing up regularly for a week, now.

Abdullah opened a small rosewood case. "Here are *ayzed* and *beyam*," he said, smiling with hooded eyes. "The one for the problem I see my lady has now. The other in case she comes to see that General Ingreid is no shield for the Brigade, but rather a millstone dragging it down to doom."

He explained the uses of the Zanj drugs. Katrini gasped by the door; Marie signed her to silence and nodded thoughtfully.

"Ingreid hasn't the brains of a sauroid," she said thoughtfully. "Go on."

"My lady has partisans of her own," Abdullah said. "Those loyal to her family. Your mother is well-remembered, your father more so."

"Few real vassals. The Seat controls my family estates, so I can't reward followers. Fighting men have to follow a lord who can give gold and gear and land with both hands. And I'm held here without easy access to anyone but Ingreid's clients and sworn men."

Abdullah spread his hands. "Funds may be advanced," he said. "Also messages carried. Not for any treasonous purpose, but is it not your right? By Brigade law does not a *brazaz* lady of your rank have a right to her own household, her own retainers?"

Marie nodded slowly. "We'll have to talk more of this," she said.

CHAPTER FOUR

"Right up ahead, ser," the Scout said. "Turn right off t'road, up to the *kasgrane,* loik."

The Expeditionary Force was winding its way through a countryside of low rolling hills, mostly covered with vineyards and olive trees and orchards; pretty to look at, even with the leaves all down, but awkward to march through. Villages grew more frequent as they approached Old Residence, and the *kasgrane*—manor-houses— were unfortified and often lavishly built with gardens and ornamental waterworks, the country-residences of the city magnates. The light airy construction showed that most of them would have been empty in winter anyway, but many of the villagers had headed for the security of city walls as well. There hadn't been any serious war here in generations, but peasants knew down in their bones that there was usually not much to choose between armies on the march. Either side might loot and rape, perhaps kill and burn. Better to hide in a city, where only one side was likely to come and where commanders were more watchful.

Raj nodded and tapped Horace's ribs with his heels. His escort trotted behind him, along the cleared space beyond the roadside ditch. Past infantry swinging along, their uniforms patched but glad to be out of the mud of the river bottoms, past guns and ox-wagons and more infantry and the hospital carts with the tooth-grating sounds of wounded men jolting over ruts in the crude gravel pavement of the road. Better than two hundred men down with lungfever, too; there'd be more, unless he got them under shelter soon. The nights were uniformly chilly now, the days raw at best, and it rained every second day or so. They'd come more than four hundred kilometers in only a month. The men were worn out and the dogs were sore-pawed.

And I've got the second-biggest city in the Midworld to take at the end of it, Raj thought grimly. Old Residence was only a shadow of what it had been in its glory days six hundred years ago, when it was the seat of the Governors and capital of the whole Midworld basin. There were still four hundred thousand residents, and it was the center of most of the trade and manufacture in the Western Territories.

They passed the head of the column; beyond that were only the scouting detachments, combing the hills ahead and around the main force to make sure there weren't any surprises in wait. A platoon of the 5th Descott waited at the turn-off.

The private laneway was narrow, but better-kept than the public road, smooth crushed limestone and bordered by tall cypress trees. It wound upward through vineyards whose pruning had been left half-finished, some vinestocks cut back to their gnarled winter shapes and some with the season's growth still showing in long bare finger-shoots. Untended sheep grazed between them on the sprouting cover crop of wild mustard. The kasgrane at the heart of the *finca,* the estate, was two stories of whitewashed stone and tile roof. The tall glass-paned doors on both stories showed it to be a summer residence; so did the hilltop location, placed to catch the breeze. The windows were shut now, and smoke wafted from the chimneys.

More came from the elaborate tents pitched in the gardens. Wagons and carriages and the humbler dosses of servants and attendants crowded about, and a heavy smell of many dogs. A resplendent figure in sparkling white silk jumpsuit and cloth-of-gold robe waited at the main entrance to the manor. A jeweled headset rested on his thin white hair, and the staff in his hand was topped by an ancient circuit board encased in a net of platinum and diamonds. It was the Key Chip of the Priest of the Residential Parish, symbol of his authority to Code the Uploading of souls to the Orbit of Fulfillment and the ROM banks of the Spirit. The vestments of the archsysups, sysups and priests around him made a dazzling corona in the bright noonday sun.

The pontiff raised staff and hand in blessing from the steps as Raj drew up. A bellows-lunged annunciator stepped forward:

"Let all children of Holy Federation Church bow before *Paratier,* the seventeenth of that name, Priest of the Residential Parish, servant of the servants of the Spirit of Man of the Stars, in whose hands is the opening and closing of the data gates."

Raj and his officers dismounted. They and Suzette touched one knee to the ground briefly; Raj had the platinum-inlaid mace of his proconsular authority in the crook of his left elbow. That meant he was the personal representative of the Governor—and in the Civil Government the ruler was supreme in spiritual as well as temporal matters. Instead of kneeling, he bowed to kiss the prelate's outstretched ring-hand. The ring too held a relic of priceless antiquity, a complete processing chip set among rubies and sapphires.

an FC-77b6 unit, Center remarked. **generally used to control home entertainment modules.**

"Your Holiness," Raj said as he straightened.

The Priest was an elderly man with a face like pale wrinkled parchment, carrying a faint scent of lavender water with him. His eyes were brown and as cold as rocks polished by a glacial stream.

"*Heneralissimo Supremo* Whitehall," he replied, in accentless Sponglish. "I and these holy representatives of the Church—"

The assembled clerics were watching Raj and his followers much as a monohorn watched a carnosauroid; not afraid, exactly, but wary. Few of them looked full of enthusiasm for a return to Civil Government rule. The Church had been the prime authority in Old Residence under the slack overlordship of the Brigade Generals. None of them had any illusions that the Civil Government would be so lax. And the Governors were also unlikely to allow the Priest as much autonomy; the Chair believed in keeping the ecclesiastical authorities under firm control.

"—and of the Governor's Council—"

The civilian magnates. The Council had been important half a millennium ago, when the Governors ruled from Old Residence. There was still a Council in East Residence, although membership was an empty title. Evidently the locals had kept up the forms as a sort of municipal government.

"—are here to offer you the keys of Old Residence." Literally: a page was coming forward, with a huge iron key on a velvet cushion.

"My profound thanks, Your Holiness," Raj said.

Quite sincerely; the last thing he wanted to do was try to take a place ten times the size of Lion City by storm. He turned an eye on the assembled magnates.

"I'm pleasantly surprised at the presence of you gentlemen," he went on. "Especially since I'd heard the barbarian General had extorted hostages and oaths from you."

Paratier smiled. "Oaths sworn under duress are void; doubly so, since they were sworn to a heretic. These excellent sirs were absolved of the oaths by Our order."

Raj nodded. *And I know exactly how much* your *word's worth,* he thought. Aloud: "However, the heretic garrison?"

Paratier looked around. He seemed a little surprised that Raj was speaking openly before his officers; a bit more surprised that Suzette was at his side.

"Ah—" he coughed into a handkerchief. "Ah, they have been persuaded . . ."

Lion City, Raj thought, *did some good after all.*

"Sir, *please* get on the train!"

Hereditary High Colonel Lou Derison shook his head. "The General appointed me commandant of Old Residence. Here I stay."

"Lou," the other man said, stepping closer. "We lost Strezman and four thousand men in Lion City. We can't *afford* another loss of trained regulars like that. There are only five thousand men in the garrison; that isn't enough to hold down a hostile city *and* defend the walls. But in the field, it may be the difference between victory and defeat. Once we've beaten the *grisuh* in battle, Old Residence will open its gates to us again—it's a whore of a city, and spreads its legs for the strongest."

Behind the junior officer a locomotive whistle let out a screech, startling Derison's dog into a protesting whine behind him. The little engine wheezed, its upright boiler showing red spots around the base, where the thrall shoveled coal into the brick arch of the furnace. Ten cars were hitched by simple chain links to the engine, much like ox-wagons with flanged wheels and board sides marked *8 dogs/ 40 men.* These were all crowded with soldiers, the last of the Old Residence garrison. Most had left during the day and the night before. The tracks ran westward though tumbledown warehouses and then through the equally decrepit city wall. The driver yelled something incoherent back toward the clump of officers.

Derison shook his head again. "No, no—you do what you must, Torens, and I'll do what *I* must. Goodbye, and the Spirit of Man of This Earth go with you."

Major Torens blinked, gripped the hand held out to him and then turned to jump aboard the last and already moving car. The wheels of the locomotive spun on the wood-and-iron rails, and the whole train moved off into the misty rain with a creaking, clanging din that faded gradually into echoes and the last mournful wail of the whistle.

Derison sighed and put on his helmet, adjusting the cheek-guards with care. His armor was burnished and there was a red silk sash beneath his swordbelt, but the weapons and plate had seen hard service in their day.

"Come, gentlemen," he said. "We ride to the west gate."

A dozen men accompanied him, his sons and a few personal retainers. One spoke:

"Is that wise, sir? The natives are out of order."

Derison straddled his crouching dog, and it rose with a *huff* of effort. "A man lives as long as he lives, and not a day more. We'll greet this Raj Whitehall like fighting men, under an open sky, not hiding in a building like women."

Massed trumpets played in the entrance to Old Residence. Horace skittered sideways a few steps, and threw up his long muzzle in annoyance. Army dogs expected trumpets to *say* something, and these were just being sounded for the noise. The walls were tall but thin, and some of the crenellations had fallen long ago. There were two towers on either side of the gate, but no proper blockhouse or thickening of the wall. There had been kilometers of ruins first, before they came to the defenses. Some pre-Fall work; most of what the unFallen built with decayed rapidly, but the rest did not decay at all. Rather more of ordinary stone and brick, heavily mined for building material. Those would date from the third or fourth post-Fall centuries, when the Civil Government had been ruled from here and included the whole Midworld basin.

The wall itself had come later, a century or two—when the population of the city had shrunk and the situation had gotten worse. Old Residence fell to the Brigade about two generations after that.

There was no portcullis, just thick timber and iron doors. The roadway opened out into a plaza beyond, thick with a crowd whose noise rolled over the head of the Civil Government column like heavy surf. This was still a *big* city. The street led south towards the White River, but hills blocked its way, covered with buildings. The giant marble-and-gilt pile of the Priest's Palace off to his left; not just the residence, but home for the ecclesiastical bureaucracy. Further to the right the rooftop domes of the Old Governor's Palace showed, with only a little gold leaf still on the concrete, and the cathedron and Governor's Council likewise—they were all on hilltops, and the filled-in area between them would be the main plaza of the city. The rest was a sea of roofs and a spiderweb of roads, and the familiar coalsmoke-sweat-sewage-dog scent of a big city. There were even cast-iron lamp-stands by the side of the main road for gaslights, looking as if they'd been copied from the three-globe model used in East Residence. Which they probably had been.

Delegations lined the street on either side; from the Church, from the great houses of the magnates, from the merchant guilds and religious cofraternities. Holy water, incense and dried flower-petals streamed out toward the color-party around Raj; with music clashing horribly, and organized shouts of *Conquer! Conquer!* That was a Governor's salute and highly untactful, because Barholm would have kittens when he heard about it—as he assuredly would, and soon.

Also waiting were a group of Brigaderos nobles, looking slightly battered and extremely angry. Raj and his bannerman and guards swung out of the procession and cantered over to the square of white-uniformed Priest's Guards who ringed them. The soldiers had shaven skulls themselves, which meant they were ordained priests.

"Who are these men?" Raj barked to their officer, pitching his voice slightly higher to carry through the crowd-roar.

"The heretic garrison commander. Thought he'd left with the rest, but they were heading this way. We have them in custody—"

"Where are their swords?" Raj asked.

"Well, we couldn't let prisoners go armed, could we?" the man said.

"Give them back," Raj said.

He turned his head to look at the white-uniformed officer when the man started to object. The weapons came quickly, the usual single-edged, basket-hiked broadswords of the barbarians. The Brigaderos seemed to grow a few inches as they retrieved them and sheathed the blades. Most of them looked as if they'd rather use them on the priest-soldiers around them.

"High Colonel Derison?" Raj asked, moving Horace forward a few paces.

"General Whitehall?" the man asked in turn.

Raj nodded curtly. The Brigadero drew his sword again and offered it hilt-first across his left forearm; the younger man by his side did likewise. Raj took the elder's sword, and Gerrin Staenbridge the younger; they flourished them over their heads and returned the blades. By Brigade custom that put the owners under honorable parole. He hoped they wouldn't make an issue of their empty pistol-holsters, because he didn't have any intention of returning *those*.

"My congratulations on a wise decision," he said.

Actually, staying on here was either a pointless gesture or cowardice. He didn't think the High Colonel was a coward, but it was a pity he'd decided to stay if he was merely stupid. Raj wanted all the unimaginative Brigade officers possible active in their command structure.

Derison inclined his head. "Your orders, sir?" he said.

"*My* orders are to convey you to East Residence," Raj replied. Derison senior seemed taken aback, but a flash of interest marked his son's face. "You'll be given honorable treatment and allowed to take your household and receive the revenues of your remaining estates."

He'd also probably be shunted off to a manor in a remote province after Barholm had shown him around to put some burnish on the victory celebrations, and his sons and younger retainers politely inducted into the Civil Government's armies, but there were worse fates for the defeated. All Brigaderos nobles who surrendered were being allowed to keep their freedom and one-third of their lands. Those who fought faced death and their families were sold as slaves.

"In fact," he went on, "I'd be obliged if you'd do something for me at the same time."

Derison bowed again. Raj reached into his jacket. "Here's the key to Old Residence," he said. "Please present it to the Sovereign Mighty Lord with my complements, and say I decided to send it to him in the keeping of a man of honor."

The Brigadero looked down at the key—which was usually, for ceremonial purposes, left in the keeping of the Priest—and fought down a grin.

"Colonel Staenbridge," Raj went on formally.

"*Mi heneral?*"

"See that these nobles are conveyed to suitable quarters in the Old Palace, and guarded by our own men with all respect."

"As you order, *mi heneral.*"

Courtesy to the defeated cost nothing, and it encouraged men to surrender.

And now to work, he thought.

"Have any of you ever heard the story of Marthinez the Lawman?" Raj asked.

He stood looking out of the Old Palace windows down to the docks. The gaslights were coming on along the main avenues, and the softer yellow glow of lamps from thousands of windows; both moons were up, the fist-sized disks half hidden by flying cloud. The picture was blurred by the rain that had started along with sundown, but he could just make out the long shark shapes of the Civil Government steam rams coming up the river, each towing a cargo ship against the current.

No complaints about the Navy this time, he thought. *Have to look up their commander.* The room was warm with underfloor hot-air pipes, and it smelled of wet uniforms and boots and tobacco.

Raj turned back to the men around the semicircular table. All the Companions, some of the other battalion commanders, and Cabot Clerett, who couldn't be safely excluded.

"Ah, Marthinez," Ehwardo Poplanich said. Suzette nodded. Her features had the subtle refinement of sixteen generations of East Residence court nobility, able to show amusement with the slightest narrowing of her hazel-green eyes. The rest of the Companions looked blank.

"Marthinez," Raj went on, pacing like a leashed cat beside the windows, "was a Lawman of East Residence." The capital had a standing police force, rather an unusual thing even in the Civil Government.

Someone laughed. "No," Raj went on, "he was a very *odd* Lawman. Completely honest."

"Damned unnatural," Kaltin said.

"Possibly. That's what got him into trouble; he blew the whistle on one of his superiors who'd taken a hefty bribe to cover up a nasty murder by a . . . very important person's son."

Nods all around the table.

"Well, it would have been embarrassing to bring him to trial, so he was thrown in the Subiculum."

That was the holding gaol for the worst sort of criminal. Usually the magistrates eventually got around to having the inmates given a short trial and then crucifixion or hanging or fried at the stake, depending on which crime had been the last before their capture. On the other hand, sometimes they just lost the name in the shuffle. A lifetime in the Subiculum was considerably worse than death, in most men's opinion. Sometimes the loss was deliberate.

"As you can imagine, he wasn't very popular there. Four soul-catchers"—kidnappers who stole free children for sale as slaves—"decided they'd beat him to death the very first night, since he'd put them in there.

"But," Raj went on with a carnivore grin, "Marthinez was, as I said, a fairly unusual sort of man. When the guards came in in the morning, the soul-catchers mostly had their heads facing backward or their ribs stove in. Marthinez had some bruises. So they took him away to the solitary hole for a week, that's the standard punishment for fighting in the cells . . .

"And as they were dragging him off through the corridors, he shouted: *You don't understand! I'm not trapped in here with you. You're all trapped in here with me!*"

"He made," Raj concluded, "quite a swath through the inmates until Ehwardo's grandfather pardoned him and made him Chief Lawman."

Raj halted before the central window, tapping one gauntleted fist into a palm. "General Ingreid thinks he as me trapped." He turned. "Just like Lawman Marthinez, eh?"

Kaltin nodded. "I don't like losing our mobility, though," he said. Which was natural enough for a cavalry officer.

Raj went on: "Kaltin, it's not enough to *beat* the Brigade. Believe me, you can have a good commander and fine troops and win battle after battle and still lose the war."

hannibal, Center said. Raj acknowledged it silently. He was still a little vague on precisely when Hannibal had fought his war—it didn't seem like pre-Fall times at all—but Center's outline of the campaign had been very instructive. Cannae was a jewel of a battle, as decisive as you could want. Even more decisive than the two massacres Raj had inflicted on the Squadron last year—except that Hannibal's enemies hadn't given up afterwards.

"To win this war, we have to do two things. We have to get the civilian population here to actively support us."

There were snorts; Raj acknowledged them. "Yes, I know they've got no more fight than so many sheep, most of them—six centuries under the Brigade. But there are a *lot* of them.

"Second and most important, we've got to make the Brigade *believe* that they're defeated. To do that, we have to get as many of them as we can in one spot; all the principal nobles and their followers, at least. And then we have to kill so many of them that the remainder are convinced right down in their bones that fighting us and death are one and the same thing. The best way I can think of doing that is persuading them to make head-on attacks into fortified positions."

Gerrin raised a brow. "That assumes they will," he said. "I wouldn't. I'd entrench a large blocking force and send a mobile field army to attack our forward base in the Crown and mop up the areas we marched through."

Raj snorted. "Yes, but Gerrin—you're not a barb." He jerked a thumb out the window. "According to the latest intelligence, Ingreid has about a hundred thousand men rallying to his banner; that's most of the regular army of the Brigade, and all of their first-line reserves.

"First, remember that the Brigade are a minority here. They're going to be worried about native and peasant uprisings, the more so since we've occupied Old Residence—which doesn't mean anything of military importance by itself, but the *people* don't know that. They'll be impressed.

"Second, they're stripping their northern frontier. The Stalwarts and the Guard will be raiding, even in winter. Especially since the Ministry of Barbarians is subsidizing them to do exactly that."

He went to the frame and ran his hand across the map of the Western Territories at the latitude of Carson Barracks, a little south of Old Residence.

"Most of the Brigaderos live north of here; it was the first area they overran, back when, and it's where most of them settled. The southern part of the peninsula was conquered more gradually, and the barbs are very thin on the ground there. So they'll be anxious about their homes and families in the north, looking over their shoulders, eager to get it over with and go home. The Brigade doesn't have the sort of command structure which can ignore that type of sentiment.

"Third, one hundred thousand men are going to be camping here, in the middle of a countryside which we shall systematically strip of every ounce of food we can. You know the Brigade; they could no more organize a supply system from the rear on that scale than they could fly to Miniluna by flapping their arms."

"There's the railroad to Carson Barracks," Gerrin Staenbridge said thoughtfully. "With that, they can draw on the whole Padan Valley." He turned to whisper to Bartin for a moment. "Yes, I thought so. *Just* capable of handling the necessary tonnage, but without much margin."

Raj nodded. "Something will be done about that. So they're going to be cold, and wet, and hungry, and after a while a lot of them will be sick, too. They'll be thinking of their nice warm manors and snug farmhouses and hot soup by the fire.

"They'll *have* to attack. And we have to be *ready*. Now, gentlemen, here's how we're going to do that. First, since we're not blessed with a contingent from the Administrative Service, I'm appointing Lady Whitehall legate for civil affairs. Next—"

CHAPTER FIVE

"Most should recover," the Renunciate Sister said.

Suzette nodded, stopping for a moment by one man's bedside. His face glistened with sweat, more than the mild warmth of the commandeered mansion's underfloor heating system could account for. He gave her a weak smile as a helper propped him up and lifted the bowl of broth to his lips. The air was full of a medicinal smell, mostly from the pots of water laced with mint and eucalyptus leaves boiling on braziers in every room and corridor. A low chorus of racking coughs sounded under the brisker sounds of orders and soup-carts.

"Lungfever is most serious when the body is debilitated," the Renunciate went on, as they walked out of the room. "Cold, exhaustion, or bad food. With warmth, rest, careful feeding and plenty of liquids, most of these men should be fit for light duty in Holy Church's cause within a month."

Which would give the equivalent of a whole battalion back to Raj. Suzette nodded, smiling.

"You've done wonderful work," she said.

The Renunciate sniffed. "The Spirit was with us, Lady Whitehall," she said tartly.

Church healers accompanied any Civil Government army; these had been with Raj for going on three years now.

"But please tell the *heneralissimo* that men who sleep in cold mud while they're too tired to eat properly *will* get sick."

"What is the meaning of this?" the merchant demanded. "Out of my way, you peasants!"

He tried to push past the infantrymen standing in the doorway of his warehouse. The peon soldiers spoke no Spanjol and would have ignored him in any case. He walked into the crossed rifles as if into a stone wall, rebounding backward with a squawk. The

270

morning sun glinted brightly on the honed edges of their bayonets as they swung up to *present*, the points inches from his chest. There was a four-dog carriage behind him, and two mounted servants armed with swords and pistols, as well as a crowd of his clerks and storesmen. None of them seemed likely to get him through into his place of business this day.

"Messer Enrike," a soothing voice said.

Enrike turned; Muzzaf Kerpatik was coming around the corner of the tall building with an officer in Civil Government uniform.

"Messer Kerpatik, am I to be robbed, after all your assurances?" the merchant demanded.

Rumor had it that Kerpatik was Raj's factotum for purchasing, an enviable post. It was plain to see he at least was no Descotter—small and slim, dressed in dazzling white linen with the odd fore-and-aft peaked cap of the southern border cities of the Civil Government, along the frontier with the Colony. His Sponglish had the sing-song accent of Komar.

"Of course not," the Komarite soothed. "Just some precautions."

"Precautions against *what?*" Enrike demanded.

Muzzaf whispered in the officer's ear. The man barked an order in Sponglish, and the squad sloped arms and wheeled away from the door. The others guarding the big wagon-gates of the ware-house remained, but the employees filed into the front section of the building.

Enrike snorted as he settled into the big leather armchair behind his desk. One of the clerks scuttled in to throw a scoopful of coal into the cast-iron stove in one corner, and a maidservant brought in kave and rolls.

"Precautions against unauthorized sales," Muzzaf said. "You'll find that all bulk-stored wheat, barley, maize, flour, rice, beans, preserved meats and so forth have been placed under seal. First sale priority goes to the authorized purchasing agents of each battalion, at list prices." He pulled a paper out of his jacket and slid it across the desk. "Soldiers are free to buy additional supplies retail, of course."

"Outrageous!" Enrike said, scanning the list. "These prices are robbery!"

"Reasonable for bulk sales," Muzzaf replied. "And payable in gold or sight-drafts on Felaskez and Sons of East Residence." The latter were as good as specie anywhere on the Midworld.

"Not reasonable in the least, given the situation," Enrike said. "I hope your General Whitehall doesn't think he can repeal the laws of supply and demand."

He gave a tight smile; the Brigade's nobles were mostly economic illiterates as well as actual ones. Enrike and his peers had done very well out of that ignorance, although it caused no end of problems when the Brigade tried to set policy.

"Oh, no," Muzzaf said amiably. "And in any case, he has in myself and others advisors who can tell him exactly how to *manipulate* supply and demand. Marvelous are the ways of the Spirit, placing to hand the tools that Its Sword has need of. Incidentally, Lady Whitehall has been appointed civic legate. Any complaints will be addressed to her."

Enrike's face fell. Muzzaf went on: "You'll note that after military requirements are met, each household is to be allowed to purchase a set amount once weekly. Also at list price."

"How do you expect to enforce *that?*"

"Without great difficulty," Muzzaf said. "Considering that we *know* how much each of you has on hand." Enrike's face fell again as Muzzaf reeled off figures. "And what normal consumption is. Incidentally, ships will be coming in from Lion City with additional supplies of grain from the Colonial merchants' stocks which were forfeited to the State . . . we wouldn't want anything like that to happen here, would we?"

"No," Enrike whispered. The news of the massacre of the Lion City syndics had spread widely.

He had dealt with those men regularly; much of Old Residence's grain supplies were shipped in from the Crown in normal years. This fall the city's grain wholesalers had gone to huge expense to bring in more from the southern ports, or by railway from the Padan valley to the west. Everyone knew what the Skinner mercenaries had done to the Colonials of Lion City, and the unleashed common people to the wealthy.

"What the Army doesn't need, we'll hand out at the list prices in retail lots," Muzzaf went on. "Just to prevent baseless speculation and hoarding, you understand."

"I understand," Enrike said, between clenched teeth.

He would make a fair profit this year—but nothing like the killing he'd anticipated. Not even as much as he'd have made off the shortages caused by the fall of the Crown and Lion City.

Damn this easterner general and his minions! The Brigade were far easier to deal with. Grovel a little and you could steal them blind. Small chance that that would work with Raj Whitehall. He might pass for a simple honest soldier in East Residence, that pit of vipers, but a simpleton from the Governor's court could give lessons in intrigue to Carson Barracks.

As for fooling Suzette Whitehall . . . he shuddered, and covertly made the Sign of the Horns with his left hand against witchcraft.

"*Watch* that," Colonel Grammeck Dinnalsyn said.

The officer in charge of the detail nodded nervously and stepped closer to inspect the bracing at the top of the wall. Twin timber-and-iron booms ran out on either side, with counterweighted wood-framed buckets on cables running over common block and tackle arrangements. The whole mass creaked and groaned alarmingly as the full bucket of dirt and rubble from outside the wall rose. Inside the wall ox-teams heaved at the cables, digging their hooves into the dirt as the long stock-whips cracked over their shoulders. The ton-weight of wet soil and rock groaned up to wall-level, then down to the stone as men hauled it in with hooked poles. Others sprang to the top of the load and unhooked the support cables, fastening them to the set running over the inner braces.

"Lock down the pulleys!" the officer Dinnalsyn had warned said. "Chocks. Take up the strain and *sheet her home.*"

Iron wheels squealed against their brake-drums as the bucket lurched up and out over the inner side of the wall. It went down the inner side in jerks as the men at the levers let cable pay out from the winches. When it thumped down the ox-teams heaved again, to tip it over. Hundreds of laborers jumped forward with shovels and mattocks and wheelbarrows, clearing it out and beginning to spread it as a base-layer along the inside of the stone wall. More cranes were operating up and down the length of it, and laborers by the thousands. A step-sided earth ramp was growing against the ancient ashlar blocks of the fortification. Just in from it more work-gangs demolished buildings and hammered rubble and stone into smooth pavement; still more were resurfacing and widening the radial roads further in. Masons labored all along the wall, replacing the top courses of stones and repairing the parapets.

That would enable men and guns to shift quickly from one section of the outer walls to another, and let troops from a central reserve move swiftly. It was amazing what you could do in a few weeks, with enough hands and some organization.

The building contractor beside the officer shook his head; looking at the ant-hive of activity inside the wall, and the scarcely smaller swarm outside digging a deep moat.

"Amazing," he said, in slow Sponglish with a strong Spanjol accent. The eastern and western tongues were closely related but not really mutually comprehensible. "How you get . . . what you say, organized so quick? Your Messer Raj—"

Cold glances stopped him. The troops referred to their commander that way, but it was not a privilege widely granted.

"—*excuzo,* your General Whitehall, he must understand such thing."

Dinnalsyn shrugged. "He understands what needs to be done, and who can do it," he said.

The contractor nodded enviously. *He* spent most of his time dealing with clients who thought they knew his job better than he did because they could afford to hire him. Working for someone who didn't try to second-guess you was a luxury he coveted.

"How you get those riff-raff to *work* so hard?" he went on, looking at the laborers.

Soldiers were doing the overseeing and technical work; artillerymen, from the blue pants with the red stripes down the legs. His own skilled men were shoring and buttressing and timber-framing. The work-gangs who dug and lifted were townsmen also, but *dezpohblado* factory-hands and day-laborers, mostly.

"Bonus to the best teams, plus standard wages. We're paying a tenth silver FedCred a day," Dinnalsyn said.

The contractor's lips shaped a silent whistle. "You paying *cash?*" he said.

Dinnalsyn nodded. The wage-workers of Old Residence were not peon serfs like the peasants of the countryside, precisely—but their employers mostly paid them in script good only at stores the bosses owned. That let them set prices as they pleased, which meant the workers were usually short by next payday and had to borrow against their wages . . . also from their employers, and at interest.

"You going to get a lot of complaints about that," the contractor said with the voice of experience. Most of his business was with the same magnates.

"No," Dinnalsyn said. His smile made the contractor swallow nervously. "I don't think we'll get many complaints at all."

"What's that?" Lieutenant Hanio Pinya said.

His patrol of the 24th Valencia Foot were dog-weary with an uneventful night of walking the streets. Restless, too. They'd gotten used to thinking of themselves as real fighting men, after Sandoral and the Southern Territories and the campaign in the Crown. A month of warm barracks and good food and new uniforms had put a burnish on the horrors of the forced march down from Lion City. Messer Raj himself had complimented the infantry battalions on their soldierly endurance. Nothing had happened since except wall-duty, unless you counted drunk soldiers asking *Guardia* patrols directions to the nearest knocking-shop or bar . . . and after real soldiering, even an infantry officer got tired of being a pimp in uniform.

"Prob'ly some bitch havin' a fight with 'er old man, sir," the platoon sergeant said hopefully. Their bivouac wasn't very far away.

The screams were louder, more than one voice, and there was a hoarse deep-toned shouting beneath them. It all sounded as if it was coming from indoors, not far down the brick-paved street.

"*Come* on," Pinya snapped. "Messer Raj said we're to keep strict order here."

The patrol lumbered into a trot behind him, their hobnails clashing in the darkened street.

Dorya Minátili screamed with despair and faltered a step as she fled out the door of her home. The soldiers outside had the same uniform as the ones inside. Out of the corner of her eye she could see a long sword swing up, and a hand grabbed at her braid.

The men in the street moved past her. The hand released her

hair, and she heard an odd wet *thunk* sound behind her. More soldiers pounded up the steps and through into the house. She turned, trembling. The one who'd been chasing her was lying on the steps, pinned to the stone by a long bayonet. His sword clattered down into the street, spinning. The soldier who had killed him twisted the rifle and pulled the blade out, long and red-wet in the moonlight, blood gushing from the wound and the twitching corpse's mouth and nose. All the other houses on the street were barred and shuttered, and this neighborhood wasn't quite affluent enough to afford gaslights. The girl began to tremble again as she noticed that the uniforms were not quite the same. These soldiers didn't have the chainmail neck-flaps on their helmets, and they wore armbands with a large red letter G. They were short dark clean-shaven men, not tall and fair like the others. An officer with a drawn sword led them; he held a bullseye lantern in the other hand.

Lieutenant Pinya shouldered the girl aside and pushed into the room. The 1st Cruisers trooper inside had been standing behind an older woman he'd bent over a table, getting ready to mount her; as the *guardia* burst in he tried to pull up his pants and go for his sword simultaneously. One man buttstroked him in the gut; another chopped his rifle stock down on the man's neck. He grunted and collapsed, while the woman scuttled away to a civilian lying groaning in a corner. Someone had been screaming rhythmically upstairs; the sound broke off in male shouts and heavy thumping.

A man came rumbling down the stairs, another 1st Cruisers trooper. Still alive and conscious, but from the way he moaned and flopped as he tried to crawl, not in very good shape.

Behind him two infantrymen carried a wounded civilian; young, with a deep cut in one leg. The men had twisted a pressure-bandage over it, but blood leaked through it already. Behind the wounded man came a girl, younger than the one who'd run out into the street. This one had a thrall collar on her neck and was buck-naked; in her mid-teens and not bad looking, probably the housemaid. More soldiers prodded another Cruiser ahead of them with their bayonets, and a corporal brought up the rear with a sack and a big ceramic jug, the type the local white lightning came in.

"Oh, *shit*," the lieutenant said.

Garrison duty back in the Southern Territories hadn't been *that* bad. A little boring, maybe. Now he'd be up all night explaining things to everyone, right up to Major Felaskez or even higher. Sober, the 1st Cruisers were pretty good soldiers and disciplined enough you could forget they were Squadrones barbarians. Three weeks on *Guardia* duty had taught him that with a few drinks under their belts they tended to revert to type; also that when drunk they couldn't tell a sow from their sisters, and either would do as well.

The corporal waved the bottle and sack, which clinked like silverware. "Guess these fuckin' barbs figured they'd get drunk and laid and get paid for it too, El-T," he said cheerfully. A chance to beat up on cavalrymen was a rare treat in a footsoldier's life. "Nobody else upstairs. Looks like they were just gettin' started, but this might not be the first house."

A voice called from the rear of the house. "Door to the alley's broke in, sir."

"Toryez, go get the medic, fast," the officer said. "Sergeant, patch the civilians. *Get* these shits trussed."

Soldiers pulled lengths of cord out of their belts and tied the prisoners' hands before them, then immobilized them by shoving the scabbards of their swords through the crooks of their elbows behind their backs. One of the prisoners began mumbling in Namerique at increasing volume, but the sergeant silenced him with a swift kick between the legs.

"Outside," Pinya said, jerking a thumb. "Roust out the neighbors, show 'em the dead barb and the prisoners so they'll sound the alarm next time."

Proclamations were one thing, but example was the best way of demonstrating that the Civil Government commanders really were ready to defend the locals against their own men.

He turned to the civilians. Both the men looked as if they would live, although it was touch-and-go for the younger man if the medic didn't arrive soon. The middle-aged woman looked dazed, and the housemaid suddenly conscious of her nakedness; she snatched up a towel and tried to make it do far too much.

"*Hablai usti Sponglishi?*" Pinya said. Blank looks rewarded him. Then the girl stuck her head around the open front door and spoke:

"I do," she said. "A little."

Her accent was heavy, but the words were understandable. "What will happen to those men?" she asked.

"Crucifixion," Pinya said bluntly. "We'll need your statements. And I want you to translate for me to your neighbors."

The girl looked at him with glowing eyes. He straightened and sheathed the sword. "Names?" he began.

"*Heneralissimo Supremo*, we yielded our great city to save it, not to see it destroyed!" the head of the Governor's Council said.

He was standing. All the petitioners were, except for the Priest Paratier, who'd been given a chair at the foot of the table. Raj sat at its head, watching them over steepled fingers with his elbows propped on the arms of his armchair. Motionless troopers of the 5th Descott lined two walls of the long chamber; the fireplace on the inner wall was burning low, hissing less loudly than the mingled rain and sleet on the outer windows. Suzette sat at his right, with clerks taking down the conversation.

"You yielded," Raj said softly, "because you knew what happened to the last city that tried to resist the army of the Sovereign Mighty Lord Barholm. The army also of the Spirit of Man."

A cleric leaned forward; he was red-faced with anger, but throttled his voice back when Paratier laid a restraining finger on his sleeve.

"*Heneralissimo,* you implied that you would be moving on to fight the Brigade, not staying here and making us the focus of their counter-attack."

Raj smiled, a cold feral expression. "No, Reverend Arch-Sysup, your own wishes were father to that thought. I said nothing of the kind."

"Peace, my son," Paratier said. His voice had faded with age, but he adjusted his style to suit rather than trying to force it. The whisper was more compelling than a shout. "Yet would not the Spirit of Man grieve if the priceless treasures within these walls, the relics and records of ancient times, were destroyed by the fury of the heretic and the barbarian?"

Raj inclined his head. "Precisely why I don't intend to allow the barbarians within the walls, Your Holiness," he said briskly. "As you may have noticed, we've been making energetic preparations to receive them."

"Throwing the city into chaos, you mean, *Heneralissimo* Whitehall," a civilian magnate said. "Overthrowing good order and discipline and encouraging all sorts of riot and tumult."

The cost of his rings and the diamond stickpin in his cravat would have kept a company of cavalry for a month, and the jewelled buckles of his shoes were the purchase-price of remounting them.

Raj smiled openly. "Messer Fedherikos, I think you'll admit that my troops are quite disciplined. So I presume you mean we've been employing the common people of the city on necessary works of defense, and worse still paying them in cash and on time. They've shown great zeal in the cause of the Civil Government of Holy Federation."

His eyes raked the petitioners. Few of them met his gaze; Paratier's eyes did; they were as calm and innocent as a child's—or a carnosauroid's.

"Do you gentlemen suppose your own commons might react to attempted treachery the way those of Lion City did after their community returned to the Civil Government?"

The naked threat clanged to the ground between them like a roundshot.

Raj's voice continued like a metronome. "Of course, there's no possibility of treachery here. We're all loyal sons of Holy Federation Church." Well, one of the Sysups was a *daughter* of Holy Church, but no matter. "And since nobody is considering treachery, I'm showing my trust for the citizens of Old Residence by declaring a general mobilization of the populace. For labor service, or for the militia which I'm forming—to include all private armed forces in the city."

There was a shocked intake of breath. That would leave the Church and the magnates helpless . . . helpless, among other things, against a popular uprising unless Raj's troops guarded them. Also helpless to deliver the city to Ingreid the way they'd delivered it to Raj.

these persons will follow instructions until situation changes drastically, Center said. Outlines glowed around most of the petitioners—most importantly, around Paratier. Red highlights marked others, **these individuals will resist necessary measures, probability 94% ±3.**

Which of them are truly *loyal?* Raj enquired.

probability of any of indicated subjects remaining loyal to the civil government unless under threat or directly coerced is too low to be meaningfully calculated.

Exactly what I expected. The only difference is that some have enough guts to be actively treasonous and some don't.

you learn quickly, raj whitehall.

No, I've lived in East Residence, he thought sourly.

Raj noted those marked as most dangerous; best detain those immediately. One or two flinched as his eye stopped at their faces.

"My son, my son," Paratier intoned. "I shall pray for you. Avoid the sin of rashly assuming that your program is debugged. The Spirit has given you great power; do not in your pride refuse to copy to your system the wisdom others have been granted by long experience."

Raj stood, leaning forward on his palms. "Your holiness, messers, I am the Sword of the Spirit of Man. The Spirit has chosen me for Its military business, not as a priest. In spiritual matters, I will of course be advised by His Holiness. In military affairs, I expect you *all* to do the will of the Spirit—Who speaks through me.

"And now," he went on, "if you'll excuse me. General Ingreid is heading this way with the whole home-levy of the Brigade, and I'm preparing for his reception."

CHAPTER SIX

The countryside outside Old Residence had a ghostly look. Colors were the gray-brown of deep winter, leafless trees and bare vines. Nothing moved but an occasional bird, or a scuttling rabbit-sized sauroid. Raj had ordered every scrap of food and every animal within two days' hard riding brought in to Old Residence or destroyed, and every house and possible shelter torn down or burned. The broken snags of a village showed at the crossroads ahead, tumbled brick and charred timbers, looking even more forlorn than usual under the slash of the rain. The two battalions rode through silently, the hoods of their raw-wool cloaks over their heads. Bridles jingled occasionally as dogs shook their heads in a spray of cold water.

Raj reined in to one side with the two battalion-commanders. The two hundred Skinners with him were jauntily unconcerned with the weather; compared to their native steppes, this was balmy spring. Many of them were bare-chested, not even bothering with their quilt-lined winter jackets of waterproof sauroid hide. The regulars looked stolidly indifferent to the discomfort. Anxious for action, if anything; men who don't like to fight rarely take up the profession of arms, and these troopers hadn't lost a battle in a long time. He had Poplanich's Own with him, and two batteries—eight guns. The other unit was the 2nd Cruisers. No artillery accompanied them, but each man had a train of three remounts, and the dogs carried pack-saddles with loads of ammunition and spare gear. The mounts were sleek and glossy-coated. Fed up to top condition with the offal from Old Residence's slaughterhouses, where the meat from the confiscated livestock was being salted and smoked.

The trumpet sounded and Poplanich's Own swung to a halt. The Skinners straggled to a stop, more or less, which was something of a concession with them. The 2nd Cruisers peeled off to the north, taking a road that straggled off into the hills.

Spirit, but I hate war, Raj thought, looking at the ruined village.

It would be a generation or more before this area recovered. If somebody cut down the olive trees and vineyards for firewood, which they probably would, that would be three generations of patient labor gone in an afternoon. Rain dripped from the edge of his cloak's hood. He pushed the wool back, and the drops beat on his helmet like the tears of gods.

Ehwardo was looking after the Cruisers. "*Thought* you had something in mind," he said mildly. "Even if you didn't say."

Raj nodded. "Even the Brigaderos won't neglect to have Old Residence full of spies," he said. "No point in making things easy for them."

"Tear up the railroad before they get here?" Ehwardo asked.

"By no means," Raj chuckled. "Ludwig's men will lie low and scout while the Brigade completes their initial movements. Railroads," he went on, "are wonderful things, no matter how the provincial autonomists squeal about 'em. The whole Civil Government should go down on its knees and thank the Spirit that His Supremacy Governor Barholm has pushed the Central Rail through all the way to the Drangosh frontier—the fact that the Colony has river-transport there has been a ball and chain around our ankles in every war we've ever fought with them."

Ehwardo raised his brows.

Raj went on: "You can do arithmetic, Ehwardo. One hundred thousand Brigaderos. Fifty thousand camp followers, at the least; a lot of them will be bringing their families along. Say, one and a quarter kilos of bread and half a kilo of meat or cheese or beans a day per man, not to mention cooking oil, fuel . . . and preserved vegetables or fruit, if you want to avoid scurvy. Plus feeding nearly a hundred thousand dogs, each of them eating the same type of food as the men but five to ten times as much. Plus twenty or thirty thousand oxen for the wagon trains from railhead to camp, all needing fodder. That's over a thousand tons a *day,* absolute minimum."

"So we wait for them to get here and *then* cut the railway," Ehwardo said. "Still, there are countermeasures. Hmmm . . . I'd station say, twenty or thirty thousand of their cavalry along the line for patrol duty. Easier to feed them, easy to bring them up when needed, and fifty or sixty thousand men would invest the city just as well as a hundred thousand. A hundred thousand's damned unwieldy as a field army anyway."

Raj smiled unpleasantly. "Exactly what I'd do. Ingreid, however, is a Brigadero of the old school; he has to take his boots off to count past ten. And not one of his regimental commanders will want to be anywhere but at the fighting front. Furthermore, all the foundries capable of building new locomotives are in Old Residence, and so are the rolling mills capable of turning out new strap-iron to lay on the rails."

The general turned to the younger commander. Ludwig Bellamy was a barbarian himself, technically—a noble of the Squadron. He looked the part, a finger taller than Raj, yellow-haired and blue-eyed. His father had surrendered to Raj for prudence sake, and because of a grudge against the reigning Admiral of the Squadron. Ludwig had his own reasons for following Raj Whitehall, and he'd managed to turn himself into a very creditable facsimile of a civilized officer.

"Ludwig, this is an important job I'm giving you. Any *warrior* can charge and die; this needs a soldier's touch, and a damned good soldier at that. It's tricky. Some of Ingreid's subordinates are capable men, from the reports." *For which bless Abdullah,* he thought. "Teodore Welf, for example, and Carstens."

He laid a hand on Bellamy's shoulder. "So don't cut the line so badly that it's obviously hopeless. Tease them. Let a trickle get through, enough to keep Ingreid hoping but not enough to feed his army. Step it up gradually, *and don't engage the enemy.* Run like hell if you spot them anywhere near; they can't be everywhere along eight hundred kilometers of rail-line. Keep the peasants on your side and you'll know exactly where the enemy are and they'll be blind."

Ludwig Bellamy drew himself up. "You won't be disappointed in me, Messer Raj," he said proudly.

The three officers leaned towards each other in the saddle and smacked gauntleted fists in a pyramid. Ehwardo shook his head as Bellamy and his bannerman cantered off along the line of the 2nd Cruisers, still snaking away north into the gray rain.

"I don't think you'll be disappointed in him either," he murmured. "You have the ability to bring out abilities in men they didn't seem to have, Whitehall. My great-uncle called it the ruler's gift."

"Only in soldiers," Raj said. "I couldn't get civilians to follow me anywhere but to a free-wine fiesta, except by fear—and fear alone is no basis for anything constructive."

"You're doing quite well in Old Residence," Ehwardo pointed out.

"Under martial law. Which is to civil law as military music is to music. I've gotten obedience in Old Residence, with twenty thousand guns at my back, but I could no more rule it in the long term than General Ingreid could understand logistics." Raj smiled. "Believe me, I know that I'm really not suited to civil administration. I know it as if the Spirit Itself had told me."

correct.

Ehwardo grunted skeptically, but changed the subject. "And now lets get on to that damned railway bridge," he said. "I don't feel easy with nobody there but those Stalwart mercenaries."

Raj nodded. "Agreed, but there was nobody else to spare before the walls were in order," he said.

The rail bridge crossed the White River ten kilometers upstream from Old Residence, the easternmost spot not impossibly deep for bridge pilings. Without it, the Brigade armies would have to go upstream to the fords to cross to the north bank—the south bank

of the river held only unwalled suburbs—which would delay them
a week or two and complicate their supply situation even further.
A strong fort at the bridge could be supplied by river from Old
Residence, and would give the Civil Government force a potential
sally port to the besiegers' rear.

They heeled their dogs forward, the heavy paws splashing in
the mud.

Antin M'lewis whistled silently to himself through his teeth and
sang under his breath:

> When from house t'house yer huntin',
> ye must allays work in pairs—
> Half t'gain, but twice t'safety ye'll find—
> For a single man gits bottled
> on them twisty-wisty stairs,
> An' a woman comes n' cobs him from be'ind.
> Whin ye've turned 'em inside out,
> n' it seems beyond a doubt
> As there warn't enough to dust a flute,
> Befer ye sling yer hook, at t' housetops take a look,
> Fer 'tis unnerneath t' tiles they hide t' loot—

The forest ahead was dripping-wet, and the leaf-mould slippery
as only slimy-rotten vegetation could be. M'lewis noted proudly how
difficult it was to see his men, and how well the gray cloaks blended
in with the vegetation and shattered rock. He made a chittering noise
with tongue and teeth—much like the cry of any of the smaller
sauroids—and twenty soldiers of the Scout Troop rose and moved
forward with him, flitting from trunk to trunk. They halted at his
gesture, among broken rocks and wire-like native scrub. Every one
of them was a relative or neighbor of his, back in Bufford Parish.
Every one of them a bandit, sheep-lifter and dogstealer by hereditary vocation. Following those trades demanded high skill and steady
nerves in not-very-lawful Descott County, where every *vakaro* and
yeoman-tenant carried a rifle and knew how to use it.

He had no doubt of their abilities. Nor of their obedience. Antin
M'lewis had risen from trooper to officer and the Messer class by
hitching his star to that of Messer Raj . . . after nearly being flogged
for theft at their first meeting. The Scouts—unofficially known as the
Forty Thieves—had a superstitious reverence for a man that lucky.
They also had a well-founded respect for his garotte and skinning knife.

Visibility was limited; rain, and ground-mist. He could see the
railway track disappearing downward toward the river, switching back
and forth to the southwest. On the tracks and the road beside them
marched mounted men, in columns of fours. Heading toward him,
which meant toward Old Residence.

"Message to Messer Raj," he said over his shoulder. "Two . . . make that four hunnert men 'n column approachin'. Will withdraw an' keep 'em unner observation."

"Couldn't tell who theuns wuz, Messer Raj," the messenger said. "Jist they'z marchin' in column, ser."
observe, Center said.

The fort on the north side of the railway bridge was a simple earthwork square with a timber palisade. White water foamed just west of it, where the stone pilings of the bridge supported the heavy timberwork arches. Mist filled the surface of the water, turning and writhing with the current beneath. A column of Brigaderos cavalry had ridden onto the southern approaches; more stretched back into the rain, a huge steel-glistening gray column vanishing out of sight. The ironshod wheels of guns thundered on the railway crossties, light brass muzzle-loading fieldpieces.

The Stalwarts within the fort were boiling to the walls; asleep or drunk or huddled in their huts against the chill for far too long. They'd probably had scouts out on the south side of the river, and the scouts had equally probably simply decamped when the Brigade host thundered down on them.

A rocket soared up from the fort. The smoke-trail vanished into the low cloud; the *pop* of the explosion could be heard, but the colored light was invisible even from directly below. As if that had been a signal, hundreds of figures boiled down over the wall and to the skiffs and rowboats tied to a pier below the bridge. They wore the striped tunics of Stalwart warriors under their sheepskin jackets. Equally national were the light one-handed axes they pulled out to chop at the painters tying the light boats to the shore. Chopping at each other as well, as panicked hordes fought for places in the boats. Some of the craft floated downstream empty as would-be passengers hacked and stabbed on the dock, others upside down with men clinging to them, still others crowded nearly to sinking. Arcs of spray rose into the air as those hacked down with oars on the heads of men trying to cling to the gunwales.

Still more Stalwarts tore up the track toward Raj's vantage-point, their eyes and mouths round O's of effort. They scattered into the woods on either side of the track. There were barrels of gunpowder braced under the bridge, with trains of waxed matchcord linking them. Nobody so much as looked at them.

The viewpoint switched to the fort itself. An older man climbed down the wall facing the bridge and began to trudge toward the Brigaderos. His graying hair was shaved behind up to a line drawn between his ears; he had long drooping mustaches, a net of bronze rings sewn to the front of his tunic and cut-down shotguns in holsters along each thigh. Raj recognized him. Clo Reicht, chieftain of the Stalwart mercenaries serving with the Expeditionary force.

"*Marcy, varsh!*" he called, as he came up to the leading enemy, a lancer officer in richly-inlaid armor. *Mercy, brother-warriors,* in Namerique.

Points dropped, jabbing close past the snarling muzzles of the war-dogs. Reicht smiled broadly, his little blue eyes twinkling with friendliness and sincerity. His hands were high and open.

"I know lots about Raj-man," he said. "He tells Clo Reicht all about his plans. Worth a lot. Take me to your leader."

Shit, Raj thought, pounding a fist into the pommel of his saddle.

He'd taken one more gamble with his inadequate forces. This time it hadn't paid off.

Raj blinked back to the outer world, to the weight of wet wool across his shoulders and the smell of wet dog. Ehwardo and M'lewis were staring at him, waiting wide-eyed for the solution. *The Governor shouldn't send us to make bricks without straw, that's the solution,* he thought. With enough men . . .

"The Stalwarts bugged out," he said crisply.

He looked from side to side. There were laneways on either side of the low embankment of the railway, and cleared land a little way up the slopes of the hills. The ground grew more rugged ahead, but nowhere impassible; behind him it opened out into the rolling plain around the city itself.

"The Brigaderos vanguard is over the bridge and coming straight at us. Courier to the city, please." A rider took off rearward in a spatter of mud and gravel.

"Retreat?" Ehwardo asked. M'lewis was nodding in unconscious agreement.

Raj shook his head. "Too far," he said. "If we run for it we'll lose cohesion and they can pursue without deploying, at top speed, and chop us up. Therefore—"

"—we attack, *mi heneral,*" Ehwardo said. He took off his helmet for a second, and the thinning hair on his pate stuck wetly to the scalp as he scratched it. "If we can push them back on the bridge . . ."

Raj nodded. He could turn it into a killing zone, men crammed together with no chance to use their weapons or deploy.

"Two companies forward, deployed by platoon columns for movement," he said. Tight formation, but he'd need all the firepower possible. "Three in reserve, guns in the middle."

He stood in the saddle and shouted in Paytoiz: "*Juluk!* You worthless clown, are you drunk or just afraid?"

The Skinner chief slid his hound down the hillside out of the forest and pulled up beside Raj. "Long-hairs come," he said succinctly. "You run away, sojer-man?"

"We fight," he said. "You keep your men to the sides and forward."

The nomad mercenary gave a huge grin and a nod and galloped off, screeching orders of his own. Around Raj, Poplanich's Own split its dense formation into a looser advance by four columns of platoon strength, spaced across the open way. A brief snarl of trumpets, and the men drew the rifles out of the scabbards to rest the butts on their thighs. Dogs bristled and growled in the sudden tension, and the pace picked up to a fast walk. What breeze there was was in their faces, so there shouldn't be any warning to the enemy from that.

Good scouting meant the five-minute difference between being surprised and doing the surprising.

"Walk-march, *trot.*"

They pushed forward, a massed thudding of paws and the rumble of the guns. Over a lip in the ground, and a clear view down through the hills to the white-gray mist along the river, with the bridge rising out of it like magic. The railroad right-of-way between was black with men and dogs, dully gleaming with lanceheads and banners. The double-lightning flash of the Brigade was already flying over the little fort as the host streamed by, together with a personal blazon—a running wardog, red on black, with a huge silver W. The house of Welf; intelligence said Teodore Welf led the enemy vanguard. The Brigadero column was thick, men bunched stirrup to stirrup across all the open space. Young Teodore was risking everything to get forces forward quickly, up out of the hills and onto the plain.

Precisely the right thing to do; unfortunately for the enemy, even a justified risk was still risky.

The trumpet sounded. The platoon columns halted and the dogs crouched. Men stepped free and double-timed forward, spreading out like the wings of a stooping hawk. Before the enemy a few hundred meters ahead had time to do more than begin to recoil and mill, the order rang out:

"Company—"

"Platoon—"

"Front rank, volley *fire, fire.*"

BAM. Two hundred men in a single shot, the red muzzle-flashes spearing out into the rain like a horizontal comb.

The rear rank walked through the first. Before the echoes of the initial shout of *fwego* had died, the next rank fired—by half-platoons, eighteen men at a time, in a rapid stuttering crash.

BAM. BAM. BAM. BAM.

The field-guns came up between the units. "If they break—" Ehwardo said. The troopers advanced and fired, advanced and fired. The commanders followed them, leading their dogs.

"If," Raj replied.

The guns fired case-shot, the loads spreading to maximum effect in the confined space. Merciful smoke hid the result for an instant, and then the rain drummed it out of the air. For fifty meters back from the head of the column the Brigaderos and their dogs were a carpet of flesh that heaved and screamed. A man with no face staggered toward the Civil Government line, ululating in a wordless trill of agony. The next volley smashed him backward to rest in the tangled pink-gray intestines of a dog. The animal still whimpered and twitched.

Men have a lot of life in them, Raj thought. Men and dogs. Sometimes they just died, and sometimes they got cut in half and hung on for minutes, even hours.

The advancing force had gotten far enough downslope that the reserve platoon and the second battery of guns could fire over their heads. Shock-waves from the shells passing overhead slapped at the back of their helmets like pillows of displaced air. Most of the head of the Brigaderos column was *trying* to run away, but the railroad right-of-way was too narrow and the press behind them too massive. Men spilled upslope toward the forested hills. Just then the Skinners opened up themselves with their two-meter sauroid-killing rifles. Driving downhill on a level slope, their 15mm bullets went through three or four men at a time. A huge sound came from the locked crowd of enemy troops, half wail and half roar. Some were getting out their rifles and trying to return fire, standing or taking cover behind mounds of dead. Lead slugs went by overhead, and not two paces from him a trooper went *unh!* as if belly-punched, then to his knees and then flat.

The rest of his unit walked past, reloading. Spent brass tinkled down around the body lying on the railroad tracks, bouncing from the black iron strapping on the wooden stringers.

Raj whistled sharply, and Horace came forward and crouched. *Got to see what's going on,* he thought, straddling the saddle and levelling his binoculars as the hound rose.

Then: *damn.*

Hard to see through smoke and mist, but there was activity down by the fort. Men with banners galloping out amid a great whirring of kettledrums. The enemy column had been bulging naturally, where advancing ranks met retreating. The party from the fort was getting them into order, groups of riding dogs being led back and men in dragoon uniforms jogging left and right into the woods. A trio of shells from the second battery ploughed into the knot of Brigaderos, raising plumes of dirt and rock, rail-iron and body-parts. When those cleared the movement continued, and the Welf banner still stood. Raj focused his glasses on the fort's ramparts; Center put a square across his vision and magnified, filling in data from estimation. A man in inlaid lancer armor with a high commander's plumes. Another with a halter around his neck and two men standing behind him, the points of their broadswords hovering near his kidneys. Clo Reicht, pointing . . .

Pointing at me. A man might not be recognized at this distance by unaided eyes, but Horace could.

The press on the bridge behind the fort had halted. Two low turtle-shaped vehicles were coming over it, slowly, men and animals rippling aside to let them pass. Steam and smoke vomited from low smokestacks; the Brigade wasn't up to even the asthmatic gas engines the Colony and Civil Government used for armored cars, but steam would do at a pinch. Another curse drifted through his mind. Someone had had a rush of intelligence to the head. The cars were running on flanged wheels that fitted the tracks. Sections of broader tire were lashed to their decks. A few minutes work to bolt them onto the iron hubs, and they'd be road-capable. Now *that* was clever.

"Ehwardo!" Raj shouted.

"No joy?" the Companion said.

"No. They began to stampede, but whoever's in charge down there is starting to get them sorted out."

A lancer regiment was extracting itself from the tangle and forming up. Guns went *thump* from the fort, and a roundshot came *whirrr-crash*, bouncing up into the air again halfway between the lead spray of enemy dead and the Civil Government's line. More and more riflemen were returning fire, some of them in organized units. The Brigaderos troops were brave men, and mostly trained soldiers. They didn't *want* to panic, and they knew the real slaughter started when one side or the other bugged out. Once somebody started giving orders, they must have been relieved beyond words.

"If that's Teodore Welf, Ingreid Manfrond had better look to his Seat later," Ehwardo said.

"And we'd better look to our collective arse right now," Raj said.

He glanced at the sky, and called up memories of what the terrain was like. More bullets cracked by, and a cannonball hit a tree upslope from him and nearly abreast. The long slender trunk of the whipstick tree exploded in splinters at breast height, then sagged slowly away from the track, held up by its neighbors.

"He's got enough brains to reverse their standard tactic," Raj said. "Those dragoons will try and work around our flanks, and the lancers will charge or threaten to to keep us pinned."

"Rearguard?" Ehwardo asked.

It was obviously impossible to stay. There had been a chance of rushing the bridge if the enemy ran, but if they didn't the brutal arithmetic of combat took over. There were just too many of the other side in this broken ground. Their flanks weren't impassible to men on foot, and the ground there provided plenty of cover.

"I'll do it, with the guns and the Skinners." He held up a hand. "That's an *order*, major. Take them back at a trot, no more, and a company or so saddled up just inside the gate. We'll see what happens. M'lewis, get your dog-robbers together. Courier to Juluk—"

the Skinner chieftain "—and tell him I need him now. Captain Harritch!"

The artilleryman in charge of the two batteries heeled his dog over.

"Captain Harritch, put a couple of rounds into the railbed now, if you please"—because he did *not* want those armored cars zipping up at railroad speeds on smooth track—"and then prepare to limber up. Here's what we'll do . . ."

Everyone here looked relieved to hear orders, as well. Now, if only there was someone to tell *him* what to do.

"Now!" the battery-lieutenant said.

Sergeant-Driver Rihardo Terraza—his job was riding the left-hand lead dog in the gun's team—heaved at the trail of the gun. The rest of the crew pushed likewise, or strained against the spokes of the wheels. The field-gun bounced forward over the little rise in the road.

spiritmercifulavatarssaveus, but the barbs were *close* this time. Not four hundred meters away, dragoons and lancers and a couple of their miserable muzzle-loading field-guns pounding up the road in the rain, which was getting worse. They had just time enough to check a little as the black muzzles of the guns rose over the ridge, appearing out of nowhere. There were other Brigaderos crossing the rolling fields, but they were much further back, held up by stone walls and vineyards tripping at their dogs.

The breechblocks clanged. Everyone leapt out of the path of the recoil, opening their mouths to spare their ears.

POUMF. POUMF. POUMF. POUMF.

Instantaneous-fused shells burst in front of the Brigaderos. *Juicy,* Terraza thought with vindictive satisfaction. He'd been with this battery for five years, since the El Djem campaign, when they only brought one gun of four out of the desert. He knew what cannister did to a massed target like that.

"Keep your distance, *fastardos,*" he muttered under his breath as he threw himself at the gun again.

Back into battery; he could feel his thigh-muscles quivering with the strain of repeated effort, of heaving this two-ton weight of wood and iron back again and again. The rain washed and diluted his sweat; he licked at his lips, dry-mouthed. Raw sulfur-smelling smoke made him cough. A bullet went *tunnnggg* off the gun-barrel not an arm's length from his head, flattening into a lead pancake like a miniature frisbee and bouncing wheet-wheet-wheet off into the air.

Their own barbs were opening up, Skinners who stood behind their shooting-sticks and fired with the metronome regularity of jackhammers. Something big blew up over toward the enemy, one of their caissons probably. That might be the Skinners, or the battery's own fire. No time to waste looking and Spirit bless *whatever* had done it; it gave the barbs something to worry about except trying to give Rihardo Terraza an edged-metal enema.

POUMF. POUMF. POUMF. POUMF.

"Limber up!" the lieutenant shouted.

This time the team caught the trail before the gun quite finished recoiling—risking crushed feet and hands, but it was a *lot* easier than hauling the gun by muscle force alone. Faster, too, which was the point right now. They kept the momentum going and the trail up, the muzzle of the gun pointing slightly down, and ran it right back to the limber. That was a two-wheeled cart holding the ready-stored ammunition and the hitch for the team. The steel loop at the end of the trail dropped on the lockbar at the rear of the limber with an iron *clung.*

Terraza ignored it; slapping the lockpin through the bar was somebody else's job. His little brother Halvaro's, in point of fact. It was the lieutenant's job to tell him where to go, and Captain Harritch's to decide where that was, and Messer Raj to look after everything. Rihardo's job was to get this mother where it was supposed to be. He sprinted forward to the head of the six-dog hitch and straddled the saddle of the left-hand lead. The right-hand lead—right-one—wurfled and surged to her feet at the same instant.

"*Hadelande, Pochita!*" he shouted to her. Pochita was a good bitch, he'd raised her from a pup and trained her to harness himself. She knew how to take direction from the lieutenant's sword as well as he did, and took off at a gallop. The team rocked into unison.

The lieutenant was pointing directions with his saber; off to the right as well as moving rearward, to knock back a flanking party of barbs that were getting too close and frisky. Off they went, a bump and thunder over the roadside ditch, and then up the rocky hillside in a panting wheeze. As soon as they'd moved out of the way the second battery opened up from a thousand meters back; the Skinners saddled up too, moving along with them. All four guns and the two spare caissons with extra ammunition. Which they would need before they saw Old Residence again.

Something hit a rock to his right with a monstrous *crack* and an undertone of metal ringing. Cast-iron roundshot from one of the barb guns, and dead lucky to be this close to a moving target. Fractions of a second later the whole team lurched, and he nearly went over the pommel of his saddle.

Pochita was down. With both her hind legs off at the hocks; the roundshot had trundled through, spinning along the ground and ignoring everything else. She whimpered and floundered; shock was blocking most of the pain, but she couldn't understand why her legs didn't work. She was a Newfoundland-Alsatian cross, a mule-dog, with big amber colored eyes. The huge soft tongue licked at him frantically as he hauled on his reins with his left hand and scrabbled for the release-catch of her harness with his right.

It gave, but he had to draw his saber and slash her free from the right-number-two dog. He clapped his heels to his mount and the team moved forward again, only to lurch to a halt once more.

"Pull up, pull up!" his brother Halvaro shouted.

Rihardo looked back over his shoulder. Pochita had tried to follow the team—she was the best dog he'd ever trained, and the most willing. Even with blood spurting from both her severed rear legs she'd tried, and fouled the limber; the last pair of dogs were almost dancing sideways in their efforts not to trample her. Pochita writhed, her body bent into a bow of agony.

"*Fuck* it!" Rihardo screamed. Rain flicked into his face, like tears. "I wouldn't pull up if it was *you* either, *mi bro.*"

He hammered his heels into the ribs of left-one. The ironshod wheel of the limber rolled over Pochita's neck, and the gun-wheel over her skull. The team jerked, and something broke with a noise like crackling timber. Halvaro was standing in his position on the limber, looking back in horror, when the shell exploded. It crumped into the earth right of the moving battery, and a hand-sized fragment of the casing sledged the young gunner forward, tearing open his back to show the bulging pink surface of the lungs through the broken rib.

Halvaro landed in front of the limber's wheels, falling down between the last two dogs of the hitch. Rihardo turned his face forward with a grunt; he ignored the second set of crackling noises as the wheels went over his brother's back and chest.

"Into battery, rapid fire!" the lieutenant said.

"Right, let's get out of here," Raj said. "They're holding back now they've lost their field guns."

He cased his binoculars; it was two hours past noon, good time for a fighting retreat begun early in the morning. The Brigaderos were scattered over a couple of thousand meters of front to the westward. The ones trying to work through the fields would be slower than Raj's guns trotting home down the road. For the first time that day he noticed the damp chill of soaked clothing; he uncorked an insulated flask and sipped lukewarm kave, sweet and slightly spiked with brandy. *Bless you, my love,* he thought: Suzette had insisted on him taking it, even though he'd planned to be back in Old Residence by noon. He offered the last of it to the artillery captain.

"*Grahzias, mi heneral,*" the young man said. He finished it and wiped his eyes, peering westward. "Those brass guns of theirs aren't much," he went on.

The two batteries had limbered up, replacing a few lost dogs from the overstocked teams on the spare caissons. They rumbled into a fast trot. The Skinners lounging about rose, fired a few parting shots and mounted, all except for one who'd decided the roadway was a good spot to empty his bowels.

"True, Captain Harritch," Raj said, as the officers reined about and followed the guns. The dogs broke into a ground-eating lope. "The problem is their determination."

Poplanich's Own seemed to be still bunched around the railway gate into the city.

What can Ehwardo be thinking of? Raj thought irritably.

"Open the bloody *gate*, you fools!" Ehwardo Poplanich screamed upward at the wall above him.

Rain spouted out of the gutters on the parapet above, falling down on the troops. He could feel the dogs getting restless behind them, and the men too—retreating was the harshest test of discipline.

A militiaman peered through a tiny iron-grilled opening in the gates at head height. "Go around to the north gate," he said, with an edge of hysteria in his voice. "We *heard* the fighting. We're not going to let the Brigade into our city just to save *your* asses, easterner."

Rifles bristled from the top of the gate. Captured weapons distributed to the city militia, but deadly enough for all that. The rain-gutters could pour boiling olive oil and burning naptha, as well . . . and there was no telling what a mob of terrified civilians would do. They'd put militia on watch in the daytime, when nothing was expected to happen, so that real soldiers could put their time to some use. Another calculated risk because they were shorthanded . . .

Raj pulled up. "*What* is going on here?" he barked. Horace barked literally, a deep angry belling.

Ehwardo made a single, tightly controlled gesture toward the peephole. Raj removed his helmet.

"This is General Whitehall," he said, slowly and distinctly. "Open—the—gate—immediately."

"Whitehall is *dead*," the man quavered. "We heard it from the fugitives. Dead, wiped out with both battalions, *dead*."

That with Raj, a complete cavalry battalion and eight guns waiting in the roadway. All because one or two cowards had bugged out from the retreat, and these street-bred militia had chosen to believe them. Ehwardo was swearing quietly beside him. The whole thing had cost *time*. If Poplanich's Own had been inside he could have rolled the guns and Skinners in with a fair margin of safety. Even if the gates opened right now, it would be chancy; the pursuit was coming in hell-for-leather at a gallop. Bells were ringing in there behind the city walls; the alarm had been given, but it might be fifteen minutes or more until the word got to a real officer.

"Get a runner to headquarters," Raj snapped at the peephole. No time to think about that. No time to think about what he was going to do to the men responsible for this ratfuck.

"Ehwardo, we'll have to see off the ones snapping at our heels before anything else. Deploy into line crossing the axis of the road, with center refused. Captain Harritch, both batteries in support, if you please; two guns in the center and the rest on the flanks. Juluk—"

The rain had died away to a fine drizzle. The land close to the city was mostly flat, and Raj had ordered every scrap of cover cut or demolished out to two kilometers from the walls. He was facing east, down the railway and its flanking road, paved this close to the city. Off to his left was the river, narrowing and turning north about here, with a high bluff in its bend about two kilometers away. Trumpet-calls were spreading out the men of Poplanich's Own, smooth as oil spreading on glass.

Good training, Raj thought. Only a fool wouldn't be nervous in this situation, but the motion was as calm and quick as drill. The column reversed, each dog turning in its own length. Each company slanted out into the fields like the arms of a V, with the platoons doing likewise, then pivoted out into line. Less than eight minutes later the six hundred men of Poplanich's Own were trotting back east in extended open order, a double rank nearly a kilometer long.

A clump of lancers led the Brigaderos' pursuit, about a thousand strong, cantering down the roadway on dogs winded from the uphill chase. The forest of upright lanceheads stirred like a reedbed in a breeze as the thin blue line of Civil Government troopers came toward them at a round trot. Beside Raj, Ehwardo nodded to himself.

"Wait for it," he said quietly to himself.

The distance closed, and the lancers spurred their tired dogs into a lumbering canter forward, charging in a clump.

"Now!"

The trumpet sounded five notes. Company buglers repeated it, and the dogs sank on their haunches to halt, then to the ground. The men ran forward half a dozen paces and sank likewise, front rank prone and second kneeling.

"Fire!"

The range was no more than two hundred meters now, close enough to see men's faces if their visors were up. Close enough to hear the bullets striking armor. The flung-forward wings of the Civil Government formation meant that every man could bring his rifle to bear. The two field guns in the center next to the commanders began firing as well, with their barrels level with the ground, firing case shot. The hundreds of lead balls sounded like all the wasps in the world, until they struck the mass of men and dogs. That was more like hailstones on tile. After the third volley the survivors turned to run, but their dogs were tired and fouled by the kicking masses of the dead and dying. Units were coming up the road behind them, dragoons and lancers mixed, rushing to be in at the kill the renewed firing indicated.

The killing went on. From behind a hillock, the Skinners rode out. Some dismounted to shoot; others swooped in, firing their giant rifles point-blank from the saddle and jumping down with knives in either hand, darting out again with choice bits of loot. The Brigaderos at the rear of the pileup began to halt and seep out sideways into the fields again. The Skinners followed, fanning out into the fields. Men ran from the menace of their fire.

"The Brigaderos really need to work on their unit articulation," Raj said coldly. "Those regiments of theirs are too big to react quickly. They get caught up in their own feet when something unexpected happens fast."

Shells went by overhead and burst over the roadway. Shrapnel sleeted down into the mass of enemy troopers caught between the windrows of dead in front of the battalion line and the clumps of riders dribbling in from the rear.

"We can . . . oh, shit," Ehwardo said.

A black beetling shape loomed up out of the rain, casting mounted men aside from either edge of its hull like the coulter of a plow. It was about eight meters long and three wide, and as tall as a tall man in the center of its rounded sheet-iron hull. Smoke and steam billowed from the stack toward the rear; the rain hissed when it struck that metal. More steam jetted from under the rear wheels, a steady *chuff-chuff-chuff*. A light cannon nosed out from the bow, through a letterbox-type slit. Small ports for rifles and pistols showed along its sides.

"*Scramento*," Raj echoed.

Someone back at the bridge had had the car manhandled across the gap they'd torn in the track, then sent it zipping up the undamaged section. A few minutes back behind the last hill to bolt the road wheels over the flanged ones, and it was ready. Now it rattled and wheezed its way forward, and Brigaderos troops followed as if pulled by the twin black lightning-bolts in the red circle on its bow slope.

Only the gun on this side of the railway embankment could bear. The crew were already working on the elevation and traverse wheels of their weapon. It bucked and slid backward; the shell kicked up a gout of dirt from the embankment beside the armored car. The vehicle slewed sideways, skidded, and came back onto the pavement, picking up speed.

"Nothing left but cannister!" the gun-sergeant screamed, as he dashed back to the caisson.

Men were switching their aim to the car. Sparks flew as bullets spanged and flashed off the surface, but even the brass-tipped hardpoints wouldn't punch through. The hatch on top clanged down, leaving the commander only the slots around it. The armored car didn't have the firepower to actually kill all that many troopers. It could break their position, and their cohesion, and that would be all she wrote. The 15mm rounds from the Skinners' sauroid rifles probably would penetrate, but they were out on the flanks . . . and they'd probably consider this his business, even if they were looking this way.

It *was* his business. "Follow me!" he shouted, and slapped his heels into Horace's flanks.

Men followed him—no time to check who—and the hound raced forward at a long gallop, belly to the earth. The iron juggernaut grew with frightening swiftness; it must be travelling at top-dog speed. His shift moved Horace aside, into the ditch. The cannon slewed around, trying to bear on him, then flashed red. Cannister whistled past his left ear, and Horace leaped as if a fly had stung him. A ball had nicked the dog's rump, and then they were inside the shot cone. Behind him a dog bleated in shock, and then he was hauling on the reins. Horace scrabbled, dropping his hindquarters almost to the ground to shed momentum, and whirled. Raj judged distance and launched himself— onto the hull of the armored car, his right hand slapping onto a U-bracket riveted to the hull. It closed like a mechanical grab, and he felt the arm nearly wrenched from its socket as his eighty kilos of mass was jerked out of the saddle and slapped flat against the upper front hull of the armored car.

Rivet-heads hammered into his chest, and the air went out of him with an agonized wheeze. His waist was at the edge of the turtleback, and his legs dangled perilously near the spinning spokes of the front wheel.

And any second the commander would stick his head out of the hatch and shoot him like a trussed sheep, or one of the bullets that were clanging off the hull would hit him.

His left arm came up and clamped onto the next U-bracket. The wool of his cloak tore as his shoulders bunched and hauled him higher. The bucking, heaving passage of the hard-sprung car over the rough roadway flung him up and down on the boilerplate surface of the hull. He scrabbled with his right foot, and got it over the edge of the upper curve of the hull and braced against a handhold. *Now* he could free a hand. The revolver stripped free of the holster with a *pop as* the restraining strap snapped across.

M'lewis was riding alongside the other side of the car—Spirit knew how—leaning far over with his rifle thrust out one-handed into the drivers slit. The sound of the shot was almost lost in the groaning, grating noise of the car's passage. He could feel it lurch under him suddenly, then he was almost flung free as it banged over the road-side ditch and into the field. The cannon slewed, trying to bear on M'lewis as hands inside hauled the body of the driver away from the controls.

That gave Raj a space. Hanging three-quarters on the forward hull, he jammed his revolver through beside the barrel of the cannon and squeezed off all five rounds as fast as his finger could pull the trigger. The minute the hammer clicked on a spent chamber he threw himself back, curling in mid-air as he would have if he'd lost the saddle while jumping a hedge.

Rocky ground pounded at him, ripping and bruising. Something

whanged against his helmet hard enough to make the last series
of rolls completely limp. He could still see the armored car lurching forward, out of control now as the bullets ricocheted inside its
fighting chamber. The prow hit a wall of fieldstone and crumpled,
the heavy vehicle bucking up at the back and crashing down again.

What followed seemed quite slow, although it must have taken
no more than fifteen seconds in all. The rear third of the car blew
apart, the seams of the hull tearing loose in a convulsive puff of
escaping steam as the boiler ruptured. That must have sent the fuel
tank's kerosene spraying forward into the fighting compartment,
because flame gouted yellow through every slit and joint in it. The
stored ammunition went off, and probably the last vaporized contents of the fuel tank at the same instant. The car exploded in a
ball of white flame. Bits and pieces of iron plating and machinery
rose and pattered down all around him.

Something cold and wet thrust into the back of his neck. Horace's
nose; Raj grabbed at the stirrup and hauled himself erect, feeling
his knees trembling and clutching at his midriff. Skin seemed to
be missing from a fair section of his face, but none of the major
bones were broken. The Brigaderos were in full retreat. Streaming
back east, dog, foot and guns with the Skinners whooping in pursuit.
Trumpets played; from his left a battalion of Civil Government cavalry
came around the city wall at a gallop and began to deploy into line.
He shook his head to clear it—a mistake—and managed to make
out the banner of the 5th Descott.

"Ser."

Raj looked up; it was Antin M'lewis, still in the saddle. "Ser, yer
all roight, then?"

"I'll live," Raj said, spitting out blood from a cut lip and feeling
his teeth with his tongue.

None loose . . . He looked back at the road. Poplanich's Own
was moving forward, all except the banner group. They were halted
around something in the roadway. Raj walked that way, one arm
braced around the pommel of his saddle for support. Ehwardo's
dog was lying dead in the roadway, neck broken and skull crushed.
Ehwardo lay not far from it. His left side from the floating ribs
down was mostly gone, bone showing pinkish-white through the
torn flesh, blood flowing past the pressure-bandages his men tried
to apply. From the way the other leg flopped his back was broken, which was probably a mercy. The battalion chaplain was
kneeling by his side, lifting the Headset from the last touch to
the temples.

Raj knelt. The older man's eyes were wandering; not long, then.
They passed over Raj, blinked to an instant's recognition. His lips
formed a word.

"I will," Raj said loudly, leaning close.

Ehwardo had a wife and four children; including one young boy who would be alone in a world decidedly unfavorable to the Poplanich *gens.*

The eyes rolled up. Raj joined as all present kissed their amulets, then stood.

"Break off," he said harshly to the Senior Captain. "Sound recall. The gate will be open, this time."

Suzette drew up on her palfrey Harbie, beside the banner of the 5th. "Oh, damnation," she said. "He was a good man."

Raj nodded curtly. *He would have made a better Governor than Barholm,* he thought.

no. Center's mental voice fell flat as stone. **he would have been a man of peace, nor would he have had the ruthlessness necessary to break internal resistance to change.**

Don't we need peace? Raj thought. *Can't anyone but a sicklefoot in human form hold the Chair?*

peace can only come through unity. barholm clerett is an able administrator with a strong grip on power, able to cow the bureaucracy and the nobility both, and he will not rest until bellevue is unified. therefore he is the only suitable governor under present circumstances.

And I have to conquer the Earth for him, Raj thought bitterly. *Him and Chancellor Tzetzas.*

bellevue, Center corrected. **earth will come long after your time. otherwise, essentially correct.**

Both units' trumpets sang in a complex interplay. Men wrapped the body of Ehwardo Poplanich and laid him on a gun-caisson; others were collecting loose dogs and the wounded, and enemy weapons.

After a moment, Raj spoke aloud: "I'm bad luck to the Poplanich name," he said.

"It's not your fault, darling," Suzette murmured.

"Didn't say it was," he replied, in a tone like iron. "Didn't say it was."

The gates were open. Regulars lined the roadway, saluting as Raj rode in, and again for Ehwardo's body. The militia stood further back, expressions hang-dog. Troopers of Poplanich's Own spat on them as they rode by, and the townsmen looked down meekly, not even trying to dodge.

Gerrin Staenbridge was waiting just inside the gate; standing orders forbade him to be outside the walls at the same time as Raj.

"The city's on full alert," he said. Then: *"Damn"* as he saw the commander of Poplanich's Own.

His eyes went back to the militia who'd barred the gate. "What's your orders concerning them, *mi heneral?"*

Raj shrugged. "Decimation," he said flatly.

"Not all of them?"

"Some of them may be of use later," Raj went on. "Although right now, I can't imagine what."

CHAPTER SEVEN

A color party and escort met Teodore Welf at the main north gate of Old Residence. He exchanged salutes with the officer in charge of it, a man younger than himself with a hook in place of his left hand. He was small and dark in the Eastern manner, smelling of lavender soap and clean-shaven, smooth-cheeked—almost a caricature of the sissified *grisuh*. Apart from that hook, and the cut-down shotgun worn holstered over one shoulder, and the flat cold killer's eyes. His Namerique was good but bookishly old-fashioned, with a singsong Sponglish lilt and a trace of a southron roll to the R's, as if he'd spoken it mainly with Squadron folk.

"Enchanted to make your acquaintance, Lord Welf," he said. "Blindfolds from here, I'm afraid."

Teodore tore his gaze from the rebuilt ramparts above, and the tantalizing hints of earthworks beyond the gate. He could see that the moat had been dug out; the bottom was full of muddy water, and sharpened stakes. The edge of the cut looked unnaturally neat, as if shaped by a gardener, but the huge heaps of soil that should have shown from so much digging were entirely missing. The distinctive scent of new-set cement mortar was heavy, and sparks and iron clanging came from the tops of the towers; smiths at work.

The soft cloth covered his eyes, and someone took the reins of his dog. Normal traffic sounds and town-smells came beyond, with a low murmur at the sight of the Brigade banner beside him. An occasional shout to make way, in accented Spanjol. Once or twice a member of the escort said something; Teodore had trouble following it, although he spoke the eastern tongue well. The men around him pronounced it with a nasal twang, and many words he'd never read in any Sponglish book. The feeling of helplessness was oddly disorienting, like being ill. Mounted troops went by, and the rumbling of guns passing over irregular pavement. Minutes passed, even with the dogs at a fast walk; Old Residence was a *big* city.

By the time the echoes changed to indicate they'd pulled out into the main plaza, Teodore Welf was getting a little annoyed. Only the thought that he was *supposed* to be annoyed kept it within bounds. Someone was drilling men on foot in the plaza, and he recognized enough Sponglish swearwords to know that whoever it was was not happy with them. If Raj Whitehall was trying to make soldiers out of Old Residence militia, then probably all parties concerned were quite desperately unhappy. The thought restored some of his cheer as he was helped to dismount and guided up steps with a hand under his elbow. One of the other emissaries stumbled and swore.

Cold metal slid between the blindfold and his skin, light as the touch of a butterfly.

"Be *quite* still, now," the lilting voice said next to his ear.

The cloth fell away, sliced neatly through. He blinked as light returned. The faded, shabby-at-the-edges splendor of the Governor's Council Chamber was familiar enough. They went through marbled corridors with high coffered ceilings and tall slim pillars along the sides, and into the domed council hall itself. The rising semicircular tiers of benches were full, with the Councilors in their best; carbide lamps in the dome above reflected from the white stone and pale wood. Teodore stiffened in anger to see that the Brigade banner had been taken down from behind the podium, leaving the gold and silver Starburst once more with pride of place.

There were a few other changes. The guards at the door were in Civil Government uniform of blue swallowtail coat and maroon pants and round bowl-helmets with chainmail neckguards. The Chair of the First Citizen was occupied by a man in an officer's version of the same outfit; on a table beside him was a cushion bearing a steel mace inlaid with precious metals.

Whitehall, the Brigade noble thought. He clicked heels and inclined his head slightly; the easterner nodded. A woman sat on the consort's seat one step below him; even then, Teodore gave her a second glance that had little to do with the splendor of her East Residence court garb. *Woof,* he thought.

Then the general's gray eyes met his. Teodore Welf had fought in a thunderstorm once, with a blue nimbus playing over the lanceheads and armor of his men. The skin-prickling sensation was quite similar to this. He remembered the battle at the railroad bridge and along the road, the eerie feeling of being watched and anticipated and never knowing what was going to hit him next.

He shook it off. His General had given him a task to do.

". . . and so, Councilors, even now the Lord of Men is willing to forgive you for allowing a foreign interloper to seize and man the fortifications which the 591st Provisional Brigade has held against all enemies for so long. Full amnesty, conditional on the eastern troops leaving the city within twenty-four hours. We will even allow the enemy three days' grace before pursuit, or a week if they agree to leave by sea and trouble the Western Territories no more.

"Consider well," the Brigade ambassador concluded, "how many kilometers of wall surround this great city, and how few, how very few, the foreign troops are. Far too few to hold it against the great host of the Lord of Men, which even now makes camp outside. Take heed and take His Mightiness' mercy, before you feel his anger."

Raj smiled thinly. *Not a bad performance*, he thought. A good many of the Councilors were probably sweating hard right now. This Teodore Welf certainly looked the part, with his sternly handsome young face and long blond locks falling to the shoulderplates of his armor. He'd spoken like an educated man, too—fought like one, in the skirmishes with the vanguard of the Brigadero army. The two other officers beside him were older, scarred veterans in their forties. Their speeches had been shorter, and their Spanjol much more accented.

"Most eloquent," Raj said dryly. "However, Lord Welf, *I* speak for this noble Council; as one of their member"—his family were hereditary Councilors in the Civil Government, a minor honor there—"and as duly appointed commander of the armed forces of the Civil Government of Holy Federation, under the orders of the Sole Rightful Autocrat Barholm Clerett. Against which and whom the 591st Provisional Brigade is in a state of unlawful mutiny. You are the foreigner here. General Forker was a rebellious vassal—"

In soi-disant theory the Brigade held the Western Territories as "delegates" of the Chair; a face-saving arrangement dating back to the original invasion, when General Teodore Amalson had been persuaded to move into the Western Territories after harassing East Residence for a generation. Old Residence had already been in the hands of a "garrison" of barbarian mercenaries for a long lifetime before that. Old Amalson had solved *that* problem with blunt pragmatism; he'd killed all their leaders at a banquet and massacred the rank-and-file next day.

"—and your marriage-kinsman Ingreid Manfrond is not even a vassal, being a usurper. Let me further point out that neither you Brigaderos nor any other barbarians built this city or its walls—you couldn't even keep them in repair. It has returned to its rightful rulers, and we intend to keep it. If you think you can take it away from us, you're welcome to try, with hard blows and not with words. Siegecraft is not something the Brigade has ever excelled at, and I predict you'll break your teeth on this nut before you crack it. Meanwhile you'll be camping in the mud and getting sick, while the people rise up behind you and the northern savages burn your undefended homes.

"Go back, Lord Welf," Raj went on. "Use your eloquence on your compatriots. Tell them to end their rebellion now, while they have their lives and land, before they're hunted fugitives cowering in caves and woods. Because the Sovereign Mighty Lord has entrusted me with the task of reducing the Western Territories and all in them to obedience. Which I will do by whatever means are necessary."

"So, what's this Whitehall fellow like?" Ingreid Manfrond said.

Ingreid and Teodore and Carstens were alone now. Teodore put his booted feet up on the chest. The servant clucked and began unbuckling the mud-splashed greaves; another handed him a goblet of mulled Sala with spices. The commander's tent was like a small house and lavishly furnished, but it already had a frowsty smell. The young man frowned; Ingreid *was* a pig. *And he doesn't know anything about women,* he thought. *The way he treats Marie is* stupid. Dangerously stupid.

It wouldn't do to underestimate Ingreid, though. There was a boar's cunning in the little eyes.

"Whitehall?" Teodore said. As a relative by marriage to the General, he could leave out the honorifics in private. "About my height, looks to be around thirty. Dark even for an easterner, but his eyes are gray. A real fighting man, I'd say, from the way he's built and from the look of his hands and face—a saddle-and-sword man, not a hilltop commander. Doesn't waste words; told me right out that if we want the city, we can come and fight him for it. And . . . Lord of Men, you've got a real war on your hands. This is a man who warriors will follow."

Ingreid grunted thoughtfully, his hand caressing the hilt of his sword. "They say he has the demon's luck, too."

"I don't know about that, but I saw his wife—and they say she's a witch. I can believe it."

Ingreid shook his head. "We'll break him," he said, with flat conviction. "No amount of luck means a turd when you're out-numbered twenty to one." His shoulders hunched unconsciously, the stance of a man determined to butt his way head-first through a brick wall or die trying.

Carstens and the young officer exchanged a glance. *I had him outnumbered and he killed two thousand of my best men,* Teodore thought. He doubted Whitehall had lost more than a hundred or so. Of course, at that rate the Civil Government army would run out of men before the Brigade did . . . but victory bought at such a price would be indistinguishable from defeat.

"What about the Civvies?" Carstens put in. "He can't hold the city with only twenty thousand men if the natives don't cooperate with him."

"The Council?" Teodore snorted. "They won't crap without ask-ing his permission, most of them. Scared of us, but more scared of him because he's in there with them. We might do something with the Priest, though. Whitehall's been leaning on the Civvie gentry pretty hard, they thought they'd watch the war like spectators at a bullfight and he's not having any of that."

Carstens nodded. "I've got some tame Civvie priests hanging around," he said. "We can get messages over the wall."

Ingreid flipped a hand. "You handle it then, Howyrd," he said. "Get me an open gate, and you're *Hereditary* Grand Constable." Carstens grinned like a wolf; that would give his sons the title, if not necessarily the office.

"Land?" he said. "I'd need more of an estate, to support that title."

"Those Councilors must have a million or two acres between them. The ones who stick to Whitehall will lose their necks—and you get your pick, after the Seat."

Teodore nodded thoughtfully. "And do I have your authority to oversee the encampment?" he asked.

Both the other officers looked at him. "Sure, if you want it," Ingreid said.

It was routine work. Almost servant's work . . . "We're going to be here a while," Teodore said. "Better to get it right. I don't want us wasting men, we've already lost too many through Forker's negligence."

"Eight camps?" Ingreid Manfrond said, peering at the map the younger man unrolled. "Why eight?"

Teodore Welf cleared his throat. "Less chance of sickness if we spread the troops out, Lord of Men," he said. "Or so the priests say."

It was also what Mihwel Obregon's *Handbook for Siege Operations* said, but Teodore wasn't going to tell his monarch the idea came out of a book, and a Sponglish book at that. He hadn't taken everything in it all that seriously himself, when he read it—but since meeting the Civil Government's army, their methods looked much more credible.

Howyrd Carstens nodded, walking to the tent-flap and using his telescope on the walls of the city two kilometers distant.

"Sounds good," he said. "With twelve regiments in every camp, we'll have enough to block any Civvie thrust out of the city more than long enough for the others to pile in."

"You think they'll dare to come out?" Ingreid said, surprised.

Teodore tossed back his mulled wine and held the goblet out for more. "Let's put it this way, kinsman," he said. "When we've got Whitehall's head on a lance, I'll relax."

"Have you *seen* those handless cows at drill, *mi heneral?*" Jorg Menyez said bitterly. "What're they good for, except getting in the way of a bullet that might hit someone useful?"

Raj chuckled without looking up from the big tripod-mounted binoculars. From the top of the north-gate tower the nearest enemy encampment sprang out at him, the raw reddish-gray earth of the berm around it seeming within arm's reach.

"Others have been known to say the same thing about our infantry, Jorg," he said, stepping back. "Grammeck, tell me what you think of those works."

The artilleryman bent to the eyepiece. The tower-top was

crowded; in the center was a sandbagged emplacement for the 200mm mortar, and movable recoil-ramps had been built near the front, timber slides at forty-five degree angles. Field-guns could run up them under recoil and return to battery by their own weight, saving a lot of time in action. A counter-weighted platform at the rear of the tower gave quick access to ground level.

Raj forestalled his infantry commander with a raised hand.

"I know, I know. Still, we have to work with what we've got. I'm going to call for volunteers from the militia; since they'll get full rations and pay—"

"We can afford that?" Jorg said.

"The Priest has agreed to pay a war-levy on ecclesiastical property," Raj said. "I expect about ten thousand men to step forward." They'd been drilling forty thousand or so, and employment was slow in a besieged city.

"We'll take the best five thousand of those. From that, cream off a company's worth for each of your battalions, younger men with no local ties. We'll enlist them, and you can begin full-time training. We've enough spare equipment for that many. At the least, they can stand watch while real soldiers sleep; I suspect we're going to get constant harassing attacks soon."

He grinned. "And just to make you entirely miserable, you can also provide cadre for the rest; that'll be about eight battalions of full-timers, armed with Brigade weapons. Again, they can replace regular infantry on things like *guardia* duty."

Jorg sighed and nodded. Grammeck looked up from the binoculars.

"That looks uncomfortably like one of our camps," he said. "Although they're rather slow about it—a full week, and not finished yet."

"It's straight out of Obregon's *Siege Operations*" Raj said. "Siting, spacing and outer lines—although the street layout inside isn't regular. But digging is servant's work, to Brigaderos. They've got some competent officers, but it isn't institutionalized, with them."

He squinted at the distant earthworks. The air was raw and chill, but the iron-gray clouds were holding off on rain, for once.

"I suspect they'll dig faster soon," he went on.

Junpawl the Skinner moved another half-inch, sliding on his belly through the slick mud. It was deep black, the second hour after midnight with clouds over the stars and both moons down. The Long Hair camp was mostly silent about him, and the nearest light was ten minutes walk away—only the great chiefs had enough firewood to spare for all-night blazes. He drew the long knife strapped to his bare thigh; he'd stripped down to his breechclout for this work, and smeared himself all over with mud, even taking the brass ring off his scalplock. Cold wind touched his back; good, the dogs for this tent were upwind ten meters away . . . and he'd held ox-dung under his armpits, a sure disguise for man-scent.

The canvas back of the tent parted under the edge of the knife, a softer sound than the guylines flapping in the breeze. The Skinner stuck his head through, flaring his nostrils, letting smell and hearing do the work of eyes. Four men, two snoring. Fast asleep, as if they were at home with their women—faster asleep than any Real Man ever slept, even dead drunk. He grinned in the darkness, eeling through the meter-long slit, careful not to let it gape. A breeze could wake a man, even a Long Hair. Inside, his bare feet touched pine-boughs; that was why the enemy rustled when they turned in their sleep.

His fingers moved, feather-light as he touched bodies to confirm positions. The Long Hairs slept huddled together for warmth, wrapped in many rich wool blankets like a chief's women, pinning their own arms. Their swords and rifles were stacked at the door of the tent— out of reach. These were indeed men who ate grass, like sheep. Only Skinners lived as Real Men should, on the steppe with their families in tents on wagons, following the herds of grazing sauroids. Hunting and war were a Real Man's work.

Slowly, moving a fraction of an inch at a time, Junpawl's left hand crept toward a face. Warm breath touched his palm. Fingers and thumb clamped down with brutal suddenness across nose and lips, pinning them closed; the blackened knife in his right hand drove down at an angle. It was heavy steel, just sharp enough—not so sharp that bone would turn the edge. It made nothing of the muscle and cartilage of the Long Hair's neck, grating home in the spine. The body flopped once, and blood poured up his forearms, but the massive wound bled the Long Hair out almost at once. The beard-less face went flaccid under his hand; it must be a young man, barely old enough to ride with the war-host.

Junpawl waited, knife poised, ready to slash and dive out of the tent. The man next to the corpse turned over, muttered in his sleep and began to snore again. The nomad mercenary sliced off one of the dead man's ears and tucked it in the pouch at his waist; one silver piece per left ear, that was what the Big Devil Whitehall would pay. Ah, that one was a *frai hum,* a Real Man in his spirit! You could buy a lot of burn-head-water with a silver piece, many fat women, lots of chocolate or ammunition.

He stepped over the sleeping man and squatted down near the second pair, carefully wiping his hands on a corner of the blanket so the next victim wouldn't feel blood dripping on his face.

He'd kill only two of the four in the tent. *Cadaw d'nwit,* a night-gift for the Long Hairs to wake up to. His giggle was utterly soundless.

The joke was worth missing the other two silver pieces. Besides, he'd stop in one more tent tonight on his way out of camp.

Delicate as a maiden's kiss, the Skinner's hand sank toward the sleeping Brigadero's face.

CHAPTER EIGHT

"I suspect we're going to get very sick of this view before spring," Raj said. *It's only a couple of weeks since the Brigaderos arrived and I'm sick of it already.* The strategic arguments for standing on the defensive were strong. He still didn't like it.

He bent to the eyepiece of the brass-and-iron tripod-mounted binoculars. The gun-redoubt the enemy were building—slowly, since they'd gotten reluctant to move outside their walls at night—was mostly complete. Walls of wicker baskets full of earth, loopholed for the heavy siege guns. The guns themselves were rolling out of the nearest of the fortified camps, soda-bottle shaped things on four-wheeled carriages, drawn by multiple yokes of oxen.

The chanting of the morning prayer had barely died; the breaths of the command group on the tower were puffs of white, although there had been no hard frost. Bells rang from the hundreds of cathedrons and churches throughout the city. Silvery fog lay on the surface of the river behind the roof-crowned hills of Old Residence. Steam rose from the kave mugs most of the officers held.

Kaltin Gruder took a bite out of a pastry. "If one has to fight in winter," he said, "this is actually not bad. Clean sheets, hot meals, running water, women. As long as the food holds out, of course."

Muzzaf Kerpatik nodded. "Two ships came in last night under tow," he said. "Eight hundred tons of provisions, and another two hundred thousand rounds of 11mm from Lion City."

Raj glanced up at the black-uniformed naval commander. The sailor cleared his throat:

"Their batteries on the south shore aren't much, at night," he said. "The channel's fairly deep on the north side, we just steam up and they try to hit the sound of our engines. Which is difficult enough if you're *used* to dealing with sound on water."

Tonhio Lopeyz, Raj reminded himself.

"Good work, Messer Commodore Lopeyz," he said, nodding.

Provisions aren't tight yet, he thought. Plenty of beans and bullets, but he needed *men.* What he could do with another five or six thousand veteran cavalry . . .

"What sort of rate of fire do you think they can get with those siege pieces, Grammeck?" he asked.

Dinnalsyn looked up from his plotting table. "Oh, not more than one shot per half hour per gun, *mi heneral,*" he said. "Their crews look like amateurs, mostly—I think they keep those guns in storage between wars. Probably only a few real gunners per tube. Still, a day or so and six guns firing those forty-kilo round-shot would bring any hundred meters of wall down, even with the earthwork backing we've put in. Curtain walls like this—" he stamped a foot "—just can't take the racking stress." Which was why they'd been replaced with low earth-backed walls sunk behind moats, in the Civil Government and Colony. The western Midworld was considerably behind the times.

There was a rattling bang from the rear of the tower. The Y-beams creaked as the platform came level with the parapet, and the crew manhandled a 75mm field gun forward onto the flagstones. A gunner waved a flag from beside it, and the platform sank as oxen on the ground below heaved at their traces and compensated for the pull of the counterweights. The timber platform bumped rhythmically against the stones of the tower's inner wall as it went down. The gun-crew trundled the weapon into position on the wooden disk that waited for it. Behind the wheels were long curving ramps; ahead of them rope-buffered blocks. The gunners slid marlinspikes through iron brackets sunk into the circular wooden disk and heaved experimentally. There was a grating sound from the "lubricating" sand beneath the planks, and the weapon pivoted, the muzzle just clearing the crenellations of the parapet.

"Will the structure take it?" Raj asked.

"I think so," Dinnalsyn said cautiously. "We've got the floors below this braced with heavy timbers." He looked at the Brigaderos. "Amateurs. Hasn't it occurred to them to check trajectories? Height *is* distance."

No, Raj thought. *But then, it wouldn't have occurred to* me *unless Center had pointed it out.*

The second gun slid into position. Dinnalsyn looked to the towers left and right of his position; the guns there were ready too.

He touched off a smoke rocket. The little firework sizzled off northward, its plume drifting through the cold morning air. Center looked out through Raj's eyes at the smoke. Glowing lines traced vectors across his vision.

"Colonel," Raj said quietly. "Bring that gun around another two degrees, and you'll make better practice, I think."

Dinnalsyn relayed the order. "We lost a great cannon-cocker when you were born to the nobility, *mi heneral,*" he said cheerfully, bending his eyes to the binoculars. Then: "*Fwego!*"

The gunner jerked his lanyard. The gun slammed backwards, rising up the tracks behind its wheels, paused for a second as mass fought momentum, then slid downward with a rush to clang against the chocks. Bitter smoke drifted with the wind into the eyes of the officers at the side of the tower. They blinked, and a spot of red fire flashed for an instant in the center of a blot of black smoke over the Brigadero redoubt. A second later one of the enemy siege cannon fired, a longer duller *booom* and cloud of smoke. Almost at the same instant there was a splintering crash from far below, and the stone of the tower trembled beneath their feet.

A brass shell casing clanged dully on timber as the crew of the field gun levered open the breech of their weapon.

None of the men on the tower commented on the enemy hit. Dinnalsyn turned to the battery commander at the plotting table. "Triangulate," he said.

The captain moved his parallel setsteels across the paper, consulted a printed table and worked his sliderule. The solution was simple, time-to-target over set ranges to a fixed location. Center could have solved the problem to the limit of the accuracy of the Civil Government guns in a fraction of a second—but that *would* start looking excessively odd. Besides, he didn't want men who needed a crutch. Come to that, neither did Center.

The captain called out elevations and bearing for each gun in the ten tasked with this mission. A heliograph signaller clicked it out in both directions, sunlight on a mirror behind a slotted cover.

"Ranging fire, in succession," Dinnalsyn said.

From east to west along the wall guns spoke, each allowing just enough time to observe the fall of shot. Raj trained his own field glasses. Oxen were bellowing and running in the open center of the Brigadero redoubt, some of them with trails of pink intestine tangling their hooves. Men staggered to the rear, or were dragged by their comrades. More were still heaving at the massive siege guns, hauling in gangs of two dozen or more at the block-and-tackle rigs that moved them into and out of position.

"Five round stonk," Dinnalsyn's voice said, cool and dispassionate. "Shrapnel, fire for effect, rapid fire. Fire."

This time the four towers erupted in smoke and flame, each gun firing as soon as its mate had run back into battery and was being loaded. The rate of fire was much higher than the guns could have achieved firing from level ground; in less than a minute forty shells burst over the enemy position, a continuous rolling flicker. Smoke drifted back from the towers, and covered the target. A rending *clap* and ball of yellow flame marked a secondary explosion as one of the siege-gun caissons went up. Four more explosions followed at half-second intervals, and the huge barrel of one of the siege guns flipped up out of the dust and smoke. When the debris cleared the

Brigaderos position looked like a freshly-spaded garden mixed with a wrecker's yard.

Raj bent to the binoculars. Nothing moved in the field of vision for a few long seconds. Then dirt stirred, and a man rose to his feet. He had his hands pressed over his ears, and from the gape of his mouth he was probably screaming. Tears ran down his dirt-caked cheeks, and he blundered out over the mound of earth and into the zone between the bastion—the former bastion—and the city. Still screaming and sobbing as he lurched forward, until a rifle spoke from the wall. Raj could see the puff of dust from the front of his jacket as the bullet struck.

"Five round stonk, contact-fused HE," Dinnalsyn said. "Standard fire, fire."

The guns opened up again, the steady three rounds a minute that preserved barrels and broke armies. Most of the shells tossed up dirt already chewed by the explosion of the stacked ammunition. Several knocked aside the heavy siege guns themselves, ripping them off their iron-framed fortress mounts. Whoops and cheers rang out from the Old Residence wall as troops and militiamen jeered and laughed at every hit. The noise continued until Raj turned his head and bit out an order that sent a courier running down the interior stairs to the wall.

"Nothing to cheer in brave men being butchered by an imbecile's orders," he said.

"Better theirs than ours, *mi heneral,*" Kaltin said.

Silence fell. The gunners took the opportunity to swab out the bores of their weapons, clearing the fouling before it bound tightly to the metal. A mounted man with a white pennant on his lance rode out from the central Brigaderos camp. That would be a herald asking permission to remove the dead and wounded, formal admission of defeat in this . . . he couldn't quite decide what to call it. "Battle" was completely inappropriate.

"True, Kaltin," Raj said. "However, remember that every time you fight someone, you teach them something, if they're willing to learn. *Somebody* over there will be willing to learn. Play chess long enough with good players and you get good."

Somebody over there had read Obregon's *Siege Operations*, at least. Not the supreme commander, or they wouldn't have committed this fiasco.

"Our army is already pretty good. We have to work *hard* to improve. All the enemy has to do is learn a few basics and it would double their combat power."

It would be a race between his abilities and the enemy's learning curve.

He remembered Cannae again. The perfect battle . . . but even Hannibal had needed Tarentius Varro commanding on the other side.

"Long may you live and reign, Ingreid Manfrond," Raj whispered.

Some of the other officers looked at him. He explained: "There are four types of commander. Brilliant and energetic; brilliant and lazy; stupid and lazy; and stupid and energetic. With the first three, you can do something. With the last, nothing but disaster can result. I think Ingreid Manfrond has shown us which category he belongs to. Let's just hope he's energetic enough to hang on to power."

"I *told* you that would happen!" Howyrd Carstens shouted.

"Watch your mouth!" Ingreid roared back.

"I told you that would happen, *Lord of Men*," Carstens said with heavy sarcasm.

A sharp gasp came from the cot between them. Both men stepped back. Teodore Welf lay on it, a leather strap between his teeth. A priest-doctor with the front-to-back tonsure of a This Earth cleric gripped the end of a long iron splinter with tongs and pulled steadily. The metal stuck out of the young man's thigh at a neat forty-five degree angle. For a second it resisted the doctor's muscles, then came free with a gush of blood.

"Let it bleed for a second," the doctor said. The flow slowed, and he swabbed the wound with a ball of cotton dipped in alcohol, then palpated the area and probed for fragments and bits of cloth. "Looks clean, and it all came out," he said. "As long as the bone doesn't mortify, you should be up and around in a while. Stay off it till then or you'll limp for years."

He passed his amulet over the puncture and then cleaned it with blessed iodine. The patient grunted again as it touched him, then stared as the bandage was strapped on.

"This will ease you."

Teodore shook his head. "No poppy. I need my wits." He glared up at the two older men, sweat pouring down his face, but he waited until the doctor was gone before speaking.

"You're both right," he said. "Carstens, we fucked up. You were right. Lord of Men, you're right—we're pressed for time."

"I suppose you've got a suggestion?" Ingreid said, stroking his beard.

The boy was a puppy, but he was brave and had his wits about him—and he was a Welf. That meant a wise General would give him respectful attention, because the Welfs still had many followers. It also meant a sensible General should allow him full rein for his bravery. An honorably dead Welf would be much less inconvenient after the war than a live, heroic one. He scowled, and his hand clenched. *Damn* the wench for miscarrying, just when he was too busy to plow her again. Her hips were good enough and she looked healthy; what had gone wrong? A son of his and hers would unite the branches and be unassailable, an obvious choice for election when he grew too old to hold power. His older sons would be ready to step in to the high offices around the Seat.

"All right," he said. "What's your idea?" He held up a hand. "No more about detaching troops to guard our rear. If I let regiments go, the whole host will start to unravel, screaming for a garrison here and a detachment there. I need them here, under my eye—too many can't understand that this war is more important than raids on the border."

"Lord of Men, the Civvies just showed us that you can throw a rock harder from a hill." Teodore jerked his chin at the map across the tent room. "Here's what I propose—"

An hour or so later, Ingreid nodded slowly. "That sounds like it will work," he said.

"It had *better* work," Howyrd Carstens said. "Unless you like the taste of dog-meat."

Now I know why our ancestors left the Base Area, Ludwig Bellamy thought. *It was that or freeze to death.* They were between Old Residence and Carson Barracks; away from the sea, the winters were harder. Frost every night now, and the rains were half-sleet. His men slept huddled next to their dogs for warmth, dreaming of the orange groves and date-palms of the Southern Territories. And the Base Area up north was even colder than this. No wonder each succeeding wave of invaders was more barbaric—their brains had had longer to freeze in the dark.

He smiled to himself, noticing he'd shaped the thought in Sponglish. When he fought with his own hands or took a woman, or prayed to the Spirit, Namerique still came first to him. For subtle wit or pondering strategy, Sponglish was more natural.

"No prisoners," he said quietly. His voice carried in the cathedron stillness of the oak forest. "No survivors."

Dogs crouched and men squatted by them, united in a tense carnivore eagerness as they heard the mournful whistle of the approaching locomotive. Open fields ran from the forest edge, black soil with cold water and a little dawn-ice in hollows; the winter wheat was a bluish sheen on the surface of it. They were north of the railroad, the embankment sweeping from southwest to northeast a kilometer away. It crossed a small stream on a single stone-piered wooden bridge, and the train and its escorting armored car had stopped there, checking carefully under the piers. He brought up the binoculars, watching the Brigade dragoons splashing through thigh-deep icy water as they poked and prodded and checked below the surface. The smell of cold and wet plowed earth and leaf-mould and dog filled his nostrils as he watched, the scent of the hunt.

They climbed back up, some to the armored car running on flanged wheels, others to the rear car of the fifteen hitched to the locomotive. Black smoke billowed from the stack; he could see the thrall shoveling coal with a will—warmth for himself, as well as power for the engine. The chuff of the vertical cylinders carried across the fields, and a long shower of sparks shot out from under the heavy timber frame as the bell-cranks drove the four coupled wheels of the engine against the strap iron surface of the rails. The locomotive lunged forward, jerked to a halt as the chain came taut, then bumped forward again as the cars slid up in turn and rammed the padded buffer bar at the rear of the coal cart. A ripple of collisions banged each of the cars together, leaving the whole mass coasting forward at less than walking pace. The process repeated itself several times before the train began to move in unison with the linking chains taut.

The armored car slid ahead more smoothly, holding down its speed to match the train it escorted. It took the better part of a kilometer for the train to reach the speed of a galloping dog. Which put it about—

Whump.

The armored car's front wheels crossed the tie he'd selected. The mine was nothing complicated; a cartridge with the bullet pulled, stuck into a five-kilo bag of black powder. A board with a nail in it rested over the bullet, and the whole affair was carefully buried under the crosstie. The car's forward motion carried it squarely over the charge before the gunpowder went off. It flipped off the track and landed upside down, the piston-rods on its underside still spinning the wheels for an instant despite the buckling of the frame. Then orange-white flame shot out of every opening in the hull; the black iron mass bucked and heaved in the center of the fire as ammunition went off in bursts and spurts.

More sparks shot out from under the locomotive's wheels as the panic-stricken driver threw the engine into full reverse. The freight cars had no brakes, however; the whole mass plowed into the rear of the locomotive, sending it plunging off the tracks even before it reached the crater. The middle cars of the train bucked into the air as the sliding weight met the suddenly immobile obstacle ahead. The rear end cracked like a whip, sending the last two cars flicking off the track and crashing to the ground with bone-shattering force.

"Charge!" Ludwig shouted.

The trumpet sounded, and the 2nd Cruisers poured out of the wood with a roar. A few of the Brigade warriors in the caboose staggered free of the wreckage in time to meet the sabers; then the troopers were jumping to the ground and hammering their way into the wrecked train. He looked east and west. The scouts blinked mirror-signals to him. All clear, no other trains in sight.

"Bacon!" a company commander shouted back to Ludwig. "Beans, cornmeal and hardtack, pig-lard."

Shots ran out as his men finished off the last of crew and escort. Ludwig frowned.

"Steel, you fools," he roared.

They needed to conserve ammunition, since the enemy stores were useless to them—although any powder they captured was all to the good. *Good lads, but they still get carried away now and then,* he thought.

The peasants they'd gathered up were edging out of the woods too, several hundred of them. Ludwig grinned to himself; they were welcome to what his men couldn't load on their spare dogs—and they'd hide it much more thoroughly than the raiders could, since they knew the countryside. A squad was down by the bridge, prying stones loose from the central pier with picks and stuffing more linen bags of gunpowder into it.

"Fire in the hole!" one shouted, as they climbed back out of the streambed.

A minute later the dogs all flinched as a pillar of black smoke and water and stone erupted from the gully. The timber box-trestle that spanned the creek heaved up in the center and collapsed in fragments. Boards and bits of timber rained down across half the distance between the wreck and the bridge. Ludwig noticed that his sword was still out; he sheathed it as a man staggered by under a load of sides of bacon and dropped two for his dog. Loads of food were going on the pack-saddles even as the animals fed. Like most carnivores, war-dogs could gorge on meat and then fast for a considerable time without much harm. Today they'd bolt a man-weight of the rich fatty pig-flesh each.

The first of the peasants arrived, panting. They were ragged men, lumps of tattered cloth and hair, more starved-looking even than usual for peons in midwinter. The Brigade quartermasters had simplified their supply problems by taking as much as possible from areas within wagon-transport distance of the railroad, not waiting for barged loads at the Padan River end of the line.

"Thank you, lord," the peon leader said, bowing low.

His followers went straight for the tumbled cars; some of them stuffed raw cornmeal from ripped sacks into their mouths as they worked, moaning and smacking, the yellow grain staining their beards and smocks.

"The *Gubernio Civil* comes to free you from the Brigade," Ludwig said. "Consider this a beginning. And you don't have to wait for us; you can take more yourselves."

"How, lord?" the serf headman asked. Peasants were already trotting back to the woods, with sacks on their backs. "We have no weapons, no gunpowder. The masters have swords and dogs and guns."

"You don't have to blow up the tracks," Ludwig said. "Come out just before dark. Unspike the rails from the crossties, or saw them through. Wait for the trains to derail. Most of them have only a few soldiers, and few have armored cars for escort. For weapons . . . you have flails and mattocks and scythes. Good enough to kill men dazed by a wreck in the dark. Most of the real Brigade warriors are off fighting at Old Residence, anyway."

And if they got too paranoid to run trains at night, there went half the carrying capacity of the railroad.

The peon headman bowed again, shapeless wool cap clutched to his breast. "Lord, we shall do as you command," he said. The words were humble, but the feral glint in the peasant's black eyes set Ludwig's teeth on edge.

Captain Hortez came up as the peasant slouched off. "Ready to go, sir," the Descotter said. He looked admiringly at the wreck. "That was sneaky, sir, very sneaky."

"I must be learning the ways of civilization; that really sounds like a compliment," Ludwig said. "It did stand to reason the Brigaderos would eventually start checking bridges."

"What next?"

"We'll try this a few more times, then we'll start putting the mine *before* the bridge. Then when they're fixated on looking for mines near bridges, we'll put them nowhere *near* bridges. After, we'll start over with the bridges. And we can just tear up sections of track."

Rip up the iron, pile it on a huge stack of ties, and set a torch to it. Time consuming, but effective.

"And the slower they run the trains so they can check for mines—"

"—and the more carrying capacity they divert to guards—"

"—the better," Ludwig finished.

"A new sport," Hortez said. "Train wrecking." Flames began to rise from the wooden cars as troopers stove in casks of lard and spilled them over the wood. Hortez looked at the line of peons trudging back towards the forest. "The peasants are getting right into the spirit of this, too. Pretty soon they'll be doing more damage than we are. Surprising, I thought the Brigadero reprisals would be more effective."

"As Messer Raj told me, you can only condemn men to death *once*," Ludwig said. "Threats are more effective as threats. Once you've stolen their seed corn and run off their stock and burned down their houses, what else can you do?"

Hortez chuckled. The bannerman of the 2nd Cruisers came up, and Ludwig swung his hand forward. The column formed by platoons, scouts fanning out to their flanks; they rode south, down into the bed of the stream. The brigade call-up had been most complete along the line of rail, too. The local home guards were graybeards or smooth-cheeked youths. Mostly they lost the scent if you took precautions . . . possibly they *really* lost it, although the first few times groups chasing them had barreled into ambush enthusiastically enough.

"I wouldn't like to be a landowner around here for the next couple of years, though," the Descotter officer said.

Ludwig Bellamy remembered the way the serf's face had lit. *Spirit, we'll have to fight another campaign to put the peons back to work after we beat the Brigade.* No landowner liked the idea of the peasantry running loose. A pity that war could not be kept as an affair among gentlemen.

Solve the problems one at a time, he reminded himself. Victory over the Brigade was the problem; Messer Raj had assigned him part of the solution, disrupting their logistics.

Whatever it took.

CHAPTER NINE

"Now that was really quite clever," Raj said. "Not complicated, but clever."

He focused the binoculars. The riverside wall was much lower than the outer defenses, but he could see the suburbs and villas on the south shore of the White River easily enough. Most of it was shallow and silty, here where it ran east past the seaward edge of Old Residence. Once the Midworld had lapped at the city's harbor, but a millennium of silting had pushed the delta several kilometers out to sea. He could also see the ungainly-looking craft that were floating halfway across the four-kilometer breadth of the river.

Both were square boxes with sharply sloping sides. A trio of squat muzzles poked through each flank; in the center of the roof was a man-high conning tower of boiler plate on a timber backing. A flagpole bore the double lightning-flash of the Brigade.

"How did they get them into position?" Raj said. There was no sign of engines or oars.

"Kedging," Commodore Lopeyz said. He pulled at the collar of his uniform jacket. "Sent boats out at night with anchors and cables. Drop the anchors, run the cables back to the raft. Cable to the shore, too. Crew inside to haul in the cables to adjust position."

"Nothing you can do about them?" Raj said.

"Damn-all, general," the naval officer said in frustration. He shut his long brass telescope with a snap.

"They're just *rafts*," he went on. "Even with those battering pieces and a meter and a half of oakwood on the sides, they draw less water than my ships, so I can't get at them. I'd have to ram them a dozen times anyway, break them up. They're floating on log platforms, not a displacement hull. Meanwhile if I try exchanging shots, they'd smash my steamers to matchwood before I made any impression—those are forty-kilo siege guns they mount. *And* they're close enough to close the shipping channel along the north bank."

As if to counterpoint the remark, one of the rafts fired a round. The heavy iron ball carried two kilometers over the water, then skipped a dozen times. Each strike cast a plume of water into the sky, before the roundshot crumpled a fishing wharf on the north bank. The cold wind whipped Raj's cloak against his calves, and stung his freshly shaven cheeks. He closed his eyes meditatively for perhaps thirty seconds, consulting Center. Images clicked into place behind his lids.

"Grammeck," he said, squinting across the river again. "What do you suppose the roofs of those things are?"

The artilleryman scanned them carefully. "Planking and sandbags, I think," he said. "Shrapnel-proof. Why?"

"Well, I don't want to take any cannon off the walls," Raj said thoughtfully. "Here's what we'll do." He took a sketchpad from an aide and drew quickly, weighting the paper against the merlon of the wall with the edge of his cloak.

"Make a raft," Raj said. "We've got half a dozen shipyards, that oughtn't to be any problem. Protect it with railroad strap-iron from one of the foundries here, say fifty millimeters on a backing of two hundred millimeters of oak beam. No loopholes for cannon. Put one of the mortars in the center instead, with a circular lid in segments. Iron segments, hinged. Make three or four rafts. When they're ready, we'll use the same kedging technique to get them in range of those Brigadero cheeseboxes, and see how they like 200mm mortar shells dropping down on them."

"*Ispirito de Persona*," Dinnalsyn said with boyish delight. "Spirit of Man. You know, that'll probably work?"

He looked at the sketch. "*Mi heneral,* these might be useful west of the city too—the river's deep enough for a couple of kilometers, nearly to the bridge for something this shallow-draft. If I took one of those little teakettles they use for locomotives here, and rigged some sort of covered paddle . . ."

Raj nodded. "See to it, but after we deal with the blockading rafts. Muzzaf, in the meanwhile cut the civilian ration by one-quarter, just in case."

"That will be unpopular with the better classes," the Komarite warned.

"I can live with it," Raj said.

The laborers would still be better off than in most winters; a three-quarter ration they had money to buy was considerably more than what they could generally afford in slack times. Of course, the civilian magnates would be even more pissed off with Civil Government rule than before . . . but Barholm had sent him here to conquer the Western Territories. Pacifying it would be somebody else's problem.

"Hmmm. Commodore Lopeyz, do any of your men have small-boat experience?" Two of the rams were tied up by the city docks, upstream of the enemy rafts and unable to move while they blocked the exit to the sea.

"A lot of them were fishermen before the press-gang came by," the sailor said.

"Gerrin, I want a force of picked men from the 5th for some night work. The Brigaderos don't seem to be guarding that boatyard they built the rafts in. Train discreetly with Messer Lopeyz' boatmen, and in about a week—that'll be a two-moons-down night, and probably overcast—we'll have a little raid and some incendiary work."

"General Whitehall, I love you," Gerrin said, smiling like a downdragger about to bite into a victim.

"On to the next problem," Raj said. "Now—"

"Whitehall will get us all *killed*," the landowner said. "We'll *starve*."

His Holiness Paratier nodded graciously, ignoring the man's well-filled paunch. He knew that Vihtorio Azaiglio had gotten the full yield of his estates sent in to warehouses in Old Residence. Whatever else happened, nobody in his household was actually going to go hungry. Azaiglio was stuffing candied figs from a bowl into his mouth as he spoke, at that. The room was large and dark and silent, nobody present but the magnates Paratier had summoned. That itself would be suspicious, and Lady Suzette and Whitehall's Komarite Companion had built a surprisingly effective network of informers in the last two months. They must act quickly, or not at all.

A man further down the table cleared his throat. "What matters," he said, "is that the longer we obey Whitehall, the more likely Ingreid is to cut all our throats when he takes the city. The commons have made their bed by throwing in with the easterner—but I don't care to lie in it with them."

"Worse still, he might *win*," a merchant said. Paratier recognized him, Fidelio Enrike.

Everyone looked at him. Azaiglio cleared his throat. "Well, umm. That doesn't seem too likely—but we'd be rid of him then too, yes. He'd go off to some other war."

"He'd go, but the Civil Government wouldn't," Enrike said. "The Brigade are bad enough, but they're stupid and they're lazy, most of them. If they go down, there'll be a swarm of monopolists and charter-companies from East Residence and Hayapalco and Komar moving in here, sucking us dry like leeches—not to mention the tax-farmers Chancellor Tzetzas runs."

Azaiglio sniffed. "Not being concerned with matters *of trade*, I wouldn't know," he said.

It had been essential to invite Azaiglio—he was the largest civilian landowner in the city—but Paratier was glad when one of his fellow noblemen spoke:

"Curse you for a *fool*, Vihtorio, Spirit open your eyes! Carson Barracks always listened to us, because we're *here*. East Residence is a month's sailing time away if the winds are favorable. Why should they pay attention to us? What happens if they decide some other frontier is more important a decade from now when they're fighting the Colony, and pull out their troops and let the Stalwarts pick our bones?"

Everyone shuddered. An Abbess leaned forward slightly, and cleared her throat.

"Seynor, you are correct. No doubt the conquest was a terrible thing, but it is long past. The Brigade *needs* us. It needs our cities—" she nodded to Enrike "—because they have no arts of their own, and would have to squat in log huts like the Stalwarts or the Guard otherwise. They need our nobility because they couldn't administer a pig sty by themselves."

"They *are* heretics," another of the nobles said thoughtfully.

"They may be converted in time," the Abbess said. "East Residence would turn all of Holy Federation Church into a department of state."

There were thoughtful nods. The civilian nobles of the Western Territories in general and the provinces around Old Residence in particular had turned having the second headquarters of the Church among them into a very good thing indeed.

"The Civil Government was a wonderful thing when it was run from here," Enrike said. "As I said, being the outlying province of an empire run from East Residence is another matter altogether. Effectively, *we* run the Western Territories under the Brigade—who provide us with military protection at a price much more reasonable than the Governor's charge."

"Not to mention the way Whitehall's stirred up the commons and the petty-guilds against their betters," someone said irritably. "The Brigade always backed us against those scum."

Paratier raised a hand. Silence fell, and he spoke softly into it: "These temporal matters are not our primary concern. Love for Holy Federation Church, the will of the Spirit of Man of the Stars—these are our burden. Raj Whitehall is zealous for the true faith, yet the Handbooks caution us to be prudent. If General Ingreid takes this city by storm, he will not spare the Church."

Needless to say, he wouldn't spare anyone else either.

"However, if he were to receive the city as a gift from us— then, perhaps we might appease him with money. This war will be expensive."

The Brigade troops had to be paid and fed from the General's treasury while they were in the field. It was full right now, Forker had been a miser of memorable proportions and had fought no wars of note, but gold would be flowing out of it like blood from a heart-stabbed man. The conspirators looked at each other uneasily; there was no going back from this point.

"How?" Enrike asked bluntly. "Whitehall's got the militia under his control."

"His officers," the head of the Priest's Guard said. "But not many of them."

"The gates are often held by these battalions of paid militiamen he's raised," the Abbess said thoughtfully.

There were forty thousand of the militia, but most of them were labor-troops at best. Half of them had volunteered when Raj Whitehall called; a thousand of the best had gone into the regular infantry battalions. From the rest he had culled seven battalions of full-time volunteer troops, uniformed and organized like Civil Government infantry but armed with captured Brigaderos weapons. The training cadre came from his regulars, but the officers were local men.

The Priest's Guard officer snorted. "Every one of the battalion commanders he appointed is a rabid partisan of Whitehall's," he said. "I've checked, sounded a few of them out very cautiously."

Paratier nodded. "Many men of sound judgment, devoted to Holy Church, were considered for those positions," he said thoughtfully. "Yet every one ready to take Our counsel was rejected."

The officer nodded. "It's unnatural. You can't *lie* to him, to Whitehall. He looks at you and, well, he can *tell.*" The priest-soldier touched his amulet. "There's a shimmer in front of his eyes sometimes, have you noticed? It's not *natural.*"

The Priest coughed discretely. "Yet men change. Moreover, not all of the officers chosen for those battalions were hand-picked by the *heneralissimo.* He is but one man, with much to do."

The others leaned forward.

"Fun while it lasted," Grammeck Dinnalsyn said dismally.

Raj nodded. The first set of Brigaderos gun-rafts had burned and exploded spectacularly when the mortar shells dropped on them—and the steamers had brought in cargo ships unhindered for several weeks.

Today was a different story. It was a cold bright day, with thin streamers of cloud high above, cold enough to dull scent. The water-spouts and explosions across the river were clear and bright, like miniature images in an illustrated book. The long *booom* of heavy guns echoed flatly, and huge flocks of wintering birds surged up out of the reeds and swamps at the sound. The new enemy rafts had their sloping sides built up smoothly into peaked roofs, and the whole surface glinted with the dull gray of iron. Hexagonal plates of it, like some marble floors, as thick as a man's arm and bolted to the heavy timber wall beneath. A mortar-shell struck one as he watched. It exploded, and the water surged away from that side of the raft in a great semicircle. When the smoke cleared and the spray and mud fell, the iron was polished brighter, but barely scarred.

A port opened in the armored side of the raft, and the black muzzle of a fortress gun poked through. The hole in the center was twice the width of a man's head. Red flame belched through the cloud of smoke. The forty-kilo shot struck the side of the Civil Government mortar-raft only a thousand meters away. White light sparked out from the impact, and a sound like a monstrous dull gong. The smaller mortar raft surged backward under the impact.

More roundshot were striking around the mortar raft, raising plumes of water or bouncing off the armor.

"The son of a whore's keeping his rafts fairly close to the shore batteries, too, in daytime," Dinnalsyn said. "Enough hits and they'll break the timber backing or spall off fragments on ours."

Raj sighed. "Recall them," he said. "This isn't getting us anywhere."

Dinnalsyn nodded jerkily, and signed to his aide. Rockets flared out over the water. After a few minutes, the mortar rafts began to back jerkily, as the crews inside winched in the cables and paid out on the ones attached to the anchors set closer to the southern shore.

"*Losien,*" Dinnalsyn said: sorry. Then more thoughtfully: "Although . . . *mi heneral,* if we put a chilled-iron penetrating cap on the mortar shells, maybe a delay fuse . . . or I could . . . hmmm. I know the theory, with a little time I could set up a rifling lathe for some of the big smoothbores we found here. Fire elongated solid shot with lead skirts like the siege guns back home—we use cast steel from the Kolobassian forges, of course, but I could strengthen the breeches of these cast-iron pieces with bands. Heat some squared wrought-iron bars white-hot and then wind them on—"

"Good man," Raj said, clapping him on the shoulder in comradeship. "Delegate it, though, don't get too focused on this one aspect. And this sort of move and counter-move can go on indefinitely."

observe, Center said.

The real world vanished, to be replaced with the glowing blue-white curved shield of Bellevue seen from the holy realm of Orbit. Blossoms of eye-searing fire bloomed against the haze of the upper atmosphere. They came from dots that fell downward, dodging and jinking. Fingers of light touched them and they died, but others survived, penetrating deeper and deeper until some went down into the night side of the planet below. Down to the grids of light that marked cities, and then sun-fire billowed out in circles, rising in domes of incandescence toward the stratosphere . . .

Raj shook his head. "Muzzaf," he said. "Two-thirds rations for the populace again. Grammeck, what really has me worried is the area southeast of the wall. Meet me in the map room this afternoon, and we'll go over it."

Sweet incense drifted over the pounded dirt of the cleared zone between the inner face of the wall and the buildings of Old Residence. A hundred meters wide, it stretched on either side of them like a wavering road. Much of it was as busy as a road; men marching, or exercising their dogs, or supply wagons hauling rations and ammunition. This section was the 24th Valencia Foot's, and they were inducting their recruits, the ones who'd survived probationary training.

The new men stood in ranks, facing the wall and the rest of the battalion, with the unit standard beside the commander and Raj. The colors moved out to parade past the files, and the unit saluted them—both arms out rigidly at forty-five degrees with the palms down and parallel to the forearm, the same gesture of reverence that they would have used for a holy relic passing in a religious procession. The banner was commendably shot-riddled and many times repaired; it had *Sandoral* embroidered on it, and *Port Murchison*.

The battalion chaplain gathered up his materials, a tiny star-shaped branding iron and a sharp knife. The unit commander was Major Ferdihando Felasquez, a stocky middle-aged man with a patch over one eye, legacy of a Colonist shell. He had a riding-crop thonged to his wrist.

That was how the oath was administered. *I swear obedience unto death, though I be burned with fire, pierced with steel, lashed with the whip.* A taste of salt, the brand to the base of the thumb, a prick on one cheek with the knife, and a tap on both shoulders with the riding crop. Some officers didn't bother with it personally, but Raj had had the same scar on his thumb since he turned eighteen and took up the sword.

"Captain Hanio Pinya, isn't it?" Raj said, as the men went back to parade rest.

"*Ci, mi heneral,*" the younger man said, stiffening slightly, obviously conscious of the newness of the Captain's two stars on his helmet.

Felasquez spoke: "I'm forming one extra company," he said. "Putting about half recruits and half veterans in it, and splitting the rest of the new men up among the others."

"How are they shaping?" Raj asked.

"Not bad, *seyor,*" the newly promoted captain said. "They're all over eighteen and below twenty-five, all over the minimum height, and they can all see a man-sized cutout at five hundred meters and run a couple of klicks without keeling over. Better raw material than we generally get."

They all nodded. Infantry units usually got peons sent by their landlords in lieu of taxes, or whatever the pressgang swept up when a unit was ordered to move and had to make up its roster.

"Odd to have so many townsmen," Felasquez said. "Although some of them are peasants who got in before the enemy arrived. No clerks, shopkeepers or house servants—all farmers or manual laborers."

The three men moved down the ranks. The recruits were all looking serious now—taking the oath did that to a man—and they'd had enough drill already to remain immobile at parade rest. With Old Residence to draw on there had been no problem equipping everyone up to regulation standards, and better than the sleazy junk that garrison units often got stuck with at home. Blanket roll over the left shoulder, wrapped around with the waxed-linen sheet that was part of the squad tent. A short spade or pickaxe stuck through the leather bindings, its head just showing over the shoulder. Spare socks, pants and knitted-wool pullover inside the blanket roll. Bandolier with seventy-five rounds, and twenty-five more in a waxed cardboard box. Three days' allowance of hardtack. Rifle and bayonet; roll of bandages; gun-oil and cleaning gear; cup, bowl and spoon of enameled iron; share of the squad's cooking gear . . .

"And by the way," Raj said, when the officers returned to the standard. "We've managed to get a satisfactory reloading shop set up, so double the usual firing practice and collect all your spent brass. Work them hard."

"They'll sweat, *mi heneral*," Felasquez promised. "Although I'd prefer to get them out under canvas 'til the new men shake down. They'll pick up Sponglish faster with no distractions, too."

"Ingreid might object to maneuvers," Raj replied dryly. "Wall duty will give them some experience of being shot at, at least." The Brigaderos had been infiltrating snipers within range of the wall by night and picking off the odd man.

Felasquez cleared his throat and rested one hand on the pole of the battalion standard.

"Men," he said, in a clear carrying voice. "You are no longer probationers, but members of the 24th Valencia Foot. For two hundred and fifty years, this flag has meant men not afraid of hard work or hard fighting. May the Spirit of Man of the Stars help you be worthy of that tradition. You will now have the honor of an address by our *heneralissimo supremo*, Raj Whitehall."

A brief barking cheer echoed off the surface of the fortification wall. Raj stepped forward, his hands clasped behind his back.

"Fellow soldiers," he said; the cheer was repeated, and he waved for silence. "I've been called the Sword of the Spirit of Man. It's true the Spirit has guided me . . . but if I'm the hilt of the Spirit's sword, my troops are the blade. These veterans—" his stance stayed the same, but he directed their attention to the ranks behind him "—have marched with me from the eastern deserts to the Western Territories, and together we've broken everyone who tried to stop us. Because the Spirit was with us, and because we had training and discipline that nobody could match."

The soldiers made no sound, but Raj could almost feel the pride they radiated. *Poor bastards,* he thought. Every fifth man in the 24th had died in the trenches at Sandoral. Mostly from artillery, with no chance to strike back.

"Victory doesn't come cheap," he went on. "But none of us has been killed running away." Even the 5th's retreat from El Djem hadn't been a bugout. Tewfik's men had been glad enough to break contact. "If you can become worthy comrades of these men—and it won't be easy—then you'll have something to be proud of."

Or you'll be cripples, or bodies in a ditch, he thought, looking at the young men. Only the knowledge that he shared the danger he sent them into made it tolerable.

"One last thing. Before you enlisted, probably only your mothers loved you." He allowed himself a slight smile.

"Now that you're wearing this—" he touched his own blue jacket "—probably not even your mothers will, any more. And that's no joke. We guard the Civil Government, but damned little gratitude we get for it. Gratitude is nice; so is plunder, when we find it— but that's not what we fight for. There's precious little faith or honor in this Fallen world; what there is, mostly wears our uniform. We fight for Holy Federation, for our oaths . . . and mostly, for each other. The men around you now are your only family, your only friends. Obey your officers, stand by your comrades, and you've nothing to fear from anyone who walks this earth."

"Put your *backs* into it," Howyrd Carstens shouted.

"You put *your* fuckin' back into it," the soldier growled back at him. "I'm a free unit brother, not a goddam peon!"

The Brigade-colonel jumped down from his dog. Sweating, muddy, stripped to the waist despite the chill, the soldier backed a pace. Carstens ignored him. Instead he walked past to the head of the cable and grabbed the thick hemp rope, hitching his shoulder into it.

"Now *pull,* you pussies," he roared.

Men, dogs and oxen strained. The siege gun began to inch forward, over the last steeper section of the hastily-built road. With a groaning shout the teams burst onto the surface of the bluffs. It was full dark, lit only by a few carefully shuttered lanterns. And by the flare of the occasional Civil Government shell, landing in the entrenchments at the eastern face of the hill. Everyone ducked at the wicked *crack* of the 75mm round going off, but the shrapnel mostly flayed the forward surface of the hill with its earthwork embankments and merlons of wickerwork and timber.

"That's how to do a man's job, boys," Carstens said, panting and facing the others.

Most of the troops on the line had collapsed to the ground once the heavy cannon was on the level hilltop. Their bodies and breath steamed with exertion; the dogs beside them were panting, and the oxen bawled and slobbered. Men ran up to hitch new cables to the iron frame of the gun's mount and lead the animals back down the slope for the next weapon. Winches clanked, dragging the gun across the log pavement laid on the hilltop, an earthquake sound as multiple tons of iron thundered over the corrugations. The soldiers gave Carstens a tired cheer as they looped up the heavy ship's hawser they had used for haulage.

"And keep your jackets on," Carstens called after them. A chill was always a danger when you sweated hard and then stopped in cold weather. There were too many men down sick as it was.

"Yes, mother," a trooper shouted back over his shoulder—the same one who'd challenged his superior to get down in the dirt with them. The men were laughing as they trotted down the uneven surface, dodging around the wagons that followed the gun with loads of ammunition and shot.

His escort brought up his dog, and he took down the cloak strapped to the saddle and flung it around his shoulders. His heart was still beating fast. *Not as young as I was,* he thought.

The area ahead looked like a spaded garden in the dim light. Earth was flying up from it, as thousands of men worked to dig the guns into the edge of the bluff facing the city. A dozen positions faced the wall two kilometers away, each a deep narrow notch cut into the loess soil of the bluff from behind and then roofed over; other teams worked on the cliff-face itself, reinforcing it with wicker baskets of earth and thick timbers driven down vertically. Behind the guns were bunkers with beam and sandbag covers, to hold the ammunition and spare crewmen. As he watched, the latest gun was aligned with its tunnellike position and a hundred men began heaving on ropes. Those were reaved through block-and-tackle at the outer lip of the position, in turn fastened to treetrunks driven deep into the soil. The monstrous soda-bottle shape of the gun was two meters high at the breech, and nearly ten meters long. It slid into position with a jerky inevitability, iron wheels squealing on rough-hewn timber.

Carstens followed it, to where Ingreid and Teodore waited under the lip of the forward embankment. Just then an enemy shell plowed into the face beyond. Dirt showered up and fell back, pattering on the thick plank roofing overhead. He bowed to the Brigade's ruler and exchanged wrist-clasps with the younger nobleman.

"Glad to see you on your feet," he said.

Teodore nodded, then waved a hand toward the city. "Our oyster," he said. "A tough one, but we've got the forks for it."

Carstens peered through his telescope. The white-limestone walls were brightly lit by Civvie searchlights, and he squinted against the glare. A globe of red fire bloomed, and a shell screeched through the air to burst a hundred meters to his left. Dirt filtered through between the planks overhead, and he sneezed.

"They're not making much practice against this redoubt," he said.

"Told you," Teodore said with pardonable smugness.

Ingreid barked laughter and thumped him on the back; the glove rang on his backplate with a dull *bong*.

"This time we're the ones pissing on 'em from above," Ingreid said. He took the telescope from his subordinate and adjusted it. "How long will it take?"

"We're at extreme range," Teodore said. "Wouldn't work at all without—" he stamped a heel "—a hundred meters of hill under us. With a dozen guns, and overcharging the loads—four, five days to bring down a stretch of wall."

"And we've got their supplies cut off, too," Ingreid said happily. His teeth showed yellow in a grin. "Slow-motion fighting, but you two have been doing well. When the wall comes down . . ."

"Don't like to put everything in one basket," Teodore said.

The older men laughed. "We've got another bullet in that revolver," Carstens said. "They'll all be looking this way—the best time to buttfuck 'em."

CHAPTER TEN

"I'll bloody well leave, that's what I'll do," Cabot Clerett snarled, pacing the room. It was small and delicately furnished, lit by a single lamp. The silk hangings stirred slightly as he passed, wafting a scent of jasmine.

"Cabot, you can't leave in the middle of a campaign; not when your career has begun so gloriously!" Suzette said.

"Whitehall obviously won't let me out of his sight again," Cabot said. "He doesn't make mistakes twice. And all he's doing is *sitting* here. I'll go back and tell uncle the truth about him. Then I'll collect reinforcements, ten thousand extra men, and come back here and do it *right.*"

"Cabot, you can't mean to leave me here?" Suzette said, her eyes large and shining.

"Only for a few months," he said, sitting beside her on the couch.

She seized his hand and pressed it to her breast. "Not even for a moment. Promise me you won't!"

"Let me out, my son," the priest said shortly.

"I'm no son of yours, you bald pimp in a skirt," the trooper growled. He was from the 1st Cruisers, a tall hulking man with a thick Namerique accent.

Savage, the priest thought. Worse than the Brigade, most of whom were at least minimally polite to the orthodox clergy.

The East Gate had a small postern exit, a narrow door in the huge main portal. A torch stood in a bracket next to it, and the flickering light caught on the rough wood and thick iron of the gate, cast shadows back from the towers on either side. A crackle of rifle-fire came from somewhere, perhaps a kilometer away. Faint shouting followed it; part of the continual cat-and-mouse game between besieger and besieged. Behind him Old Residence was mostly dark, the gasworks closed down for the duration as coal was conserved for heating and cooking. Lamps were few for the same reason, showing mellow gold against the blackness of night. The white puffs of the priest's breath reminded him to slow his breathing.

"I have a valid pass," he said, waving the document under the soldier's nose. There was a trickle of movement in and out of the city, since it was advantageous to both sides.

"Indeed you do," a voice said from behind him.

He whirled. A man stepped out of the shadow into the light of the torch; he was of medium height, broad-shouldered and deep-chested, with a swordsman's thick wrists. Much too dark for an ex-Squadrone, a hard square beak-nosed face with black hair cut in a bowl around his head. Major Tejan M'brust, the Descotter Companion who commanded the 1st Cruisers. The priest swallowed and extended the pass.

"Signed by Messa Whitehall, right enough," the officer said.

More of the 1st Cruiser troopers came out, standing around the cleric in an implacable ring. Their bearded faces were all slabs and angles in the torchlight; most still wore their hair long and knotted on the right side of their heads. He could smell the strong scent of sweat and dog and leather from them, like animals.

Another figure walked up beside M'brust and took the document. "Thank you, Tejan," she said. A small slender woman wrapped in a white wool cloak, her green eyes colder than the winter night. "Yes, I signed it. I *did* wonder why anyone would take the risk of leaving the city just to fetch a copy of the Annotations of the Avatar Sejermo. The man couldn't understand the plain sense of the Handbooks himself and he's been confusing others ever since."

The priest's hand made a darting motion toward his mouth. The troopers piled onto him, one huge calloused hand clamping around his jaw and the other hand ripping the paper out of his lips. He gagged helplessly, then froze as a bayonet touched him behind one ear.

Suzette Whitehall took the damp crumpled paper and held it fastidiously between one gloved finger and thumb. "In cipher," she said. "Of course." She held it to the light. The words were gibberish, but they were spaced and sized much like real writing. "A substitution code."

The relentless green gaze settled on him. Her expression was as calm as a statue, but the Descotter officer beside her was grinning like a carnosauroid. He threw back his cloak and held up one hand, with a pair of armorer's pliers in it, and clacked them.

The priest moistened his lips. "My person is inviolate," he said. "Under canon law, a priest—"

"The city is under *martial* law," Suzette said.

"Church law takes precedence!"

"Not in the *Gubernio Civil,* Reverend Father."

"I will curse you!"

The marble mask of Suzette's face gave a slight upward curve of the lips. Tejan M'brust laughed aloud.

"Well, Reverend Father," he said, "that might alarm ordinary soldiers. I really don't think my boys will much mind, seeing as they're all This Earth heretics."

The hands holding him clamped brutally as he struggled. "And," M'brust went on, "I'm just not very pious."

"Raj Whitehall is the Sword of the Spirit," Suzette said. "He *is* a pious man . . . which is why I handle things like this for him." She turned her head to the soldiers. "Sergeant, take him into the guardhouse there. Get the fireplace going, and bring a barrel of water."

"*Ya, mez,*" the man said in Namerique: *yes, lady.*

M'brust clacked his pliers once more, turning his wrist in obscene parody of a dancer with castanets. "They say priests have no balls," he said. "Shall we see?"

The priest began to scream as the soldiers pulled him into the stone-lined chamber, heels dragging over the threshold. The thick door clanked shut, muffling the shrieks.

Even when they grew very loud.

"Not much longer," Gerrin Staenbridge said.

The thick fabric of the tower shook under their feet. A section of the stone facing fell into the moat with an earthquake rumble. The rubble core behind the three-meter blocks was brick and stone and dirt, but centuries of trickling water had eaten pockets out of it. The next round gouged deep, and the whole fabric of the wall began to flex. Dust rose in choking clouds, hiding the bluffs two kilometers away. The sun was rising behind them, throwing long shadows over the cleared land ahead. The ragged emplacements along the bluffs were already in sunlight, gilded by it, and it was out of that light that the steady booming rumble of the siege guns sounded.

"Time to go," Raj agreed.

They walked to the rear of the tower and each stepped a foot into a loop of rope. The man at the beam unlocked his windlass.

"I'll play it out slow like," he said. "And watch yor step, sirs."

Gerrin smiled, teeth white in the shadow of the stone. When they had descended a little, he spoke.

"I think he was telling us what he thought of officers who stay too long in a danger zone. Insolent bastard."

The tower shook again, and small chunks of rock fell past them. Raj grinned back. "True. On the other hand, what do you suggest as punishment?"

"Assign him to the rearguard on the tower," Gerrin said, and they both laughed.

There were dummies propped up all along the section of wall the Brigade guns were battering, but there had to be some real men to move and fire up until the last minute, before they rappelled down on a rope and ran for it. All of them were volunteers, and men who volunteered for that sort of duty weren't the sort whose blood ran cold at an officer's frown.

They reached the bottom and mounted the waiting dogs, trotting in across the cleared zone. Raj stood in his stirrups to survey the whole area inside the threatened stretch of wall. The construction gangs had been busy; for an area a kilometer long and inward in a semicircle eight hundred meters deep, every house had been knocked down. The ruins had been mined for building stone and timbers; what was left was shapeless rubble, no part of it higher than a man's waist. Lining the inner edge of the rubble was a new wall, twice the height of a man. It was not very neat—they had incorporated bits and pieces of houses into it, taking them as they stood—and it was not thick enough to be proof against any sort of artillery. It was bulletproof, and pierced with loopholes along its entire length, on two floors. The ground just in front of it was thick with a barricade of timbers. Thousands of Brigadero swordblades had been hammered into them and then honed to razor sharpness.

The falling-anvil chorus of the bombardment continued behind them. The tower lurched, and a segment of its outer surface broke free and fell, a slow-motion avalanche. Very faintly, they could hear the sound of massed cheering from the enemy assault troops waiting in the lee of the bluffs.

Raj grinned like a shark at the sound. He hated battles . . . in the abstract, and afterwards. During one he felt alive as at no other time; everything was razor-clear, all the ambiguities swept away. It was the pure pleasure of doing something you did very well, and if it said something unfavorable about him that he could only experience that purity in the middle of slaughter, so be it.

"Good morning, messers," he said to the assembled officers, once they were inside the interior wall. The room looked to have been some burgher's parlor, with a rosewood table now dusty and battered. Over his shoulder: "Get the rest of them off the wall. The enemy will be expecting that about now.

"Now," he said, tapping his hands together to firm up the gloves. The juniors were looking at him expectantly.

tell them, Center said. **as i have told you, over the years.**

Raj nodded. "We're receiving a demonstration," he said, "of two things. The advantage of numbers, and the benefits of fortification."

He looked around and settled an eye on Captain Pinya. "What's the primary advantage of superior numbers, Captain?"

The infantryman flushed. "Greater freedom to pursue multiple avenues of attack, sir," he said.

"Correct. Most of the really definitive ways to thrash an enemy in battle involve, when you come right down to it, pinning him with one part of your forces and hitting him elsewhere with another. The greater your numbers, the easier that is to do. If you have enough

of an advantage, you can compel the other side to retreat or surrender without fighting at all. Those of you who were with me back
in the Southern Territories will remember that the Squadron had a
very large advantage in numbers—although they had a substantial
disadvantage in combat effectiveness.

"In fact, they could have made us leave by refusing to fight
except defensively. Keep a big force hovering some distance from
us, and use the rest to cut off our foraging parties. Pretty soon
we'd have had to either charge right into them, or starve, or leave.
Instead they obligingly charged straight into our guns themselves.

"You have to attack to win, but the defensive is stronger tactically,"
Raj went on, looking down at the map.

"It's effectively a force magnifier. So is fortification, as long as
you don't get too stuck to it. In a firefight, a man standing behind
a wall is worth five times one running toward him; one reason why
I'm known as the 'King of Spades.' You may note that here we're
outnumbered by five to one . . . but the Brigade has to attack. That
effectively puts us on an equal footing, and restores the tactical flexibility which the enemy's superior numbers denies us.

"That, gentlemen," he went on, tapping the map, "is the essence
of my plans for this action." There was a place marked for every
unit on the paper, but nobody's plan survived contact with the enemy.
"We use the fortifications to magnify the effect of our blocking forces,
which in turn frees up reserves for decisive action elsewhere, with
local superiority. I remind you that we're still operating on a very
narrow margin here. Our edge is the speed of reaction which our
greater flexibility and discipline provide. I expect *intelligent* bold-
ness from all of you."

The meeting broke up as men dispersed to their units. Staenbridge
was the last to leave.

"Kick their butts, Gerrin," Raj said.

They slapped fists, wrist to wrist inside and then outside. "My
pleasure, Whitehall," the other man said.

"Spirit of *Man*," rifleman Minatelli said.

From the second story firing platform he had an excellent view
of the city wall going down. He had lived all his life in Old Residence, working in the family's stonecutting shop. It was like watching
part of the universe disappear. The quivering at the top of the wall
got worse, the whole edifice buckling like a reed fence in a high
wind. Then the last sway outward didn't stop; at first it was very
slow, a long toppling motion. Then it was *gone*, leaving only a
rumbling that went on and on until he thought it was an earthquake and the whole city would shake down around his ears. Dust
towered up toward the sun. When it was over the wall was just a
ridge of tumbled stone, with a few snags standing up from it where
the tower had been.

A cannonball struck with a giant *crack* and fragments of stone blasted around it. The next round came through the gap, burying itself in the rubble. Minatelli had never felt so alone, even though there were men on either side of him, nearly one per meter as far as he could see. The platoon commander was a little way off, chewing on the end of an unlit stogie and leaning on his sheathed saber.

Minatelli swallowed convulsively. The man down on one knee at the next loophole was a veteran of twice his age named Gharsia. He was chewing tobacco and spat brownly out the slit in the stone in front of him before he turned his head to the recruit.

"Sight yor rifle yet?" he said.

"Nnn-no," the young man said, straining to understand.

He'd spoken a little Sponglish before he volunteered; the priest in their neighborhood taught letters and some of the classical tongue to poor children. A month in the ranks had taught him the words of command, the names for parts of a rifle and an immense fund of scatology. He still found most of the rankers difficult to understand. *Why did I enlist?* he thought. The pay was no better than a stonecutter's. The priest had said it was Holy Federation Church's work, and he'd finally gotten between Melicie Guyterz's legs the time he got to go back to the home street in uniform. The memory held small consolation. He certainly hadn't been the first one there.

"Gimme." The older man picked up Minatelli's weapon and clicked the grooved ramp forward under the rear sight, raising the notch.

"Das' seven hunnert," Gharsia said. "Aim ad ter feet. An' doan' forget to set it back when dey pass de marks."

He passed the weapon back. "An' wet der foresight," he said, licking his thumb and doing that to his own rifle.

Minatelli tried to do the same, but his mouth was too dry. He fumbled with his canteen for a second and swallowed a mouthful of cold water that tasted of canvas.

"*Gracez,*" he said. *Thanks.*

The veteran spat again. "Ever' one you shoot, ain't gonna shoot me," he said. "We stop 'em, er they kill us all."

The young man braced his rifle through the slit and watched the field of rubble and the great plume of dust at the end of it. It occurred to him that if he hadn't enlisted, he'd be at home waiting with his family—completely helpless, instead of mostly so. That made him feel a little better, as he snuggled the chilly stock of his rifle against his cheek.

"Could be worse," he heard the veteran say. "Could be rainin'." The day was overcast, but dry so far. The light was gray and chill around him, making faces look as if they were already dead.

Footsteps sounded on the wood of the parapet behind him. He turned his head, and then froze. Captain Pinya, the company commander—and Major Felasquez, and Messer Raj himself.

"Carry on, son," Messer Raj said. He looked unbelievably calm as he bent to look through the slit. A companionable hand rested on the young soldier's shoulder. "You've got your rifle sights adjusted correctly, I see. Good man."

They walked on, and the tense waiting silence fell again. "Y' owe me a drink, lad," Gharsia said. Some of the other troopers chuckled.

"Up yours," Minatelli replied. It didn't seem so bad now, but he wished something would happen.

"Upyarz!"

The white pennant showed over the edge of the western gate. That was the signal. The Brigade colonel swung his sword forward, and the regiment poured after him. They were very eager; nobody had been told why they were held here, away from the attack everyone knew was coming on the other side of the city. It had to be kept secret, only the colonel and his immediate staff, and they informed by General Ingreid himself and his closest sworn men. Sullenness turned to ardor as he gave them the tale in brief words.

"We're getting a gate opened for us, boys," he said. "Straight in, chop any easterners you see, hold the gate for the rest of the host. Then the city's ours."

"Upyarz!" the men roared, and pounded into a gallop behind him. None of them had enjoyed sitting and eating half-rations or less in the muddy, stinking camps. He didn't envy the citizens of Old Residence when the unit brothers were through with them.

The road stretched out ahead of him, muddy and potholed. The dogs were out of condition, but they'd do for one hard run to the gate. Get in when the Civvie militiamen opened it, hold it and a section of the wall. The following regiments would pour through into the city and the defense would disintegrate like a glass tumbler falling on rock. They'd take Whitehall from behind over to the east, the way the wild dog took the miller's wife.

He was still grinning at the thought when his dog gave a huge yelping bark and twisted into the air in a bucking heave. The Brigade officer flew free, only a lifetime's instinct curling him in midair. He landed with shocking force, and something stabbed into his thigh with excruciating pain. It came free in his hand, a thing of four three-inch nails welded together so that a spike would be uppermost however it lay. A caltrop . . .

"Treachery!" he groaned, trying to get up.

His knee wasn't working, and he slumped back to the roadway. Behind him the regiment was piling up in howling, cursing confusion, men sawing at the reins as dogs yelped off across the fields. Some of them were running three-legged, one paw held up against their chests. Others were down, biting frantically at their paws or flanks. Dismounted men came running forward; riding boots had tough soles, and they had little to fear from the caltrops. Two of them helped him up.

The gates were less than a hundred meters away. They did not open, but two new-cut squares in them did, at about chest height from the ground. The black muzzles that poked through were only 75mm, he knew—but they looked big enough to swallow him whole. He could even see the lands, the spiral grooves curving back into the barrels. Drawing his sword he lurched forward cursing. There was just enough time to see a thousand riflemen rise to the crenellations of the wall before the cannon fired point-blank canister into the tangled mass of men and dogs halted before them.

"Here dey come," Gharsia said.

Rifleman Minatelli squinted over the sights of his rifle. His mouth was dry again, but he needed to pee. The rubble out where the city wall had been was nearly flat, but the cannonade had lifted. The first line of Brigaderos appeared like magic as they toiled up the ramp the fallen stone made and over the stumps of the wall. His finger tightened on the trigger.

"Wait for it!" the lieutenant barked.

Poles had been planted in the rubble to give the defenders exact ranges. Minatelli tried to remember everything he'd been told and shown, all at once. Tuck the butt firmly but not too tight into the shoulder. Let the left eye *fall* closed. Pick your target.

He selected a man. The first rank of the Brigaderos were carrying ladders, ladders tall enough to reach his position.

He'd seen the heretics riding through the streets occasionally all his life. Once a child had thrown an apple at one, in the avenue near his parent's street. The big fair man had drawn his sword and sliced it in half before the rotten fruit could strike, booming laughter as the urchin ran. The motion had been too quick to see, a blur of bright metal and a *shuck* as it parted the apple in halves.

When were they going to get the order?

A rocket hissed up into the air. *Pop.*

"Company—"

"Platoon—"

"*Fire!*"

He squeezed the trigger. BAM. Loud enough to hurt his ears as two thousand rifles spoke. Smoke erupted all around the semicircle of the inner wall. The rifle whacked him on the shoulder, still painful despite all the firing-range practice he'd had. His hand seemed to be acting on its own as it pushed down the lever and reached back to his bandolier. His eyes were fixed and wide, hurting already from the harsh smoke. It blew back over his head, and the Brigaderos were still coming. The next round clattered against the groove atop the bolt. He thumbed it home and tried to aim again. Another wave of Brigaderos topped the rubble, and another one behind them— they were all wearing breastplates. The muzzle of his rifle shook.

"Pick your targets," the officer said behind him.

He swallowed against a tight throat and picked out a man—bearded and tall, carrying his rifle-musket across his chest. Tiny as a doll at eight hundred meters.

"*Fire.*"

He aimed at the ground just below the little stick-figure and squeezed again. This time the recoil was a surprise. Did the man fall? Impossible to tell, when the smoke hid his vision for a second. Men *were* falling. Dozens—it must be hundreds, the enemy were packed shoulder to shoulder in the breach, running forward, and another line behind them. How many waves was that?

"Keep aiming for the ones coming over the wall," the officer said again. "The men downstairs are firing at the ones closer. Pick your targets."

"*Fire.*"

Again. "Independent fire, rapid fire, *fire.*"

He started shooting as fast as he could, muzzle hopping from target to target. A foot nudged him sharply, bringing him back to himself with a start.

"Slow down, lad," the older man said. He fired himself, levered open the action and blew into the chamber, reloaded, raised the rifle. Without looking around he went on: "Steady, er de cross-eyed ol' bitch'll jam on yu, for shore."

Minatelli copied him, blowing into the breech. The heat of the steel was palpable on his lips, shocking when the air was so cold. He reloaded and braced the forestock against the stone, firing again, and forced himself to load once more in time with the man beside him. It was steady as a metronome; lever, blow, hand back to the bandolier, round in, pick a target—fleeting glimpse through the smoke—fire. Clots of powder-smoke were drifting over the rubble. Fresh puffs came from down among the tumbled stone; some of the barbs were firing back at them. He felt a sudden huge rage at them, stronger than fear.

"Fuckers," he muttered, reaching back again.

His fingers scrabbled; the upper layer of loops was empty. *Twenty-five?* he thought, surprised. How could he have fired twenty-five rounds already? There was an open crate of ammunition not far from him on the parapet; when he needed to he could always grab a handful and dump them into his bandolier loose.

"Fuckers," he said again, snarling this time. His shoulder *hurt.* "Where are the fucking cavalry?"

He'd spoken in Spanjol, but the men on either side laughed.

"Who ever see a dead dog-boy?" one asked.

"Dey fukkin' off, as usual," Gharsia said, spitting out the loop-hole again. "Dog-boys out ready to get dere balls shot off chargin', glory-os. I built dis wall, gonna use it an' that suit *me fine.* Dis de easy life, boy."

Bullets spattered against the stone near Minatelli's face. He fought not to jerk back, leaned forward further instead. Another wave of Brigaderos was coming through the gap, a banner waving among them. He aimed at it and shot as it passed a ranging-post. The banner jerked and fell, the men around it folding up like puppets. A lot of people must have had the same idea. He felt just as scared, but not alone any more.

"Come *on*, you fuckers!" he shouted. This time he pulled out three bullets and put the tips between his lips.

"Determined buggers," Jorg Menyez said.

Another group of Brigaderos snatched up their ladders and ran forward. A platoon along the loopholes to either side of the commanders brought their rifles up and fired; the volley was almost lost in the continuous rolling crash of musketry from the wall and of return fire from the Brigaderos outside. The group with the ladder staggered. The ladder wavered and fell as most of the men carrying it were punched down by the heavy 11mm bullets from the Armory rifles. The survivors rolled for cover, unlimbering the muskets slung over their backs.

Raj peered through the smoke. "There must be ten thousand of them crammed in there," he said.

Bullets from the ground-level loopholes were driving through two and three men. All over the rubble-strewn killing ground, rounds were sparking and ricocheting off the ground where they did not strike flesh. A great wailing roar was rising from the Brigaderos crowded into the D-shaped space, a compound of pain and fear and frustrated rage.

"They're not sending in another wave," Menyez said.

He looked about; the men holding this sector were his own 17th Kelden Foot. They fired with a steady, mechanical regularity. Every minute or so one would lurch backward as the huge but diffuse enemy firepower scored a lucky hit on a firing slit. Stretcher-bearers dragged off the wounded or the dead, and a man from the reserve platoon of that company would step forward to take the place of the fallen. Cartridge-cases rolled and tinkled on the stone, lying in brass snowdrifts about the boots of the fighting men.

Raj nodded slowly. He turned and caught the eye of an artillery lieutenant who stood next to a tall wooden box. An iron crank extended from one side, and copper-cored wires ran from the top into a cellar trapdoor next to it. Raj raised a clenched fist and pumped it down twice. The young gunnery officer grinned and spun the crank on the side of the box. It went slowly at first, then gathered speed with a whine. The corporal beside him waited until he stepped back panting, then threw a scissor-switch on the box's other side. Fat blue sparks leapt from it, and from the clamps on top where the cables rested.

✧   ✧   ✧

For a moment, rifleman Minatelli thought the wall under him was going to fall as the city's ramparts had. The noise was too loud for his ravaged ears to hear; instead it thudded in his chest and diaphragm. He flung up a hand against the wave of dust and grit that billowed toward his firing slit, and coughed at the thick brickdust stink of it as it billowed over him. The explosions ran from left to right across the D-shaped space before him, earth and rock gouting skyward as the massive gunpowder charges concealed in the cellars of the wrecked houses went off one after another. The Brigaderos on top of the charges simply disappeared—although for a moment he thought his squinting eyes caught a human form silhouetted against the sky.

Silence fell for a second afterwards, ringing with the painful sound that was inside his ears. His mouth gaped open at the massive craters that gaped across the open space, and at the thousands of figures that staggered or crawled or screamed and ran away from them. Then the big barrels of pitch and naphtha and coal-oil buried all around the perimeter went off as well, the small bursting charges beneath them spraying inflammable liquid over hundreds of square meters, vomiting the color of hell. Wood scattered through the rubble of destroyed buildings caught fire. Men burned too, running with their hair and uniforms ablaze. Men were running all over the killing zone, running to the rear.

They're running away! Minatelli thought exultantly. The lords of the Brigade were running away from *him,* the stonecutter's son.

He caught up his rifle and fired, again and again. Then, grinning, he turned to the villainous old sweat who'd been telling him what to do.

The veteran lay on his back, one leg crumpled under him. The bullet that killed him had punched through his breastbone and out through his spine; the body lay in a pool of blood turning sticky at the edges, and more ran out of the older man's mouth and nose. Dry eyeballs looked up at the iron-colored sky; his helmet had fallen off, and the cropped hair beneath was thin and more gray than black.

"But we won," he whispered to himself. His mouth filled with sick spit.

A hand clouted him on the back of his helmet. "Face front, soljer," the corporal snarled.

Minatelli started, as if waking from a deep sleep. "Yessir," he mumbled. His fingers trembled as they worked the lever of his weapon.

"Happens," the corporal went on. He bent and heaved the body closer to the wall, to clear space on the parapet, and leaned the dead man's fallen rifle beside the loophole. "I towt de ol' *fassaro*'d live for'ver, but it happens."

"Yessir."

"I ain't no sir. An' watch watcha shootin', boy."

✧   ✧   ✧

Rihardo Terraza grinned as he helped manhandle the gun forward. He could see through the firing slit ahead of them; the gun was mounted at the very edge of the new wall, where it met the intact section of the original city fortifications.

The Brigaderos were trying to fall back now, but they weren't doing it in the neat lines in which they attacked. They were all trying to get out at once—all of them who could still walk, and many of them were carrying or dragging wounded comrades with them. That meant a pile-up, as they scrambled over the jagged remains of the city wall. The ones closest were only about fifty meters away, when the muzzle of the gun showed through the letterbox hole in the inner wall. Some of them noticed it.

PAMMM. Firing case-shot. Everyone in the crew skipped out of the way as the gun caromed backward and came to a halt against rope braces.

"One for Pochita, you *fastardos,*" Rihardo shouted, leaping back to the wheel.

Four other guns fired down the line; the other battery at the opposite end of the breech in the city wall opened fire at the same moment. The crowds of Brigaderos trying to get out halted as the murderous crossfire slashed into them, while the massed rifles hammered at their backs.

Best bitch I ever trained, Rihardo thought, coughing in the sulfur stink of the gunsmoke. His eyes were stinging from it too.

PAMMM.

"One for Halvaro!"

Gẹrrin Staenbridge gave Bartin's shoulder a squeeze. They were waiting in the saddle, riding thigh-to-thigh.

The younger man flashed him a smile. Then the massive thudding detonations of the mines came; they could see the pillars of earth and smoke, distant across the intervening rooftops. The gates creaked, the ten-meter-high portals swinging open as men cranked the winches. This was the river gate, the furthest south and west in Old Residence you could get. The bulk of the anchoring redoubt loomed on their left, and beyond it the river wall. Behind them was one of the long radial avenues of the city, stretching in a twisting curve north and east to the great central plaza. It was packed solid with men and dogs, four battalions of cavalry and twenty guns.

The gates boomed against their rests. Gerrin snapped his arm forward and down. Trumpets blared, and the 5th Descott rocked into a gallop at his heels. The gate swept by and they were out in the open, heading west along the river road. Cold wind cuffed at his face, and the sound of thousands of paws striking the gravel road was an endless thudding scuff. The ragged-looking entrenchments of the Brigade siege batteries were model-tiny ahead and to the right.

And directly to the right the plain was covered with men, marching or running or riding, a huge clot of them around the gaping
wound in the city's wall where the guns had knocked it down. Almost
to the railway gate and that was opening too. . . .

He clamped his legs around the barrel of his dog and swung to
the bounding rhythm of the gallop; his saber beat an iron counterpoint to it, clanking against the stirrup-iron. Distance . . . *now*. A
touch of the rein to the neck and his dog wheeled right and came
to a halt, with the bannerman by his side and a score of signallers and runners. The column behind him continued to snake its
way out of the gate; the ground shook under their paws, the air
sounded with the clank of their harness. Riding eight men deep,
each battalion spaced at a hundred yards on either side of two
batteries of guns. His head went back and forth.

Smooth, very smooth, he thought. Especially since there hadn't
been time or space to drill for this in particular. They'd decided
to keep each battalion stationary until the one in front was in full
gallop, and that seemed to have worked. . . .

The time it took a dog to run a kilometer and a half passed.

"Now," he said.

Trumpets sang, and the great bar of men and dogs came to a
halt—tail-end first, as the last battalion out of the gate stopped with
their rear rank barely clear of the portals. Another demanding call,
picked up and echoed by every commander's buglers. He turned in
his saddle to see it; he was roughly in the middle of the long column,
as it snaked and undulated over the uneven surface of the road. It
moved and writhed, every man turning in place, with the commanders
out in front like a regular fringe before a belt. Spaces opened up,
and the whole unit was in platoon columns. A third signal, and
they started forward at right angles to the road, front-on to the
shapeless mass of the Brigaderos force.

It looked as if the enemy had ridden most of the way to the wall,
then dismounted for the assault. Now the great herd of riderless
dogs was fouling any attempt to get the men who hadn't been
committed to face about. More harsh brassy music sounded behind
him, discordant, multiplied four times. The platoon columns shook
themselves out, sliding forward and sideways to leave the men riding
in a double line abreast toward the enemy. And . . . yes, the most
difficult part. The men to his right, near the gate, were holding their
mounts in check. To his left the outer battalions were swinging in,
the whole formation slantwise to the wall with the left wing
advanced as they moved north.

Too far to see what Kaltin was doing, as he deployed out of the
railway gate to the north of the breach. Presumably the same thing,
and that was *his* problem, his and Raj's. He could rely on them
to do their parts, just as he could rely on Bartin to keep the left
wing moving at precisely the speed they'd planned.

The mass of Brigaderos ahead of him was growing with shocking speed. That was the whole point, hit them before they could recover from the shock of the disaster in the breach—and before the vastly larger bulk of their forces could intervene.

He heeled his dog into a slightly faster canter, to put himself in plain view. "Bannerman, trumpeter," he said, pulling his dog up to a walking pace. "Signal *dismount and advance.*"

The long line did not halt exactly in unison—that was neither possible nor necessary with a force this size, and the command lagged unevenly as it relayed down to the companies and platoons—but there wasn't more than thirty seconds difference between the first man stepping off the saddle of his crouching dog and the last. There was a complex ripple down the line as each unit took its dressing from the standard, and the battalion commanders and bannermen adjusted to their preplanned positions. Then the four battalions were walking forward in a staggered double line with rifles at port arms.

The guns stopped and turned to present their muzzles to the enemy a thousand meters away. All except the splatguns; they were out on the left wing, insurance in case the enemy reacted more quickly than anticipated. Metallic clanging and barked orders sounded. A series of *POUMF* sounds thudded down the line, sharpening to *CRACK!* behind him and to the right from the muzzle blast of the nearest guns. The first shells hammered into the enemy. The first fire came from them; he could hear the bullets going by overhead, not much menace even to a mounted man at this range. Unless you were unlucky. The cannon were settling down into a steady rhythm. Dogs milled about ahead of them, some shooting off across the rolling flatland in panic. More and more rifle-muskets thudded from the enemy, tiny puffs of dirty smoke. Here and there a man fell in the Civil Government line, silent or shouting out his pain. The ranks advanced at the same brisk walk, closing to fill in the gaps.

Eight hundred meters. "Sound *advance with volley fire by ranks,*" Gerrin said quietly. Kaltin should be in place behind them, anvil to the hammer.

BAM! And nearly fifteen hundred rifles fired in unison. The front rank checked for ten seconds, aim and fire and eject and reload, and the rear rank walked through, on another ten paces, stopped in their turn. *BAM-BAM-BAM-BAM*, an endless stuttering crash. The front rank again. More men falling, but the disciplined rifle fire was stabbing into the Brigaderos like giant hay knives into a pile of fodder. He was closer to the breach in the wall now, close enough to see that it was still jammed with men trying to retreat. The ones outside were trying too, running across from his right to left, but there was nowhere to go. The two sallying forces had met at the westernmost junction, facing about to put the trapped force in a box.

"At the double!"

✧   ✧   ✧

The inside of the mortar-raft was hot, thick with the choking scent of overheated metal and burning coal. The little locomotive engine wheezed and puffed at the rear of the enclosure, shoving the heavy box of iron forward. The chain drive-belt from its flywheels ratcheted against the shaft across the stern, and water from the covered paddle-wheel spattered against the board partition that separated the engine from the gap in the raft's floor.

Commodore Lopeyz stuck his head out of the top hatch, wondering bitterly why he'd volunteered for this. *Because everyone else seemed to be volunteering for* something, he thought dryly.

The cold air flowing over the top of the slope-sided box was shocking after the fetid heat inside. The wind was in his face as he went up the narrowing White River at a walking pace. It carried the long black plume of smoke from the stack behind him, to where the other two rafts followed in his wake. None of them was doing more than four knots . . . but they hadn't far to go, and it was a minor miracle none of them had broken down. The surface of the river was steel-gray, with small whitecaps now and then as the breeze freshened. The land to the right, on the north back, was rising; he could see little over the levee beside the stream, except the three hundred meter tabletop of the bluffs where the Brigaderos siege battery was located.

They were level with it now, turning northwest with the bend in the river. The raft shuddered and slowed under him, fighting the current that grew stronger with every meter upstream. He dropped a few steps down the ladder and signalled to the engineer; no use trying to talk, when the hiss of steam and roar of the furnace blended with the sound of the paddles beating water into froth and made the inside one bath of noise.

The engineer pulled levers; his sweat-glistening attendants hovered over the drive-belts, the improvised part of the arrangement. The right-hand paddle wheel went faster, and the left-hand one slowed. Slowly, clumsily, the mortar raft began to turn its nose in toward the bank. He climbed back up the ladder to judge the water ahead; his hands and feet moved carefully on the greasy iron. The other craft were copying him, and the channel was deeper on the north shore. They moved in further, slowing, until the levee loomed ahead and nearly cut off their view of the bluff a kilometer inland.

He signalled again, waving his arms down the ladder. The engines groaned and hissed to silence. The sudden absence of noise was shocking, like the cool air that funneled down through the hatchway. The black gang leaned wheezing on their shovels, next to the wicker coal-bins; they and the engineers were both stripped to their trousers and bandannas, black as Zanjians with the coal-dust and glistening with heavy sweat. So were the ships' gunners grouped around the mortar. Crewmen swarmed out of the other hatches and the anchors splashed.

"Ready?" he called to the gunners.

Their officer nodded. Over the squat muzzle of the mortar was a pie-shape of iron on a hooped frame. The gunner reached up and unfastened a bolt, and one segment of the pie fell down, hinged on the outer curved frame. Gray daylight poured into the gloom of the hold, and a wash of cold air that smelled of water and silty mud.

Lopeyz pushed his head out the hatchway again. The other two rafts were anchored alongside, only ten and thirty meters away. Wedge-shaped gaps showed in their top decks as well.

"Two thousand two hundred," he called, estimating the distance to the enemy gun emplacements.

He levelled his glasses; plenty of activity up there, but only a few of the ant-sized figures were turning towards the river. Lopeyz grinned to himself. The Brigaderos had cleverly dug their guns into the loess soil, presenting impossible targets for the Civil Government artillery in Old Residence. They had also made it impossible to move the big smoothbores in a time of less than hours.

"*Fwego.*" He opened his mouth and jammed his palms against his ears.

SHUMP.

The raft bobbed under him, and ripples floated away from it in a near-perfect circle. Hot air snatched at his three-cornered hat. Smoke billowed through the hold, sending men coughing and gasping. More swept across the upper deck in the wake of the man-high oblong of orange fire that belched out of the mortar's 20cm tube. He blinked against the smoke and watched the blurred dot of the forty-kilo mortar shell rise, hesitate and fall. It plunged into the riverward slope of the bluffs. A second later earth gouted up in a huge plume that drifted and fell in a rain of finely divided dirt. These shells had a hardened tip made by casting them in a water-cooled mould, and the fuses were set for a delay after impact.

"Up three, increase charge one bag," he shouted down past his feet into the hold.

The crew spun the elevating screw and the stubby barrel of the mortar rose. The loader wrapped another donut of powder onto the perforated brass tube at the base of the shell, and three men lifted it into the muzzle.

SHUMP.

This time it arched over the lip of the bluff, into the flat area behind the enemy guns. Lopeyz raised his binoculars and grinned like a downdragger. Men were spilling over the edge of the bluffs, some picking their way down the steep brush-grown slopes, others plunging in their haste. Still more were running eastward, down the gentler slope of the bluff to the rear, where the Brigaderos had shaped the earth into a rough roadway. He could hear shouting; it must be very loud, to carry this far—and his ears were ringing from engine-noise and the firing of the mortar.

"Correct left one," he said. The crew turned the iron traversing screw one full revolution, and the mortar barrel moved slightly to the left. "Fwego."

SHUMP.

Right into the gun positions along the lip of the bluff facing Old Residence.

"Fire for effect!" he barked. The other rafts cut loose as well. *SHUMP. SHUMP. SHUMP.* A pause. *SHUMP. SHUMP. SHUMP.* Ragged clouds of smoke drifted upriver with the breeze. The edge of the bluff began to come apart under the hammer of the shells.

The Brigaderos rifles went into the cart with a clatter. Rifleman Minatelli straightened with a groan and rubbed his back; it had been a *long* day. The sun was setting behind the ruined, gutted Brigaderos position on the bluff to the west, tinging it with blood—which was appropriate. The air was getting chilly, but it still smelled the way he was learning went with violent death; like a latrine, mixed with a butcher's shop where the offal hasn't been cleaned away properly. A sour residue of gunpowder mixed with it all. It wasn't quite so bad here in the open fields beyond the breach in the wall, where the wind blew. Some distance off, a company of cavalry sat their saddles, rifles across the pommel and eyes alert.

A wail came up from the field nearby. The Brigade had offered a truce in return for permission to remove their wounded and dead. That had turned out to mean friends and often family coming to look through the bodies when the Civil Government troops had finished stripping them of arms and usable equipment. Or bits of bodies, sometimes. Minatelli swallowed and hitched the bandanna up over his nose. A little further off big four-wheeled farm wagons piled with dead were creaking back to the enemy lines. The priests said dead bodies bred disease; Messer Raj was pious that way, and the word was he was happy to see the Brigaderos taking them off for burial.

One of the women keening over a body looked his way. "Why?" she shouted at him. "What did we ever do to you? Why did you come here?" She spoke accented Spanjol, but probably didn't expect him to understand.

The young private pulled down his bandanna. "I was *born* here, you stupid bitch," he growled, and turned away.

The other members of his squad laughed. There were six all told of the eight who'd started the day; Gharsia dead, and one man with the Sisters, his collarbone broken by a bullet. They moved on, leading the two-ox team, and stopped by another clump of bodies. These had been ripped by canister, and the smell was stronger. Minatelli let his eyes slide out of focus; it wasn't that he couldn't watch, just that it was better not to. He bent to begin picking up the rifles.

"Fuckin' *Spirit!*" one of his comrades said. It was the squad corporal, Ferhanzo. "Lookit!"

Thumbnail-sized silver coins spilled from a leather wallet the dead Brigadero had had on his waist belt. Whistles and groans sounded.

"Best yet," the corporal said, pouring the money back into the wallet and snapping it shut. "Here."

He tossed it to Minatelli, who stuffed it into a pocket. The young Old Residencer was the best of them at arithmetic, so he was holding the cash for all of them. *They're treating me different,* he thought.

It hit him again. *I got through it!* He'd been scared—terrified—but he hadn't fucked up. *He* was a veteran now.

That made him grin; it also made him more conscious of what was at his feet. That was a mass of cold intestines, coiled like lumpy rope and already turning gray. Insects were walking over it in a disciplined column, carrying bits off to their nest, snapper-ants with eight legs and as long as the first joint of his thumb. He retched and swallowed convulsively.

"Hey, yu shouldda been ad Sandoral," one of the other men said slyly. "Hot nuff tu fry 'n egg. Dem wogs, dey get all black 'n swole up real fast, 'n den dey pops lika grape when yu—"

Minatelli retched again. The corporal scowled. "Yu shut yor arsemout'," he said. "Kid's all right. Nobody tole yu t' stop workin'."

The platoon sergeant came by. "Yor relieved," he said. "Dem pussy militia gonna take over. We all get day's leave."

" 'Bout time," the squad corporal said.

The noncom had volunteered his squad for very practical reasons; he finished cutting the thumb-ring off the hand of the corpse at his feet before he straightened.

"C'mon, boys, we'll git a drink 'n a hoor," the corporal said.

"I, uh, just want some sleep," Minatelli said.

The front of his uniform was spattered with blood and other fluids from the bodies he'd been handling. He should be hungry, they'd had only bread and sausage at noon, but right now the thought of food set up queasy tremors in his gut. A drink, though . . . And the thought of a woman had a sudden raw attractiveness. It was powerful enough to mute the memory of the day gone by.

The corporal put an arm around his shoulders. "Nu, best thing for yu," he said. "Wash up first—the workin' girls got their standards."

The Priest of the Residential Parish entered the door at the foot of the long room as if he were walking to the great altar in the cathedron, not answering a summons sent with armed men. His cloth-of-gold robes rustled stiffly, and the staff in his hand thumped with graceful regularity as he walked toward the table at the other end of the chamber. The inner wall was to his left, a huge fireplace with a grate of burning coals; to his right were windows, closed against the chill of night. He halted before the table that spanned the upper end of the room and raised his gloved hand in blessing.

Got to admire his nerve, Raj thought. *He has balls, this one.*

"Why have you brought me here, my daughter?" Paratier said. "A great service of thanksgiving for the victory of the Civil Government and the army of Holy Federation Church is in preparation."

He stood before the middle of the long table. Behind it sat Suzette, flanked by scribes and a herald; Raj was at one comer, his arms crossed. The walls of the room were lined with troopers of the 5th Descott, standing at motionless parade rest with fixed bayonets. Evening had fallen, and the lamps were lit; the fireplace on the interior wall gave their bright kerosene light a smokey coal-ember undertone on the polished black-and-white marble of the floor and the carved plaster of the ceiling. The Priest looked sternly at Suzette, then around for the seat that protocol said should have been waiting for him. Raj admired his calm assumption of innocence.

"The Spirit of Man of the Stars was with us this day," Suzette said softly. "Its will was done—but not yours, Your Holiness."

"*Heneralissimo* Whitehall—" the Priest began, in a voice as smooth as old oiled wood.

"Lady Whitehall is acting in her capacity as civil legate here," Raj said tonelessly. "I am merely a witness. Please address yourself to her."

Spirit, he thought. He had known good priests, holy men—the Hillchapel chaplain when he was a boy, and a goodly number of military clerics since. Priest-doctors and Renunciates; even some monks of the scholarly orders, in East Residence.

Paratier, however . . . there seemed to be something about promotion beyond Sysup that acted as a filter mechanism. Perhaps those with a genuine vocation didn't *want* to rise that high and become ecclesiastical bureaucrats.

"Bring in the first witness," Suzette said.

A door opened, on the table side of the wall beyond the fireplace. A man in the soiled remnant of priestly vestments came through in a wheeled chair, pushed by more soldiers. His head rolled on his shoulders, and he wept silently into the stubble of his beard.

"What is this?" Paratier boomed indignantly. "This is a priest of Holy Federation Church! Who is responsible for this mistreatment, abominable to the Spirit?"

"I and officers under my direction," Suzette said. She lifted a cigarette in a long holder of sauroid ivory. "He was apprehended attempting to leave the city and make contact with the barbarian generals. The ciphered documents he carried and his confession are entered in evidence. Clerk, read the documents."

One of the men sitting beside Suzette cleared his throat, opened a leather-bound folder, and produced the tattered message and several pages of notes in a copperplate hand.

"To His Mightiness, General of the Brigade, Lord of Men, Ingreid Manfrond, from the Priest of the Residential Parish, Paratier, servant of the servants of the Spirit of Man, greetings.

"Lord of Men, we implore you to deliver us from the hand of the tyrant and servant of tyrants Whitehall, and to forgive and spare this city, the crown of your domains.

"In earnest of our good faith and loyalty, we pledge to open to you the east gate of Old Residence and admit your troops, on a day of your choosing to be determined by you and Our representative. This man is in my confidence and bears a signet—"

"Produce the ring," Suzette added.

A box was opened; inside was a ring of plain gold, set with a circuit chip.

"—which is the mark of my intentions. With Us in Our determination to end the suffering and bloodshed of Our people are the following noble lords—"

Paratier thumped his staff on the marble flags. "Silence!" he said, his aged voice putting out an astonishing volume. "How dare you, adulteress, accuse—"

"The prisoner will address the court with respect or he will be flogged," Suzette said flatly.

Paratier stopped in mid-sentence, looking into her eyes. After a moment he leaned on his staff. Suzette turned her gaze to the man in the wheeled chair.

"Does the witness confirm the documents?"

"Yes, oh, yes," the priest whispered. "Oh, please . . . don't, oh please."

"Take him away," Suzette said. "Prisoner, do you have anything to say?"

"Canon law forbids the judicial torture of ordained clerics," Paratier snapped. After a moment he added formally: "Most Excellent and Illustrious Lady."

"Treason is tried under the authority of the Chair, and witnesses in such cases may be put to the question," Suzette pointed out.

"This is Old Residence; no law supersedes that of Holy Federation Church within these walls. Certainly not the fiat of the Governors!"

"Let the record show," Suzette said coldly, "that the prisoner is warned that if he speaks treason again—by denying the authority of the Sole Rightful Autocrat and Mighty Sovereign Lord Barholm Clerett, Viceregent of the Spirit of Man of the Stars upon Earth— he will be flogged and his sentence increased."

Paratier opened his mouth and fell silent again. "Does the prisoner deny the charges?"

"I do. The documents are forged. A man under torture will say whatever will spare him pain."

Suzette nodded. "However, torture was not necessary for your other accomplices, Your Holiness. Bring them in."

Seven men filed in through the door, their expressions hangdog. A light sheen of sweat broke out on Paratier's face as he recognized them; Fidelio Enrike, Vihtorio Azaiglio, the commander of the Priest's Guard . . .

"Let the record show the confessions of these men were read," she said. "Prisoner, you are found guilty of treasonable conspiracy with the enemies of the Civil Government of Holy Federation. The punishment is death."

Paratier's lips whitened, and his parchment-skinned hand clenched on the staff. Raj stood and moved to Suzette's side.

"But," she went on, "on the advice of the *Heneralissimo Supremo* this court will temper the law with mercy."

A pair of priests came forward; these were easterners themselves, military chaplains attached to the Expeditionary Force.

One carried a plain robe of white wool. The other bore a copy of the Canonical Handbooks, a thick book bound in black leather and edged with steel.

"You are to be spared on condition that you immediately take the oath of a brother in the Order of Data Entrists," she said. "From here you will be taken to the mother-house of your Order in East Residence. There you may spend your remaining years in contemplation of your sins."

The Data Entrists were devoted to silent prayer, and under a strict rule of noncommunication.

Paratier threw down his staff violently. "This is Anne Clerett's doing," he hissed.

For the first time since the Priest entered the room, Suzette's face showed an expression; surprise. "The Consort's doing?" she said.

"Of course," the old man said bitterly. "She and her tame Arch-Sysup Hierarch were trying to foist the absurd doctrine of the Unified Code on Holy Federation Church. As opposed to the *true* orthodox position, that the Interface with humanity is an autonomous subroutine only notionally subsumed in the Spirit Itself."

"You are in error, Brother Paratier," Suzette said helplessly, shaking her head. To the priests who stood on either side of him: "Proceed."

When the new-made monk had stalked out between his guards, she turned to the six magnates.

"As agreed, your lives are spared in return for your testimony." She paused. "Your property and persons are forfeit to the State, as are those of your immediate families. Clerk, announce the sentences."

The room filled with silence as the prisoners were herded out; some defiant, others stunned or weeping. When the commander of the detachment had marched his men out, Raj rested one thigh on the table beside his wife and laid a hand on her head, stroking the short black hair, fine as silk.

"Thank you," he said. "Of all my Companions, the best."

Suzette rose to her feet, so suddenly that the heavy chair clattered over behind her. She flung her arms around Raj. Startled, he clasped her in turn, feeling the slight tremors through her shoulders. She spoke in a fierce whisper, her face pressed to his neck:

"Anything for you, my love. *Anything.*"

CHAPTER ELEVEN

"Well, now we can see what they've been building," Raj said. "You know, I'd like to get ahold of the man over there who's been coming up with these clever ideas."

"Whh . . . what would you do to him?" the new Alcalle of Old Residence said. He shivered slightly in the breeze; it was another bright cold day, but the wind was still raw from the last week of drizzle.

"Give him a job," Raj replied. "I can use a man that clever."

He bent to look through the tripod-mounted heavy binoculars. The . . . whatever-it-was had just crept out of the Brigade camp, the one that straddled the local railway leading north. In normal times the line carried coal from the mines thirty kilometers to the north. He'd ordered those closed—the pumps disassembled and the shafts flooded—before the enemy arrived, although there had been some coal stacked on the surface. Now the enemy had come up with a completely different use . . .

The railroad battery was mounted on the wheels of several rail cars. They had been bolted together with heavy timbers, and more laid as a deck. On that went three forward-facing smoothbore fortress guns, firing twenty kilo shot. Over the guns in front was a sloping casement; he estimated the iron facing was at least two hundred millimeters, backed by thick beams. The sides and top were covered in hexagonal iron plates, probably taken from the gun-rafts on the south shore of the lake. The whole assemblage was too wide to be stable on the one and a half meter gauge of the railroad, so hinged booms extended from either side of the mass. They rested on wheeled outriggers made from farm wagons, but reinforced and provided with iron shields to the front. The battery was pushed by a single locomotive, itself protected by the mass of wood and iron ahead of it.

"What do they intend to do with it?" Gerrin Staenbridge asked.

observe, Center said.

The scene before him jumped, with reality showing through as a ghostly shadow. At five hundred meters the battery stopped its slow forward crawl. The slotted ports on the forward face opened, and the muzzles of the fortress guns showed through. Flame and smoke bellowed out, and solid shot hammered into the north face of the wall, into the gate towers, at point-blank range.

Then darkness fell across the vision, as the sun descended. The Brigaderos crew scrambled to unchock the wheels of the battery, and it crept laboriously backward as the straining engine tugged it safely within the gates of the earth-bermed camp.

Raj nodded. "Bring it up to close range," he said. "Batter the fortifications during the day, withdraw it at night."

The Brigaderos had gotten very nervous about leaving their camps during the hours of darkness, with the Skinners roaming free.

"Hmmm." Grammeck Dinnalsyn considered it. "Shall I start an interior facing wall?"

"No," Raj said, smiling slightly. "With the guns at close range, they could cover any assault through a breach—batter down anything we threw up, and give close support to the storming party. In fact, with the outer wall down they'd command the whole city down to the harbor; it's all downhill from here."

"Sir." Cabot Clerett stepped forward. "Sir, I'll assemble a forlorn hope. With heavy fire support from the walls, we should be able to reach the casement with satchel charges before it gets to close range."

The young major glanced aside at Suzette. The rest of the officers were glancing at *him;* that was a suicide mission if they'd ever heard one.

"No, Major Clerett," Raj said, his smile broadening. "I don't think I'll give the Sovereign Mighty Lord cause to remove me from my command just yet." *By killing his heir* went unspoken.

His smile grew broader still, then turned into a chuckle. The Companions and dignitaries stared in horrified amazement as it burst into a full-throated guffaw. Cabot Clerett went white around the lips.

"Sir—" he began.

Raj waved him to silence. "Sorry, major—I'm not laughing at you. At the enemy, rather; whoever came up with this idea is really quite clever. But it's a young man, or I miss my guess. Colonel Dinnalsyn, how many field guns do we have within range?"

"Twelve, *mi heneral,*" the artilleryman said. His narrow face began to show a smile of its own, suspecting a pleasant surprise. "But they won't do much good against that armor."

"I don't think so either," Raj said, still chuckling. "So we'll wait . . . yes."

In an eerie replay of Center's vision, the battery halted at five hundred meters from the north gate. Some of the civilians on the tower edged backward unconsciously as the crew edged down behind the shields rigged to the booms and began hammering heavy wedges behind the wheels. Others took out precut beams and used them to brace the casement itself against the surface of the roadbed; that would spread the recoil force and make the battery less likely to derail its wheels. The Brigaderos worked rapidly, shoulders hunched against the knowledge that they were within small-arms range of the defenses—and that while the iron shields on the boom and outrigger might protect them from rifle bullets, they would do nothing if shrapnel burst overhead.

Hammers sounded on wood and iron, then were tossed aside as the soldiers completed their tasks and dove gratefully back into the shelter of the casement. The previous attempts to force a battery near the walls of Old Residence had given the Brigaderos a healthy respect for the artillery of the Expeditionary Force.

Raj tapped Dinnalsyn on the shoulder with his fist. "Now, Colonel, if you'll have your guns concentrate on the roadbed, just behind that Brigadero toy—"

Dinnalsyn began to laugh as well. After a moment, the rest of the Companions joined in, whooping and slapping each other on the back; Suzette's silvery mirth formed a counterpoint to the deep male sound. Only the civilians still stared in bewilderment and fear. Cabot Clerett was not laughing either, although there was an angry comprehension in his eyes.

POUMPF.

The field-gun mounted on the tower strobed a turnip-shaped tongue of flame into the darkness. The *crack* of the shell exploding over the stranded railroad casement was much smaller, a blink of reddish-orange fire. Like a lightning-bolt, it gave an eyeblink vision of what lay below. The casement itself was undamaged save for thousands of bright scratches in the heavy gray iron of its armor. The locomotive was still on the tracks, although a lucky shell had knocked the stack off the vertical boiler. Black smoke still trickled out of the stump, but without the pipe to provide draught over the firebox, there was no way the engine could pull enough air over the firebox to raise steam.

Not that steam would have done any good. For fifty meters back from the locomotive, the tracks were cratered and twisted, the wooden rails and ties smashed to kindling and the embankment churned as if by giant moles.

When the second shell burst over them, the soldiers trying to repair the track under cover of darkness bolted for the rear, throwing down their tools and running for the safety of the camp. Bodies and body-parts showed how well that had worked before, in daylight—and since the guns on the towers of the city wall were already sighted in, the darkness was no shield. No shield to anyone but the Skinners lurking all around; tonight the price of ears had been raised to a *gold* piece each.

A carbide searchlight flicked on from the main gate, bathing the casement and the men around it. A thousand Brigaderos dragoons were grouped there, trying to protect the casement and the gunners within from the savages roaming the night. The only way to do that was to bunch tightly . . . which made them a perfect target now, as the guns opened up with a five-shell stonk and two battalions of infantry volleyed from the towers and wall. The dragoons peeled away from the casement, at first a few men crawling backward from the rear ranks or running crouched over, then whole sections of the regiment throwing down their weapons and pelting for the rear. Fire raked them; it would have been safer to wait in whatever cover they could claw from the ground, but men in panic fear will run straight into the jaws of death. Even though death was the fear that drove them.

By the time the searchlight had been shot out by a Brigadero luckier or more skillful than the rest, only the regiment's commander and a small group around him remained. He turned and began to walk stolidly away, the banner flapping at his side. They disappeared into the darkness; a few seconds later the doors of the casement swung open, and the gunners dropped to the ground in a tight clump. They hesitated for a few seconds, then began running north after the retreating colonel.

Half a minute later firing erupted from the darkness itself, the long muzzle-flashes of Skinner rifles lancing out from positions along the embankment. A screeching followed, like saws biting through rock, a flurry of lighter gunshots from Brigaderos rifle-muskets and pistols. Then only screaming, diminishing until it was a single man sobbing in agony. Silence fell.

"Sir," Cabot Clerett said stiffly, bracing to attention.

Only he and Suzette and Raj remained on the parapet, beside the crews of the two guns and their commander. The parapet was darkened against the risk of enemy snipers, lit by the pale light of a one-quarter Miniluna.

"Sir, I request permission to destroy the enemy casement," Cabot went on, his voice as stiffly mechanical as the compressed-air automatons in the Audience Hall in East Residence.

"By all means, Major Clerett," Raj said.

He had been leaning both elbows on one of the crenellations of the parapet. When he straightened up, the moon turned his face to shadow under the helmet brim, all but the gray eyes that caught a fragment of the light. The younger man could see nothing but cold appraisal in them. Imagination painted a sneer beneath.

"It wouldn't do to let them reoccupy it tomorrow," Raj said. "They did enough damage to the gates as it was."

Suzette moved forward. "I'm sure Cabot will do a splendid job," she said, smiling at him.

Cabot Clerett clicked heels and inclined his head. "Messa."

And nobody will even notice, he thought savagely, as he clattered down the tower stairs to the guardhouse at the base. *It'll be the cherry on the cake of another brilliant Whitehall stratagem. Nobody but Suzette will realize what I did.*

Two Skinners were standing on top of the casement when he arrived at the head of a company of the 2nd Life Guards. They watched silently, leaning on their long rifles, as he lit the rag wrapped around the neck of a wine bottle full of coal oil and tossed it through the open hatch. Another followed, and yellow flame began to lick through the hatchway and the gunports and observation slits.

"Better get out of the way, sir," Senior Captain Fikaros said.

Cabot nodded silently; they rode back to the gate. Men were already at work on it, cutting out the cracked timbers and mortizing in fresh, nailing and hammering. He stood and watched silently as the casement burned; the timbers of its frame were fully involved now, and the iron was beginning to glow a ruddy color around the holes were flame pulsed with a rhythm like a great beast breathing. The munitions must have been stored in metal-clad boxes, probably water-jacketed, because it was fifteen minutes before the first explosion. A few of the iron plates flew free, and the heavy casement jumped as fire jetted out of every opening. Then the whole vehicle disappeared in a globe of orange-red fire that left afterimages blinking across his retinas for minutes. The shock wave pushed at him, sending him staggering against the rough surface of the gate. Men within shouted in alarm as the tall leaves of the doors rattled against their loosened hinges.

"Hope those Skinners had enough sense to get off," Fikaros said. He laughed. "A tidy end to a tidy operation. I wonder how many more siege guns the enemy has?"

"Enough," Cabot Clerett said tonelessly. "Return the men to quarters, Captain."

"Sir. Care for a drink in the mess, Major?"

"For a start, Captain."

"Spirit *damn* them," Raj said with quiet viciousness. "I *need* those reinforcements."

The windows were open, to catch the first air of the early spring afternoon. It was still a little chill, but on a sunny day no more than made a jacket comfortable. The air smelled cleaner than usual in a city; coal was running short, even for cooking-fires.

"How many does that make?" Gerrin Staenbridge said. "Landings in the Crown as a whole."

Jorg Menyez shuffled papers. "Five regular infantry battalions," he said. "Ordinary line units, suitable enough for garrison work. And seven battalions of regular cavalry. The 10th Residence, 9th and 11th Descott Dragoons, 27th and 31st Diva Valley Rangers, the 3rd Novy

Haifa, and the 14th Komar. Plus about six batteries of artillery, say twenty to twenty-four guns."

"Good troops," Raj said. "And as much use in the Crown as they would be in bloody East Residence—or Al Kebir, for that matter."

"You've got plenary authority as Theatre Commander," Gerrin pointed out.

Raj indicated a pile of letters, his correspondence with the commanding officers of the reinforcements. His teeth showed slightly in a feral smile of tightly-held rage.

"I've got power of life and death over the whole Western Territories—in theory," he said. "Half of them didn't even reply. The other half said they can't get into a city *surrounded* by a hundred thousand troops."

"Odd, since we've no problem getting small shipping in every night," Staenbridge said.

Antin M'lewis nodded. "Ser," he said. "Me boys could git hunnerts in by land, any night ye name. Them barbs is stickin' real close-loik ter their walls."

"The fix is in," Dinnalsyn said.

Raj nodded. "Informally, I've had word from Administrator Historomo. The battalion commanders are under word-of-mouth instruction from the Chair not to place themselves under my orders. They're not under *anyone's* orders, really, although for most purposes they seem to be doing what Historomo says. He's got them split up in penny packets doing garrison work his militia and gendarmes could handle just as well."

He swore again, bitterly. "With another four thousand cavalry I could *end* this bloody war before wheat harvest." That would be in four months. "Without them, it may take *years*."

"The Brigaderos are in pretty poor shape," Staenbridge said judiciously. "They must have lost twenty thousand men in those attacks over the winter—probably thirty thousand all told, if you count the ones rendered unfit-for-service."

"And they're losing hundreds every week to general wastage," Menyez said. "They've had a visit from Corporal Forbus."

M'lewis nodded, and there was a general slight wince. Cholera in a winter camp was a nightmare. "Them camps is smellin' high," he said. "An' their dogs is in purly pit'ful shape."

"They still outnumber us five to one," Raj said. "We're losing men too, to snipers and harassing attacks. Not as many, but we didn't have as many to start with. Jorg, what about the militia?"

"Limited usefulness only, *mi heneral*," Menyez said. "The full-time battalions can hold a secure fortified position with no flanks, but I wouldn't ask more of them. The part-timers aren't even up to that. Local recruits in our regular infantry units have settled in splendidly . . . but that's largely because we took only the best and in small numbers."

Raj nodded. "Where's Clerett?" he asked.

"Ah . . ." someone coughed. "He was at luncheon with Lady Whitehall and some of his officers, I think."

"Well, *get* him here,"

He paced like a caged cat until the younger man arrived. When he did, Raj kept his face carefully neutral.

"Sir." Clerett saluted with lazy precision.

"Major," Raj replied. He indicated the map boards with a jerk of his head. "We were going over the general position, now that winter is coming to an end."

Cabot looked at the maps. "Stalemate," he said succinctly.

"Correct," Raj replied. *He's no fool, and he's learned a great deal,* he thought carefully. Judging a man you disliked was a hard task, calling for mental discipline. "We are now considering how to break it. Specifically, we need the four thousand cavalry currently sitting in the Crown."

"With their thumbs up their bums and their wits nowhere," Gerrin Staenbridge added.

Cabot Clerett's face was coolly unreadable. *He* has *learned,* Raj thought.

"Sir?" the younger man prompted.

Raj returned to his chair and sat, kicking aside the scabbard of his saber with a slight unconscious movement of his left foot. He paused to light a cigarette, drawing the harsh smoke into his lungs, then pulled out a heavy envelope from the same inner pocket that had held the battered platinum case.

"Under my proconsular authority, I'm promoting you to Colonel." He held out the papers; Clerett took them and turned the sealed envelope over in his hands.

A *pro forma* murmur of congratulations went around the table. Cabot Clerett bowed his head slightly in formal acknowledgement. The promotion meant less to the Governor's nephew than to a career officer, of course.

"I'm also detaching you from command of the Life Guards. You will proceed to Lion City immediately, and take command of the forces listed in your orders—essentially, all the cavalry and field-guns in the Crown. Pull them together, put them through their paces for a week or so, improvise a staff. Then move them out; the Brigade hinterlands have been pretty well stripped of troops, so there shouldn't be much in your way. Use your discretion, but get those men and dogs near here as quickly as possible. Then communicate with me; we'll use the river-barges, slip the troops in at night."

"Sir." Cabot smiled, a slow grin. A major independent command . . . and given because the reinforcing units would obey *him*. Since he was the heir, they'd better. "Sir, do you think it advisable to trap another four thousand men here behind the walls?"

"I do," Raj said dryly.

The militia and the regular infantry between them could hold the city walls against anything but an all-out attack. With fourteen thousand Civil Government cavalry, he could take the mounted units out and use them as a mobile hammer to beat the enemy to dust against the anvil of the fortified city.

Cabot tucked the unopened envelope into the inner pocket of his uniform jacket.

"I'm to proceed to Lion City, mobilize and concentrate the cavalry and guns, form them into a field force, and rejoin the main Expeditionary Force, using my discretion as to the means and place?" he said.

"Correct, colonel."

"Immediately?"

"As soon as possible."

"I believe I'll be able to proceed tonight," Cabot said cheerfully. "If you'll excuse me, sir? I have some goodbyes."

Raj ground out the cigarette savagely as the Governor's nephew left the room.

"Was that altogether wise?" Gerrin murmured.

"Perhaps not," Raj ground out. "But it's the only bloody thing I could think of." He looked around. "Now let's get on with the planning, shall we?"

"Glad to see you again, Ludwig," Raj said.

Ludwig Bellamy grinned. The expression was not as boyish as it had been four months ago. His face had thinned down, not starved but drawn closer to the strong bones.

"Glad to be back, *mi heneral,*" he said.

They turned their dogs and rode inward from the gate where the last of the 2nd Cruisers was entering; it was pitch-black, overcast and with no moon. Dim light came from the lanterns on the gate towers above, and from shuttered lanterns in the hands of some of the officers. The heavy portals boomed shut behind them, and the locking bars shot home in their brackets with an iron clanking.

"Captain M'lewis did excellent work getting us past the enemy pickets," Ludwig went on.

"Warn't hardly nao problem," M'lewis said. "Them barbs ain't stirrin' by noight."

"We could smell them," Ludwig said. "Although what they've got left to crap, I don't know."

Raj rode in silence for a few moments. An occasional sliver of light gleamed from a second-story window, as some householder cracked a shutter to check what was going by outside. The dogs' paws beat on the pavement, a scud-*thump* sound, in time with the creak of harness among his escort. Bellamy's men had theirs stuffed with rags to muffle noise. A mount sneezed and shook its head with a jingle of bridle irons.

"The railroad's wrecked, then?" he said at last.

"They're repairing segments with plain wood rails," Ludwig said; pride showed in his voice. "And hauling trains with oxen. The whole area's up in arms, peasant revolt and famine, with three or four regiments beating the bush for *insurectos*. We swung north, and they're trying to run wagon trains from the Padan River down to the camps here. Also we saw troops heading north, toward the frontier; the peasants gave us rumors about Guard and Stalwart raiding, and pirates along the coast."

Raj nodded. "Scavengers around a dying bull," he said. "Commodore Lopeyz has sunk three corsairs in the last month, found them hanging about just over the horizon." One hand indicated the delta of the White River to their left. "What with one thing and another, I think the enemy will be forced to make a move soon."

"How's the supply situation, sir?"

"Not bad, but getting worse. We've enough to keep the men and dogs on full rations for now, although the civilians are being shorted. No famine, though."

Apart from the odd body found dead in a doorway in the morning, but that happened in any city, under siege or not.

"What'll they do?"

"I'm not sure . . . but they'll do something. Soon."

"No!" Ingreid Manfrond said, sweeping the map aside.

His eyes were bloodshot as he glared at the other Brigade commanders.

"Lord of Men—" Teodore Welf began.

"Shut up, you puppy!" Ingreid roared. "You lost me twenty thousand men with your last bright idea."

Teodore stepped back from the table, clicked heels—his armor clanked too—and gave a stiff bow before leaving. Ingreid stared after him; it was a breach of protocol to leave the General's presence before permission was granted. Most of the other officers looked elaborately elsewhere; a few looked calculating, wondering if the triumvirate was breaking up. The weak spring sunlight came through the tentflap with a gust of air, ruffling the maps on the table. The sour smell of the camp was worse, men with runny guts and dogs too.

"Your Mightiness," Howyrd Carstens said, "he was right this time. We've got to deal with this new army." His thick calloused thumb swept over to the Crown, then up the peninsula from Lion City.

"They're over the Waladavir," he said. "Our arse is hanging in the breeze like a bumboy's, and if he heads southwest and cuts us off from the Padan valley we're fucked—how many men are dismounted already because we can't bait their dogs?"

"You think I should send Welf off, with his mother's milk still wet on his lips?" Ingreid said. "Give him fifteen regiments?"

His voice was no longer a roar, but still hoarse with anger. He snapped his fingers, and a servant came forward with wine. It was too early in the day . . . but he needed it. The raw chill of this damned winter had gotten into his bones.

I'm not sixty yet, he thought. I *can out-ride and out-fight any of them.* But the price kept going up every year.

Carstens shook his head. "Whoever you want," he said. "Send me, or go yourself. Take twenty thousand men, the ones with the best dogs and the fewest troopers down sick. That'll still leave us with seventy thousand fit for service here, more than enough to blockade the city. Stamp on this little Civvie column—there can't be more than four regiments' worth. Then come back here."

Ingreid shook his head. "I'm not splitting our forces," he said. "I'm through underestimating Whitehall, Spirit of Man of This Earth curse him. What we'll do is—"

He began giving his orders, pointing with a stubby finger now and then.

Carstens hawked and spat on the ground when he was finished. "Might work," he said. "Anyway, you're the General."

Ingreid was conscious of their eyes on him. A proper General led the warriors of the Brigade to victory. So far he'd lost two-score regiments in battle, and half as many again to sickness. It wasn't a distinguished record . . . and his grip on the Seat was still new and uncertain.

"I *am* the General," he said. "And I'll have Whitehall's skull for a drinking cup before the first wheat's reaped this year."

CHAPTER TWELVE

"He's up to *something*," Raj said. The setting sun glittered red on the lancepoints of a regiment of Brigaderos cuirassiers moving at the edge of sight. "Something fairly substantial."

Once more they were gathered on one of the north gate towers; Suzette looking a little pale from the lingering aftermath of influenza and some woman's problem she wouldn't tell him about, curled up under a mound of furs.

"Movin' troops," M'lewis added, nodding. Parties of his Scouts were out every night, collecting information and the ear-bounty. "Looks loik back 'n forth, though."

Gerrin and Ludwig Bellamy bent over the map table. "Well," the older man said thoughtfully, "Ingreid's done bloody silly things before. Hmmm . . . moved about ten thousand men from the south bank of the river to the north, and none of *them* have been moved back."

"Ingreid's trying hard to be clever," Raj said absently, tapping his jaw with a thumb. "He's going to do something—no way of hiding that—but he doesn't want us to know where."

"All-out assault?" Ludwig Bellamy said.

"Possibly. That would cost him, but we can't be strong enough all along scores of kilometers of wall. With his numbers, he could feint quite heavily and then hit us with the rest of it somewhere else."

A crackle of tension went through the officers, like dogs sniffing the spring air and bristling. Raj looked out again at the enemy camps; blocks of men and banners were moving, tiny with the distance.

observe, Center said.

The vision was a map, with counters to represent troops and arrows for their movements.

Are you sure? Raj thought.

probability 82% ±5, Center replied. **examine the movements of artillery.**

"Ah," Raj said aloud. "He's moving the *men* around, but the *guns* have been going in only one direction."

The other men were silent for an instant. "Foolish of him," Staenbridge said.

Ludwig nodded. "I think he's short of draught oxen," he said. "Probably they've been eating them. Shortsighted."

"Then here's what we'll do," Raj said. "Jorg, select the best eleven battalions of your infantry, and hold them in readiness down by the river docks. You'll command. Move the rest up here to the northern sector. Gerrin, I want you here with me. Ludwig, you'll take the armored cars and all the cavalry except the 5th and 7th—"

When he finished, there was silence for a long moment.

"That's rather risky, isn't it?" Gerrin said carefully. "I think it's fairly certain we could stop Ingreid head-on."

Raj smiled grimly. *What's that toast?* he asked Center: it was something from one of the endless historical scenarios his guardian ran for him.

"A toast, messers," he said, raising his cup. "*He fears his fate too much, and his desserts are small, who will not put it to the touch—to win or lose it all.*"

"Where're we going, Corporal?" rifleman Minatelli murmured.

The 24th Valencia were tramping down the cobblestoned streets toward the harbor in the late-night chill. They were still blinking with sleepiness, despite a hurried breakfast in their billets. Men with torches or lanterns stood at the streetcorners, directing the flow. It was dark despite the stars and moons, and he moved carefully to avoid treading on the bootheels of the man in front. The cold silty smell of the river estuary was strong, underneath the scent of wool uniforms and men. Occasionally a window would open a crack as the folk inside peered out at the noise below. Trapped and helpless and wondering if their fate was to be decided tonight . . .

"How da fuck should I know?" the corporal snarled. "Jest shut—"

"*Alto!*"

"—up."

Almost as helpless as I am, Minatelli thought.

Although he had his rifle. That was comforting. The Battalion was all around him, which was still better. And Messer Raj always won his battles, which was more comforting still—everyone was sure of that.

Of course, the last battle—his first—had shown him you could get killed very dead indeed in the middle of the most smashing victory. Gharsia's lungs and spine blasted out through his back illustrated quite vividly what could happen to an experienced veteran on the winning end of a one-sided slaughter.

It wasn't worrying him as much as he thought it should, which was cause for concern in itself.

The long column of infantry stumbled to a halt in the crowded darkness.

"Stand easy!" The men relaxed, and a murmur went through the lines. "Silence in the ranks."

Minatelli lowered his rifle-butt to the stones and craned his neck. He was a little taller than average, and the street's angle was downward. The long rows of helmeted heads stretched ahead of him, stirring a little and the dull metal gleaming in the lamplight; the furled Company pennants ahead of each hundred-odd, and the taller twin staffs at the head where the color sergeants held the cased national flag and battalion colors. Another full battalion was passing down the street that crossed the one from the 24th's billet, marching at the quickstep.

"Something big on," he muttered out of the corner of his mouth to the corporal.

Officers walked up and down beside the halted column. Another battalion was marching down behind them, crashing to a halt at a barked order when they saw the 24th blocking their way. Breath steamed under the pale moonlight.

"Doan' matter none," the corporal whispered back, without moving his head. "We jest go where we're—"

The trumpet rang sharply. Men stiffened at the sound.

"Attent-*hun*. Shoulder . . . *arms*."

"—sent."

Minatelli came to and brought the long Armory rifle over his right shoulder, butt resting on his fingers. The trumpet sounded again. He wished the corporal hadn't sounded a little nervous himself.

"Alo sinstra, waymanos!" *By the left, forward.*

His left foot moved forward automatically, without his having to think about it. Hobnails gritted on the cobbles; they were wet and slippery with the dew, although morning was still a few hours off. Marching was easy now, not like at first. The problem with that was that it gave him time to think. Where *were* they sending everyone? Because from the sound, there must be at least four or five battalions on the move, all infantry. They'd been turned out with full kit—but no tents or blanket rolls, only one day's marching rations, and two extra boxes of ammunition each in their haversacks.

They marched through the Seagate and onto the road by the wharves. It was a little lighter here, because the warehouses were backed up against the wall and left more open space than the streets. Most of the docks were empty, looking eerie and abandoned with starlight and moonlight glittering on the oily surface of the water. They halted again at the fishing harbor, upstream from the berths where the deep-hulled ocean traders docked.

"Company E, 24th Valencia," a man called softly.

Captain Pinya turned them left from the battalion column onto a rickety board wharf. Boats were waiting alongside the pier, fishing smacks and ship's longboats and some barges with longboats to tow them. Men waited at the oars, in the ragged slops sailors wore; there were others directing the infantry, in Civil Government uniform but with black jackets, and cutlasses by their sides—marines. The company commander stepped down into a long-boat, followed by the trumpeter and bannerman.

The lieutenant of Minatelli's platoon hopped down into a barge. "Sergeant, get the men settled," he said.

"*Come* on, straight-leg," one of the marines snarled at Minatelli. He was holding a painter snubbed around a bollard, anchoring the flat-bottomed grain barge to the wharf. "*Get* your asses in it. I've got to help *row* this bleeding sow."

The corporal clambered down. "About all yu good fur, fishbait," he said. "Yu herd da man, boys. Time fur a joyride."

"Easy, girl," Robbi M'Telgez said. "Easy, Tonita." His dog wuffled at him sleepily ·from the straw of her stall. The corporal turned up the kerosene lamp and rolled up his shirtsleeves, taking the currycomb and beginning the grooming at the big animal's head. Tonita's tail thumped at the ground as he worked the stiff brush into the fur of her neck-ruff. It was not time for morning grooming, still hours too early, but the dog didn't mind. Most of the other mounts were still asleep, curled up in their straw. The stable smelled of dog and straw, but clean otherwise; the animals were all stable-broken, and waited for their trip to the crapground. It was a regular stable, requisitioned from a local magnate when the 5th was billeted.

M'Telgez felt the dog's teeth nibble along his shoulder in a mutual-grooming gesture as he worked over her ribs. The task had a homey familiarity, something he'd done all his life—back home on the farm, too; the M'Telgez family owned five saddle-dogs. He'd raised one from a pup and taken it to the army with him; Tonita was his second, bought with the battalion remount fund as a three-year old, just before the Southern Territories campaign. War was hard on dogs, harder than on men. Idly, he wondered what his family would be doing right now. Pa was dead these two years; his elder brother Halsandro had the land. It was a month short of spring for Descott, so the flocks would be down in the valley pasture.

Probably the women would be up, getting breakfast for the men; his mind's eye showed them all around the wooden table, spooning down the porridge and soured milk.

Ma and Halsandro's wife and his sisters, they'd spend the day mostly indoors, spinning and weaving and doing chores around the farmyard. The water furrow for the garden would need digging out, it always did this time of year, so Halsandro would be at that with the two hired men. He'd send Peydro and Marhinz, the younger

M'Telgez boys, down to the valley pens to guide the sheep and the family's half-dozen cattle out for the day. They'd be sitting their dogs, shivering a little in their fleece jackets, with their rifles across their thighs. Talking about hunting, or girls, or whether they'd go for a soldier like their brother Robbi . . .

"Hey, corp," someone called from the stable door. He looked up. "Turnout, an' double-quick loik, t'El-T says."

M'Telgez nodded and gave the currycomb a final swipe before hanging it on the stable partition. Tonita whined and rose as well, sniffing at him and rattling the chain lead that held her bridle to the iron staple driven into the wall.

"Down, girl," M'Telgez said, shrugging into his jacket. He picked up his rifle and turned, away from the plaintive whining. "Nothin' happ'nin'."

You couldn't lie to a dog. They smelled it on you.

"Everything is ready?" Suzette asked.

The Renunciate nodded stiffly. Her face might have been carved from oak, but there was a sheen of sweat on her upper lip. Around them the church bustled; the regular benches had been carried out, and tables brought in instead to fill the great echoing space under the dome. Doctors were setting up, pulling their bundles of instruments out of vats of boiling iodine-water and scrubbing down. The wax-and-dust smell of a church was overlaid with the sharp carbolic stink of blessed water.

"Down to the stretchers and bandages," the nun replied. "For once, there is no shortage."

Suzette nodded and turned away. They'd commandeered a dozen buildings along the streets leading off from the plaza, and all the city's remaining hansom-cabs for ambulances. Plenty of priest-doctors as well, although the Expeditionary Force's own medics would direct everything, having the experience with trauma. Time between injury and treatment was the most crucial single factor, though. More of the wounded would live . . . provided Raj won.

He will, she told herself. A twinge in her belly made her grimace a little. Fatima put a hand under her elbow.

"I'm fine," she said, conscious that she was still pale. The pain was much less, and the hemorrhaging had stopped. Almost stopped.

"You shouldn't have," Fatima whispered in her ear.

"I couldn't take the chance," Suzette said, as softly. "I couldn't be sure whose . . . there will be time."

She straightened and nodded to her escort at the door. They were looking a little uneasy at the preparations. It was odd, even the bravest soldier didn't like looking at an aid station or the bone-saws being set out.

"Back to headquarters," she said.

✧   ✧   ✧

"Kaltin, you and the 7th Descott are the only reserve on the whole west section of the walls," Raj said.

They stood around the map, watching his finger move and cradling their kave mugs. *I'm trying to fill a dozen holes with six corks,* he thought. Another shoestring operation . . . He went on:

"Ludwig can watch the east with the bulk of the cavalry until it's time. Gerrin and I are up here in the north with the 5th and nine battalions of regular infantry, but you're *it* over there—you and the militia. They're not that steady, and even a fairly light attack will spook them. Keep them facing the right way."

"Count on it," the scar-faced man said, slapping fists.

"I am. *Waya con Ispirito de Hom.*"

Raj straightened and sighed as Gruder left. "Well, at least we're getting good fighting weather," he said.

The windows showed the ghostly glimmer of false dawn, but the sky was still bright with stars. Yesterday's rain was gone, although the ground outside the walls would still be muddy. Nothing would limit visibility today, though.

"I hope you messers are all aware how narrow our margins are, here," Raj said. "The blocking force has to *hold.*" He nodded at the infantry commanders. "And the rest of you, when the time comes, *move.*"

"It seems simple enough," one said.

Raj nodded grimly. "But in war, the simplest things become extremely difficult. Dismissed."

The men filed out, leaving only him and Suzette in the big room. "You'd be more useful back at the aid station," he said. "Safer, too. This is too cursed close to the walls for comfort."

Suzette shook her head. "East Residence would be safe, my love. I'll be here," she said.

"Mamma, an' ye'll nivver see the loik of *that* comin' down t' road from Blayberry Fair," one of the Descotter troopers on the tower murmured.

The rolling northern horizon was black across an arc five kilometers wide. The Brigade was coming, deployed into fighting formation; the front ten ranks carried ladders and the blocks behind had their muskets on their shoulders and bayonets fixed. The sun was just up, and the light ran like a spark in grass from east to west across the formation as it hove into view, flashing on fifty thousand steel points. They chanted as they marched, a vast burred thunder, timed to the beating of a thousand drums. Between the huge blocks of men came guns, heavy siege models and lighter brass fieldpieces, hauled by oxen and dogs and yet more columns of Brigaderos warriors.

"Now, this isn't particularly clever," Raj said lightly.

To himself he added: *But it just may work.* Brute force often did, although it was also likely to have side-effects. Even if Ingreid won this one, he was going to lose every fifth fighting man in the Brigade's whole population doing it.

"Counter-battery?" Dinnalsyn asked.

"By all means," Raj said.

"Lancers to the fore," Gerrin Staenbridge noted.

The dull sheen of armor marked the forward ranks; they'd left the polearms behind, of course. Muskets were slung over their backs.

"Those lobster-shells will give them some protection," Raj said. "From fragments and glancing shots, at least."

The gunners' signal-lantern clattered. The chanting of the Brigaderos was much louder, rolling back from walls and hills:

"*Upyarz! Upyarz!*"

Raj swallowed the last of his kave and handed the cup to the orderly; he shook out his shoulders with a slight unconscious gesture, settling himself to the task.

"Since I'm handling the towers," Gerrin said. "I'd appreciate it if you could be ready to move the reserves sharpish, Whitehall," he went on dryly.

"I'll do my best," Raj replied with a slight bow.

They grinned at each other and slapped fists, back of the gauntlet and then wrist to wrist.

"Right, lads," Raj said, raising his voice slightly.

Pillars of smoke were rising into the cold bright dawn air from the towers, stretching right and left in a shallow curve to the edge of sight. Gunsmoke, from the fieldpieces emplaced on them—the infantry on the walls hadn't started shooting yet. The *POUMPF* . . . *POUMPF* of the cannonade was continuous, a thudding rumble in the background. Behind it the sharper *crack* sound of the shells bursting was muffled by the walls. As he spoke a huge *BRACK* and burst of smoke came from one tower far to the west, where a heavy enemy shell had scored a lucky hit. Another came over the wall with a sound like a ship's sails ripping in a storm and gouted up a cone of black dirt from the cleared space inside the walls. The sulphur smell of powder smoke drifted to them, like a foretaste of hell to come.

"The whole Brigade's coming this way," Raj went on. "Most of our infantry went out upriver to take them in the flank. Pretty well all the cavalry's going to go out the west gate and take them in *that* flank.

"The problem is," he went on, rising slightly onto his toes and sinking back, "is that all that's left to hold them while that happens is us . . . and the rest of the infantry on the walls, of course."

He raised one hand and pointed at the north gate towers, his left resting on the hilt of his saber. "Colonel Staenbridge and Captain Foley each hold a side of the gate, with a company of the 5th. The rest of you—and me—have to stop whatever gets over the walls. If we do, it's victory. If we don't . . ."

He paused, hands clasped behind his back, and grinned at the semicircle of hard dark faces. Things were serious enough, but it was also almost like old times . . . five years ago, when he'd commanded the 5th and nothing more.

"You boys ready to do a man's work today?"

The answer was a wordless growl.

"Hell or plunder, dog-brothers."

"Switch to antipersonnel," Bartin Foley said briskly.

The front line of the Brigaderos host was only three thousand meters away. The rolling ground had broken up their alignment a little, but the numbers were stunning; worse than facing the Squadron charge in the Southern Territories, because these barbs were coming on in most unbarbarian good order. The forward line gleamed and flickered; evidently they'd taken the time to polish their armor. It coiled over the low rises like a giant metallic snake. Fifty meters behind it came the dragoons, tramping with their bayoneted rifles sloped. He could make out individual faces and the markings on unit flags now, with the binoculars. Most of the heavy guns were far behind, smashed by the fieldpieces mounted on the towers or stranded when the shelling killed the draught-oxen pulling them. Also further back were columns of mounted men, maybe ten thousand of them—ready to move forward quickly and exploit a breach anywhere along the front of the Brigade attack.

Terrible as a host with banners, he thought—it was a fragment from the Fall Codices, a bit of Old Namerique rhetoric. The banners of the enemy flapped out before them in the breeze from the north. Hundreds of kettledrums beat among them, a thuttering roar like blood hammering in your ears.

POUMPF. The gun on his tower fired again. The smoke drifted straight back; Foley could see the shell burst over the forward line of Brigaderos troopers and hear the sharp spiteful *crack.* Men fell, and more airbursts slashed at the front of the enemy formation. Guns fired all along the line, but not as many as there might have been. Half the 75s had been kept back to support the cavalry. The duller sound of smoothbores followed as the brass and cast-iron cannon salvaged from storage all over Old Residence cut loose, firing iron roundshot. He turned the glasses and followed one that landed short, skipped up into the air and then trundled through the enemy line. Men tried to slap aside or dodge, but the ranks were too close-packed. Half a dozen went down, with shattered legs or feet ripped off at the ankle.

The ranks closed again and came forward without pause; the fallen ladders were snatched up once more. The smoothbores were much less effective than the Civil Government field guns, and slower to load—but there were several hundred of them on the walls. Their gunners were the only militiamen in this sector, but they ought to be reliable enough with the bayonets of the Regulars near their kidneys . . . The defenders' artillery fired continuously now, lofting a plume of dirty white smoke over the wall and back towards the city. A few of the Brigaderos siege guns had set up and were firing over the heads of their troops; more of their light three-kilo brass pieces were wheeling about to support from close range.

Foley ignored them; he'd developed a profound respect for the Brigade's troopers, but their artillery was like breaking your neck in the bath—it could happen, but it wasn't something you worried about.

They must have lost two, three thousand men already, Foley thought.

"Spirit, they really want to make our acquaintance," he said. "I knew I was handsome, but this is ridiculous." The lieutenant beside him laughed a little nervously.

Rifles bristled along the forward edge of the tower. More would be levelling in the chambers below his feet, and along the wall to either side. The city cannon were firing grapeshot now, bundles of heavy iron balls in rope nets. It slashed through the enemy, and they picked up the pace to a ponderous trot. Approaching the outermost marker, a fine of waist-high pyramids of whitewashed stones—apparently ranging posts weren't a trick the Brigade was familiar with. One thousand meters.

"Wait for it," he whispered, the sound lost under the rolling thunder of the cannonade.

The Brigaderos broke into a run. Foley forced his teeth to stop grinding; he touched the stock of the cut-down shotgun over his back, and loosened the pistol in his holster. At all costs the Brigade mustn't take the gate, that was why there were companies of the 5th in the towers on either side. Gerrin was in overall command of the wall, all he had to worry about was this one tower and the hundred and fifty odd men in it. The troopers were kneeling at the parapets, and boxes of ammunition and hand-bombs waited open at intervals. Nothing else he could do . . .

"UPYARZ! UPYARZ!"

The front rank of dismounted lancers pounded past the whitewashed stone markers. A rocket soared up from the tower on the other side of the gate and popped in a puff of green smoke.

"Now!"

Along the wall, hundreds of officers screamed *fwego* in antiphonal chorus. Four thousand rifles fired, a huge echoing *BAAAMMMMM* louder even than the guns. The advancing ranks of armored men wavered, suddenly looking tattered as hundreds fell. Limply dead, or screaming and thrashing, and flags went down as well. Foley caught his breath; if they cracked . . .

"UPYARZ! UPYARZ!"

They came on, into the teeth of a continuous slamming of platoon volleys. And behind them, the first line of dragoons halted. The long rifle-muskets came up to their shoulders with a jerk, like a centipede rippling along the line. Their ranks were three deep, and there were thirty thousand of them.

"For what we are about to receive—"

Everyone on the tower top ducked. Foley didn't bother—he was standing directly behind one of the merlons, with only his head showing.

Ten thousand rounds, he thought. The front rank of the dragoons disappeared as each musket vomited a meter-long plume of whitish smoke. *Even so you'd have to be dead lucky—*

Something went *crack* through the air above his head. Something else whanged off the barrel of the cannon as it recoiled up the timber ramp and went *bzzz-bzzz-bzzz* as it sliced through a gunner's upper arm. The man whirled in place, arterial blood spouting.

"Tourniquet," Foley snapped over his shoulder. "Stretcher-bearers."

The next rank of Brigaderos dragoons trotted through the smoke, halted, fired. Then the third. By that time the first rank had reloaded.

"Lieutenant," Foley said, raising his voice slightly—the noise level kept going up, it always did, old soldiers were usually slightly deaf— "see that the men keep their sights on the forward elements."

It's going to be close. I wish Gerrin were here.

"Damn," Raj said mildly, reading the heliograph signal.

"Ser?" Antin M'lewis asked.

He was looking a little more furtive than usual, a stand-up fight was not the Forty Thieves' common line of work, but needs must when the demons drove.

"They've put together a real reserve," Raj said meditatively.

Somebody over there had enough authority to control the honor-obsessed hotheads, and enough sense to keep back a strong force to exploit a breakthrough. Gunsmoke drifted back from the walls in clouds. He wished the walls were higher, now—even with the moat, they weren't much more than ten or fifteen meters in most places. Height mattered, in an escalade attack. He grew conscious of M'lewis waiting.

"I can't send Ludwig out until they've committed their reserve," Raj explained. M'lewis wasn't an educated man, but he was far from stupid. "Twenty thousand held back is too many of them, and too mobile by half. Got to get them locked up in action before we can hit them from behind."

M'lewis sucked at his teeth. "Tricky timin', ser," he said.

Raj nodded. "Five minutes is the difference between a hero and a goat," he agreed.

A runner trotted up and leaned over to hand Raj a dispatch.

Current stronger than anticipated, he read. *Infantry attack will be delayed. Will advance as rapidly as possible with forces in bridge-head. Jorg Menyez, Colonel.*

"How truly good," Raj muttered. He tucked the dispatch into his jacket; the last thing the men needed was to see the supreme commander throwing messages to the ground and stamping on them. "How truly wonderful."

"We'll proceed as planned," Jorg Menyez said firmly.

"Sir—" one of the infantry battalion commanders began.

"I know, Major Huarez," Jorg said.

He nodded down towards the river. The last of Huarez' battalion was scrambling out of their boats, but that gave them only six battalions ashore—less than five thousand men. The rest were scattered along the river with the sailors and marines laboring at the oars.

"Commodore Lopeyz," Menyez said. "I'm leaving you in command here. Send the steamboats back for the remainder of the force." Rowing had turned out to be less practical than they'd thought from tests conducted with small groups. Speeds were just too uneven. "Assemble them here. As soon as three-quarters are landed, the remainder is to advance at the double to support me. Emphasize to the officers commanding that no excuses will be accepted."

Translation: *anyone who hangs back goes to the wall.* Of course, if the scheme failed they were all dead anyway, but it didn't hurt to be absolutely clear.

He took a deep breath of the cold dawn air. Off a kilometer or so to the east the walls of Old Residence were hidden, but they could hear the massed rifles and cannon-fire well enough. A hazy cloud was lifting, as if the city were already burning. . . . Below him were what he had. A few thousand infantrymen, second-line troops officially. Peons in uniform, commanded by the failed younger sons of very minor gentry. Ahead was better than four score thousand Brigade warriors.

"Fellow soldiers," he said, pitching his voice to carry. Whatever he said would go back through the ranks. With appropriate distortion, so keep it simple.

"Messer Raj and our comrades need us," he said. "If we get there in time, we win. Follow me."

He turned, and his bannermen and signalers formed up behind him. Normally company-grade officers and above were mounted, but this time it was everyone on their own poor-man's dogs. "Battalion columns, five abreast," he said. "Double quickstep."

The Brigadero emplacements on the bluff above were ruined and empty, but there would be *somebody* there. Somebody to report.

"*Hadelande!*" he snapped, and started toward the sound of the guns.

"Follow me!" Raj called.

He touched his heel to Horace's flank. The trumpet sang four brassy notes, and the column broke into a jog-trot; he touched the reins lightly, keeping his dog down to the pace of the dismounted men behind him. The fog of black-powder smoke was thick, like running through heavy mist that smelled of burning sulfur. The wall to his right was almost hidden by it despite the bright sun, towers looming up like islands. The noise was a heavy surf, the continuous crackle of rifle-fire under the booming cannon. A louder *crack* sounded as a forty-kilo cannonball struck the ramparts, blasting loose chunks of stone and pieces of men.

Messengers and ambulances were moving in the cleared zone behind the walls. Now they saw men running, unwounded or nearly so. The fugitives shocked to a halt as they saw the Starburst banner and Raj beneath it; everyone recognized Horace, at least.

"You men had better rejoin your unit," Raj said. They wavered, turned and began scrambling back up the earth mound on the inside of the wall.

Raj opened the case at his saddlebow, calming the restless dog with a word as a shell ripped by overhead to burst among the outermost row of houses behind. Through the binoculars he could see the rough pine-log ends of scaling ladders against the merlons of the wall, and infantrymen desperately trying to push them aside with the points of their bayonets. Any defender whose head was above the stonework for more than a second or two toppled backward; there must be forty or fifty blue-clad bodies lying on the earth ramp, most of them shot through the head or neck. The defenders were pulling the tabs of hand-bombs and pitching them over the side; more showered down from the towers a hundred meters to either side, thrown by hand or from pivot-mounted crossbows.

A dozen more scaling ladders went up, even as smoke and flashes of red light above the parapet showed where the bombs were landing among men packed in the mud of the moat, waiting their turn at the assault.

"Deploy," Raj said. The trumpet sang, and the 5th faced right in a double line, one rank kneeling and the one behind standing. A ratcheting click sounded as they loaded their weapons. "And fix bayonets." It would come to that, today.

"Captain, can those splatguns bear from here?"

"Just, sir," the artilleryman said.

The multi-barreled weapons were fifty meters behind the firing line, itself that distance from the wall. The crews spun the elevating screws until the honeycombed muzzles rose to their limit.

Raj drew his sword and raised it. The bullets that had sent sparks and spalls flying all along the parapet under assault halted as Brigaderos helmets showed over the edge, masking their comrades' supporting fire. The Civil Government soldiers rose themselves, firing straight down; but the first wave of Brigaderos were climbing with their pistols drawn. In a short-range firefight single-shot rifles were no match for revolvers. Smoke hid the combatants as dozens of five-shot cylinders were emptied. Seconds later the unmusical crash of steel on steel sounded as scores of the barbarians swarmed over the parapet, sword against bayonet.

"Wait for it."

One moment the firing platform above was a mass of soldiers in blue uniforms and warriors in steel breastplates, stabbing and shooting point-blank and swinging clubbed rifles. The next it held only Brigaderos, the defenders pitching off the verge and into the soft earth of the ramp below, or retreating into the tower doors. A banner with the double lightning flash of the Brigade waved triumphantly.

"*Fwego!*" His sword chopped down.

BAM. Then *BAM-BAM-BAM-BAM,* crisp platoon volleys running down the line. A long *braaaap* four times repeated from the splatguns.

Time shocked to a halt for a second. There were hundreds of Brigaderos jammed onto the fighting platform of the wall, and most of them did not even know where the bullets that killed them came from. Many were looking the other way, waving on comrades below or hauling up the assault ladders to lower down from the wall. The whole line of them shook, dozens falling out and down to crash with bone-shattering force. Some of the Civil Government soldiers who'd jumped down were still moving, it was soft unpacked earth below on the ramp and a grazing impact, but doing it with thirty kilos of steel on you was another matter altogether.

Half the enemy were still up, even with the splatguns punching four-meter swaths through the packed ranks. A few had time to fire revolvers or begin the cumbersome drill of loading their rifle-muskets—both about as futile as spitting, but he admired the spirit—before the next rattle of volleys hit them. The splatguns traversed, snapping out their loads with mechanical precision.

"Cease fire," Raj said. "Marksmen only."

Silence fell as the trumpet snarled; the best shots in each squad stepped forward a pace and began a slow crackle of independent fire at anyone unwise enough to climb the ladders and show his head over the parapet. The Civil Government troops in the towers at each end of the breach were cheering as they fired and lobbed handbombs. That meant the enemy were giving back from the foot of the wall, although the slamming roar of noise continued elsewhere. And incredibly a few of the infantry who'd tumbled down from the fighting platform were up and forming a firing line at the base of the earth ramp. Raj heeled Horace forward; a young officer was limping down the improvised unit of walking wounded, hustling men with the slack faces of battle-shock into line, slapping them across the shoulders with the flat of his saber. Here was someone who also had the right instincts.

"Lieutenant," Raj said.

He had to repeat the command twice before the young man heard;

when he turned his eyes were wide and staring, the iris swallowed in the pupil.

"Cease fire, lieutenant."

"*Ci, mi heneral.*"

"Good work, son." The younger man blinked. "Now get them back up there. Anyone who can shoot."

"Back up, sir?" The lieutenant was shivering a little with reaction. He looked at the earth ramp above, littered with enemy bodies, two deep in places. A fair number of bodies in blue-and-maroon uniforms, too. One was crawling down the timber staircase that rose from the flat cleared zone to the ramparts, leaving a glistening trail behind him.

"Back up," Raj said. He scribbled an order on his dispatch-pad and ripped it off. "Get this to your battalion commander."

Telling him to thin his troops out to cover the bare patch; probably unnecessary, but it never hurt to be careful. There were already some riflemen from the towers up above fanning out onto the rampart, firing out at the enemy or pitching bodies down into the moat—the right place for them, let the Brigaderos get an eyeful.

"Hop to it, lad."

A dispatch rider pulled up in a spurt of gravel. "Ser," he said, extending a note from his gauntlet.

Estimate ten thousand mounted enemy reserves moving eastward with artillery, it said. *Remaining ten thousand dismounting and preparing to advance southeast toward wall. Gerrin Staenbridge, Colonel.*

"Well, that's that," Raj muttered. "Verbal acknowledgement, corporal."

Another messenger, this one on foot. "Sir, barbs on the wall, east four towers—Malga Foot's sector. Major Fillipsyn says they'll be over in a minute."

"Lead on," Raj replied.

"Messenger," he went on, as the command group rode back toward the 5th's waiting ranks. "To Major Bellamy. *Now.*"

The enemy had ten thousand men in reserve to exploit a breakthrough. He had six hundred-odd to plug the holes.

"Battalions to form square," Jorg Menyez said.

The trumpeters were panting, like all the rest of them—they'd come better than a kilometer at the double quickstep, all the way up from the riverbank, over the railway embankment, looping north and west until they were almost in sight of the eastern gate of Old Residence. They still managed the complex call, repeating it until all the other units had acknowledged. A final prolonged single note meant *execute.*

The 17th Kelden Foot were in the lead; they swung from battalion column to line like an opening fan. So did the 55th Santander Rifles at the rear. The units on either side slid like a pack of cards being stacked, the eight-deep column thinning to a much longer

column of twos. Five minutes, and what had been a dense clumping of rectangles eight ranks broad and sixty or so long was an
expanding box, shaking out until it covered a rectangle three hundred men long on each side. The fifth battalion stayed in the center
as reserve.

Here's where we see if they can do it, Menyez thought, his lips
compressed in a tight line.

This sort of thing was supposed to be the cavalry's work. Infantry
were for holding bases and lines of communication. He'd said often
enough that that was wrongheaded; now he had a chance to prove
it . . . or die. Worse, the whole Expeditionary Force would die.

He swept his binoculars across the front of the enemy formation,
counting banners. The air was very clear, crisp and cool in his lungs,
smelling only of damp earth. The city was a pillar of gunsmoke,
rising and drifting south. Sparkling, moving steel was much closer,
rippling as the enemy rode over the rolling fields, bending as they
swung to avoid an olive grove.

"About ten thousand of them, wouldn't you say?" he said to his
second in command.

"Eight to twelve," the man replied. "Three regiments of lancers,
the rest dragoons and thirteen . . . no, sixteen guns."

"Runner," Menyez said. "To all battalion commanders. Fire by platoons at any enemy fieldpiece preparing to engage at one thousand
meters or less."

That was maximum range for the three-kilo bronze smoothbores
the enemy used, and well within range for massed fire from Armory
rifles. No artillery here to support *him,* curse it. A few rounds of
shrapnel were just the thing to take the impetus out of a Brigade
lancers' charge.

"For the rest, standard drill as per *receive cavalry.*"

"*Los h'esti adala cwik,*" his second said as the messenger trotted
off: *they're in a hurry.* The Brigaderos were coming on at a round
trot, and it looked as if the dragoons intended to get quite close
before dismounting.

"Ask me for anything but time, as Messer Raj says," Menyez said,
clearing his throat.

That was one good thing about an infantry battle. He drew a deep
breath, free of wheezes for once. At least there weren't any *dogs*
around, not close enough to affect him.

"They'll probably come at a corner first," he went on. That was
the most vulnerable part of an infantry square, where the smallest
number of rifles could be brought to bear. "They *do* seem to be
in a bit of a rush."

Private Minatelli wasn't aware of hearing the trumpet. Nevertheless,
his feet were ready for the order when it was relayed down to his
platoon; *prone and kneeling.*

The men ahead of him flopped down, angling their bodies like a herringbone comb. He went down on his left knee, conscious of the cold damp earth soaking through the wool fabric of his uniform trousers. This had been a vineyard until someone grubbed up the vines for firewood, and shattered stumps of root still poked out of the stony loam amid the weeds. Now that they were halted he could hear the battle along the city walls, the boom and rattle of it muffled by distance and underlain by a surf-roar of voices.

His own personal Brigaderos were much closer. Hidden by a fold in the ground, but he could see the lancepoints. There looked to be an almighty lot of them. . . .

Omniscient Spirit of Man, he thought as they came over the crest of the rise like a tidal wave. There were *thousands* of them, big men in armor on huge Newfoundlands and St. Bernards. Pounding along in perfect alignment with lances raised, three ranks deep, heading straight for the front right corner of the square. Right at *him.* Fifteen hundred meters away and still far too close, and getting closer every second. His arms seemed to raise his rifle of their own volition, and it took an effort that left his hands shaking to snap it back down to rest on the ground.

"Set sights for four hundred meters."

The order went down the ranks. Minatelli snapped the stepped ramp forward under the rear sight with his thumb, lifting the leaf notch to the second-to-last position; for more than that, it had to be raised vertically and used as a ladder-sight. Four hundred meters still seemed awfully close.

"Fire on the command."

Feet tramped behind him. He looked back for a moment; two companies of the reserve battalion were lining up across the V-angle of the square's corner. Minatelli hoped none of them would fire too low—even standing, the muzzles would be only a half-meter over his head. When he turned his head back the Brigaderos were close enough to turn his mouth even drier. Picking up speed; they were going to start their gallop at extreme rifle range, get through the killing zone as quickly as they could. He could hear the drumbeat sound of the massed paws, feel it vibrating through the ground. The armor was polished blazing-bright, hurting his eyes under the early morning sunlight. Banners and helmet-plumes streamed with the wind of the riders' speed; the long lanceheads glittered as they swung down into position.

"UPYARZ!"

"Wait for it."

The officer sounded inhumanly calm; Minatelli took a long breath and let it out slowly. If he missed, that was one more sauroid-sticker coming at *him.* Another breath.

"Aim."

The rifle came up and the butt snuggled into his shoulder. Let the weight of the bayonet drop it a little, aim at the dog's knees. Ignore the open snarling mouths.

"Fire!"

BAM. A hammer thudding into his shoulder. And *crack* as hundreds of bullets went over his head. Reload. The deadly beauty of the lancers' charge was shredding, dogs falling and men flying in bone-shattering arcs. *BAM* and more of them were down. Adjust the sights. *BAM.* Charge coming forward in blocks and chunks, piling up where galloping dogs didn't have enough time to avoid the dead and wounded—heavy dogs with an armored man on their backs weren't all that nimble. *BAM* and the Brigade standard was down, and a lancer dropped his weapon and bent far over to snatch it off the ground. *BAM* and his body smashed back over the cantle of his saddle; a couple of dozen infantrymens' eyes must have been caught by the movement.

Thank the *Spirit* for a stiff breeze to carry off the powder-smoke, otherwise he'd be firing blind into a fogbank by now.

BAM. The metal of the chamber was hot against the callus on his thumb as he pushed home another round. The kick was worse, the rifle hit you harder when the barrel began to foul. Dogs snarling, a sound like all the fear in the world, fangs as long as daggers coming closer to his face. Lancepoints very close . . .

BAM. BAM. BAM.

"Back and wait for it!" the company commander barked.

Spirit damn it, where are Jorg and Ludwig? Raj thought.

Up the street, the Brigaderos paused as they saw the improvised barricade of overturned wagons and tables. They were a mixed group, dismounted lancers and dragoons . . . Then an officer shouted and they came pounding down the pavement with their rifle-muskets leveled. Probably planning to reserve fire until the last minute. Not a good decision, but there weren't any in their situation.

Nor in his, now that the enemy were over the walls.

"Pick your targets, make it count," the captain said. Rifles bristled over the barricade. "Now!"

The volley slammed out, the noise echoing back from the shuttered buildings on either side. At less than a hundred meters, with the Brigaderos crammed into a street only wide enough for two wagons to pass, nearly every bullet hit home. Men fell, punched off their feet by the heavy bullets. The survivors paused to return fire, hiding the chaos at the head of their column with a mantle of powder-smoke. Into it fired the splatguns in the buildings on either side of the barricade, taking the whole length of the street back to the cleared circuit inside the walls in a murderous X of enfilade fire. The *braaaap* sounded again and again.

Damned if I like those things, Raj thought as the smoke lifted a little. The head of the roadway was covered in bodies, many still moving. The splatguns were certainly effective, but they made the whole business too mechanical for his taste.

you need not worry. Center's voice held a cold irony. **if you fail here, men will hunt each other with chipped flint before the next upward cycle begins.**

Did I say I wouldn't use them? he thought.

"That's that for the moment," he went on aloud. "They'll be back soon."

He ducked into the commandeered house they were using as forward HQ. His spurs rang on the oak boards as he climbed the stairs to the second story.

"Still not spreadin' out, ser," the Master Sergeant there said, pointing without lowering his binoculars.

Raj levelled his own glasses through the window. The Brigaderos were over the wall in three places, and the numbers were enough to make his belly clench. The defenders in the towers were still holding out, keeping up their fire on the enemy-held sections of the wall. Despite that more and more of the barbarians were coming over, and they'd dropped knotted ropes and ladders down to the earth ramp backing the wall. The only good news was that they didn't seem to know what to do once they got down. Most of them were milling around, returning fire at the towers. A thousand or so were pushing directly in at the houses where the 5th had taken refuge, standing and exchanging fire with the riflemen hidden in door and window and garden wall.

They were probably a mix-and-mash from dozens of units, he decided, and no senior officers had made it over the defenses yet. Plenty of aggression—you'd expect that from men who'd kept on coming through the killing zone and the moat and the wall—but nobody directing them.

That changed as he watched. A new banner went up on the wall, and he could hear the roar from the Brigaderos. A running wardog, red on black, over a silver W. Teodore Welf's blazon.

What they should *be doing is enlarging their breach and taking the gate from the rear,* he thought. Once they had a gate, the city was doomed. *Welf's clever. On the other hand, he's also young. . . .*

"Get my personal banner," he snapped over his shoulder. He reached around to take the staff, then blinked as he saw it was Suzette handing it to him.

"I put the bannerman on the firing line," she said.

The carbine slung from her shoulder clacked on the polished wood of the staff. Raj swallowed and nodded, before he braced the pole out the forward window of the parlor and shook the heavy silk free. It slithered and hissed, snapping in the wind and chiming— a flying sauroid picked out in gold scales on the scarlet silk, with a silver Starburst behind it all.

The stiff breeze swung it back and forth, then streamed it out sideways. Raj ducked down and pulled Suzette with him as bullets pocked the limestone ashlars around the window.

"I don't think the Whitehalls are all that popular around here," he said.

"Provincials," Suzette replied, rounding out her vowels with a crisp East Residence tone. "What can one expect?"

"I'm a monkey from the wilds myself," Raj answered her grin, pushing away the knowledge of what the heavy bone-smasher bullets from the enemy rifle-muskets could do to a human body. Hers, for example.

Instead he duckwalked below the line of the windows to one in the corner and looked out. The amorphous mob of the Brigade vanguard was turning into something like a formation. Welf's banner was down among them now, and he and his sworn men—probably a cross between a warband and a real staff—were pushing the remnants and individual survivors of the storming party and the 5th's greeting into line and behind what cover there was, even if only the heaped bodies scattered in clumps across the broad C-shaped arc of the cleared zone they held. As soon as that was done they started forward . . . right towards his HQ.

Perils of a reputation, he thought dryly. Teodore had a personal mad on with him; also he was probably apprehensive about leaving Raj in his rear.

"Runner," he said sharply. "Compliments to Captain Heronimo, and shift all splatguns to the front immediately." Suzette handed him a glass and sank down beside him, back to the wall; he drank the water thirstily.

"Young Teodore is a clever lad," he said absently. The fire directed at the houses was thickening up, growing more regular. "But he's making a mistake. He should leave a blocking force and peel back more of the wall, go for the gates."

Suzette touched him lightly on the knee. "Can we stop them?"

"Not for long," he said. "Not for very long at all."

"Your Mightiness," the courier said, as he spat the reins out of his teeth.

One hand held a pistol, the other a folded dispatch. His dog stood with trembling legs, head down and washcloth-sized tongue lolling as it panted.

"Report," Ingreid Manfrond said. Howyrd Carstens took the paper.

"Lord of Men," the dispatch rider said, "High Brigadier Asmoto reports we couldn't break their square—it's advancing, slowly. More infantry coming up from the river, marching in square, about as many again but strung out in half a dozen clumps. The High Brigadier requests more troops."

"No!" Manfrond roared. "Tell him to *stop them.* They're only foot soldiers, by the Spirit. Go!"

The man blinked at him out of a dirt-splashed face and hauled his dog's head around, thumping his spurred heels into its ribs. The beast gave a long whine and shambled into a trot.

Another rider galloped up and reined in, his mount sinking down on its haunches to break. "Lord of Men," he said. "From Hereditary Colonel Fleker, at the eastern gate. Sally."

"How many?" Manfrond barked.

"Still coming out, Your Mightiness. Thousands, mounted troops only—and guns, lots of guns. They punched right through us."

The Brigade's ruler sank back in the saddle, grunting as if belly-punched. Beside him Howyrd Carstens unlimbered his telescope and peered to the southeast. They were on a rise a kilometer north of the point where the assault had carried the defenses; the action over to the west was mostly hidden except for the rising palls of powder-smoke, but they could see the northeast corner of the city walls.

"I *told* you the wall was too fucking easy," he rasped. "Here they come, guns and all."

Ingreid snatched the instrument, twisting the focus with an intensity that dimpled the thin brass under his thick-fingered grip. The first thing he saw was Brigade troops scattering, a thin screen of mounted dragoons. Some of them were firing backward with their revolvers. Then the head of a column of enemy troops came into view, loping along in perfect alignment at a slow gallop. A half-regiment or so came into view—a battalion, they called it—and then a battery of four guns, then more troops . . .

"Get the message off to Teodore to withdraw now," Carstens said. "I'll get the flank organized."

"Withdraw?" The telescope crumpled in his hands, and the weathered red of his face went purple. "Withdraw, when we've *won?*"

"Won *what?*" Carstens roared. "We've got our forces split three ways, thousands of them on the other side of the bloody *wall,* no gate, and eight thousand of the enemy coming out to corn-cob us while we look the other way!"

"Shut up or I'll have you cut down where you stand!" Ingreid roared. "Get down there and hold them off while Welf finishes Whitehall."

Carstens stared at him incredulously, then looked down the hill. The bulk of the Brigade force—sixty or seventy thousand men—was jammed up against the face of the Old Residence northern wall, what he could see of it through the smoke. Most of the men were firing at the walls and the towers, the ones who weren't dying in the moat. Artillery ripped at them, and thousands of rifles. A section of the wall a thousand meters long was quiet, in Brigade hands . . . except that the towers were still mostly holding out. The north gate was a colossal scrimmage, the moat *full* of bodies. He looked over at the enemy force. Already cutting in west, their lead element was north of the main Brigade force under the walls. Carstens could play through what happened next without even trying; the guns—must be fifty of them—pulling into line and the Civvie cavalry curving in like a scythe.

"Get Teodore out of there, you fool," he said. "I'll try and slow down the retreat."

"UPYARZ!"

Raj rose and shot the Brigadero in the face. He toppled backward off the ladder, but the one below him raised his musket one-handed through the window, poking up from below the frame. Raj felt time freeze as he struggled to turn the weapon in his left hand around. He could see the barbarian's finger tightening on the trigger, when something burned along the ribs on his right side. Suzette's carbine, firing from so close behind him that the powder scorched his jacket.

The Brigadero screamed; his convulsive recoil sent the bullet wild, *whtaanngg* off the hard stone of the wall. Suzette stepped forward, her face calm and set. She leaned out and fired six times, pumping the lever of the repeating carbine with smooth economy. Behind her the Master Sergeant was pulling the friction-fuse tab on a handbomb; he shouldered her aside without ceremony as the last shot blasted the helmet off a dragoon climbing up toward the Whitehall banner. The bomb arched down and exploded at the base of the ladder. Men screamed, but the heavy timbers remained, braced well out from the wall. Raj and the noncom set the points of their sabers against the uprights and heaved with a shout of effort. Steel sank into wood, and the ladder tilted sideways with a gathering rush.

"Stairs!" someone shouted.

Raj left Suzette thumbing rounds into the tube magazine of her Colonial weapon and led a rush to the head of the stairs. There were three rounds left in his revolver; Center's aiming-grid slid down over his vision, and he killed the first three men to burst up the stairwell. The fourth stumbled over their bodies because he refused to release the rifle-musket in his hands. Raj kicked him in the face with a full-force swing of his leg. Bones crumpled under the toe of his riding boot, feeling and sounding like kicking in thin slats in a wooden box. The man after that swung a basket-hilted sword at Raj's knees. Raj hopped over it, stamped on the barbarian's wrist as he landed, and thrust down between neck and collarbone. Muscle clamped on the blade, almost dragging it from his hand; then half a dozen troopers were shooting down the stairway on either side of him, or thrusting with their long bayonets.

"Watch where yer shootin', fer fuck's soik!" a Descotter voice shouted up to them.

Muzzle-flash showed crimson in the murk from below, and the flat crash of steel on steel sounded for an instant.

"Watch who ye lets in t'fuckin' door, ye hoor's son," the Master Sergeant shouted back.

Raj dragged breath back into his lungs; powder-smoke lay in wisps through the shattered furniture of the parlor. *We're not going to stop the next one,* he thought with sudden cold clarity.

"Raj." Suzette's voice was raised just enough to cut through the background roar. "Who are those men?"

He stepped to the side window. Just visible to the left—the west—were troops marching down the cleared zone behind the walls. They wore Civil Government uniforms, but there *weren't* any troops in that direction except the infantry holding the north wall, who had all they could cope with and more right now. And none of the Regulars in his command marched that sloppily. They weren't marching at all, not double-timing, they were *running*. Running like men fleeing a battle, except that they were running straight into one.

Raj was fairly sure Teodore Welf was still alive, from the speed of the reaction. A block of Brigaderos peeled off from the stream coming over the wall and swung out to confront the—

Militia, Raj realized. *It's the local militia.*

The confused-looking group halted and gave fire; too ragged to be a real volley, a long staccato flurry. The Brigaderos heading for them returned it, but they didn't bother to stop. They charged, while the militiamen fumbled with ramrods and percussion-caps. Raj gave a silent whistle of amazement; the city troops *didn't* disintegrate in panic. Some did, running back along the way they'd come, but most stood to meet the gray-and-black tide. They were going to be slaughtered when it came to hand-to-hand, but they were trying, at least.

"Ser," the Master Sergeant said at his elbow. "Got a bunch've t'locals comin' up behind us, say they wants t'help, loik."

The seamed, scarred face of the noncom looked deeply skeptical.

"Bring them forward, sergeant," Raj said. "By all means. Beggars can't be choosers."

Ludwig Bellamy reined in. "Cease fire!" he shouted, and the trumpets echoed it. The last of the enemy ahead were hoisting reversed weapons, or helmets on the muzzles of their rifles. "Get these men under guard."

Silence fell, comparative silence after the roar he'd grown accustomed to over the last two hours. He waved his bannerman forward, and they rode past the last Brigaderos holdouts within the walls of Old Residence and down the wall toward Messer Raj's command post.

Bellamy looked around. "Spirit *of Man,*" he swore.

The carnage around the gate had been bad. Probably more bodies than here. It had taken a fair amount of time to get the way unblocked. But this *looked* every bit as bad; smelled as bad, as far as he could tell through a nose already stunned into oblivion today. The whole two-hundred meter width of cleared ground inside the wall was carpeted with bodies, no matter how far they rode; black-and-gray uniformed Brigaderos dragoons, armored lancers, men in the blue and maroon of the Civil Government. Stretcher-bearers had to step on the dead to get at the wounded, and there were thousands. More bodies hung from the walls, or carpeted the earth ramp where the enemy had tried to retreat when they realized what was happening outside. Occasionally a patch of living Brigaderos sat with their hands behind their heads, or putting field-dressings on their own wounded.

He stopped at a mound of dead gathered more thickly around a banner of a running wardog; the pole still canted up from the earth, but the bodies were two and three deep in a circle around it. Armor rattled.

"Stretcher bearers!" he called sharply, reigning aside. A pair trotted over. "This one's alive."

"Sir. Orders are for our wounded first."

"This is an exception," Ludwig bit out. The man's armor was silver-chased and there had been plumes in his helmet. "Get him to the aid station, *now.*" Although from the amount of blood and the number of bullet holes, it might be futile.

The three-barred visor was up, and the face inside it was enough like Ludwig Bellamy's that they might have been brothers. It was something far more practical that prompted his action, though. If that was Teodore Welf, he had two presents for Messer Raj today.

He swore again when they finally pulled up in front of the forward HQ building. The stone facing looked as if it had been *chewed*. Men were sitting in the windows, or leaning against the walls, looking a little lost. Another stood in the main entranceway. A tall man, his face black as a Zanjian's with powder-smoke. Suzette Whitehall stood beside him with her arm around his waist.

Ludwig Bellamy drew rein and saluted. "*Mi heneral,*" he said.

Raj grinned, a ghastly expression in the sooty expanse of his face. When he removed his helmet, there was a lighter streak along the upper part of his forehead.

"Took you long enough," he said.

Bellamy motioned a man forward; he dismounted and laid a flag at Raj's feet. "It's the flag of Howyrd Carstens, Grand Constable of the Brigade," he said. "We would have brought the head, but . . ." Ludwig shrugged. A 75mm shell had landed close enough to Carstens that there really wasn't much left besides the signet ring they'd identified him with.

CHAPTER THIRTEEN

"It seems a good deal of trouble to go to, to hang me healthy," Teodore Welf said; his voice was low, because it hurt to breathe deeply.

He was sitting propped up in the big four-poster bed, swathed in bandages from neck to waist, one arm immobilized in splints. A priest-doctor in the ear-to-ear tonsure of a Spirit of Man of This Earth cleric stood by the bedside, glaring at Raj and Suzette and the Companions; he was of the Brigade nobleman's own household, allowed in during the after-battle truce. It was a cold spring night, and rain beat at the diamond-pane windows, but a kerosene lamp and a cheerful fire kept the bedroom warm. The flames lit the inlaid furniture and tapestries; also the hard faces of the fighting men behind Raj.

"I'm a thrifty man," Raj said, in Namerique almost as good as Teodore's Sponglish. "I've no intention of hanging you, or anything else unpleasant."

"Excellent, your excellency: I've had a surfeit of unpleasantness just lately," the young nobleman said. "Did you take Howyrd, too?"

"The Grand Constable? I'm afraid he died holding the rearguard."

Welf sighed. "Spirit have mercy on the Brigade," he said.

"I doubt that the Spirit will, just now, since the Spirit has tasked me with reuniting civilization and you're trying to stop me," Raj said.

The young Brigade noble looked at him; his eyes went a little wider when he saw the flat sincerity in Raj's.

"Particularly since the Spirit has given you Ingreid Manfrond for a ruler," Raj concluded.

Teodore was a young man, and still shaken by the wounds and the drugs the surgeons had given him. His agreement almost slipped out.

Raj nodded. "We'll talk more when you're feeling better," he said, and raised a brow at the priest.

The cleric bowed his head grudgingly. "Lord Welf will live," he said. "Fractured ribs, broken arm and collarbone, and tissue damage. Much blood loss, but he will walk in a month. The arm, longer."

A servant came in with a tray bearing tea and a steaming bowl of broth, dodging with a squeak as she met the high-ranking party going out through the same entranceway. Nothing spilled on the tray despite her skittering sideways, a feat which required considerable dexterity and some risk of dumping the hot liquids on her own head. Raj absently nodded approval as they tramped down the corridor. It wasn't far to his own quarters; Teodore Welf was one ace he intended to keep quite close to his chest.

"I suppose you've got some use for him?" Gerrin Staenbridge said, as they seated themselves around the table. Orderlies set out a cold meal and withdrew. "Apart from making sure that Ingreid doesn't have the use of him, that is."

Raj nodded. "Any number of uses. For one thing, while he's here he can't replace Manfrond—which would be a very bad bargain for us."

Staenbridge laughed, then winced; there was a bandage around his own head. "I imagine he's not too charitably inclined toward the Lord of Men right now," he said. "About as much we were toward our good Colonel Osterville down in the Southern Territories."

Kaltin Gruder drew the edge of his palm across his neck with an appropriate sound. Gerrin nodded.

"I might have *done* that, if we'd had a war down there after you left," he said to Raj. "He'd have gotten us all killed."

Raj nodded. "Young Teodore probably does feel like that," he said judiciously. "Something we can make use of later, perhaps. Now, to business."

Jorg Menyez opened a file. "Ten percent casualties. Fifteen if you count wounded who'll be unfit-for-service for a month or more. Unevenly distributed, of course—some of the infantry battalions that held the north wall are down to company size or less."

"The 5th's got five hundred effectives," Staenbridge said grimly.

Raj nodded thoughtfully. "Ingreid lost . . . at least twenty-five thousand," he said.

"Plus five thousand prisoners," Ludwig interjected, around a mouthful of sandwich. "From their rearguard, mostly—they fought long enough to let the rest get back to their camps, but we had them surrounded by then. None of them surrendered until Carstens died, by the way."

"All of which leaves us with about seventeen thousand effectives, and Ingreid with nearly sixty thousand," Raj said. If the Brigade hadn't had fortified camps to retreat to he would have pursued in the hope of harrying them into rout. He certainly wasn't going to throw away a victory by assaulting their earthworks and palisades.

"Still long odds, but their morale can't be very good. What I propose—"

A challenge and response came from the guards outside the door, and then a knock. Raj looked up in surprise.

"Message from Colonel Clerett, *mi heneral,*" the lieutenant in charge of the guard detail said.

"Well, bring it in," Raj said. He'd left standing instructions to have anything from Cabot Clerett brought to him at once.

"Ah—" the young officer cleared his throat. "It's addressed to Messa Whitehall."

"Well, then give it to *her,*" Raj said calmly. He kept his face under careful control; there was no point in frightening the lieutenant.

The younger man handed the letter to Raj's wife with a bow and left with thankful speed. Suzette turned the square of heavy paper over in her fingers, raising one slim brow. It was a standard dispatch envelope, sealed by folding and winding a thread around two metal studs set in the paper, then dropping hot wax on the junction and stamping it with the sender's seal. Silently she dropped it to the table, put one finger on it and slid it over the mahogany toward Raj.

A bleak smile lit his face as he drew his dagger and flicked the thin edge of Al Kebir steel under the wax. The paper crackled as he opened it. There was nothing relevant in the first paragraphs . . . the others looked up at his grunt of interest.

"Our dashing Cabot fought an action outside Las Plumhas," he said. A sketch-map accompanied the description. "He's got the four thousand cavalry with him, and twenty-seven guns. Met about ten thousand of the Brigaderos, and thrashed them soundly."

Nice job of work, he thought critically. Got them attacking with a feigned retreat—barbs usually fell for that—and then rolled them up when they stalled against his gun line. *Our boy has been to school.*

"What!"

The roar of anger brought the others bolt upright in surprise; Raj was normally a calm man. His fist crashed down, making the cutlery dance and jingle.

"The little *fastardo!* The clot-brained, arrogant, purblind little *snot!*" Raj's voice choked off; there were no words adequate for his feelings.

Suzette's fingers touched his wrist; the contact was like cool water on the red-hot heat of his anger. He drew a deep breath and continued reading, lips pulled tight over his teeth.

"Our good Colonel Clerett," he said at last, throwing down the paper—Suzette scooped it up and tucked it into a file of her papers— "has decided that it's pointless to join us here. Instead he's going to head straight southwest across the Brigade heartland, wasting the land, and head for Carson Barracks to draw *off* Ingreid's main force and free up the situation."

The shocked silence held for a full minute. Then Gerrin Staenbridge spoke: "You know, *mi heneral,* that might just work."

Raj gulped water and spoke, his voice hoarse. "It might work if *I* was leading the detachment. I might've told *you* to do that if *you* were leading it. Cabot Clerett—"

observe, Center said.

Reality faded, to be replaced by a battlefield. He had an overhead view, of three hills held by ragged squares of Civil Government soldiers. Columns of smoke rose from each, as rifles and cannon fired down into a surging mass of Brigaderos that lapped around like water around crumbling sandcastles. As he watched the wave surged up over one of the squares, and the neat linear formation dissolved into a melee. That lasted less than a minute before nobody but the barbarians was left alive on the hilltop. Those men turned and slid down the slope in a charge like an avalanche to join the assault on the next formation.

A flick, and he saw Cabot Clerett standing next to his bannerman. A dozen or so men were still on their feet around him. Cabot's face was contorted in a snarl that would have done credit to a carnosauroid. He lunged forward and drove the point of his saber through a barbarian's chest. Six inches of metal poked out through the back of the Brigadero's leather coat. The blade was expertly held, flat parallel to the ground so that it wouldn't stick in the ribs. It still took a moment to withdraw, and a broadsword came down on his wrist. The sword was sharp and heavy, with a strong man behind it. The young noble's hand sprang free; he pivoted screaming, with arterial blood spouting a meter high from the stump. The bannerman behind him drove the ornamental bronze spike on the head of the staff into the chest of the swordsman who'd killed Clerett, then went down under a dozen blades. The Starburst trailed in blood and dirt as it fell.

probability 57% ±10, Center went on dispassionately.

Raj blinked back to reality, feeling the others staring at him.

"Well," he said calmly, "the way I figure it, there's about an even chance or a little more he'll get himself killed and his force wiped out."

Kaltin filled his wineglass. "You've taken the odd risk yourself, now and then," he pointed out.

Raj shrugged, loosening the tense muscles of his shoulders. "Only when it's justified. We don't *need* to take risks now. With those four thousand men, I can wrap this war up in a year or two. The Western Territories have waited six hundred years for the reconquest, a year won't make any difference."

Kaltin's right, he thought. *A couple of years ago I'd have done the same thing myself.* For a moment he felt Center's icy presence at the back of his mind, wordless.

"Anyway," Ludwig said thoughtfully, "they'll have to detach a pretty big force to deal with Cabot. That should give us an opportunity."

"Expensive if it costs four thousand of the Civil Government's elite troops," Raj said. He shrugged. "Let's deal with the situation as it is. Bartin, bring the map easel over here, would you?"

"Most Excellent mistress, there's been a terrible disaster!"

Marie looked up from the pile of samples the merchant was showing her.

"News from the front?" she said tonelessly.

The steward shook his head and continued in his Spanjol-accented Namerique. "No, the main granaries down by the canal, mistress."

He wrung his hands; Marie stood and swept out of the room, up the grand curving staircase to the rooftop terrace. It was a clear spring night in Carson Barracks, smelling as usual faintly of swamp. Some previous General had bought an astronomical telescope. Marie had ordered it brought out of storage and set up here, on the highest spot in the city; she wasn't allowed out of the palace much, but she could *see* the whole town. When she put her eye to the lens the squat round towers of the grain storage leapt out at her. Smoke was billowing out of their conical rooftops, red-lit by the flames underneath. The warehouses were stone block, but the framing and interior partitions and roofs were timber . . . and grain itself will burn in a hot enough flame.

One of the towers disintegrated in a globe of orange fire that swelled up a hundred meters above the rooftops. Burning debris rained down on the surrounding district, and on the barges and rail-cars in the basins and switching-yards near the end of the causeway.

Flour will not only burn: when mixed with air, as in a half-empty bulk storage bin, it is a fairly effective explosive.

"Manhwel," she said crisply to the steward, standing and drawing her shawl about her bare shoulders against the slight damp chill. The ladies-in-waiting were twittering and pointing about her. "Send all the Palace staff but the most essential down to help fight the flames."

"At once, Most Excellent Mistress," he said.

"The rest of you, back to your work. Don't stand there gaping like peasants."

All of them surged away, except Dolors and Katrini. And Abdullah, bowing with hand touching brows and lips and heart, a slight smile showing teeth white in his dark beard. He didn't say a word: none was necessary. Thanks to a few gallons of kerosene and a few loyal Welf followers, and the Arab's timing devices, Carson Barracks was now in no state to stand a siege. With harvest four months off, the central provinces around the rail line to Old Residence devastated, and every city short of food as winter stocks dwindled, it would probably be impossible to resupply to any meaningful degree.

"And Manhwel, send my personal condolences immediately to General Manfrond."

There was a fairly good courier service between the capital and the forces in the field. Her lip curled. Good enough for her to learn how *that fool* Ingreid Manfrond was wasting his fighting men. Every second family in the Brigade was in mourning for a father, a son, a husband. With Teodore prisoner and Howyrd Carstens dead, he'd be even worse.

We cannot win this war, she told herself. *And if Manfrond remains General, he will destroy the Brigade trying to.*

The flames were mounting higher, and the red glow was beginning to spread as timbers from the explosion caught elsewhere, for thousands of meters around. Bells clanged and ox-horn trumpets hooted, but Carson Barracks was a city of women and old men and servants now.

Ingreid Manfrond must go . . . and there would be revenge for her mother and for the House of Welf. The servant shivered as he watched her smile.

She motioned Abdullah closer as the steward left. The guards at the corners of the terrace were well out of earshot.

"I suppose you'll be reporting as well," she said. He shrugged expressively. "Those devices you showed us worked well."

"They are of proven worth, my lady," he murmured, bowing again.

"Everything I've done has been my own decision," Marie said after a moment, looking at his bland expression. "Why do I get this feeling that you're behind it?"

"I merely offer advice, my lady," he said.

"We're like children to you, aren't we?" she said slowly.

He must be conscious that the guards would hack him in pieces at her word, but there was a cat's ease in the way he spread his hands.

"There is much to be said for the energy of youth, Lady Welf," he said.

"Send my regards to Teodore," she went on. "Tell him I was right about Manfrond."

"He's definitely pulling out," Raj said.

The windows of the conference room were open to the mild spring day; the air smelled fresh and surprisingly clean for a city. Buds showed on the trees around the main plaza—those that hadn't been cut for firewood during the siege—and a fresh breeze ruffled the broad estuary of the White River, past the rooftops of the city. A three-master was standing downstream, sails shining in billowing curves of white canvas as she heeled and struck wings of foam from her bows. Pillars of smoke marked the Brigade camps on the distant southern shore, where excess supplies and gun-rafts burned.

"Cautiously," Jorg Menyez said. "The troops on the south shore are guarding his line of retreat southwest of here, along the rail line." He traced a finger on the map. "And north of the city he's withdrawing from the eastern encampments first."

Kaltin Gruder rubbed the scarred side of his face. "We could try and snap up moving columns," he said.

Raj shook his head. "No, we want to speed the parting guest," he said. "From the latest dispatches, Clerett is ripping through everything ahead of him."

A few of the Companions looked embarrassed; the dispatches were all addressed to Lady Whitehall.

Raj cleared his throat. "I'd say our good friend Ingreid 'Blind Bull' Manfrond isn't retreating, to his way of thinking—he's charging in another direction. Right back toward his home pasture at Carson Barracks, against an opponent he thinks he can get at in the open field."

And very well may, if Center's right, Raj thought. It was so tempting . . .

"You plan to let him withdraw scot-free?" Tejan M'Brust looked unhappy, his narrow dark face bent over the map, tapping at chokepoints along the Brigade's probable line of retreat.

"Did I say that?' Raj replied, with a carnosaur grin. "Did I? Commodore Lopeyz, here's what I want you to do . . ."

They're holding hard, Raj thought.

The terrain narrowed down here, a sloping wedge where the railway embankment cut through a ridge and down to the river. A kilometer on either side of him hills rose, not very high but rugged, loess soil over rock. Trees covered them, native whipstick with red and yellow spring foliage, oaks and beeches in tender green like the flower-starred grass beneath. The air smelled intensely fresh, beneath the sulfur stink of gunpowder.

Just then the battery to his left cut loose; some of the aides and messengers around him had to quiet their dogs. Horace ignored the sound with a veteran's stolid indifference; in fact, he tried to sit down again.

"Up, you son of a bitch," Raj said, with a warning pressure on the bridle.

Three shells burst over the Brigaderos line ahead of him, two thousand meters away. They were three deep across the open space, with blocks of mounted troops in support and a huge mob of dogs on leading lines further back, their own mounts. He trained his binoculars; the forward line of the enemy fired—by troops, about ninety men at a time—turned, and walked through the ranks behind them. Fifty paces back they halted and began to reload, while the

rank revealed by their countermarch fired in turn and then did
the same. His own men were in a thinner two-rank formation about
a thousand yards closer, giving independent fire from prone-and-
kneeling and advancing by companies as the barbarians retreated.
It gave their formation a saw-toothed look; once or twice the
mounted lancers behind the dragoons had tried to charge, but the
guns broke them up.

The enemy were suffering badly, paying for their stubborn courage.
Neither side's weapons were very accurate at a thousand meters,
but the Civil Government troops didn't have to stand upright and
stock-still to reload. Still, a steady trickle of wounded came back,
born by stretcher-bearers and then transferred to dog-drawn ambulances. Their moaning could be heard occasionally, from the road
that wound by the hillock he'd selected to oversee this phase.

Cost of doing business, he told himself. He'd not have paid this
sort of butcher's bill just to hustle the enemy on their way, though.

More firing came from the wooded hills on either side, an irregular
crackling rather than the slamming volleys of open-field combat. That
was bad country, tangled gullies overgrown with brush, steep hill-
sides and fallen timber. Jorg's infantry were pressing forward on either
flank, but it was slow work. Up close and personal, as the men
put it.

Antin M'lewis pulled up. "Ser," he said. "Barbs gettin' tight-packed
back terwards t'bridge. Them fish-eaters is in position."

Raj nodded. An aide puffed on his cigarette and walked over
to touch it to the paper fuse of a signal rocket; quite a large one,
as tall as a small man with its supporting stick. The missile lit
with a dragon's hiss and a shower of sparks and smoke that sent
the aide skipping back and the dogs to wurfling and sneezing in
protest. Their eyes followed it, faces turning up like sauroid chicks
in a nest when the mother returned. At a thousand meters height
it popped into a ball of lesser streamers, a huge dandelion-fluff
that held for a moment and then drifted northward with the breeze,
losing definition as it went.

"That's it," Lopeyz said, from the conning tower of the first
steamboat. "Slip the cables."

The reddish smoke of the rocket drifted away. A wailing screech
from the whistle of his craft echoed back from the bluffs, and the
three mortar-boats chuffed into the current. Here the river was tending
as much north as west, and the water ran faster. Their converted
locomotive engines wheezed and clanged; he looked down between
his feet and saw the sweat-gleaming bodies of the black gang as
they shoveled the coal into the improvised brick hearths around the
firedoors. To his right on the north bank of the river he could hear
the firefight going on in the woods, and see the drifting smoke of
it. A little further on, and the river narrowed. The banks were black

with men and dogs, the rail bridge swarming with them like a moving carpet of ants—he could see that even a kilometer away.

Panic broke out at the sight of the Civil Government riverboats, shouts and screams and a vast formless heaving. The bridge locked solid as men tried to stampede to the south bank and safety. Bullets began to sparkle off the wrought-iron armor of the three boats, some of them punching through the thinner metal of the smokestacks with a distinctive *ptunggg* sound. He swung a metal plate across the opening, leaving only a narrow slit for vision, and shouted down the hatchway.

"Reduce speed to two knots!"

The central channel was deep here, but narrow, and there were sandbanks and snag-heads all around. He looked back; the other two craft were following in line, the black coal-smoke pouring from their stacks and the river frothing in the wake of their paddles. Just then a monstrous *tchunggg* made the interior of the gunboat ring like a bell. Lopeyz clutched for a handhold and looked around.

"Four-kilo shot," his first mate shouted over the engine noise. The helmsman hunched his shoulders and kept his eyes firmly ahead.

Lopeyz nodded. Light field piece firing roundshot, no menace to the gunboats . . . unless they got really lucky and took off a smokestack, in which case the furnaces wouldn't draw and he'd lose steam. The danger was less unpleasant than the thought of how it would foul up the mission. *I have been around Raj Whitehall too long,* he thought.

The earthwork fort holding the north end of the bridge came into view. The sides were gullied with the winter rains and poor maintenance, but it was still occupied, and the enemy had moved heavier guns in. Fortress models throwing forty and sixty-kilo solid shot, which *was* a threat to the gunboats.

"Prepare to engage," he called.

The gunners in the forward part of the hull loaded a round into the mortar, one set for delayed explosion. At the same instant a flash of red showed on the ramparts of the fort. About a second later a plume of water five meters high erupted off the port bow as the cannonball struck.

"Range one thousand. Let go the anchors, engines all stop." Silence struck ears accustomed to the groan and clank of the engine, broken by the sounds of water and of venting steam from the safety valve. There was an iron clank as a wedge-shaped segment of the deck armor over the muzzle of the mortar was released and swung down.

"*Fire!*"

"Spirit," Raj murmured to himself.

POUMF. The field-gun fired again, and the crew cheered as the shell struck just short of the bridge. It hammered into ground covered with men and dogs, gouting up a candle-shape of dirt and body-parts. The crowding down there was so bad that the empty space filled at once, pressure from the sides forcing men in like water into a splash-hole. All along the ridge overlooking the narrow ledge of floodplain Civil Government troops stood and fired down into the dense mass, working their levers with the hysterical exultation that a defenseless target brings. The bulk of the enemy were far too closely packed to use their weapons, even if they had the inclination. More guns came up; they'd been slowed by the press of surrendering men and riderless dogs behind.

The fort by the bridge was broken and burning. So was the center span of the bridge itself, the wooden trestle licking up flames that were pale in the bright midmorning sun. The heads of men and dogs showed in the water. The swift current swept most of them downstream, toward the tidal estuary and the waiting downdraggers. More followed them into the water by the minute. . . .

"Cease fire!" Raj shouted.

There hadn't been much fight in the Brigaderos since they realized the bridge was under attack behind them. A splatgun bounced up, unlimbered and cut loose down the slope into the enemy. A pocket opened for a second, where the thirty-five rounds punched in together.

"Cease fire, Spirit-dammit, sound *cease fire!*" Raj shouted again.

The bugles sang again and again, and the sound began to relay down the other units. The Civil Government soldiers were packed almost shoulder to shoulder above their opponents as well, and the firing began to die away reluctantly. As the noise died, the movement below did as well. Ten minutes later the cries of the wounded were the loudest sound; he could see thousands of faces turning toward him, toward the Starburst banner amid the guns.

"White parley flag," he said to an aide. "Find an officer. Unconditional surrender, immediately, but I guarantee their lives and personal liberty if nothing else." He had better uses for troops this good than sending them to the mines.

"Well, Ingreid's down to what, fifty thousand by now?" Gerrin Staenbridge said.

"Four thousand dead, four thousand surrendered, from their rearguard—roughly," Bartin Foley said, looking at his notepad.

The commanders were sitting around a trestle table. Below them squads of prisoners were picking over the field, collecting the dead and the weapons under the supervision of Civil Government infantry. Wagonloads of enemy wounded and plunder groaned up the switchback road, and packs of captured dogs. Artillerymen and artisans from Old Residence were swarming over the railway bridge and repairing the damage; the sound of sawing and hammering drifted back along with the endless rushing sound of the river against the stone pilings. Still more prisoners were at work repairing the earthworks of the fort. Even the artillery might be salvageable; those cast-iron and cast-bronze pieces were hard to damage.

Raj swallowed a mouthful of bread and sausage and followed it with water. "Grammeck, how long on the bridge?"

"Ready by tomorrow if we push it," the artilleryman said. "No real structural damage."

Raj nodded. "Kaltin, how many dogs did we capture?"

"More than we can use or feed," the Companion said. "Eight, nine thousand, not counting the ones who're better shot. Why?"

He raised a hand. "All right," he said. The others leaned forward. "As you may have guessed, I don't intend to give Ingreid a free passage home. If he gets behind the fortifications of Carson Barracks, we could be here for years—and it'd be cursed hard to cut off its communications, not with the river so close."

Staenbridge rubbed a hand along his jaw, rasping the blueblack stubble. "An open-field encounter?" he said. "Fifty, fifty-five thousand men . . . chancy."

Raj shook his head and smiled, weighing down the corners of a map with plates and cups. "I've no intention of fighting unless he obliges me by attacking a strong position head-on . . . and I think even the Lord of Men has realized *that's* a mistake."

The others chuckled and watched intently as Raj's finger traced the line of the railway between Old Residence and Carson Barracks, four hundred kilometers to the southwest in the valley of the Padan.

"He has to withdraw along this line . . . well, he *could* march straight to the nearest riverport on the Padan, but that's not what he'll do. This stretch of country along the line of rail is bare and the railway is useless for anything substantial, thanks to Ludwig here." The ex-Squadrone blushed. "He'll have to bring in wagon trains from areas with supplies—and at the worst time of year, too."

"Ah, *bwenyo*," Kaltin Gruder said. "A razziah, eh?"

"Hmmm." Gerrin pursed his lips. "Still, we'd have only six thousand men," he pointed out. "Difficult to coordinate and not much if we *do* have to fight."

"Not nearly enough," Raj agreed. "We'll need eleven thousand rifles and all the field guns as a minimum. Jorg, we'll take nine battalions of your infantry."

The Kelden County nobleman looked up, blinking in surprise. "My boys can march," he said. "But they're bipeds, *mi heneral.*"

"Not on dogback they aren't," Raj said. That's why I asked how many dogs we captured." He held up his hands against the storm of protest.

"I know, I know; it takes years to train a cavalryman, he practically has to be born at it. I don't expect them to be able to fight mounted, or maneuver, or switch from mounted to dismounted action quickly—I don't expect them to do anything but stay on the beasts, then get off and form up on foot for infantry action. Mounted infantry, not cavalry."

Jorg Menyez closed his mouth on the protest he had been about to make and sat silent for a second. Then he nodded. "Yes, they can do that," he said.

Raj rapped his knuckles on the rough boards. "Spirit willing and the crick don't rise," he said. "Pick the best, leave the units that got hardest-hit during the assault behind. Put a good solid man in charge, he can recruit up to strength locally. Not likely to be any real fighting around here for the rest of the campaign, anyway.

"We'll divide into three columns," he went on. "Gerrin, Kaltin and Ludwig to command, fifteen guns each. Bare minimum supplies, no tents, no camp followers, no wheeled transports except the ammunition limbers for the guns. Put six hundred rounds of 11mm per man on pack dogs, three days' hardtack, and that's about it."

He drew a straight line on the map along the railway. "That's Ingreid." Three X's, one ahead of the Brigade force and two more on the south and left of it. "That's us. Just enough skirmishing to keep them slowed down."

A big army was a slow army anyway, and if they were forced to deploy, they'd be slower still. Every day cross-country increased their supply problems. Raj stretched out a hand with the fingers splayed, then pulled it back toward himself and clenched them.

"We'll stay close enough together to keep in supporting distance," he said. "Cut off all foragers, and retreat sharpish if a substantial force tries to attack. If Ingreid stops and lunges for us, we can all close up and pick our spot. Either he breaks his teeth on us by attacking entrenchments front-on, or he has to resume marching toward Carson Barracks—in which case we resume harassment. With any luck, by the time he gets to his capital he'll be starving."

"What about their right flank?" Gerrin asked, tracing an arc to the north of the railway line.

"Our good and faithful Colonel Clerett's up there, burning and killing," Raj said. "From the reports, I expect him to reach Carson Barracks long before Ingreid does. Also, I'll put the Skinners on that flank. Juluk will enjoy that."

"Spirit help the civilians," Jorg said. Raj shrugged.

"Fortunes of war—and Skinners consider killing civilians poor sport when they've got Long-Hairs at hand," he said. "When we all get where we're going, we can link up with Clerett, which will give us fifteen or sixteen thousand first-rate troops . . . and Ingreid should be considerably weaker by then. Any questions?"

A murmur of assent. "I want to be moving by tomorrow," he went on. "Here's the disposition of units—"

CHAPTER FOURTEEN

The long gentle ridge above the roadway was covered in peach trees, and the whole orchard was in a froth of pink blossom. The scent was overpoweringly sweet, and rain-dewed blossoms fell to star the shoulders and helmets of the troopers sitting their dogs beneath. Grainfields stretched down to the roadway and rolled away beyond, an occasional clump of trees or a cottage interrupting the waist-high corn or thigh-high wheat. Ploughed fallow was reddish-brown, pastureland intensely green. The sun shone bright yellow-orange in a cloudless sky, with both moons transparent slivers near the horizon. A pterosauroid hovered high overhead, its ten-meter span of wings tiny against the cloudless sky; toothed feathered almost-birds chased insects from bough to bough above the soldiers, chirring at the feast stirred up by the paws of the dogs. Occasionally one would flutter to a stop, cling to bark with feet and the clawed fingers on the leading edge of their wings, and hiss defiance at the men below.

"We look like a bunch of damned groomsmen riding to a wedding," Kaltin Gruder said, brushing flowers off his dog's neck. The officer beside him chuckled.

Half a kilometer to the north and a hundred meters below, a train of wagons creaked slowly eastward. Oxen pulled them, twenty big white-coated beasts to the largest vehicles, land-schooners with their canvas-covered hoops; they ranged from there down to the ordinary humble two-wheeled farm carts pulled by a single pair. Kaltin whistled tunelessly through his teeth as he moved his binoculars from east to west. Most of the people with the convoy were obviously natives, peasants in ragged trousers and smocks. More followed, driving a herd of sheep and slaughter-cattle in the fields beside the road—right through young corn and half-grown winter wheat, too.

There were other men on dogback, though, with lobster-tail helmets and black-and-gray uniforms. Riding in columns of twos on either

392

side of the convoy, and throwing out small patrols. One group of four was riding up the open slope below towards the orchard.

"About two hundred dragoons," he said, and began to give brisk orders. That was just enough to make sure that no band of disgruntled peons jumped the supply train. Not enough to do anything useful today.

A bugle sounded; the Brigaderos scouts hauled frantically on their reins as three hundred men rose to their feet and walked in line abreast out of the orchard. Another two companies trotted down and took up position across the road ahead of the convoy, blocking their path back towards the main Brigade army.

"Now—" Kaltin began, then clicked his tongue.

The Brigade kettledrums whirred. The civilians were taking off straight north through the grainfields; if the commander of the convoy escort had any sense, he'd be doing the same. Instead the barbarians fired a volley from the saddle—not a round of which came anywhere near the Civil Government force, although he could hear bullets clipping through the treetops five meters overhead—drew their swords, and charged.

"More balls than brains," the battalion commander said, and called to a subordinate.

Further back on the ridge, guns crashed. Shells ripped by overhead and hammered up ground before the charging Brigaderos. At four hundred meters the riflemen cut loose with volley fire. Thirty seconds later the survivors of the Brigade charge were galloping frantically in the other direction, or holding up reversed weapons. All but their leader; he came on, sword outstretched. At a hundred meters from the Civil Government line his dog stumbled and went down as if it had tripped, legs broken by shots fired low.

"Let's see what we've got," Kaltin said, touching a heel to his dog's flank.

He rode up to the fallen man. *Boy,* he thought. Only a black down on his pale cheeks; on his hands and knees, fumbling after his sword. Kaltin leaned down and swung the point of his saber in front of the boy's eyes.

"Yield," he said.

Blinking back tears of rage, the young man stood and offered his sword across his forearm.

"I am hereditary Captain Evans Durkman," he said, and flushed crimson when his voice broke in mid-sentence.

Down below the troopers of the 7th Descott were proceeding in businesslike fashion. The oxen were unharnessed and driven upslope with whoops and slapping lariats. Men stood in the wagons to load sacks of cornmeal and beans and dried meat and sausages onto strings of dogs with pack-saddles. An even louder whoop told of a wagon filled with kegs of brandy; there were groans as a noncom rode up and ordered the tops of the barrels smashed in and the pale liquor dumped on all the remaining vehicles. Less than five minutes after the action began, the first brandy-fueled flames licked skyward. A few minutes after that, the whole train was burning. Sullen prisoners smashed their own rifles against the iron tyres of the wagon wheels under the muzzles of the Descotter guns.

"You won't get away with this, you bandit," the extremely young Brigadero growled in passable Sponglish.

Several of the men around Kaltin chuckled. He smiled himself; not an unkindly expression, but the scars made it into something that forced the younger man to flinch a little beneath his bravado.

"If you mean that force of fifteen hundred men who was going to meet you," he began.

Just then a faint booming came from the northeast, echoing off the low hills. It took the Brigadero a few moments to recognize the sound of a distant cannonade, and then he went chalk-white under his pale skin.

"—that's them," Kaltin finished. "Now your boots, young messer."

The other man noticed that the prisoners were barefoot; he surrendered his own grudgingly, watching in puzzlement as the footwear were thrown onto the roaring bonfire that had been a wagon a few minutes before.

"We don't have time or troops to guard you," Kaltin said helpfully to the hangdog group of prisoners. "And I doubt Ingreid has mounts, weapons or footwear to spare—to say nothing of food. So if you've got any sense, you'll all start walking home right now. I'm sure your mother will be reassured to see you, Hereditary Captain Durkman."

He sheathed his sword and gathered up his reins. The Brigadero burst into sputtering Namerique; Kaltin spoke a little of that language, mostly learned from his concubine Mitchi. Judging by the terms for body parts, most of what the youngster was saying was obscenities. Several of his older subordinates grabbed him by the arms. *They* probably understood exactly what the alternative to release was for an inconvenient prisoner, and were surprised they were still alive.

Markman shook them off. "When are you going to stop hiding and skulking?" he said hotly. "When are you going to come out and give battle like honest men?"

Kaltin grinned as he turned his mount eastward. "We are giving battle," he said over his shoulder. "And we're winning."

He turned and chopped a hand forward. "*Waymanos!*"

"Well, this is something new," Bartin Foley said.

The road was a churned-up mass of mud and dung and dogshit; exactly what you would expect after a major army passed by. The litter of discarded baggage was about what he'd become accustomed to, after the first week. One of the main problems had been preventing the men loading themselves down with non-essential loot. Some of it *had* been fairly tempting—even a silver bathtub, for the

Spirit's sake! Masses of servants and thralls and camp followers as well, not just whores but families.

This time it was guns, their barrels glistening under the quick spring rain. The bronze glittered more brightly as the clouds split and watery sunlight broke through. Twenty of the guns were light field-pieces; three were heavier, not quite siege guns but nearly . . . and that must be about all of Ingreid's remaining artillery, counting what had bogged down in fords and fallen off bridges and broken its axles before getting this far.

"They're over here, sir," Lieutenant Torridez said.

The ruts didn't stop at the edge of the road; in fact, it was difficult to say just where the road had been, in the swath of trampled and churned devastation cutting southwest through the fields. Only the line of the railway embankment made it certain. There was a good deal of swamp and forest hereabouts, and drainage channels in the cleared fields. The three hundred Brigaderos squatting with their hands behind their heads were in what had probably been a pasture in better days.

"Found them sitting here," Torridez went on. "Didn't give us any trouble at all."

Foley wrinkled his nose slightly at the smell, and made a mental note to make sure the priests were checking on the mens' drinking water. Dysentery like this was the last thing they needed. The two Civil Government officers pulled up beside an older man; he was wearing back-and-breast armor, although the troops in the field were dragoons. He rose, blinking watery gray eyes at the young man with the hook; his head was egg-bald, and his face had probably been strong before fever and hunger left the skin sagging and ash-colored.

"Colonel Otto Witton," he said hoarsely.

"Captain Bartin Foley," the younger man replied in careful Namerique. "This is your regiment?"

Witton laughed, then coughed wrackingly. "What's left of it," he said. "The ones who didn't bug out last night." He laughed again, then coughed until he retched. "We're the rearguard, officially."

Foley touched his lips with his hook. "Colonel, you *may* be in luck," he said. "I'm sending back an escort with our walking wounded." The Brigadero nodded, as aware as he of the other option. "However, there are a few things I'd like to know . . ."

Witton grunted and spat red-flecked spittle into the mud. "Ask away. A brother and a son I've lost because that pig-ignorant sauroid-fucker Manfrond bungled this war into wreck, and Teodore Amalson's whole legacy with it. Outer Dark, *Forker* might have done better."

"The Spirit of Man is with General Whitehall," Foley said. "Now, what we'd like to know is—"

The sound from the edge of the swamp was nearly half a kilometer away, and still loud enough to stun. The form of it was something halfway between a gobbling shriek and a falcon's cry, but the volume turned it into a blur in the background, like the stones in a watermill. The creature charged before the last notes died. Its body was seven meters long and it had the rangy lethality of a bullwhip. Half the length was tail, and most of the rest of it seemed to be head, split in a gape large enough to engulf half a man's torso. It was running on its hind legs, massive yet agile, thick drumsticks pushing the clawed eagle feet forward three meters for each bounding birdlike stride. The forelegs were small by comparison, but they each bore clawed fingers out-stretched toward the prey. Mottled green scales covered the upper part of its body; the belly was cream, and the wattles under its throat the angry crimson of a rooster's comb.

The stink of decay had brought it out of the swamps where it hunted hadrosauroids. The target was the three hundred disarmed Brigaderos, and it would plow into them like a steam-powered saw through soft wood. A big carnosaur like this would kill until everything around was dead before it started feeding, then lie up on the kills until the last shred of rotting meat was engulfed.

"Dismount, rapid fire, *now!*" Foley shouted, his voice precise and clear and pitched high to carry.

A hundred men reacted smoothly, only the growling of anxious dogs making it different from a drill. The first shot rang out less than twenty seconds later. Foley could see bullets pocking the mud around its feet, small splashes amid the piledriver explosions of mud and water each time the three-toed feet hit the ground. More were striking the outstretched head, but a sauroids brain was smaller than a child's fist, in a large and very bony skull. Then a lucky shot hit the shoulder girdle and bounced down the animal's flank. It was far from a serious wound, but it stung enough to make the carnosaur think—or to trigger one of the bundles of hardwired reflexes that passed for thought.

It spun in place, tail swinging around to lever it and jaws snap-ping shut with a sound like a marble statue dropping on flagstones as it sought the thing that had bitten it. That put it broadside-on to Foley's company, and he could *hear* the bullets striking, a sound like hailstones hitting mud. Most of them would be brass-tipped hardpoint sauroid killers. The beast swung around again and roared, breaking into a fresh charge. Foley clamped his legs around the barrel of his dog and drew his pistol, aware as he did so that he might as well kiss the beast on the snout as shoot it with a handgun. Ten meters from the firing line—a body length—the carnosaur's feet stopped working; one slid out in front of it, the other staying behind instead of moving forward for the next stride. The long head nosed down into the soft dirt, plowing a furrow toward them.

The jet-colored eyes stayed open as the three-ton carnivore slid to a halt barely a meter away. The troopers went on shooting, pump-ing four or five rounds each into the sauroid; that was experience, not nervousness.

Foley quieted his dog, fighting to control his own breathing. He'd done his share of hunting for duty back home in Descott, although he'd never much enjoyed it. But Descott was too arid to support many big carnivores, the more so as the grazing sauroids had all been shot out long ago. A pack of man-high sicklefeet, of which there were plenty, were just as dangerous. But not nearly so nerve-wracking.

"Sorry for the interruption," he said, turning back to Otto Witton. The Brigadero's hands were still making grasping motions, as if reaching for a nonexistent gun.

"They ah, they usually don't—"

"—come so near men," Foley finished for him. "Except when we make it safe for them by killing each other off."

Which happened fairly often: one reason why it was so easy for land to slip back into barbarism. Once a tipping-point of reduced population was reached the native wildlife was impossible to keep down. How anyone could think that the Spirit of Man was of *this* Earth was beyond him, when Man was so obviously unsuited to living here. It probably wasn't the time for a theological controversy, though.

"Thank you," the older man said. He inclined his head toward his men, most of them too exhausted even to run when the carnosaur appeared.

"*Danad,*" Foley said in his native tongue: *it's nothing.*

Witton took a deep breath, coughed, and began: "Ingreid's got about—"

"Ser," Antin M'lewis said. " 'Bout six thousand of 'em, workin' ter ourn left, through thet swamp."

Raj nodded, looking southeast. The main force of the Brigade host had shaken itself out into battle formation, although that had taken most of the morning. The countryside here was almost tabletop flat, planted in grain where it wasn't marsh. There were still an intimidating number of the enemy, stretching in regular blocks from one end of sight to another, but they were advancing very slowly. Noon sun cast back eye-hurting flickers from edged metal and banners, but there was a tattered look to the enemy formations even at this distance.

"Is it my imagination," Gerrin said, focusing his binoculars, "or are they even slower than usual?"

"One-third of them aren't mounted any more," Raj replied.

They both grimaced; scouts had found charred dog-bones in the Brigaderos' campfires, the last couple of days. That was not quite cannibalism, but fairly close for a nobleman bred to the saddle. The enemy might be barbarians, but they were gentlemen of a sort. It probably came no easier to them than it would to either of the Descotters, or to any Messer.

"Well, we've cost them a day," Gerrin said.

"Indeed. Grammeck, stand ready to give them a quick three-round stonk when they get in range, then pull out.

"Jorg." Raj raised his voice slightly; Menyez was on his long-legged riding steer, and the beast liked dogs no better than its master. "Get the infantry back, mounted and moving."

"We'll backpedal?" Staenbridge said.

Raj shook his head. "Take the cavalry, loop over and have a slap at that flanking column," he said. "M'lewis, you and the Forty Thieves accompany. We'll cover your flank. Don't push unless you take them by surprise; if you do, run them into the marsh."

Gerrin nodded, tapping on his gauntlets and watching the Brigade army. "Maybe it's my classical education," he said, "but don't you get a sort of unfulfilled feeling at winding up a campaign without a grand climactic battle?"

"I certainly think Ingreid would like to go out in a blaze of glory rather than lose to runny guts and no rations," Raj said. "Personally, it's my ambition to set a new standard someday by winning an entire war without ever actually fighting. This one, you'll note, is not over yet."

The five thousand Civil Government troops along the gunline stood, turned and marched smartly to the rear as the trumpets blared. They were not exactly on a ridge, this terrain didn't have anything worthy of the name, but there was a very slight swelling. Enough to hide the fact that they'd mounted and ridden off, rather than just countermarching and ready to reappear as they'd done half a dozen times.

"And it's only another week to Carson Barracks," Raj said.

"Ten days, if Ingreid doesn't speed up," Gerrin replied. "See you at sundown, *mi heneral.*"

Raj stood for a moment, looking at the advancing army. *Waste,* he thought. *What a bloody waste.*

He didn't hate Ingreid Manfrond for resisting. Raj Whitehall knew that it was absolutely necessary to reunite Bellevue, but the Brigaderos didn't have his information. You couldn't blame the Brigade's ruler for wanting to defend his people and hang onto his position. It was the man's sheer lack of *workmanship* that offended Raj.

CHAPTER FIFTEEN

"General."

Cabot Clerett's salute was precise. Raj returned the gesture. "Colonel."

They walked into the tent and sat, waiting silently while the orderly set out watered wine.

"A first-class encampment," Raj said.

It was: right at the edge of the causeway that carried road and railway to Carson Barracks, and hence commanding the canal as well. Clerett had dug the usual pentagonal fort with ditch and bastions, but he'd worked a small Brigadero fort into one wall, making the position very strong. It smelled dismally of swamp and the stingbugs were something fierce, but the men and dogs were neatly encamped, drainage ditches and latrines dug, purifying vats set up for drinking water. He'd made it larger than necessary, too; with some outlying breastworks, it would do for the whole force at a pinch and as long as they didn't have to stay too long.

"However, Ingreid should be here in about a day or so," Raj went on.

Cabot leaned forward. The past few months had fined down his face and added wrinkles to it as well; he looked older than his years now, stronger, more certain of himself.

Not without justification, Raj thought grudgingly. It had been a daredevil campaign, but apart from the recklessness of the concept quite skillfully managed. The man could command.

"And we're between him and his capital!" Clerett said, striking the table with his fist. The clay cups skittered on the rough planks of the trestle, which looked as if they'd been salvaged from some local stable. "We've got him trapped."

"Well, that's one way of looking at it," Raj nodded. "Or you might say that he'll have us between his field army and the garrison of Carson Barracks, who together outnumber us by about five to one."

399

Clerett's hand clenched on the table. "I consider it absolutely essential," he said, his voice a little higher, "to maintain my force in its present position. If Ingreid gets behind the fortifications of Carson Barracks, he can bring supplies in through the swamp channels, or move troops out—it could take years to complete this conquest if we were to allow that."

"Reconquest," Raj said, sipping some of the sour wine and looking out the open flap of the tent. "It's a reconquest."

The sun was setting over the swamps, red light on the clouds along the horizon, shadow on the tall feathery-topped reeds. The milk-white fronds dipped and billowed across the huge marsh, tinged with blood-crimson. Above them the sky was darkening to purple.

"You consider it *absolutely essential?*" he went on. Clerett nodded curtly, and Raj smiled. "Well, then it's fortunate I agree with you, isn't it, Colonel?"

Clerett nodded again, looking away. He still needed to do that, not experienced enough to hide his expression completely. "I've been in correspondence with Marie Manfrond—Marie Welf, she prefers— since I got here last week," he said neutrally.

"Excellent; so have I. Or rather, so has Lady Whitehall."

"Suz—Lady Whitehall is here?" Clerett asked. His hand tightened on the cup.

"Indeed. So we're aware of the supply situation in Carson Barracks." *And I hope she's not aware of dissension in our ranks,* Raj added to himself. Maintaining psychological dominance over a proud and intelligent barbarian like Ingreid's unwilling wife was difficult enough.

Clerett cleared his throat. "What about Ingreid? I've got about a week's supplies."

"I've got three days. Ingreid doesn't *have* a supply situation . . . but he's a stubborn fellow, and he may be learning. We wouldn't want to have him move north up the Padan and entrench in Empirhado or one of the riverport towns."

Clerett shook his head. "No more sieges," he agreed.

"Well." Raj stood. "I'd better see to settling the main force," he went on. "If you'd care to join us for luncheon tomorrow, we could settle plans."

There was something pathetic in the way Clerett thanked a man he hated for the invitation.

"I hope you're feeling well," Raj said.

Teodore Welf looked from Raj's face to Suzette's, to the Companions grouped around the table. The Expeditionary Force was digging in outside, and this inn at the head of the causeway had been selected as the praetorium at the center of the encampment.

"Thank you, Excellency," he said. "The dog-litter wasn't too uncomfortable, and the ribs are healing fine. The priests say I can ride now." His arm was still in a cast and strapped to his chest, but that was to be expected. "Although at the rate I've been going this past year, my skeleton is going to look like a jigsaw puzzle."

Raj nodded; broken bones were a hazard of their profession. "I've brought you here to discuss a few things," he said. Young Teodore had talked a little with him, rather more with Ludwig Bellamy and some of the Companions, and Suzette had ridden by his litter a good deal.

He nodded at the pile of letters before the Brigadero noble. "You can see your cousin Marie doesn't think much of Ingreid Manfrond's stewardship."

Teodore nodded cautiously, running his good hand through his long strawberry blond hair. "I may have made a mistake supporting Manfrond for General," he admitted. "In which case the marriage was an . . . ah, unnecessary sacrifice."

"Let's put it this way," Raj said. "Ingreid Manfrond came at me with rather more than a hundred thousand fighting men—about half the home-levy of the Brigade, and the better half. Right now, between disease, desertion and battle, in the siege and the retreat, he's down to about forty-five thousand, all starving. While we're stronger than we were when we started."

Teodore nodded, tight-lipped. Raj went on: "Now, let's say Ingreid has the sense to retreat, heading for the north or even the Costa dil Orrehene in the far west. He'd be lucky to have twenty thousand by the time he reached safe territory where I'd have to let him break contact. Personally I think every man with him would die or desert before then. But say he did, and raised another hundred thousand men, stripping your garrisons in the north. That'd be the last of your fighting men this generation. Do you think he'd do any better in a return match?"

Teodore hesitated for a long moment. "No," he said finally.

Center's grid dropped down around the young man's face, showing heat distribution, capillary flow, pupil dilation.

subject teodore welf is sincere, probability 96% ± 2.

"Ingreid Manfrond isn't the only noble of the blood of the Amalsons," Teodore said. Beads of sweat showed on his forehead, although the evening was mild.

Raj nodded again. "There is that," he said. "But honestly now, could any of the likely candidates—could you, for example—do more than prolong the war even more disastrously for the Brigade—given the situation as it now exists?"

The pause was much longer this time. "No, curse you," he said at last, his voice a little thick. "Ingreid's tossed away the flower of our strength and handed you half the Western Territories on a platter. The south and the coastal cities will go over to you like a shot; there are hardly any Unit Brothers down there anyway. We'd end up squeezed between you and the Stalwarts and Guard to the north and ground into dogmeat. It might last one year, maybe two or three, but that's it."

subject teodore welf is sincere, probability 91% ±3, Center said. **high probability of mental reservations to do with period after your departure.**

Teodore sighed and relaxed in his chair. "Anyway, *I* don't have to worry about it anymore, Excellent Heneralissimo."

Raj grinned, a disquieting expression, and jerked his chin toward the door. "On the contrary," he said. "Outside there is a saddled dog, with that priest of your household on another. This," he slid a paper across the table, "is a safe conduct through our lines."

The blue eyes narrowed in suspicion. "Your terms, Lord Whitehall?"

"No terms," Raj said, spreading his hands. "I make you a gift of your freedom. Do with it what you will."

The Brigadero picked up the paper and examined the seals, gaining a few seconds time. "How do you know I won't advise Ingreid to resist and tell him what I know of your dispositions?" he said.

"I don't," Raj replied. "But I'm fairly sure of your intelligence . . . and your regard for your people." *Also of your hatred of Ingreid and regard for the fortunes of the House of Welf, but let's be polite.*

An orderly came in with Welf's sword-belt. The weapon was in its scabbard, the flap neatly buckled over the butt of the revolver opposite it. Teodore stared at him wonderingly as he stood to let the man buckle it about him. Then his face firmed, and he made a formal bow.

"Messer Heneralissimo, Messa Whitehall, messers," he said, and turned on his heel to walk out into the gathering darkness.

"That was a bit of a risk," Jorg Menyez said soberly.

"About a nine-tenths chance I'm right," Raj said. He looked around at the Companions and his wife. "And now we can expect another guest."

"Ser."

Raj shot upright, hand going to the pistol beneath his pillow. Suzette sat up beside him, a gleam in the darkness of the room. The voice came again from outside the door.

Raj padded over to it, pulling on his uniform trousers. "Yes?" he said, walking out into the ready room.

"Shootin' in t' barb camp," M'lewis said.

"The Skinners?"

"Barb guns, ser," the ferret-faced scout said. There was burnt cork on his cheeks and a black knit cap over his hair; the testimony was first-hand. "Purty heavy, then dyin' away."

"Shall I beat to arms, *mi heneral?*" Tejan M'Brust asked; he was officer of the night watch.

Raj blinked and looked out the window. Maxiluna three hands-breadths from the horizon, near the Saber. Four hours until dawn.

"No," he said. "Let the men get their sleep." To M'lewis. "Keep an eye on things, but don't interfere unless they move out of their camp."

Raj waited impassively, seated at the head of the long table. It was an hour short of noon; formalities with safe-conducts and protocol had eaten the hours since dawn. The common room of the inn was severely plain, whitewashed stone walls, hearth, long table, all brightly lit through tall windows flung open to the mild humid air. The inlaid platinum mace of office lay in front of Raj; his personal banner and the Starburst of Holy Federation stood against the wall behind him, but otherwise he hadn't made any effort to fancy it up. Some of the officers standing behind and to either side of him were talking softly. Cabot Clerett was stock-still but fairly quivering with tension. Once or twice Raj thought he was actually going to walk out on the ceremony, and only a word from Suzette in his ear calmed him down a little.

At last a snarl of Brigade kettledrums sounded outside, answered by a lilt of bugles. Boots crashed to earth as the honor guard presented arms. Bartin Foley's clear baritone announced:

"Her Illustriousness, Marie Welf, Provisional Regent of the Brigade. His Formidability, Teodore Welf, Grand Constable of the Brigade."

Foley marched through, saluted, and dropped to parade rest beside the door.

"The *Heneralissimo Supremo;* Sword-Bearing Guard to the Sovereign Mighty Lord and Sole Autocrat Governor Barholm Clerett; possessor of the proconsular authority for the Western Territories; three times hailed Savior of the State, Sword of the Spirit of Man, Raj Ammenda Halgren da Luis Whitehall! The Heneralissimo will receive the Regent and Grand Constable. Enter, please."

The two young Welfs walked in proudly, Marie's hand resting on her cousin's good arm. Raj raised a mental eyebrow as he watched the woman's cold hawk-face; beautiful enough, but Ingreid might as well have taken a sicklefoot to his bed, if it had been against her will. They halted across the table from him; Teodore bowed, and Marie made a formal curtsey. Silence fell, until breathing and the low tick of a pendulum clock in one corner were the loudest sounds.

Raj took the victor's privilege. "What of General Ingreid Manfrond, who I assumed ruled the Brigade?" He kept his voice carefully neutral.

"Ex-General Ingreid has been deposed by the assembly-in-arms," Teodore said, meeting Raj's eyes levelly. "For treasonous incompetence. Civilian authority has been vested in Marie Welf as nearest in blood to the last legitimate General, and military authority in myself. Ingreid Manfrond was placed under arrest last night. Unfortunately, he killed himself before he could be brought for trial."

Raj nodded; Marie Welf *was* wearing a black ribbon on one arm in formal token of mourning. She was also wearing the ceremonial laser-pistol of the General's over a gown stiff with gold embroidery and silver lace.

"I take it this embassy is recognition of defeat?" Raj went on.

Two more stiff bows. This time Marie spoke, in a husky contralto. "*Heneralissimo,* as the Brigade's armies are still in the field, I request terms of surrender equivalent to those given the Squadron nobles who surrendered before the final battles in the Southern Territories."

Ah, shrewd, Raj thought. Technically reasonable, and it would preserve two-thirds of the landholdings of individual Brigade members, rather than the one-third he'd been granting up to now.

"I'll certainly recommend those terms to the Sovereign Mighty Lord," Raj said judiciously. Whoever ended up as Vice-Governor out here was going to need the Brigaderos in a not-too-sullen mood. "And I'm sure those of my officers with influence at court will as well."

That was Cabot Clerett's cue. After an embarrassing pause, he spoke in a tone suggesting that the words were being dragged out of concrete:

"I will certainly recommend that course to the Sole Rightful Autocrat."

Raj resumed: "Unfortunately, pending confirmation from East Residence all I can accept is unconditional surrender."

Marie stiffened, but Teodore leaned over to whisper in her ear. "Very well," she said bleakly, and drew the ancient laser. She stepped forward to lay it on the table before Raj; Teodore followed with his sword.

Raj nodded, smiling. It took several years off his face. "I'll have rations sent to your camp immediately, Grand Constable," he said. "We'll return the men to their homes as rapidly as possible. Please, be seated."

Suzette went round the table to draw Marie Welf to a chair. "I have been looking forward to meeting you in person," she said. "This is Colonel Clerett, nephew to the Governor . . ."

The citizens of Carson Barracks watched in silence as Raj Whitehall rode through the gates, following the Starburst flag of the Civil Government. Their silence seemed more stunned than hostile, as they crowded thickly before the low squat buildings and the barbaric ornament of gilded terracotta; lines of infantry kept them from the pavement. Paws thudded, the ironshod wheels of the guns rumbled over granite paving blocks and the hobnailed boots of marching foot soldiers crashed down. The column was thick with banners, color-parties representing all the units. The cheering started as the color party trotted into the central square; it was packed with the orderly ranks of the Expeditionary Force. Bannermen peeled off to stand before their comrades as Raj rode on to the steps of the palace, beneath the three-story columns shaped in the form of Federation landing boats.

The noise beat at him like surf as he pulled Horace to a halt. Teodore Welf stood to hold his bridle as he swung down; Raj waited until Suzette's fingers rested on his swordarm before he began to climb the steps. The mace of office and symbol of the proconsular power was in the crook of his left elbow, responsibility heavier than worlds. The Companions followed him in a jingle of spurs on marble.

He stopped at the top of the stairs, turned to face the assembled ranks and held up his right hand for silence. It fell slowly.

"Fellow soldiers," he began. Another long swelling roar. "I said when we started this campaign a year ago"—*was it that long since Stern Isle?*—"that you needn't fear to face any troops in the world. You've met an army ten times your numbers, and beaten it utterly. Your discipline, your courage, your endurance have won a victory for the Civil Government that men will remember for ever. I'm proud to have commanded you."

He bowed his head in salute. This time the sound of his name beat back from the high buildings surrounding the square like thunder echoing down a canyon.

"*RAJ! RAJ! RAJ!*" Helmets went up on rifles, bobbing in rhythm to the chant. Yet when he raised his hand again, silence fell as if the sound had been cut off by a knife-blade.

"And the first thing I want you to do with your donative of *six* months' pay—" he cut off the gathering yell with a gesture "—is drink to our fallen comrades." That sobered the crowd a little.

"The Spirit has uploaded their souls to Its net. For the Spirit's sake, and theirs, and mine, remember that this land and these people are now also subjects of the Civil Government of Holy Federation, not our enemies." He smiled and made a broad gesture. "Remember that, and have fun, lads—you've earned it. Dismissed to quarters!"

He turned through the great bronze doors with an inward sigh of relief. The Spirit knew the men deserved the donative, and congratulations from their commander, but he'd never liked public speaking. Worse, there was always the risk some overenthusiastic imbecile would start hailing him with Gubernatorial honors, which rulers far less suspicious than Barholm Clerett would neither forget nor forgive.

The dying cheers were faint inside the great hall. Here the only soldiers were those who lined the red-carpeted passageway to the high seat of the Generals. They snapped to attention and presented arms as Raj passed by; he was conscious of six hundred years of history looking down from the walls. Six hundred years since Teodore Amalson conquered Old Residence and started this building; nearly that since his grandson finished it. Never in all that time had men in the uniform of the Civil Government entered here armed. That was not the only first today. Star Spirit priests proceeded him, swinging their censers of incense and chanting. Behind the seat the double lightning-flash of the Brigade was hidden by a huge Starburst banner. Other banners lay piled on the steps, Brigade battle-flags.

It was all highly symbolic, and from their stunned expressions the Brigade nobles who made up most of the audience appreciated every nuance. Raj paced up to the Seat, treading banners underfoot. Suzette stopped at the lower Consort's seat; Raj turned at the top of the dais and raised the mace of office. Save for the soldiers braced to attention, every head sank low in bow or curtsey, holding the posture until he sank back to the cushions.

"The Western Territories have returned to the care of Holy Federation, forever," he said. "And now, gentlemen, we have a great deal to do."

CHAPTER SIXTEEN

"Spirit, has it only been a month?" Raj said, looking down the table. The staff meeting had taken several hours, and it was not the only official gathering of his working day. "Middle age and Bureaucrat's Bottom is creeping up on all of us."

"Good work, Muzzaf." He tapped the sheaf of billeting and supply files before him. "Without you, we'd have had to do *all* this ourselves."

The slimly elegant Komarite bowed in his chair. "Willingly I suffer the emplumpment of the civil service in your cause," he said.

The Companions grinned; a few groaned in sympathy.

"One of us should escape," Gerrin Staenbridge said, leaning back and puffing on his cheroot. "Somebody's going to have to deal with the west coast."

Nods of agreement: the Forker family still had many partisans on the Costa Dil Orrehene, beyond the Ispirito mountains. A good many of them had refused to come in and swear allegiance.

"None of you," Raj said, "I'm going to quarter Juluk and his Skinners out there until they see the merits of law, order and submission."

After a moment's silence, Jorg Menyez spoke. "Now that is what they call an *elegant* solution," he said with a slow smile. His infantry were in charge of keeping order in the billeting zone, which was a fair definition of "utter futility" where Skinners were concerned.

"Kaltin, you *will* be getting out of town," Raj went on. "The Stalwarts have been making trouble north of Lis Plumhas. I want you to take your 7th, the 9th and 11th Descott Dragoons, 27th and 31st Diva Valley Rangers, the 3rd Novy Haifa, and the 14th Komar and go put a stop to it. You'll pick up fifteen thousand Brigade troops from the northern garrisons; don't hesitate to listen to their officers, they've had experience with the savages."

Kaltin nodded eagerly, then paused. "Ah, those are mostly Clerett's troops, aren't they?"

"No, they're the Civil Government's troops," Raj said coldly. "And it's about time they were reminded of it. Since Colonel Clerett prefers to remain in the city"—*and sniff around my wife, damn him*—"I'm sending them with you."

His tone returned to normal. "Incidentally, no prisoners, and you're authorized to counterraid across the frontier once you've disposed of those on our soil. With Stalwarts, you have to speak in a language they understand."

"I'd have to swear eternal brotherhood with them before killing them, to make them really comfortable," Kaltin said. "Actually, I'm fairly glad to get away from my own household right now."

A chuckle ran through the other men. "You really should slow down," someone said. "You'll wear yourself away to a sylph."

Kaltin gave him a look of affronted virtue. "It's Jaine, the little mophead I rescued from the Skinners? It turned out she was some sort of fifth grand-niece of the family I'm billeted with here."

"That's a problem?" Raj asked.

"No, floods of happy tears and she's off to the kinfolk and I'd be a fool to object, wouldn't I? Only Mitchi turns out to have gotten attached to the girl and she's moping and blaming *me*."

"Get her pregnant, man," Tejan M'Brust said.

"She *is* pregnant. Have you ever slept with a woman who pukes every morning?" Gerrin made a *tsk* sound. "Easy for *you* to say. In any event, I'm glad to be on my way back to the field."

"Quickly," Raj said. "And take the Forty Thieves with you."

Antin M'lewis looked up; his men were enjoying themselves in Carson Barracks, and only a few had been caught as yet.

"The Honorable Fedherko Chivrez is coming to join us," Raj said. "As the Governor's representative in the field." At the others' blank look: "He was Director of Supply in Komar back a couple of years."

Muzzaf Kerpatik swore sharply in a Sponglish whose sing-song Borderer accent was suddenly very strong.

Kaltin frowned. "Not the cheating bastard who tried to stiff us on the supplies just before the El Djem raid?"

"Just the one. And the one you and Evrard ran out a closed window headfirst, then held while Antin here started to flay him from the feet up."

"It worked," Kaltin pointed out.

Raj nodded. "And I still want both of you out of town when he arrives, which could be any time."

"Chivrez is Tzetzas' dog," Muzzaf cut in. "And the Chancellor never forgets an injury."

"Agreed," Raj said. "See to it you're gone by this time tomorrow." The two men left.

"If there's nothing else?"

Ludwig Bellamy coughed politely. "Ah, *mi heneral*, Marie and Teodore would like a word with you this evening. Confidential."

Raj raised a brow, caught by something unusual in the young man's tone. "By all means," he said.

"I thought I might be there," Ludwig said. "And possibly Gerrin?"

Raj leaned back in his chair. "They requested that?" he said, his eyes narrowing slightly.

Ludwig flushed slightly and looked at his fingernails. "No, it was just a thought."

"Then I'll see them alone in my private office in—" he consulted a watch "—twenty minutes. If that's all, messers? Not you, Gerrin."

When they were alone: "What was that in aid of, do you know?"

"Not really," the other man said, taking out a small ivory-handled knife and trimming a fingernail. "Ludwig has been talking to me of late . . . and not for the sake of my winsome charm, worse luck. I think he's worried about this administrator they're sending out; he's convinced it would be a mistake to replace you so soon, if that's what he's going to do."

"I was never much good at overseeing civilians," Raj pointed out.

"These Brigaderos are scarcely that, my friend. They're used to a strong hand. *And* they respect you, which they wouldn't some lard-bottomed penpusher from East Residence. Things need to settle down here. A year as proconsular governor would be a good idea; five would be better."

"A year might be advisable but it's unlikely, and five is neither," Raj replied. It was firm Civil Government policy never to unite military and civil command except in emergencies.

He tapped a thumb against his chin. "Ludwig's also been seeing a good deal of the late Ingreid Manfrond's widow, hasn't he?"

"My delectable young Arab conduit to the gossip pipeline tells me so. Ludwig's been hunting with Teodore a good deal, too. Hadrosauroid heads and deep conversation. I don't think you have to fear conspiracy; Ludwig's still of an age for hero-worship, and you're it."

"Conspiracy against me, no," Raj said. "Hmmm. Ludwig and Marie . . . that might not be a bad thing, in the right circumstances."

Those being a new address in East Residence for Marie Welf . . . or Bellamy, as she would be then. Teodore would probably be welcomed there also, encouraged to have the revenues of his estates shipped east, given lands and office, and never, never allowed west of the Kelden Straits again.

"In any case, stick around, wouldn't you?"

Raj's private office was fairly small; he'd never felt comfortable working in a room that had to be measured in hectares. It gave off the bedchamber he shared with Suzette, which *was* that sort of place, and he supposed it must have been a maid's on-call room before the Palace changed hands. He'd had the plain walls fitted with bookcases and map-frames, and a solid desk moved in. Right now the overhead lantern and the low coal fire made it seem cozy rather than bleak, and he smiled as he welcomed the two young Welf nobles. The smile was genuine enough. Teodore was a like- able young spark, an educated man in his way, and he had the makings of a first-class soldier. Marie was just as able in her own way, if a bit alarming.

And she'll probably lead poor Ludwig a devil's dance, he thought, but that was—might be—Bellamy's problem.

"Be seated, please," he said. "Now, you had something you wished to discuss with me?"

The two Brigaderos glanced at each other. He nodded. "That door gives on to my bedchamber, and it's bolted from the other side," he said encouragingly. "The other door leads to a corridor with a guard party ten meters away. It's quite private."

Marie gripped the arms of her chair. "*Heneralissimo Supremo*," she said, in fluent but gutturally accented Sponglish, "we have come to discuss the future of the world . . . starting with the Western Territories."

Raj leaned back in the swivel-mounted seat. "Illustrious Lady, I'd say that particular issue has been settled rather definitely."

"No, it hasn't," Marie replied. "You've said you want to unite the Earth."

"Bellevue," Raj corrected. "I've been *instructed* to unite the planet Bellevue, yes." Exactly by whom he'd been instructed was some- thing they had no need to know.

"We believe—almost all the Brigade now believes—that you've been sent by the Spirit to do just that," Marie said passionately. There was a high flush on her cheeks, and her eyes glowed. "How else could you have defeated the greatest warriors in the world with a force so tiny?"

Teodore coughed discreetly; his sword-arm was out of its cast, although still a little weak. "I think I can speak for the Brigade's fighting men," he said. "That's about their opinion too, although not everyone puts it down to the Spirit. Some of them just think you're the greatest commander in history."

"I'm flattered," Raj said dryly. "The Sovereign Mighty Lord has many able servants, though."

"To the Outer Dark with Barholm Clerett!" Marie burst out. "We've all heard of his ingratitude to you, his suspicion and threats—and we've all heard of his other servants, Chancellor Tzetzas and his ilk who'd skin a ghost for its hide."

Teodore leaned forward. "Barholm didn't conquer the Western Territories," he said. "You did. We're offering you the Brigade, as General—and with the Brigade, the *world*. You want to unite it? We'll back you, and with you to lead and train us *nothing* can stop us. Your own troops will follow you to Hell; they already have, many times. That'll give you the cadre you need. In five years you'll march in triumph into East Residence; in ten, into Al Kebir. Your Companions will be greater than kings, and your sons' sons will rule human kind forever!"

Whatever I expected, it wasn't this, Raj thought.

Marie was leaning forward, fists clenched at her throat and eyes shining. Raj looked from one eager young face to the other, and temptation plowed a fist into his belly. The taste was raw and salty at the back of his throat. He kept most of it off his face, but neither of the Brigaderos were fools. They exchanged a triumphant glance, and would have spoken if he had not held up a hand.

"If—" he cleared his throat. "If you wouldn't mind waiting for me in the conference room, messer, messa?"

"I could do it," he whispered into the hush of the room. Aloud: "I *could.*"

It wouldn't even be all that difficult. The Western Territories were naturally rich, and they had at least a smattering of civilized skills among the native aristocracy and cityfolk. The Brigade hadn't known how to use them, but he would. Grammeck Dinnalsyn could have the factories here producing Armory rifles in a few months. Lopeyz was a better fleet commander than any Barholm had on the payroll. They could snap up Stern Isle and the Southern Territories before winter closed the sea lanes. That would give them sulfur, saltpeter, copper and zinc enough. Modern artillery would be more difficult, but not impossible.

In a year he would have a hundred thousand men trained up to a standard nobody on Bellevue could match. The Skinners would flock to his standard. With men like Muzzaf to help organize the logistics and a fleet built in the shipyards of Old Residence and Veronique, they could—

observe, Center said.

—and Raj Whitehall rode through the streets of a ruined East Residence. Crowds cheered his name with hysterical abandon, even though the harbor was filled with fire and sunken hulks.

Chancellor Tzetzas spat on the guards who dragged him before the firing squad. Barholm wept and begged. . . .

Maps appeared before his eyes; blocks and arrows feinting and lunging along the upper Drangosh. The towers of Al Kebir burning, and one-eyed Tewfik kneeling to present his scimitar. Fleets ramming and cannonading on a sea of azure, and the white walls of cities he'd only read of, Zanj and Azanian. The Whitehall banner floated above them.

Raj Whitehall sat on a throne of gold and diamond, and men of races he'd never heard of knelt before him with tribute and gifts . . .

. . . and he lay ancient and white-haired in a vast silken bed. Muffled chanting came from outside the window, and a priest prayed quietly. A few elderly officers wept, but the younger ones eyed each other with undisguised hunger, waiting for the old king to die.

One bent and spoke in his ear. "Who?" he said. "Who do you leave the scepter to?"

The ancient Raj's lips moved. The officer turned and spoke loudly, drowning out the whisper: "He says, *to the strongest.*"

Armies clashed, in identical green uniforms and carrying his banner. Cities burned. At last there was a peaceful green mound that only the outline of the land showed had once been the Gubernatorial Palace in East Residence. Two men worked in companionable silence by a campfire, clad only in loincloths of tanned hide. One was chipping a spearpoint from a piece of ancient window, the shaft and binding thongs ready to hand. His fingers moved with sure skill, using a bone anvil and striker to spall long flakes from the green glass. His comrade worked with equal artistry, butchering a carcass with a heavy hammerstone and slivers of flint. It took a moment to realize that the body had once been human.

Raj grunted, shaking his head. *Couldn't my sons*—he began.

any children of yourself and lady whitehall will be female, Center said relentlessly. **genetic analysis indicates a high probability of forceful and intelligent personalities, but the probability of any such issue maintaining stability after your death is too low to be meaningfully calculated.**

I could pick a successor, adopt—

irrelevant, Center went on. **the ruling structure of the civil government will never voluntarily submit to rule from outside— and you would represent a regime centered on the western territories. to force submission you would be compelled to smash the only governmental structure capable of ruling bellevue as anything but a collection of feudal domains. this historical cycle would resume its progression toward maximum entropy at an accelerated rate upon your death.**

Better for civilization that I'd never been born, Raj thought dully. The residue of the visions shook him like marsh-fever.

in that scenario, correct. Center's voice was always wholly calm, but he had experience enough to detect a tinge of compassion in its overtones. **i pointed out that your role in my plan would not result in optimization of your world-line from a personal perspective.**

Raj shook his head ruefully. *That you did,* he thought.

Voices sounded from the bedchamber, raised in argument. The bolt shot back and Cabot Clerett came through behind a levelled revolver—one of Raj's own, he noticed in the sudden diamond-bright concentration of adrenaline. The younger man was panting, and his shirt was torn open, but the muzzle drew an unwavering bead on Raj's center of mass.

"Traitor," Clerett barked. His heel pushed the door closed behind him. "I suspected it and now I can prove it."

Raj forced himself out of a crouch, made his voice soft. "Colonel Cabot, you can scarcely expect to shoot down your superior officer in the middle of his headquarters," he said. "Put the gun down. We'll all be back in East Residence soon, and you can bring any charges you please before the Chair."

Which will believe anything you care to say, he thought. With a competent general as heir, Raj Whitehall became much more expendable.

"Back to East Residence," Cabot laughed. His face was fixed in a snarl, and the smell of his sweat was acrid. "Yes, with a barbarian army at your back. Your henchmen may kill me afterwards, but I'm going to free the Civil Government of your threat, Whitehall— if it is the last thing I do."

The door opened behind Clerett and Suzette stepped through; she was dressed in a frilled silk nightgown, but the Colonial repeating-carbine in her hands had a well-oiled deadliness. Clerett caught the widening of Raj's eyes as they stared over his shoulder. The trick is old, but the breeze must have warned him. He took a half-step to the side, to where he could see the doorway out of the corner of his eye and still keep the gun on Raj.

Suzette spoke, her voice sharp and clear. "Put the gun down, Cabot. I don't want to hurt you."

"You don't know—you didn't hear," Cabot shouted. "He's a *traitor.* He's even more unworthy of you than he is of the trust Uncle placed in him. I'll free *both* of you from him."

A sharp rap sounded at the other door. Everyone in the study started, but Cabot brought the gun back around with deadly speed. He was young and fit and well-practiced, and Raj knew there was no way he could leap the space between them without taking at least one of the wadcutter bullets, more likely two or three.

"*Mi heneral,* the Honorable Fedherko Chivrez has arrived." Gerrin's voice was as suave as ever; only someone who knew him well could catch the undertone of strain and fear. "He insists that you grant him audience at once to hear the orders of the Sovereign Mighty Lord."

Cabot's snarl turned to a smile of triumph. His finger tightened on the trigger—

—and the carbine barked. The bullet was fired from less than a meter away, close enough that the muzzle-blast pocked the skin behind his right ear with grains of black powder. The entry-wound was a small round hole, but the bullet was hollowpoint and it blasted a fist-sized opening in his forehead, the splash of hot brain and bone-splinters missing Raj to spatter across his desk. Clerett's eyes bulged with the hydrostatic shock transmitted through his brain tissue, and his lips parted in a single rubbery grimace. Then he fell face down, to lie in a spreading pool of blood.

Strong shoulders crashed into the door. Raj moved with blurring speed, snatching the carbine out of Suzette's hands so swiftly that the friction-burns brought an involuntary cry of pain. He pivoted back towards the outer doorway.

Gerrin and Bartin Foley crowded it; others were behind, Ludwig and the Welfs. Among them was a short plump man in the knee-breeches and long coat and lace sabot that were civilian dress in East Residence. His eyes bulged too, as they settled on Cabot Clerett.

Raj spoke, his voice loud and careful. "There's been a terrible accident," he said. "Colonel Clerett was examining the weapon, and he was unfamiliar with the mechanism. I accept full responsibility for this tragic mishap."

Silence fell in the room, amid the smell of powder-smoke and the stink of blood and wastes voided at death. Everyone stared at the back of the dead man's head, and the neat puncture behind his ear.

"Fetch a priest," Raj went on. "Greetings, Illustrious Chivrez. My deepest apologies that you come among us at such an unhappy time."

Chivrez' shock was short-lived; he hadn't survived a generation of politics in the Civil Government by cowardice, or squeamishness. Now he had to fight to restrain his smile. Raj Whitehall was standing over the body of the Governor's heir and literally holding a smoking gun.

He drew an envelope from inside his jacket. "I bear the summons of the Sovereign Mighty Lord and Sole Autocrat," he said. "Upon whom may the Spirit of Man of the Stars shower Its blessings."

"Endfile," they all murmured.

A chaplain and two troopers came in and rolled the body in a rug. Chivrez cut in sharply:

"The body is to be embalmed for shipment to East Residence." Then he cleared his throat. "You, General Whitehall, are to return to East Residence immediately to account for your exercise of the authority delegated to you. Immediately. All further negotiations with the Brigade will be conducted through me and my staff."

"You won't do it, will you, sir?" Ludwig Bellamy blurted.

Raj looked at the bureaucrat's weasel eyes.

observe, Center said.

He saw those eyes again, staring desperately into the underside of a silk pillow. The stubby limbs thrashed against the bedclothes as the pillow was pressed onto his face. After a few minutes they grew still; Ludwig Bellamy wrapped the body in the sheets and hoisted it. Even masked, Raj recognized Gerrin Staenbridge as the one holding open the door.

The scene shifted, to the swamps outside Carson Barracks. The same men tipped a burlap-wrapped bundle off the deck of a small boat. It vanished with scarcely a splash, weighed down with lengths of chain and a cast-iron roundshot weighing forty kilos.

"Of course I'll go," Raj said aloud. He looked at Chivrez and smiled. "You'll find my officers very cooperative, and dedicated to good government," he said.

Raj's smile grew gentle as he turned to Suzette; she stared at him appalled, her green eyes enormous and her fingers white-knuckled where they gripped each other.

"It's my duty to go," he went on.

observe, Center said.

This time the scene was familiar. Raj lashed naked to an iron chair in a stone-walled room far beneath the Palace in East Residence. The glowing iron came closer to his eyes, and closer . . .

chance of personal survival if recall order is obeyed is less than 27% ±6, Center said, **chance of reunification of bellevue in this historical cycle is less than 15% ±2 if order is refused, however.**

"It's my duty to go," Raj repeated. His head lifted, from pride and so that he wouldn't have to see Suzette's eyes fill. "And may I always do my duty to the Spirit of Man."

V
THE SWORD

To Jan

The Planet
BELLEVUE
In the Age of Raj Whitehall
c. 1184 After the Fall

N

Drangosh Campaign

East Residence

Oxhead Mts.

CIVIL GOVERNMENT

COLONY

border

Centrail rail

Main Ghor Canal

Sandoral

Raj's
pontoon
bridge

Colonial
siege lines

Raiding force retreats

Badlands

DRANGOSH RIVER

Gruder
sets
ambush

X Osterville's camp

Ain el-Hilwa

+ Raj's camp

Tewfik leads detachment to pursue raiders

Raj's and Tewfik's
final meeting

Badlands

Raiding groups

Raiding groups

limit of irrigation zone

Tewfik pursues

Raj's
landing point

temporary railroad

ruins
of Gurnyca

supply base

Colonial
pontoon
bridge

Main Ghor Canal

N

Desert

Border
Forts

Al Kebir

one-hundred kilometers

CHAPTER ONE

"Raj?" Thom Poplanich muttered.

Then, slowly: "Raj, how old are you?"

Raj Whitehall managed a smile. "Thirty," he said.

The perfect mirrored sphere of Sector Command and Control Unit AZ12-b14-c000 Mk. XIV's central . . . being . . . showed an image which seemed to give the lie to that. It wasn't the gray hairs or the scars on the backs of his hands that made him seem at least forty, or ageless.

It was the eyes.

Thom looked at his own image. Nothing at all had changed since that moment when he'd frozen into immobility, five years ago. Not the unhealed shaving nick on his thin olive cheek, or the tear in his floppy tweed trousers from a revolver bullet.

life is change, Center said. The voice of the ancient computer was like their own thoughts, but with a vibrato overtone that somehow carried a sense of immense weight like a pressure against the film of consciousness. **even i change.**

Raj and Thom looked up, startled. "Center? You're alive?" Thom asked.

No words whispered in their skull. Thom looked at his friend. *Raj looks like an old man.*

I haven't changed a hair, outwardly . . . but that's the least of it. Five years of mental communion with the machine that held all Mankind's accumulated knowledge. Five years, or eternity. He thought of his life before that day, and it was . . . unimaginable. Less real than the scenarios Center could spin from webs of data and stochastic analysis.

The two men gripped forearms, then exchanged the *embrahzo* of close friends. Thom could smell coal-smoke and gun-oil on the wool of his friend's uniform jacket, that and riding dogs and Suzette Whitehall's sambuca jasmine perfume.

The scents cut through the icy certainties Center's teaching had implanted in his mind. Unshed tears prickled at his eyes as he held the bigger man at arm's length.

"It's good to see you again, my friend," he said quietly.

"Yes, that's . . . well, I came to say goodbye."

"Goodbye?" Thom asked sharply.

"That's right," Raj said, turning slightly away. His eyes moved across the perfect mirrored surface of the sphere, that impossibly reflected without distorting. "Things . . . well, Cabot Clerett, the Governor's nephew" —and heir, they both knew— "was along on the campaign. There were a number of difficulties, and he, ah, was killed."

"Spirit of Man of the *Stars*," Thom blurted. "You came back to East Residence after *that*? Barholm was suspicious of you anyway."

Raj gave a small crooked smile and shrugged. "I didn't reconquer the Southern and Western Territories for the Civil Government just to set myself up as a warlord," he said. "Center said that would be worse for civilization than if I'd never lived at all."

an oversimplification but accurate to within 93%, ±2, Center added remorselessly. Over the years their minds had learned subtlety in interpreting that voice; there was a tinge of . . . not pity, but perhaps compassion to it now. **the long-term prospects for restoration of the federation, here on bellevue and eventually elsewhere in the human-settled galaxy, required raj whitehall's submission to the civil authorities. too many generals have seized the chair by force.**

Thom nodded. The process had started long before Bellevue was isolated by the destruction of its Tanaki Spatial Displacement net. The Federation had been slagging down in civil wars for a generation before that, biting out its own guts like a brain-shot sauroid. The process had continued here in the thousand-odd years since, and according to Center everywhere else in the human-settled galaxy as well.

"Couldn't Lady Anne do something?" he asked. Barholm's consort was a close friend of Raj's wife Suzette, had been since Anne was merely the . . . entertainer was the polite phrase . . . that young Barholm had unaccountably married despite being the Governor's nephew. The other court ladies had turned a cold shoulder back before Barholm assumed the Chair; Suzette hadn't.

"She died four months ago," Raj said. "Cancer."

A brief flash of vision: a canopied bed, with the incense of the Star priests around it and the drone of their prayers. A woman lying motionless, flesh fallen in on the strong handsome bones of her face, hair a white cloud on the pillow with only a few streaks of its mahogany red left. Suzette Whitehall sat at the bedside, one hand gripping the ivory colored claw-hand of her dying friend. Her face was an expressionless mask, but slow tears ran from the slanted green eyes and dripped down on the priceless snowy torofib of the sheets.

"Damn," Thom said. "I know she wanted every Poplanich dead,

but . . . well, Anne had twice Barholm's guts, and she was loyal to her friends, at least."

Raj nodded. "It was right after that that I was suspended from my last posting—Inspector-General—and my properties confiscated. Chancellor Tzetzas handled it personally."

"That . . . that . . . he gives graft a bad name," Thom spat.

Raj smiled wanly. "Yes, if the Chancellor didn't hate me, I'd wonder what I was doing wrong."

A flash from Center; a tall thin man in a bureaucrat's court robe sitting at a desk. The room was quietly elegant, dark, silent; a cigarette in a holder of carved sauroid ivory rested in one slim-fingered hand. He signed a heavy parchment, dusted the ink with fine sand, and smiled. A secretary sprang forward to melt wax for the seal . . .

Raj nodded. "I expect to be arrested at the levee this afternoon. Barholm's worried—"

Thom laid a hand on Raj's shoulder. The muscle under the wool jacket was like india rubber. It quivered with tension.

"You *should* make yourself Governor, Raj," he said quietly. "Spirit knows, you couldn't be *worse* than Barholm and his cronies."

Raj smiled, but he shook his head. "Thanks, Thom—but if I have a gift for command, it's *only* for soldiers. Civilians . . . I couldn't get three of them to follow me into a whorehouse with an offer of free drinks and pussy. Not unless I had a squad behind them with bayonets; and you *can't* govern that way, not for long. I'd smash the machinery trying to make it work. Barholm is a son-of-a-bitch, but he's a *smart* one. He knows how to stroke the bureaucracy and keep the nobility satisfied, and he really is binding the Civil Government together with his railroads and law reforms . . . granted a lot of his hangers-on are getting rich in the process, but it's working. I couldn't do it. Not so's it'd last past my lifetime."

observe:

—and they saw Raj Whitehall on a throne of gold and diamond, and men of races they'd never heard of knelt before him with tribute and gifts . . .

. . . and he lay ancient and white-haired in a vast silken bed. Muffled chanting came from outside the window, and a priest prayed quietly. A few elderly officers wept, but the younger ones eyed each other with undisguised hunger, waiting for the old king to die.

One bent and spoke in his ear. "Who?" he said. "Who do you leave the keyboard and the power to?"

The ancient Raj's lips moved. The officer turned and spoke loudly, drowning out the whisper: "He says, *to the strongest.*"

Armies clashed, in identical green uniforms and carrying Raj Whitehall's banner. Cities burned. At last there was a peaceful green mound that only the outline of the land showed had once been the Gubernatorial Palace in East Residence. Two men worked in companionable silence by a campfire, clad only in loincloths of tanned hide. One was chipping a spearpoint from a piece of an ancient window, the shaft and binding thongs ready to hand. His fingers moved with sure skill, using a bone anvil and striker to spall long flakes from the green glass. His comrade worked with equal artistry, butchering a carcass with a heavy hammerstone and slivers of flint. It took a moment to realize that the body had once been human.

Raj shivered. *That* was the logical endpoint of the cycle of collapse here on Bellevue, and throughout what had once been the Federation; if it wasn't prevented, there would be savagery for fifteen thousand years before a new civilization arose. The image had haunted him since Center first showed it. It felt *true*.

"Spirit knows, I don't *want* Barholm's job," he went on. "I like to do what I do well, and that isn't my area of expertise. The problem is getting Barholm to understand that."

barholm's data gives him substantial reason for apprehension, Center pointed out. **not only does raj whitehall have the prestige of constant victory, but more than sixteen battalions of the civil government's cavalry are now comprised of ex-prisoners from the former military governments.**

Squadrones and Brigaderos; Namerique-speaking barbarians, descendants of Federation troops gone savage up in the desolate Base Area of the far northwest. They'd swept down and taken over huge chunks of the Civil Government, imposing their rule and their heretical Spirit of Man of This Earth cult on the population. Nobody had been able to do anything about it . . . until Barholm sent Raj Whitehall to reconquer the barbarian realms of the Military Governments.

Governor Barholm had officially proclaimed Raj the Sword of the Spirit of Man. The prisoners who'd volunteered to serve the Civil Government had seen him in operation from both sides. They *believed* that title.

"Then stay here!" Thom said. "Center can hold you in stasis, like me—hold you until Barholm's dust and bones. You've done all you can, you've done your duty, now you *deserve* something for yourself. It won't further the reunification of Bellevue for you to commit suicide!"

probability of furthering the restoration of the federation is slightly increased if raj whitehall attends the levee, Center said.

"I must go. I *must*. I—"

Raj turned back, and Thom recoiled a half step. The other man's teeth were showing, and a muscle twitched on one cheek. "I . . . there's been so much dying . . . I *can't* . . . so many dead, so many, how can I save myself?"

"They were enemies," Thom said softly.

"No! Not *them*. My own men! I used men like bullets! There aren't one in three of the 5th Descott Guards remaining, of the ones who rode out with me against the Colony five years ago. Poplanich's Own—raised from your family estates, Thom—had a hundred and fifty casualties in one battle, and *I* was leading them."

Thom opened his mouth, then closed it again. Center cut in on them, an iron impatience in its non-voice:

leading is the operative word, raj whitehall. you were leading them. observe:

"Back one step and volley!" Raj shouted, hoarse with smoke and dust.

Around him the shattered ranks firmed. Colonial dragoons in crimson djellabas rode forward, reins in their teeth as they worked the levers of their repeating carbines. The muzzles of their dogs snaked forward, then recoiled from the line of bayonets.

BAM. Ragged, but the men were firing in unison.

"Back one step and volley!" Raj shouted again.

He fired his revolver between two of the troopers, into the face of a Colonial officer who yipped and waved his yataghan behind the line of dragoons. The carbines snapped, and the man beside Raj stumbled back, moaning and pawing at the shattered jaw that dangled on his breast.

"Hold hard, 5th Descott! *Back one step and volley.*"

Raj blinked back to an awareness of the polished sphere that was Center's physical being. That had been too vivid: not just the holographic image that the ancient computer projected on his retina; he could still *smell* the gunpowder and blood.

if you had not struck swiftly and hard, the wars would have dragged on for years. deaths would have been a whole order of magnitude greater, among soldiers of both sides and among the civilians. as well, entire provinces would be so devastated as to be unable to sustain civilized life.

Images flitted through their minds: bones resting in a ditch, hair still fluttering from the skulls of a mother and child; skeletal corpses slithering over each other as men threw them on a plague-cart and dragged it away down the empty streets of a besieged city; a room of hollow-eyed soldiers resting on straw pallets slimed with the liquid feces of cholera.

"That's true enough for a computer," Raj said.

Even then, Thom noted the irony. He was East Residence born, a city patrician, and back when they both believed *computer* meant *angel* he'd doubted their very existence. That had shocked Raj's pious country-squire soul; Raj never doubted the Personal Computer that watched over every faithful soul, and the great Mainframes that sat in glory around the Spirit of Man of the Stars. Now they were both agents of such a being.

Raj's voice grew loud for a moment. "That's true enough for the Spirit of Man of the Stars made manifest, true enough for *God*. I'm not God, I'm just a man—and I've done the Spirit's work without flinching. But I'd be *less* than a man if I didn't think I deserve death for it." Silence fell.

"They ought to hate me," he whispered, his eyes still seeing visions without need of Center's holographs. "I've left the bones of my men all the way from the Drangosh to Carson Barracks, across half a world . . . they ought to hate my *guts*."

they do not, Center said. **instead—**

A group of men swaggered into an East Residence bar, down the stairs from the street and under the iron brackets of the lights, into air thick with tobacco and sweat and the fumes of cheap wine and *tekkila*. Like most of those inside, they wore cavalry-trooper uniforms—it was not a dive where a civilian would have had a long life expectancy—but most of theirs carried the shoulder-flashes of the 5th Descott Guards, and they wore the red-and-white checked neckerchiefs that were an unofficial blazon in that unit. They were dark close-coupled stocky-muscular men, like most Descotters; with them were troopers from half a dozen other units, some of them blond giants with long hair knotted on the sides of their heads.

There was a general slither of chairs on floors as the newcomers took over the best seats. One Life Guard trooper who was slow about vacating his chair was dumped unceremoniously on the sanded floor; half a dozen sets of eyes tracked him like gun turrets turning as he came up cursing and reaching for the knife in his boot. The Life Guardsman looked over his shoulder, calculated odds, and pushed out of the room. The hard-eyed girl who'd been with him hung over the shoulder of the chair's new occupant. The men hung their sword belts on the backs of their chairs and called for service.

"T'Messer Raj," one said, raising a glass. "While 'e's been a-leadin' us, nivver a one's been shot runnin' away!"

— they do not hate you. they *fear* you, for they know you will expend them without hesitation if necessary. but they know raj whitehall will lead from the front, and that with him they have conquered the world.

"Then they're fools," Raj said flatly.

"They're men," Thom said. "All men die, whether they go for soldiers or not. But maybe you've given them something that makes the life worth it, just as you have Center's Plan to rebuild civilization throughout the universe."

They exchanged the *embrahzo* again. Thom stepped back and froze, his body once again in Center's timeless stasis.

Raj turned and took a deep breath. "Can't die deader than dead," he murmured to himself.

CHAPTER TWO

The great corridor outside the Audience Hall shone with the delicate colored marble and semiprecious stone that made up the intaglio work of the floor. The walls were arched windows on the outer side, and religious murals on the inner—icons of the Saints, lives of the martyrs, stars, starships, Computers calling forth Order from Primeval Chaos. Though the day was overcast, hidden gaslights threw a bright radiance through mirrors.

Soldiers in the black uniforms and black breastplates of the Life Guards stood along the walls every few paces, rifles at port; officers had their swords drawn and the points resting at their boots. The uniforms were Capital-crisp, but the faces under the plumed helmets were closed and watchful—square beak-nosed faces, dark and hard, on men slightly bowlegged from riding as soon as they could walk. The Life Guards were recruited from the Barholm family estates back in Descott county, from vakaros and yeoman-tenant *rancheros*. When Descotters ate a man's salt they took the responsibilities seriously, in the main.

Suzette adjusted Raj's cravat, beneath the high wing collar of the dress-uniform jacket. There was a fixed, intent look on her face. Raj recognized it; it was the look you got when the overall situation was completely out of control, so you focused on the immediate skill you *could* master. Suzette had been brought up in East Residence, and her family had been patrician for fourteen generations. Court etiquette—and the intricate currents of court intrigue—were as much her heritage as the saddle of a war-dog or the hilt of a saber were to him.

He'd seen the same look on a Brigade trooper's face, adjusting the grip on his sword and the angle of the blade—as he rode into the muzzle of a cannon loaded with grapeshot.

Three of his Companions were standing around, with similar expressions. *They* were looking at the Life Guards, and figuring the odds on a firefight if an order came through to arrest Raj on the spot. *Not good*, he thought.

"Relax," he said quietly. "There isn't going to be any trouble here today."

The party around Raj Whitehall stood in a bubble of social space, lower-ranking courtiers and messengers either avoiding their eyes or staring fascinated at the famous General Whitehall; for the last time, if rumor was correct. Many of them were probably thinking how lucky they were never to have risen so high. The stalk that stood out above the others was the first to be lopped off.

Which is why the Civil Government doesn't rule the whole Earth, as it should, Raj thought with an old, cold anger.

correct, Center replied. Then it added pedantically: **bellevue. earth will come later.**

The crowd parted as a man came through. He wasn't particularly imposing; no more than twenty-one or so, and slimly handsome. His left arm ended at a leather cup and steel hook where the hand should have been. His uniform was standard issue for Civil Government cavalry, blue swallowtail coat and loose maroon breeches, crimson sash under the Sam Browne belt; all tailored with foppish care, but travel-worn and stained with sea salt in places. He carried his round bowl helmet with the chainmail neck-guard and twin captain's stars tucked under his left arm. The right fist snapped to his chest as he saluted, then bowed to Suzette.

"Messer Raj," he said. "My lady Whitehall." A smile as he glanced past them to the other Companions. "Dog-brothers."

"Spirit," Raj said mildly, shaken out of his strait preoccupation with what would probably happen in the next half-hour. "I thought you were back in the Western Territories with the 5th, Bartin."

Not to mention with Colonel Gerrin Staenbridge; Bartin Foley had gotten into the 5th as Gerrin's protégé-cum-boyfriend. He was far more than that now, of course.

"Administrator Historiomo decided," the young officer said, voice carefully neutral, "that since the Brigade survivors in the Western Territories were cooperating fully, a number of units were surplus to garrison needs."

"Which units?" Raj said.

Bartin cleared his throat. "The 5th Descott Guards," he said.

Raj's Own, as they liked to call themselves.

"The 7th Descott Rangers, 1st Rogor Slashers, Poplanich's Own, and the 18th Komar Borderers," he went on.

The cavalry units most closely associated with Raj, and the ones commanded by the men who'd become his Companions, the elite group of close comrades he relied on most.

"In addition, the 17th Kenden County Foot, and the 24th Valencia," he continued.

Jorg Menyez commanded the 17th: a Companion, and the Civil

Government's best infantry specialist, able to turn the despised foot soldiers into fighting men of sorts. The 24th . . . *Ferdihando Felasquez.* Good man . . .

"And last but not least, the 1st and 2nd Mounted Cruisers."

Recruited from the defeated barbarians of the Squadron, after Raj crushed them in a single month's campaign back in the Southern Territories, three years ago. They'd always been warriors; under civilized instruction, they'd also become quite capable soldiers. The commander of the 1st Cruisers, Ludwig Bellamy, had made the same transition; but as a Squadrone nobleman he also regarded himself as Raj's personal liegeman. Tejan M'Brust, the Descotter Companion who'd taken over the 2nd Cruisers, probably thought the same way— although he wasn't supposed to, being a civilized man.

"They're all," Bartin went on, with a slight smile, bowing over Suzette's hand, "on their way back. Together with the field artillery. I came ahead on one of the steam rams, but everyone should be here in a day or three, if the weather stays fine."

Beside Raj, Colonel Dinnalsyn pricked up his ears. The artillery specialist had hated being separated from his beloved weapons. He'd trained those crews himself.

Joy, Raj thought. It just *happened* to look like Raj's own personal army was heading back to the East Residence at flank speed.

Antin M'lewis cracked his fingers. "What happen t'Chivrez?"

The Honorable Fedherko Chivrez had been sent out to take command of the Western Territories after Raj conquered them—and had arrived to find the Governor's promising young heir Cabot Clerett dead at Raj's feet, with a smoking carbine in Raj's hand.

Suzette gave him a single cool violet look from her slanted eyes and then turned them away, her face the unreadable mask of an East Residence aristocrat.

Raj remembered Cabot's eyes bulging, as Suzette shot him neatly behind the ear, in the instant before his trigger finger would have punched an 11mm pistol round through Raj's body. Chivrez had seen; Chivrez had been Director of Supply in Komar back five years ago, and had tried to withhold supplies from Raj's men. Two Companions named Evrard and Kaltin Gruder had run him out a closed window headfirst, then held him while Antin M'lewis started to flay him from the feet up. Raj had gotten the supplies and won the campaign.

The trouble with that sort of method was the long-term problems. On the other hand, if Raj *hadn't* gotten those supplies, his troops would have been wiped out by the Colonials in the desert fighting. You paced yourself to the task, and if the task got done you worried about secondary consequences later.

"Ah." Bartin Foley considered the tip of his hook. "Well, Messer Chivrez seems to have betrayed the Governor's trust and absconded with some of the Brigade's treasures."

observe, Center said.

A bedroom in the palace of the Generals of the Brigade, in the Western Territories. Chivrez thrashing, his arms and legs held down by four strong men, another pressing a pillow over his face. The stubby limbs thrashed against the bedclothes. After a few minutes they grew still; Ludwig Bellamy wrapped the body in the sheets and hoisted it. Even masked, Raj recognized Gerrin Staenbridge as the one holding open the door.

The scene shifted, to the swamps outside Carson Barracks. The same men tipped a burlap-wrapped bundle off the deck of a small boat. It vanished with scarcely a splash, weighed down with lengths of chain and a cast-iron roundshot weighing forty kilos. Gerrin raised a meter-diameter blazon of the Brigade's sunburst banner, crafted in silver and gold with the double lightning flash across it picked out in diamond.

"Pity," he murmured. "Not bad work in a garish sort of barbarian way, and it would buy a good many opera tickets and dinners at the Centoyard back home. Ah, well—authenticity."

He tossed the disk after the bureaucrat's body. It sank with a popping bubble of marsh gas. Somewhere off in the swamps a hadrosauroid bellowed.

Antin M'lewis grinned uneasily as the Companions exchanged glances. They knew, of course . . . but he wasn't quite sure if Messer Raj knew. They were all of the Messer class by birth themselves; he'd levered himself up into it by hitching his star to Messer Raj's wagon. *Ye takes t'risk a' fallin', too,* he thought.

M'lewis had started off as a Bufford Parish bandit, a sheep stealer by hereditary profession, and made even that most lawless part of not-very-lawful Descott County too hot for him. Enlistment had been the alternative to a rope—or a less formal appointment with a knife. He'd met Raj over a little matter of a peasant's pig gone missing despite a no-foraging order. One look had told him this was a man who had to be either served or killed, and he'd made *his* decision. It had led him near enough to death more times than he could count, and also to advancement beyond his dreams.

On the other hand, one of the things that surprised him about gentlemen born was how bad they were at making use of their advantages. There were good points to a rough upbringing. One of them was being able to say the unsayable.

"Ah, ser," he suggested, leaning forward and whispering, "what wit' t' lads comin' in s'soon, mebbe we'uns ud better dip out loik—come back wit' better company inna day er two?"

Raj spoke in a clear, conversational tone, without looking around: "I'm attending this levee as ordered by the Sovereign Mighty Lord, Captain M'lewis. You may do as you please."

M'lewis spat on the intaglio floor. *Spirit. Mebbe I should a' stayed in sheep-stealin'.*

He followed nonetheless; he might have been born a thief, but he'd eaten this man's bread and salt.

A metal-shod staff thumped the floor, and the tall bronze panels of the Audience Hall swung open. The gorgeously robed figure of the Janitor—the Court Usher—bowed and held out his staff, topped by the Star symbol of the Civil Government.

Suzette took Raj's arm. The Companions fell in behind him, unconsciously forming a column of twos. A Life Guard officer stepped forward.

"Your weapons, Messers," he said, his face expressionless.

Raj made a chopping gesture with his free hand, and the forward rustle of the Companions died. He handed over ceremonial revolver and court sword. This time it was Bartin Foley who whispered in his ear:

"A company of the 5th arrived *with* me, sir. If you're arrested . . ."

"Captain Foley, the Sovereign Mighty Lord's orders will be *obeyed* by all troops under my command—is that clear?"

observe, Center whispered in his mind. Raj, in a cell, darkness and the flickering light of lanterns. Rifle-fire from the halls outside, flat slapping echoes off the stone, and the turnkey's shotgun pointed through the bars at Raj's face, the hammer falling as he jerked the trigger . . .

"I've served my Governor and the Spirit of Man to the best of my ability," Raj added. "I chose to assume that the Governor, upon whom be the blessings of the Spirit always, will see it the same way."

The functionary's voice boomed out with trained precision through the gold-and-niello speaking trumpet:

"General the Honorable Messer Raj Ammenda Halgern da Luis Whitehall, Whitehall of Hillchapel, Hereditary Supervisor of Smythe Parish, Descott County! His Lady, Suzette Emmaenelle—" *None of his other titles,* Raj noted. He'd been officially hailed *Sword of the Spirit of Man* and *Savior of the State* in this room.

He ignored the noise, ignored the brilliantly decked crowds who waited on either side of the carpeted central aisle, the smells of polished metal, sweet incense, and sweat. The Audience Hall was two hundred meters long and fifty high, its arched ceiling a mosaic showing the wheeling galaxy with the Spirit of Man rising head and shoulders behind it. The huge dark eyes were full of stars themselves, staring down into your soul.

Along the walls were automatons, dressed in the tight uniforms worn by Terran Federation soldiers twelve hundred years before. They whirred and clanked to attention, powered by hidden compressed-air conduits, bringing their archaic and quite non-functional battle lasers to salute. The Guard troopers along the aisle brought their entirely functional rifles up in the same gesture.

The far end of the audience chamber was a hemisphere plated

with burnished gold, lit via mirrors from hidden arcs. It glowed
with a blinding aura, strobing slightly. The Chair itself stood four
meters in the air on a pillar of fretted silver, the focus of light
and mirrors and every eye in the giant room. The man enChaired
upon it sat with hieratic stiffness, light breaking in metallized
splendor from his robes, the bejeweled Keyboard and Stylus in his
hands. A tribal delegation was milling about before it, still speaking
through its hired interpreter.

The linguist's face was professionally bland, but occasionally a
look of horror would cross his features as he moved his lips,
working out Sponglish equivalents of the mountaineers' singsong
native tongue:

"Hjburni-burni-burni—"

"Humbly we beseech you, O Sovereign Mighty One, Sole Autocrat,
our poverty prevents other than our traditional border auxiliary
duties—"

Center broke in: **more accurately rendered: back off, stonehouse-
chief, or we'll see what terms the colony offers its border
auxiliaries—we're closer to al kebir than east residence.**

"Hjurni-burni-burni, burjimi murjimi urgimi—"

"In our humble huts in the mountains, we seek only to till our
poor fields in peace—"

we're your allies and *you* **pay** *us* **for guarding the passes;**

"—kuljurni ablurni hjurni-burni Halvaardi burri murri—"

"—and surely there are closer, richer lands which need the attention of your talented administrators—"

**—so the next tax collector who asks for "earth and water" from
the halvaardi gets thrown down a well to find plenty of both.**

Barholm made a slight gesture with one hand, and the tribesfolk
were ushered out, protesting, amid a ripe stink from the butter they
used to grease their braids. One of the wooden clocks they carried
on their belts gave its mechanical *kuku, kuku* as the pillar that
supported the Chair sank toward the white marble steps; at the rear
of the enclosure two full-scale statues of gorgosauroids rose to their
three-meter height and roared as the seat of the Governor of the
Civil Government sank home with a slight sigh of hydraulics. A faint
whine sounded, and the arc lights blazed brighter. At the center of
the mirrors' focus Barholm blazed like a shape of white fire.

Raj took three paces forward and went down in the ceremonial
prostration—the full prostration, since his former titles were stripped
from him. He rose and knelt the prescribed three times; by his side
there was a quiet rustle of silks and lace as Suzette sank down with
an infinite gracefulness.

"What punishment," Barholm boomed, his voice amplified by the
superb acoustics of the Audience Hall, *"is fit for him who was foremost in Our trust? Yea, what baseness is more base, what vileness
more vile, than one into whose hand the Sword of the State has been*

entrusted—when that most wretched of men turns the Sword against the very root and foundation, the Coax Cable of the Spirit—"

In East Residence, rhetoric was the most admired of the arts— far ahead of, for instance, military or administrative skill; infinitely more so than engineering. A speech like this could go on for hours, when the entire content could be boiled down to "kill him."

The semicircle of high ministers stirred behind their desks. The tall slender form of Chancellor Tzetzas turned sharply to hiss General Gharzia, Commander of Eastern Forces, into silence; the elderly soldier was listening to a messenger—a courier in tight leathers, not a court usher or an aide. From the floor, Raj watched Gharzia's face congeal like cooling lard. He didn't have to pay attention to what Barholm said, he knew how that would end . . .

Gharzia rose and circled to Tzetzas' side. The Chancellor tried to shake off the hand that plucked at his sleeve, then turned to listen with a tight, controlled fury that would have frightened Raj if he'd been in Gharzia's shoes. People who seriously annoyed the Chancellor tended to have accidents, or develop severe stomach problems, or be killed in duels.

Raj had never seen Tzetzas frightened before. It was a far less pleasant experience than he would have thought; whatever his other vices, nobody had ever even accused the Chancellor of cowardice. To make him interrupt the ceremony of triumph over his most hated rival, it had to be something massive.

"And—" Barholm noticed the movement to his right and broke off, flipping up the smoked-glass eyeshield. "Tzetzas! *What* do you think you're doing?"

The raw fury in his voice made Tzetzas check half a step. The Governor was the Spirit's Viceregent on Earth; if he ordered the Guards to cut the Chancellor to pieces on the steps of the Chair, they would obey without hesitation. That had happened in past reigns, more than once. Wise Governors remembered that those reigns had been short . . . but Barholm Clerett had been growing more and more unstable since his wife died.

"Sovereign Mighty Lord," Tzetzas said, his voice a cool precision instrument, handled with faultless skill. "I deserve your anger for my boorishness. Yet concern drives your servant. The Colony has invaded our territories; news has arrived by heliograph."

There was a chain of stations between the frontiers and East Residence; high-priority messages could be relayed in hours, where couriers would take days or weeks. Only the Colony and the Civil Government possessed such means, on Bellevue.

"You interrupt me for a *raid*?"

The Bedouin and the Civil Government's Borderers had been stealing girls and sheep and cutting each other up over waterholes since time immemorial. It was a peaceful week that passed without a minor skirmish, and there were several *razziah* a year from either side.

It usually didn't even cause a ripple in the profitable trade carried on between the more civilized urban element on both sides of the frontier.

Tzetzas threw himself down on his knees. "Not a raid, Sovereign Mighty Lord. Invasion. The Settler of the Colony himself, Ali— and his one-eyed brother and general, Tewfik. They have taken Gurnyca."

A low moan swept through the Audience Hall. That was the largest city on the lower Drangosh river and the closest major settlement to the eastern frontier.

The mad anger disappeared from Barholm's face, as cleanly as if cut with a knife. A minute later, so did the eye-hurting brilliance of the arc lights. By contrast, the Audience Hall seemed black.

"The levee is closed," Barholm said, in a flat carrying voice.

There were yelps of protest from petitioners. The officer of the Life Guards barked an order, and hands rattled on stocks as the rifles came to present-arms.

"An immediate meeting of the State Council will be held in the Negrin Room," Barholm said into the sudden stillness. "All others are dismissed."

Raj rose to one knee. "Sovereign Mighty Lord," he said calmly. "Does the Sole Autocrat wish my presence?"

Barholm paused, looking over his shoulder. "Of course," he said. A snarl broke through the mask of his face. "Of course!"

"*Sayyida,*" the man said, bowing with hand to brows, lips and heart; his dress was the knee breeches and jacket of an East Residence bourgeois, but his tongue was the pure Syrian Arabic of Al Kebir, capital of the Colony. "Peace be with you."

"And upon you peace, Abdullah al'Aziz," Suzette Whitehall replied in the same language, the rolling gutturals falling easily from her tongue.

Her maids had replaced the split skirt, leggings, and blond wig of court formality with a noblewoman's day-robe; she wrote as she spoke, glancing up only occasionally. The steel nib of the pen skritched steadily on the paper.

"Are you ready?" she said.

"For the Great Game?" the Arab replied, smiling whitely in his neatly trimmed black beard. "Always, my lady."

"Good. Here are papers, and a sight-draft on Muzzaf Kerpatik."

The Whitehalls' chief steward, among other things. A Borderer from the southern city of Komar, and no friend of any Arab, but also not likely to let personal feelings interfere with his work.

"My instructions, *sayyida?*"

"Proceed at once to Sandoral on the Drangosh. Military intelligence for my lord, if it presents itself; for myself I wish full information on the higher officers of the garrison and the local nobles:

THE SWORD

loves, hates, histories, feuds, alliances. Also any information from the Colony."

He took the papers and repeated the bow, using the documents for added flourish. "I obey like those multiplex of wing and eye who served Sulieman bin'-Daud, my lady," he said cheerfully. "That city I know of old." He'd done similar work for her the last time Raj commanded in the East, four years before.

"See that nobody stuffs you into a bottle," she added dryly, dropping back into Sponglish.

"I shall be most careful," he replied in the Civil Government's tongue, faultless down to the capital-city middle-class crispness of his vowels. "There is yet much to be done to repay my debt to you, my lady. And," he added with a cold glint in his dark eyes, "to those Sunni sons of pigs in Al Kebir, also."

Druze were few on Bellevue; less, since the Settlers had decided to purify the House of Islam a generation ago. Those sniffed out by the mullahs could count themselves lucky to be sold as slaves to the sulfur mines of Gederosia. The path from there to Suzette Whitehall's household and manumission had been long and complex . . .

"Your family are provided for?" Abdullah nodded. "Go, then, thou Slave of God," Suzette said, once more in Arabic, playing on the literal meaning of the man's name. "Thy God and mine be with thee."

"And the Merciful, the Lovingkind with thee and thy lord, *sayyida*," he replied, and left.

"Fatima," Suzette went on.

"Messa?"

"Take this to the Renunciate Sister Conzwela Dihego; she's second administrative assistant for medical affairs to the Arch-Sysup of East Residence. It's an authorization to mobilize priest-doctors and medical nuns, with the necessary supplies and transport for immediate dispatch to Sandoral."

"Wasn't she with us in the Western Territories?" the Arab girl asked.

"Yes; and Anne got her that job on my say-so when we got back." Suzette sighed; she missed Anne. "Quickly. And send in Muzzaf."

The Companion sidled through the door as Fatima left; the opening showed a controlled chaos of packing. He was a short slight man, with the dark complexion of a Borderer and a singsong Komarite accent. He was dressed in jacket and breeches of white linen, the little peaked fore-and-aft cap of his region, and a sash which nearly concealed the pepperpot pistol and pearl-handled gravity knife he preferred. He bowed deeply, a gesture much like Abdullah's.

Nearly a thousand years of conflict had left the Borderers much resembling their enemies of the Colony, though it was a killing matter to suggest it aloud.

"Messa Whitehall," he said, showing white teeth against his spiked black chin-beard. Like everyone else in the household, he was reacting to the news of Raj's reinstatement with almost giddy relief. "We campaign again?"

"Yes," Suzette said.

She pushed a document across the table with a finger. "One of your relatives is contractor for the East Residence municipal coal yards, isn't he?"

Muzzaf nodded; men from Komar and the other Border cities were prominent in trade all over the Civil Government, and in the new joint-risk companies.

"Subcontractor, Messa. The primary contract is farmed to an . . . associate of Chancellor Tzetzas." He took up the paper and whistled silently. "That is a great *deal* of coal."

"Subcontractor is good enough. Have him release that amount to the Central Rail; and drop a suggestion with their dispatching agent that they begin to accumulate rolling stock *immediately.* Sweeten the suggestion if you have to."

"Immediately."

They exchanged a smile; Chancellor Tzetzas had confiscated all Raj's wealth . . . all that he had been able to find, at any rate. Neither the Chancellor nor Raj knew exactly how much the Whitehalls had had; Raj left such things to Muzzaf and Suzette . . . and they had anticipated the evil day long before. Raj knew how to handle guns and men, and even politics after a fashion, but money could also be a useful tool.

Silence fell as the steward left, broken only by the scritching of the pen and the faint thumps and scraping of the packing in the outer chambers. On the bed behind her were Raj's campaigning gear: plain issue swallowtail jacket of blue serge, maroon pants, boots, helmet, saber, pistol, map case, binoculars. Beside it was her linen riding costume and a captured Colonial repeating carbine, her own personal weapon . . . and the one, she reflected, that had disposed of the Clerett's heir.

A pity, she thought absently, tapping her lips with the tip of the pen before dipping the nib in the inkwell again. *A very pleasant young man.*

And easy to manipulate. Which had been crucial; like his uncle, he'd been mad with suspicion against Raj. With envy, too, in young Cabot's case: of Raj's reputation, his victories, his hold over his soldiers, and his wife.

A pity she'd had to kill him. Particularly just then. Shooting people was a crude emergency measure . . .

Which reminded her. She crossed to her jewel table and reached beneath for a small rosewood box. A tiny combination lock closed it, and she probed at that with a pin from a brooch.

Yes, the crystal vials of various liquids and powders within were all full and fresh—there was a slip of paper with a recent date inside to remind her, one of Abdullah's many talents.

You never knew what sort of help Raj would need . . . whether he knew it or not.

"You *will* triumph, my knight," she whispered to herself, closing the box with a click. "If I have anything to do with the matter."

CHAPTER THREE

Governor Barholm stood while the servants stripped off the heavy robes; apart from Raj, they were the only people in the chamber who didn't look terrified . . . and they didn't have to watch the Governor's face. A sicklefoot had that sort of expression, just before it pivoted and slashed open its prey's belly with the four-inch dewclaw on one hind foot.

The Negrin Room was three centuries old. Walls were pale stone, traced over with delicate murals of reeds and flying dactosauroids and waterfowl; there was only one small Star, a token obeisance to religion as had been common in that impious age. The heads of the Ministries were there: Chancellor Tzetzas, of course; General Fiydel Klostermann, Master of Soldiers; Bernardinho Rivadavia, the Minister of Barbarians; Mihwel Berg of the Administrative Service; Gharzia, Commander of Eastern Forces. The courier from the east as well.

It was strange not to see Lady Anne Clerett, the Governor's wife. Barholm didn't have anyone he really trusted now that she was dead, and it was affecting his judgment.

"Heldeyz," Barholm snapped. "*Give* us the report, man."

Ministerial couriers were men of some rank themselves, but it was still strange how unintimidated Heldeyz looked, even facing the stark fury in Barholm Clerett's eyes. His own were fixed and distant, in a face still seamed by trail dust.

Barholm went on fretfully: "I *don't* know why Ali has done this. The treaty after the last war was generous to a fault—particularly since we *won* the war. The gifts of friendship . . ."

observe:

Sweating slaves heaved at bundles of iron bars, heaping them on the flatbed rail-cars and lashing them down. One slipped and fell to the paving stones of East Residence's main station. A bar snapped across; as a clerk bustled over a guard rolled the broken end beneath his boot.

"Spirit," he said in a tone of mild curiosity. The interior of the fracture showed a gray texture. "That's not wrought iron, it's *cast.*"

Cast iron came straight from the smelting furnace; it was hard, brittle and full of impurities. Only after treatment in a puddling mill did it become the ductile, easily worked material so valuable for machinery and tools.

The clerk cleared his throat. "I think you'll find," he said significantly, "that the Chancellor has inspected the manifests quite carefully."

The guard grinned; he was a thin man with a long nose and a pockmarked face, an East Residencer by birth with all the ingrained respect for a good swindle that marked that breed. He brushed his thumb over the first three fingers of his right hand. The clerk smiled back.

"Sovereign Mighty Lord," Raj said. "I think you'll find that quality, quantity, and delivery dates on our tribute—pardon, our gifts of friendship—to the Colony have been below the Treaty terms."

Figures scrolled before his eyes, and he read them in an emotionless monotone worthy of Center.

Barholm blinked. He turned his eyes on Tzetzas, and a fine beading of sweat broke out on the Chancellor's olive face. "Sole Autocrat," the minister said, spreading his hands. "When contracts are handed out, something always sticks—so many layers of oversight, so many hands—you know—"

The Governor's fist struck the table. Gold-rimmed *kave* cups bounced and clattered in their saucers.

"I know who's responsible for seeing that the payments were met!" he roared; suddenly there was the slightest trace of Descott County rasp in his Sponglish. "You *fool,* I don't expect you to work for your salary alone, but I *did* expect you to know enough not to piss in our own well! D'you have any idea what this war is going to cost in lost taxes and off-budget funding?"

He paused, and when he continued his voice was calm. "You'd better have some idea, because you're going to pay the overage—personally."

"Sovereign Mighty Lord," Raj said. "Right now, I think we'd better concern ourselves with the state of the garrisons on the Drangosh frontier."

Barholm snapped his fingers. "Gurnyca had a garrison of—"

"Ten thousand men, Sole Autocrat," Mihwel Berg said helpfully. "At least, ten thousand on the paybooks."

Chancellor Tzetzas busied himself with his papers. When Barholm spoke, it was to General Gharzia.

"General," he said, his voice soft and even, "tell me—and if you lie, it would be better for you if you had never been born—how many troops were *actually* on the strength of the Gurnyca garrison? In what condition?"

Gharzia licked his lips, going gray under the tanned olive of his skin. "Two thousand, Sovereign Mighty Lord. In . . . ah, poor condition."

Somebody had been collecting the pay of the missing eight thousand. All eyes turned to the Chancellor.

The ruler turned back to the courier from the east. "Now, Messer Heldeyz," he said evenly. "Your report, please."

"Yes, Sole Autocrat."

Heldeyz stared at his hands. "I met the Colonials fifty klicks south of Gurnyca," he began. "They—"

observe, Center said:

Terrible as an army with banners. Bartin Foley had quoted that to Raj, once; it was a fragment of Old Namerique, from the codices that survived the Fall.

There were plenty of banners in the forefront of the Colonial host that crossed the Drangosh. The green flag of Islam, marked with the crescent, or with the house blazons of regiments and noble *amirs*. The peacock-tail of the Settlers; that meant Ali was present in person. And a black pennant marked with the Seal of Solomon in red. *Tewfik.* Ali's brother, disqualified from the Settler's throne because of the eye he'd lost in the Zanj Wars, but the Colony's right arm nonetheless.

Raj recognized the terrain instantly; he'd campaigned out east himself, five years ago. Generations of the Civil Government's soldiers had taken their blooding in that ghastly lunar landscape of eroded silt, and all too many left their bones there. Just north of the border and the river forts, by the look of it, in one of the locations where the right—the western—bank was too high for irrigation. In consequence nothing grew there, except for a few bluish-green native shrubs.

The oily-looking greenish-gray waters of the Drangosh were a kilometer and a half across. A bridge of boats had been built across it, big river-barges of the type used for trade up and down the river from Sandoral to Al Kebir and the far-off Colonial Gulf. *Good engineering,* Raj thought; as good as the Civil Government's army, or a little better. The barges were lashed together with huge sisal cables as thick as a man's waist; then timbers and planks were laid across to make a deck, and pounded clay half a meter thick on top of that to give the men and animals a firm surface. There were even straw balustrades on either side, chest high, to keep the beasts from spooking at the water curling up around the blunt prows of the barges.

Men flowed across in a steady stream: Colonial dragoon *tabors,* battalions, riding in column of fours, mainly. Mounted on slender Bazenjis and greyhounds, lever-action repeating carbines in scabbards by their right knees, scimitars or yataghans at their belts, bandoliers over the chests of their faded scarlet djellabas. The sun glittered on the polished spikes of their conical helmets, and the pugarees wound about them fluttered in the breeze. Between the blocks of cavalry came guns: light pompoms, quick-firers throwing a two-kilo shell from a clip magazine; field guns, much like the Civil Government's 75mms; and heavier pieces drawn by oxen. Those were cast-steel muzzle-loading rifles, heavy pieces up to 150mm, siege guns. And there was transport, light dog-drawn two-wheel carts, heavy wagons pulled by sixteen pair of oxen.

Officers directed the traffic with flourishes of their nine-tailed ceremonial whips, each thong tipped with a piece of jagged steel.

Where— Raj thought. Center's viewpoint shifted to the western bank.

In the Colony's army, as in the Civil Government's, infantry were usually second-line troops, good enough to hold forts and lines of communication. Ali—Tewfik, probably—had sent his over first, and they were hard at work. Swarms of men stripped to their loincloths or pantaloons, burned from their natural light brown to an almost black color, swinging picks and shoveling dirt into the baskets others hauled. They moved over the land like disciplined ants, and a pentagonal earthwork fortress was rising around the western end of the pontoon bridge. A fairly formidable one, too; deep ditch, ten-meter walls, ravelins and bastions at the corners with deep V-notches for the muzzles of the guns. The Colony's green flag and the Settler's peacock already flapped around a huge pavilion-tent in its center. Within, ditched roadways had been laid out, and neat rows of pup tents, heaps of stores, and picket-lines for the dogs were rising.

Enough for—

"Sixty thousand men," Raj said. "Fifty thousand cavalry, ten thousand infantry or a little more to hold the bridgehead."

Heldeyz stopped, flustered. "Yes, *heneralissimo*," he said; evidently the news of Raj's demotion hadn't reached the eastern marches yet. "That's my estimate. How did you know?"

"Logistics. If Ali's planning on moving as far north as Sandoral, that's the maximum number he can supply overland from the bridgehead. Our forts at the border can hold out for six months or more, even if the Colony put in a full attack—which they won't or they couldn't put that large a field army into action. They'll have blockforces around the frontier strongpoints, but they can't use river transport to supply Ali. So they moved north and crossed upstream of the forts."

Both the Colony and the Civil Government had put generations of effort into those defenses. The giant cast-steel rifles in the forts would smash anything that tried to steam past them on the river. That ruled out supply by riverboat.

"Ali—Tewfik—must have built a railroad line to the east bank," Raj said. "But on the western shore, it'll be animal transport. Even with what they can forage, no more than fifty thousand men and riding dogs. They wouldn't bring less, not for a full-scale invasion, and they couldn't feed more."

Barholm shot Raj a considering look. "Go on," he said to Heldeyz.

The courier nodded. "I met—"

observe, Center whispered in Raj's mind:

Heldeyz knelt before a throne. It was lightly built, of cast bronze fretwork, but inlaid with gold and gems in a pattern that flared out behind the seat like a peacock's tail. A man in shimmering cloth-of-gold sat on it. Throne and man glittered when stray beams of light penetrated the lacework canopy that slaves held above it; a spray of peacock feathers sprang from the great ruby in the clasp at the front of his turban. Around the Settler stood generals and noblemen, a few Bedouin chiefs in goathair robes and ha'ik, mullahs in black, servants with flasks of iced·sherbert, crouching clerks and accountants with paper and pen and abacus. None of them came within the ring of guardsmen, black slave-mamluks with great curved swords naked in their hands, or bell-mouthed riot guns at the ready.

"Your master, the *kaphar* king, has offended me grievously," Ali said, speaking fair Sponglish. "He has violated the terms of our treaty . . . and my father's blood cries out for vengeance. No duty is more sacred. Yet Allah, the Merciful, the Lovingkind, enjoins us to peaceful deeds."

Ali's face was heavy-featured but regular, the curved beak of the nose dominating, offset by full red lips and a forked beard. His eyes were large and brown, luminous and somehow disturbing. Apart from an occasional twitching tic of his right cheek, the expression was one of mild reason.

An officer approached, going down on both knees and bowing until the point of his helmet-spike touched the glowing Al Kebir carpets that covered the ground before the Settler's pavilion and campaign-throne.

"*Amir el Mumineen*, Commander of the Faithful, the infidel emissaries from the city of Gurnyca crave the honor of your presence."

Ali's eyebrows rose slightly. He leaned back in the portable throne, and servants stepped forward to spray rosewater from crystal ewers through rubber bulbs. He sipped sherbert from a glass globe through a silver straw and waited.

"By all means, let them enter," he said gently.

The delegates ignored Heldeyz, prone on the carpet before the Settler. There were half a dozen of them, mostly in the dress of wealthy merchants, one in Civil Government uniform. They threw themselves prostrate; a gesture that only the ruler of the *Gubernio Civil* was legally due. In fact, it was forbidden to any other on penalty of death, but the Governor was in East Residence, and Ali was very much present before their gates with fifty thousand men.

"Sovereign lord," the head of the delegation mumbled into the carpet; he was an elderly man, sweating in the heat, the wattles under his chin sliding down into the expensive but dust-stained silver lace of his cravat. "Spare us."

Well, thought Raj. *That's straightforward enough.*

"Surely," the *alcalle* of Gurnyca said, "we may make amends to Your Supremacy for any offense we have unwittingly given. We are but poor merchants, not the lords of State. We have no knowledge of high matters. Yet if wrong has been done you, we are willing to pay. Surely there can be peace—who would benefit from war?"

Ali smiled. "There may be peace, if God wills. There is but one God, and all things are accomplished according to the will of God." He nodded, and added in his own tongue: "*Salaam, insh'allah.*"

One ringed hand stroked his beard, and he flicked a finger at a clerk. "You spoke of payment. The tribute from you *kaphar* ingrates is in arrears to the extent of—"

"—twenty-one hundred thousand gold *dinars*, O Lion of Islam," the clerk said. "That is not counting interest on late payments at—"

"Silence," Ali purred, a lethal amusement in his voice. "Am I a merchant, to haggle? By all means, if this is made good, let there be peace."

Even under the Colonial guns, that brought a wail of protest. "Lord, Lord," the alcalle said. "We are but one city! There is not that much gold in all Gurnyca, not if we stripped the dome of the cathedron and the fillings from our teeth."

"Both of which," Ali pointed out genially, "will be done if the city is put to the sack." He raised a hand. "It is the time of prayer. Surely, we may speak again of this later; and you shall return to your city with an escort and safe passage. In the morning, I shall give my final decision."

The scene shifted, the sun dropping toward the horizon and both moons high, looking like translucent glass against the bright stars. Date palms and orange groves stood in darkening shadow as the Gurnyca elders and Heldeyz rode their dogs through the belt of irrigated land surrounding the city. Water chuckled in the canals that bordered the fields, oxen lowed, but there was no sight or sound of human beings, no smoke from the whitewashed huts of the peasantry. Fields lay empty, scattered with tossed-aside hoes and pruning hooks; a manor stood ghostly among its gardens, with only the raucous sound of a peacock strutting along the tiled portico.

Frontier reflexes, Raj thought grimly. *They know when to make a bolt for the walls.*

There were no buildings or trees within a half-kilometer of the fortifications, only pasture and field crops; and the city defenses were first-rate. Raj remembered them well from the archives, which he'd memorized long before Center entered his life. Modernized a century ago, and then again in his father's time. A clear field of fire, good moat, new-style walls sunk behind it, low and massive. Ravelins and bastions at frequent intervals, giving murderous enfilade fire all along the circuit, with a strong central citadel near the water. The guns were cast-iron muzzle-loaders like most fortress artillery, but formidable and numerous; there were some very up-to-date rifled pieces among them.

Resolutely held by a strong garrison, the city could have held for months against the Colonial army—and it would be impossible to bypass. Taking it by siege would require full-scale entrenchments, pushing artillery positions forward inch by bloody inch, escalade trenches, until enough heavy howitzers were close to the wall and you could pound it flat. Even then, storming it would be brutally expensive. By that time, the Civil Government would have had time to mobilize its field armies in the East and march to the city's relief. It was a strategy that had worked a dozen times in the endless eastern wars.

If the garrison was up to strength and competently led.

Center's viewpoint switched to the escort, a full half-battalion of them, two hundred and fifty men. They didn't look particularly impressive at first sight, dark bearded men, many with the tails of their pugarees drawn across their faces like veils. Raj looked for telltale signs: their hands, the wear on the hilts of scimitars and carbines, the way they sat their dogs, how often they had to check or spur to keep their dressing.

These lads have been to school. Their commander was a stocky man, one of the ones with the tail-end of his turban drawn across his face. Scars seamed the backs of his hands, and another gouged down from forehead to nose . . .

. . . and his eye was unmoving on that side. *Tewfik.* Raj cursed to himself. With a glass eye for once, rather than his trademark patch. He'd met the Colonial commander once, in a parley before the Battle of Sandoral, four years ago. *What's he doing there?* It was a job for a minor emir, not the commander-in-chief.

An image flickered through Raj's consciousness, tinged somehow with irony: himself, leading the 2nd Cruisers through the tunnel under Lion City's walls.

Point taken, Raj noted dryly.

The white dust of the road shone ruddy with the setting sun, streaked with the long shadow of the tall cypresses planted by its side. They came to the outer gatehouse of the city's defenses, where the highway crossed the moat on stone arches. Civil Government troops opened the iron portals: infantrymen, slovenly-looking even for footsoldiers. Raj ground his teeth at the rust on one man's rifle barrel. They eyed the Colonial troops with the prickly nervousness of a cat watching a pack of large dogs through a window. Heldeyz saluted their officer and opened his mouth to speak.

Tewfik drew his revolver and shot the man in the face.

A red spearhead seemed to connect the Arab's hand and the guard officer's nose for an instant, and then the footsoldier jerked backward as if kicked in the face by an ox. His helmet rang against the stone of the gatehouse, the last fraction of the *clank* lost in the snapping bark of carbines as the Colonials cut loose with their repeaters. They boiled forward, screaming in a wild falsetto screech. One of the Civil Government soldiers managed to get a round off, the deeper boom of his single-shot rifle painful in the confined space. Then he went down under a Colonial officer's yataghan, still stabbing upward with his bayonet.

The fight in the gateway lasted bare seconds, leaving Heldeyz and the city fathers sitting their dogs and gaping at the litter of bodies. Puffs of off-white smoke drifted by; the Colonials were wasting no time. Dozens of them stuck their carbines through gunslits in the doors and fired blind, as fast as they could work the levers, sending a lethal hail of the light bullets to ricochet off the stone walls within. Hand-bombs and axes pounded the doors open. The rest of the Colonial force formed a dense four-deep firing line at the inner gate, thumbing reloads from their bandoliers into the loading gates of their weapons. Heldeyz's head whipped around at the high shrill scream of a Colonial bugle.

Mounted men were pouring out of the orchards that ringed the city, spurring their dogs. The animals bounded forward at a dead run, covering the ground in huge soaring leaps as they galloped with heads down and hind legs coming up nearly to their ears on every jump. Rough hands threw the courier aside as the column poured into the strait confines of the gatehouse and broke out into the cleared ground beyond; a battery of pompoms followed, their long barrels jerking wildly as the gunners lashed their dogs. Iron wheels sparked on the paving stones, and behind them the roadway was red with crimson djellabas . . .

Barholm's fist hit the table as the courier's words stumbled into silence. He didn't have Center's holographic visions to flesh them out, but there was nothing wrong with his wits.

"They *knew* the wogs were there in force and they didn't keep a better guard than that?" he said.

"Sole Autocrat, the garrison was under-strength and badly trained," Raj said quietly. "In any case, they paid for their folly."

"Yes," Heldeyz said, his eyes remote. "They paid."

observe, Center said.

The scimitar flashed in the sun. A heavy *thack* sounded, with the harsher wet popping of fresh bone underneath. The *alcalle*'s head rolled free; his body collapsed from its kneeling position, heavy jets of arterial blood splashing into the reddish mud that stained the ground. Clouds of flies lifted, then settled again. The executioner flourished his heavy two-handed curved sword ritually.

The smoke from the burning buildings covered the smell, even from the pyramid of heads the Settler's mamluks were building beside the outer gate. Few of the chained coffles of Gurnycians marching out paid much attention to it; their faces were mostly blank, eyes to the ground. Mounted Colonial guards urged them on with snaps of the *kourbash*, the long sauroid-hide whip. They were the lucky ones: pretty women, strong young men, craftsmen, and children old enough to survive the trip south to the markets of Al Kebir.

Ali pointed. "No, cut that one's throat," he said, indicating a Star priest with a thin white beard. The executioner lowered his sword.

The old man's eyes were closed; he was praying quietly as the black-robed mamluk stepped up behind him and drew the curved dagger. Ali giggled when the body toppled thrashing to the ground.

"The *halall*," he said, sputtering laughter. The ritual throat-cutting that made meat clean for Muslims to eat. "Is it not fitting, for these beasts?"

Raj noted a mullah's lips tightening at the blasphemy. Nobody spoke.

The good humor on Ali's face turned gelid as he gripped Heldeyz's face in his hand and turned it to the heaps of severed heads.

"Do you *see*, infidel?" he screamed. "Do you *see*?"

A portly man in a green turban shoved his way through the crowd. A string of prisoners followed him, mostly girls in their early teens, with a few younger boys. He prostrated himself.

"Oh guardian of the sacred ka'ba, you wished—" he began in a falsetto voice.

Ali released the Civil Government courier. "Yes, yes," he said impatiently. His hand flicked to a girl and a boy. "Those two, and don't bother me again before the evening meal." He jerked his head at his guards. "Come. Bring the pig-eating *kaphar*."

Wagons took up most of the roadway, oxen lowing under the load. Inside, in the cleared space within the walls that Civil Government law commanded, were huge heaps of spoils; officers were directing the troopers as they piled it in neatly classified heaps. Cloth, metalware, tools, coin, precious vessels from the Star churches and temples . . . Beyond, only a few buildings still stood. As Heldeyz watched, a merchant's townhouse collapsed inward about the burn-ing rafters, the thick adobe walls crumbling like mud. A ground-shaking thump, and the great dome of the Star temple followed; Raj recognized the sound of blasting charges.

"See, unbeliever," Ali went on. "The pig and son of pigs Barholm—it was not enough that he cheated me of the blood-price of my father's death, he expected me—*me*—Ali ibn'Jamal, to sit among the women and do nothing while he conquered all the world. Conquered all the world, then turned on me! Turned on the Faithful! No, *kaphar*, Ali ibn'Jamal, Guardian of Sinar, Settler of the House of Islam, is not such a fool as that.

"Tell Barholm I am coming for him." Ali's mouth was jerking, and his voice rose to a shrill scream. "Tell him I have something for him!"

Colonial soldiers were setting a sharpened stake in the ground. They dragged out the Arch-Sysup Hierarch of the Diocese of Gurnyca. He was a portly man, flabby in middle age, stripped to his silk underdrawers. The black giants holding his arms scarcely lost a step when he collapsed at the sight of the waiting impaling stake . . .

Silence fell around the table. At last, General Klosterman cleared his throat.

"Well, I don't think there's much doubt as to Ali's intentions," he said.

Barholm nodded abstractedly. "General Klosterman, how long would it take to mobilize all available field forces and meet the Colonists in strength?"

Klosterman paled. Master of Soldiers was an administrative post, but it did give the elderly officeholder a good grasp of the state of the Civil Government's defenses.

"Lord, Ali has fifty thousand of his first-line troops with him. If we summoned *all* available cavalry, we couldn't field half that in time to meet him south of Sandoral, or even south of the Oxhead Mountains . . . and forgive me, Sovereign Mighty Lord, but the troops we could summon would not be in good heart."

observe, said Center.

This time Center's projections started with a map. Raj recognized it, a terrain rendering of the Civil Government's eastern provinces. The Oxhead Mountains ran east-west, then hooked up northward; north of it was the sparsely settled central plateau, and to the south and east was the upper valley of the Drangosh and its tributary. That was densely settled in part, where irrigation was possible; elsewhere arid grazing country, with scattered villages around springs in the foothills.

Colored blocks moved, arrows showing their lines of advance. He nodded to himself; so and so many days to muster, supplies, roadways, the few railroad lines. Twenty thousand men maximum, perhaps thirty thousand if you counted the ordinary infantry garrisons called up from their land grants. And . . .

Men in blue and maroon uniforms fled, beating at their dogs with the flats of their sabers or with riding whips. A ragged square stood on a hill, with the Star banner at its center. Black puffballs of smoke burst over the tattered ranks, shellbursts, and Colonial field guns hammered giant shotgun blasts of canister in at point-blank range. Men *splashed* away from the shot in wedges. A line of mounted dragoons drew their scimitars in unison, flashing in the bright southern sun. *Five battalions*, Raj estimated with an expert eye. *Twenty-five hundred men*. Trumpets shrilled, and the scimitars rested on the riders' shoulders. Walk-march. Trot. The blades came down. Gallop. Charge. A single long volley blew gaps in their line, and they were over the thin Civil Government square. The Star banner went down. . . .

"Lord," Klosterman went on, "with humility, my advice is that we throw as many men into Sandoral and the eastern cities as we can. Ali cannot take them quickly."

Tzetzas spoke for the first time. "But he *could* bypass them," he said.

Raj nodded silently, conscious of eyes glancing at him sidelong. **observe,** said Center.

From horizon to horizon, the land burned; ripe wheat flared like tinder under the summer sun, sending clouds of red-shot black into the sky. Denser columns marked the sites of villages and manor-houses. In an orchard, peasants worked under Colonial guns, ring-barking the trees and piling burning bundles of straw against their roots.

A flicker, and he was outside a city: Melaga, from the look of the olive-covered hills around it. Raw red earth marked the siegeworks about it, a circumvallation with a high wall topped by a palisade. Zigzag works wormed inward from there, each ending in a redoubt protected by earth-filled wicker baskets. Swarms of men hauled cannon forward and dug at the earth. Guns boomed from the city walls, and men died in the siegeworks, but more took their places. Howitzers lobbed their shells into the sky, the fuses drawing trails of smoke and fire until they burst within the walls . . .

"No, that would be far too uncertain," Tzetzas went on. "Instead, well, the treasury is unusually full. We could offer Ali twice, three *times* the previous tribute."

Barholm snorted. "After we shorted him on the last agreement? I can just *see* him quietly going back to Al Kebir, demobilizing his army and waiting for the gold to arrive."

"Sovereign Mighty Lord," Heldeyz said, "he's not here for gold. He's here for blood. He's . . . he's not going to be bought off. You have to see him—"

ali would agree to the increased tribute, but remain on civil government soil, probability 97%, ±2. observe, said Center.

"Filth!" Ali screamed. He strode through the pavilions, kicking over platters filled with whole roast lambs, rice pillaus, fruits, and ices. "You call this a feast of welcome! Filth!"

The syndics of the town shrank backward, looking around with the instinctive gesture of men in a trap with no exit.

"That pig Barholm, that two-dinar Descotter hill chief who calls himself a conqueror, it isn't enough he makes me wait for my tribute, but he insults me too."

Ali stopped, smiled, relaxed. The expression was far more frightening than the bloodthirsty madness of a minute before.

"Well then, we'll have to show the *kaphar* what it means to insult the Commander of the Faithful, won't we?" he went on.

He eyed the assembled syndics with much the same expression that a farmwife would have, standing in the yard and fingering her knife as she selected a stewing pullet.

observe:

A younger Ali knelt behind a girl. Gardens bloomed around them, thick with flowers and softly murmurous with bees; the stars shone above, the only light on the rippling water of the fountain save for a few discreet lanterns. Ali had a hand on the girl's neck, pushing her face below the surface of the water as he thrust into her. He let her rise for an instant, long enough to take one breath and scream.

It bubbled out as he pushed her down again. Her hands beat against the marble of the pool's rim, leaving bloody streaks on the carved stone.

observe:

Ali sat at a chessboard, across from a grave white-bearded man. The pieces were carved from sauroid ivory and black jadeite; they played seated on cushions of cloth-of-gold, beneath a fretted bronze pergola that served as support for a huge vine of sambuca jasmine. A slender girl naked except for the filmy veil that hid half her face poured cut-crystal goblets full of iced sherbert. Droplets of condensation stood out on the silver ewer.

"Checkmate, Prince of the Faithful," the older man said. "Congratulations. This is your best game yet."

Ali looked down at the chessboard, his lips moving as he traced out the possible movements. When he moved, it was so swiftly that the serving girl had time for only the beginning of a scream.

His hand grasped the *cadi*'s white beard, and the dagger slashed it across. He threw the tuft of hair in the older man's face.

"Sauroid-lover," he screamed. "You dare to insult me?"

The old man drew himself up. "You forget yourself, Ali," he said. "I am appointed by the Settler to guide your footsteps. You must learn restraint—"

Ali moved again, very quickly. The curved dagger in his hand was hilted with silver and pearls, but the blade was layer-forged Sinnar steel, sharp enough to part a drifting silk thread. It sliced more than halfway through the *cadi*'s throat. The old man turned, his blood arching out in a spraying stream of red across the priceless silk of the cushions and the white body of the girl. Ali stood silent, panting, watching the body tumble down the alabaster steps of the gazebo. Then he turned toward the servant, smiling. Blood ran down his mustaches, and speckled his lips.

observe:

Ali sat on the Peacock Throne of the Settlers, in a vaulted room whose ceiling was an intertwining mass of calligraphy picked out in gold, the thousand and one names of Allah, the Merciful, the Lovingkind. From a glass bull's-eye at the apex, light streamed down, mellow and gold, to the tessellated marble floor. Guards stood motionless around the walls of the great circular chamber. Others dragged a man forward; he was stripped to his baggy pantaloons, a hard-muscled man in his thirties with a close-cropped beard and a great beak of a nose.

"Greetings, Akbar my brother," Ali called jovially. "How good, how very good to see your face again!"

The Settler's brother drew himself up and spat on the marbled floor. "You have won, Ali," he said disdainfully. "Yours is the Peacock Throne. Bring out the irons and have done."

"Irons?" Ali said.

That was the traditional punishment for the losers, when a dead Settler's brothers fought for the throne. Only a man complete in his limbs and organs could be Commander of the Faithful; Tewfik was disqualified because he had lost an eye in battle. A red-hot iron fulfilled the same purpose.

"Irons?" Ali said again. "Oh, may Allah requite me if I should put out the eyes of one born of the same seed, of Jamal our father."

Eunuchs brought out a stout iron framework, like a high bed-stead with manacles at each corner. Akbar began to bellow and thrash; the guards held him down with remorseless strength while the plump, smooth-faced eunuchs snapped the steel cuffs around wrist and ankle.

"Shaitan will gnaw your soul in hell if you shed a brother's blood!" Akbar yelled.

Ali stood and made a gesture. The guards saluted with fist to brow, and marched out of the great chamber.

"I? Shed your blood? Never, my brother."

Ali stood by the iron rack, stroking his beard. He pulled a handkerchief from one sleeve of his pearl-sewn robe and made as if to wipe his brother's face; when the other man opened his mouth to shout a curse Ali deftly stuffed the length of silk into it.

"There. It is unmannerly to interrupt the Settler. Do you not remember, brother, how you boasted to your captains during our brief, unfortunate civil strife—how you boasted to them that I should be sent into exile on an island in the Zanj Sea with only a mute crone to attend me? That a . . . how did you phrase it? A perverted bastard son of a diseased sheep like me did not deserve the delights of the hareem, and that the pearl-breasted beauties who served me would be shared among your *amirs*."

He clapped his hands. A line of women filed into the throne room, the long robes of their *chadors* brushing the floor and the sleeves hiding their hands.

Ali turned. "Zufika, Aisha," he said. "All of you—hide not the light of your faces."

Obediently, they dropped the filmy black cloaks to the floor. Several of them were carrying long slim knives; two bore a charcoal brazier between them, holding the metal frame with iron tongs. Others set a stool by the iron frame. Ali sank down with a satisfied sigh.

"No, I shall not shed a drop of your blood," he said. "But you surprise me, with this unseemly conduct. Don't you know it is unfitting for an entire male to look on the faces of the Settler's women?"

Zufika came forward, the knife in her hand. "Attend to it, my sweet one."

Through the gag, Akbar began to scream.

"Sovereign Mighty Lord," Raj said quietly.

Silence fell; even Barholm checked himself, dropping the finger he'd been wagging under Chancellor Tzetzas' nose.

"With your permission, lord, I'll take command in the East. Superseding the Commander of Eastern Forces and the garrison commandants."

There were nods all around the table, even from Gharzia. Right now the high command in the east was the sort of honor you took with you to an unmarked grave.

"And I'll take seven thousand cavalry *to* the border."

"Ridiculous—"

"That'll strip the garrisons of—"

"D'you want Ali to march right into East Residence—"

Raj raised his hand. "Sovereign Mighty Lord, the troops are on their way to East Residence as we speak. Most of the garrison of the Western Territories. Veteran fighters, the cream of our armies."

Barholm looked at him narrow-eyed. *And the soldiers most loyal to you.* The thought needed no words.

"That's forty-five hundred men, perhaps a little more. I'll take another two thousand of the Brigaderos prisoners who've been reequipped and organized along Civil Government lines, and some of the battalions who were with me in the Southern Territories campaign and are now attached to the Residence Area command."

Gharzia was scribbling on his pad. *"Heneralissimo—"* he began, giving Raj the title he'd been formally stripped of "—that'll still leave you well below Ali's numbers, discounting his infantry and line-of-communications troops. Shouldn't we pull back more of the Southern and Western Territories garrisons?"

Raj spread his hands. They were brown with sun, battered and nicked and callused from swords and reins, as out of place in this quiet elegant room as the man himself.

"That would take too long. Messers, Sole Autocrat, we don't have the *time.* Please understand, no matter what I do, the border area is going to get the worst working-over it's had in a century or more."

observe, Center said.

—and Colonial dragoons rode through a Borderer hamlet, tossing torches through the windows. Fire belched back, red flames and sooty smoke turning the whitewash black above the openings. Here and there a limestone lintel burned with white-hot fire as it sublimed.

—the last of a line of Arabs picked himself up off a woman and adjusted his robe. She lay motionless in the dust of the street, eyes empty, spittle running down from the corner of her mouth. The Colonial kicked her in the ribs, then called an order to the others. He had the crossed lines of a *naik*, a corporal, on the sleeve of his djellaba. Two of the troopers picked the woman up by the ankles and wrists, grunting at the limp dead weight. The naik jerked a thumb, and they dumped their semi-conscious victim head-first down the well.

—bursting charges spouted plumes of smoke and rock and pulverized dirt across the massive sloping front of the dam. It stretched two hundred meters across a U-shaped valley amid dry rocky hills, a stone-paved road on its top and stone and iron gates at one side where the tumbling water of the flume was channeled into a canal. For long moments nothing seemed to happen, and then water sprouted from the surface where the explosives had been laid. It gouted like erupting geysers, turning to rainbow splendor at the edges under the bright noon light. The sappers whooped and danced as the rushing torrent eroded the earthwork of the dam like a lump of sugar under a spout of hot tea. Then the earth shuddered as the dam collapsed in earnest, and the lake headed downstream in a roaring wall of brown silt and tumbling rocks.

"Yes, yes," Barholm said. The other advisors were silent as the two Descotters met each other's eyes.

"I think I can retrieve the situation," Raj said calmly. "Provided, of course, I have my Governor's full confidence. *Do* I have your confidence, my lord?"

Barholm's lips tightened. "Yes, yes," he said again. He snapped his fingers for a parchment, wrote, signed, extended his hand for the Gubernatorial seal. It thwacked into the purple wax with an angry sound.

He pushed it across the polished flamegrain wood of the table. Raj picked it up. It was a delegation of viceregal power, requiring all officers and officials of the Civil Government to tender him full cooperation—rare for a commander sent out into the *barbaricum*, unheard-of within the borders.

If I smash the Colonials, Raj thought—unlikely as that seemed right now—*that'll be the last strong opponent the Civil Government faces.* He'd reconquered the Southern and Western Territories; the Base Area was far away, and the Zanj states of the Southern Continent even farther. Once the Colony had been beaten back, Barholm Clerett's position would be safer than any Governor's in the past five hundred years. Safe enough that he would certainly no longer need a *heneralissimo supremo.*

"Yes," Barholm repeated. "Who could doubt that you have my *full* confidence?"

Raj stood, bowing and tucking the Gubernatorial Rescript into the sleeve-pocket of his uniform jacket.

"Then if you'll forgive me, Sovereign Mighty Lord, Messers."

His face held an abstracted frown as he left the room, ignoring the murmur behind him. Landing five thousand men and thirty guns, with all their dogs and stores, wasn't easy at the best of times. Getting them straight off the ships and headed east fast without a monumental foul-up would be real work.

disembarkation would be most efficiently achieved as follows, Center began.

CHAPTER FOUR

Corporal Minatelli clattered down the steep wooden steps into the hold of the freighter, his hobnail boots biting into the pinewood. The ship was pitching less now that the sails were furled and the steam tug was bringing it into port.

Minatelli shook his head, still a little bewildered at the sight. He'd grown up in Old Residence, in the Western Territories, and he was familiar enough with fine building. But Old Residence had shrunk steadily since the Brigade conquered it, with forest and groves and nobles' country-seats spreading over the old suburbs. These days it was just a big city.

East Residence was a *world*. It sprawled over the seven hills on all sides of its deep U-shaped harbor: houses and factories, up to the heights where gardens and marble marked the patricians' quarter and the Gubernatorial palaces. A haze of coal-smoke hung over it, a forest of masts and smokestacks darkened the water; squadrons of low-slung steam rams with their paddles churning the water, big-bellied merchantmen with grain from the Diva country of the far north, or ornamental stone and wine from Kelden, whole fleets of barges down from the Hemmar River. And all over the hills, the tracery of gaslight like fairy lights, still bright in the predawn hours.

He hoped he'd have time to see the great Star Temple that Governor Barholm had built. It was supposed to make the one in Old Residence look like a hut—and now, that seemed possible.

Minatelli's feet and body took him through the crowded hold of the troopship without more than an occasional jostle; after the cleaner air on deck, the stink of it hit him again. His eight-man section was waiting by their gear.

"What's t'word, corp?"

"We're heading east," Minatelli said.

His own Sponglish was fluent now, but it still carried the accent of the Spanjol more common in the Western Territories. He'd been recruited into the 24th Valencia when Messer Raj came to make war against the Brigade; before that his local priest in Old Residence had taught him his letters and numbers, which was one reason he'd made watch-stander and then corporal so fast. Most of the Civil Government's infantry were of peon stock, and almost all illiterate.

He made a quick check of the gear laid out on each of the straw pallets. Waterproof blanket, blanket, long sword-bayonet, cartridge pouches with seventy-five rounds, another fifty in a cardboard box, entrenching spade or short pick, mess tin, canteen, haversack, spare clothing if any, bandage packet, blessed chlorine powder for purifying water, three days' hardtack . . .

The corporal picked up one of the Armory rifles and stuck his thumb into the loop of the lever before the handgrip. A push and the block went *snick*, snapping down at the front so the grooved ramp on top led to the chamber. He peered down the barrel, raising it to the light. *No rust, not too much oil.* He snapped the lever back: *clack.* A pull on the trigger brought a sharp *click* as the pin fell on the empty space where a cartridge would lie in combat.

"Not too bad, Saynchez," Minatelli said. "Awright, git the kit on."

A chorus of grumbles. "Yor all gone soft," he said relentlessly. "Be off yor backsides soon."

He swung his own on. Webbing belt, pouches, shoulder-straps, haversack and bayonet went on like a coat; all you had to do was snap the buckle on the belt. Everything else went into the blanket roll; you rolled that up into a sausage, strapped the roll shut with leather thongs, then bent it into a U-shape and slung it over your left shoulder with the tied-together ends at your right hip. He grunted a little as it settled down, shrugging until it rode properly; you could wear blisters the size of a cup if you didn't adjust it just right.

An officer and bugler came down the main hatchway. The brassy notes of *Full Kit* and *Ready to Move Out* sounded, loud through the dim crowded spaces. The troops erupted in cursing, crowding movement, all but the most experienced veterans—*they'd* gotten ready beforehand. Minatelli grinned at his squad.

"Happy now?"

It was a lot easier to put your gear on when a couple of hundred others weren't trying to do the same, and that in a hold packed with temporary pinewood bunks.

Saynchez snorted. He was a grizzled man in his thirties, one of two in the squad who'd been out east with the 24th the last time. He'd also been up and down the ladder of rank to sergeant and back to private at least twice; it was drink, mostly.

"We goin' east fer garrison, er t'fight?" he asked.

"Messer Raj didn't tell me, t'last time he had me over fer afternoon *kave* n' cakes," Minatelli said dryly.

He wouldn't be looking forward to garrison duty, himself. Some preferred it; in between active campaigns Civil Government infantry

were assigned farms from the State's domains, with tenant families
to work them. You had to find your own keep from the proceeds, minus
stoppages for equipment. Provided your officers were honest—which
Major Felasquez was, thank the Spirit—the total came to about the
same as active-service cash pay. About what a laborer made, with more
security and less work. But it sounded *dull*, especially to a city boy
like him, and he hadn't joined up to be bored.

Mind you, some of the fighting in the Western Territories had
been more interesting than he really liked. He remembered the long
teeth of the Brigade curaissiers' dogs, the lanceheads rippling down,
sweat stinging his eyes, and the sun-hot metal of the rifle as he
brought it up to aim.

"Word is," he went on, relenting, "that t'wogboys is over the frontier.
Messer Raj's bein' set out to put 'em back."

Saynchez shaped a silent whistle. Minatelli looked at him hopefully; the far eastern frontier with the Colony was only a rumor to
him. Saynchez had been with the 24th when Messer Raj whipped the
ragheads and killed their king.

"Them's serious business," the older private said. "Them wogs is
na no joke."

"Messer Raj done whup 'em before," one of the other soldiers said.

"Serious," Saynchez said softly. "Real serious."

Minatelli slung his rifle. The bugle sounded again: *Fall in.*

A locomotive let out a high shrill scream from its steam whistle.
Its two man-high driving wheels spun, throwing twin streams of
sparks from the strap-iron rails beneath. The long funnel with its
bulbous crown belched steam and black smoke, thick and smelling of burnt tar. Behind it eight iron-and-wood cars lurched against
the chain fastenings that bound them together. They were heaped
with coal, and heavy. It took more wheel-spinning and lurching halts
before the train finally gathered way and rocked southward through
the city towards the Hemmar Valley and the long journey east.

Raj's hound Horace snarled slightly at the train. He ran a soothing
hand down the beast's neck, clamping his legs slightly around its
barrel. Other riders were having more trouble with their animals.
Hounds tended to have good nerves; it was one of their strong points.
They also tended to do exactly as they pleased whenever they felt
like it, but everything was tradeoffs. Horace moved forward at a
swinging walk, stepping high over the rails, his plate-sized paws
crunching on the cinder and crushed rock of the roadbeds.

More coal trains pulled out, building up the reserves at the stations farther east along the Central Rail; barges lay beside the dock,
heaped with the dusty black product of the Coast Range mines.
Other trains were making up, of slat-sided boxcars with *40 hombes/
8 dawg* freshly stenciled on their sides; forty men, or eight riding
dogs. The railyards sprawled along a good part of East Residence's

harbor. Barholm Clerett had built more kilometers of line than the previous ten Governors combined; whatever you said of him, he was a builder. Temples, forts, railways—the great Central Line from the capital to Sandoral completed at last—dams, canals. Much of it financed with the plunder from Raj's campaigns, and dug by captives from them.

It was a mild early-summer day, the sky blue except for a few puffs of high cloud, both moons up—Maxiluna was three-quarters full, Miniluna a narrow crescent. Like the one on the Colony's green banner, the crescent of Islam.

Raj shook his head at the thought. Beyond the moons were the Stars, and the Spirit of Man of the Stars.

Today there were more soldiers than railway men in the marshaling yard. Men heaved rectangular crates onto the bed of a railcar. Each had the Star of the Civil Government stenciled on its side, and *11mm 1000 rnds*. A group of artillerymen—they were stripped to their baggy maroon pants, but those had a crimson stripe down the outside of the leg—was manhandling a field gun onto the flatcar behind, heaving it up a ramp of planks and lashing the tall iron-shod wheels down to eyebolts on the deck. Oilcloth covers were strapped over the muzzle and breech, to keep dust and moisture out of the mechanism. Near-naked slaves with iron collars embossed with *Central Rail* were pulling in handcarts loaded with rations: hardtack, raisins, blocks of goat cheese, sacks of dried meat, barrels of salt fish. A farrier-sergeant of the 5th Descott came by leading a string of riding dogs on a chain lead snapped to their bridles; they surged away in wuffling alarm as a locomotive hooted, and the man clung until his feet were nearly off the ground.

"Pochita! Fequez! Ye bitches brood, quiet a'down, er I'll—*sorry, Messer Raj*—"

"Carry on, sergeant."

"—I'll skin yer lousy hides, *quiet* there."

The giant carnivores calmed, but their ears stayed back, and lips curled away from teeth as long as a man's finger. Few of the beasts had ever seen a steam engine before, much less ridden in a train. For that matter, few of the troopers had either, even the natives of the *Gubernio Civil*; most of them were countrymen, the cavalry from border areas or backwaters like Descott County. What the half-savage westerners he'd brought into the service thought of it, the Spirit only knew.

A platoon of infantry passed him, rifles at their right shoulders and blanket rolls over the left. He read their shoulder-flashes, and gave the officer a salute.

"Glad to have you with me again, 24th Valencia," he said. "That was good work you did at the siege of East Residence, and the pursuit."

The lieutenant at their head snapped out his sword and returned

the salute with a flourish. The men raised a deep shout of *Raj! Raj!*
Some others picked it up, until he waved them to silence. In the
relative quiet that followed, he heard a noncom cursing at a fatigue-
party:

"Didn't hear t' General tell ye t'stop workin', did ye? Move yer
butts! Put yer *backs* inta it."

*What with one thing and another, it's probably for the best there's
no time to address the men,* he thought mordantly.

A speech from the commander was customary before taking the
field, but the last thing he needed right now was the inevitable
spies—in East Residence they were even thicker than fleas and
almost as common as bureaucrats—giving a lurid description of
his troops crying him hail. Far too many Governors had started
out as popular generals; bought popularity more often than not,
but winning battles would do as well. It made any occupant of
the Chair suspicious, and usually more comfortable with mediocri-
ties holding the high military ranks.

He looked around at the bustling yard: chaotic, but things were
getting done.

"Good work, Muzzaf," he said to the man riding at his side.

The little Komarite looked up from his clipboard; there were dark
circles under his eyes. "A matter of times and distances, *solamnti,*"
he said. "No different from calculating tonnages or profit margins."
He grinned. "A pleasure working for a man who understands numbers, at that, my lord. Too few military nobles do."

Few nobles have Center advising them, Raj thought. Aloud: "I say
again, good work."

It was that: a formidable bit of organization. Railways had been
around for a long time now, but there had never been enough
of them, or enough uninterrupted kilometers of line, to move large
forces. He'd had enough to do managing the men; Muzzaf had
been invaluable once Raj explained the basic idea. This was going
to change warfare forever. Not that the railways were that much
faster than dogback yet, but they were untiring—and more
importantly, they could carry heavy supplies long distances at the
same speed as light cavalry, without draft beasts eating up their
loads or dying.

And it never hurt to acknowledge when a man did something
right, either. Another thing too many nobles did was simply snap
their fingers and expect things to fall into place. It was the engineers and administrators that made the Civil Government more than
another feudal pigsty.

Muzzaf grinned. "Half of it was your lady's labors," he said.
"Without her keeping the patricians off my back . . ." He shrugged
meaningfully.

Raj nodded. Suzette Whitehall had been born in East Residence,
to fifteen generations of city nobility. Nobody knew how to work

the system better. It was one of her manifold talents. *The wonder is she picked a hill-squireen like me,* he thought with a smile. He'd been nothing in particular then, just another land-poor Descotter nobleman making his way in the professionals like his fathers before him.

And where—

"My lady," he said.

She stood with the command group, but she turned quickly at the sound of his voice. Her smile was slight, but it warmed the slanted gray eyes; Horace crouched, and Raj stepped free of the stirrups and bent over her hand. She was in Court walking-out dress, lace skirt split at the front and pinned back to show embroidered leggings, mantilla, the works. It surprised him; he'd expected her traveling gear. Fatima was beside her, carrying a tray with a bottle of Kelden Sparkler and several long-stemmed glasses, each with half a strawberry on its ice-cooled rim.

He reached out a hand—not for the wine, it was too early for him—but for the fruit. She touched his fingers with her folded fan.

"That's ammunition, my knight," she said.

A party of officials was picking their way through the shouting chaos of soldiers and guns and dogs, heading his way. He recognized the Municipal Prefect of East Residence—the Governors didn't allow the city an *alcalle* of its own, knowing the fickleness of an East Residence mob—and he looked deeply unhappy. Raj braced himself.

"*More* time lost," he growled deep in his throat.

Suzette touched him on the arm. "A minute, darling," she said. "I expected this. That's Rahol Himentez, and he had a mob stone his townhouse when the coal ran out one winter. He's had a bee in his breeches about it ever since."

She swept off towards the dignitaries.

"—winter reserves," Raj could hear the Prefect bleating. "And the enemy's on the *Lower* Drangosh, not the Upper—"

But he stopped, and his flunkies with him, milling around as Suzette's soothing voice cut through the plaintive whine.

Beside him, Gerrin Staenbridge chuckled with admiration. "Cut off by the flying squadron, by the Spirit," he said. "Commandeered my mistress to do it, too."

One of the other officers laughed. "Small loss to you," he said. Staenbridge had an eye for handsome youths.

"Well, she *is* the mother of my heir," he pointed out, and cocked an eye toward the civil servants Suzette had intercepted. They were beginning to move back towards the headquarters building, in a sort of Brownian motion gently shepherded by the women.

Raj nodded curtly. "Right, gentlemen," he said to the circle of battalion commanders; most of them his Companions, all of them veterans. "Now, you've all got your maps?"

They did, although some of the ex-barbarians, Squadrones and Brigaderos, were looking at them a little dubiously. The Civil Government's cartographic service was one of a number of advantages it had had over the Military Governments. Unfortunately, the Colony's mapmakers were just as skillful.

"This campaign," he went on, meeting their eyes, "is what we've been training for these past five years."

"Conquering half the world was a *training exercise*?" Ludwig Bellamy blurted.

Raj nodded, with an expression a stranger might have mistaken for a smile. "No offense, Messers, but we're not fighting barbarians this time. If we hold out a sausage grinder, they're not going to scratch their heads, mutter and then obligingly ram their dicks into it while we turn the crank.

"These are disciplined troops with first-rate equipment, operating closer to their base of supplies than we will be. And they have a first-rate commander; Tewfik ibn'Jamal is nobody's fool. I've fought him twice; lost one, won one—and the time I won, Tewfik had his father Jamal looking over his shoulder and jogging his elbow. Jamal was no commander."

Gerrin nodded. "This time he's got Ali along," he pointed out. His square, handsome face was dark olive, more typical of Descott than Raj's, who had a grandmother from Kelden County in the northwest. "Ali's not only no commander, by all accounts he's a raving bloody lunatic."

"That's our only advantage, and we'll need it. Messers, no mistakes this time. We move fast, and we hit like a hammer. Gerrin, detail two hundred of the 5th to me, and I'll take them ahead on the first train. You'll be rearguard here and come in on the last with the remainder of the battalion."

He held up a hand when the other man began to protest. "I need someone here I can trust to see the plan carried out, Colonel."

"We also serve who only stay and chivvy bureaucrats," Staenbridge said.

"Ludwig," Raj went on. "We're short of rolling stock. I'm giving you the 1st and 2nd Mounted Cruisers" —the former Squadron troops— "and the 3/591, 4/591 and 5/591" —all Brigaderos from the Western Territories— "and you'll follow on dogback. Entrain your baggage, commandeer what remounts you need from the Residence Area pens, and keep to the line of rail. You can pick up supplies at the railstops; nothing on the men but their weapons and personal gear. Understood?"

Ludwig Bellamy slapped one gauntleted fist into the other. "*Ci, mi heneral*," he said, his Sponglish as pure as a native Civil Government officer; it even had a hint of a Descott Country rasp.

Nobody would mistake him for an Easterner, though. He stood a finger over Raj's 190 centimeters, and the hair cut in an Army bowl crop was yellow-blond. He'd been the son of a Squadron noble, one who surrendered to Raj to keep his lands. Ludwig had been part of the deal, a hostage for his father's good behavior. He was far more than that now. The man beside him was like enough to be his brother, and was his cousin-in-law; Teodore Welf, former second-in-command of the Brigade.

He tapped his fingers on his sword-hilt; unlike his kinsman by marriage, he kept the shoulder-length hair of a Military Government officer, and wore the basket-hilted longsword of the Brigade rather than an Easterner's saber.

"Good thinking, *mi heneral*," he said. "Some of the men . . ." He shrugged at the shrieking locomotives around them. "Well, they're not used to these modern refinements."

"True, Major Welf," Raj said. *Meaning*, he thought, *that steam engines scare them spitless.* They probably thought they were captive demons. "It'll toughen them up, too. See that they get in some drill with their Armory rifles, Ludwig."

Bellamy tossed his chin upward slightly in affirmation; with a slight start, Raj recognized the gesture as one of his own. *How times change.*

"The Brigaderos can use some hard marching," Ludwig Bellamy said judiciously. Welf shrugged unwilling agreement. "They're good shots and good riders, but a bit soft in the arse."

For that matter, there were plenty of officers in the Civil Government's armies who wouldn't dream of campaigning without half a dozen servants and a wagonload of luxuries.

Not the ones who went to war with Raj Whitehall, though.

"So." Raj turned to the other commanders. "Jorg, you and Ferdihando will bring the 17th Kelden Foot and the 24th Valencia on the next series of trains, right after me and my detachment of the 5th."

Jorg Menyez was a slender balding man, with receding brownish hair and mild blue eyes, red-rimmed as usual. He was violently allergic to dogs, the reason he'd gone into the low-prestige infantry service.

"Infantry first?" he said in mild surprise. He'd shown what foot soldiers could do if properly trained and led, but it was still odd.

"I need reliable men in Sandoral right away," Raj said. "Osterville's in charge there. Dogs aren't the most urgent priority, where dealing with Osterville's the problem."

There were a few snickers. Osterville had been sent to take over in the Southern Territories after the reconquest, when Raj was recalled in not-quite-disgrace. The command of the Fortress and District of Sandoral was quite a comedown. None of the officers who'd been with Raj had supported Osterville, for all that he was one of Barholm's Guards; that was one reason he'd lost the political struggle with Mihwel Berg of the Administrative Service. None of it was likely to make him kindly-disposed toward the *Heneralissimo Supremo.*

Menyez sneezed thoughtfully into a handkerchief. "He's supposed to have twenty thousand men there," he said. "I doubt there's half that fit for duty." Osterville would be drawing the pay of the vacant ranks; it was a common enough scam, if not on quite that scale.

"Five thousand if we're lucky, but that's more than enough to make trouble if Osterville's a mind to," Raj said. *Insane to make trouble with the Colonials over the border,* he thought absently—but he'd seen what jealousy could do to a man's mind. "Which is why I want your riflemen in place."

"*Si, mi heneral.*" Menyez frowned. "How *did* Berg manage to get Osterville canned from that post? Berg's not a bad sort, for a pen-pusher, but Osterville was one of Barholm's Guards, after all."

Raj shrugged. "He's pretty sure I did it," he said. "Spirit knows why. In any case, we'll cross Messer Osterville when we come to him. Movement: after Colonel Menyez, the remainder of the cavalry," he went on, listing the battalions. "Any questions?"

Kaltin Gruder, the commander of the 7th Descott Rangers, shrugged his heavy shoulders. Pale scars stood out against the olive tan of his face.

"*No problemo, mi heneral,*" he said. "Thrashing the wogboys has its attractions; the looting's good and I like the smell of harem girls."

Raj clenched his teeth for a moment. There were times when the task of restoring civilization on Bellevue was like pushing a boulder up a greased slope. Gruder was a professional; he wasn't supposed to be thinking like a MilGov barbarian noble or an enlisted man . . . then he caught the grin and answered it.

I talk to Center too much, he thought. *Angels have no sense of humor, it seems.*

The cool irony that touched the back of his mind was wordless, but it communicated none the less.

"Colonel Dinnalsyn, you'll space the guns out between the battalions. One last thing: we've a new issue of splatguns." There were exclamations of delight; the rapid-fire multibarreled guns were the first new weapon the Civil Government had adopted in a hundred twenty years. Raj had had them run up in the Kolobassian armories on his own authority—to Center's designs.

"Four per battalion. Remember they're infantry weapons, not guns; push them forward, and we'll give the Colonials some of the grief their repeaters and pom-poms do to us. If that's all, then, we'll get under way."

The Companions slapped fists in a pyramid of arms. "Hell or plunder, dog-brothers."

Gerrin Staenbridge watched the tall figure of the General ride away. "As I remember it, wasn't Lady Anne Clerett the one who dropped a word about Osterville in our Sovereign Mighty Lord's ear? I wonder who talked to *her*?"

They all looked in Suzette's direction. Staenbridge grinned. "Behind every great man . . ." he quoted.

"You know, Messers," he went on, drawing on his gauntlets, "I was with Messer Raj back when he took command of the 5th in the El Djem business, south of Komar. Only five years . . . and that one man has changed the world—and changed himself."

"Haven't we all," Kaltin Gruder said, touching the long scars on his face. The Colonist shrapnel that had carved those furrows had killed his younger brother, on Raj Whitehall's first independent campaign. "Haven't we all."

CHAPTER FIVE

"Damned hot," Tejan M'Brust said, using an end of his neckerchief to wipe his face.

"No shit," Ludwig Bellamy replied.

He reined aside to the verge of the road, his dog stepping wearily over the ditch and hanging its head, panting, under the shade of a plane tree.

The troopers' dogs were panting too, a massed sound like hundreds of wheezing bellows as they rode by in column of fours. A knee-high fog of dust rose from the crushed rock surface of the road; he sneezed and hawked and spat to one side. The Descotter followed suit and offered him a canteen, water with vinegar. It cut the gummy saliva and dust nicely. Bellamy drank and watched the 1st and 2nd Mounted Cruisers go by, the dogs at a fast ambling walk. Both units were under strength—they'd paid a substantial butcher's bill in the Western Territories and hadn't had time to recruit back to full roster yet—but they shaped well, to his critical eye. A few were even talking or joking as they rode, though most slumped a little, reins in one hand and eyes fixed on the rump of the dog ahead. The unit dressing was crisp, though.

"They're shaping better than the Brigaderos," M'Brust said, echoing his thought. "I don't think there's a regular cavalry unit better, my oath I don't. Not even the 5th Descott."

Ludwig nodded, grinning tiredly. His people, the Squadron, were accounted wilder than the Brigade; they'd come down from the Base Area later, and the Southern Territories they'd conquered had been a backwater. But these battalions had been longer under Messer Raj's discipline and were first-rate material to begin with, once they had childish notions about charging with cold steel knocked out of them.

For a moment the skin between his shoulders crawled, as he remembered the Squadron host advancing into volley-fire and massed artillery. The chanting, the waving banners, the sun bright on a hundred thousand swords . . . and Raj Whitehall waiting, his men a thin blue line looking as fragile and ordered as a snowflake by comparison. Waiting, then raising his sword and chopping it downward. . . .

He shook it off, removed his helmet and let the air dry his sweat-damp hair. To their left the land rose in rocky hills, dry and shimmering with heat in the summer sun. To the right were gentle slopes, citrus orchards, and then open grain-fields with peons bending over their sickles as they reaped. The dusty yellow of the wheat was like flashes of gold through the glossy green leaves of the fruit trees. More to the point, between road and orchards passed a rock-lined irrigation channel, and a slow current of water. It was dry and intensely hot here in the southern foothills of the Oxheads—the land was sloping down toward the sand deserts of the borderlands—and the sight and sound of the water was intoxicating. He squinted at the sun, then remembered to take out his watch and click open the cover; in the Southern Territories, even wealthy nobles hadn't carried them. There was no point; nobody needed to know the time that precisely, and they were impossible to keep repaired, anyway.

Civilization. "Benter," he said to the younger brother who was his aide. "Twenty minutes. Water the dogs."

He turned and heeled his dog westwards down the line of march; behind him the cool brassy notes of the trumpet sounded, and the signalers of each company passed it back. When it reached the rear of the column the last unit halted first—you had to do it that way, or the whole mass would collide with each other, like a drunken centipede. His lips quirked at the memory of his father trying to halt a mass of Squadron warriors on the move, back when he was a boy. *That* had taken the better part of an hour, even with the paid, full-time fighters of the household guard.

The three Cruiser battalions of ex-Brigaderos were full strength . . . except for their stragglers. Teodore Welf rode up, red in the face from the heat and from embarrassment.

"Major Bellamy," he said, saluting.

"Major Welf," Ludwig replied, glancing past him.

They spoke Sponglish, although the Squadron and Brigade dialects of Namerique were fairly close: regulations, and it was best to stay in the habit, since more than half the officers in their units were seconded Civil Government natives like M'Brust.

Men and dogs had collapsed in the road. Others were leading their animals from the wayside to the ditch, walking slowly with their legs straddled. A few had trotted over despite their saddle sores and lay with their heads and shoulders buried in the life-giving coolness. Ludwig frowned and jerked his head toward them.

Teodore cursed and drew his sword, spurring to the ditch. "Up and out of there, you slugs!" he shouted. The flat of the weapon whacked down on shoulders. "Purify it first, damn your arse! You can't fight with the runs!"

The soldiers stood, dripping. Officers rode up, as dust-caked as their men, and the troopers formed lines. Some led the dogs downstream; others scooped their canteens full and added the blessed purifying chlorine powder; it was a rite shared by the Spirit of Man of This Earth cult they followed and the Star Church of the Civil Government, but not all commanders were equally pious. Messer Raj insisted on the full canonical treatment—water for human drinking to be purified by powder or by ten minutes at a hard rolling boil, with no exceptions.

The Spirit favored him for it, too. It wasn't uncommon for armies in the field to lose five men to dysentery for every one killed in combat. That didn't happen to troops under Raj's command.

Welf trotted back. "Sorry, Ludwig," he said. "The Western Territories aren't this hot."

Ludwig nodded. The Western Territories were damned cold and rainy, to his way of thinking—his own ancestors had plowed through them on their way to the southern side of the Midworld Sea, and he was glad of it. Of course, even the Western Territories were warm and dry compared to the Base Area, which explained why the Brigade had stopped there; they'd been the first of the Military Governments to pull up stakes and move south.

"And your fine gentlemen aren't used to sweating this hard," he replied, smiling to take the sting out of it.

"True enough," Welf said. He flexed the arm that had been broken by a Civil Government bullet outside Old Residence, nearly two years ago. "I'd never have dared drive them this hard, back . . . well, back then."

Ludwig nodded. Even the troopers had been nobles of a sort back home, with a few hundred hectares and peons to do the work. Of course, that had its compensations: plenty of leisure to practice and hunt. So they were fine riders, and mostly good shots. The Brigade had armed its men with muzzle loaders, but rifled percussion muskets, not the flintlock smoothbores that had been the best his people could make or maintain.

"How's my fair cousin?" Teodore went on.

"Marie? Still pregnant, according to the last letter," Ludwig said. "Thank the Spirit. Otherwise she'd be trying to outdo Messa Whitehall and riding with us."

Teodore shuddered elaborately. He turned to watch a dog-cart creak up, loaded with sunstruck Cruisers, their dogs on leading-ropes behind. "Throw some water on those!" he ordered.

Ludwig put his helmet back on. The leather-backed chainmail of the pentail thumped on his neck, and sweat from the sponge-and-cork lining ran into his hair and down his cheeks, greasy and stale.

"I'm beginning to wish we'd taken the train," he said.

"Getting there's half the fun," Teodore replied, blinking red-rimmed blue eyes.

A trainload of artillery began to pull out of the East Residence station, guns and men riding on flatcars, the draft dogs in boxcars farther back from the engine. As soon as it cleared the switchpoint, the remainder of the 5th Descott jogged forward, breaking into platoons as they swarmed into the last two trains.

"*Alo sinstra, waymanos!*" *By the left, forward march.* Ten minutes, and the final platoon was loaded into its boxcar.

Gerrin Staenbridge looked around. "The last?" he said.

Muzzaf Kerpatik looked just as exhausted as he did. "The very last, *mi colonel,*" he said.

Staenbridge ran a hand over his chin, the sword-calluses rasping against the blueblack stubble. "Hard to believe." *Sleep. Razors. Food.* He didn't believe in those anymore, either.

Some sort of Palace flunky-in-uniform was wading toward him over the tracks and the litter of the three-day emergency. They'd been operating in battle mode: throw anything that breaks or isn't needed out of the way and think about cleaning up later. That included a fair bit of broken-down rolling stock, as well as dead dogs, dead draft oxen, about fifty tons of coal that had spilled in odd spots and wasn't worth the time and effort of collecting, and spare gear. Central Rail stevedore-slaves, dockworkers, and press-ganged clerks lay about in various stages of collapse.

But no soldiers. Every man, dog, gun, and round of ammunition was on its way east. *Spirit of man, I could sleep for a week.*

If that flunky meant what he thought it did—another message from some hysterical fool in the Palace who wanted his hand held—he'd be *talking* for a week. The people up on the First Hill hadn't grown any less terrified of Ali over the last couple of days, and they were still given to brainstorms, most of which started and ended with keeping more troops around to protect their own precious personal fundaments. If he'd wanted to listen to bleating, he would have stayed at home on the family estate and herded sheep.

"See you in Sandoral," he said to the little Komarite, and ran for the second train.

It was moving as he clamped his saber hand on an iron bracket and swung up onto the rear platform. This car had been tacked on at the last minute; it was the type used to carry railroad company guards through bandit country, with bunks and a cookstove inside. He'd found it parked on a siding, and be damned if he wasn't going to keep it all to himself; that way he'd stand some chance of getting a little sleep in the fifty hours or so it would take to get to Sandoral. There was some hardtack and dried sausage in his duffel—

The smell of curry startled him as he opened the rear door of the guardcar; his stomach growled a reminder of how long it had been since he ate. Fatima cor Staenbridge—the *cor* meant freedwoman— glanced around from the little stove.

"Ready in a minute, Gerrin," she said.

He opened his mouth to roar, thought better of it, and sat down, sighing and unbuckling his sword belt. *My own damned fault.* He'd rescued the girl during the sack of El Djem more or less on impulse; rather, she'd picked Bartin Foley to rescue her from a gang of Descotter troopers bent on gang rape, and he'd helped out. He'd *kept* her on impulse, too; Bartin had needed some experience with women—a nobleman had to marry and carry on his line eventu- ally, whatever his personal tastes. She'd managed to keep up in the nightmare retreat through the desert, after Tewfik mousetrapped them, which demanded some respect; she'd also gotten pregnant—whether by him or Bartin was a moot point and no matter—which was more than the wife he visited once a year for duty's sake had managed to do.

"Imp," he said.

She stuck out her tongue at him and handed him the plate. *Spirit, she's still only twenty.* He'd freed her, of course, and acknowledged the child—two, now—his wife hadn't objected at all, since by Civil Government law he could divorce her for not giving him an heir. The children had to stay with her back on the estate most of the time after they were weaned, of course, as was fitting.

He began shoveling down the fiery curry, washing it down with water and a surprisingly drinkable red. Drinkable compared to ration issue, that was. *And to think I was accounted a gourmet once,* he thought. Polo, hunting, balls, theater, fine uniforms and parades and good restaurants, handsome youths, witty conversation . . . surprising how little he'd missed them, in the five years since Raj Whitehall had been given command of the 5th Descott and sent out to teach the wogs not to raid the Civil Government borders.

I resented him then, he mused. Gerrin had been senior . . . but he'd needed a commander to bring out his best. A furious perfection of willpower possessed Raj; Gerrin could recognize it without in the least desiring to have it himself. *And it's never been boring.* Back then, he'd been so bored he'd fiddled the battalion accounts out of sheer ennui.

He finished the plate. Fatima was sitting on the edge of the bunk, eyes demurely cast down; a good imitation of humility. *What an actress. The stage lost something when she was born Colonial.* Natural talent, he supposed, plus being hand-in-glove with Suzette Whitehall in her impressionable years.

Gerrin sighed again. As far as he was concerned, sex with women was like eating plain boiled rice without butter or salt—possible, but . . . *On the other hand.* A soldier learned to make do with what

was at hand; when all you had was boiled rice, that was what
you ate.

The mournful sound of the locomotive whistle echoed through
the night. It was evening, and twilight was falling over the rolling
hills of the Upper Hemmar River. To their right the last sunlight
glittered on the surface of the river below, like a ribbon of hammered silver tracing its way through the darkening fields. The same
light caught the three-meter wings of a pterosauroid as it soared
over the water, gilding the naked skin and the short plush white
fur of its body. Higher, the hills were dusty-green with olive trees,
or carpeted with vines in their summer lushness. Terraced fields of
barley were brown-gold on the lower slopes; cypresses and eucalyptus lined the dusty white streaks of roadway and surrounded the
whitewashed adobe of villas.

Raj looked up from the maps. Center could provide better, holographic projections with all the information you needed, but he'd
been raised with paper and it still had something the visions lacked.
His father had taught him to read maps, going around Hillchapel—
the Whitehall family estate, back in Smythe Parish, Descott County—
with compass and the Ordinance Survey, until he learned to see the
ground and the markings as one.

"*Sentahvo* for your thoughts, my heart," Suzette said.

She had her *gittar* in her lap, gently plucking at the strings.

"Thinking about Descott, and Hillchapel," Raj said. "Damn, but
it's been a long time since we've seen it."

Suzette nodded. She'd fitted in surprisingly well; if she considered
it a bleak stone barn in the middle of a wilderness, she'd never said
so. Well, compared to East Residence, that was what it was; a kerosene lamp was a luxury, in Descott. Most of the County was upland
volcanic wilderness, thin forest and thinner stony pasture where you
needed ten hectares to feed a sheep. Bandit country too, and bad for
killer sauroids.

He missed it.

"This is as domestic as we get, I'm afraid," Suzette said lightly.

Raj glanced around the railroad car. It had been fitted with table
and chairs; there was a commode behind a blanket screen, a couple
of skins of wine-and-water hanging from the wall, a lantern overhead,
and a box of field rations—Suzette's version, and a vast improvement
on Army issue. One of his aides was snoring on the floor.

In a car behind, the troopers were singing—they probably thought
of it as singing, at least—in a roaring chorus:

> "We're marchin' on relief over burnin' desert sands
> Six hundred fightin' Descotters, t' Colonel, an' t'band
> Ho! Git awa', ye bullock-man—ye've heard t'bugle blowed
> The Fightin' Fifth is comin', down the Drangosh Road—"

"We're luckier than they are," Suzette said, lifting her head and looking off into the gathering night. "We're together, at least. . . . Their women have to sit and wonder. And every time someone rides up to the farmhouse door it might be a messenger with a bundled rifle and saber that's all they'll see of a lost husband, or a son."

"It's not much of a married life I've given you," Raj said.

Suzette smiled at him. "I wouldn't exchange it for any other," she replied. "I don't think you're one of those who're allowed to have a normal life, anyway."

"Not yet, at least," Raj said. *Never,* went unspoken between them.

It wasn't as if Barholm would give Raj an honored retirement, even, as a reward for victory.

i have found it unwise to use the term never, Center said.

Suzette's fingers strummed the *gittar* again. Raj pulled the greatcoat around his shoulders and let his head fall back. *Just a moment,* he thought. *A moment's rest.*

"*Git* yer arses out offen t'floor," the sergeant barked. "We'll be there anytimes."

Corporal Robbi M'Telgez blinked awake.

"Jist when I waz gittin' t'hang a sleepin' on these things," he said mournfully, picking straw out of his hair and yawning in the hot close darkness of the boxcar, thick with the smell of sweat.

The train was slowing, swaying more from side to side. All around was the flat irrigated plain of the Upper Drangosh. M'Telgez put his eye to the slats in the boxcar; it was good-looking country, dry but fit to sprout shoelaces where there was water. The wheat and barley were in, the fields being plowed for a summer crop of corn or millet; cotton and sugarcane and indigo were all well up, and there were orchards in plenty as well, mostly dates and citrus.

Good land fer the gentry, hell on farmers, he thought idly. Rich land meant poor men to work it; they'd all be peons around here. *Hotter n' blazes, too.*

They passed through a belt of country places, retreats for rich cityfolk built in an open, airy style that looked indecent somehow compared with the foursquare solidity of the houses he was accustomed to—but then, Descott was a long way north of this, and highland country too. He didn't suppose it got cold here even in winter. Then there were shanties on both sides of the rail line, crude booths of straw and reeds. He swore softly when he saw who was in them, besides refugee peasants from the countryside. Among them were men in Civil Government uniforms, only infantry, but still . . . they looked *hungry.*

"Ain't they supposed to pay 'em when they calls 'em in from t'farms?" he said.

The troop sergeant laughed sourly. "Wuz ye born yesstiday, M'Telgez?"

Trooper Smeet put his eye to a crack. "Good's a place t' croak as any," he said mournfully. "We'll a' git kilt, ye know. I hadda dream—"

The rest of the platoon threw bits of hardtack and cold bacon-rind and anything else handy.

"Ye keep sayin' thayt long 'nuff, it'll happen, yer bastid," M'Telgez said disgustedly.

Smeet grinned; he was missing his two front teeth, and his face was a brown wrinkled map of twenty years' service. "Ye knows a way 't live ferever, loik?"

Just inside the city walls the train screeched to a stop; he braced himself against the planking and shaded his eyes as the doors were thrown open.

"*Come* on," the sergeant yelled again.

The boxcars emptied rapidly, the men stretching, the dogs barking with hysterical relief. It was just as hot outside, with the dry baking heat that he remembered from the first campaign down here five years ago, but at least you could breathe in the open. M'Telgez unsnapped the lead-chain of his mount and spent a moment soothing her.

"Sooo, quiet now, Pochita, ye bitch," he said. A tongue the size of a washcloth and rough as industrial abrasive lapped at his face. "Quiet—down, girl."

Out of the corner of his eye he could see Messer Raj and the company commander and the captain in charge of the Scouts—M'lewis and his Forty Thieves were along, best to double-strap your pouch—talking earnestly. He worked faster, sliding his rifle into the scabbard at the right front of his saddle, tightening the girth and breast-straps, checking the neck-bandolier and the fastening on the saber hanging from the other side. He slid the blade free a handspan and tested the edge, then checked the loads on the revolver he had tucked into one boot-top.

Messer Raj would have a job of work for them to do, and no mistake. He'd been in the 5th Descott for five years now, and that was one thing you could rely on.

"Nice to be loved," Bartin Foley said.

"Not when they get in the way," Raj replied.

They rode at the head of the column, slowly. Cheering civilians packed the sidewalks, hysteria in their voices. Rose petals and rice showered down on the troops, as if they were a party of grooms-men bringing a bride home from her father's house. Individuals darted out to offer bottles of wine to the soldiers or, even more danger-ous, food to the dogs. *What do they think's going to happen when they stick a roast in a war-dog's face?* Raj thought, turning in the saddle to see one of the crowd reeling back and clutching a gashed-open forearm. The crowd-stink was as palpable as the blurring waves of heat that radiated back from the whitewashed adobe of the buildings and soaked the uniform coat beneath his armpits.

The noise was spooking *all* the dogs, a solid roar between the whitewashed, blank-walled, flat-roofed houses.

"Trumpeter!" Raj snarled. "Sound *Draw.*"

The sharp notes cut through the white-noise background of the crowd, as they were designed to cut through the clamor of battle. Two hundred hands slapped down on the saber hilts slung to the offside of their saddles; two hundred blades came free in a single slithering rasp, then flashed as they were brought back to rest over the shoulder. The dogs knew the calls as well as the men, and they snarled in unison, a chilling bass rumble. Long wet fangs glistened, each backed by half a ton of carnivore. War-dogs were bred for aggressiveness and trained to kill, and the bristling snake-headed posture of these indicated they were perfectly ready to do just that.

The crowd screamed and surged away; there would be deaths in the trampling . . . but not nearly as many as there would be if Ali sacked the city, which was what was going to happen if they kept getting in his way. Overhead, doors slammed shut as the wrought-iron balconies emptied. Raj heeled Horace into a trot; the bugler signaled again, and the whole column rocked into motion behind him. The iron wheels of the splatgun battery clattered behind them.

"Well, that'll make us less popular, *mi heneral,*" Bartin said.

"Popularity be damned," Raj replied, feeling some of the tension drain out of his shoulders.

They broke into the *Plaza Real*, the square that formed the center of all Civil Government cities. The usual buildings fronted it: the Star Temple with its gilded dome, the arcaded Government House, the townhouses of wealthy landowners and merchants . . . and the cavalry barracks, conveniently to hand in case of trouble. Highly unusual were the tents and shanties that had gone up all over the square, crowding right up to the ornamental fountain and gardens in its center; the sour smoke of their cooking fires lingered, and the stink of an overloaded sewer system.

"Refugees," Raj said grimly. "Must be fifty or sixty thousand of them inside the walls."

"Sandoral has fifty thousand people in normal times," Suzette said. "With that many more . . ."

Raj nodded. "We'll definitely have to do something about that."

They drew rein before the barracks, a series of two-story buildings connected by walls and iron-grille gates, enclosing a central parade ground. They smelled even worse than the rest of the city, not just the inevitable aroma of dogshit that was inescapable where cavalry were stationed, but the fetid stink of overcrowding and neglect. They *looked* neglected—gates awry, stucco flaking in damp patches from the walls. But with the units as under strength as his intelligence had it, they shouldn't be crowded—and washing was hanging from the windows, women and children too numerous for camp followers leaning out and pointing, or lounging in the doorways.

"Captain Foley," Raj said. "Dismount the men, rifles, and a watchstander and troop here. Then accompany me, if you please."

The bugle sang. The men sheathed their sabers and pulled the Armory rifles out of the scabbards. Another call, and the dogs sank to a crouch; the men stepped free of the stirrups and bent to loop their reins over the hitching rail and watering trough that lined the plaza side of the garrison buildings. A long clicking sounded as they loaded their weapons; the 5th Descott didn't carry guns for show, and when they made a threat they meant it.

An officer came out of the main gate, fastening his sword belt. Raj ran an eye over him: thirty or so, but with an older man's belly straining against the sash and belt, unshaven, the blue uniform coat stained under the armpits. He didn't expect soldiers to waste time trying to look strack in the field, but in garrison keeping neat reminded them that they *were* soldiers; it was a sign of self-respect. They had running water here, for the Spirit's sake! And every eight-man section of cavalry troopers was allowed one soldier's servant to handle routine fatigues.

Also an officer should set an example.

Just about what I expected, in short, Raj thought, a cold anger tightening its hand under his breastbone. He returned the stranger's salute.

"Captain Hamelio Pinochet, 47th Santanner Dragoons," the man said.

"*Heneralissimo* Raj Whitehall," Raj replied. "I'm here to take command, Captain."

The unfortunate officer swallowed, attempting to brace to attention. "Ah, *mi heneral,* you'll understand, with the emergency and the refugees—"

"I understand perfectly, Captain." With housing at a premium, somebody had seen the profit potential in renting out the military's spare space. "Lead on."

Milling civilians looked at them curiously as they walked through the long barracks halls; each had space for a hundred men's cots, with rooms for the lieutenants and a suite for the company commander, plus a ready room and mess. Right now they were crowded with twice that number or more of refugees; from their clothes, well enough off to be making a fortune for whoever was running this scam. A swelling murmur ran through them as Raj passed. By the time they reached the buildings still in military use, it had preceded them a little; enough for protesting feminine squeals to be fading as women were hustled out of the barracks, and for the soldiers to have made emergency repairs. Not *much* in the way of repairs. Gear was piled in heaps all over the floors, few of the men were in full uniform, and there were still cards and dice lying in some corners. The troopers stood braced at the foot of their cots, visibly willing their vital functions to cease.

Raj ignored them for a moment. Instead he stripped a rifle out of the rack by the locker at the head of a cot and worked the action. "No rust here, at least," he said mildly. Then:

"Captain Pinochet, how many men are on muster here? You're rated at four battalions." Twenty-four hundred men or so, in theory.

"Ah . . . about one thousand, sir. Most of the officers aren't, ah . . ."

"Present at the moment, yes," Raj said. "Fall the men in, if you please, Captain."

Raj crossed his arms and waited while the bugles rang. It took a very long time for the garrison troops to sort out their equipment. *Starless Dark knows what shape the infantry's in,* he thought with a mental wince. This was the elite cavalry.

"Ten'*hut.*"

The noncom's bark brought the men to a ragged attention as Raj strode out; the banner of the 5th Descott was at his back, and his personal blazon. The two companies of the 5th tramped out at the double, and fell in at his back with the smooth economy of end- less practice, the uniform crash of their hobnails sounding across the drillground and echoing back from the barracks and stables that ringed it.

Raj waited for a minute. "Men," he said at last, "I'm going to keep this short and sweet."

He pointed over his shoulder. "There's a bloody great wog army coming up the Drangosh; they're about five days' march that way. I've got troops coming in from the west, but we're going to need every man who can ride and shoot. That means *you.* Every soldier, that is. I'll be back in a few hours, and I expect to see you look- ing and acting like soldiers by then." He paused again.

"Captain Pinochet, please send runners to the remaining battal- ion officers of this command. You may inform them that any man holding the Governor's commission not present when I return may consider himself dismissed from the service." He turned his head to the bugler. "Sound *dismissed to quarters.*"

The garrison left much more quickly than they'd assembled. Raj nodded once, tapping a thumb against his chin. "I think they're getting the message," he said. "Now for Osterville."

Antin M'lewis was muttering under his breath. Raj knew the song without needing to hear words or tunes: it was an old Army ditty whose chorus went *Lovely loot/That's the thing makes the boys git up an' shoot!*

Commandant Osterville's house was a looter's dream. The outer gates were gilded wrought iron, the inner Zanj ebony studded with miniature silver sauroid heads. A chandelier of Kolobassian crystal hung overhead, to light the three-story atrium. Floor and sweeping staircases were of marble; the walls held gilt-framed mirrors and paintings; man-high alabaster urns held trailing bougainvillea . . . Punkahs swayed, moving air cooled by fountains playing over fretted stone and scented by orange-blossom.

The majordomo bowed himself out of the way—a plump eunuch with a Colonial accent. *Poor bastard can't help it,* Raj thought; but they always put his teeth on edge. Osterville had put on weight and lost a lot of hair since Raj had seen him last. He'd always been ambitious, and Capital-smooth; now he had a sour pinch to his mouth and lines between there and his nostrils. Which were turned up as if at a bad smell. There was a crowd of hangers-on by him, aides and flunkies and the battalion commanders of the garrison.

"Whitehall," Osterville said frigidly. "What the devil do you think you're doing, coming in here and giving orders outside the chain of command?"

There was a murmur of indignation from the flunkies; but the battalion commanders stayed stony-silent, with a slight unconscious withdrawal, as if Osterville had something contagious. Raj gave them a swift glance. None of them had been living on their pay here— not with Osterville's example before them, not if Abdullah's reports were true—but they didn't love the Commandant for it. Especially not now that their careers and lives were on the line.

Raj reached into his jacket. "Commandant Osterville. By Gubernatorial Rescript, I have been given command of all Civil Government troops in this area. I hereby notify you that I am assuming control."

Osterville read through the note. "I acknowledge your overall authority," he said after a moment.

Raj could see the wheels turning behind the narrow black eyes. *Whitehall's in disfavor. Even if he wins, he'll be removed.*

"But this document does *not* give you authority to interfere in the internal command structure of the units under my authority as district commandant. You may give your orders to me, and I will carry them out as I see fit."

Divided command . . . Behind Raj, the Scout Troop—the Forty Thieves—tensed; they hadn't followed the exchange, not really, but they could read the hostility in the air well enough.

M'lewis had recruited the Scouts himself. None of them were men likely to hesitate if ordered to arrest the Commandant . . . or to take him and the others out back and shoot them, if it came to that. Osterville looked past Raj and his complexion turned a muddy gray.

Disaster, Raj knew. A good chance of a firefight right here in the city, or at least wholesale passive resistance by the garrison troops. This mission balanced on a knife edge as it was . . .

. . . and Osterville wouldn't back down. Not openly; whatever else the man was, he wasn't that type of coward.

Suzette moved forward. "Hernan, Hernan," she said, tapping him on the arm with her fan. "Last time I was in Sandoral there were more interesting things than a lot of smelly soldiers." She wrinkled her nose. "Don't tell me you've become a *complete* provincial out here, my dear. And you were such a gay blade back in the City." When someone in the Civil Government put a capital on it that way, only one city could be meant.

Osterville bowed over her hand.

"*I've* been trapped on a troop train for three days. Couldn't you find a decent meal for a poor, benighted gentlewoman so far from home? And fill me in on what passes for society out here? *And* find me a decent bath and somewhere to change out of these *impossible* clothes?"

Osterville was giving a good impression of a man who had just been struck between the eyes with a bag full of wet sand, but he rallied; after all, he *had* been at Court for the better part of a decade.

"Enchanted, Messa," he said suavely. "Business, however . . ."

Suzette made a dismissive gesture. "Oh, Raj just wants some help unloading trains." She tucked her hand under his arm. "Please?"

Osterville snapped his fingers at an aide. "Luiz, draw that up; here, I'll sign it. Certainly, certainly, my dear Messa Suzette . . . trains, you say? Logistics, clerks' work."

Raj stood silently as they strolled away across the intaglio floor. His head moved back to the officers who'd been attending Osterville, with the smooth tracking motion of a track-mounted fortress gun.

"Messers," he said flatly. "I remind you that you'll be needed with your units later this afternoon in the main cavalry barracks. Good day to you. Captain M'lewis, if you please."

He turned on his heel. Faintly, he could hear:

". . . quite acceptable dessert wines, but far too sweet for table. But I've found a mountain vintage from this village in the Oxheads . . ."

CHAPTER SIX

The City Offices of Sandoral were nearly as crowded as the barracks, although they smelled of musty paper and lamp-soot and ink rather than sewage and dogshit. Clerks in knee breeches and dirty ruffled shirts were running in all directions, waving papers in the air; abacuses clicked; wheeled carts full of folders of documents rumbled over the tiled floors of the corridors. There were petitioners in plenty about, too. The clamor died as Raj shouldered through; the forty troopers of the 5th tramping behind him with their rifles at port, bayonets fixed, were a stark reminder of why Sandoral was in an emergency in the first place.

Raj strongly suspected that most of the bureaucrats would continue to think of it as a tiresome interruption of routine right up until the Settler's troops came over the wall.

Civilization, he thought sourly, watching one man blink at him through thick lenses, fingers pausing on the counting stones. *The sacred trust I defend. The reason I obey purblind idiots.*

They clattered up a broad stairway; the upper corridor was considerably less crowded, a condition enforced by several slope-browed men with cudgels. All of whom sensibly faded into doorways at the sight of the naked steel and harsh uniform clatter of hobnails.

"You can't go in there! That's Chief Commissioner Kirmedez's—"

"Siddown," M'lewis snarled at the functionary. The man sat.

Kirmedez looked up from his desk as Raj entered. He was a thin dark man with receding hair, dressed plainly with a simple cravat. His eyes widened slightly as he took in Raj and the soldiers behind him; he rose and bowed.

"Heneralissimo," he said politely. "How may I serve you?"

Raj took the measure of the man. *Honest,* he thought, *for a wonder.*

oversimplification, Center said, **but a valid approximation.** A grid snapped onto the administrator's face, with mottled patterns showing heat and the dilation of his pupils. **proceed.**

477

It was impossible to lie to Raj Whitehall . . . with an angel looking out through his eyes. He didn't like it, but it was useful, and he'd use any tool to get the job done.

Anything at all.

"Messer Kirmedez," Raj said, "Sandoral will be under siege by the Colonials within two weeks maximum. Possibly less."

Kirmedez sat and tapped the piles of documents on his desk. "*Heneralissimo*, this city cannot stand siege. We're grossly over-crowded, and the grain reserves are low."

Raj nodded. By law, a fortified border town like this was supposed to keep a year's reserve of basic foodstuffs, in return for remission of some taxes. He didn't need to ask what had happened to it.

"Exactly, Messer. I'm therefore evacuating all civilians to East Residence."

Kirmedez's hard thin face went fluid with shock for an instant. "That's impossible."

Raj allowed himself a flat smile. "On the contrary. Anyone who leaves on their own feet—or on dogback or in a carriage or by ox wagon—can take whatever they wish to carry. But whenever a troop train gets in, and I expect them at four-hour intervals, the garri-son is going to sweep up enough people to fill it for the return trip. There will be absolutely no exceptions. Messer Commissioner, you'd also better inform the citizens immediately, because the first twelve hundred will be leaving in about two hours on the train that brought me. Is that understood?"

Kirmedez closed his mouth. He stared at Raj for a full thirty sec-onds, then looked at the feral faces of the Descotter gunmen behind him.

"You mean it," he said softly.

"I'm not in the habit of making empty threats, Messer," Raj said, equally quiet.

Kirmedez nodded.

The door was open, and the word had spread swiftly. A roar sounded through the offices, shading up into a hysterical wail. Kirmedez rose and reached for a brass bell on his desk, but Raj put out one hand.

"Captain," he said to M'lewis.

The Scout commander turned and barked an order. The column in the corridor outside turned and brought their rifles up in a single smooth jerk.

"*Fwego!*"

BAM. The volley slammed into the lath and plaster of the ceiling. Chunks and dust rained down on the faces of those who'd come out of their offices, and down the open stairwell onto the crowd below.

"Reload!"

Silence fell amid the *ping* of spent brass landing on the tiles and the metallic clatter of rounds being thumbed home and levers worked.

Gray-white gunsmoke drifted down the hall and carried the stink of burnt sulfur.

Silence fell. Kirmedez's bell sounded through it. "Back to work, if you please," he called. "Messer Hantonio, step in here. We have a great deal to do."

He nodded thanks to Raj. "And they'll take it seriously, too. Good day to you, *Heneralissimo.*"

Raj raised an eyebrow; it wasn't often you met an administrator with that firm a grip on reality.

"*Bwenya Dai,*" he replied politely.

And the bureaucrat was right. There was a great deal to do, fortunately. You could forget a lot, when you had work on hand.

Chief Commissioner Kirmedez snapped his fingers impatiently. "Stop babbling, man!" His assistant fell silent.

"It doesn't *matter* if it's impossible; it has to be done anyway. Now, send out the criers. But first, send runners to all the following households."

He handed over a list. The assistant whistled. "My apologies, *patron,*" he said. "I should have thought of that."

Kirmedez nodded. "Hantonio, when this war is over, I will still be Chief Commissioner of Sandoral and District, whoever is Commandant. Those men will still be wealthy and powerful. And they will remember who gave them advanced warning to gather their personal possessions and their households for evacuation."

The assistant smiled with genuine admiration.

Kirmedez smiled back. "Favors are the grease that let the civil service wheels turn, Hantonio. Never forget it."

And Heneralissimo Supremo Whitehall has done me a favor, he thought, pausing briefly. *I wonder if he realizes it?*

"Jorg!" Raj called, pleasure in his voice.

Jorg Menyez pulled up his riding steer. It lowed, then swung a long brass-tipped horn down in Horace's face. The hound whuffled and reconsidered the grab it had been thinking of making at the long-legged riding animal's shank.

"Just in," the infantry commander said.

Behind him a column of footsoldiers poured down the street, shouldering the milling civilians aside; this time they were trying their best to get out of the way, not blocking the road with their welcome. The furled colors of the 17th Kelden Foot went by, to the steady *thrip . . . thrip* of the drum.

"The heliograph says Gerrin just boarded the last train out of East Residence, and Bellamy and his trained barbs are making good time, should be here in three days maximum."

"Spirit," Raj said, mildly surprised. "It's actually working."

Both men spat to their left and made the sign of the horns with their sword-hands; Raj touched his amulet, a circuit board blessed by Saint Wu herself a century before.

"You've seen where the infantry are kenneled?" Jorg said, anger flushing his fair-skinned face.

Raj nodded. "Think they'll be fit for anything?"

"Nothing complex, but we may be able to put some backbone into them," Jorg said. "They ought to enjoy the first part of the plan, anyway. Any trouble with Osterville?"

"No," Raj said.

Menyez hesitated, then let the bitten-off syllable stand.

The barracks-yard was far more crowded this time; all the cavalry, the ragged ill-kept lines of the infantry units, the two hundred of the 5th Descott beside Raj, and the neat formations of the 17th Kelden and 24th Valencia to either side. The sun was sinking behind the western edge of the barracks; Raj narrowed his eyes against it, seeing only the black silhouettes of the troops.

"Fellow soldiers," Raj said.

Of a sort. It wasn't these men's fault that they'd been badly commanded, but he didn't intend to let the consequences keep him from carrying out the mission. A lot of them were going to pay with their lives for their officers' slackness, before this was over.

"We've very little time. The 33rd Drangosh, the 12th Pardizia" —he listed the infantry battalions, about half the two thousand available— "will turn to and begin construction of the necessary boats and gear for a pontoon bridge to cross the Drangosh and carry our invasion force. This task will be performed under the direction of Colonel Dinnalsyn of the Artillery Corps."

A long murmur swept through the packed garrison formations. Raj stood like an iron idol, hands clasped behind his back, while the shouts of *Silence in the ranks!* controlled it. None of his veterans had moved; probably because none of them were surprised at what he intended.

"The cavalry formations based in Sandoral will immediately assume control of the gates. Only military personnel will be allowed to enter the city or approach on the main roads.

"The remainder of the infantry will begin clearing Sandoral and evacuating the civilian population to the railroad station, commencing immediately. No resistance is to be tolerated. All units will be accompanied by parties of the 5th Descott, the 17th Kelden, or the 24th Valencia.

"I'm aware that you men of the district infantry battalions have been seriously neglected. Effective immediately, all arrears of equipment, rations, and pay will be made up from the stocks in the city's treasury and arsenals. For the duration, you will be quartered inside the walls—to be precise, in the housing of the evacuated civilians."

Stunned silence sank over the parade ground. The formations rippled slightly as men turned to one another, then back to the figure standing on the stone dais. A helmet went up on a rifle among the infantry, and a voice cried out:

"Spirit bless Messer Raj!"

"Raj!"

"*Raj!*"

"*RAJ! RAJ!*"

He let it continue and build for a moment, judging, waiting until they were about to break ranks and crowd around him. A raised hand brought the sound back down from its white-noise roar, like receding surf on a beach.

"Cheer after we've beaten the wogs back to their kennels," he said. "Until then, we've a man's job of work to do. See to it."

"*RAJ! RAJ! RAJ! RAJ!*"

Corporal Minatelli turned back down the street. "*What's* the problem now?" he barked.

"Theynz warn't open up," the garrison soldier said timidly in a thick yokel burr. "They wouldn' give us no food either, when we wuz hongry. Turned us'n away frum d'doors."

Minatelli sighed. *Raggedy-ass excuse for a soldier*, he thought disgustedly. Literally; the man's buttocks were hanging out a great rent in his trousers, and the blue of his jacket was faded to sauroid's-egg color. He had a beard, too, like a barb or a wog.

"*Here's* how ye do it, dickhead. Y'ain't askin' 'em to dance, see?"

He stepped to one side and put the muzzle of his rifle against the lock. *Bam*, and bits of lead and metal pinged and whistled across the street. The ragged soldier yelped as one scored a line of red across the side of his face. Minatelli slammed the sole of his boot into the door beside the lock, and the wood boomed open against the hallway.

"What's the meaning of this?" shouted the man inside. "It's impossible—you peon scum, where's your officer? I'll have you flogged, *flogged*—"

Smack. The side of Minatelli's rifle-butt punched into the man's face. Blood spattered down the lace sabot of his shirt. The soldier chopped the butt up under the man's short ribs, and he folded over without a sound. Minatelli grabbed him by the collar and threw him out into the street.

"Anyone what ain't out in ten, gits shot!" he shouted to the crowd of family and servants. "Out, out, *out*. T'wogs is comin'!"

A torrent of civilians poured out of the townhouse door. Minatelli grinned to himself; a couple of them trampled on the head of the household before two with more presence of mind or family affection picked him up and carried him out into the crowded darkness of the street. The gas lamps were on, but the reddish light only made the milling crowd seem less human, a gleam of eyes and teeth and wailing voices in the hot night. Both sides of the street were lined with troopers, their fixed bayonets a bright line containing the shapeless movements of the crowd. Occasionally one would jab at someone who crowded too close, and a scream of pain would rise above the hubbub of confusion, fear and anger.

Minatelli's grin grew broader. Back in Old Residence, he'd been a stonecutter like his father and grandfather before him. They'd have sent him around to the servants' entrance if he so much as called on a house like this. Now he got to buttstroke one of the breed of stuck-up *riche hombes* bastards. Military service definitely had its good points.

The garrison soldier gaped at him for a slow twenty seconds. Then his crooked brown teeth showed in an answering smile. The glitter in his eyes was alarming.

"Sor!" he said, saluting smartly. Then, to his squadmates: "C'mon, boyos!"

Their boots and rifle-butts thundered on the next door down. Minatelli reloaded, slung his rifle and turned to Saynchez.

"How many, d'ye think?"

"Mebbe six, seven hundert," the older private said. "No different n'countin' sheep, a-back on me da's place. Me da ran sheep fer the squire."

"*Banged* the sheep, more like," one of their squad said, sotto voce.

"Wouldn't mind bangin' this one," another added. A feminine squeal came from the darkness.

"No fuckin' around!" Minatelli said sharply. "That's enough—move this bunch down to t'train station. *Hadelande!*"

"Tight! Get those boards *tight* before you nail them to the stringers!" Grammeck Dinnalsyn said, for the four hundredth time.

The infantryman gaped at him, then obligingly whacked at the edge of the board with his mallet. The dry wood splintered. Dinnalsyn winced, then skipped aside to let a dozen men go by with a beam. One of his officers followed, drawing lines on the timber with a piece of chalk and consulting a crumpled piece of paper in the other. A noncom stumbled after him, holding up a hurricane lantern. Both moons were up, luckily, and there were bonfires of scrap lumber scattered along the broad stretch of riverside as well. Wagons rumbled in with more wood; wheelbarrels went by loaded with mallets, nails, rope, and saws.

"Cut here, here and *here*," the young lieutenant said, giving a final slash with the chalk. Crews sprang to work with two-man drag saws.

The first pontoon was already ready to launch down by the river's edge, a simple breast-high wooden box of planks on rough-cut stringers, eight meters by twelve. The stink of hot asphalt surrounded it, as sweating near-naked soldiers slathered liquid black tar from pots onto the boards.

Dinnalsyn pulled out his slide rule. *Si. Now, the river's nine hundred meters; make it eight meters per barge, allow a reserve of ten percent, and—*

A dog pulled up beside him with a spurt of gravel. He looked up and pulled himself erect. *"Mi heneral,"* he said.

Raj nodded, his eyes light gray in the shadows under his helmet brim. "How's it coming, Grammeck?"

"On schedule, more or less."

"Will they float?"

"After a fashion, if we use enough tar and the wood swells tight. I'm going to float them as we finish them, that'll give the timber some time to soak."

"Good man," Raj said. "While you're at it, have your people run up steering oars and paddles. We'll put some of the garrison infantry to practicing maneuvering, that'll be important later. Here in the Drangosh valley, quite a few of them were probably riverboatmen before the press gang came through."

"Si, mi heneral. The Forty Thieves aren't with you?"

Raj was riding alone, save for his personal bannermen, buglers, and galloper-messengers. He nodded.

"Too much temptation in the city, under the circumstances. They're out living up to their *official* designation. M'lewis will get it done; he's a soldier, in his fashion." Raj turned in the saddle to watch the first pontoon boat being manhandled into the water. It splashed into the Drangosh and bobbed, riding unevenly. "They'll be enough?"

"Mi heneral, consider it done. I can finish the rest in time, if I get enough of the raw materials."

Raj's teeth showed slightly. "Oh, that ought not to be a problem. Poplanich's Own just detrained, they're out helping the 5th get the timber in, and we're moving quickly."

He paused. "One more thing; send out some of your people, use the garrison if you must, and confiscate every boat you can find; every fishing smack, barge, canoe, whatever. Not just here, in the suburbs and every section of the valley we can still reach."

"And *back*, ye bitches' brood."

The civilians still crowding the street wailed and stampeded; which was just fine as far as Robbi M'Telgez was concerned. Handling a lariat and a dog was second nature—his family were *rancheros*, yeoman tenants who herded on shares back in Descott—but this was tricky. One end of the braided leather rope was snubbed to the second-story end of a roof beam; the other was wrapped three times around the pommel of his saddle. Pochita sank down on her haunches and backed one tiny step at a time, and he could feel the thousand-pound body arching like a bow between his thighs. The rest of his platoon were doing likewise, one or two dogs to every rafter. The animals were used to working in unison, and they snarled beneath their panting as they hauled.

The adobe wall smoked dust for an instant and then collapsed towards them. Released from the pull, Pochita skipped back nimbly until her hindquarters touched the house on the other side of the irregular little plaza. M'Telgez coughed through the checked bandanna over his face; his dog sneezed massively and shook her head, the cheek-levers of the bridle rattling. *Got t'check 'em,* he thought. *They should be snug, not loose.*

Foot soldiers waded forward into the dust, rummaging for the planks and beams. They'd done the same thing here in Sandoral for material to build earthwork forts, in the last campaign against the wogs a few years ago; now they were tearing down rebuilt houses to make boats.

Always something new with Messer Raj.

Antin M'lewis sank closer to the earth, hugging it for shelter and trying to *think* dark like the moonless night. It was homelike, in an unpleasant sort of way; as a rustler by hereditary profession, he'd spent enough time like this back home working his way in past the *vakaros* pulling night guard on some unsuspecting squire's herds. Darkness, the dogs belly-down too in a gully a few hundred meters back, his face blacked with lamp soot or burnt cork. The wind moving into his face, so no scent went to the target or his dogs— infantry ahead here, but why take a chance, and there might be a mounted officer. Just like home.

Descott was rarely this hot, though. And most Descotter *vakaros* would be more alert than the wog ahead of him.

He eeled forward on his belly, moving every time the Colonial sentry's pacing turned him back toward this angle of approach. Useless sentry, the bugger was smoking a pipe and M'lewis could see the ember light with every draw, even smell the strong tobacco. Backlit by a watch-fire too, which must be playing hell with his night-vision.

Mother. The wog had stopped, and his spiked helmet was turning as he looked outward. He hesitated, almost taking the carbine from over his shoulder, then resumed his steady pacing. *Mother. Spirit.*

Forward another five meters. The dust was trying to make him sneeze, but Goodwife M'lewis hadn't raised any of her sons to be suicides. Now he was behind a head-high clump of alluvial clay, right where the towel-top would pass on his next circuit.

Come on, he thought. *Git yer wog arse over here. Come t'pappa.* His weight came up on his knees and one hand. The other went to the wooden toggle in his waist, callused fingers around satin-smooth pearwood. Ready. Ready. One knee bent under him, bare toes gripping the dirt.

The Colonial muttered something in Arabic and stopped. He bent, raising one foot and knocking the dottle out of his pipe on the heel of his curl-toed boot.

Thank you, Spirit, M'lewis thought, and moved very quickly. Straighten the knee, rising, right hand whipping forward and to the left in a hard sideways flick. Following the toggle and the wire it dragged, as if they were pulling him out of the dirt. Perfect soft weight on the hand, as the wire struck the left side of the wog's neck and whipped around, slapping the other toggle into his reaching left hand—practiced ten thousand times since he was a lad, and it *worked* when you had to. Wrists crossed, jam the knee into the wog's back, *heave.*

The sudden coppery smell of blood filled the night. M'lewis went down with the Colonial, abandoning the garrote that had sawn half-way through to his backbone and grabbing his equipment to muffle the clatter. Figures had started upright at the campfire; one of them seemed to be dancing a jig for an instant. The sounds were slight but definite. A meaty *thock,* the sound of a steel-shod rifle butt in the side of a head. The wetter, duller sound of steel in flesh. And once the unmistakable crackle of a breaking neck, like a thick green branch being popped. Then silence.

M'lewis jerked the garrote free and wiped it clean on the dead Arab's pugaree. The campfire was quiet when he came up, his men finishing rifling the pockets of the dead—he could have forbidden that, and he could tell a pig not to shit in the woods, too—and sitting calmly in the same positions with wog helmets on their heads. The Scout commander nodded to them as he passed, walking out into the dark and to the edge of the little cliff. There was a gully beyond it, then low eroded clay hills, and then flat farmland. Dim enough normally at two hours past midnight, except for the hundreds of neatly spaced campfires. More lights crossed the river, over to the western bank where the smoking ruins of Gurnyca lay.

He settled in with his sketchpad and pulled out his binoculars. Railroad to the riverbank; he checked, and saw fatigue parties still working on it. *Laid on t'dirt,* he noted on his pad as he sketched. No embankment or crushed-rock bedding for the ties. Emergency line, low capacity, but still enough to carry supplies. Mounds of supplies throughout the basecamp, within the normal earthworks and ditch. Ammunition boxes, shells, sacks with dogmash and dried fish and jerked meat, skins of vegetable oil, all the hundred-and-one items that an army on the march needed. Convoys were moving across the pontoon bridge even at night: wagons drawn by skinny long-legged oxen, and long guns with the distinctive soda-bottle shapes of built-up siege weapons, battering pieces. 130mm and 160mm, he decided. Rifled guns, good artillery, but bitches to move.

Rail to the river, but oxcarts over it. No grazing, except from the farms; if Ali was moving north, he'd be foraging to support his men, but once he stopped, the convoys would have to come in every day. About ten kay of troops holding the bridgehead and pontoons, sappers and line-of-communication infantry. It all looked very professional, as good as anything the Civil Government's army could do. Not at *all* like fighting the barbs out west. The MilGov barbs were full of fight, but dim as a yard up a hog's ass, most of the time. These wogs used their heads for something besides holding their turbans up.

M'lewis finished his estimate and duplicated the numbers and sketch-map. "Cut-nose, Talker," he whispered, as he eeled backward.

Cut-nose was a ratty little man, his cousin on his mother's side. They might have been brothers for looks—it was quite possible they *were* brothers, Old Man M'lewis had got around a fair bit before they hanged him—except for the missing organ. Then again, maybe they weren't close relations; no M'lewis would try to sell a dyed dog back to the man he'd stolen it from. Talker was a hulking brute from the mountains on the eastern fringe of Descott. They both had rawhide guards shrunk onto the forestocks of their rifles, and Talker had a couple of fresh severed ears on a loop of thong around his neck.

"Tak this t'Messer Raj," he said. "Swing east. Month's pay bonus iffn ye gits there afore me."

"Ser!" Cut-nose said, smiling yellow-brown with delight. Talker grunted.

M'lewis came to a crouch and headed back toward the gully and the dogs, the rest of the Scouts falling in behind him. He took the time to stamp his feet back into his boots before he straddled the crouching dog. He usually didn't bother with socks; a dollop of tallow in the boot served as well, if you didn't mind the smell.

"Ride," he said.

Messer Raj would have his news. It was bad news, as far as Antin M'lewis could see, but—thank the Spirit!—it wasn't his job to figure out what to do about it.

They swung into the saddle and followed the gully north, riding with muffled harness. Every kilometer or so he paused and headed for high ground; the eastern bank was generally a little above the level on the west, and there were few dwellers close to the main stream, if you avoided the raghead semaphore towers. Every stop showed Colonial watchfires on the other side; Ali's convoy guards, picketed all the way down his line of march northward towards Sandoral.

The third time showed something a little different. He closed his eyes for a minute before putting them to the glasses. There was a fair-sized Civil Government town on the other side of the river, and as he watched, the first of the buildings went up in a gout of flame. That gave enough light to watch the Settler's troops systematically stripping the warehouses and granaries before they put them to the torch; Ali'd be living off the land as much as he could, to spare the transport.

There was a migratory insect on Bellevue about the length of a man's thumb. Every century or so swarms of them would hatch north on the Skinner steppe and fly south, eating the land bare until they reached the empty deserts to spawn and die. Where they passed, famine followed.

Ali's men were more localized, but just about as thorough.

Barton Foley sat in the shade of the palm tree and tapped his lips thoughtfully with the end of his pencil. *Now, would* virile *go well with* while *in that stanza, or not?* he thought.

"Heads up!"

He sighed and tucked the volume back into the saddlebag. Someday he'd have the time to really write. *Someday I'll be dead,* he added sourly to himself—*although hopefully not soon*; twenty-one was a bit early even in this trade. *Maybe I'm not cut out to be a poet or a playwright.* History, now, that might be more interesting. He'd certainly got a close-up on some of it.

"More refugees?" a lieutenant asked.

"I don't think so," the young captain said thoughtfully, raising his glasses.

The picket of the 5th was two kilometers out from Sandoral: the roads were thick with refugees, heading into the city and then being routed out. It was better to intercept them a ways from the gates, to avoid crowding the roadways nearer the city. Two troops and a splatgun were enough to discourage even the most hysterical from bolting to the shelter of the walls. By now, most of them had gotten the message. There was a continuous traffic out of town too, hopeful magnates with their valuables in wagons, realistic ones with the hard cash on pack-dogs and the family in a fast well-sprung carriage.

It was easy duty, a way to rest the troops; a nice little date grove for shade, a good well for water. Some resourceful soul had a fire going and a couple of chickens roasting over it; the peons would never miss them. The smell was a pleasant overlay to the usual odors of dog and sweat-soaked wool uniforms and gun oil.

Foley wiped his face with his red-and-black checked neckcloth. *Ironic,* he thought. The 5th Descott had looted a warehouse full of them back in El Djem, the Colonial border town southwest of here. They'd just barely made it back alive from that one, after Tewfik mousetrapped them, but the scarves had become a unit trademark; it was as much as a soldier's life was worth to wear one, if he wasn't in the 5th.

The column of dust was heading in from the northwest, just now down into the flat irrigated land around Sandoral. Suspiciously regular dust, columns of it, with a thinner, wider film in front. Very much what a couple of battalions of Civil Government cavalry would make, riding hard in column with their scout-screens out ahead, all regulation and by the book. He waited until the first of the vedettes came into view, checked the silhouette and the breed of dog.

"Message to the *Heneralissimo*," he said. "The Cruisers and Welf's Brigaderos are here."

Very good time, too. No more than five days from the time they left East Residence just ahead of the first trains. Even with the railroad to supply them, it was a creditable performance, particularly if the dogs were still fit for action.

He was a little surprised. Those fair MilGov complexions were extremely pretty, but he'd doubted they could take the Eastern sun.

"Good timing," Raj said.

Ludwig Bellamy and Teodore Welf looked more like twins than ever, down to the thick coating of gray-white dust on their faces and the dark streaks of sweat through it.

"Rail convoys on schedule?" Bellamy asked.

They moved forward under the awning and collected bowls of soup and a bannock each; the line parted to let them through, but it was the same food as the troopers were waiting for. The medical staff—priest-doctors and nuns—was manning the pots, since there weren't any wounded to care for so far. Suzette dashed by, stopping long enough to thrust a cup of watered wine into Raj's hand. The others were dipping water out of a bucket; Ludwig waited politely until the others had drunk, then dumped the remainder over his head.

"I *needed* that," he said; the grin made you realize he wasn't yet thirty.

Neither am I, Raj remembered with slight surprise. He felt older, though.

Aloud, he went on: "I'll give Barholm Clerett that, he does get the trains running on time. We're expecting the last in at any moment. How are your men?"

"They'll be ready to fight after a night's sleep; and the dogs are mostly sound-footed. We took your advice and commandeered a big pack of remounts from the East Residence reserve before we left." Bellamy looked around. "You haven't been wasting time here."

There were few civilians left on the streets of Sandoral. Instead they swarmed with soldiers and dogs, wagons and carts, and an ordered chaos of movement under the harsh southern sun. The garrison infantry were doing most of the hauling and pushing, but they looked better fed, and far better dressed. A thud and plume of smoke and dust marked another house being demolished for building materials; off in the distance sounded the *heep . . . heep* of troops being drilled and a crackle of musketry practice. The artillery park filled most of the square, guns nose-to-trail with their limbers waiting behind, and Dinnalsyn's gunners giving them a last going-over.

"Speak of the devil," Bartin Foley said, smiling fondly.

A bugle sounded, and the color party of the 5th Descott came trotting into the square, the battalion banner floating beside the blue and silver Starburst of Holy Federation. Gerrin Staenbridge heeled his mount over to the clump of officers and saluted with an ironic flourish.

"*Mi heneral*, the remainder of your force, reporting as ordered." He looked around in his turn. "I see you've started the party without me."

"Just laying in the drinks and rehearsing the band, Gerrin," Raj said. "No problem getting under way?"

"No, but there might have been if I'd lingered. Our good Chancellor Tzetzas isn't happy about having the field army so far from home, at all, at all. If I hadn't taken the last of the trains, I suspect the bureaucrats would have followed me all the way here to argue with you about it."

Raj laughed harshly. "Not with Ali so close," he said. "Although our good Commandant Osterville is almost as much of a pest, in his way. And he *is* here."

"Speak of the devil," Foley said again, his voice flat as gunmetal this time.

He took Staenbridge's arm and began whispering rapidly, gesturing with the hook on his left arm. Raj caught his own name and *Suzette* once or twice.

The Commandant of Sandoral and District was pushing his way through the thronging mass in the square; not looking very happy, and unhappier by the minute at the lack of deference, from Raj's veterans and from what were supposedly his own troops.

"Whitehall," he said. "General Whitehall," he amended; Raj's face was politely blank, but several of the Companions had dropped their hands to pistol-butts or the hilts of their sabers.

"Where the Starless Dark have you been?"

Raj straightened, finished the wine, and dipped his bannock into the stew. "Well, Commandant, I've been rather busy—getting ready for the war, you see."

Somebody chuckled, and Osterville turned a mottled color. "I'll thank you to accompany me to my headquarters," he said. "We've got several things to discuss."

"If you want to talk, *Colonel*, you'll talk here and now. Because as I mentioned, there is a war impending."

Words burst from the smaller man. "You're *destroying* my city!" he barked. "I've received petitions from every man of rank in the district—"

Raj raised an eyebrow. "I don't doubt you have," he said. "Let them petition Ali. That's the alternative, and I think they'd like his methods even less than mine. In any case, as you've made clear, you're the supreme civil authority in this area; relations with the local nobility are your responsibility."

The Commandant opened his mouth and closed it again. He snapped his fingers, and an aide put a sheaf of documents in his hand.

"Perhaps you've been too *busy*," he said, "to read these dispatches from the Capital? They've been coming over the semaphore by the dozens."

Raj mopped his bowl with the heel of the bannock and plucked the papers out of the smaller man's hand. He glanced through them, chewed, swallowed.

"Oh, I've been reading them," he said.

He ripped the thick sheaf through with casual strength, tossing the fragments into the dry hot wind. They fluttered off like gulls, and one of the newly arrived dogs of the 5th snapped inquiringly at a piece as it went by.

"I have the *Governor's* authority, signed by the Sovereign Mighty Lord himself. I received it in person, from his own hands. What are a few waggling flags to *that*?"

He tossed the last of the papers to the cobbles. "And now, Colonel Osterville, if you don't have any more problems . . ."

"But I do have *this*," Osterville said. The document he produced was thick parchment, impressively sealed with lead and ribbons.

Raj raised an eyebrow. "You have a decree from the Chair, a Vermilion Order, swaying the wide earth?" he asked, using the formal terminology.

"Not exactly," Osterville said. "But you will note it's from Chancellor Tzetzas, in the Governor's name, requiring you to cease and desist from interfering with private properties and instead attend to your assigned mission."

"From the Chancellor?" Raj said, examining the parchment. He crumpled it experimentally. It was first-quality sheepskin parchment, soft and supple. "By courier, I suppose?"

Osterville nodded toward a man in his entourage. Raj looked at him, and then around.

"M'lewis. Deal with this as it deserves," he said.

"Where are the jakes?" the Scout Captain said, putting down his bowl and unfastening his sword belt.

Like most Civil Government cities, Sandoral had public lavatories, simple brick boxes connected to storm-flushed sewers. M'lewis strode over to the nearest, and back a minute later. He was holding the now brown-streaked and stinking parchment by one corner between thumb and finger. Shocked silence gripped the Commandant's party as he walked over to the courier, unfastened the flap of his message pouch, and dropped the soiled parchment inside.

"Just so the Chancellor understands exactly what weight I attach to his attempts to interfere with my mission and the Governor's authority," Raj said.

"You're mad," Osterville said softly. "Mad. Nobody—Tzetzas will eat your *heart*."

Raj's smile sent Osterville back a step. "Perhaps I am mad, Colonel. Perhaps I'm the Sword of the Spirit of Man. In either case, I'm in charge here." He produced a document of his own. "And this is your own confirmation, directing your troops to cooperate in the transport of the civilians."

He held it up, and one of the Companions leaned over to read it with interest.

"That! That was that witch, she—" On the edge of ruin, Osterville pulled himself back. He'd been about to say something that would be a public provocation to a challenge. He ran a hand through his hair. "Where is *she*? I haven't seen her since . . ."

Raj laughed, an iron sound. "Colonel Osterville, I've answered your official inquiries. You can scarcely expect me to stretch business to the point of giving you an itinerary for my wife. Now, if you'll pardon me—"

He turned, and the officers followed him. Gerrin Staenbridge paused, holding his gauntlets in one hand and tapping them into the palm of the other. For a moment Osterville feared he would slap them across his face in challenge, but the hard dark features were relaxed in a smile. He held the order Osterville had signed—the order that Suzette Whitehall had somehow charmed out of him. He read it, pursing his lips, then looked up at Osterville with an expression of feline malice before he spoke one word.

"Sucker."

CHAPTER SEVEN

It was the hour before dawn, a little chilly even in summer in the clear dry southern air. The massed ranks of the army knelt as the Sysup-Suffragen of Sandoral paced by, with acolytes swinging censers that spread aromatic blue smoke across the men. He reached out his Star-headed staff in blessing as he passed the colors of each unit, and the men extended both hands out, palms down, in the gesture of reverence. Behind the hierarch came four priests bearing a litter on which rested a cube of something clearer than crystal and taller than a man. Light swirled in it, growing and flaring until the watchers bowed their heads and closed their eyes in awe. It shone through the closed lids, through hands flung up before faces, then died away amid a murmur of awe.

Raj touched his amulet as he rose. "The Spirit is with us," he said. *Or at least Center is. What a cynic I've become.*

realist, Center corrected.

Is there a difference?

He turned to the command group. Which included, from necessity, Colonel Osterville.

"Gentlemen, my congratulations. You've managed a very complex operation in record time and with surprisingly little confusion; my particular thanks to Colonels Menyez and Dinnalsyn. Now it's time to show the wogs that two can play the invasion game. Colonel Osterville, I presume you'll wish to accompany the field force rather than remain in Sandoral?"

"I certainly will. Furthermore, I insist that the cavalry battalions of the Sandoral garrison be under my command."

Raj nodded. "By all means, Colonel. By all means."

Osterville shot him a suspicious glance, and found his face blandly unrevealing. He tugged at his mustachio thoughtfully.

colonel osterville is attempting to intuit the reason for your ready agreement, Center pointed out. **probability of success 12% ± 3.**

"Colonel Menyez, you will command the city garrison. I'm leaving you the 17th, the 24th, the garrison infantry, and three batteries of field guns. You'll also have the guns of the fixed defenses, of course."

Dinnalsyn looked up. "I've tested the militia artillery crews who volunteered to stay," he said. "Not bad at all, and the ammunition's plentiful."

Jorg Menyez nodded thoughtfully. "Any cavalry? The garrison units can stand behind a parapet and shoot, and the 17th and 24th can do anything cavalry can except ride and charge with the saber, but I could use a mobile reserve."

"I'll leave you three companies of the 5th Descott," Raj said. "That'll have to do. The field force will comprise three columns.

"The remainder of the 5th, the 1st and 2nd Mounted Cruisers, the 3/591, 4/591, and 5/591, and the main artillery reserve of thirty guns will go with me. Colonel Osterville, you'll command your garrison cavalry and two batteries. Major Gruder, you'll have the 7th Descott Rangers, the 1st Rogor Slashers, the Maximilliano Dragoons, and Poplanich's Own. Major Zahpata, you'll take your 18th Komar Borderers, the City of Delrio, and the Novy Haifa Dragoons. Plus two batteries of field guns each.

"We'll be advancing fast, close enough for mutual support; no wheeled transport except for the guns and the ammunition reserve. Spread out, live off the land; spare lives when you can, but burn and destroy everything else, so long as you can do it quickly. Let the semaphore posts stand long enough to get off messages. Portable plunder will be transferred to the central group, and from there back here to Sandoral for eventual division; do *not* allow the men to weigh themselves down with choice bits. When Tewfik comes looking for us, we're going to need every bit of mobility we can get.

"The purpose of this exercise is to create enough havoc that Ali will be forced to divert at least part of his army from the west bank of the Drangosh. We lay waste the nobles' estates; the nobles scream for protection. He can give any particular noble the chop, but he can't ignore too many of them—hopefully, he's not so much of a bloody lunatic as to forget that, at least not yet. We can't face the entire Colonial army in the field, but we may be able to give part of it a bloody nose. Move fast, and create the maximum amount of panic and alarm; that's more important than actual damage.

"Any questions?"

A few of the officers looked at each other, but none spoke. Raj slapped on his gloves. "Then to your men, Messers, and the work of the day."

Raj mounted Horace and turned the dog and his personal bannermen down the front of the assembled force. He halted before the ranks of the infantry.

"Fellow soldiers," he said, raising a hand. "I'm off to teach the wogs the price of invading the Civil Government of Holy Federation."

Silence reigned. "I can only do that if Sandoral is strongly held behind me." He pointed south. "Ali is coming, and more wogs than you can count are coming with him. If you hold these walls, we can win this war; otherwise, we all die. I'm riding out confident in the aid of the Spirit of Man of the Stars—and in your courage and discipline. Which is why, when the plunder is divided, all the infantry here will receive a full share, just as the cavalry troopers do. Are you lads ready to do a man's work today?"

The 17th began the cheering, and it spread down the line as Raj rode past, his personal flag dipping in salute as he passed each battalion's banner. The cavalry were massed on the other side of the square; you had to use a different manner with them.

He grinned as he reined in, facing the long rows of helmeted riders and the panting tongues of the dogs; they knew something was up as well, and their pricked-forward ears were mirrors of the men's excitement.

"To Hell or plunder, dog-brothers," Raj roared.

The men gave back a single exultant bark, and the dogs howled, thousands of them in antiphonal chorus, a sound that slammed back from the buildings around the plaza and made the hair crawl along the spine.

"Walk-march . . . trot."

"I might have known," Raj said, reining in on the little hillock beside the east-bank end of the bridge.

Suzette pulled up Harbie, her riding palfrey, beside Horace. The smaller dog wagged its tail and sniffed Horace's muzzle; after a moment Horace gave a snuffle in reply and turned his head away in lordly indifference.

"You do have a medical element along," Suzette said, her eyes bright with friendly mockery. She touched the first-aid kit slung from the saddlebow. "There's no reason I shouldn't join them."

The boards of the pontoon bridge rumbled as a splatgun battery crossed. Cavalry followed in columns of fours, the plate-sized paws thudding on the wooden pavement. Some of the dogs had their ears back at the unfamiliar slight swaying of the surface beneath their feet; others looked upstream or down. The men were singing, an old Descotter folktune:

"Goin' t'Black Mountain wit me saber an' me gun;
Cut ye if yer stand, shoot ye if yer run—"

"I can command thousands of armed men and not a single woman," Raj grumbled. One armed woman, he corrected himself. Suzette had her Colonial repeating carbine in a scabbard tucked under the saddle flaps before her left knee.

"Well, you did *marry* me, not *enlist* me, darling," Suzette said.

Raj snorted and returned his attention to the map. Below, the raiding force poured across the Drangosh, dogs and guns. *Twenty-five, thirty-five klicks a day,* he thought, tracing it with his finger. South and east—there was nothing close to the river to raid, but the Ghor Canal ran a little farther east, and there was a thick belt of cultivation along it. *Three or four days should bring us to . . .* A city, called Ain el-Hilwa, about halfway between here and the Colonial bridgehead opposite Gurnyca.

By that time the wogs should be well and truly terrorized.

"Scramento!" Robbi M'Telgez swore.

The carbine bullet pecked dirt from the adobe wall into his eyes. He crouched and duckwalked along it, rising slightly to peer through the branches of a flowering bush a few meters farther on. There wasn't much shooting elsewhere in the hamlet, but this was the best house; therefore the one most likely to be defended.

"Ye, Smeet, Cunarlez, M'tennin," he said. "Cover us. Five rounds rapid. T'rest fix yer stickers. We'll tak Rosalie t'breakfast."

"We'll a' git kilt," Smeet muttered. "Hunnert meters, dog-brothers. I gits t'winda on 't lef." He blew on the round he loaded into the chamber.

M'Telgez drew the bayonet—nicknamed Rosalie from time immemorial—from the left side of his belt beneath the haversack and clipped it beneath the muzzle of his rifle. There was a multiple rattle and click as the other men of his squad followed suit.

The house ahead was bigger than most in the sprawling settlement along the irrigation ditch; probably the local headman's. It was about a hundred meters upstream from the burning wreckage of the *noria,* the water-powered millwheel that filled the distributory network of irrigation ditches. A small square house of two stories, blank whitewashed adobe below, a few narrow windows above, and most of it was courtyard enclosed by a wall. It hadn't been constructed as a fortress; it had been a long time since Civil Government troops came this far, and none of the local villages even had a defensive perimeter. From what he knew of raghead custom, the wogs built this way to keep neighbors from seeing their women. But it *functioned* perfectly well as a minor strongpoint.

"Hadelande!" he shouted, and vaulted the wall.

The three men he'd designated cut loose, firing as rapidly as they could work the levers and reload. The heavy bullets knocked dust-spouting holes in the mud brick around the windows, or went through—most of them went through, it was only fifty meters and everyone in the 5th ought to be able to hit a running man in the head at that range—beating down the enemy fire. A light bullet still pecked at the dust between his feet. He suppressed his impulse to leap and yell, concentrating on running.

The six Descotters flattened themselves by the doorway. No sense waiting there; it would just give someone upstairs time to think about dropping something unpleasant on them. He was suddenly conscious of his dry gummy mouth, the sweat trickling down from neck and armpits under his uniform jacket, the sound of a chicken clucking unconcerned out in the dusty yard. M'Telgez held out three fingers, two, one.

He and the next trooper stepped out and fired at the lock. They were lucky; nothing hit them when the crude wooden mechanism splintered. The other four fired a round each through the datewood planks while he and his partner stuck their bayonets through the gaps between and lifted the bar out of its brackets. The door burst inward, and they were through.

It was an open space of packed earth with a well in the center and rooms about it. An open staircase came down from the second story opposite him, and men were leaping down it. One pointed a long-barreled flintlock *jezail.*

It boomed, throwing a plume of smoke. Someone behind him yelled—yelled rather than screamed, so that couldn't be too serious. Armory rifles banged, and the other man with a firearm toppled from the stairs; he had a repeating carbine, which showed that this squad had a proper sense of target priorities. Then a wog was rushing at him, swinging a long scimitar.

Clang. M'Telgez caught the sword on his bayonet, and it skirled down the forearm-length of steel until it caught in the brass cross-guard. He let the inertia of the heavy sword push both weapons downward, and punched across with the butt of his rifle. It smacked into the Arab's bearded face with a crackle of breaking bone, a crunching he could feel through his hands. The Colonial pitched sideways, spinning and fouling the man behind who was trying to pull a double-barreled pistol out of the sash around his ample belly. His mouth opened in an "O" of surprise as M'Telgez spun his rifle around and lunged, driving his bayonet through the Arab's stomach and a handspan out his back.

There was a soft, heavy resistance, a feeling of things crunching and popping inside. He twisted sharply and withdrew, a few shards of white fat clinging to nicks in the blade of the bayonet. Blood spattered out; the wounded man's eyes rolled up in his head and he collapsed backward.

The men of the 5th waited an instant, taking cover behind the mudbrick columns that supported the second story of the house. M'Telgez reloaded his rifle and raised three fingers, then jerked them towards the stairs. Three men ran up them and through the open arched door at the top. A shadow moved at the corner of his eye. He whirled, just in time to see it was a veiled and robed woman with a big earthenware pot raised over her head in both hands. M'Telgez raised the muzzle of his rifle as his finger curled on the trigger, and the bullet smashed the vase into shards, leaving her standing with her hands spread and eyes wide.

He pivoted the rifle and jabbed the butt into her stomach. Air whooped out of her and she collapsed to the ground. The Descotter put a boot in the small of her back and pinned her to the dusty earth.

"Anythin' up thar?" he called sharply.

"Nothin'," a voice answered him. "Jist sommat wog kids."

"Bring 'em down," he called. "Rest a yer dog-brothers, search it. Look unner t'roof tiles, t'hearthstone, shove yer baynit inna any chink ye see. Nuthin' heavy, jist coin an' sich."

Which was a pity; cloth and tools and livestock would all fetch a good price back in the *Gubernio Civil* if they had time to send them back, not to mention the wogs themselves. A good stout wog would bring six or seven silver FedCreds sold to the slavers who usually followed the armies, a quarter the price of a riding dog. He'd picked up some coin that way in the Southern Territories. M'Telgez banked half his pay and most of his plunder with the battalion savings account; he had an eye on a little place back in the County when he'd done his twenty-five years. There were two schools of thought on that—some held that you had about one chance in four of living that long in the Army, so it made more sense to spend it on booze and whores as it came.

Robbi M'Telgez had noticed that troopers who thought that way tended to be careless, and to make up a large share of the discouraging statistics. Besides, his family could use the money too, if it came to that.

The three men he'd sent up came down again, one holding a small wooden box. "Found 'er in t'rafters, loik," he said, grinning broadly. "Coin, by t'Spirit."

Looking on the bright side, the wogs hadn't had time to really hide much.

Another herded a group of children, the oldest leading or carrying the younger. They set up a wail at the sight of the bodies in the courtyard, then surged back again when one of the troopers scowled and flourished his bayonet. Thumping and crashing sounds came from the ground floor, as the rest of the squad searched.

"Git t'kiddies out an' a-down by t'church, t'mosque, whatever." Orders were to spare noncombatants and the unresisting. "Yer!" He shouted through the ground-floor door. "Whin yer finished, set t'cookin' oil around."

That would start the fire nicely. He took a deep breath and exhaled, letting the tight belly-clamping tension of action fade a little. A pissant little skirmish, but he'd been in the Army seven years now, since he turned eighteen, and he knew you could die just as dead that way as in a major battle.

"And Smeet, plug that."

Trooper Smeet had a tear in the side of his jacket, and it was sodden and dripping. " 'Tis nuttin'," he said. "We'll a' git kilt anyways—"

"Did I *asks* yer?" M'Telgez said, scowling. "Did I?"

"Co'pral half a year and already drunk wit' power," Smeet said, grinning with an expression that was half wince. He was coming down off the combat-high too; often you didn't really feel a minor wound until you had time to think about it. He leaned his rifle against a wall and shrugged out of his webbing gear and jacket. "I bin co'pral six, seven times—t' feelin' don't last nohows, dog-brother."

There was an ugly flesh wound along his ribs, only beginning to crust. One of his comrades washed it from his canteen, then applied the blessed powder and sealed, the priest-made bandage they all carried in a pouch on their belts. Smeet yelped and swore; the stuff stung badly, and many of the less pious men wouldn't use it on a cut unless you stood over them. M'Telgez wasn't much of a Church-going man, but Messer Raj insisted on following Church canons in such things, which was good enough for him.

The attending trooper used his bayonet to cut off one of the tails of Smeet's jacket, ripping it in half and using it to bind the padding over his ribs.

"An' git t'priest at it, soon as, or ye'll feel me boot up yer arse," M'Telgez warned. Smeet was a good enough fighting man, but he tended to be slack about kit and such.

M'Telgez looked down at the woman and smiled.

Pillars of black smoke stood out against the northern horizon. The smell drifted down with the wind, full of the unpleasant smells of things that should not burn. White-hot, the noon sun burned most color out of the land, turning the reaped grainfields to a pale yellow dust. Blocks of alfalfa and *berseem*-clover were almost eye-hurtingly vivid, and the odd patch of fruit trees or olives cast shade dense and black and sharp-edged. Where the 7th Descott Rangers waited beside their dogs, there was welcome shade from rows of eucalyptus on either side of the road, but the air was still and very hot. Insects shrilled in the dust, and a few tiny pterosauroids swooped after them, their long triangle-tipped tails flickering as they scooped cicadas into their needle-toothed little jaws.

The men squatted patiently beside their mounts, the gun teams lying down in their traces, satisfied after their drink in the roadside canal. The beasts looked glossy-coated and strong despite the heat and hard work; the all-meat diet of plundered Colonial stock agreed with them, after the usual mash of grain and beans eked out with bones and offal. Kaltin Gruder stood, eating grapes from the bunches in the helmet he held reversed in his left hand, waiting with the same stolidity as his troopers.

He ate more grapes and smiled. He'd soldiered against the Military

Governments in the west without passion, and as much occasional mercy as advisable. He was a noble of the Civil Government, a Descotter, and a professional; war was his trade, the only trade unless he wanted the Church or to go home to the County and chase rustlers. The Colonials, though . . . his younger brother had died from a Colonial shellburst, in the El Djem campaign. He rubbed one thumb down the deep parallel scars that seamed the left side of his face.

This was personal.

The sound of paws came from the north, and the whistle of the pickets in their ambush positions passing them through. The scouts trotted up to him, sitting easily with their rifles across their thighs. The lieutenant who led them saluted.

"*Seyhor,*" he said. "Sir. About two thousand of them; many carriages and dogs, and a substantial number of armed men."

"Regulars?"

"*Ferramenti, danad, seyhor,*" the young officer replied. "I'd swear, nothing, sir. Household guards, no twenty in the same livery."

That was the advantage of counter-attacking. Most of the military nobles, the *amirs,* and their *ghazis* would be over on the west bank, with Ali—all the ones who had any desire to fight and die for Islam, at least. Ali had gotten overconfident.

Still, it wouldn't do to emulate his mistake. Fighting for their homes and families could make even rabble desperate.

"Company commanders," he said.

Back along the road men shifted as the word passed down, fastening their webbing, here a man checking his rifle or tightening the girth on a dog. The mounts took their cues from their masters, keeping a well-drilled silence, but they bristled. The unit commanders gathered around Gruder's banner.

"The objective," he said, crouching and drawing in the dirt with a twig, "is a column of refugees about half a klick north. They're coming at fair speed for civilians, but we've gotten ahead of them. We'll debouch, deploy—so—and put in an attack. Captain Morinez, bring your guns along at the trot, if you please.

"The general order is to kill anyone who resists; let the rest run, as long as they do it on foot. We'll take provisions, spare dogs—I want to put the ammunition reserve in pack-saddles—and any high-value loot." He dumped the grapes out of his helmet and buckled it on. "Burn or smash whatever we don't take. Oh, and we're not taking any hundred-pound bundles of loot, either, so wooers be swift—or refrain."

There was a harsh chuckle, and nods. This was a military picnic so far; it wouldn't stay that way, but there was no reason not to make the most of it while they could.

"Hell or plunder, dog-brothers." He straddled his dog Fihdel and his feet found the stirrups as it rose. "Boots and saddles, gentlemen."

❖   ❖   ❖

"Approximately one hundred seventy-seven thousand four hundred FedCreds. Gold," Muzzaf Kerpatik added. "That's allowing for the usual discounts on sales."

Raj grunted noncommittally, leaning one hand against the tentpole. It was a captured tent, from the baggage train Kaltin had overrun; they'd leave it behind in the morning. He looked out across the camp—not much of one, just the picket lines of staked-out dogs, the men cooking around their campfires. Odd to be in a camp where you heard more Namerique than Sponglish, but the central group was mostly MilGov troopers. *Fruits of conquest.* That was the true spoil of war; peace in the lands he'd retaken, and their fighting men here defending the Civil Government.

The MilGov soldiers, the ex-warriors of the Squadron and Brigade, were happy enough. An easy campaign so far, under leaders they trusted; they were warriors by birth and professional soldiers by the trade he'd given them, and indifferent to who they fought.

The sun was setting in the west, over toward the Drangosh thirty kilometers distant. It was hazed with burning, crops and buildings and towns; the raiding force had smashed a path of devastation a hundred kilometers southward. He could smell the smoke, faint under the cooking and dog odors of a war-camp.

"How much of that plunder is from Osterville's group?" Raj asked.

"Ah, unfortunately Colonel Osterville's battalions have had poor luck. Less than two thousand from them."

A chuckle ran around the table behind him. "I don't think," Raj said, "the men are going to find it amusing that Osterville's boys are holding out on them. Particularly given the recent service records, respectively."

"Raj, darling," Suzette said. "*Do* come and sit down. Or pace like a caged dog, but make up your mind."

He shrugged a little sheepishly and returned, sitting and taking up a drumstick. It was sauroid, but tasted pretty much like the chicken that was the alternative. As usual, Suzette had managed to find something better than you had any right to expect in the field; of course, the pickings were good. He stoked himself methodically.

"You don't like this, do you, darling?" Suzette said.

"No," Raj said. "I'm a thrifty man. The looting's good here because this area hasn't been fought over in a long time. It'll be generations recovering."

"Which will weaken the Colony," Gerrin Staenbridge pointed out.

He'd managed to shave and find a clean uniform, which was a minor miracle when they were all living out of saddlebags. *Every man pays the price he will for what he values,* Raj thought. Gerrin dressed for dinner the way he dressed line for a charge, with finicky care, as a mark of civilization.

"That's assuming the stalemate continues out here," Raj said. "The

Civil Government of Holy Federation is the legitimate ruler of *all* humankind. The Colonials included."

Staenbridge raised an eyebrow: "Well, it hasn't had much luck enforcing that for millennia or so," he pointed out.

During which time the Colonials had besieged East Residence twice and the Civil Government had reached as far as Al Kebir once.

"I don't like it either," Bartin Foley said.

They looked at him, and the younger man dropped his eyes to the cut-down shotgun on the table before him, his single hand slowly reassembling the clean, oil-gleaming parts. They went together with smooth clicks and snaps, and he slid it into the harness he usually wore over his back.

"It's not real soldiers' work, harrying peasants like this," he went on doggedly.

Gerrin and Raj nodded in chorus, and smiled at the coincidence. "Not good for morale, really," Raj said. "Not too much of it."

"Gets the men thinking like bandits," Staenbridge agreed.

Suzette shook her head. "Such perfect knights," she said with gentle mockery. Then: "Ah, Abdullah."

The Druze entered with two suspicious troopers at his heel, their bayonets hovering not far from his kidneys, and Antin M'lewis to one side. He bowed: "*Sayyid. Sayyida.*"

Raj leaned back in the captured folding chair, some *amir*'s hunting equipment. *I'll be damned. I didn't expect to see him alive again, I really didn't.* Suzette had an eye for picking reliable servants, though.

"That's all, men," he said to the troopers. They hesitated, and his tone grew dry. "I can handle one Arab, thank you." They saluted, threw Abdullah a warning glance, and wheeled smartly out.

Damn, this living legend shit can get wearing. The men wouldn't leave him alone for a moment, watching, listening, guarding. Damn their dear loyal souls. What was he, an invalid?

you are their talisman, Center said. **without you they would feel themselves lost.**

I'm only one man, Raj thought/protested. *And I've got competent officers.*

belief is its own reality.

Abdullah pulled documents from his ha'aik. He also accepted a goblet of watered wine; his particular brand of exceedingly eccentric shi'a Islam had some liberal notions.

"Lord," he began. "Ain el-Hilwa is swollen to bursting with refugees. Perhaps a hundred and seventy, a hundred and eighty thousand in all. They crowd the city and the suburbs outside the wall."

Raj nodded. That was no surprise. The spy's long brown fingers moved dishes to tack down the map and papers against the warm breeze of evening.

"The garrison includes ten thousand men of the Settler's regulars and the *ghazis* of the local *amirs*, but of these no more than two hundred are of single *tabors*." *Banners*, the Colonial equivalent of the Civil Government's battalions, although usually a little smaller. "The rest have been sent on detachment to the Settler's army across the Drangosh.

"Likewise, their officers quarrel. The provincial *wali*, Muhmed bin Tarish, is a court favorite; he hides among his women and sends messages commanding the men to stand fast within the walls. Haffez al'Husseini, the most senior of the military officers, is a veteran of the Zanj wars, but slowed by his wounds. He—"

The report flowed on, full and concise; units, strengths, weapons, dispositions, guns, the state of the fortifications and the water supply (which was good, since the city straddled the Ghor Canal). Center drew holographic projections over the map.

Abdullah's voice ceased. The others waited, in a silence filled by the flutter of canvas in the wind and the muted sounds of the camp; a dog howling, the brass of a trumpet calling, a challenge and response at an outlying vedette. Ten minutes later Raj blinked.

"Yes," he said, softly, to himself. "That should do." He looked up. "Excellent work, Abdullah. You won't regret it."

Abdullah bowed. "My life is to serve, *sayyid*."

Raj waved a hand. "If your son still wants that cavalry ensign's commission—and I'm still around and in command when he turns sixteen—it's his."

A very rare honor for one not of the Star Church; although Abdullah's faith allowed its adherents to freely observe the ceremonies of other religions, where advisable. The Druze bowed again, more deeply.

"Gerrin," Raj went on. "We'll be concentrated by 0900 tomorrow?"

"All except for Osterville," Staenbridge said. "But he's—"

"—closer nor he said, ser," M'lewis put in. "Nobbut six klicks east."

Raj nodded. "Here's what we'll do. Bartin, write this up. At dawn—"

CHAPTER EIGHT

"Allahu Akbar! Gur! Gur!"

The band of Colonials swept out of a side street in the maze of alleys. The morning sun burned bright on their scimitars and spiked helmets; beneath their djellabas they had wound tight linen strips, the winding-sheets of men determined to seek Paradise in battle with the unbelievers.

The main street was narrow and crooked as well; only one file of troopers was between Raj and the attack. Horace spun beneath him with a roaring growl, and his hand swept out saber and pistol. A grid of green lines clamped down over his vision, and the outlines of the Colonial troopers glowed. One strobed; the one with his carbine in his hands. Still a hundred paces away: a long pistol-shot but not impossible for a skilled man on dogback to make with a shoulder-weapon. And the Arab looked good. . . .

Raj moved his wrist. A red dot settled on the Colonial's midriff. His finger squeezed the trigger. *Crack.* The carbineer flipped over the cantle of his saddle. *Crack.* Another down. Place the dot and the bullet went where Center indicated it would. *Crack—crack—crack.* The revolver was empty, and the Colonials were through.

A clang of steel on steel as a scimitar met his saber. He flexed his wrist to let the sharply curved blade hiss by, then cut back-hand across the Arab's face. A second was barreling in with his blade upraised. Horace lunged with open mouth for the Bazenji's throat. Raj stabbed, and the point of his weapon went in below the breastbone. He ripped it free with desperate strength, wheeling. Suzette's carbine clanged and nearly dropped from her hands as she used it to deflect a cut. Raj rose in the stirrups and chopped down-ward; there was a jar like the blade hitting seasoned oak, and a splitting sound. It nearly wrenched from his hand, sunk to brow-level in the Colonial's skull, but the weight of the falling body pulled the metal free.

There had been no time for fear. Something contracted in a hard knot under his ribs when he saw his wife clutching at her upper arm.

"It's nothing, light cut," she said.

He checked; in the background rifles barked as the troopers put down the dogs of the dead Arabs where they stood snarling over their masters' bodies. She was right; she held a dressing over the superficial wound while he tied it off.

"Damn, that was too close," he said. "Anyone else wounded?"

His bannerman had gashed fingers where he'd used the staff to block a cut. Suzette heeled Harbie closer and went to work on that. The sergeant of the color-party was looking at him wide-eyed.

"Spirit, ser," he blurted. "Five dead wit' five shots!"

Raj felt a flush of embarrassment. He wasn't actually a first-rate pistol-shot; the sword was his personal weapon of choice, and with that he was very good. With Center's eerie trick, you didn't *have* to be good. He didn't much like the experience. It was too much like being a weapon yourself, in another's hand.

Whatever works, he thought.

precisely.

"Keep moving," he said sharply.

The suburbs of Ain el-Hilwa were burning already, as the Civil Government troops shot and hacked their way through the crowds who ran screaming towards the gates. Shells went by overhead in long ripping-canvas arcs, to crash on the massive stone-faced walls behind the moat. It was a wet moat, full of canal water, right now dark with the heads of refugees swimming across; and getting no help from the garrison. The gates were jammed tight with a press of humanity.

"Forward!" he said again. "Dammit, bugler, sound *Advance at speed!*"

The brazen scream cut through the white noise of the crowds, the gathering roar of the flames. Sheer press of numbers was slowing the advance despite complete surprise. The people ahead *wanted* to get out of the way of the sharp blades and snarling meter-long jaws and rifle fire; they *couldn't*.

Should have stayed in their houses, he thought—or in the sprawling city of reed shanties and tents outside the suburbs. There was no wisdom in panic.

A field gun bounced up behind him. The crew pulled the trail free of the limber and spun it around, running it forward with the long pole held up and the nose of the gun down. They pushed it through the front line of Civil Government troopers and let the trail fall.

"Stand clear!" the gun commander said. He skipped aside himself and pulled the lanyard.

Pomph. The shock of discharge slapped at him, bouncing back and forth from the narrow walls.

So did the hundreds of lead shot in the canister charge. Men—
and women and children—splashed away from the spreading scythe
of it.

"*Waymanos!*" Raj shouted again. "Forward!"

The buildings dropped away on either side as they came out into
the broad cleared area around the moat. Cannon and pompoms were
firing from the walls, but most of the shots went overhead, into the
belt of houses, helping with the work of destruction. In the gates,
the garrison were firing down into their own people, dropping
handbombs and pouring burning naphtha from the murder-holes over
the arched entrances to clear the press. The gates swung shut, and
the bridges over the moats gaped as hinged sections were pulled up.

"Damn," Raj said aloud. "Runner, to battalion commanders. Get
the fires going and pull back."

A shell burst twenty yards ahead. Raj stood in his stirrups and
brought out his field glasses, sweeping along the walls. Chaos, but
active chaos—groups in the crimson djellabas of Colonial regular
troops, infantry from the looks of them, and the white-and-colored
patchwork of city militia. More and more of the fortress guns were
getting into operation, too.

He turned Horace to the rear. "Come on, let's get out before the
fires spread."

He was conscious of a few odd looks. Technically, this was a
defeat—they hadn't been able to rush the gates, despite the shambolic
panic of the Colonial garrison's response. Raj grinned a little wider.

A reputation for having something up your sleeve could be quite
helpful. Even when you *did* have something up your sleeve.

Suzette was flexing her arm, wincing only a little, as they turned
and trotted back through the smoke and noise. Shells whirred by
overhead; ash and bits of debris fell into the dirt streets about them.

I'm almost *glad that happened*, Raj thought. Something sounded
an interrogative at the back of his mind. *I was beginning to wonder
whether I'd lost my capacity for strong emotion.*

i am not contagious.

The hell you're not, Raj thought. *For example, I wouldn't have
dared to talk this way to an angel a few years ago.* He looked down
at the city. *For another, I wouldn't do what I'm going to do to
Osterville a few years ago. Even to Osterville.*

**ah. that is the effect known as "life," raj whitehall. and it is
contagious; not only that, but fatal. for all of us.**

"Should be ready in about three hours, *mi heneral*," Dinnalsyn
said.

The gunner and Raj stood together outside the earthworks, five
kilometers from Ain el-Hilwa. Two thousand troopers and as many
press-ganged Colonial refugees dug steadily, hauling the dirt from
the growing ditch upslope in baskets, buckets, helmets, and cloth

slings improvised from coats. The sun was high, and the men sweated as they worked; an hour on and an hour off, with the off spent standing guard or watering and feeding the dogs. The earthwork fort was two hundred meters on a side, a standard marching camp with a ditch as deep as a standing man, an earthwork rampart as high inside with a palisade on top, and bastions at the corners and gates with V-notches for the guns. The air was full of the smell of sweat and freshly turned earth.

He walked over to the edge. "Found that buried cask of beer yet, dog-brothers?" Raj called in Namerique.

The big fair men in the nearest section groaned laughter. "Don't worry, lord," one yelled back. "By the Spirit of Man of This Earth, we'll have a grave big enough for all the enemy we kill if it takes us all day."

Raj waved as he turned away. *Not bad,* he thought. Back home, these men scorned digging in the earth as fit for peons and women; real men fought, hunted, and drank. They'd learned something of soldiering, then—granted he'd had to kill about a third of the adult males in their nations to get their attention, but they were learning.

Within the enclosure medics were setting up, and tents being pitched in neat rows along the streets; everything necessary for a mobile military city of five thousand men. It could be made more elaborate the longer they stayed, but by midafternoon the camp would be ready to defend. It was said, not without truth, that watching a Civil Government army encamp was more discouraging for barbarians than fighting a battle with them. The Colonials wouldn't be intimidated, but they'd know exactly how hard it was to storm this sort of earthworks.

"Good, Grammeck," he said. "Keep pushing it. Gerrin, once we've got the wall up, let all these Colonials go—it won't hurt the troops to finish up by themselves. Kaltin, you've got overwatch—"

"Ser," his color-sergeant said.

Raj looked around. A party of Civil Government officers was riding up; not his own, Osterville's banner. Raj waited in silence.

"General," Osterville said.

"Colonel," Raj replied. Formally: "Colonel Osterville, I'm ordering you to bring your command within the walls of this encampment."

Osterville sneered, a rather theatrical expression. "I'll have to deprive you and Messa Whitehall of that pleasure. As Commandant of the Military District of Sandoral, our authority is concurrent. These commands remain separate, and *I'm* not afraid of that lot of wogs over there."

He pointed; his own four battalions were setting up camp on a hill no more than a kilometer from the walls. Beyond that was a dense pall of smoke, as the ruins of the suburbs beyond the wall smoldered. Not coincidentally, there was an orchard and pleasant little country villa on the hill.

"I warn you," Raj went on, stroking his chin, "that the Colonials may try to sally. Your position is more vulnerable than mine."

Osterville spat—toward the city, which made the gesture ambiguous. "They're scum, with incompetent officers. Obviously, or they'd be over the river with Ali, wouldn't they?" His voice took on a faint hectoring, lecturing note. "Look at the way they reacted when we attacked this morning. As I said, *I'm* not afraid of them, and neither are my men. We're staying where we are."

"By all means, Colonel Osterville," Raj said mildly. "Perhaps it's advisable, all things considered."

From the ranks of officers around Raj a loud whisper continued the thought: "Considering what our men would do to those garrison pussies who've been shorting the take."

Osterville's head whipped around, finding a wall of bland politeness. He saluted and pulled his dog around, with a violence that brought a protesting whimper as the cheek-levers of the bridle gouged.

"Ser." A messenger this time, from the heliograph detachment who'd been setting up a relay back to the bridgehead. "Message from Colonel Menyez."

The silence grew tense. Raj read. "Ali's arrived," he said. "And tried the usual. So far—"

observe, Center said.

"Noisy beggars," Major Ferdihando Felasquez said.

The Colonial army was parading past the walls of Sandoral, fifty thousand strong. *Tabor* after *tabor* of mounted men in crimson djellabas and pantaloons, in a perfect order that rippled with the rise and fall of the trotting dogs. Between the blocks of men came guns, light pompoms and 70mm field pieces, with heavier siege weapons behind. Beyond that, on a hillock just out of medium artillery range, an enormous tent-pavilion in brilliant stripes was already going up. From the tallest pole flew the green crescent banner and the peacock of the Settlers.

And over it all came an inhuman pulse of drums, like the beating heart of some great beast. Beneath that the clang of cymbals and the brazen scream of long curled trumpets.

Felasquez tapped his gauntlets against his thigh. "Should we send them a few love-notes?" he asked. "Some of the heavier pieces on the wall could reach that far."

"No," Jorg Menyez said, scanning down the line of units with the big tripod-mounted field glasses. "We're playing for time, so there's no sense in poking the sauroid through the bars. Ah, yes. Notice something?"

He stepped aside and Felasquez bent to the eyepieces. A forest of banners was going up before the Settler's pavilion. "Ali, Hussein the Wazir, the Grand Mufti of Sinnar, the Gederosian Dervishes . . . wait a minute."

Menyez nodded. "No Seal of Solomon. Tewfik's not here."

"Unless they want us to think that."

"No, that's not the way Colonials think."

Felasquez nodded. "I'd still feel easier if you weren't splitting up so much of the 24th Valencia," he went on.

"The garrison infantry need stiffening; we haven't had enough time to work them into first-class shape."

"You can't stiffen a bucket of spit with a handful of lead shot," Felasquez said.

Menyez clapped him on the shoulder. "It's not as bad as all that. They're trained men, sound at bottom; they've just been neglected recently. Standing behind a parapet and shooting is about the easiest type of combat for 'em. They just need some examples. How're the militia-gunner volunteers showing?"

"Pretty well; still have to see how they stand fire, of course. But the ones who stayed were the ones who *wanted* to fight. A lot of them were with us when we fought Jamal, five years ago."

Along the walls of Sandoral men stood to the parapet and looked out the merlons, but their numbers were sparse. Most of the garrison stood to in the cleared space within the walls, or waited in their billets. Apart from them the city was a ghostly place, where little moved but rats and cats almost as feral.

"It's all waiting now," Menyez went on, "and I want my supper. Runner; message to the *Heneralissimo*—"

This time the viewpoint shifted to a point on the rail line west. Raj recognized it: a long viaduct over a gully that was a torrent in the winter and spring. The burning remnants of the wooden trestle bridge lay scattered below.

A long file of Colonial dragoons rose from prayer and rolled up their issue rugs. Naiks and rissaldars screamed at them, and they returned to their work—hacking through the ties of the railway line. As each section of track came loose, they carried it at a run to one of the bonfires that blazed at intervals down the line and threw it on. The dry wood flared up like tinder, and in the heart of the furnace-heat he could see the thin strap iron turning cherry-red and then yellow, slumping and twisting into a mass of metallic spaghetti that would have to be carted to the forges and rolling-mills as scrap.

Raj nodded to himself, tight-lipped. No surprise; a railroad was the best military target there was. But it had taken generations to get the line from Sandoral to East Residence completed; until Barholm Clerett came to the throne and Raj reconquered the territories to the west, there always seemed to be a more urgent short-term priority.

The Colonials were doing a good professional job of the wrecking, and there were a lot of them.

✧   ✧   ✧

Dust smoked up from the road. Sweat dripped off the twenty-hitch train of oxen as they strained at the trek-chain. The big tented wagon rolled forward, its axles groaning, man-high wheels turning at the steady, inexorable pace that would take it ten kilometers a day and neither more nor less. It was one of a line of two dozen, between them taking up several kilometers of road; all of them had the Crescent pyrographed on the wood of their sides, and the Peacock stenciled on their tilts.

The load was sacked grain, and bales of a repulsive-looking dried fish; even in the holographic vision he could imagine the mealy, oily smell of it. *Advocati*, the staple dog-fodder of the Drangosh valley, a sucker-mouthed parasitic bottom-feeder with no backbone. Dogs would eat it, just; even slaves would refuse it if they could. As he watched, the oxen halted as the drivers snapped their whips. Men with baskets of grain and dried alfalfa pellets went down the train, dumping loads by the draft cattle.

The escort sank down and unlimbered the goatskin water-bottles at their waists, stacking their light lever-action rifles. Infantry, with short curved falchions at their belts rather than the scimitars of the cavalry. Tewfik wouldn't be wasting his best men on duty like this, but here was about a platoon of them. The drovers were civilians, slight men in ragged clothes.

A voice called, and drovers and soldiers alike knelt in the dust, performing the ritual washing and unrolling their mats. A call, and they knelt to distant Sinnar, the holy city where the first humans on Bellevue had landed, bringing a fragment of the ka'ba from ruined Mecca.

A Colonial officer with gold-rimmed spectacles and a green-dyed beard stood beside a hole. It was outside the walls of Sandoral—he could see the city in the middle distance—but outside ordinary artillery range. There were several hundred Colonials working in the hole, mostly stripped to their loincloths, but they had the look of soldiers. Probably engineers; the Colony had whole units of them, rather than expecting line units to be able to double up at need, the way the Civil Government did. He'd never seen men work harder, or with more skill.

Picks were flying; plank ramps went down into the hole, and wheelbarrows came up at a trot, full of earth. The dirt was piled neatly in heaps not far away; other men were filling sandbags from the heaps. Still more shaped timber, raw beams from orchards around the city, or seasoned timber salvaged from houses. A knocked-down floor of planks waited to be assembled.

A bunker, Raj decided. *Cursed large one, too. Probably for Ali.*

Raj blinked, conscious of the eyes on him. They were all used to his . . . spells of inattention . . . by now.

He cleared his throat. "Ali's reached Sandoral and he's digging in around the city. So far he hasn't mounted an assault—bringing up his siege train, at a guess. He's got the full fifty thousand men with him; it must be straining his supply of wagons and fodder to keep them fed. Tewfik's banner isn't with the main army."

There was a stir at that. "What do we do, *mi heneral?*" Staenbridge asked.

"We dig, and we wait."

"Wait for what?"

"For the wogs" —he nodded toward Ain el-Hilwa— "to take the bait. In which case, we—"

The officers waited in silence, a few taking notes. "Is all that clear?" Raj finished.

"No reserve?" Staenbridge asked.

"Not this time; it's a calculated risk, but so's this whole expedition."

He turned and looked at the Arab city, surrounded by the smoldering wreck of its suburbs, crammed to the very wall with refugees.

"Either this will be easy, or it'll be impossible," he said.

probability of action proceeding according to current projections, 78% ± 7, Center said helpfully.

"I'd put it at about three to one on easy," he went on. "If not, we'll just have to react fast."

> *"When you go by the Camina Bellica*
> *As thousands have traveled before*
> *Remember the Luck of the Soldier*
> *Who never saw home anymore!*
> *Oh, dear was the lover who kissed him*
> *And dear was the mother that bore;*
> *But then they found his sword in the heather,*
> *And he never saw home anymore!"*

"Ser." Antin M'lewis was Officer of the Day; he slipped into the circle around the fire. "Major Hwadeloupe t'see yer."

Raj finished the mouthful of fig-bread and dusted his hands, leaning back on the cushions—someone had salvaged them from a nearby Colonial mansion, and they were all resting on them and the Al Kebir carpets from the same source. A roast sheep on rice had been demolished, and they were punishing the sweetmeats and pastries the Colonials were famous for. The wine was too sweet, even diluted, but nobody was drinking all that much of it anyway; they knew him better than that. The firelight played on the faces around it, bringing out scars on Kaltin Gruder's as he leaned forward to light a twig and puff a cheroot alight.

"By all means, Antin, bring him along," Raj said.

Hwadeloupe commanded the 44th Camarina Dragoons, one of Osterville's battalions.

"An'. ser . . . he's got 'is men out there. Hunnerts of 'em, not too far."

"Keep an eye on them, Captain."

The strong male voices were roaring out the next verse, the one that had gotten the song officially banned centuries ago. It was a truth the Governors preferred that the Army not be too conscious of:

"When you go by the Camina Bellica
From the City to Sandoral,
Remember the Luck of the Soldier
Who rose to be master of all!
He carried the rifle and saber,
He stood his watch and rode tall,
Till the Army hailed him as Governor
And he rose to be master of all!"

"Glad you could join us," Raj said as Hwadeloupe strode up. "No, no, no salutes in the mess, Major. Have some wine."

The soldier-servant handed him a mug of half-and-half, watered wine. He gripped it distractedly, a middle-aged man with the marks of long service on the southern border on his leathery face.

"*Mi heneral,* if we could speak privately?"

"I have no secrets from my officers and Companions, Major." Not *quite* true, but it was a polite way of telling Hwadeloupe that he couldn't expect to hedge his bets.

"Ah . . . sir, I would like to transfer my battalion to your command—to this encampment, that is."

The rest of the command group had fallen silent; Suzette kept strumming her *gittar,* but softly. Without the song, the minor noises of the camp came through: dogs growling, a challenge from the walls, the iron clatter of a field gun's breechblock being opened for some reason.

"If I might ask why?" Raj went on implacably.

Hwadeloupe stood very straight. "Sir. Colonel Osterville thinks there's no risk from the garrison of Ain el-Hilwa. But I know you don't think so, and I see your men still have their boots on, and your guns are limbered up. Colonel Osterville may be right. On the whole, though, when he and you disagree, I'll bet on you. With respect, sir."

Raj shoulder-rolled and came erect. "I can always use good men," he said. "And I don't think you'll regret that decision. Captain M'lewis will show your men to their bivouac area within the earthworks."

"Ah, sir. There's one other matter." Hwadeloupe kept his eyes fixed over Raj's shoulder. "We have, ah, a considerable quantity of booty with us. Just picked up, you understand. We'd like to turn it in now to the common fund, as per your standing orders."

Raj raised an eyebrow; one of Gerrin's expressions, and very useful in situations like this. "That's odd, Major. We've had several smaller parties in from Colonel Osterville's camp, and they've all had some late-arriving booty to turn in too." He extended his hand. "No hard feelings. M'lewis will settle your people in."

"I'll see to that myself, if it's all the same to you, *mi heneral*," Hwadeloupe said, taking the extended hand in his own. "And thank you, sir."

Raj returned to his cushion beside Suzette. "That's about two hundred in all," he said.

"Separating the sheep from the goats," Staenbridge replied. "Or those too stupid to live from the remainder."

Foley frowned. "Some of them are staying over there to follow orders," he pointed out.

"My dear," Gerrin said, "what's that saying—from the Old Namerique codexes—"

Foley was something of a scholar. " '*Against Fate even the gods do not fight,*' " he quoted.

"Exactly."

Raj nodded and leaned back, his head not quite in Suzette's lap. Both moons were out and very bright, bright enough to interrupt the frosted arch of stars. Her fingers wandered over the strings.

> "*It's twenty-five marches to Payso*
> *It's forty-five more to Ayaire*
> *And the end may be death in the heather*
> *Or life on the Governor's Chair*
> *But whether the Army obeys us,*
> *Or we serve as some sauroid's fare*
> *I'd rather be Lola's lover*
> *Than sit on the Governor's Chair!*"

Cut-nose Marhtinez lay in the dark and breathed quietly. He was ten meters from the walls of Ain el-Hilwa, outside the north gate. An overturned two-wheel cart hid him; the bodies of the two dogs who'd been drawing it until they met a cannonball were fairly ripe after a day in the hot sun, and so was the driver: black, swollen, the skin split and dripping in places, like a windfallen plum. He'd had about seven FedCreds in assorted silver in his pouch, though.

The night was fairly dark, only one moon in the sky and that near the horizon. The starlight was enough for him to see men moving on the walls—and they were moving without torches. He could even hear some wog curse when he ran into something and barked his chin. A whistling and dull thudding followed, about the sound you'd expect one of those nine-barbed whips the wog officers used to make. The yelp of pain that followed was strangled, and the next slash brought no sound at all.

Quiet's a whorehouse on payday, he thought scornfully. It was a good thing there weren't any Bedouin scouts with the Ain el-Hilwa garrison. Those sand-humpers were too good for comfort.

Cut-nose moved his head slightly. The star he was using was still a fingerbreadth above the horizon. An hour and a bit short of dawn, call it an hour and twenty minutes.

He moved backward out of the wrecked cart, keeping it between him and the wall. Nothing on his body clinked or reflected light, and his hands and face were blacked; Mother Marhtinez might not have known exactly who his father was, but she hadn't raised any fools. Pause, move, pause, until he was behind a snag of ruined wall, still hot enough from the fire to feel on his skin. He picked up his rifle—nothing but a hindrance and a temptation in the blind where he'd spent the night—and eeled cautiously back to his dog.

Captain M'lewis was waiting there. Cut-nose grinned ingratiatingly. He didn't have much use for officers, and still less for a promoted ranker who might be a kinsman. He did have the liveliest respect for Antin M'lewis's wits, his wire garrote, and the skinning-knife he wore across the small of his back beneath the tails of his uniform jacket. All the Forty Thieves—the Scouts—had a standing invitation to go out behind the stables and settle things with knives if they felt they couldn't obey someone who wasn't Messer-born.

So far only one fool had taken M'lewis up on it; he was on the rolls as a deserter. Nobody had found the body. *Good riddance,* Cut-nose thought. The Scouts beat regular duty all to hell. Less boring, more plunder—a *lot* more in some cases—and no more dangerous. M'lewis wasn't the charge-the-barricade type.

"They're movin', ser. Gittin' ready, loike," he said in a soft whisper, directed at the ground—nothing to carry far.

M'lewis nodded. "Messer Raj was expectin' it, an' t'scouts at t'other gate says th' same," he observed. "Here, git this t'him fast."

"Sir."

Kaltin Gruder's voice. Raj rolled out of his blankets; Suzette was already reaching for her carbine. He fastened his weapons belt. His boots were already on; if the men had to sleep in them, so could he.

"Message from M'lewis just got in."

A Scout was behind the battalion commander. "Ser. Noise in t'wog town. I weren't more 'n ten meters off, an' heard it plain. North gates."

The ones nearest Colonel Osterville's camp. Raj took the message and read it. "Boots and saddles, please. Quietly. We'll deploy as arranged."

"Line of march?"

"Scout troop has pickets along it. They'll signal with shuttered lanterns."

Raj could hear the noise spreading; not very loud, no shouting, but a long-drawn out clatter as men rousted out of uneasy sleep and saw to their equipment. The Companions arrived, and the other battalion commanders. Shapes in the night, dimly lit by the embers of the fire, a feeling of controlled anxiety. He grinned into the dark. A night march. Difficult. An invitation to disaster, with any but very experienced troops. The handbooks were full of bungled night attacks, men firing on their comrades, whole battalions wandering off lost, irretrievable disaster.

"Barton," he said. "What's that toast again?"

" 'He fears his fate too much, and his deserts are small, who will not put it to the touch—to win or lose it all.' "

"Exactly. Messers, to your units. *Waymanos!*"

An orderly brought up Horace; he put a foot in the stirrup and swung into the saddle. The headquarters party fell in around him, bannermen and buglers and gallopers. Men blinked and dogs yawned cavernously; the wet *clomp-clomp* sound of jaws snapping closed rippled through the dark streets. Iron-shod wheels rattled on dirt as the 75s and splatguns moved. He cantered down the east-west notional laneway of the camp, the *wia erente*, keeping to the side. Men and dogs were moving the same way, the lead element of the 5th, followed by the 1st and 2nd Cruisers. The other gates were all open as well, flanked by lantern-bearing pathfinders. Thousands of heavy paws thumped the earth, an endless rumbling sound.

Flat terrain, mostly. Nothing between him and Osterville's camp but four kilometers of fields, with the occasional orchard or shallow ditch. The objective was on the same side of the Ghor Canal, thank the Spirit, even *Osterville* wasn't stupid enough to put an obstacle that needed bridging between him and the only supports available. *Keep in column,* he decided. In column they could move down the laneways, at a fast walk. Once deployed into line their speed would drop by four-fifths.

The night was still quiet, almost chilly in the last moments of predawn; overhead the arch of stars was a frosted road leading to infinity. The command group rode silently, no need for talk unless something went very wrong. The palms that lined the roadway were black silhouettes against the sky. He looked over his shoulder to the west and caught the faintest rim of peach-pink there.

He reined Horace sideways into the fields, a hunching scramble through the ditch, then stood in the stirrups to look. Nothing but a few watchfires from Osterville's camp. The north gates of the city were hidden by the western wall. Flags rippled behind him, his personal banner and the Star. Over his shoulder he could see the other gates of the camp, now; the spiked-log barricades were pulled aside, and a steady stream of men and dogs and guns was pouring out. Not a single jam-up, not a voice raised ... *damn, but these are good troops.*

Three columns, each about half a kilometer apart, each a little over two thousand strong. And—

" *'The gates flew back, and the din of onset sounded,'* " Bartin murmured.

"More Old Namerique?" Raj said.

"From the Fall Codexes," the young man replied.

When the Fall began, books had died with the machines that recorded them—the Church called it the Great Simplification. In the first generation the survivors wrote down as much as they could, most of it in Old Namerique, the official language of the Federation. Bits and pieces survived, even a thousand years later.

The gates of Ain el-Hilwa had certainly flown back with a vengeance.

"One hell of a din, too," Raj said; even at more than three kilometers, it was louder than the noise his own men were making.

Then light winked from the parapet of the low-set city wall, and a deep whirring sound crossed the sky. A dull booming echoed, and under it the sharper sound of the exploding shells. The winking lights, scores of meters apart, rippled from east to west across the north face of the city. Heavy rifles, aimed at Osterville's camp. The shells seemed to be contact-fused rather than airburst, but it would still be an unpleasant way to wake up, and there were a lot of those guns.

The white dust of the road stretched out ahead of him. The dawn was just touching the western horizon behind him, but there was a sudden flare of white light stabbing north toward Osterville's position, arc-searchlights from the city wall. *My, all the modern refinements*, Raj thought. Intended to light up the Civil Government position for the attackers and blind any defenders looking toward the city.

Dun and off-white, men were running up the long gentle slope toward the smaller Civil Government camp. On foot, mostly, with gun teams among them, pulling the light five-shot pom-poms the Colonials favored for close support. They were shouting, too, high wailing shrieks. Raj unclipped his binoculars and brought them to his eyes, body adapting to the swing of his dog's trot with the unconscious skill of a lifetime.

Only half a kilometer from the walls. And they didn't dig in at all. Osterville had been *very* careless.

A stutter of gunfire broke out from Osterville's camp, building rapidly. Raj could imagine the chaos, men rushing half-dressed from their blanket rolls, grabbing up the rifles stacked by their campfires. Red light winked from the hilltop, muzzle flashes like fireflies in the dark; the sun was just edging over the horizon.

The Colonials were making some effort to deploy, spreading out in an irregular mass—more a thick skirmish order than a real firing line. The pom-poms wheeled about and opened up, firing uphill. The *CRACK-CRACK-CRACK-CRACK-CRACK* of the clip-loaded weapons sounded through the dawn, and their little one-kilo shells burst upslope in petals of fire. The return fire was building fast, panicked, with no ordered crash of volleys. Smoke began to shroud the hilltop, from the defensive fire and the incoming Colonial shells, and—

"Bugging out already," he said. In the long-shadowed light of dawn he could see a trickle of mounted men heading north from Osterville's encampment. "Ludwig, how many of the Colonials would you say?"

"Seven or eight thousand at least, *mi heneral.*"

Raj nodded thoughtfully. The whole garrison of Ain el-Hilwa, or near enough. Attacking Osterville's position was actually not a bad idea—he would have tried it, in their position—but sending everyone haring out of the gates like this? *No more sense than a bull carnosauroid in breeding season,* he decided.

"Captain Foley, the signal."

Barton swung down out of the saddle and stuck the launching-stick of a small rocket in the dirt.

Fisssssth. The little rocket soared into the paling sky and burst with an undramatic *pop.* Red and blue sparks shot out in a perfect round puffball. Behind Raj trumpets sang in harsh antiphonal chorus. The long column dissolved as units spurred out left and right, like a huge fan snapping open. It was lighter now, light enough to tell a dark thread from a white, the traditional dividing line between night and day. Light enough for the men to move across the fields without much trouble, at least.

The other columns were following suit. Ten minutes, and there was a continuous two-deep line moving northeastwards with his banner at the center. Not parade-ground neat—the line twisted and curled a little around obstacles, with fifty meters or so of gap between each battalion. The guns pulled through, heading east and a little south, setting up by groups of batteries on prechosen hillocks. The Colonials were fully occupied, their front ranks within two hundred meters of Osterville's position and moving in fast. Close enough to use their carbines, and a huge snapping crackle went up from their front ranks; not *only* from their front ranks, either—they were losing men to friendly fire, if he was any judge.

"Sound *Prepare for Dismounted Action,*" he said.

The bugles sang again, taken up and relayed down the line. Men pulled the rifles from the scabbards before their right knees, resting the butts on their thighs.

"Are they bloody *blind?*" Staenbridge asked in amazement, looking at the Colonials.

"No, just very preoccupied, and extremely badly led," Raj said.

There were probably individual men in the Colonial force who could see what was happening, but it was a scratch put-together

and whoever had done the putting hadn't arranged for signals and
gallopers. A penalty of taking all your best troops along in a single
expeditionary force; what was left to defend against a counterstroke
wasn't up to much.

Six hundred meters, Raj thought.

**five hundred eight-eight and decreasing to nearest enemy
element. five hundred eighty. five seventy-six.** Center provided
a numbered scale on the whole Colonial formation; their right wing
was just out of extreme rifle-shot.

More of Osterville's men were bugging out, but that wouldn't be
visible to the wogs. A slamming close-range firefight ran in a C all
around the front of the hill, as the larger Colonial force overlapped
the Civil Government forces upslope. Most of the pom-pom shells
were flying right over the hill, dangerous only to the deserters
streaming northward—who deserved whatever they got. The Colonial
rifle fire was uneven; their men were pumping out their seven-shell
magazines and then pausing to reload. That had to be done by
pushing one round at a time through the loading gate in the side
of the weapon, which evened things out a little, but Osterville's fire
was dropping off noticeably, as the Colonials beat down his men
by sheer weight of numbers.

Five hundred meters. "Sound *Dismounted Advance.*"

The buglers sent the message down the lines: a four-note preparation, twice repeated, then a single sustained note taken up by the
signalers in unit after unit. Six thousand dogs crouched. Not quite
in unison, but nearly so within battalions. The men stepped free
of the stirrups without pausing, and the dogs rose and walked behind,
still in ranks as regular as the men's. A good cavalry battalion drilled
six hours a day, six days a week for this moment, until the signals
played directly on the nervous systems of men and mounts. Raj turned
his binoculars to the far right of his line: Hwadeloupe's men were
badly under strength, but they were carrying it off quite well.

A long clatter as the men loaded. Raj's head went back and forth;
the troops were advancing at a steady walk, the splatguns trundling
forward with the soldiers, two per battalion. They were light enough
for the crews to manhandle them like that; they looked much like
field guns, but each was actually thirty-five double-length rifle barrels
clamped in a tube. He watched as one crew let the trail thump to
the ground and loaded. One man swung the lever down, another
inserted an iron plate with thirty-five rifle cartridges, the lever went
back up with a thump. Waiting for the order—but they were
artillerymen and very good at estimating ranges. He chopped out
his palm. The buglers took it up. All up and down the line men
checked a half-pace. And . . .

"*Halto!*"

Officers ducked ahead and spread arm and drawn saber to mark
the firing line. Another bugle call and the front rank dropped to

the ground and the men behind them went to one knee, right elbow resting on it. The platoon commanders and senior noncoms walked quickly between the two ranks for a moment, checking that the sights were adjusted for the range. The muzzles quivered as each trooper picked a target. The dogs crouched; only the mounted officers, Company-grade and above, marked the line. Company pennants and battalion banners too, of course; the men took their dressing from the flags.

Raj took a deep breath. It was a peculiar exultation, like handling a fine sword with perfect balance; the pleasure that came only from a difficult task performed exactly as it should be.

Some of the enemy were turning now, firing frantically. Far too late. The trumpets spoke again, preparing men for the order:

"Fwego!"

BAMMMbambambambabam . . . Six thousand rifles fired within a few seconds of each other. A discordant medley of battalion trumpeters sounded the *Fire by Platoon Volleys.* BAM. BAM. BAM. Rippling down the formation. Front line prone, second rank kneeling. Front rank fire-and-reload, second rank fire-and-reload, a steady pounding crackle. The dawn wind was from the east, blowing the new fogbank of powder smoke backward in tatters. The smell was overwhelming in the fresh morning air: a sharp unpleasant reek of burnt sulfur and stinging saltpeter. The smell of death.

The splatgun crew spun the crank at one side of the breechblock. *Brraaaap.* A long splat of sound as the thirty-five rounds snapped out. *K-chung* as the lever went back and the plate was lifted out by the loop on its top, a rattle as another was slapped home and the lever worked. *Brraaaap. Brraaaap.* Three hundred rounds a minute. An ancient design, ancient before the Fall, from man's first rise; primitive enough that men in these days could build it. The priests said that Man had been perfect, before the Fall. Raj had always been a believer; it was obscurely disturbing that part of that perfection was better and better mechanisms of slaughter.

He threw the thought aside, with a touch to the amulet blessed by Saint Wu; there was the work of the day to be done. Raj turned and cantered down the line. The Civil Government formation was at right angles to the Colonial formation, like the crossbar on a "T." The whole weight of its fire was crashing into the end of the Arab line. And most of the Civil Government cavalrymen could *hit* a man-sized target at three hundred meters, many of them at twice that range. Even if they missed, their 11mm bullets would run the entire length of the enemy line, with good odds of hitting *something.* The Colonials were melting away, men smashed to the ground by the heavy hollowpoint bullets with massive exit wounds that bled them out in seconds, or tore limbs from bodies.

He paused behind one of the ex-Brigadero units. A noncom was walking down the line, slapping men across the shoulders with the flat of his saber when they instinctively rose to fire standing. *Problem,* Raj though. They'd trained on muzzle-loading rifle muskets. You had to stand to reload those, tearing open the paper cartridge and pouring the powder down the barrel. They were excellent shots even by Descotter standards, but not used to getting under cover—and even at this range, some of the Colonial carbine-bullets would hit standing men. A few snapped by him.

Ludwig Bellamy rode up. "It's a slaughter, *heneralissimo,*" he said enthusiastically. "Teodore—Major Welf—asks permission to remount his battalion and charge—"

"Denied," Raj said sharply.

Welf had been a very tricky opponent in the Western Territories, but he was still a Brigadero at heart and had a lingering fondness for cold steel. The Civil Government military style was economical of men where it could be, not having so many trained soldiers to expend.

"I'm not going to waste men on this lot." He raised the binoculars again. "Besides, about now—"

There was boiling confusion all down the front of the Arab army. A knot of mounted officers around a huge green banner was galloping toward the threatened flank, with more courage than sense. At their head was a portly gray-bearded man waving his ceremonial lash and shouting furiously, probably trying to pull units out of line and get them to face front left. Small chance of that, since Osterville's men were still firing from *their* front, besides which most of them probably hadn't realized what was happening, and facing about would put the morning sun directly in their eyes.

The enemy bannerman went down. Seconds later half a dozen of the officers around him did, and then the elderly man with the whip punched backward over the cantle of his saddle. His dog whipped about and sniffed him, then sank down on its haunches and howled.

"—they're going to bug out."

It started with the men in sight of the dead commander. They broke like a glass pitcher dropped on a stone floor, and fled back toward the city. Bullets kicked up dust around their feet like the first raindrops of a storm, and littered the ground with bodies. That unmasked the central part of the Colonial host, and for the first time they could see exactly what it was that had devoured the left wing of their army. And the steady, unhurried volleys punched out, from a Civil Government line marked by a growing tower of smoke that made their position clear even a kilometer away. The Arabs disintegrated like a rope unraveling from the left end, men throwing away their weapons to run screaming for the city gates. Droves piled up at ditches that a man could leap easily, as the first tripped and the men behind trampled on them.

"*Spirit,* sir—if we charge now—"

"Major Bellamy, all that charging now would do is give *them* an opportunity to hurt *us*." He looked around. "Messenger to Major Gruder: advance from the left in line, by battalions, pivoting on . . ." —he considered— "on the 3/591st." You had to start moving the outside of a line first, or the whiplash effect would leave the outermost man running.

"Are we going to let them back into the city, *mi heneral?*" Ludwig Bellamy asked, crestfallen.

Raj smiled unpleasantly. "By no means, Major. By no means."

"Range three thousand. Up three. And a bit. Contact fuse. Load."

Grammeck Dinnalsyn raised his eyes from the split-view rangefinder. Three batteries were deployed along the slight rise: twelve guns. Another three were a few hundred meters farther on, setting up amid the outer spray of the dead Colonials. Dismounted men were trotting by in waves as the left flank of the Civil Government force swung in to pin the retreating Colonials against the walls of Ain el-Hilwa, but that was no concern of the artillery today; they weren't tasked with supporting the dogboys. The riflemen were firing as they advanced, independent fire in a continuous crackle all up and down the line. The sun sparkled on the bright brass of the spent cartridge cases.

Breechblocks clattered as the big 75mm shells were passed from the limber and rammed home. The crew stood aside as the master gunner clipped his lanyard to the trigger and payed it out.

"Ranging gun, shoot," Dinnalsyn said.

Battery commander's work, really, but enjoyable, and he rarely got a chance to do it these days. The gunner jerked sharply.

POUMPH. A long jet of smoke shot out from Number One of A Battery. The gun threw itself backward in recoil, the trail gouging a trough in the clay. The crew jumped forward as soon as it came to rest, grabbing the trail and the tall wheels and running it back to the original position.

Dinnalsyn raised his binoculars. A tall plume of black dust sprouted from the roadway outside the northeast gate of the city, like an instant poplar that bent in the breeze and dispersed as the dirt scattered.

"Excellent," he said. "Batteries, range."

The thick tubes of the guns rose as the gunners spun the elevating screws under the breeches.

Excellent shooting on the first try, and it was excellent to serve under a commander who *understood* what artillery could and could not do.

The other two batteries were tasked with the northwestern gate, a bit farther—near maximum effective range. Their ranging gun fired seconds after his, and the gout of dirt flung skyward was a hundred meters short. Even that trial shot told, flinging parts of men and equipment skyward. Both roads into Ain el-Hilwa were black with running men, and more every second. They tried again, and the next round fell neatly before the open gates.

"Airburst, three-second fuse, shrapnel, load."

Blue-banded shells from the limbers, passed forward hand to hand three times; gun crews had redundant members to replace casualties in action. Not that there looked to be much counterfire this time. The master gunners pulled the ring-shaped blockers out of the noses of the shells, arming the fuses. Into the narrow hole went a two-pronged tool they carried chained to their wrists, to adjust the timers. A brass ring on the fuse turned, listing the time in seconds; within, drilled beechwood turned in a perforated brass tube, exposing a precisely calculated length of powder-train.

"Number one gun ready!"

"Number two gun ready!"

"Number three gun ready!"

"Number four gun ready!"

"Battery A ready!"

"Batteries will shoot, for effect. On the word of command."

He raised his free hand, the other holding his binoculars. *Use your judgment*, the general had said. Men were running through, but that was the first spray of them. He waited, gauntleted hand in the air. The gates were narrow, and so were the arched bridges that carried the roadways over the city moat. You *wanted* city gates to be a chokepoint, for defensive reasons, and Ain el-Hilwa had excellent fortifications. Routed, the Arab troops were not going to wait while they were marshaled through with maximum efficiency. Every man for himself meant a tie-up.

Sure enough, the roadways were black with men and great fans of them were spreading out along the edge of the moat. He chopped his hand downward.

"Now!"

POUMP. The first gun fired. A precise twenty seconds later the second followed. *POUMP. POUMP. POUMP.* By the time the last gun fired, the first had been pushed back into battery and was ready to fire again. A steady two rounds a minute, to conserve barrels and break armies. No problem, with the men fresh. Pushing the ton weights of metal around was hard work, but they were trained to a hair and the day was young.

Four *crack* sounds downrange, as the shells burst. Ragged black smokeballs in the air over the crowd at the gates; below them panic, as the shells' loads of musketballs scythed forward in an oval pattern of destruction.

POUMP. POUMP. POUMP. POUMP. This time one of the rounds hammered into the dirt before exploding, a faulty time-fuse. No great problem this time; the crater made the pileup greater. He shifted his glasses to the other gate. The spread of shell was wider there, some far enough from the gate to kick up dust, but you expected that at extreme range.

The general cantered up with his staff and messengers. He paused for a moment, leaning on the pommel with both hands and studying the artillery. *Strange man*, Dinnalsyn thought. He saw too much, knew too much. Knew as much about guns as he did himself, and was better at judging distance and trajectories; a cannon-cocker's skills, not a talent you expected in a hill-squireen out of Descott. And he never *forgot* anything, never missed a detail—as if angels were whispering in his ear. There were those strange little trances, too. Grammeck was city-born to a merchant family, and prided himself on his modernity, but there might be something in the tales of Messer Raj being touched by the Spirit.

"I could do better execution with more tubes, *mi heneral*," he said.

They had fifty-five guns along, and they were all reconcentrated now that the raiding parties had joined forces.

Raj shook his head, his stone-hard face still turned to the gates where men screamed and died and the corpses tossed under the hammer of the shells.

"Not for this," he said. "We don't have the ammunition to expend."

True; they were limited to what they'd brought along. He made a mental note to shift things around to even out the reserve supplies between batteries before they broke camp. A glance at his watch told him it was still early, barely 0800.

"And speaking of which," the general went on, "give them another three rounds per gun and cease fire. Another few minutes and the guns on the walls will have you registered here."

As if to punctuate the thought, a heavy shell buried itself in the earth a hundred meters ahead of them and exploded, throwing clods of dirt as far as the second hillock.

"And then limber up and get out of range," Raj said.

"*Si, mi heneral.*"

seventy-six rounds per gun, Center said.

Ah, Raj thought. About his own offhand estimate. Strange, that so much of Center's advice was a refinement of what he'd have done anyway.

of course. otherwise i would not have selected you.

Which was reassuring. There were times he doubted he was the same man who'd blundered into the centrum beneath the Gubernatorial Palace.

that youth would be gone forever by now in any case.

Raj shrugged and looked down at the field of battle with a mixture of distaste and the sensation a farmer had looking back over an expanse of grain cut and stooked in good time. The Colonials had finally gotten their gates shut and the cannon on the wall active;

but that left most of their garrison trapped outside the wall and exposed to fire.

"Signal cease-fire. And get a truce flag ready."

"What terms?" Staenbridge said.

"The usual. Parole not to participate further in this campaign, and one gold FedCred per head."

One advantage of fighting the wogs was that they and the *Gubernio Civil* had been locked in combat so long they'd developed an elaborate code of military etiquette and generally observed it for sound reasons of mutual long-term advantage. One provision often used was releasing prisoners on parole, when the alternative was killing them for want of time and facilities. It put them out of action for the remainder of the war in question, and was about as profitable as selling them for slaves, which was the other choice. Granted that they could be used on some *other* frontier, which freed up troops to be used against you; on the other hand, both powers had an interest in keeping the barbarians at bay.

and the cause of civilization is served, as well.

Kaltin Gruder came up. Raj nodded. "Nice turning movement, Kaltin."

"Work of the day, *mi heneral.* Are we going to take their parole?"

Raj nodded. Kaltin's mouth tightened, but he nodded unwillingly.

"Ali might not keep it," he pointed out. Reluctantly: "Of course, it wouldn't *matter*, with these handless cows."

"There are no bad soldiers, Kaltin, only bad officers. But these have had their morale fairly thoroughly shattered, and they won't be any use to anyone for a good long while. See to it."

Another party rode up; this one included a number of bandaged and bleeding men. The most senior seemed to be a captain; Raj didn't recognize him, which probably meant he was from Osterville's command.

captain fillipo swarez, 51st mazatlan.

Thank you, Raj thought. Aloud: "Captain Swarez."

The man blinked at Raj through red-rimmed, exhausted eyes, holding his bandaged arm against his chest to limit the jarring of his dog's movement.

"General Whitehall. I am reporting as senior officer in . . . as senior officer of the other field force battalions."

Raj raised an eyebrow. "Major Gonsalvez?"

"Dead, sir."

"Colonel Osterville?"

observe:

A brief vision this time: Osterville's muddy sweating face, bent low over the neck of his dog and slashing behind with his riding crop. A string of remounts followed, and several servants, and pack dogs with small heavy crates strapped to their carrying saddles.

Swarez spat. "That for the *hijo da puta!* Nobody saw him after the shelling started, and his dogs and personal servants are missing."

One of the lieutenants behind him spoke. "*Heneralissimo,* let me send a patrol after him—let me *take* a patrol after him. I guarantee, he'll never trouble you again."

Growls of assent rose from the survivors; their mounts snarled in sympathy, scenting their masters' mood. *No zealot like a convert,* Raj thought.

He shook his head. "Messer Osterville" —he omitted the military rank— "suits me well enough where he is." He looked back at the captain.

"Captain Swarez, how many survivors?"

"Six hundred in all, sir. Two hundred wounded."

Half Osterville's original force, but that included several hundred who'd defected to Raj during the night, and the Spirit alone knew how many who'd bugged out this morning.

"How many of those in your 51st Mazatlan?"

"Two hundred twenty-six. Fit for duty, that is, sir."

Which meant they'd kept together fairly well. "All right. Tell the remainder that those who wish may transfer to your unit, or to any of my other battalions that'll take them—some of them are severely under strength. Have everyone ready to move shortly."

Swarez saluted, relief on his face. A soldier's battalion was his home and family, and his had just been spared from disbandment. The other survivors could count themselves lucky to have open slots waiting for them.

Raj watched the party with the white flag riding up to the gates of Ain el-Hilwa. He doubted the negotiations would take long; they'd be too hysterically thankful not to face a storm and sack, which they now lacked the men to stop. Say until noon to get the wounded sorted, police up and destroy the enemy weapons, collect the ransom . . .

Demand some fast sprung wagons as part of it, he decided. There were good roads all the way from here to the bridgehead opposite Sandoral. Then . . .

"Meeting of the command group at midday," he said. "Now let's get this wrapped, gentlemen."

He looked down at the field again before he reined about. A good workmanlike day's effort. Unpleasantly final for several thousand Colonials.

It wasn't going to stay this easy. This was a sideshow so far. Ali's main attention was focused on Sandoral.

CHAPTER NINE

"Fwego!"

Corporal Minatelli opened his mouth and put his hands over his ears. His firing slit was close enough that the fortress gun would hurt his hearing if he didn't.

BOOOOMM.

"Reload, canister!"

The big soda-bottle-shaped fortress gun surged backward on its pivot-mounted carriage, muzzle wreathed in smoke. The wooden friction blocks squealed against their screw tighteners as they slowed the multitonne weight of cast iron and steel. It slowed to a stop at the end of the low ramped carriage, and the militia crew sprang into action. Two men leaped in with a bundle of soaked sponges on a long pole and rammed it down the barrel. There was a long *shhhhhhhhhhh* as the water met hot metal and flashed into steam. They pulled the pole out and flipped it, presenting the wooden rammer head. Two more men were lifting the round in, a big dusty-looking linen bag of coarse gunpowder nailed to a wooden sabot, with a tin canister full of lead balls on the other end.

Minatelli shuddered as he turned away. Canister from a light field gun was bad enough. Canister from a 150mm siege weapon . . .

The gun rumbled like thunder as the gunners released the blocks and it ran down the carriage to lift the iron shutter and poke its muzzle out the casement wall. Bronze wheels squealed as the four men at the rear threw themselves at the handspikes in response to the master gunner's hand signals. The gun carriage was mounted on a pivot in the center, with the front and rear running on wheels that rested on an iron ring set into the concrete floor.

"Bring her up two—they'll be trying again," the master gunner said. He accompanied it with hand signals, for the ones who had lumps of cotton waste stuffed in their ears. His crew spun the big elevating wheel at the breech two turns, and the massive pebbled surface of the gun elevated smoothly at the muzzle.

Keep to your trade, Minatelli told himself, stepping up to the firing parapet. He usually didn't have much time for militia, but these gunnery boys knew their business. He peered through; the sunlight made him squint, after the shade of the wall platform with its overhead protection of timber and iron. The stone of the wall was cool against his cheek.

Outside, six hundred meters from the wall, the wog trench was still swarming. Men were dragging away the dead and wounded, the smashed gabions, wickerwork baskets with earth inside them. He could see flashes of heads and shoulders as picks and shovels swung. The trench was big, a Z-shaped zigzag running back to the main wog bastion twelve hundred meters out; that was a continuous earthwork fort all the way around the city now. Cannon flashed from it, and he could feel the massive stone-fronted walls tremble rhythmically under him as the heavy solid shot pounded selected spots. Dust puffed up, making him sneeze. He wiped his nose on his sleeve and spat.

There were hundreds of the assault trenches worming their way toward the walls, but this one was his section's particular tribulation.

The enemy guns boomed again. One bolt struck right beneath him, and his rifle quivered against the stone it rested on with a harsh tooth-gritting vibration. It would be difficult for them to make a breach; Sandoral's walls were twenty meters thick counting the earth backing, and sunk well behind the moat so that only a lip showed . . . but it would happen in time.

Shells screeched by overhead, exploding behind him among the empty houses. The ragheads didn't seem to be worrying about ammunition supplies. He'd helped defend the walls of Old Residence against a hundred thousand Brigaderos, twice the number that the wogs had, but this felt worse. Back then they'd had Messer Raj, and the MilGov barbs had wandered around with their thumbs up their bums while the Civil Government force wore them down. The towel-heads weren't that kind of stupid.

He hopped down and walked along the space of wall his section held, and the platoon of garrison infantry they were supporting. One of those was stretched out on the walkway, most of the top of his head missing and brains spattered all over his firing niche.

"*Fuck* it!" Minatelli screamed. "You—y'fuckhead—didn't y'*tell* him?"

The dead man's corporal looked up. "Couldn't make 'im listen."

The wogs had big bipod-mounted sniper rifles working from their forward lines, single-shot weapons as heavy as the sauroid-killers the Skinner nomads used. They had telescopic sights, too.

"Well, git t'body out of t'way," Minatelli said angrily. Two of the man's squadmates dragged it away as it dribbled. Bad for morale to have corpses lying around if you didn't have to. It was a pity you couldn't remove the smell; it was hot and close here, and the blood began rotting almost at once.

Everyone else was keeping their head away from the firing slit until told. Rifles were lying in the flat stone bottoms of the slits, with their levers open to keep the chambers as cool as could be. Each niche had a couple of wooden strips set into troughs in the stone, with rows of holes drilled in the wood. Each hole held a cartridge, base-up and ready to hand. Two thousand-round ammunition crates rested on ledges between firing positions, their tops loosened and the protective tin-foil curled back to show the ten-round bundles, one hundred bundles per box. Buckets of water and dippers hung from iron hooks; there was a wooden box of hand bombs by every man's firing position, round cast-iron balls the size of an orange, with a ring on top to arm the friction fuse. There were even some spare rifles in a rack, for the men disarmed by the jams that would be inevitable once firing got heavy and the weapons heated up.

The only thing missing was enough men to fill all the firing niches, plus the reserve that doctrine called for. What they had was one rifleman for every three slots, one man for nine meters of front. The Colonials had enough troops to attack anywhere along four kilometers of wall, without warning.

The lieutenant blew his whistle. Men tensed, thumbing rounds into their rifles and working the levers to shut the actions. Minatelli sprang back into his niche and licked his thumb to wet the foresight. Enemy pom-poms raked the line of firing slits. The infantry-man jerked his head down and squeezed his eyes shut as grit blasted through his, then blinked them open.

"Make 'em count, boys!" he shouted. "Thems *cavalry* you're shootin'."

Men were swarming out of the forward Colonial works, men in djellabas and spiked helmets. Their carbines were slung; most carried long ladders, and some lugged small mortars with folding grappling hooks and reels of cord attached. Others pushed wheeled bridging equipment to get them across the moat. Pairs carried little cohorn mortars, adapted to hurl grappling hooks at the end of a reel of iron cable.

Spirit, there's a lot of them. His narrow slit showed *thousands*, and more pouring out of the trenches like ants out of a kicked-over burrow.

White-painted iron stakes marked the ranges outside. The ramp sight on the rear of Minatelli's rifle was set for four hundred meters. He steadied the forestock against the stone and curled his finger around the trigger, taking a deep breath. The first enemy crossed by the four-hundred-meter-mark, two files holding a ladder between them. He dropped the sight onto the front-right man, let it down to the man's knees, and stroked the trigger. A soft click sounded as the offset, the first slack, took up.

Gentle, like it was a tit, he told himself, and squeezed.

Bam. The wog stopped as if he'd run into a stone wall and dropped, the ladder sagging and swinging broadside onto the city defenses as his teammates staggered and tripped. *Last one I know for certain,* Minatelli thought. Rifles barked in a stuttering crash all along the wall, smoke erupting from the slits. Men in the attacking force fell, and other men replaced them. Minatelli worked the lever of his rifle and thumbed in rounds. Spent brass tinkled around his feet.

BOOOOMMM. The big cannon a few meters down took him by surprise this time; he'd been too involved in his personal war to notice the master gunner's orders. He did see the result, as the malignant wasp-whine of the canister round spewed out its hundreds of ten-gram lead balls. It caught the mouth of the assault trench with a fresh wave of ragheads just clambering over the gabions. They vanished, swept away in the storm of hundreds of marble-sized shot. Dust and fragments of wicker spurted up all over the face of the trench. When the dust cleared, the dirt was covered with a carpet of men pulped into an amorphous mass, a mass that still heaved and moaned in places.

"Reload, canister!"

Minatelli himself reloaded, pausing to snap the ramp under his rear sight down to two hundred meters. The rifle was foul after more than two dozen shots, and the metal scorched his callused thumb as he shoved home the next round. The recoil was worse now too, and his shoulder would be sporting a fine bruise tomorrow, assuming he was here to feel it. Massed carbine fire pecked at the rock outside, some of it uncomfortably close. A round whined through the firing slit, the flattened lead going *whip-whip-whip* as the miniature metal pancake sliced air. It could slice him as easily. He bounced back up, picked a target, fired, ducked back down to reload.

Spirit. He was glad he was in here and not out there. There were as many wogs down as moving.

"Hold 'em, boys, or we're all hareem guards!" he called, and fired again.

Again. The cannon fired a third time, or was it the tenth? No way to tell. Smoke hung dense and choking, turning the ground outside the walls into a fog-shrouded mystery where crimson shapes dashed and bunched. The Colonials were nearly to the edge of the outer works, kicking their way through the caltrops—triangles of welded nails scattered through grass deliberately left to grow knee-high. Some distant part of Minatelli was amazed that men would slow down in the face of rifle fire to avoid getting a nail in the foot, but many did.

Then the cannon from the projecting bastions cut loose. Each V-shaped protrusion took hundreds of meters of wall in enfilade, dozens of cannon sweeping the ground with loads of heavy canister. Most of them were carronades, short big-bore weapons like gigantic shotguns. Not much range, but they didn't need it.

Minatelli paused to let his rifle cool a bit with the lever open, gulped water from a bucket down a throat as raw as if it had been reamed out with a steel brush. Drops fell on the metal of the breechblock and sizzled. When the smoke cleared enough for him to see again, he reloaded and aimed at one of a pair of Arabs dragging a wounded comrade back with them. He shot, reloaded . . .

"Cease fire! Cease fire!"

The bugles reached him where the shouted command did not. His finger froze on the trigger, and he worked the lever and caught the ejected shell. His fingers were black with powder residue, and it coated his lips, tasting of sulfur when he licked them. There were more dead wogs outside than he could count, coating the ground in sprays and swaths back toward the enemy works, bobbing in the moat below amid the wreckage of wooden bridging equipment and ladders. More up and down the foot of the wall. In places the carpet of bodies stirred and moaned; there were so many he could smell the blood-and-shit stink of ripped-open bodies all the way up here.

He took another drink of water and left his rifle lying on the stone firing slot, lever open. "Sound off!" he called. Then he trotted over to the platoon commander's station.

"Sor! Two dead, three wounded serious." That included the two sections of garrison infantry his eight men were overseeing. "Ev'ryone else ready for duty."

The lieutenant was a good enough sort, a bit young. He looked out through the slit next to him and returned his unused revolver to its holster. Perhaps because he *was* young, he spoke aloud:

"They thought they could rush us. No respect."

"Plenty now, sor."

The young officer nodded, unconsciously smoothing down a wispy mustache. "Yes. Now they'll try starving us out."

Spirit, Minatelli thought.

There hadn't been much but men, dogs, weapons, and ammunition in the trains that brought them east. Sandoral had been full of hungry refugees for a week before they got here, and the invasion had disrupted the harvest.

"Messers, to fallen comrades."

As youngest of the senior officers present, Bartin Foley gave the toast in the three-quarters diluted wine. They all drank.

"Messers, the Governor." Raj gave that, and they tossed aside the clay cups.

As if to remind them of the fallen, a man screamed from the tent nearby where the wounded were being tended. Casualties had been light by every reasonable standard except that of the men whose own personal flesh had been torn and bones been shattered. Suzette was present, but her sleeves were rolled to the elbows and there was still blood spattered down the front of her jacket.

"I gather we won't be trying to take Ain el-Hilwa, *mi heneral,*" Staenbridge said.

"Of course not; what would we do with it?" Raj said. He tapped the map on the table before them. "Messers, we'll split up into the same three raiding parties—Major Swarez, you'll accompany the center group with me" —Osterville's ex-follower nodded—"and Major Hwadeloupe, you'll be attached to Major Gruder's command.

"We'll head south by southeast along this axis." He traced it on the map. "Keeping west of the Ghor Canal."

"Our objective is the railway?" Staenbridge said, tracing it with one finger.

The scouts had given them a definite bearing; it came straight west from the main Colonial line along the Gederosian foothills.

observe, Center said.

A train screeched to a halt, sparks fountaining out from the tall driving wheel of the locomotive. It was a new machine, painted in black and silver, with Arabic calligraphy along the sides in gilt paint and up the tall slender smokestack. Behind it were a dozen cars, the last an armored box with a pom-pom mounted on a turntable behind a shield; thirty or so riflemen poked their weapons out of slits in the boilerplate that sheathed it. The other cars held sections of track, already spiked to cross-ties, piled up in stacks and secured by chains. Another train halted behind the first. This one had boxcars full of men and tools.

They boiled out, their officers waving the ceremonial lash and shouting; there was more noise than a comparable group of Civil Government soldiers would have made, but no more confusion. Teams jogged forward and undogged the chains holding the first train's cargo. They set up a light folding crane and lowered the sections of pre-formed track to the ground; other teams lifted them with iron hooks and trotted forward, keeping step with a wailing chant.

Ahead of the two trains was a section of wrecked track a quarter-kilometer long. Engineers gave the roadbed a quick check with levels and transit; gangs of workers shoved the burnt, twisted ties and rails to one side. The prefabricated sections were dropped in place and the hookmen went back for another load at the same steady trot. Another team slewed the tracks into alignment with long poles like gunners' handspikes and bolted them together.

Raj shook his head. "There aren't enough of us, and we don't have enough time," he said. "The Colonial sappers can repair track faster than we can tear it up—until Tewfik can get back here. The major bridges will be heavily guarded. But we want him to *think* we're a threat to the railway line, and by all means tear up any stretch you reach."

"What news from Sandoral?" Staenbridge said.

"Ali put in a quick attack when he arrived in force, and when that didn't work he tried a full assault with engineering and artillery support. Total losses of four to five thousand, including wounded too badly hurt to return to duty soon. Our casualties were very light."

"My, my. I wouldn't like to be on Ali's staff right now,"

Visions crawled beneath the surface of Raj's vision; beheadings, impalements. Ali was quite mad.

"Gerrin," he said, "neither would I. He's still got forty thousand effectives, not counting his infantry garrisons." They had seven thousand cavalry, and three thousand infantry in all.

"More goblets than bottles at this banquet," Staenbridge agreed.

If there wasn't enough wine to fill all the glasses at table, beyond a certain point juggling the liquid from one glass to another wouldn't help.

"We might take their supply dump at the railhead," Dinnalsyn said thoughtfully. "That would embarrass them considerably."

"It's fortified, and there are ten thousand men in there," Raj said. "Not first-rate troops, but they're expecting trouble and they've got considerable artillery."

They all nodded. You might be able to take a position like that by a sudden unexpected *coup de main,* or if it was held by barbarians too dim to take the proper precautions. Not otherwise, not with a larger enemy field force free to operate against your rear.

"If that's all, gentlemen, we'd better see to business. Tewfik's banner hasn't been reported back at Sandoral either."

The main column trotted down a roadway through the early morning cool. It was twenty feet broad, well-graded dirt surfaced with gravel, winding down through terraced barley fields from a low ridge planted with a mix of olives and almond trees. Gullies running down toward the flat were full of reddish-green native scrub; a flock of sheep-sized bipedal grazing sauroids fled honking and gobbling into the bush as the troops passed. Dew still laid the dust on the rolling hillside. Beyond were flat fields, irrigated and intensively cultivated. The villages were deserted, ghostly, not a human or a domestic animal in sight. The peasantry had had warning enough to flee by now, driving their herds before them.

Raj finished a pear and tossed the core aside, squinting ahead. Then he stiffened and flung up one hand.

"*Halto.* Silence in the ranks."

The bugles snarled, and the column came to a dead stop in less than three strides. Silence fell, broken only by the occasional jingle of harness as a dog shifted.

There. A dull thudding sound, like a large door being slammed far away. It echoed, and was repeated. Again. Again.

"Artillery, by the Spirit," Staenbridge said softly.

Raj nodded, closing his eyes to concentrate.

civil government field guns, Center said. **two batteries, approximately 8.7 kilometers south-southeast of your present position.**

"Well, that's something serious," Bartin Foley observed flatly.

Ain el-Hilwa had been the only action hot enough to need artillery support so far. The officers around Raj exchanged glances, and so did the men in the long ranks zigzagging back up the hill. The military picnic was over.

"Kaltin," Raj said. That was where Kaltin Gruder's *kampfgruppe* was operating.

He called up the maps of the area. A low ridge on either side, running east-west, more flat ground to the south.

"Sound *Reverse Front*," he said. "Then *Trot*."

The bugle screamed again, and the dogs turned in place. They waited the thirty seconds necessary to turn the gun-teams and broke into a rocking trot back up the slope.

"Messengers to the raiding parties, immediate concentration here," Raj began. "Colonel Staenbridge, establish your banner there" —he pointed to the notch where the road crossed the hill— "with a firing line on the reverse slope, ready to move up. Major Bellamy, that'll be your 1st and 2nd, and the 1/591st. Gerrin, anchor your left there" —he pointed to a reservoir— "and re-fuse your right with the raiding parties as they come in. Grammek, get your guns on the reverse crest too, but keep the teams close."

The artilleryman nodded. That was dangerous—risking immobilizing the weapons if the teams were injured—but gave essential seconds of extra time if you had to pull out fast.

"No fieldworks, but put up some quick sangars for the splatguns. Suzette, have those Church people ready to triage the wounded and move them back immediately; we won't be staying. Captains M'lewis, Foley, I'll be taking a company of the 5th and the Scouts forward with me. And one splatgun. Questions?"

Heads shook. "Good. To your positions, please. Gerrin." Staenbridge reined in. "I've got an unpleasant feeling we'll be coming back faster than we go. Be ready to stop them hard." Even veteran troops could turn unsteady if it looked like a rout.

Staenbridge nodded; they leaned toward each other and slapped fists, inside of the wrist and then back. "We'll be here, *mi heneral*."

Raj met Suzette's eyes for a moment. No words were necessary. *"Waymanos!"*

They trotted through a land silent and deserted, warming towards the crippling heat of a Drangosh Valley summer morning. Raj's little force rode in column, with a spray of pickets out ahead. The dogs kept up a steady canter-trot-walk-trot-canter, eating the kilometers. Their tongues lolled, but their ears were pricked forward, all but Horace's, which were a hound's floppy style. The guns sounded much closer now, thudding bangs. The terrain hereabouts was mixed, fingers of high *doab* running from the clay bluffs along the Drangosh into the lower, flatter country to the east that extended past the Ghor

Canal to the foothills of the Gederosian Mountains. From the sound, the guns were firing on the next ridge south.

All the men had heard the sound before, and most of the dogs. The troopers rode with their rifles across their thighs.

Whistles came from up ahead. One of the Scouts came down the road at a quick lope.

"Courier comin', ser," he said.

The messenger's dog was panting. He pulled a sweat-dampened paper from a jacket marked with the shoulder-flashes of the 7th Descott Rangers. A smell of scorched hide came from the leather scabbard in front of his right knee, the smell a hard-used rifle made when it was slapped into the sheath still hot.

"Ser," he said, "Major Gruder reports we'ns ran inta a patrol. Thought't were a patrol, turned out t'be more wogs'n we could handle."

Raj read quickly; it was a request for reinforcements, with a quick sketch map of the action. He shook his head. Kaltin was a first-class tactician, but he had a tendency to over-narrow focus, to lock his teeth in a situation and try to beat it to death.

"My compliments to Major Gruder, and tell him I'll be there shortly. And to be ready to move position, quickly."

"Ser!"

"Barton, bring them up to a lope."

The messenger pulled his mount around and clapped heels into its flanks. The sound of the guns grew sharper as the ground rose. He could see powder-smoke rising above the higher terrain to the south. A trickle of wounded passed them, riding-wounded leading dogs with more badly injured men slung over them—it was all you could do, in a situation like this.

POUMPF. POUMPF. POUMPF. The guns were firing steadily; he could see them now, spaced out amid spindly native whipstick trees on the ridge. They were firing from the top crest, the crews pushing them back every time they recoiled. Raj pulled off the roadway, leaning forward in the saddle as Horace took the ditch with a bound and swung up the hill.

Kaltin Gruder met him. "Ran into a patrol," he said. "Company strength—one *tabor*. I jumped them, more of them came up, I called in my raiding parties, then even *more* showed up. There's a battle group of two thousand down there now, and they're not stopping for shit. These aren't line-of-communications troops. Regular cavalry, and good ones."

Raj grunted in reply, sweeping his binoculars over the slope below. It was sparsely wooded with whipsticks, tall spindly trees with branches that drooped up and away from the main stem on all sides, dangling fronds of featherlike leaves.

POUMPF. POUMPF.

The eight guns on the ridgeline kept up their steady shelling, the pressure-wave of the discharges slapping at faces and chests. At least twenty Colonial artillery were firing in reply from the lower ground to the front, half pom-poms and half 70mms. They weren't attempting a counter-battery shoot, just searching the edge of the treeline to try and beat down the fire of the Civil Government riflemen. All across the open ground Colonial dragoons were moving forward on foot, line after line of them in extended skirmish order.

Gruder went on: "I've got the 7th in the center, with Poplanich's Own and the 1st Rogor to the right and left and the Maximilliano over there."

He pointed to the east, where smoke and the steady crackle of small arms indicated action. "Whoever the wog commander is, he knows his hand from a hacksaw—started trying to work around my flanks as soon as he got a feel for the depth of my firing line here. I moved the Maximilliano out to extend the line, but it thinned me here badly."

Raj nodded curtly. Gruder's three battalions—a thousand men or so, all under strength—were keeping up a steady crackle of independent fire. Down below figures in red djellabas were scattered on the ground or hobbling, limping, and crawling back toward the guns and the banners grouped around them. Advancing against veteran riflemen cost heavily. A splatgun gave its ripping *braaap* and a file of Colonials nearly a thousand meters away went down as the spread of rifle bullets hit them. Several of the enemy guns shifted aim; Raj could see the splatgun team trundling their light weapon to a new position just ahead of the pompom and field gun shells.

But more and more of the Colonials were making it to their own firing line close to the woods. Their repeaters were just as deadly as the heavier Civil Government weapons at ranges under a hundred meters, and they fired much faster. A haze of off-white powder smoke was drifting away from the thickening Colonial position. Even as he watched, several platoons rose and dashed forward for the woods. Many fell, but others went to ground in the scrub along the edge of the savannah. Once in among the trees, their repeaters would slaughter men equipped with single-shot rifles.

"We can crush them like a tangerine if you swing in with the main force, *mi heneral*," Gruder said.

Kaltin does *tend to get too focused*, Raj thought. His own mind was moving in cool precise arcs and tangents, like something scribed on a drawing-board by an engineer's compasses and protractors. Like a mental analogue of the way you felt when fencing; perhaps a little like the way Center felt all the time, if Center had subjective experience.

He felt more alive than anywhere else. It was a pity he could only feel this on the battlefield, that his art could only be practiced as men died. There were times when he lay awake at night, wondering what that said about him. But not now. Not now.

"No, Major, a full-scale meeting engagement isn't what I have in mind. If there's one Colonial battle group around, there's going to be others."

He considered for a few seconds. "This will have to be quick. We'll withdraw by leapfrogging battalions. Move Poplanich's Own back half a klick to that rise, and the guns. You'll take the 7th and the others back to join the main force. I'll hold the rearguard." Gruder didn't like retreating. "M'lewis, detach two men to each of the battalion commanders to guide them to the main-force position. Follow with the rest."

Gruder nodded briskly; he didn't like it, but that would make no difference to his obedience. Antin M'lewis turned and barked orders. Pairs of men galloped off.

"Trumpeter!" Raj went on. "Relay. Half-kilometer withdrawal. On the signal."

The complex call went out, was echoed. A single long note followed.

The battery on the rise fired one last *stonk* and let the guns roll downhill to their limbers. The teams snatched up the trails and slapped them on; retaining pins went home with an iron clank, the six dogs of each team rose, and the guns set off down the open slope at a trot. Three men rode the offhand dogs of the team; there were two seats on the gun axles and two on the limber, and the remainder had dogs of their own. Up from the savannah came the splatguns, hauled by four-dog teams; lighter, they overtook the field pieces despite the smaller draft.

The crackle of small-arms fire intensified. "Barton. We'll give the wogs a going-away present. Standing saddle-volley, use the crestline. Place the splatgun."

Company A of the 5th was nearest to full strength, eighty men, only forty down from regulation. They fanned out behind Raj, heeling their dogs a meter and a half downslope. The dogs turned and faced the crest, then crouched. The men crouched with them, squatting. It was an inelegant and uncomfortable posture—you couldn't let your full weight rest on the dog—but the men moved into a flawless double line with the ease of a housewife slapping dough for tortillas. Three-meter spacing between each, and the rows staggered so that the rear row matched the intervals in the front. He looked at their faces: stolid, immobile under the film of sweat, a few chewing tobacco and spitting. Every one of them knew what was about to happen.

Below, the Colonials hesitated a crucial handful of seconds when the fire from the Civil Government troops ceased. Just long enough to let them dash back to their waiting dogs. Center unreeled numbers as the depleted battalions trotted up the slope, rallied, and cantered northward. He winced slightly. Those units had been under strength before. A lot of them were still down there in the burning grass and shattered whipstick trees, and would never leave. Long curled trumpets sounded, shriller than his own. Half the Colonials turned and started to jog back towards their dogs. The others opened fire on the retreating raiders; not many went down, but some men and dogs fell out of line.

"Reacting fast," Raj murmured.

The Colonial commander was sending his mounted reserve forward, galloping up the hill. Two *tabor*, a little under three hundred men, with a pair of pom-poms galloping behind. Galloping guns was risky, especially on uneven ground like this. A few men, wounded or just extremely brave, had stayed behind among the dead. One rose to a knee and shot the off-lead dog of a pom-pom team. It collapsed, biting at its wounded leg. The gun slewed around, then tipped over and spun. The massive torque spun through the trail and the harness, turning the team into a thrashing pile of twisted metal and shredded meat that bounced downslope and scattered the dismounted Colonials who followed.

Raj watched the mounted Colonials approach. Numbers scrolled across his vision. The Arabs were keening as they charged. If they could prevent his men from breaking contact . . .

500 meters. 450. 400.

"Now!" he barked.

"Tenzione!" Bartin Foley called, his clear tenor pitched a little higher to carry. The men rose from their squat to stand straddling their dogs. The long Armory rifles came up to their shoulders in smooth curves, the muzzles dead level except for the minute individual quivers as they picked their targets. The slope had concealed them, and to the enemy it must have appeared as if the heads and shoulders popped up out of nowhere.

The Colonials reacted with veteran reflexes, crouching in the saddle and sloping their scimitars forward. Their dogs bounced into a full gallop, throwing themselves forward to get through the killing zone as fast as possible.

"Fwego!" Foley's sword chopped down in a bright arc.

BAM. Eighty rifles fired within a half-second of each other. *Braaaaaap.* The splatgun fired from its position in enfilade to one side.

The charging Colonials seemed to stagger. Dogs went down all across their front. It was only three-hundred-odd meters, and at that distance most of the 5th's long-service men could hit a running man, not to mention a thousand-pound dog. Men flew out of the saddle, and rear-rank dogs leaped and twisted desperately to avoid the thrashing heaps ahead of them.

"Rear rank, *fwego!*"

BAM.

"Reload!"

"Front rank, *fwego!*"

BAM.

"Reload!"

Braaaaap. Braaaaap.

"Rear rank, *fwego!*"

BAM.

Braaaaap. The crew worked the splatgun like loom-tenders in one of the new steam-driven factories. Its load struck like case-shot, but far faster and more accurate.

A Colonial trumpet brayed and drums sounded. The mounted Colonials withdrew, leaving their dead and wounded; the thick screen of dismounted men down in the woods ceased to wait for their comrades to bring up their dogs and started up the slope once more. Field gun shells went overhead with a ripping-canvas sound.

He's putting in an enveloping attack, Raj decided, feeling through the movements for the enemy commander's mind. *He's decided this is a sacrificial rearguard.* Half the enemy were mounted already; the dismounted thousand or so would swamp a small rearguard like this in moments, and then the Arab troopers could pour after the fleeing Civil Government soldiers. They were lighter men on fast desert-bred dogs, slender-limbed Bazenjis; they would catch what they chased, and with a two-to-one edge in numbers and more in guns the issue could not be in doubt.

"*Waymanos,*" Raj said.

The dogs rose under the men and turned, and the splatgun crew hitched their weapon and leaped to the saddles and limber-seats. Ten seconds later Company A was moving downslope and north at a trot that turned into a rocking gallop.

They were two hundred meters away when the dismounted Colonials crested the hill. Carbine bullets cracked around their ears; the bannerman's staff jerked in his hand, and a man went out of the saddle with a coughing grunt.

"Don't mask their fire," Raj cautioned.

Foley flicked his saber to the left, and the block of men shifted course. Raj leaned forward against the rush of hot air, the banner snapping and crackling next to him. He looked back; the Colonials were re-forming on the hill, mounting up as their comrades led their dogs forward. North were flat open fields, marked with dust plumes where the retreating Civil Government battalions moved north toward his main force. A slight rise topped by a mosque and grove of cypress trees stood about a kilometer ahead.

Metal flashed there. Raj looked over his shoulder again. The Colonials were coming now, in solid blocks of mounted men; moving at a fast trot and deployed in double line abreast, for speed when they had to go into action. *Sensible.* They'd had a bloody nose twice this morning. He took a quick squint at the sun; 1100 hours. And about now . . .

There was a puff of smoke from the cypress grove ahead. A whir went by overhead, like heavy canvas being ripped in half. A malignant *crack* behind, and another puff of smoke, as the time-fused shell burst over the charging Colonials.

"Hope none of them fire short," Bartin Foley shouted, grinning.

Raj felt himself showing teeth in response. "Take them home, Bartin," he called.

He shifted the pressure of his knees and turned Horace directly for the left end of the formation ahead—Poplanich's Own, four hundred men strong. Plus two batteries of 75s, now firing as fast as the gunners could ram the shells home, reckless both of the barrels and the ammunition supply. Rounds whined by overhead and burst, in the air, or throwing up fountains of dirt if the time fuse failed. He crouched over the dog's neck and set his teeth as the battalion's splatguns opened up; no need to look behind. Closer, and he could see the two staggered rows of men in prone-and-kneeling formation. Then rifles came up and the steady BAM . . . BAM . . . of platoon volleys started. The smoke was thick enough to half-mask the troops as he pulled up in a spurt of gravel by the battalion commander's position.

The Colonials were closer than he expected, four hundred meters but wavering under the unexpected hail of fire. *Yes, about two thousand of them still,* Raj thought; and their artillery was coming over the hill, pompoms and field guns both.

As he watched, blocks of mounted Colonials veered to left and right, moving to flank the Civil Government blocking force. Without prompting, each battery ceased fire for an instant and heaved its guns around to deal with the new threat; the flanking forces moved farther out, but the Colonials in front seemed to disappear. Raj read their trumpet signals: *Dismount* and *At the Double.* The line shrank as the dogs crouched, then turned into a long double rank of men on foot coming forward at a uniform jog-trot.

"In a moment, Major Caztro," Raj said.

The Major—he was a cousin on his mother's side of the late Ehwardo Poplanich—nodded.

"The gunners aren't happy about it," he said.

"Better grieving than dead," Raj said dryly, taking a drink from his canteen; the day was already very hot.

"And . . . *now!*" he said. The major relayed the order to his buglemen.

The gunners fired a last round from their weapons. He could hear one sergeant cursing as he wrenched the breechblock free and tossed it to one of his men. Then he jammed a shell backwards into the opening, stuck a length of slowmatch into the hole where the fuse would normally go, and lit it with the last of the stogie clamped between his lips.

"Fire in the hole!" the noncom shouted. It was echoed down the gun line. "Ten seconds!"

The troopers were already double-timing back to their dogs and swinging out the rear of the cypress grove around the mosque.

"Retreat by platoon columns, at the gallop!" Major Caztro shouted.

Raj looked to either side as he touched his heels to Horace's ribs. The flanking parties were still well back, and the main Colonial force were just remounting and kicking their beasts into a gallop—which must be rather frustrating for them.

The noon sun was blinding-bright. The white dust of the road reflected its heat, and sweat rolled down his forehead out of the sodden sponge-and-cork lining of his helmet. Horace was panting, his black coat splotched with dust. Raj uncorked his canteen and rubbed a little of the water into the dog's neck; if it went down with heat prostration, he was deeply out of luck. Another check behind: the Colonials were coming on fast, but they were staying in line and bringing up their guns with them.

Cautious, but smart, Raj decided.

Barreling in hell-for-leather might have caught him quicker, but he'd already given them the back of his hand twice. There was nothing to show that he didn't have the battalions who'd retreated from the meeting engagement waiting at intervals to mousetrap an unwary pursuit.

Which is our margin, he knew. The Colonials would have won a flat-out gallop.

"How far, *mi heneral?*" the major asked, swerving his dog over to Raj's side.

"Just under seven kilometers," he said. The nearest Colonials were half a klick back, now. "Twenty minutes at this rate."

Caztro looked back as well. "Just long enough for them to get convinced we're going to run all the way to Sandoral?"

"Exactly, Major."

If everyone hasn't bugged out when Kaltin's men came in hell-for-leather.

"*Halto!*"

Raj pulled Horace to a stop, then let him crouch to the ground. His wheezing pant sounded half-desperate, and he was a strong-winded dog. Some of the others were collapsing outright; men brought buckets of water and sloshed them across the moaning, gasping animals. Raj pulled off his sweat-damp neckerchief and turned to trot for the command group below the crest of the hill.

"They're right on my heels," he said.

And everything looks klim-bim, he thought, with a wave of relief so enormous that he felt slightly dizzy. The ground was good—he'd picked it himself—and Gerrin hadn't been wasting his time. The men were spread out along the ridge, well back from the crest and invisible from the other side. Officers lay prone at the top, with their flags furled and laid flat among the scattered olives;

inconspicuous rock and earth sangars had been prepared for the
guns and splatguns. Back north behind him there was an aid station
waiting for field surgery, and relays of men were bringing up buckets of water from the irrigation canal. Kaltin's battalions had watered
their dogs and moved up into the firing line, all but Poplanich's
Own; two more were on the far right flank, waiting still mounted.
Farther north, a small force trotted away dragging brush on the
end of their lariats to simulate the dust of a much larger body
retreating towards Sandoral.

"And they're coming on like there was no tomorrow," Staenbridge
said.

Raj knelt beside him and looked south. The Colonials were
advancing at a round trot, deployed for action in two double-file
lines with their guns and command group between.

"Message to Colonel Dinnalsyn," Staenbridge went on. A runner
bent near. "My compliments, and the first stonk should be directed
at the enemy artillery, before it has a chance to deploy."

Raj looked up and down the long curving line. "Guns?" he said.

"Splatguns forward, and the bulk of the field guns to either side."
Staenbridge pointed downslope, to a clump of greenery around a
small manor house. "Masked battery there."

Raj's breathing slowed. "Good work keeping everything calm when
Kaltin's men came galloping in," he said.

"He had them well in hand, and Suzette and her helpers were
there with bandages and water," Staenbridge said judiciously. "I doubt
anyone in this army would dare panic while she was looking."

Raj nodded. *Still good work, Gerrin.* He leveled his binoculars and
took another swig from the canteen, remembering to follow it with
a salt tablet; the last thing he needed was heat prostration.

leading elements at 2300 meters, Center said helpfully. **closing
rapidly.** A set of numbers appeared in the upper right corner of
his vision, scrolling down as the enemy trotted nearer.

"Wait until their scouts stumble over us?" Staenbridge said.

"Agreed."

Damned if I'm needed here at all, he thought ruefully. *I could
go take a nap.*

you are the source of overall direction, Center reproved. **you
have chosen and trained competent subordinates.**

I'm not the only one, Raj thought.

"Keep the initial reception low-key," he added aloud.

A screen of scouts preceded the Colonial main body. A dozen of
them came loping up the roadway toward the crest, eyes restless. Raj
saw their officer half-check as he neared, looking to right and left.
What spooked him—

it is too quiet. no birds or pterosauroids except the scavengers.

Raj looked up. Huge wings circled at the limit of vision, supporting long-beaked heads and patient, hungry eyes. Slightly lower were

the true birds men had brought with them from lost Earth, crows and naked-necked vultures.

Damn. "I wonder what they do when there's no war?" he said.

Staenbridge looked up too for an instant. "When isn't there war?"

The Colonial scouts came closer. Their leader spurred over the crest of the rise not a hundred meters from Raj, and froze in horrified shock, his bearded mouth dropping open into an O of surprise.

Braaaap. A splatgun fired point-blank, and the scouts went down into a tangle of kicking, howling dogs and wounded men. Troopers swarmed over them in a flurry of shots and bayonet thrusts. Several broke for the rear. Picked marksmen were stationed along the crest; they fired with slow care. One Colonial went down, another . . . and then the third, already crouched wounded over his saddle.

Raj turned his binoculars to the Colonial banner; it was his first glimpse of the enemy commander. A square middle-aged face beneath the spired helmet, dark and hawk-nosed, with a gray-shot forked beard. Not Tewfik, but a junior product of the same hard school. *Come on, be a good wog,* Raj thought urgently.

He'd done it by the book twice now, stopped and deployed when meeting a rearguard. Both times it had cost him time, time for the enemy force which had ravaged his country to escape with their plunder. And there were those dust plumes. If he did it again, the Civil Government troops might escape altogether. Overruning a small rearguard without putting in an attack on foot would force him to spend lives, but that was a cost of doing business.

Yeş. The Colonial trumpets brayed and the enemy force rocked into a slow gallop, the front rank drawing scimitars and officers their pistols.

"He's going to try and roll right over us," Staenbridge said with a cruel smile. "But this pitcher will find himself catching, nonetheless."

Raj nodded tersely. He looked to the right. "You kept the . . ."

"1/591st as strike reserve—they're at full strength, their dogs are fresh, and they're fond of the sword," Staenbridge said. He turned back to the front. "Not long now."

750 meters. 700 meters. 650 meters.

Raj nodded. Staenbridge jerked a hand at the signalman, who bent to touch his cigarette to the blue paper of the rocket. It arched skyward and went *pop.*

The banners of eleven battalions rose over the crest of the ridge in a single rippling jerk. Four thousand men rose and took six paces forward, the front rank dropping to one knee and the rear standing. Gunners heaved at the tall wheels of their weapons until the muzzles showed over the ridge. Splatgun crews pulled the concealing bushes away from their dug-in weapons.

The Colonial formations halted as if they had run into a brick wall. They were all veteran troops, and they realized instantly and gut-deep what the sight before their eyes meant; it meant they had all just been sentenced to death.

The battalions opened fire independently, but within a few seconds of each other. All the enemy were on the long gentle upslope, which meant that even if a bullet was over head-height when it reached the enemy formation—high trajectories were inescapable with black-powder weapons—there would probably be someone in front of it before it struck the earth. The platoon volleys rippled up and down the Civil Government line in an instant fogbank of dirty-gray gunsmoke, an endless BAM*bambambambambam* of sound. Brass sparkled in the bright sunlight as the troopers worked their levers and ejected the spent rounds. A steady, metronomic round every six seconds; forty thousand rounds in a minute. The four splatguns per battalion added half as many again.

The masked battery down on the flat opened fire simultaneously with the riflemen above, since they didn't have to manhandle their guns into position. The range was nearly point-blank; eight shells fired at minimum elevation whistled down the corridor between the first and second waves of the Colonial force. Two burst early, slashing shrapnel into the backs of the men and dogs of the first wave. One arched over and burrowed into the soft alluvial soil, sending up a nearly harmless plume of black dirt that collapsed and drifted on the wind. Five airburst within a hundred meters of the enemy command group amidst the limbered-up guns. Five black puffballs, each with a momentary snap of red fire at its heart. The green banner went down, and there was a circle of wounded dogs snapping at their hurts around the place where it lay in the dust.

Ten seconds later, the forty-eight guns of the massed artillery reserve fired from either end of the ridge. Their fire wasn't nearly as accurate as the masked battery; the range was longer, and the gunners had less time to estimate the range and adjust their pieces. The shells were contact fused. Many gouged the earth short, or fell long; both did damage enough. The score or so that fell on target hammered into the Colonial artillery train, still tied to limbers and teams. Dogs died or were wounded into howling agony—and a half-tonne of berserk carnivore was much more hindrance than a dead beast. Ammunition limbers exploded in globes of red fire, flipping wheels and barrels and bits of men dozens of meters into the air. Even then the crews of the surviving guns tried to unhitch them and swing the muzzles around to bear on the enemy who were slaughtering them.

Futile. The crews were within easy small-arms range of the ridge; dozens went down in the few seconds he watched. More shells burst among them, and overhead as the Civil Government artillery switched to time-fused shells that flailed them with shrapnel from above. More ammunition limbers exploded. He saw Colonial artillerymen cut dogs loose from their surviving teams and spur to the rear; officers who tried to stop them were ridden down. The whole crimson-uniformed mass was in full flight, those who could still move. The men on the fastest dogs were first, with the dismounted running or limping or dragging themselves afterwards.

Smoke drifted across the Civil Government line, thick even though a stiff breeze was blowing. Crewmen crawled forward from the splatguns, staying low and calling targets and distances back to their fellows. Officers directed the troopers' volleys with their swords.

Gerrin Staenbridge raised an eyebrow at Raj, who nodded. Another signal rocket hissed skyward, and this time the starburst puff of smoke was blue. A trumpet snarled six notes out on the right flank of the Civil Government force, and the cry of *cease firing* ran down the battalions on that end of the line. The 1/591st trotted their dogs over the ridge and down the slope, speed building. The swords came out in a single ripple of sun-struck silver as the speed of the charge built. Slowly at first—those were big men on heavy dogs, huge-pawed Newfoundlands and Alsatians sixteen hands at the shoulder. They growled as they charged, a sound like massed millstones grinding away in a cave, and the men shouted:

"UPYARZ! UPYARZ!"

"Nicely done," Raj said. "Oh, *nicely* done."

The charge swept down the hill and crashed through the flank of the disintegrating Colonial formation. The ex-Brigaderos held their ranks with fluid precision, stabbing and hacking and shooting with the revolvers most of them wielded in their left hands; the dogs were well enough trained to need no guidance but knees and voice and their place in ranks. The lighter Arab cavalry would have had trouble meeting a charge like that mounted at the best of times. With half their men down and unit cohesion gone, they reacted the way a glass jar did dropped on a flagstone floor. Men spattered in every direction; the 1/591st rode through their line, rallied to the trumpet call, dressed ranks and charged through again in the opposite direction. Hundreds of dismounted Colonials were holding up reversed weapons or helmets, asking quarter.

The barbarians in Civil Government service were whooping like boys as they cantered up the slopes again, despite a few empty saddles; shaking bloodied swords in the air and chanting their guttural Namerique war cries.

"Damn, but that's frightening," Raj said, shaking his head and scanning the enemy.

"Frightening?"

"One mistake, and two thousand disciplined troops with an able commander get creamed."

"*Their* mistake, fortunately."

Raj nodded grimly. "*Un*fortunately, Tewfik has enough men that he can afford to make a mistake—and he won't make this one again. If we make one mistake like this, the campaign is lost and so is

Sandoral and the war. We'd lose everything south of the Oxheads as far west as Komar."

Staenbridge blinked. "It must hurt, thinking ahead like that all the time," he said. "General pursuit, *mi heneral*? I think we can take the lot of them, here."

Raj nodded. "That would be best. I hate to see so many good soldiers wasted like this, though."

wait. listen.

"Wait," Raj said automatically. Then: "Sound *Cease Fire* and *Silence in the Ranks*."

Staenbridge looked at him oddly, then signed to the trumpeters. The call rang out, and silence fell—silent enough so that the sounds of wounded men and dogs were the loudest things on the battlefield.

And off to the northeast, a muffled thudding sound, very faint.

"Guns," Staenbridge said. "You've got good ears, *mi heneral*."

distance 18 kilometers.

An hour or two at forced-march speed. "All a matter of knowing what to listen for," Raj said. Center had to use his ears, but it could pay attention to *everything* they detected, however faintly. "We went looking for Tewfik, and we've bloody well found him, haven't we?"

"You think that's him?" Staenbridge said.

"It's another battle group of Colonial cavalry meeting one of the raiding parties I called in," Raj said. "And where there's two, there'll be more. Tewfik's here, and if he's got less than twenty thousand men with him, I'm a christo. He's probing to find out where we are, and once he knows he'll pile on."

He tapped one fist into the palm of the other hand. "Messenger, ride to the sound of the guns; that's probably Major Zahpata's group. Tell him to withdraw as quickly as possible and rejoin on the route north. Gerrin, let's get ready to move out of here, and do it *now*. Hostile-territory drill."

"We have to move anyway," Raj said, preparing to rein Horace around.

The doctor's shoulders slumped. Suzette moved over two steps and laid her blood-spattered hand on Raj's knee. The dog bent its head around and snuffled at her. She shoved it gently away as she looked up at her husband.

"We'll do what's necessary," she said. He nodded wordlessly and pulled on the reins with needless force.

Suzette moved back to the line of wounded. *Not this one*, the Renunciate's eyes said.

Suzette looked down at the soldier sweating on the litter. His olive face was gray with shock, his eyes squeezed tightly shut. There was a tourniquet around the upper thigh of his right leg, and a pressure bandage over a wound below the ribs. He *might* have survived the leg wound, although he'd have lost the limb—there were fragments of bone sticking out of the mass of red-and-gray flesh below the tight-wound cloth. There was a faint sewer smell from the stomach wound, though.

"Here, soldier," she said in Namerique—from his coloring the man was MilGov. "Take this, it'll help with the pain."

The blue eyes fluttered open, wandering, the pupils dilated. She lifted a shot-glass sized dose of liquid opium to his lips; enough to knock a war-dog out, and fatal for a man.

Better than leaving them for the Colonials, she thought. It was bleak comfort.

"Yes!" Major Hadolfo Zahpata said. "Pour it on, *compaydres.* Give those wogs hell!"

He walked down the firing line—more like a C with the wings bent back, now. *Fifteen hundred if it's a man,* he thought, squinting into the bright sunlight. *I have perhaps three hundred fifty. And we had to run into them facing the sun.*

Twigs fell on his uniform coat from the apricot trees of the little orchard, cut by the bullets of the Colonial dragoons to his front. More went overhead with flat cracking sounds; he looked down and saw the left sleeve of his jacket open to the elbow, sliced as neatly as by a tailor's shears. One millimeter closer, and . . .

They were advancing by squad rushes across the open grainfields; several hundred were behind the lip of an irrigation ditch about a hundred fifty meters to the front. That gave them cover, which was very bad. His guns were firing over open sights, trying to suppress them, which meant that they had to more or less ignore the steady flow of men *over* the embankment and into the open ground—although, thank the Spirit, they had knocked out the brace of pom-poms there. And the enemy were working around his flanks, both of which were now re-fused.

A body of the enemy stood to charge. A few meters down the line a splatgun crew slammed another iron plate of rounds into their weapon and spun its crank. *Braaaaap.* Two more of the rapid-fire weapons joined it. The Colonials staggered, the center punched out of their ranks. Company and platoon officers redirected the troopers' fire, and volleys slammed out. The Arabs sank back to the ground, opening fire once more. A splatgun crewman went *ooof* and folded over at the middle, dropped, his legs kicking in the death-spasm. Another stepped up from the limber to take his place. Bullets flicked off the slanting iron shield in front of the weapon with malignant sparks.

Thank the Spirit for the splatguns, and for Messer Raj who made them, Zahpata thought. He was a pious man—most who lived on the Border were—and Messer Raj was living proof that the Spirit of Man of the Stars watched over Holy Federation. *Despite our sins,* he added, touching his amulet.

A Colonial shell screeched overhead to explode behind him. There was a chorus of screams after it, men flayed by the shrapnel, and howls from wounded dogs. A revolver banged, putting down the crippled or dangerously hysterical among the animals. Beside him his aide ducked involuntarily at the shell's passage. Zahpata smiled and stroked his small pointed black chin-beard.

Spent brass lay thick around the troopers prone in the shade of the fruit trees; wasps and eight-legged native insects crawled over the shells, intent on the windfallen apricots scattered in the short dry grass. Their sickly sweet scent mingled with the burnt sulfur of powder smoke and the iron-and-shit smell of violent death.

"I'm glad to see you're not concerned, sir," the aide said as Zahpata lowered his binoculars and leaned on his sheathed saber.

Zahpata smiled thinly; the aide was his nephew, something not uncommon in the Civil Government's armies and very common in the 18th Komar Borderers. All of them were recruited from the same tangle of valleys in the southern Oxheads five hundred kilometers west of here, and half the battalion were relatives of one sort or another. The aide—his mother was Zaphata's older sister—was a promising youngster, but inexperienced at war. Except for the continual war of raid and skirmish and ambush with the Bedouin along the frontier, but all Borderers were born to that.

"I am not as concerned, *chico*, as I was before I saw that," he said, pointing. "The unbeliever commander must be so delighted at the prospect of our destruction he did not notice."

He pointed. The aide leveled his own binoculars, squinting against the sun. Zahpata knew what he was seeing; a line of slivers of silver light. Sun on sword-blades.

"Are they ours?"

"Would reinforcements for the sand-thieves advance with drawn blades?" Zahpata asked. By the length of front, that was two battalions—his City of Delrio and Novy Haifa Dragoons, reconcentrating as he'd ordered before this began. Doubtless they'd stepped up their pace to the sound of the guns. "In a moment—"

There was a frantic flurry of trumpet-calls from where the enemy commander's banner stood. Zahpata grinned like a war-dog scenting blood as the Colonial artillery ceased fire and began to limber up with panic speed.

"Sound *Fix Bayonets!*" he said.

The bugle's brassy snarl sounded. Surprised, men checked their fire for an instant; then there was the long rattle and snap as the blades came out and the men slid them home. The enemy had checked their advance; now they rose and turned to retreat. Fire slashed into their backs. Out in the fields beyond, the two Civil Government battalions glinted again as the sabers came down and the charge sounded.

"Sound *General Advance with Fire and Movement*," he said

happily. A good many enemies of the Spirit were going to the Starless Dark today.

The troops rose and dressed their ranks by company and battalion standards; the men at either end of the line double-timed to turn their C into a bracket with the open end facing the enemy. *Hammer to the anvil,* he thought. The oncoming battalions spread wider, and their artillery wheeled about to unlimber and open fire.

Zahpata frowned. *Hope they're not overconfident.* Any shells that overshot would be coming straight at his men; and if he had many casualties from friendly fire, there would be floggings.

An orderly led up his dog; Zahpata put one hand on the saddlehorn and vaulted up. A whistle brought his head around.

The messenger was a Descotter, with the shoulder-flashes of the 5th. "Ser," he said, in the grating nasal accent of his home County. "T'*heneralissimo* sends his compliments, an' yer t'rejoin immediate— on t' road headin' north. Fast, loik, ser."

Zahpata's aide moved his dog closer as the major read the slip of paper the messenger pulled out of his glove.

"Messer Raj has been *defeated*?" he asked incredulously.

"Don't be more of a fool than your mother made you, Hezus," Zahpata snorted, reading. "Ah—a great victory. Another infidel group, defeated with small loss."

He wrote on the reverse of the first message. "My compliments to the *heneralissimo,* and we expect to intersect the northern road at . . ." What was the heathen name? Ah, yes. ". . . at Mekrez al-Ghirba."

That should put him on an intercept course, or even get there ahead of time. The messenger saluted, pulled his dog's head around, and clapped his heels to its ribs.

"If we're not defeated, sir, why are we pulling back?"

Zahpata looked at the eager young face and sighed inwardly. The boy was here as a military apprentice, and you expected the young to be fools. *Although Messer Raj was only a few years older when he had his first independent command.*

"Messer Raj met and defeated one enemy column; perhaps two thousand men, twenty-five hundred. With twenty guns. We met and defeated another—fifteen hundred men, ten guns. What do you think will happen next?"

"Oh," the aide said.

Zahpata clouted him alongside the head, half-affectionately; his helmet *bonged.* "Live and learn, boy—or don't learn and die." He looked around. "Messenger, to battalion commanders. 18th Komar will lead; City of Delrio follows, Novy Haifa to rear. Scout-screens on all sides, maximum alertness. *Hadelande!*"

CHAPTER TEN

It was dark, with the sun down and only Miniluna in the sky. The earth gave back the day's heat, radiating from the bare clay of the badlands in the Drangosh bend; the darkness turned the ochers and umbers of the canyons to a uniform gray. Pterosauroids cheeped and mewed overhead, swooping after night-flying insects; Raj caught a gleam from the huge round eye of one, a vagrant trace of starlight. Earth-descended bats passed more silently. Off in the tangle of gullies and sinkholes something roared on a rising note, ending in a pierced-boiler screech; there was a rattle along the lines of dogs as the big animals raised their heads and cocked ears toward it. Some carnosauroid; they were hard to eliminate, in any area without a dense population, and the Civil Government force was into the belt of uncultivated land that extended from just west of Ain el-Hilwa along the river north to the border.

Raj sat, wrapping his officer's cloak around his shoulders and looking up at the stars that stretched in a thick frosted band across the sky. The Stars where man had once dwelt, before the Fall—and would again, if Center's plan succeeded.

The unFallen had the powers of gods, Raj thought. *Yet from what Center tells me, they were still men—not sinless, as the Church teaches. They had their wars and their intrigues, as we do; their tragedies and defeats, as we do.*

true, the voice in his mind said. **my analysis is that such are inherent in the nature of your species.**

Raj leaned back against the clay and lit a cheroot. *What's the point, then?* he asked. *If all I'm doing is letting people make mistakes on a bigger scale and a broader canvas?*

Center was silent for half a minute. **this is a difficult question, and one at the limits of my powers of analysis. i was not constructed so as to be capable of philosophical doubt.**

Another pause. **in your terms: the fall represented a limitation** of human choice due to suboptimal decisions. the greater capacities of a unified and technologically advanced civilization free humans from the determinism of nature. both their triumphs and their failures become matters of choice.

Ours aren't?

only to a very limited degree. the vast majority of humans on bellevue are peasants, because you lack the productive capacity to organize yourselves otherwise. this precludes forms of government and social organization less authoritarian, because the civilized regions depend too heavily on coercion to produce the surplus on which cities and a literate leisure class depend. if the fall continues, even agriculture-based societies will collapse and maximum entropy will be reached at a hunter-gatherer level. the survival of human life on this planet will then be in doubt.

As if to illustrate the point, the carnosauroid's retching scream sounded again through the night.

a new civilization may eventually emerge; but it will lack any continuity with the ancestral culture. and fifteen thousand years of savagery means hundreds of generations of human lives without the opportunity to exercise their capacities.

Raj nodded. Peasants were old at forty, and every day in their lives was pretty much the same, except when something went badly wrong. The Church said it was punishment for men's sins—which seemed to be literally true in Center's terms as well—but there was no reason for the punishment to go on forever.

He shivered slightly, despite the warmth of the earth at his back. *The fate of the human race for the next fifteen millennia rests on me, then. And our chances of pulling it off are no better than even.*

correct.

He stood and flicked the stub out into the darkness, a solitary ember that arced away and was lost in the night. He turned. Behind him the command group was gathering about the pool of light cast by a kerosene lantern, the undershadow putting the bones of their faces into hard relief. They were unfolding maps, munching on hardtack and pieces of jerked meat; their smiles and eyes looked as feral as so many war-dogs in the yellow light.

"Well, sooner started, sooner finished," Raj said. He strode into the light. "Right, gentlemen. Tewfik's main force is rather smaller than I'd expected—about sixteen thousand men, according to Captain M'lewis's report."

"Countin' banners, sir. Couldna' git closer. Them wogs is screened tighter 'n a cherry inna raghead's hareem."

Everyone nodded. Colonial units were less standardized in number than their Civil Government equivalents. One reason for that was a deliberate attempt to make it harder for observers to get a quick, accurate tally of a Colonial army's numbers by counting the unit standards.

"We'll take sixteen thousand as a ballpark figure—which worries me, Messers. We're here" —he put his finger on a spot west of Ain el-Hilwa— "and we have to cut the bend of the Drangosh to get back to our bridgehead opposite Sandoral. I hope you all realize that after leaving Ali's main army—"

He moved his finger to the west bank, and north almost to Sandoral, then south again to the Colonial pontoon bridge.

"—he could have dropped forces off to cross the river and take up blocking positions *north* of us."

By their expressions, the thought was an unpleasant surprise to a few of the battalion commanders—although not to his Companions.

"That depends on Tewfik's estimate of our numbers and intentions. We'll let the men rest another hour, then start out at Maxiluna rise." With both moons in the sky, there would be more than enough light for riding. "We'll make use of every hour of darkness we can; it'll be cooler, too.

"Colonel Staenbridge," he went on, "you take the three companies of the 5th and lead the way. Spread out but move fast. Captain M'lewis, you'll be the scout screen for the scout screen. Gerrin, if you run into anything you think you can handle, punch through. If not, go around if *that's* possible, screening our retreat. Major Zahpata, you and your 18th Komar will follow in column of march right behind. Exercise normal caution, but rely on Colonel Staenbridge for your intelligence. Gerrin, if you run into anything you *can't* handle, Major Zahpata is to move up immediately and support the 5th at your direction. Understood?"

Both men nodded. *At least I don't have to wonder who'll take orders from whom,* Raj thought thankfully. That sort of thing had nearly gotten him killed in the Southern Territories campaign, at the hands of the late unlamented Major Dalhousie. The problem was that the Civil Government didn't have permanent field armies or a structure above the battalion level—large concentrated field forces were too tempting to ambitious generals. By now, all these men had been on campaign with him long enough to work smoothly together, and he'd disposed of the purblind idiots, one way or another.

"The rest of you will be following in double column up these roads," he said, tracing the route northwest with two strokes of his finger. "They're never more than a kilometer apart, so you'll be close enough for mutual support. If Colonel Staenbridge runs into a major block-force, you'll flank and go round—taking a lick at them from the rear in passing. Boot their arse, don't pee on them; we *cannot* afford to get tangled up in a meeting engagement."

"My oath no," Staenbridge said mildly, still studying the map. "Not with Tewfik and sixteen thousand wogs after our buttocks."

"Exactly."

"What's the source of our intelligence on these pathways through the badlands?" Zahpata asked.

Raj had drawn those in himself. "Personal sources, Major. You may rely on them." *Center can do more with my eyes than I can,* he added silently.

"Major Gruder, I have a special tasking for your command. Otherwise, the order of march will be as follows—"

When the other officers dispersed to their units, Raj lead Kaltin Gruder out into the mouth of the notch.

"Kaltin, I want you to execute a battalion ambush on Tewfik's lead elements here," he said.

Gruder squinted up at the eroded clay hills, comparing them with his memory of the same scene by daylight. "Good ground," he said. "And we've given them a couple of bloody noses—he'll be more cautious this time."

"Probably. Time is exactly what I want you to gain; but *not* at the price of your battalion. Understood?"

Gruder nodded. Raj went on: "Tewfik knows he has two ways to win this campaign. The quick way is to catch us and smash us up before we get back to Sandoral. He's got numerical superiority, but it'd still be expensive. On the other hand, a quick victory is always preferable; the sooner you win, the less time the other side has to come up with something tricky. The slow way is to chase us back into Sandoral and starve us out. So he'll probably be willing to take a swipe at you to save time, but it won't be a reckless one."

Raj reached a space of flat sand, coarse outwash detritus from the bluffs above. He smoothed it further with his boot and drew his sword to sketch in it.

"This is your position. More or less of a very broad V, with the open end facing south. Have your men dig rifle pits at the foot of these hills; I'll detail the City of Delrio to help before they pull out. Scatter the dirt, and it'll be difficult for them to estimate your numbers before they get close. I suggest you place them by companies like this." He traced lines. "With your dogs reasonably close to hand, here and along here. I'll also have the Delrio leave you their splatguns—that'll give you eight total. Put them down here—here—here—here, in pairs."

His sword marked spots along the face of the V. Gruder frowned. "Down on the flat?"

"They're not artillery, Kaltin—those are bullets they're shooting, not shells."

Gruder nodded thoughtfully; a bullet was dangerous all along its trajectory if it was fired at a formation with any depth. Fired from above, it either hit the target it was aimed at or plunked harmlessly into the dirt; fired on the level, it went much farther.

"That'll give you crossfire from both infantry and splatguns, like this." The tip of Raj's saber traced X marks across the sand.

"Now," he went on, moving the sword to left and right on either side of the notch, "this terrain is pretty well impassable to formed bodies of troops. Certainly to artillery. Put observers *here* and *here*. Tewfik may try to work dismounted troopers around your flanks in those areas. If he does, block them with your reserve company—it ought to be easy, in that ground.

"Over here, about twenty klicks, is the only other path suitable for artillery and large formations of troops. That's where he'll go when he decides he can't just rush you out. Put a relay of men between here and there; when his flanking force gets there, pull out."

He raised his head and met the other man's eyes, his own flat and hard. "I give you *no discretion* concerning that. When his men reach there, you bug out. Understood?"

"*Si, mi heneral,*" Gruder said. He grinned. "I have learned something over the past five years."

"I certainly hope so, because I can't spare you *or* your battalion," Raj said.

"Hmmm. Artillery here?" Kaltin's saber pointed to the apex of the V.

"Yes, and start the guns out first. Also, walk all that ground tonight, and have your company commanders do it too. Ranging marks, all the bells and whistles."

"*Si.*" Kaltin studied the improvised sand-table. "I'll have them come and look at this, too. You have a good memory for terrain, *mi heneral.*"

Which was true, and even more so with Center's assistance. "*Waya con Ispirito del Homme,*" Raj said. They gripped forearms. "Get me an extra half-day."

"The Spirit with you also, General. Consider it done."

Tewfik ibn'Jamal, *Amir* of the Host of Peace, lowered his binoculars and cursed. Arabic was the finest of all languages for that, as for all else—as would be expected for the language God chose to dictate His word in—but the rolling, guttural obscenities did not relieve his feelings.

"And may the fleas of a thousand mangy feral dogs infest the scrotum of the *kaphar* general Whitehall," he concluded.

Ahead was a broad slope five thousand meters across at its mouth, narrowing down to barely a hundred where the roadway snaked into the badlands. The hills behind and to either side were not high, but they were steep as the sides of houses, crumbly adobe scored and riven by the rare cloudbursts of the Drangosh Valley winter. The roadway was graded dirt—a secondary road. The main highway—Allah torment in the flames of Eblis the souls of the engineers who laid it out—ran parallel to the Ghor Canal, through the populated districts farther east and towards Ain el-Hilwa. *That town of fools and dotards.*

Taking that would mean two days' delay, more than enough time for the invaders to scuttle back to the walls of Sandoral—and take any hope of concluding this accursed war quickly with them.

Another *tabor* of dismounted troopers trotted up into the V, angling for the enemy's foremost position on that side—if they could dislodge the outer rim, they could unravel it up the foot of the hills. A steady *braaaap . . . braaaap* sounded, and men fell. Figures in crimson djellabas dropped into the hot white dust of the valley floor, to lie still or twitching and moaning. He could see puffs of dust where the bullets struck, smoke pouring from the positions of the new rapid-fire weapons, a steady crackle and bang from the rifle-pits where the infidel troopers kept up a continuous hail of well-aimed fire. A pom-pom galloped up to support the soldiers.

The rapid-fire weapons from both sides of the V shifted to it. The dogs of its team went down in a tangle, and the gun's long slender barrel slewed around in futility. He watched a survivor drag a wounded comrade into its shelter. Bullets fell on it like a rain of hail to ricochet off in sparks and whining fragments.

In the gun-line directly before him crews heaved at the trails of 70mm field guns and pom-poms. More smoke billowed out as they fired, a ripple of red tongues of fire from left to right. Dirt fountained skyward along the enemy lines, and a spare team was galloped out to retrieve the pom-pom and the wounded.

"Can you not suppress those Shaitan-inspired weapons?" he asked.

His artillery chief shrugged unwillingly. "Insh'allah," he said. "*Amir*, whatever they are, they do not recoil as artillery pieces do—so they can be deeply dug in. All we see is the muzzle and the top of an iron shield. To make good practice we must draw close—and you saw the result of *that*. Also they have a battery of field guns above, with a two-hundred-meter advantage in height. If I push our gun line forward, they will come under artillery fire from the heights as they try to deploy, as well as from small arms."

"Move guns to the left, concentrate on the outer arm of the enemy defenses."

"As the *Amir* commands," the gunner said.

Tewfik turned back to the map table. Sweat dripped from the points of his beard onto the thick paper, reminding him of how thirsty he was. The goatskin *chaggal* at his side was half-empty; his men's would be worse, and there was no source of good water sufficient for fifteen thousand men within a half-day's ride.

"Muhammed," he said, and one of his officers bowed. "Sound the recall."

"Another push and we will be through, *Amir*," the man said stubbornly.

"Another push and we will lose another hundred men dead," Tewfik said. Just then a pair of stretcher bearers trotted by. Their burden moaned and tried to brush at the flies crawling on the ruin of his face. "Or like *that*. I do not continue with a plan that has failed."

"I obey."

"And start men moving here." He traced a line to the eastward on the map. "The going's passable for men on foot. Put some of those Bedouin hunters to use; the sand-thieves do nothing but sit on their arses and eat better men's food. They should know the footpaths. Work around toward the rear of the enemy position.

"Anwar," he went on. "You will take the reserve brigade and go" —he moved the finger in a looping circle far to the west— "twenty kilometers. A tertiary road—passable for wheels, according to the reports. Push all the way through to open country on the other side of these badlands, secure the route, and I will follow. Mutasim, you will put a blocking force across the mouth of this deathtrap; I'll leave you thirty guns. When the *kaphar* pull out, pursue, slow them if you can; we'll see if whoever Whitehall left in charge has sense enough to flee quickly as we flank him."

Mutasim scowled. "So far we have accomplished little," he said, tugging at his beard.

"There is no God but God; all things are accomplished according to the will of God," Tewfik said. He fought the urge to grind his teeth. "We were sent to stop the enemy's ravaging of our land; this we have done. We will pursue him. If we catch him, we will destroy him; if not, we will besiege him in Sandoral, which has not the supplies to support his men for long. In a week, they must begin to eat their dogs—which destroys all hope of mobility. After that, it is merely a matter of time. This was a damaging raid, no more. Insh'allah."

"As God wills," the others echoed.

"Go. Move swiftly."

The officers departed, and trumpets began to sound. Only the aides, messengers, and the *Amir*'s personal mamluks were left, silently awaiting his will. Tewfik stood and stared up the valley again, unconsciously fingering his eyepatch. It had never stopped him seeing into the heart and mind of an enemy commander before. *Whitehall, Whitehall, what is your plan? What dream of victory do you cherish in your secret heart?*

That was what bothered him. He remembered the El Djem campaign; he'd caught Whitehall there, beaten him—although the fighting retreat had been stubbornly effective, preventing him from finishing the young *kaphar* commander off without paying a price that seemed excessive. He'd bitterly regretted that decision a year later, when the Colony's forces met Whitehall's army.

May the Merciful, the Lovingkind, have pity on your soul, my father, he thought. Jamal had been a hard man and a good Settler, but no great general. *You ordered that we attack directly into the* kaphar *guns, and we paid for it,* Tewfik thought bitterly. Jamal had paid with his head, the House of Islam with thousands of its best troops and a legacy of civil war. All Whitehall's doing; it had been a good day's work for Shaitan when Whitehall had been born among the infidels of the House of War instead of a believer.

Since then Whitehall had made war in the West, while Tewfik repaired the Host of Peace and prepared for the next round of battle. This time there should be no doubt about the outcome. He had overwhelming numbers, and even Ali wasn't going to force him into the sort of error their father had made.

Yet the Faithful had good intelligence sources in the western realms. Tewfik had followed Whitehall's campaigns closely, and spoken with eyewitnesses. *Why this raid?* By bringing his force out from beyond Sandoral's walls, Whitehall had exposed them to the risk of defeat— without any countervailing chance of decisive victory. True, he had ravaged rich lands; true, he had inflicted stinging tactical reverses on the Muslims. *Our losses were greater than his. But we can absorb them without strategic consequence, and he knows this.* Nor were burnt-out villages in this one little corner of the Settler's domains any sort of strategic loss; yes, a tragedy for those who suffered, and enough to wake screams of rage from the nobles whose estates were ravaged, but nothing mortal. At least once in the past *kaphar* hosts had ravaged their way to the walls of Al Kebir itself, and the House of Islam still stood—there were vast and rich lands south and east of the capital to draw on. This was nothing by comparison.

Whitehall must have *something* in mind, something decisive. But *what?*

Tewfik plucked at his beard again. "He threw as many troops as he could into Sandoral before we reached the walls," he muttered to himself. "Yet it would have been better to send one-third as many, and use the other trains for supplies." Sending all the civilians out of the fortress city had been a shrewd move, but not enough. And why so many cavalry, when the issue would be settled by fighting from behind strong works?

"He has too many troops to hold the walls, and not enough food to feed the numbers he brought—yet not enough men to meet us in the field."

Three pounds of food per man per day, fifteen per dog; Whitehall knew the importance of logistics as well as any man. What was his plan?

There was something else here, something beyond a young *kaphar* chieftain with a genius for war. The infidels whispered that their false god rode at Whitehall's elbow.

He shrugged off the notion. There was no God but God. "Insh'allah," he said again, snapping his binoculars back into the case at his waist. "We waste no more time."

"Hadelande!"

Robbi M'Telgez pulled the rifle free from the scabbard and kicked his feet free of the stirrups. Dirt clouted the soles of his boots as

Pochita crouched; he turned and ran up the crumbly slope, coughing in the dust Company A kicked up in their scramble. He chopped
the butt of his rifle into the dirt to help the traction, feeling the
dirt sticking to the sweat on his face, blinking his eyes against the
sting and thanking the Spirit for the chain-mail avental riveted to
the back of his helmet. It might or might not turn a swordstroke,
but the leather backing of the mail protected your neck from the
sun pretty good.

Captain Foley reached the top and his bannerman planted the
company pennant. The officer stood with arm—hook arm—and sword
outstretched, to give the alignment. M'Telgez flopped down on his
belly and crawled the last three paces to the ridgeline, because bullets
were already cracking overhead. *Got guts, that one,* he thought.

Foley stayed erect until the unit was in place, then went to one
knee only a little back from the crest. Some men in other units gave
them a hard time for having the colonel's boyfriend as company
commander. He didn't care weather Foley banged men, women, bitch-
dogs or sheep—as long as he knew his business, which he did.

There were plenty of wogs making for the same crestline from
the other side, hundreds of them. The slope was steeper there,
though; he could see clumps of them falling back in miniature
avalanches of rocks and clay, down to where their dogs milled
about in the dry streambed below. Others were prone on the slope,
firing at the Civil Government banners that had appeared on the
ridge above. M'Telgez flipped up the ladder sight mounted just
ahead of the block of his Armory rifle and clicked the aperture
up to 800 meters.

"Pick your targets!" the ensign in command of his platoon shouted.

He did, a wog with fancywork on his robe walking around at
the base of the hill and followed by signalers. A long shot, and tricky
from up here, but he had the ground for a firm rest. He worked
the rifle into the dirt, fingers light on the forestock, and took up
the first tension on the trigger.

"Fwego!"

BAM. Eighty rifles fired. The butt punched his shoulder; a measurable fraction of a second later the wog in the fancy robe folded
sideways under the hammering impact of the heavy 11mm bullet.
He fell, kicking. *Not goin' t'git up, neither,* M'Telgez thought. Not
with a hollowpoint round blowing a tunnel the size of a fist through
his stomach and intestines. The Descotter whistled tunelessly through
his teeth as he worked the lever and reloaded, the spent brass tin-
kling away down the slope to his rear. Most of the others had picked
closer targets; bodies were sliding back down the steep slope. Live
ones, too, as the more sensible wogs decided that toiling slowly up
a forty-degree slope of crumbling dirt under fire wasn't the way to
a long life.

BAM. He picked another hard target, a Colonial prone behind a slight ridge and firing back. The djellaba blended well with the clay, but he aimed up a little. The wog jerked up seconds later, clawing at his back. Lever, reload.

"Five rounds, independent fire, rapid, *fwego.*"

M'Telgez's hand went back to his pouch; he pulled four bullets out of the loops and stuck their tips between his lips like cigarettes. Another went into the chamber, and he snapped the ladder-sight back down to the ramp.

Damn. There were too many wogs who'd decided to chance it. *Bam.* One down. Out one of the rounds between his lips. *Bam.* A miss, but the target yelled and danced sideways. *Bam.* Head shot, and the spiked helmet went end-over-end downslope in a splash of blood and brains. *Bam.* Couldn't tell, smoke too thick. *Bam.*

The oncoming enemy wavered, then fell back; most of them turned over onto their backsides and tobogganed down the slope, controlling the slide with their feet. There were boulders and rocks enough at the bottom to take cover behind, if they were careful.

"Dig in!"

The order came down the line. M'Telgez cursed; like most cavalry troopers, he hated digging—back home in Descott, a *vakaro* resented any sort of work that couldn't be done from the saddle. Resignedly, he spoke to his squad:

"Even numbers! Odd numbers on overwatch. C'mon, lads, 'tain't yer dicks yer grabbin', put yer backs inta it."

He reached to the back of his webbing belt and undid the leather pouch that held the head of his entrenching tool. It was a mattock-and-pick if you put the head in the central hole, a shovel if you put it into the slot behind the broader section. He unhooked the wooden handle that hung from his belt by the bayonet on his left side and knocked it into the main hole. A few swift blows cut through the hard crust of the adobe; it came up in chunks, and he piled those and handy rocks ahead of him, working down the slope behind to make a cut that would let him lie comfortably and fire through a couple of notches.

The afternoon was savagely hot, and the sweat ran down his body in rivulets that he could feel collecting where his shirt and jacket met the webbing belt. The damp cotton drill cloth clung and chafed. A carbine bullet went by overhead now and then with a malignant wasp-whine, encouraging him. A man came by with extra ammunition slung in canvas bandoliers from the pack-dogs; M'Telgez snagged an extra fifty rounds and cut a notch to support them with a few quick strokes of the mattock.

"M'Telgez! Report to the captain!"

Shit. Jest whin I wuz gettin' comfortable, loik, the corporal thought resignedly. "Smeet, y'got it fer now. Don't fook up too bad, will yer?"

"We'll a' git kilt, but it'll na be *my* fault, corp," the older trooper said cheerfully.

M'Telgez wiped his hands on the swallowtails of his jacket and picked up his rifle, then stepped-slid downhill a pace or two; running crouched, his head was below the ridgeline. The crunch of entrenching tools in the dirt marked his passage, and the steady crackle of fire from the alternate numbers keeping up harassment against the wogs. He also passed a few dead men; head and neck wounds were generally quickly fatal.

"Ser," he said when he came to the company pennant.

Barton Foley braced his pad across his knee with the point of his hook and wrote. "You have the way back to battalion, Corporal?"

"Yesser," M'Telgez answered.

He had a good eye for that sort of thing; and it was an officer's job to remember what his men could do.

"Detail one man of your squad to accompany you, and take this to Colonel Staenbridge."

"*No problemo, seyhor.*" He'd take M'tennin, the lad was young, eager and a good shot. Smeet could handle the squad—he was a good junior NCO, when there was no booze around. Drunk, he didn't know a sow from his sister or an officer from an asswipe.

"Verbally, add that we can handle it for the present but would appreciate reinforcements. Report back immediately with his reply— and watch out, there may be wogs in these ravines."

M'tennin screamed.

M'Telgez took one look over his shoulder and clapped his heels to Pochita's ribs. The thing already had the younger man's shoulders in its jaws and one clawed foot hooked into his dog's side, ripping downward in a shower of blood and fur and loops of pink-gray gut. Pochita needed no urging; she brought her hindpaws up between her front and leapt off in a bounding gallop, teeth bared, ears flat, and eyes rolled back, right down the narrow floor of the canyon. Her rider whipped his head around as something screeched behind him, a sound like a steam-whistle gone berserk.

He could *smell* its breath, like a freshly-opened tomb in hot weather. It was bipedal and longer than a war-dog, probably heavier, but it ran with a birdlike stride—lightly, on the toe-pads of its three-clawed feet, so lightly that the shotgun blast of dirt and stones spraying back from each impact was a surprise. The body was a dusty orange-yellow, striped irregularly with vivid black; the open mouth was mottled purple and crimson. Teeth the size of his fingers reached for him, and the clawed forefeet on either side. Behind it another much like it—hunter's reflex told him they were probably a mated pair—was tearing at the bodies of M'tennin and his mount with impartial gluttony. Its muzzle went skyward, the long narrow jaws dislocating as it swallowed a leg and hip.

"*Hingada tho!*" M'Telgez screamed. "Fuck ye!" The carnosauroid shrieked back at him, another carrion-scented blast.

His rifle was in the crook of his left arm. He snatched the pistol out of his boottop with his right and thrust it backward, not three meters from the thing's mouth. Even so half the rounds missed. Three did hit; none of them seemed to do much good. A blood-fleck appeared on the shiny black skin between the angry red of the nostrils, and one fang shattered into fragments of ivory. That got the beast's attention, at least; it spun sideways for an instant, snapping and rearing on one leg as the other slashed at whatever had struck it.

Then it realized *he* had hurt it. Some of the bigger carnosauroids were too dumb to do anything but kill and eat; the smaller agile ones like this could be a lot smarter. There was more than simple hunger in the cry it gave as it bounded after him once more, body horizontal and long slender tail snapping behind it at the tip like a bullwhip.

"Fuck *me*," M'Telgez muttered through a dry mouth, and hurled the revolver at the beast. *That* hadn't been such a good idea.

He leaned left and then right as Pochita took the curves of the narrow gully at dangerous speed. The carnosauroid didn't let little things like turns slow it down; it just ran right up the wall of the cut, letting momentum keep it upright with its head parallel to the ground for an instant. The man wound the sling of his rifle around his right forearm with desperate speed. He'd have only one chance, and that wasn't much with a single-shot rifle. Reloading at the gallop . . . he might as well try to fly like a pterosauroid by flapping his arms.

The sides of the gully opened out a little. The carnosauroid screamed again and speeded up, half-overtaking the fleeing human.

Right. Likes t'knock yer over afore it bites.

Normally holding the long Armory rifle out one-handed would have made M'Telgez's arm tremble. Now it was steady, everything diamond-clear to his sight. Even the sideways lunge of the predator seemed fairly slow, an arc drawn through the air to meet the questing muzzle of his weapon.

Bam. The shock of recoil was a complete surprise, hard pain in his arm. The weight of the carnosauroid slammed into Pochita's haunches, and the dog skittered in a three-sixty turn before resuming its gallop. The torque of the outflung rifle nearly dislocated M'Telgez's shoulder, but the pain was negligible next to the horrifying knowledge that he'd failed. Footfalls still ripped the earth behind him, only a little further back—and Pochita's tongue was hanging out in exhaustion.

He rounded another curve—

—and nearly ran into a screen of mounted men in blue jackets and round bowl-helmets. Their guns flicked up, but their eyes were behind him.

"Shoot, ye dickheads!" he screamed, as his dog braced its forelegs and sank down on its haunches to stop.

They didn't. Bent over his pommel, gasping and wheezing, M'Telgez looked behind to see why.

The carnosauroid lay prone not five meters behind him, its muzzle plowing a furrow in the dry gritty dirt. One leg was outstretched and the other to the rear, as if it had done the splits in mid-stride. Tail and head beat the ground in an arrhythmic death-tattoo, then slumped into stillness. A neat hole drilled in the yellow scales just behind and above one ear-opening showed why.

"Well, fuck me," M'Telgez mumbled again. It took three tries to return his rifle to the scabbard, and two to get his canteen open.

"There's one'll na try it, dog-brother," one of the troopers said admiringly. Two rifles cracked as the corpse of the sauroid went through another bout of twitching, the jaws clashing with an ugly wet metallic sound. Carnosauroids took a good deal of killing.

A jingling and thump of paws sounded in the draw; the battalion standard came up. M'Telgez pulled himself erect with an effort and saluted.

"Colonel, message from C-captain Foley," he said. "Ah, we're, ah—"

"Take it easy, lad," the Colonel said, not unkindly, looking at the dead predator and then at M'Telgez's dog. "You had a close shave, there, Corporal."

M'Telgez followed the lifted chin. Pochita's tail was half-missing, ending in a bloody stump; now that the dog wasn't running for its life it was trying to twist around and lick the injury. He dismounted and reached automatically into his saddlebags for ointment and bandages, a cavalry trooper's reflex, and a lifelong *vakaro*'s.

One bite closer . . . he thought. The image must have been clear on his face, because the Colonel leaned down and clapped him on the shoulder.

"Good shot," he said. "Anything with this?"

"Ah, t'Captain 'uld want some reinforcements, loik," M'Telgez said. In an effort to clear his mind: "We'nz goin' t'push through 'em, ser?"

In many line outfits that might have been insolence; Descotters had an easy, unservile way with their squires, though. And he was a long-service man with a good record.

"No, Messer Raj knows a way around," Colonel Staenbridge said. "We just have to block them while the main force gets through. I'll come myself. Lead the way, Corporal."

M'Telgez looked around at the bewildering tangle of blind canyons, sinkholes, and ragged hills. *The Spirit* must *be wit 'im,* he decided. Which was a comforting thought.

"Cheer up, lad," Staenbridge said, as the column formed up and passed the dead predator.

One of the troopers tossed him a fang as long as his hand, with a lump of bloody gum still on the base. M'Telgez dropped it into his haversack; it'd be something to show the girls, cleaned up and worn around his neck on a thong. Might as well get something out of that; that poor *fastardo* M'tennin wasn't going to, not even a burial. There wouldn't be anything left of him or much of his dog by the time they got there.

"Cheer up. Could have been worse—it could have been wogs."

M'Telgez looked down at the four-meter length of tiger-striped deadliness lying in the dirt. He nodded. That was true enough. The carnosauroid had only wanted to kill and eat him.

Wogs might have taken him alive.

"Good," Raj said. "That was clever of Tewfik, but he had to split his covering force up into too many detachments—there are a lot of badlands out there."

Staenbridge nodded. "Only two or three hundred men on the route we actually took," he said. "Still, it might have gotten sticky if we couldn't go around—they had an excellent position. How *did* you know that section of earth was thin enough to cut through behind them?"

An angel told me, and it *could tell the thickness of the gully walls by measuring how inaudible sounds passed through,* Raj thought sardonically. He wondered what Staenbridge would make of the explanation. Raj didn't understand a word of it himself.

sound waves are—

Forget it. I know it works, I don't have to know how or why.

"Lucky guess, Gerrin." The tone ruled out any further questions. "We're about—"

two point six kilometers.

"—two and a half klicks from the bridgehead, now. This is going to be tricky."

"You expect Tewfik to catch us crossing?" Staenbridge said, raising a brow.

"No, but he's not the only competent commander in the Colonial army, and he'll be in heliograph contact with their main body. What I want you to do is—"

CHAPTER ELEVEN

"Come on lads, put your *backs* into it," Colonel Jorg Menyez shouted. "Messer Raj needs this finished and ready to go by full sunrise!"

Arc lights hissed and kerosene lanterns cast their softer light across the chaos on the riverbank quays of Sandoral. Miniluna and Maxiluna were both on the horizon, paling to translucence as the sun cast bands of yellow and purple up into the fading dusk of night.

At least it's a little cooler, the infantry officer thought. That should speed things up. He'd had the preparations going on all night, what could be done without attracting attention.

There was no more point in trying for silence now, not with two thousand men splashing and clattering as they moved the big box-like pontoon barges into position. Most of the supports had been beached along Sandoral's long waterfront, just outside the river wall. Teams of men grunted and heaved, some pushing, others prying with beams and planks. One by one the square shapes surged out into the river, then jerked to a halt as the anchor-ropes caught them. Other ropes were payed out and men hauled in groaning unison to pull the barges to the growing eastern end of the bridge. North of it was a line of cable floating between barrels; each marked a line dropping down to an anchor on the riverbed. Naked boatmen swam out with more lines to secure the barges to the cable.

As each was tied off against the current, notched beams went into the cutouts in the bulwarks, and sections of planking were pegged down on top. Men scrambled forward to the next even while the mallets were still pounding on the one they ran on; water slopped over the upstream side as the weight of scores of infantrymen and their burdens of timber and cordage rested on the end barge alone. Down in the hulls others threw buckets of water overside and screamed abuse at the work teams above.

A long hollow *boooom* sounded from the southward, from where the nearest part of the Colonial siege line had anchored itself with an earthen fort on the riverbank. A long whirring crash followed, and men froze as a heavy roundshot hit the water and skipped like a thrown rock across the surface of the water by a playful boy. Once . . . twice . . . three times, and the final plume of water was shorter than the others. The Drangosh drank down the big cast-iron ball as easily as it would the boy's pebble. Menyez blew out the breath he had not been aware of holding.

Two kilometers. A little too far. There were ironic cheers from some of the men, and the hammering clatter of work resumed. He looked eastward. The bridge was nearly to the other shore, where a company of infantry was heaving at winches anchored in the dirt, hauling the last few barges. *Nice fast piece of work,* he thought. It helped that they'd done it before, of course.

Booooom. A little sharper this time, a rifled piece. The sound of the shell was higher as well. It came much closer, only a few hundred meters south, but struck the water only once. A tall fountain of spray reached skyward, high enough that its top was touched red by the light of the sun rising in the west.

"Close, but that only counts with handbombs," he said.

Far off and faint, trumpets spoke on the eastern bank. A message began to flicker in from the heliograph station there, as the light strengthened enough for the tripod-mounted mirrors to catch it.

The problem was that there were other heliograph relays farther down the river—Colonial ones.

"Come on, *mi heneral,*" Menyez said under his breath.

He looked back over his shoulder at Sandoral. The city was eerily quiet, hardly even a thread of smoke marking the hushed stillness of the morning. Not even a cock crowing; all the chickens had gone into the stewpots several days ago.

And nearly the whole garrison out here working on the bridge, he added to himself. Pretty soon that thought was going to occur to somebody else.

Ali ibn'Jamal lowered his telescope. "My so-brilliant brother has let them escape," he said bitterly. "Allah requite him for it. And their bridge of boats is nearly finished to receive the ravagers of the House of Peace."

Everyone else in the clump of nobles and commanders maintained a tight silence. A cool morning wind ruffled robes and beards and the peacock and egret plumes in turbans and helmets, but many of them were sweating nonetheless.

Cowards, Ali thought, and raised the telescope again. The *kaphar* were working like men possessed on their bridge, getting the surface laid before Whitehall appeared. Tewfik was going to let him ride back into Sandoral like a conquering hero!

"Commander of the Faithful."

It was one of the cavalry generals, a protégé of Tewfik's. *Who cannot be Settler. But who could rule from behind the Peacock Throne, with a puppet Settler.* It had happened before.

The man knelt and touched his forehead to the floor. "The deserters have told us the *kaphar* are on half-rations—they have been for a week. With another eight thousand men and eight thousand dogs within the walls, they will eat their stores bare in a few days. Then the city must fall."

Eight thousand. Tewfik hadn't killed more than a few hundred of them, after they spent more than a week ravaging his lands. *His* lands! *I do not want them to surrender. I want them to* die.

Of course, they could die after they surrendered . . . but if he allowed them terms, it would be unwise to break them. Not with Tewfik and his officers so close around him—not when they absurdly, blasphemously valued a word given to an unbeliever.

He raised the telescope again. It was incredible how quickly the infidels had gotten their bridge put back together. Cannon were firing from the walls of the earth fort around him, but doing no damage— the range was so great that only sheer luck or divine intervention would land a shell where it could accomplish anything.

They must have their whole garrison working on that, Ali thought. He could see them clearly now that the sun had risen.

Ali smiled suddenly. Those watching his face flinched and looked away, then forced themselves to turn their heads back; it was not safe to be unaware of the ruler's moods.

Ah, Tewfik my brother, you did not think of that. All his life he had been in Tewfik's shadow in matters of war; blundering and hacking his way through the complex problems of the battlefield in confusion, while Tewfik cut to victory with a lambent clarity. But this time, he was the one to see.

"You," he said to the kneeling officer. "Ubaydalla Said. I order an assault on the walls—an immediate assault. Rise, take command of the forward troops, and execute my commands."

"I hear and obey, Settler of Islam," the officer said. He paused thoughtfully. "That is an excellent suggestion. But the preparations—"

It was the expression on his face that moved the Settler; the surprise, that Ali could have come up with a workable plan. He plucked the ceremonial whip out of the man's belt and lashed him across the face with it. An upflung hand saved Said's eyes from the nine pieces of jagged steel on the ends of the thongs, but blood dripped heavily into his beard and from his gashed mouth.

"Are you a coward as well as a fool, pig? Are you *deaf*? I said immediately! If you have time to prepare, so will the enemy! And you are to lead the attack, personally."

"As God wills," the officer said quietly. He bowed again, blood dripping on the priceless carpets, and wheeled away sharply, calling for his subordinates.

❖   ❖   ❖

A whistle blast jarred Corporal Minatelli out of exhausted sleep. It was much like waking up after a payday in Old Residence. For a moment he lay blinking in puzzlement. It must be Star Day, why were they calling him to work at the quarry already?

The whistle went on and on, sharp repeated calls. A trumpet joined in, sounding: *Stand to, Stand to* over and over again. Then he knew exactly where he was: on the parapet of the wall at Sandoral, with hot white sunlight slashing through the firing slits. He erupted up out of his blanket roll and grabbed his rifle and webbing in either hand, running to his duty station. His muscles ached from a night of hard labor, and the two hours of sleep seemed to have dumped a skullful of hot sand behind his eyes. He was hungry too, mortally hungry with the aching need of a man who had been using twice as many calories as he took in. None of it mattered.

He buckled his belt and leaned back slightly from the wall to make sure that everyone in the squad was at their posts—seven men to hold a section of wall that had been undermanned with forty. Seven men and the six militiamen left of the dozen that usually operated the big gun to his left. Probably the rest of the walls were just as empty. Spirit!

"Oh, *scramento*," he said as he knuckled the crust out of his eyes and looked out the slit.

From left to right across his field of vision the Colonial earthworks were belching jets of smoke with lances of red fire at their hearts; the siege guns were cutting loose. Underneath their deep booms he could hear the sharper sounds of the field guns in the forward bastions, and the rapid *pom . . . pom . . . pom* of the quick-firers. Much of the ground between the Colonial outworks and the city moat and wall was still covered by bloating bodies, and the ripe oily stink was thick—the wog commanders had refused the usual truce to remove the dead. That didn't seem to be slowing down the men who boiled out of the forward ends of the assault trenches any.

In the days since the first attempt at an escalade, the Colonials had braved constant sniping to rig overhead covers for the last few hundred meters of the trenches—platforms of palm logs and sandbags that wouldn't stop a heavy shell but did quite well against rifle bullets and case shot. Now the last ten meters or so of that were jerked down, and the soldiers in crimson came out like red warrior ants. They didn't seem to be as well organized this time, but there were an awful lot of them.

"Ready for it," Minatelli called, clearing his eyes with the thumb of one hand. The fabric of the fortifications quivered underneath him as the heavy solid shot rammed into the granite facing of the concrete-and-rubble wall. Dust quivered up from every crack and crevice. He took an instant to gulp water from a dipper, stale and welcome as a mother's love.

The wogs were running forward with their long ladders, built to cross the moat and not break even at an acute angle to the ground. The walls of Sandoral were not very high; they could not be, and be thick enough to resist modern rifled cannon. Others carried grapnel-throwing mortars.

"Now!" he shouted, and fired. Shots were crackling out all along the walls, and the deeper roar of cannon.

Booom. The fortress gun fired. A swath of the enemy went down, but the scratch crew were cursing with the shrillness of panic as they struggled to reload and relay the huge piece; there just weren't enough of them. Minatelli fired again and again, as fast as he could work the lever—worry about overheating and extraction jams later. Wogs fell, to lie among the bloated, swollen remnants of the previous attack, but they kept coming. Grapnels thumped out of the mortars and blurred up to the ramparts, trailing snakes of cable with knotted hand- and footholds. A shadow fell across his eyes as a ladder toppled toward the wall, slanting out to the ground beyond the moat. He dropped his rifle on the stone ledge for a moment and reached into a bin, pulling out a hand bomb and snagging the ring on top on a hook set into the wall. A quick jerk freed the ring, and the bomb began to hiss as the friction primer within burned.

Toss. A vicious *crack* over towards the base of the ladder. Men fell, and the heavy eucalyptus poles of the construct swayed. A dozen men cut loose with their repeaters at Minatelli's gunslit. Thousands were kneeling all along the edge of the moat, bringing the fighting platform under direct aimed fire. A little way down from Minatelli a lucky pom-pom shell blasted right into a gunslit and exploded; an instant later so did the hand bombs in the bin there, blowing chunks of stone and flesh out into the moat and back down into the cleared zone below the city walls. He ducked down and back as ricochets buzzed through the narrow space, then dashed to the next slit. A file of wogs was already running up the ladder—it was no steeper than some stairways—toward the roof of the fighting platform overhead. He fired again and again. Men fell tumbling off the ladder and down into the foul water of the moat; some of them bobbed limply, others swam for the shore.

Boom. The fortress gun cut loose again, and another swath of wogs went down back toward the assault trench—but there were far too many already near the wall. Almost at the same time an enemy shell struck right underneath the muzzle of the gun. The huge banded barrel jumped backwards; a trunnion cracked, and the weapon pivoted sideways with a squeal of ripped bronze and crackling timbers. A gunner's legs were caught in the way, and the man smeared against the pavement and the iron guide-ring like liver paste on bread.

More carbine rounds flicked at Minatelli's firing slit. He ducked back again, fixed the bayonet on his rifle, then slung it across his back. He filled his hands with hand bombs, slipping his fingers through the rings to carry them—dangerous, but fuck *that* right now for a game of soldiers.

"Saynchez! Hold 'em!" he screamed, and ran back down the covered walkway to the dismounted gun.

The other five militia gunners were standing gaping, looking at their dead comrade.

"Get yor fukkin' *guns*," Minatelli screamed. His hands were full, so he kicked one of the gunners in the arse to get his attention; the man whirled, gaped, then went for his personal weapon. The gunners were equipped with shortswords, revolvers, and double-barreled shotguns: just the thing for the sort of short-range scrimmage that was all too likely in a moment. He could hear boots on the roof overhead.

"The wogs is over the wall," Minatelli shouted, and leaped for the top of the gun.

There was a circular hole above it, with an iron ladder and an octagonal observation-point of timber and boilerplate above, usually for the master gunner. Minatelli scrambled up it, stuck his head out of the hatch, and began throwing hand bombs. There were wogs clambering up onto the roof of the fighting platform by the score— though many were cut down by the enfilade fire of the light swivel guns on the bastion towers to either side—and thank the *Spirit*, none of them looking at him!

The cast-iron bombs clattered on the stone flags; he ducked back down as they burst with rending *crang* sounds, and bits of casing peened off the outside of the observation point. He rose again and threw the last of them; wogs were shooting at him from the outer edge, pausing at the top of their scaling ladders.

He dropped back down. Case shot hammered the boilerplate outside as a swivel gun tried to sweep the ramparts clear.

"*Hingada tho!*" he cursed at the unseen gunner in the tower, and dropped back to the gun. He could feel the heat of it through the soles of his hobnailed boots.

"Follow me!" He jumped down to the decking with a clash and spark of nails on the concrete.

The militia gunners ran behind him as he dashed back. A wog with his carbine slung and a long curved knife between his teeth swung down from the lip of the overhead, hung by both hands and jacknifed himself in to land on the very edge of the platform, with a fifteen-meter drop behind him. Minatelli shouted and lunged; he had just time enough to meet the Colonial's eyes, black and unafraid. The man was trying to draw the revolver tucked through his sash when the point of Minatelli's bayonet thumped into his chest. The steel didn't penetrate the breastbone, but it was enough to send the man backward over the edge, snarling in frustration.

Another landed beside him. A militiaman fired his shotgun from behind Minatelli, powder scorching his side. The spreading buckshot caught the wog in the gut, blasting him over the edge with his limbs flailing like a jointed doll. Another was hanging from the lip of the roof—it was deliberately made with an overhang beyond the fighting platform below, to make this sort of thing difficult. Minatelli lunged again, this time between the dangling legs. The wog let go with a scream and plunged downward. His drop revealed another kneeling above, aiming a carbine. Minatelli fired from the hip; the Colonial threw himself backward out of the line of fire.

The infantryman pivoted. Two of the militiamen were down, and a pair of wogs he hadn't even noticed stood on the deck. Two more were fighting another; one blocked his scimitar with the barrel of his shotgun, then reeled away wailing over fingers hanging by threads of flesh. That gave his comrade time enough to draw a revolver and fire five times with the muzzle almost pressed against the Arab swordsman's back.

The body hit the ground with a thump. The survivors of Minatelli's squad were at their firing slits, shooting and throwing hand bombs. No, one was stabbing outward with his bayonet. The corporal started towards that slit, hands reloading his rifle of their own volition. The last militiaman shouted from behind him, warning in the tone.

Minatelli turned. Another wog was coming at him, carbine clubbed. He caught it on the bayonet, pivoted the rifle and buttstroked the wog in the face; turned with frantic speed and caught another through the throat with the point. The militiaman was at his side, but more and more wogs were dropping down to the firing platform, some coming through the observation hatch over the gun. His men turned from the firing slits. He shouted to them to rally.

Something flashed very brightly, and there was a soft floating sensation. A heavy pressure. Blackness.

Raj drew up beside Menyez at the western end of the pontoon bridge. The infantry commander grabbed at his stirrup-iron. "Wogs over the wall," he said. "Everything's committed—no more reserve!"

"I'll handle it," Raj replied. "Organize this end and get the remainder and the artillery concentrated in the plaza. *Waymanos!*"

The lead cavalry were coming over the bridge at a round trot, the fastest safe pace.

"Bugler," Raj snapped. "Sound *Charge!*"

The man obeyed instantly, but his eyes went wide. The troops responded as if the call were playing directly on their nervous systems, clapping their heels to their dogs and plunging forward. The floating bridge rocked and shuddered under the sudden impact of thousands of half-tonne dogs accelerating to their running pace. Howls and shouts rose over the massive thudding and creaking; Raj ignored them, drew his sword and spurred Horace across the Maidan, the empty space by the riverside, to the main water gate. It was broad, thank the Spirit; more than broad enough for cavalry to take in four-abreast column, and there was a wide straight avenue from there to the *Plaza Real*.

He looked westward, squinting into the sun and straining to hear the sounds of combat from the city walls. Green arrowed vectors painted themselves over his vision.

major penetrations at these locations.

"There!" he yelled, pointing with his sword.

Gerrin Staenbridge went by with the banner of the 5th Descott; his reply was a flourish of his own saber, and the men followed his abrupt curve with fluid precision.

"There!" Raj directed the next battalion. "There! There!"

A fourth. "Follow me!"

Not only over the wall, they're into the bloody city, Staenbridge thought, as the column of the 5th Descott burst out of the street into the harsh light of the open ground just inside the city wall. Broad stairways angled up from the roadway to the fighting plat-form; right now they were swarming with Colonials, their crimson djellabas a solid blotch of color in the dark shade, an occasional helmet-spike or officer's plume glinting. More were milling about on the ground at its foot, the survivors of the first wave. They were disorganized—not many in any unit would have made it this far—but that wouldn't last. Men who'd made it through the killing ground outside and over the wall in the first wave would be too aggres-sive to sit around waiting for orders.

"Deploy in line of companies!" he roared. Buglers relayed the order every man half-expected.

The column of mounted troopers pouring out of the mouth of the street split on either side of him, fanning out like the arms of an outstretched capital Y with his banner as the dividing point. In thirty seconds they were in a line facing the wall, and moving forward three hundred strong.

"Dismount! Fix bayonets!"

The dogs crouched and the men stepped free, drawing their rifles from the scabbards. Steel glinted as the long blades snapped home.

"Advance with fire, volley fire by platoon ranks!"

BAM. The men moved forward at the double. Colonial officers were hustling the wogs at the foot of the wall into makeshift firing lines, moving them forward in turn. *Can't give them room to deploy.* He'd be outnumbered too badly if he did. Unless more troops arrived up from the river, and he couldn't count on that.

BAM. BAM. BAM. The 5th could double forward and volley-fire at the same time, something possible only with endless practice. There weren't many Colonials at the foot of the wall . . . yet . . . and more of them were reloading than firing, pulling rounds out of the loops across their chests and thumbing them through the loading gates of their carbines. Men fell on both sides, stumbling out of his line, flopping backward when the heavy 11mm Armory rounds punched them in the Colonials ahead.

A sound of iron wheels on flagstones. A splatgun crew wheeled their weapon around and ran it forward. Staenbridge pulled his dog aside.

"The stairway!" he barked.

The master gunner nodded and spun the elevating screw down to maximum. The honeycombed muzzle of the weapon rose like the nose of a hunting dog sniffing the wind. Two more crewmen moved the trail to his direction as he crouched over the breech. He snarled satisfaction and spun the crank.

Braaaaap. Thirty-five rounds punched into the mass of Colonials on the stairway. A bubble of dead and dying sprang into existence in the thick crowd, instantly filled as more pressed down from above. *Braaaap.*

Staenbridge spurred back to his banner, dismounted. The rest of the command group followed. He drew his revolver, tossed it into his left hand, then drew his saber and filled his lungs. Bartin was beside him, hook ready, his double-barreled coach gun in his good hand. Their eyes met for an instant.

"*Charge!*" he shouted, and broke into a run forward.

With a bellow, the 5th Descott threw themselves after their Colonel.

"Charge!" Raj barked.

The trumpeter sounded it; the brassy clamor echoed back from the silent walls of the houses on either side.

"UPYARZ! UPYARZ!" the men bellowed in reply.

Raj snarled silently and leaned forward, point outstretched beyond Horace's neck. The 1/591st filled the street from wall to wall; some of them were riding down the sidewalks, inside the line of plane trees and gaslights that separated the brick walkway from the granite paving blocks of the street. The heavy paws of the big Newfoundlands made a drumming muffled thunder, and the column filled the road for better than two hundred meters back. Even at a slow gallop it was insanely risky; he gritted his teeth against the memory of what men looked like after a hundred war-dogs trampled over them.

Just have to be careful.

Horace was a little ahead of the pack, beside Raj's personal bannerman; the battalion standard and Teodore Welf were to one side. Ahead was a thin scattering of Colonials, running down the road; except for the ones turning to run away when they saw that juggernaut of huge black dogs and white fangs, bared swords and shouting barbarian faces. One officer—a high-ranking one, from the spray of plumes at the front of his helmet—had managed to find a dog, in Civil Government–issue harness. It was highly restive under its new rider. Dogs were like that; you had to train with them a good long while before they accepted you, if they had any spirit.

He was keeping the reins and the cheek-levers they controlled tight, and slapping at men's shoulders with the flat of his scimitar as he hustled them into a semblance of a firing line.

His eyes grew wide as he saw Raj's banner. He turned to meet the onrush, drawing an ornate silver-inlaid revolver with his other hand. He clapped spurred heels to the dog's flanks; it bounded forward and a little to one side, crabbing against the ruthless skill of the rider as he forced it forward.

"Whitehall!" he cried in Arabic. "Shaitan waits for thee, Whitehall— and God is great!"

Crack. The bullet scorched past Raj's face. *Going to have a coal miner's tattoo from that one,* a distant corner of his mind recorded. The Arab had bleeding wounds across his face in a nine-line pattern, but his eyes were utterly intent. One well-placed shot or slash, and the heart would be out of the Civil Government force.

All the rest of his attention was on the point of his saber. Luck as well as skill saved the Colonial; his restive dog jibed at the last instant, and the swords crossed in a unmelodious skirring of steel on steel. Nimble, the Colonial's dog pivoted in its own length and started back to avoid the trampling rush of the Brigaderos. The dismounted men ahead had no such option. They managed one volley, an eruption of smoke and red fire. The whole front of the attacking line seethed as men and dogs went down across the fifteen-meter front. Men arched through the air to smash with bone-shattering force against the hard stuccoed stone of the house walls or crumple on the pavement; one landed with gruesome accidental accuracy on the crossbar of a gaslight and hung impaled and twitching like a shrike's prey on a thorn.

But there was too much momentum behind the charge for a single volley to halt, and many of the wounded dogs kept their feet. The light 10mm bullets of the Colonial carbines were deadly to men, but it took a lucky hit to kill a twelve-hundred-pound dog with one shot. Riderless dogs were almost as dangerous as the ones with swordsmen on their backs; one seized a Colonial by the head in its half-meter mouth and flipped him over its tail with one flex of its massive neck. The rear files squeezed by the thrashing chaos of the front rank, and the thin Colonial line went down in a flurry of swordstrokes and two-inch fangs.

The Colonial officer was very much alive. He took aim again; Raj threw himself down on the right side of his dog, holding on to the pommel with one heel. A trick a Skinner nomad had taught him, and it paid off . . . the pistol bullet went snapping through the air where his body had been an instant before. He drew his pistol and shot underneath Horace's belly, into the stomach of the Colonial's dog. The animal hunched itself up in an astonishing leap that made the Arab release the gun and grab for the reins; then two 1/591st troopers were on him. The scimitar flashed against the heavy MilGov broadswords for one stroke, two, three; he slashed one trooper across the face even as the other slammed his heavy blade through the Arab's stomach.

Raj heaved himself upright. That had been *close*. For a moment there were no wogs in sight except the ones running away—and running away from a dog in a straight line was a losing proposition. Then they were out into the cleared zone just inside the wall. The main city gate—the one with the railway entrance—was just to his right; it was wreathed in smoke, but the Civil Government's banners were still flying above it, and the cannon mounted there were a constant rolling *booom* of thunder. Ahead of him a thin line of Civil Government troopers—the three companies of the 5th he'd left as the main reserve—were holding against a growing tide of wogs pouring down from their foothold on the wall. Just barely holding, and not for long; the Colonials had lost all unit cohesion coming over the wall, but they were forming up again like crystals accreting in a saturated solution, and more every minute.

The 5th's volleys rang out, crisp and unhurried, but as he watched, they were losing men like a sugar lump under a stream of hot tea.

Teodore Welf drew rein beside him as the 1/591st fanned out into line. "Dismount?" he asked.

Raj shook his head. "Not enough time. We've got to hit them before they get organized."

These MilGov knights liked cold steel, and this was the situation for it. The whole scene in front came in glimpses, flashing through gaps in the drifting clouds of sulfurous smoke. More every second, as cannon and rifle fire pumped it out. Bullets went by with an ugly *crack* sound. Five men down the line a trooper gave a grunt and toppled slowly out of the saddle.

A captain of the 5th dashed up, breathless. "Sir?"

"Get them out of the way, Fittorio, then re-form on my left and give me fire support. Welf, get those splatguns out to the right now we've got room for them. *Move!*"

The bugles sounded. The Descotters ahead gave one last volley and turned, moving back at the double. The ragged line of Colonials beyond them gave their yelping cheer and charged in turn, unaware of what awaited behind. Unaware until the bugle sang, and the dogs of the Brigaderos howled in unison. The screams of their riders were only slightly more human. There was just space enough to build up momentum, but plenty of room to deploy in the drill manual's double line. The cavalry came looming up out of the smoke, big men on big dogs, their swords bright. They crashed into the dismounted Colonials like a baulk of timber swinging at high speed; men went down, slashed and stabbed and bowled over by sheer momentum.

Now we see how well their training has sunk in, Raj thought. Aloud: "*Halto!* Dismount, fix bayonets, forward with fire and movement, independent fire!"

One or two of the troopers vanished into the throng ahead, eyes fixed and froth dripping from their mouths. The rest halted and stepped off their crouching dogs, sheathing swords and drawing their firearms—although some might not have, if the dogs hadn't stopped automatically. *Click,* and the long bayonets snapped onto the Armory rifles. The men walked forward in a steady line, not quite straight—more like a very shallow C—taking their dressing from the battalion standard and Raj's beside it. The front of their formation showed level for an instant, then vomited smoke. The sheet of fire smashed into the Colonials clustered at the base of the stairway.

The detachment of the 5th moved into place on the left flank, swinging in like a hinged door. The splatguns wheeled by at a trot and unlimbered, pushing into place to cover the gap between the end of the line on his right and the bare ground around the gate, swept by fire from the bastion towers.

Raj took a step forward. "Charge!" he shouted.

The troopers leveled their bayonets and ran in pounding unison; he ran along with them. The Colonials wavered, and then fled. *The bayonet's a terror weapon,* Raj knew. It didn't really *kill* all that many people, not in this age of breech-loaders, but there were times when it could make men *run.* Or try to run; the stairway that slanted down along the wall was too jammed with men for the ones on the ground to make much headway. Figures in crimson djellabas began to fall from the stairs in ones and twos, caught and squeezed out when the pressure from above and below forced the thick torrent of men to buckle sideways.

"*Halto!* Volley fire!"

The order relayed down the chain of officers. One rank knelt, the other firing over their heads. The rifles came up, aiming upward into the press. BAM. BAM. BAM. Rippling down the line, rounds whanging and keening off the stone, punching through three and four men at a time.

"Platoon column," Raj roared. "Welf, feed them up after us—you men, follow me!"

"To hell with *that,*" the young MilGov noble said, and relayed the command. A column of forty troopers formed, with the banners only a few ranks from the front.

"*Hadelande!*"

"*Upyarz!*"

Many of the first Colonials went down with the bayonets in their backs. The troopers to the rear of the column fired over their comrades' heads, up the broad stairway. From the foot of it, six hundred men did likewise, and the splatguns with their muzzles raised to maximum elevation. Trapped, the Colonials on the stair turned to fight.

Raj found himself shoulder to shoulder with Teodore Welf; bayonets bristled on either side of them, and the banners waved behind. *Up a step.* Raj caught a scimitar on the guard of his saber, shot under it into his opponent's body. It tumbled down underfoot, and he nearly went over himself, with no room for his feet. An Armory rifle shot next to his ear, leaving it ringing. He threw himself back into swordsman's stance, right foot forward, and lunged again. Again. Welf was fighting with a long dagger in his right hand, using the heavy single-edged broadsword in his left like a ribbon saber; blond hair flew about his shoulders as he howled some Namerique war chant with every other breath. Fire swept the stairs ahead of them; Raj's hair crawled on the back of his neck at the thought of what would happen if somebody aimed a little low.

Or if these wogs had the time to reload. One did. Center's green aiming-grid slapped down across Raj's vision, outlining the figure in strobing light. He moved the red dot onto the center of mass and pulled the trigger, and the man spun away with the carbine flying out of his hands. Another target designated; he turned slightly, the pistol outstretched, squeezed the trigger. It was a hand bomb beginning its arc downward towards him, an impossible target . . . impossible without Center. Left-handed, at that. The iron sphere exploded less than a meter from the thrower when the bullet struck it.

A lot of men had seen that, seen his arm like a pointer and the result. It was close enough to a miracle as no matter, to anyone with practical experience of firearms. Welf shouted:

"Spirit with us! Spirit of Man for Messer Raj!"

The Brigaderos behind him took it up; and some of the stubborn fight went out of the Colonials ahead. More and more were running back up, trying for the grappling lines and ladders over the walls. Raj chanced a look over his shoulder; more banners in the open ground beneath the wall: the 18th Komar, the 7th Descott. The stone was slippery underfoot, slippery with red rivulets running down from above. Fire from the ground was raking the firing platform above, deliberately built with little rear cover.

Not often you actually see that, see ground running with blood. The last time had been in Port Murchison, when Conner Auburn's fleet had sailed into his ambush.

Suddenly he was staggering onto level ground, the fighting platform on the wall; fire from below ceased, and a huge cheer went up as the bannermen waved their flags back and forth. Bodies heaped the pavement. Men poured out of the bastion towers before and behind him, shooting and wielding bayonet and rifle butt, shotguns and clubbed ramrods for the gunners. Ladders toppled as men thrust with poles or the points of their bayonets, through the firing slits and from the roof above.

Silence fell—comparative silence: only the cannonade and the screams of the wounded that littered the platform and stairs and the ground on both sides of the wall. He stepped up to a gunslit and looked out. The Colonial artillery was firing again; shells whined by overhead and crashed into the city behind.

"Get—" he turned and croaked; then stopped, realizing that he didn't recognize the man holding his banner. There were always volunteers for that job, and a continuous need for them. One of the runners was still there, though, reloading his pistol with a hand that dripped blood. "Verbal order to the battalion commanders. Pull their men back into cover. Get me Menyez. And then get that seen to."

"Ser."

The staircase was emptying; men rushed up it to take positions at the firing slits. Others helped or carried the wounded back below; the enemy went over the side to fall like bundles of discarded clothing to the hard-packed earth below. Except that bundles didn't scream on the way down, sometimes . . . *Well, no time for niceties.*

A voice spoke in Namerique: "Otto, this whore's son is alive—shoot!"

Raj looked up sharply and said in the same language: "Check there isn't one of ours alive under there first, man."

The big trooper braced himself and then began dragging bodies away by their legs; two of his comrades waited to either side, bayonetted rifles poised, and an ensign joined them with his revolver drawn. Half a dozen of the bodies were Colonial regulars, the remainder Civil Government infantry—24th Valencia, by the shoulder-flashes.

24th's been taking it on the chin, Raj thought. *They died hard, though, by the Spirit.*

Suddenly he had time to notice his own panting exhaustion, and the way his harness seemed to squeeze at his ribs. He felt for the canteen at his belt and found it empty, the bottom half ripped open in a flower of jagged tinned iron. Somebody made a joke as he tossed it aside, and he felt his testicles trying to draw up. He wasn't afraid of death, much—it was more that he had so much to *do*—but there were some wounds that were much more terrifying. A trooper handed him another canteen and he rinsed out his mouth, spat, and drank; it was water cut with vinegar, cutting through the dust and phlegm in his throat.

"*Tenk,*" he said—the Namerique word for thanks—and handed it back.

He started to wipe his mouth on the back of his sleeve, then stopped when he realized it was still sodden with blood. There was a little less on his left arm, so he used that instead. Now he could feel the sting of a half-dozen minor wounds, mostly superficial cuts, and a couple of bone-bruises. He broke open the revolver, ejected the spent brass and reloaded, then cleaned his saber a little, enough to resheath it. A trooper swore from the pile of dead.

"This one *is* alive, and he's one of ours!"

Raj moved over. His brows rose; that looked like a minor miracle. The infantryman was even more covered with blood than Raj, although—just like the stuff all over Raj—most of it didn't seem to be his own. A huge bruise covered one side of his face; a rifle lay beside him, the butt shattered and bayonet bent. The rings of a half-dozen handbombs were still on his fingers.

Raj whistled silently, and a number of the cavalry troopers nodded. He went on one knee and extended his hand; someone put another canteen in it, and he used that and his neckcloth to wipe some of the crusted blood from the man's face. He was young, no more than his early twenties, and rather light-skinned.

corporal minatelli, Center supplied. **enlisted in old residence two years ago. literate, watch-stander.** Details from the service record ran through his mind with the icy certainty of the ancient computer's data-transfer.

Damn, if he's as good as he looks, make that Ensign *Minatelli,* Raj thought.

The noncom's eyes snapped open, and he started violently, hand reaching for the knife in his boot. Raj caught it with irresistible strength.

"Easy there, fellow soldier," he said.

Minatelli controlled a dry retch. Raj checked his pupils; no noticeable difference in the dilation, so the concussion couldn't be too bad. A day's weakness and a bad headache. Lucky: any blow strong enough to knock you out was a real risk to life and limb.

"Sor," he said. The situation seemed to be sinking in. "Anyone else, sor?" he said hoarsely, with a clipped Spanjol accent under the Army dialect of Sponglish.

Definitely Ensign Minatelli, Raj decided. He looked up at the 1/591st junior officer with a question in his face.

"One other, sir—we're giving him first aid now. Looks fairly bad but he might make it."

"Sorry, son," Raj said.

"Spirit," Minatelli whispered. "Did our best, sor, but t'ere was just too many."

"You did fine, soldier. You held them long enough for us to get here."

He slapped the young man gently on the shoulder and rose. Teams of stretcher bearers were coming up the stairs at a run, now that they were a little clearer. A messenger preceded them.

"Ser. From Colonel Staenbridge—wogs back on their sida t'wall. Same frum Major Belagez."

That was a relief, though not unexpected. This had been the most dangerous penetration, the one nearest to the main gate.

"Raj!"

He looked around quickly; it was Suzette, with Fatima in tow and a Renunciate nun-doctor, who was bending over the wounded men being loaded onto the stretchers. Raj looked down at himself . . . well, it *was* a little alarming. She finished helping tie off a bandage and picked up her kit, walking over to him with a determined expression.

"It's not mine," he said, slightly defensive.

"Well, what about *this*?" she asked.

Raj looked down in genuine surprise. There was a long slash down his right arm, starting just above the wrist and running to his elbow. He worked the fingers. Not deep enough to really hurt, and it was with the grain of the muscle anyway. The soft scab broke and fresh blood oozed out along the path the scimitar had traced. *Must have been a good one,* he thought absently. They had some really fine swordsmiths in Al Kebir and Gedorosia, who made blades you could cut through a floating scarf of *torofib*-silk with; ones that would keep the edge when they hacked through bone.

"Take that jacket off right now."

Suzette's voice was determined. Raj obeyed automatically, and caught some of the soldiers concealing grins. *All part of the legend,* he thought resignedly. Even Horace had his place in it, and they all had to follow their roles willy-nilly. He swore mildly as she swabbed out the cut with iodine and washed down the arm before bringing out a roll of bandages.

"Is all that necessary?" he said.

"It *should* have some stitches," she said tartly. "Try not to use it too hard."

"I'll try," he promised. Then he smiled. "I couldn't let you be the only one to collect a scar from this campaign, now could I? Think of my reputation."

She gave an unwilling snort of laughter. "Your reputation will suffer even more if you get killed doing a lieutenant's work. Let the younger men have a chance."

"When you stay home and do embroidery, my dear, it's a deal."

He levered himself erect from his seat on a ledge and looked up. *0900,* he thought. Less than two hours past dawn.

Looking down from the fighting platform, he saw that the cleared ring inside the walls was mostly empty. Except for the enemy dead, of course. *Burial parties.* He'd look in on the wounded . . . *Get those fires under control.* The Colonial shelling had started more; luckily, Sandoral was mostly a city of adobe, brick, and stone with tiled roofs supported by arches—timber had always been expensive here, and he'd ripped out most of it for the bridge.

"Back to work," he said, and walked toward the staircase. Flies rose in a buzzing cloud from the stone, amid the faint sweetish smell of blood beginning to rot in the hot morning sun. A severed hand lay almost in his path; he started to kick it aside, then shook his head and walked down the stairs.

The flags crackled in the wind as his bannermen followed.

CHAPTER TWELVE

Suzette was pale. Fatima looked up in alarm; neither of them was a stranger to field-hospitals after all these years, so it couldn't be that. With a shudder, the Arab girl remembered her first time here, the first battle, four years ago. *Then* there had been huge wooden tubs set up at the feet of the operating tables, to hold the amputated limbs. And they had been full, all that endless day. Bartin had lost his hand that day; she'd held his shoulders down while the surgeon worked.

This was mild, by comparison. Only a few dozen shattered limbs to come off, with plenty of time to dose the worst cases with opium. A few hundred others, and more than half would live. But Suzette *did* look ill as she walked among the cots set up in the main chamber of Sandoral's cathedron. The air smelled of old incense and wax, under the stink of disinfectant and blood.

She was still Messa Whitehall. She finished the conversation, turned on her heel, and walked without running to the door. Fatima followed, grabbing up a towel. Retching sounds came from the cubicle; it was a priest's vesting room, in normal times. Suzette knelt and vomited into a bucket. Fatima hurried up beside her and handed her the towel, then went back for water.

"I don't understand it," Suzette said, wiping her face and slumping back in the chair.

Fatima put a hand on her forehead. "You're not running a fever, Messa."

"No, I'm not. And I feel fine, most of the time; just these last couple of mornings I—" She stopped. "What *date* is it?"

"Second of *Huillio*. Why do you want to . . . oh!"

Suzette's eyes went round. She turned her head slowly and met Fatima's gaze. The younger woman's mouth dropped open; she squeaked before managing to get out a coherent word:

"I thought . . . I thought you couldn't, that is—" She stopped in embarrassment.

"No, there wasn't enough time," Suzette said dazedly. Then her face firmed. "This is *not* to go beyond these walls, understand?"

"Of course, Messa," Fatima said soothingly. "But wouldn't Messer Raj want to know?"

"Not while he's got so much to worry about," Suzette said.

The flat rooftop terrace of Sandoral's District Offices made an excellent observation post, being close to the river and higher than the tops of the maidan wall; it was also far enough in from the defenses that Colonial shells were unlikely to land in the vicinity. The noon sun pounded down, turning the blue tile of the floor pale, drawing knife edges of shadow around the topiaries and pergolas. City administrators had held their receptions here, amid the potted bougainvillea and sambuca jasmine that had already begun to wilt without care. The iron heel plates of the officers' boots sounded on the floors, harsh and metallic. A heliograph station occupied one corner, and a map table and working desk had been set up by the railing nearest the river.

"Well, he's not wasting any time," Raj said.

Through the tripod-mounted heavy binoculars the east bank showed plainly. Tewfik's seal-of-Solomon banner waved from the highest ground; around it several thousand men worked with pick and shovel.

Grammek Dinnalsyn was using a telescope, also mounted; he made a few precise adjustments to the screws and sketched on a pad.

"That's not intended for his whole force," he said. "About three, four hundred men, perhaps."

Raj nodded agreement and took another bite of his sandwich. *Which reminds me . . .*

"Jorg," he said. "You've had your men on half-rations while we were away?"

"*Si*. Mostly hardtack and jerky, some fish and dried fruit."

"The whole command is back on full rations as of now," he said. "Bait the dogs properly, too. Muzzaf, get me a complete inventory of supplies. And fuel."

"*Si*," the little Komarite said. "*Seyhor*, I can tell you immediately— we have less than a week's supply at that rate of expenditure."

"Excellent," Raj said with a smile. The others looked at him oddly. "I presume Ali knows?"

"The outlines," Menyez said. "We've had a few deserters, mostly from the garrison units. Presumably they've 'taken the turban' and told him what they know."

Raj nodded thoughtfully. "Any the other way?"

"Three—two from their transport corps, claim to be Star Church believers conscripted for supplies. The other's a Zanj."

The Colony had conquered some of the outlying city-states there, but was fiercely resented. The Zanj were of different race than most of the Colonials, and followed a branch of Islam the conquerors thought heretical.

"They're probably spies, of course," Menyez concluded. "I've kept them in close confinement."

"I'll talk to them; I can usually get the truth out of a man," Raj said. He was conscious of sidelong glances; another part of the myth, that it was impossible to lie to Messer Raj. *It is when Center's looking through my eyes,* he thought. "In any case, it doesn't matter what Ali knows. Or even what Tewfik knows."

Barton Foley pointed. "They're bringing men across."

Everyone raised their glasses. An overloaded fishing skiff labored across the current, on a trajectory that would land it just south of Sandoral's walls on the western bank. Heads and V-marks of ripples showed where dogs on lead-halters swam in the boat's wake. On the riverbank it had left, men were building an earth ramp down to the water's edge and putting together a raft from bits and pieces, date-palm logs and thin boards that looked as if they'd come from some sheep fence.

"It'll take him a while to get his men back to Ali," Gerrin Staenbridge said, examining his nails. The way the Civil Government forces had scavenged up every small boat and all available materials was handicapping their enemies badly. "You have something in mind, don't you, *mi heneral?*"

Raj grinned at him. "Possibly. Can you think what?"

Staenbridge shook his head. Raj nodded amiably.

"And that's an excellent thing too," he said. "Because you're an extremely perceptive officer, and you have *all* the information. If you can't figure it out, probably Tewfik can't either. Gentlemen, I want you to spend the rest of today and tomorrow reorganizing. Don't let your men settle in too tight—I want full readiness to move at a moment's notice. Those units that've been hit hard, do the necessary shifting around immediately. Weapons maintenance, ammunition issues, the lot—again, immediately, please. Understood?"

Nods. "Grammeck, this afternoon I want to go over some matters with you; bring the complete plans for the pontoon bridge, please. If there aren't any questions, Messers?"

There was obviously one burning one, but nobody was going to ask it. Jorg Menyez remained when the others had left the flat rooftop.

"Colonel?" Raj asked. It wasn't like Jorg to talk for reassurance sake. He was obviously a little embarrassed.

"*Heneralissimo,*" he said. "Ah . . . I thought you'd want to know about Osterville."

"Osterville?" Raj asked. It was an effort to remember the man; he hadn't thought of him since Ain el-Hilwa. *And good riddance.* "It's enough that he isn't here, making trouble."

"No, he won't be doing that," Menyez said. "It was unpleasant, but as you said, it was necessary."

Raj looked at him. Menyez flushed. "All right, *mi heneral*. I destroyed the letter and your seal, and he went into the Drangosh with a sixty-kilo roundshot tied to his ankles . . . but I still don't like it."

Raj nodded. "Of course, Jorg." *Only Suzette has my seal.* "I understand."

He shivered slightly, despite the heat of the day.

A dot of red light arched over the wall, trailing fire through the darkness. *Thud.* It exploded among the vacant houses—hopefully vacant houses—and a column of fire rose into the night. Another spark. *Thud.*

"That makes six the past hour," Raj murmured to himself.

in the past fifty-five minutes thirty seconds, Center added. **harassing fire.**

"Ali's obviously decided to starve us out," Raj agreed.

An image drifted across his eyes: his own emaciated body, still living, naked and covered with weals and burns. Pairs of dogs were hitched to chains attached to each ankle and wrist. The drivers urged the dogs forward slowly, gradually taking up the slack. Ali ibn'Jamal sat watching, pounding his fist on the arm of his portable throne and laughing with pleasure, licking his full lips. Tewfik stood to one side, arms crossed and a look of faint disgust on his face, echoed by most of the noblemen and officers around him. Behind him a gallows stood skeletal against the sky, with the bodies of the Companions dangling from it—by meathooks through their ribs. Several of them were still writhing . . .

Raj made a grimace of distaste. "Even by the standards of Mihwel the Terrible, Ali is a prime case."

a subjective judgment, but accurate. child-rearing practices among the colonial royal family are conducive to severely dysfunctional personalities.

A step sounded on the tiles behind him. There had been no challenge and response from the sentries on the stair below, so it could be only one person.

Suzette leaned on the railing beside him, looking out over the city and the glistening water. "Full circle, my love," she said. "Sandoral, and a battle to come."

"And men dying unexpectedly," he said.

She turned her face towards him, drawn and pale beneath the moons. "Osterville couldn't lead and wouldn't follow and wouldn't get out of the way and let you work, either. Can you imagine the sort of havoc he'd have created back here, with everything depending on Jorg keeping things running smoothly? We'd have ended up *swimming* across, while Osterville tried to make everyone do things his way."

"Jorg—"

"Jorg is good man and a good officer, but he doesn't have your talent for facing men down—especially not men higher on the chain of command. You know that." A little anger crept into her voice: "How many better men have been killed on this campaign so far?"

Raj smiled ruefully and shook his head. "You always could out-argue me," he said. A shrug. "I just don't like having a fellow officer killed like that. It's the sort of thing Tzetzas does."

Suzette sighed. "I don't like it either," she said quietly. "But it had to be done."

Raj nodded. They watched another Colonial shell come over the walls.

"It's cold," Suzette said in a small voice.

Raj extended his arm and the long military cloak he wore. Suzette came under it and laid her cheek against his chest.

"We can't afford any mistakes this time, can we?" she said after a moment.

"No," Raj replied. He looked up at the moons. They'd be rising late, tomorrow evening. *Victory or death,* he thought. *All men die, but this has to be done.* "Let's turn in."

"Precisely this bearing," Raj said.

He drew a line in the dust with the stick. Behind him the artillerymen staked down their frame—two sets of rigid beams at right angles, with a slanted piece across the arms. They aligned it with the mark in the dust; once it was firmly in place, they pushed the gun up the slanted fronting of the frame and tied off the wheels at a chalk mark on the wood.

"Range is exactly 3,525 meters," Raj said. "Load contact, two-second delay."

"Sir," the gunner said, giving him a glance.

How could you know? Raj read in his face. And a trace of awe; men knew he didn't make empty boasts.

Raj walked on to the next gun's position as the iron clang of the breechblock sounded behind him. All fifty-eight surviving field guns were lined up just inside the north wall of Sandoral, all up on the frames; all aligned along the precise vector he'd drawn in the dirt for them. Every single one, as far as Center could judge, was now aiming at the exact midpoint of earth above Ali's command bunker, behind the Colonial outworks—where he invariably retired after the sunset prayer. All the fortress guns in the fixed positions on the wall were aligned as well, those of them that would bear on the target.

Irregularities—wear on the rifling of guns, slight differentials in shell loading and drag, whatever—would spread the projectiles. It ought to be an unpleasant surprise, nonetheless.

Dinnalsyn looked back at the long row of guns. "Think we'll get him, *mi heneral?*"

"No," Raj said. "That's a very secure bunker. The last thing I want to do is put Tewfik in full command. But it'll certainly get his attention, and Ali's got a short temper. If I know my man, he'll do something stupid."

The limbers stood in a row five meters behind the guns, the dog teams in traces and lying down.

"Are the rafts ready?" Raj said.

"Ready and waiting, sir," Dinnalsyn said. "The planking and decking from the pontoon bridge was exactly as much as we needed . . . I suppose that's no coincidence?"

"You might say that," Raj replied. He clapped him on the shoulder. "Stay ready for it."

The last of the cavalry battalions on special duty were sitting by the wall, finishing their evening meal: beans and pigmeat and onions, dished out from kettles over camp fires and scooped up with tortillas. It was the 5th Descott. They were professionals enough to concentrate on eating, but he could feel the tension crackling off them. He walked over and made a beckoning gesture. They crowded around him and crouched or sat at his hand signal; only about three hundred fifty left—and the battalion had been at double strength when he took it west to fight the Brigade.

"All right, dog-brothers," he said quietly. That forced them to listen carefully and lean closer; it also made each man feel as if he was talking to that one alone, as an individual. "You've guessed that something's up. Two hours after sundown—"

The sun was just touching the western horizon.

"—the guns are going to cut loose with a five-round stonk. The second the last gun fires—but not before—you give the wogs five rounds rapid. Then you come back down from the wall, ride your dogs to the docks, get on the rafts and off we go."

He paused a moment. "You're all fighting men and all Descotters," he went on. "My father and grandfather and great-grandfather fought the wogs, and so did yours."

Nods; Descotter *rancheros* held their land on military tenure, paying their tax in men rather than money. Fathers and sons and brothers followed each other into the same battalions time out of mind; comrades were neighbors at home, officers the squire's sons.

"There's a lot of Descotter blood and bone buried around here. Now we have a chance to end it." That caused a rustle, men coming forward in their crouch and leaning on their rifles. "If we win this one, we break them—not just push them back, but wreck them for all time. If we lose . . ." He grinned. "Well, we haven't done much losing while we've been together, you and I, have we?"

A low snarl of agreement. "Everything depends on the wogs thinking we're still here, at least for a while. You'll move back to the docks quickly and you'll do it quietly, and with no foul-ups. Understood?"

Gerrin Staenbridge stepped forward. "You can count on us, *mi heneral*," he said solemnly. Another growl from the ranks.

"Keep it quiet, keep it quiet," Ensign Minatelli said.

There were only fifteen men left in his platoon, now—several of them lightly wounded—so it wasn't very different from running his squad. The star on the front of his helmet still felt like a weight of lead to his spirit, though. They formed up outside their bivouac, in the forecourt of what had been a nobleman's house. Minatelli walked down his platoon, giving everything a final check. The men's haversacks were full, three days' rations—smoked pork and hardtack, dried apricots and figs—and extra ammunition in their blanket rolls.

"Company G, fall in."

The men found their places by instinct, in column of twos back from the company pennant. It was *dark* outside: the city gaslights were out, of course—nobody left to shovel coal and tend the tank-farms—and all torches and fires had been forbidden.

Just as well, he thought. It was frightening how few of them were left; the main Colonial attack had come right over their sector of the wall yesterday. Forty men in the company, barely a full platoon.

The battalion colors came by, and Major Felasquez carrying a shuttered bull's-eye light. His one eye gleamed a little as he turned, stopped for a brief murmur with Captain Pinya and stepped closer to the men.

"All right, lads," he said, a little louder.

Don't expect the wogs could hear even if we shouted, Minatelli thought. *On the other hand, it gets everyone thinking* quiet.

"We've had enough from the towel-heads; now we're going to give it back, the way the monkey gave it to the miller's wife, by surprise and from the rear. Mind your orders, do it right, and with the Spirit's help and Messer Raj's plan, we'll whip them." He stepped back. "24th Valencia Foot—*Waymanos!*"

The column moved forward jerkily; it was strange to the point of being dizzying not to step off to the beat of the drum, and the troops had been told not to march in step. The uniform clash of hobnails on stone pavement was like nothing else on earth, and it carried. Instead they walked, with an occasional quiet curse as somebody stepped on the heels of the man ahead. Guides stood at intersections, their lanterns the only light in the deserted city. Minatelli kept his hand on the hilt of his new sword and ignored the eerie quietness.

Through the river gate the darkness lifted a little; a one-quarter Miniluna and the stars reflected off the rippled surface of the water. Gravel crunched, then planks boomed a little under their boots. The column halted.

"24th Valencia?" someone asked ahead, a dim figure against the water. "*This* way."

They waited; the men ahead melted away company by company. "Company G, this way."

The men scrambled through the knee-high water and into the barge; it was one of the boxlike constructs he'd helped to cobble together out of wood salvaged from wrecked houses. A long steering-oar marked the notional stern, and there were men standing to the sweeps on either side, six to a flank. They had only a single shuttered lantern to work with, but despite the darkness and the crowding only an occasional thump and oath marked someone tripping as they clambered down from the planking to the hold of the crude vessel.

"You'll be pulling the outermost raft," Captain Pinya said.

"That one, sir?" Minatelli said, pointing.

"That's right, Ensign."

Ensign. Spirit. My folks will never believe it.

He shook himself back to the present. There were so many more ways to fuck *up* at a higher rank. Right now, that could get *everyone* killed.

He saluted and climbed down himself, a little awkward with no rifle on his shoulder and a sword and pistol at his belt. He turned around as soon as he was at the bow, making sure everyone's equipment was blacked as ordered. *Right. Nothing showing but eyeballs.*

"Cast off," he said quietly.

The ropes were undone and the barge began to drift. "That way," he said, pointing.

The rowers were from the Sandoral District garrison; they'd all had some experience moving these damned things around. They dug their clumsy oars into the water and heaved, grunting. One step forward, lower the oar, haul it one step back. Minatelli thumped the boards beside him softly to keep the beat, peering ahead to his target. It was almost invisible until they were on top of it, two sections of the pontoon bridge decking with some timbers in between.

"*Halto,*" he said.

Hands and poles on the raft fended them off and turned the barge around. Ropes were made fast to both sides of the stern, and then the barge released to drift slowly downstream. It halted with a slight jerk, held by the cables that anchored the row of rafts. Minatelli looked back along them, back to the shore and the black silhouette of the city wall. The sun had been down at least an hour and a half. More and more of the pontoon barges and every other type of boat available on the Sandoral docks—the ones that hadn't had a chance to get upstream when the news of the invasion got here—put out into the darkening water, anchoring or sculling up to the rafts. The docks were a moving carpet of men, helmets and furled banners and the muzzles of slung rifles.

Not long now.

"Rest easy, boys," he said. "Rest a bit."

"Gently, gently," Suzette whispered.

The infantrymen assigned as stretcher bearers were well-meaning but clumsy. There were enough of them to manhandle the stretchers into the bottom of the barge and fit them into the crude racks the carpenters had made, turning them into improvised bunk beds. The wounded were dosed heavily with opium to dull the pain of movement, but now and then a man would moan in his delirium. The Renunciates and priest-doctors moved quickly among them, checking pulses.

"Spirit have mercy, this one's dead," a nun said.

"Leave him be," Suzette replied. *Damn.*

The final load came from the carriages and handcarts they'd pressed into service as ambulances.

She looked west, towards the ramparts.

"Drop it in, don't throw it!" Jorg Menyez hissed.

An officer relayed the order. Endless files of infantrymen passed sacks of hardtack and crates of dried meat and fruit from hand to hand, out from the wagons to the end of the pier. Once there, they knelt and let their burdens drop into the water. The current caught them, the hardtack floating for a few minutes before waterlogging dragged it down with a scatter of bubbles, the pierced casks and boxes sinking faster.

A good thing this is fresh water. There would be downdraggers in a feeding-frenzy if they tried this in a harbor. Doubtless the plesiosauroids out in the deeper water would be feeding full tonight, as it was.

"Colonel. Major Tormidero sends 'is compliments, and is 'e to load tha wine?"

"No," Menyez said, biting off the *damned fool* with an effort. "Tell him Ali's men may drown their sorrows as they wish, if they don't fear Allah's wrath."

But not a scrap of food will they find in Sandoral, he thought with hard glee. He sneezed into his handkerchief, not too badly; there weren't any dogs in the immediate neighborhood. It was pitch black. He looked anxiously over the river to the Colonial fortlet planted where the pontoon bridge had been. Evidently *they* hadn't seen anything unusual, either. *It's a siege. They don't* expect *anything to happen.*

"Spirit, but this is a madman's gamble," he whispered to himself, lips barely moving. The only chance at victory . . . but what a chance.

"And what a story to tell the grandchildren, if we pull it off!"

If they didn't . . .

✧   ✧   ✧

Ali ibn'Jamal took another handful of rice and grilled lamb, belching politely. It was surprisingly good, considering what the cooks had to work with; the army was on preserved rations wagoned up from the bridgehead. His own cook had priority on what little the foragers were bringing in, of course. The bunker had been made quite homelike: silk tapestries and silk-and-gold thread Al Kebir carpets, embroidered cushions about low tables of chiseled brass, incense in crescent-shaped burners on tripods about the walls. The lamplight had been turned down to a civilized level, and zebec and zither played melodiously from behind a screen in one corner. Ali ate, and held out his hands for the slave to wash with rosewater and towel dry.

"Your appetite should be better, Tewfik my brother," he said, and belched again. "Think of how the *kaphar* pigs within Sandoral's walls would drool and slaver at the sight of such a feast!"

Tewfik turned from a low-voiced conversation with his officers. "Indeed, Settler of the House of Peace," he said. "They are very short of supplies. That is why I fear some new trick of this Shaitan's-seed Whitehall."

Ali scowled for a moment, then gestured expansively. "Whitehall is trapped," he said. "He cannot sortie—our men outnumber his and are strongly entrenched; our rear, even, is protected by great works, even though no relieving force of any numbers can approach. He cannot build his bridge of boats again, with your fort and its guns covering the opposite bank. What can he do but starve?"

"Commander of the Faithful, I do not *know* what he can do. And that is what—"

"My lord." One of the duty officers of the Settler's guard came up to Tewfik and bowed. "You commanded that we notify you: the infidel have launched a signal rocket from the walls. One blue starburst."

A gun boomed in the distance. They all ignored it; the Colonial artillery was lobbing a steady round every twenty minutes into Sandoral, to keep the infidels from sleeping easily.

Another boom, and another; and the explosion of a shell, far too close. Another junior officer dashed down the stairs into the bunker.

"From the walls!" he shouted. "Lords, *all* the *kaphar* guns are firing from—"

"Fwego!"

Grammeck Dinnalsyn swept his saber downward. POUMPH. The first of the field guns vomited a long tongue of red flame into the night, backlighting the cloud of smoke that swirled away from the muzzle. Like a ripple, the line of explosions swept down the row of guns, repeated fifty-eight times. The noise was deafening, shock-waves echoing back from the high flat surface of the city wall like pillows of hot air smacking into face and chest. Already the stairways were showing running men, the militia gunners; one per gun on the walls, each to pull the lanyard on a weapon pre-laid on its target.

The first field gun had already fired its second round by the time the last piece discharged at the other end of the line. The crews moved with smooth, metronomic precision. The guns couldn't recoil, up on the elevating frames—although he hated to see the trails overstressed like this; it was asking for trouble later. Each piece had a stack of five extra shells next to it, with preset fuses. Swing the lever and wrench the breech aside; the brass shell clanged out, with a puff of sulfur-reeking smoke. Loader shoved the next round in, breechman pushed the interrupted-screw block home and slapped the lever down, master gunner clipped his lanyard to the toggle, and *fire.*

Six rounds, and silence except for the ringing of abused ears. The master gunners of the two central pieces slashed the ties holding the wheels to the elevating frames with their swords, and the pieces ran down the sloped timbers. The crews snatched up the trails before the pieces could slow, running them back to the limbers and slapping the locking-rings down. The pins went home with an iron clank, men leaped into the saddle or swung onto the axletree seats, and the guns rumbled off down toward the docks at a round trot. An instant later the sound changed to a hard rattle as the metal rims of the wheels rose onto the cobblestones. The maneuver was repeated again and again, each gun out from the first two cutting loose and limbering up to follow.

Dinnalsyn neck-reined his dog around. The guns were vanishing into the night, and small-arms fire crackled from the ramparts above. Alone but for his aides and messengers, he saluted the walls.

"Here's to you, *heneralissimo,*" he said. "I don't know how the hell you manage it, but it's never dull. *Waymanos!*"

He clapped heels to his dog.

Corporal M'Telgez was acutely conscious of Messer Raj standing quietly behind him as the artillery bellowed. It was blacker than a meter up a sauroid's butt here on the wall's fighting platform; and it smelled of old death, rotting blood and bits of bodies. He willed himself to ignore the smell, and the feeling of confinement—he was a dog-and-saddle man, not a mole or a town-dweller—and the far more nerve-wracking presence of the *heneralissimo.* Not that he was one to interfere with a man doing his work, far from it. It was just a little disconcerting to have Messer Raj and the Colonel and the Captain all pick *your* spot to pause when the balloon went up. There was a gap in the gabions he'd picked earlier for his first aiming point. Invisible in the darkness now, but pretty soon—

"*Fwego!*"

The stubby mortars on the towers chugged. Starshells burst over the wog entrenchments, throwing a flickering blue-white magnesium light. He exhaled and squeezed the trigger. *Crack.* His rifle punched his shoulder. He worked the lever and reached for one of the rounds in the wooden holder beside his hand. *Crack.* A Colonial gun fired from the forward trenches. He adjusted his sights and aimed for it, with any luck a round might ricochet off the barrel and into one of the crew. *Crack. Crack. Crack.*

"Cease fire! Rearward, on the double!" he called out.

His squad was closest to the staircase. They double-timed down it, through the hot dark and the faint reflected light of the starshells, while the field guns blazed away to their right. Eyes and teeth glimmered from the dogs crouching in neat rows in the open space within the walls; they were too well trained to move when they'd been told to stay, but the noise made them eager and uneasy. They rose with a surge as their riders straddled them. M'Telgez's feet found the stirrups, and he slid his rifle into the scabbard, taking the reins in tightly with his left hand. More and more men poured down the stairways by the gates, until the whole battalion was mounted.

No trumpet calls, but the men fell in—every dog knew its place by smell, if nothing else. M'Telgez saw the shadowy length of the battalion standard go by, and an arm flash up. He tapped his heel to Pochita's flank, and the whole column broke into a fast walk that turned into a slow loping trot. They moved south of the last of the guns, under the arc of the last shells, then turned eastward toward the docks. The sky ripped above them. M'Telgez felt his shoulders hunch; his hindbrain knew what that meant, only too well.

CRUMP. A heavy shell sledged into the empty space behind him. Seconds later dirt pattered down out of the air. At least they weren't firing airburst; it must be too difficult with no observation of the fall of shot. *CRUMP. CRUMP. CRUMP.* The last one fell on a gun that was moving parallel to the column of the 5th Descott, and the limber went up too in a huge ball of red-orange flame. Men screamed and dogs wailed ahead of him. An officer rode out; his pistol cracked as the dogs were put down, and the men swung up behind comrades, no time for first aid now. *CRUMP. CRUMP. CRUMP.* More shells went by overhead and blasted into the upper stories of empty houses. Adobe brick and fragments of roof tiles and burning planks cataracted into the streets. He kept his head down and followed the man ahead of him, hoping that the officers knew where they were going. Shells were coming overhead in a continuous stream, but a whole city was a big target.

Mother, he thought. This was worse than a battle; then you could *do* something.

Horace knew he was being ridden toward another boat ride. He turned nose-to-tail and circled. Raj cursed, but he didn't bother yanking on the reins; you could pull until the levers gouged a hole right through his cheeks, and Horace wouldn't pay much attention. Instead he let the knotted reins fall on the pommel and leaned forward, thumping the hound's neck with the flat of his hand.

"Come *on*, you son of a bitch," he said firmly. "We've got places to go and things to do. Stop this nonsense."

Horace lowered his ears and head and turned, breaking into a shambling trot. Raj's banner snapped in the night air; the Colonial shells went by overhead with their mechanical wails, a continuous diminuendo punctuated by the crash of the bursting charges. He pressed with his heels as a barricade of brick and burning rubble closed the way. Horace took it in a single long leap, then checked a pace to let the others come through. Heat slapped at him as they passed over the flame; a dog yelped suddenly as it stepped on a hot ember.

Raj grinned into the darkness. *Well, we certainly got their attention,* he thought.

all colonial guns are firing at maximum speed, Center noted. **even with ample ammunition reserves, this will degrade performance and shorten the life of the barrels.**

Raj nodded. Wasteful. The hotter a gun got, the worse the wear on the lands of the rifling. After a while it had to be sent back to the foundry to have a new sleeve fitted into the barrel and rifled, and it was never quite as good after that. The third time it had to be scrapped.

"Want to do the honors, *mi heneral?*" Jorg Menyez said.

He waved to the lines of slowmatch that snaked away among the warehouses and boatyards of Sandoral's docks. The raw smell of kerosene and gunpowder was thick in the air.

"Dinnalsyn assures me that it will all go off at about the same time."

Raj looked around with grim satisfaction. When the warehouses and shipyards went up, it would also take all the remaining timber in Sandoral suitable for boats or rafts or bridging materials. Ali might get the city, but he was damned if there'd be anything immediately useful in it when he did. No food, no building materials.

"I wouldn't dream of denying you the pleasure, Jorg," Raj said.

Menyez ceremoniously puffed on his cigarillo and applied the end to the slowmatch. It lit with a sullen hiss and trail of blue smoke.

"And now we bid farewell to beauteous Sandoral: land of exotic giant cockroaches, intolerable sticky heat-rash, and picturesque, hairy wogs with razor-sharp gelding knives," the infantryman mock-quoted. East Residence had enough of a middle class to support a tourist trade, mostly steamboat excursions to the Bay Islands. Guidebooks were common, too. *"Hadios, mi heneral."*

It probably did the men good to see their commanders relaxed and confident. *It does me good. Jorg's usually a worrier. Morale's*

probably as high as it should be. Possibly higher than it should be . . .
Now who's worrying?

"*Hadios,* Jorg. See you downriver."

He turned Horace. Raft after raft was heading downstream, casting off behind its towing-barge. Sweeps tossed up small chuckling
ripples of green water, a faint sheen under the crescent of Miniluna.
As each loosed its ties to the anchor cables, another cluster of dogs
and guns would trundle out across the linked rafts to the outermost. War-dogs whined as chain staples fastened their bridles to pins
in the decking; the wheels of guns and limbers were lashed down,
and another raft and barge combination was under way. Beyond the
rafts boats speckled the water, sloops and ferries, and score after
score of the pontoon barges.

Messengers trotted up, reported, left. *Damn. Amazing. Only one
traffic jam.* And that caused by rubble blocking a street and the
battalion assigned to it swerving into another's route. Paws and
feet and wheels filled the night with a low rumble of purposeful
noise, none of it as loud as the whistle and crash of two hundred Colonial guns bombarding the city. More starshells lightened
the sky to the west, Colonial this time, put up so their artillery
had better visibility.

"Shall I order a cease-fire?"

"No, Hussein," Tewfik replied, also in a whisper.

The central roof of the bunker had caved in, but the beams had
not given way completely. They sagged to the floor, their jagged
breaks splintered, like bone-white teeth. Dry dirt poured down still,
pooling and spreading; soldiers dug bodies out of the pile, some
wounded and some dead, and carried them up the stairs. Ripped
down and stamped in a pile, the tapestries still smoldered from the
burning kerosene that falling lamps had sprayed across them—sprayed
across men, as well.

Although not, unfortunately, across my brother, Tewfik thought.
It would be a disaster if Ali died just now. It might be salva-
tion if he were struck down by an incapacitating injury; the longer,
the better. *There is no God but God, and all things are accomplished according to the will of God.* But sometimes it was difficult to understand His tactics. He wrinkled his nose at the smell
of burning carpets. More waste. The cost of them was enough to
pay a brigade of cavalry for a year, and now they would be
replaced. Transport would be commandeered to replace them, while
the guns ate a month's reserve of ammunition.

"*Amir,* we will lose guns soon if we keep up this rate of fire,"
the officer warned. "The barrels are so hot we'll have cook-offs during
reloading."

"Reduce the rate, but not so much that *he*" —he nodded to the
other chamber of the bunker; Ali's sputtering curses could still be

heard there, and occasionally a woman's scream— "will notice. Better to shoot the lands out of the barrels than have more executions."

The officer stroked his beard and leaned close. "*Amir,* it is time to consider if the House of Peace can stand, with this man at the head of it."

Tewfik stared into the other man's face for a moment; the brown eyes met his single one unflinching. *Good. I have no cowards on my staff.*

"He has no sons," he said quietly. "Nor do I."

"The Prophet Muhammed had no sons; but many rulers sprang from his daughters."

"And many wars sprang from the claims of his daughters' descendants and the orthodox caliphs, beginning with Kharballa," Tewfik pointed out. That had started a split that echoed down millennia, not even ending with the Last Jihad. "There are also too many nobles with enough of the Settler's blood to make a fair claim. Ali is no fool, he's killed the only ones with indisputable claims or great ability, or both. If we have civil war now, the *kaphar* and the Zanj and the northern savages will race each other to pick our bones. We must continue."

"For the present."

"For the present," Tewfik agreed. *Until Ali alive becomes more a menace to the House of Islam than Ali dead,* went unspoken between them. "Now go, and have the gunners reduce their rate of fire by one-third. On my authority."

I control the Host of Peace, but I cannot rule, he knew bitterly. Not in his own name. If only there were a male heir, a regency might be possible—but there was not. The mullahs would not issue the Friday prayer for one-eyed Tewfik; men would not obey, not without a soldier standing behind them. He would shatter what he most wished to preserve, if he tried that.

"Insh'allah."

The acrid gloom of the bunker was stifling. Left hand on the hilt of his yataghan, he strode up the stairs, past the protective curves and the intermediate guardroom. The blue-white sputtering light of starshells made him slit his eyes at the dark motionless bulk of Sandoral's low-slung walls. They mocked him from behind the moat, tantalized him. Men and dogs labored to bring the ammunition forward to the siege guns from the bombproofs set behind the main line, along pathways sunk into the ground with protective berms on either side. The gunners toiled, stripped to the waist, their faces and torsos black with powder smoke. Many had balls of cotton wool stuffed in their ears, but they courted deafness as well as death with every shot. It did not stop the smooth choreographed sequence of laying, swabbing, loading, ramming, firing.

A heavy shell bit a section out of the firing parapet in a clap of orange flame and rumble of sound. Water spurted up where the stone fell into the moat, leaving a ragged gap in the concrete core. No fire replied from the city.

"Was that your plan, Whitehall, to weaken our artillery? Did you know how my brother would respond to your taunt?"

The stonk on the command bunker had been wickedly well-placed. Whitehall was well served, good officers, brave and well-trained troops, well equipped. *Does he know us well enough to predict that my brother would waste ammunition and guns like this?* He nodded. Certainly.

"Yet it cannot affect the outcome of the war," he mused.

Could it be cover for another raid? Unlikely. With a pontoon bridge for rapid withdrawal and a secure fortified base, Whitehall had still been unable to do more than divert him temporarily. Now the land across the river was unfit to support moving troops. What could the infidel accomplish with the smaller number of men they could smuggle across the river now?

That was the problem. He did not know.

"Lord *Amir*. The Settler requires your presence."

Tewfik ground his teeth. *He has beaten enough women to feel brave again,* he thought. *Now he must play at commander. And waste my time!*

With an enemy like Whitehall, time was one thing you never had a surplus of. From all reports, Barholm Clerett was almost as difficult a master to serve as Ali ibn'Jamal—but at least he was far away.

The little galley Raj was using as his HQ had been some rich merchant's toy before war came to Sandoral, or perhaps belonged to a landowner with estates on the riverbank who wanted to be able to commute to his townhouse in the district capital. For a moment Raj wondered where he was, that little provincial oligarch. On the road west, grumbling in his carriage with a nagging wife and the nurse fussing with the children and a train of baggage carts behind? Perhaps already in East Residence, imposing on some distant relative or dickering with a lodging-keeper not at all impressed by anything from beyond the walls of *the* city. Or caught on his country property by Colonial raiders, and now tumbled bones in a ditch.

We must be making ten klicks per hour, he thought.

a range of 9.7 to 10.1, averaging 9.9 overall, Center said.

Tonight and tomorrow to reach their destination, traveling with the current. The men in the barges and boats were sculling, but more to keep station and direction than for propulsion. There were enough in each vessel to change off at frequent intervals, too.

"Over to Major Bellamy," Raj said, pointing.

The galley came about sharply, bringing a protesting whine from

Horace and Harbie on the foredeck. The crew were all ex-boatmen and used to the shattering labor at the oars; one side dug theirs in hard, the other feathered, and the man at the tiller pushed it over. The slender boat turned in almost its own length and stroked eastward. Beside a raft crowded with troops and dogs it halted; Raj leaned over the side, one hand on the rail.

"There's your destination, Major," he said, pointing southward, downstream. "Remember the timing's crucial."

Bellamy waved back wordlessly, his bowl-cut blond hair bright in the darkness. His rowers bent to their work, and several of the other barges followed. Raj's galley curved back toward the main body of the straggling armada, like a sheepdog with its flock.

More like a pack of carnosauroids, Raj thought, watching the dull glint of moonlight on the barrels of the field pieces on a raft.

Suzette came up beside him, a cigarette glowing in its holder of carved sauroid ivory. "The waiting's the hardest part," she said.

"No, just the longest," Raj said. "Having to send others out, that's hardest."

She put an arm around his waist and leaned her head on his shoulder.

CHAPTER THIRTEEN

"Stake the dogs," Ludwig Bellamy said.

His second-in-command blinked at him. "It's more than a kilometer to the objective," he said in surprise.

"Ni, migo," Bellamy said in Namerique. "Walking that far won't kill us."

He shook his head as the man walked away to spread the order by whisper. Messer Raj had taught his Squadrone followers that fighting on foot was no disgrace, but they'd still rather ride ten kilometers than walk one.

He squinted at his map; an aide lit a match and held it over the paper. Messer Raj had penciled in the route with his own hands. *Yes. That's the gully.* There was a roadway of sorts along the river's edge, but it was entirely too visible from the other side, back around Sandoral. His scouts gathered around, holding the reins of their dogs.

"Lead the way," he said, tracing out the branchings of wash and ravine. "It's only a klick; but keep an eye out for wog pickets."

He looked up at the bulk of the unit; nearly everyone was ashore from the beached barges and rafts, although many were soaked to the waist. Water squelched in his own high boots. The last few came in sight, holding their rifles and bandoliers over their heads as they waded to the muddy riverbank.

"Fall them in," he said quietly.

The 1st Mounted Cruisers formed up in ranks four deep, and the rabble of militia gunners behind them. They'd have no part in the immediate action, but they were important if everything worked right.

"Migos, Messer Raj trusts us to do this job right without holding our hands. Let's show him he's right. Keep it quiet and move quickly."

"Right face. At the double, forward *march.*"

They swung off into the night, rifles at the trail. Bellamy trotted up along the line to the head, where the battalion banner was. His aide was leading his dog, back at the rear; the men would march with

595

a better will if they saw the commander on foot too. Some of them grinned and shook their rifles in the air as he passed.

They're pumped, Bellamy decided. This had all the earmarks of one of Messer Raj's sauroid-out-of-the-helmet tricks. They trusted their leader's luck. And they hated being cooped up inside walls, no matter how strong.

He looked ahead. *You have to earn your luck.* It was much darker here, where most of the sky was blocked out by the clay walls of the badlands on either side. They panted up steep slopes, scrambled down others, slogged through sand and deep dust that sucked at their boots, splashed through a few wet spots where water from the spring floods still lay. Men panted, sweated, cursed in low voices. The ground rose toward the hills where the road from the east met the river, where Tewfik had planted his fortlet.

A scout came cantering back and pulled his dog up on its haunches. "As you thought, Lord," he said, leaning down. He was one of the old-fashioned ones, with his hair pulled up in a knot at the side of his head. "There is only a shallow ditch and berm on the landward side—my dog could jump it. And all the cannon point to the water."

Bellamy grunted with relief. Messer Raj had said that was the logical thing for Tewfik to do, but you couldn't count on an opponent having good sense.

He paced back along the column, personally giving the command to halt. The battalion came to a stop with a few lurches that ran one group of men onto another's heels, but nothing major. The company commanders gathered around him.

"Come," he said, leading them westward up a final line of ridge. Beyond was rolling open ground, sparsely bushed with thorny native scrub and some cacti. "There."

In the open, the moonlight was enough to make the Colonial works plain enough. He used his binoculars: not much of a ditch, and there were no obstacles—no timbers studded with old sword-blades, no thorn zariba. Doubtless those would have been added in time, but there had been no time. Across the water red specks crawled through the air and the endless flat thudding of the bombardment continued. There were enough fires in Sandoral now to cast a reddish glow across the great river, expanding and uniting into columns of flame without men to fight them.

"Spread your men out along this ridge, and order fixed bayonets," Bellamy said. "Every man may load his rifle, but no reloading once we're into the enemy camp."

Nods, enthusiastic from the *Squadrones,* less so from the Civil Government officers seconded to the battalion. Fighting at close quarters in the dark, friendly fire would be a greater threat than the enemy. Their repeaters gave them an advantage in a close-range firefight, anyway. Better to rely on impetus and cold steel.

"Nothing fancy," Bellamy said, repeating Messer Raj's words. "Just raise a shout and go in on my signal."

Across two hundred meters of open ground. But the Spirit was with them, and the initiative.

He lay on the ridgeline. "Uncase the colors," he said to his bannermen; they pulled the leather tubes off the standards and gently shook the heavy silk free, taking care to keep both flags—the unit and the Civil Government blazon—below the ridgeline. To either side came rustling, crunching sounds as the men filed up company by company. Starlight glittered as they fixed their bayonets and then lay prone at the word of command. He could see one or two praying, among those closer; others were waiting, stolid or eager as their temperament took them.

And I don't think of glory, he realized. A few years ago that would have been his main concern in a situation like this; that men see him add honor to his name. *Now I'm just worried that nothing go wrong.* Messer Raj was right: civilization was contagious. It was more efficient than the old ways, but it took much of the color out of life. He swallowed water and vinegar from his canteen and loosened his sword in its scabbard, flipped open the cylinder of his revolver and checked the loads.

Marie will enjoy hearing about this. His Brigadero wife still thought war was glorious, and envied warriors. She'd probably have made a good soldier if she'd been born male—her cousin Teodore certainly did—provided she survived the seasoning. *I'd rather go through a battle than pregnancy, at that.* Strange to think of having children—legitimate children; byblows by peon girls didn't count. Stranger still to think of them growing up in East Residence; nobody had said he couldn't move back to the family estates in the Southern Territories, but he could take the hint.

He grinned. That would be terminally dull, anyway. At least Marie could sit out the war in a city with plenty of balls and theater and opera, or bullfights and baseball stadiums.

If we win this war, will there be wars for my sons to ride to? Possibly not; and was that a good thing, or the end of all honor?

Thud. Thud. Thud. There were explosions across the river, along the docks of Sandoral. Plumes of red fire rose into the night, spreading with startling suddenness. In less than thirty seconds the whole waterfront went up in a wall of flame, as the time-fused incendiaries caught among kerosene-soaked wood and spilled cooking oil. There was enough underlight to see the pillars of smoke, roiling and black and red-tinged by the fires.

He took a deep breath. *"Gittem!"* he roared, the old Squadron war shout. The trumpeters were playing *Charge,* over and over again, a raw brazen scream.

The flags went forward. The 1st Mounted Cruisers rose to their feet and threw themselves forward at a pounding run, their bayonets leveled. Ludwig Bellamy ran at their head, sword held forward like a pointer.

"GITTEM! GITTEM!" they bellowed.

Wogs all looking at the show, he thought with hammering glee. The wall stayed empty for long seconds. Then a few carbines began to crack, muzzle flashes like fireflies in the night. Men fell, but not many. He jumped down into the ditch, felt the jar as his boots landed in the muck at the bottom, scrambled in the chunky raw adobe of the berm. It was less than man-height; a Colonial appeared on the top, aiming a long-barreled revolver downward. It snapped a spike of fire, and the bannerman with the battalion standard went down. Somebody else grabbed it up, used the butt as a climbing-prop. Ludwig braced one hand on the berm and chopped with his saber, felt the edge slam into ankle-bone. The Colonial toppled and rolled down toward him, shrieking and trying to draw a dagger. Ludwig slammed the guard of his sword into the man's face and climbed over his body onto the top of the berm.

Cookfires lit the interior of the fortlet, and the glare of burning Sandoral across the river. Men in crimson djellabas streamed back from the gun line that faced the water, firing as they came. Ludwig gave a quick glance to either side; the berm's broad top was solid with his men. Company commanders were planting their pennants, platoon officers taking three steps forward and turning to face their men with outstretched arm and sword as a bar to give their commands the dressing.

"Sound *Kneel and Stand,*" he snapped.

The front rank dropped to one knee and leveled their rifles. The men behind them stood and aimed. Here and there a trooper dropped as the Colonial fire began to thicken a little, falling forward to tumble loose-limbed to the foot of the berm. He waited an instant, until the target had time to thicken.

"*Fwego!*" Ludwig shouted. Then: "*Charge!*"

BAM. One long sound, like a single impossibly long shot. A bright comb of fire reached out towards the dim shapes of the Colonials, five hundred threads of it. On the heels of the volley the troopers ran forward through the thick curls of smoke, their steel glinting red in the reflected light. The Colonials wavered, then ran back the way they'd come, screaming their panic. A few stood and fought, emptying their carbines and drawing their scimitars, but they died quickly—spitted on dozens of points, beaten down with the butt, simply trampled.

Ludwig slashed at a man crawling out of a pup tent, hurdled another. Up the slope to the gunline that was this fortlet's main purpose, set here to command the river and prevent the rebuilding of the pontoon bridge. The guns had been dug in, set in revetments with V-shaped notches forward for their barrels. One group of Colonials, braver or better-led than the rest, was trying frantically to manhandle a pom-pom around to face the menace from the rear. He stopped, braced his legs and began to fire. *Crack. Crack. Crack. Crack. Crack.* Two men down in the confusion around the light gun, and then his troopers were past. Steel clashed on steel for a moment, replaced by the butcher's-cleaver sound of metal slamming into flesh.

Silence fell. 1st Cruiser troopers were standing on top of the fortlet's western wall, firing down—firing at the backs of the fleeing survivors of the post's garrison.

"Sound *Rally*," Ludwig said. "Benter," he went on to his younger brother. "To Captain Marthinez, and his Company A is to man the parapet. Get me a count of the casualties. Hederbert, find those militiamen and put them on the guns, right now. Mauric, see that those dead wogs are all really dead."

He walked as he spoke, over to the flagstaff before the Colonial commander's tent. The dead man lying by the flagstaff was probably the tent's owner, by the scrollwork on his djellaba; he'd been hit by three or four Armory 11mm rounds, and was very thoroughly dead. The smell of death was spreading on the cool night air, like raw sewage and a butcher's shop combined. Ludwig slashed the cord of the flagpole with his saber. The green banner of Islam fluttered to the ground; he used it to clean the sword before sliding it back into its scabbard.

His bannerman needed no prompting. Seconds later, the blue-and-silver Starburst of Holy Federation fluttered up the rough staff and streamed out, almost invisible in the darkness.

Let Ali take a look at that, *when he gets tired of shelling an empty city,* Ludwig thought, grinning.

The Cruisers cheered at the sight of the flag, man after man taking it up, shaking their rifles in the air or putting up their helmets on the points of their bayonets:

"Hail! Hail! *Hail! Hail! HAIL! HAIL!*"

Ludwig felt a rush of pride: less than six minutes from the moment he'd given the order to charge. Then he looked up at the flag. *The banner of the Gubernio Civil,* he thought. Four years ago most of these men had fought against the army that Messer Raj led under that banner. There were perhaps half a dozen Sponglish-speaking natives of the Civil Government in the 1st Mounted Cruisers; the rest were MilGov and heretic to a man.

And here they were, crying the banner hail as if . . . *well, it is their own. Now.* Messer Raj had given them that.

Mustafa al-Kerouani jerked himself awake and checked his watch. Good, it was still a few minutes until the next status check. He bent to the eyepiece of the telescope and waited. Nothing from the relay to the north, the second from the siege lines around Sandoral. He frowned. They should give him three flashes from their carbide lantern; that was regular procedure. Allah might be merciful if they were all asleep, but neither their *tabor* commander nor Tewfik would. Besides, there was the honor of the engineering corps to consider. What were they, real soldiers or the *fellaheen* conscripts of infantry, who couldn't be trusted to remember to wipe their arses with their left hands unless an officer reminded them every time they shat?

He reached out and squeezed the handgrip of his own lantern. The slotted shutters over the front clacked open, revealing the brilliant chemical light amplified by the hemisphere of mirror behind it. Three long, two short—*acknowledge.*

Nothing. He swore again, looking around the little hilltop camp. A dozen men, eight of them sleeping, around a low-coal campfire with a brass *kave*-pot standing over it on an iron stand. Their riding- and pack-dogs, picketed out on a line. Two sentries, the telescope, heliograph, lanterns for night work, and their personal baggage. One of dozens strung between the bridgehead at Gurnyca and the Settler's headquarters outside the *kaphar* city. Paralyzingly boring duty; there weren't even any of the infidel *fellaheen* left around here, which meant no fresh provender except for some sauroid meat, and no women.

Three long, two short. Still no acknowledgment. *Ibrahim ibn'Habib is a lazy, wine-swilling son of a pig, but he isn't that negligent.* Best send someone over to take a look.

Mustafa blinked out into the darkness where the sentry paced. The bright light killed his night vision, but he could see the outline.

"Moshin?" he said. The other man was Qahtan ash-Shabaai, and much taller. "Moshin, take your dog and check those bastards on Post Three. They must be asleep, or dead."

"Dead," Moshin said—but it was not Moshin's voice, and the word was so thickly accented that he could barely understand it.

Mustafa al-Kerounai reached for his sidearm. He felt the bayonet that punched through his jaw, tongue and palate only as a white flash of cold. Then the point grated through brain and blood vessels within his skull, and the world ended in a blaze of light.

Antin M'lewis withdrew the blade with a jerk. Around him there was a flurry of movement; bayonets and rifle butts struck, and the pick end of an entrenching tool went into the back of a sleeping man's skull with the sound an axe made striking home in hard oak. Talker stamped on a neck with an unpleasant crunching sound, like a bundle of green branches snapping. Dogs wuffled and snarled, dragging at their picket chain as they smelled death. He ignored them and swiveled telescope and signal lantern around on their mountings. The alignment was marked in chalk on the fixed baseplate of the equipment, and he had the code for *acknowledge 0100 hours all is well* on his pad. He clacked it out carefully and waited for the return signal.

Good. There it was. They *still* didn't suspect anything. He used one tail of his uniform jacket to shield his hand and picked up the pot of *kave*, pouring a cup into his messtin.

"Throw summat more wood on t'fire," he said. It might arouse suspicion if the sentinel fire went out during the night. He tossed aside the spiked Colonial helmet. " 'N git back ter yer dogs. We'ns'll see how many more of t' wogs is overconfident."

"Fwego!"

BAM. The single massive volley turned the supply convoy's night encampment into a mass of screaming men and howling dogs, with the oxen's frantic bawling as accompaniment. Major Peydro Belagez smiled, a cruel closed upturn of the lips. He could see the scene quite well, with the watchfires as background.

BAM. Men rose from their blankets and slapped backward instantly, punched down by the heavy Armory bullets. BAM. Maddened by pain and the smell of blood, an ox-team pulled over the wagon to which they'd been tethered and ran off into the night. The wagon's tilt fell across a fire and the dry canvas flared up brightly.

"Forward, *compaydres*," he said.

The two companies of the 1st Rogor Slashers moved forward in line, with a crackle of platoon volleys. Less than thirty Colonial troops had guarded the convoy, and they were infantry—support troops, hardly fighting men at all. The few who lived ran into the night, or knelt and raised their hands in surrender.

As Belagez watched, the platoon commanders called the cease-fire. Two surviving Colonials bolted when they saw the Civil Government troops more clearly; their dark complexions and the shoulder-flashes made it clear they were Borderers, men whose feud with the Colony was old and bitter. A bet was called, and two troopers stepped forward and knelt, adjusting the sights of their rifles. The running Colonials jinked and swerved as they fled; the two Slashers fired carefully. On the third shot one of the Arabs flopped forward, shot through the base of the spine. His face plowed into the dirt, mercifully hiding the exit wound. The other went down and then rose again, hobbling and clutching his thigh as if to squeeze out the pain of his wounds.

"Hingada thes Ihorantes!" the first rifleman said. Death to the Infidel, the Slashers' unit motto. "You should do better than that, Huan!"

"Malash. The Spirit appoints our rising and our going down," the other man grunted. He breathed out and squeezed the trigger. *Crack.* Measurable fractions of a second later, dust spurted from the back of the Arab's djellaba. He went down and sprawled in the dirt.

Meanwhile the others had been rounded up. They sat, hands behind their heads, staring at their captors with the wide-eyed look of men who wanted very badly to wake from an evil dream and couldn't. The toppled wagon was burning fiercely now, with a thick

flame that stank like overdone fish three days dead to begin with—
advocati, no mistaking the stench. Sun-dried, they were oily enough
to burn like naphtha.

Belagez pointed with his saber. "Get moving—push the other
wagons over and tip them into the fire. Break open those crates,
that'll be hardtack." The Colonial version came in thin sheets about
the size of a man's hand; it would burn too, in a hot fire.

He switched to Arabic, accented but fluent enough. "You, you
unbelieving sons of whores. Get to work."

The teamsters and surviving guards joined his men in heaving
more of the supplies onto the growing blaze. Another wagon toppled
onto it, and the smell of frying apricots joined the stink, enough
to make his stomach knot a little. The blaze would be visible for
kilometers, but there was nobody alive to witness it—not unless a
survivor or two from the last convoy they'd hit had run very fast.
The twenty-wagon parties had been spaced quite evenly at four-
kilometer intervals along the road, commendable march-discipline
and very convenient for the battalions the *heneralissimo* had landed
on the west bank. He looked at his watch; it was bright as day
now, and hot enough to make him step back.

0300. This would be their last, they'd have to ride hard to make
the rendezvous with the river flotilla by dawn. He certainly didn't
want to miss the end of this campaign. The fire grew swiftly; his
men were in a hurry too, and the prisoners worked very hard.

Idly, he wondered if they knew they were building their own
funeral pyres. Probably. Still, it was the Spirit's blessing that men
were reluctant to abandon hope while they still breathed.

"*Oh night that was my guide
Oh night more loving than the rising sun
Oh night that joined the lover
To the beloved one,
Transforming each of them into the other.*"

Raj opened his eyes, then started awake. Suzette laid aside her
gittar and smiled at him, handing over a cup of *kave*.

"This yacht has all the conveniences, my love," she said.

"What—"

"Absolutely nothing has happened except what you said would.
Belagez and the other landing parties made rendezvous. The Colonials
have no idea what's going on—we're moving faster than the news.
It's noon."

"Ah."

He took the cup and sipped. He felt less jangled than usual on
waking, less of the sense that something catastrophic had happened
and had to be turned around immediately. *How long has it been
since I slept without worry?* he thought.

Five years, one month seven days. defining "worry" as your subtextual intent rendered the term.

Thank you very much, he thought. Aloud: "Thank you, my sweet. You must have fended them off like a mother sauroid on a rookery."

Suzette smiled; not her usual slight enigmatic curve of the lips, but widely as if at some private joke. She shook her head.

"You've had five years to train them, Raj; and they're good men. They wanted you to rest while you could. They can carry out your orders, but we all want—need—you to be at your best when you're needed. Besides" —she dimpled slightly— "you look so young and vulnerable when you're asleep."

Raj laughed softly. *I'm committed,* he realized. *One turn of pitch and toss, winner take all.* It would either work or it wouldn't, and if it didn't he wouldn't be around to worry about it. There was nothing behind them but Ali and his fifty thousand men, barring the road to the border.

"What was that song?" he asked, finishing the coffee. Suzette poured him another and handed him breakfast—toasted hardtack, but she'd found some preserves for it, somehow.

"Very old. My tutor taught it me when I was a girl; Sister Maria, that was."

"Doesn't sound religious," Raj said.

the song is derived from the devotional poetry of st. john of the cross, Center said. **the musical arrangement was made approximately two thousand four hundred years ago on earth.**

"Ahem." A voice from behind the door of the little stern cabin, out on deck. "I hate to interrupt this touching domestic scene, but . . ."

"Coming, Gerrin," Raj said ruefully.

He stamped into his boots and fastened on his equipment, then scooped up the map he'd been working on late into the night. The sun outside was blinding, the shadow of the awning above hard-edged and utter black by comparison. Raj blinked out over the sparkling green waters of the Drangosh. For a kilometer either way, out of sight behind bends in the high banks, it was covered with rafts and barges and boats. With men and guns and ammunition . . . *nine thousand men.* Nine thousand, to decide the fate of empires. *Nine thousand men relying on* me *to pull it off.* The thought was less crushing than usual. *If there was any force this size on Earth—*

bellevue.

—*Bellevue, then, you pedant, this was it.*

Raj smiled. Staenbridge and the other battalion commanders grinned back at him. Bartin Foley chuckled.

Raj raised his brows. "Your thoughts, Captain?"

He spread the rolled paper on the deck; the officers and Companions crowded around it, kneeling, staking down the corners with daggers.

"*Mi heneral,* I was just thinking how much less pleasant this morning must be for our esteemed friend Tewfik, when he finds out we've left the party and stiffed him with the drink tab."

A snarling ripple of laughter went around the map. "True enough." Raj rested one hand on his knee and spread the fingers of the other over the map. It was his drawing, with Center supplying a holographic overlay for him to work with. "Gentlemen, this is our latest intelligence on the enemy's bridgehead camp and the pontoon bridge over the Drangosh. You'll note—"

Bompf. The little mortar chugged, and a grapnel soared up through a puff of smoke.

Why? Tewfik thought. The fires had raged all through the night, as if the *kaphar* did not care that the city burned around their ears. No fire from the walls and towers, not all through the night and the bombardment. Now they were ignoring his herald under a flag of truce, for the whole hour since dawn. *Since I could finally free myself from my brother's whining and threats.*

The sun was bright in the east, eye-hurting. He shaded his eye with one hand, the other hooked through the back of his sword belt. The breeze blew from the river and fluttered his djellaba; it snapped out the blue-and-silver Starburst of the Federation from the gate towers of Sandoral, as well. The air was heavy with the sickly scent of things that should not burn—one of the constants of war. He had smelled the same in Gurnyca, and in burnt-out cities down on the Zanj coast. Worse, once, when they had shelled a warehouse full of holdouts in Lamoru and the dried copra inside had caught fire.

"Lord Amir, a lucky sniper from the wall—"

"I do not think this is a plot to assassinate me, Hussein," Tewfik said. *Allah alone knows what it is, but not that, I think.*

Men climbed up the cable the mortar had thrown. The first of them had a stick with a white rag attached to it thrust through the shoulder harness of his webbing gear; a flag of truce, by the one and only God. Let Whitehall respect it; he had a name for being scrupulous in such things.

The men climbed in through a narrow window high above the bridge that carried the railway over the moat and through the city wall. Tewfik waited with iron patience. A mirror flashed from the parapet.

Tower apparently empty, he read. He clawed at his forked beard, nostrils flaring instinctively as if to smell out a trap. More silent waiting, until there came the muffled *thud* of an explosion behind walls, and very faintly, a scream.

The officers around him tensed. A half-minute later, the mirror blinked again.

Boobytrap, six casualties. Tower deserted. Walls deserted. No enemy in sight.

A hubbub of oaths and excitement broke out around him; the word spread along the siege lines as the great gates swung open and revealed the dogleg passage beyond. A long slow roar like heavy surf welled up, as men climbed out of the entrenchments and onto the gabions, and others dashed from the tents and the cooking-fires behind.

"The city is ours!" someone shouted. "The *kaphar* have fled!"

Tewfik felt a great hand reach into his chest and squeeze. Azazrael's wings brushed darkness over his eyes. Almost, he prayed that the dark angel would come for him now; surely this would count as dying for the Faith, in the Holy War. Hussein and one of his mamluks cried out in shock and rushed to support him; he brushed them aside and staggered forward to the edge of the main works.

Fled? he thought. "Fled? Where? Northeast, to the valleys of the Borderers? To hide in their mud-built forts and make little raids, while we bottle them up with one-tenth of our strength and march to the gates of East Residence with the rest? Whitehall?"

"But . . ." The aide's face was fluid with shock. "If not north, then where?" He looked at his commander's face, and fear replaced the shock. "What is it, Lord *Amir*?"

"Kismet," Tewfik said. "Fate. If not north, then south . . ."

"But, Lord *Amir*, the message stations, the outposts along the road—we have heard nothing!"

"Exactly." He whirled. "Hussein. Twenty men, each with three led dogs. Kill the dogs with haste if they must, but make such speed as men may. To the commandant of the railhead camp; maintain maximum alertness, enemy in your vicinity."

Hussein gaped. Tewfik seized him by the shoulder-straps of his harness and shook him. "Fool born of fools, the entire raid across the Drangosh was a diversion—their bridge a disguise for boats and rafts to *float their force south.*"

"May the Lovingkind have mercy upon us!"

"Go!" He turned to the others. "Sound the alert. Mobilize the cavalry, *all* of it—"

"Lord *Amir*," one officer said urgently. "The Settler . . ."

The Settler, who will delay for hours before he grasps the necessities. And with him every one of the great noble houses, and the orders of the Maribbatein and ghazis, all of whom will jealously insist on being consulted before a major move is made.

He raised his hands. "Allah! One day! That is all I ask of You, *one day.*"

Never had he prayed with such sincerity.

CHAPTER FOURTEEN

"Messers, the garrison is ten thousand men, not counting civilian laborers."

The Companions bent over the sand-map for the last briefing. Antin M'lewis hung back slightly, although his scouting this afternoon had provided the last-minute updates. Considerations of social rank aside, he didn't have a line command; his men would be split up and acting as trail guides for the actual units.

Raj went on, pointing with his sword. The wet sand allowed a surprising amount of detail; he'd spent about an hour getting it right, just possible with Center to overlay holograms and make each motion perfectly efficient. The long shadows of evening brought it out well.

"As you can see, it's a square earth fort; two-meter ditch, two-meter palisade and earth rampart, chevaux-de-frise in the ditch. Pentagonal bastions at each corner, gun lines along the fighting parapet, and four gates at each of the compass points. The railroad leads in from the east, and the pontoon bridge out from the west side. There are ten-meter watchtowers on either side of each gate; the gates are spiked timber barriers. Most of the artillery is concentrated in the bastions, which are as usual higher than the main berm; they bear along each wall."

"Ten thousand men," Jorg Menyez said thoughtfully. "*Heneralissimo*, that's a Starless Dark of a lot of firepower."

Raj nodded. "If we let them apply it, which we won't. They're line-of-communications troops, railroad labor battalions and engineers and supply specialists. Also they're not expecting us. We're not going to give them time to get ready, either; and there's one last little surprise to distract them.

"We're here." He moved his sword point north on the sand map, tapping a point on the east bank of the Drangosh. "Less than two klicks north of the objective as the pterosauroid flies. We'll move separately, by battalion columns, marching on foot, as follows."

He named the battalions, moving from left to right, east to west. "17th Kelden County Foot and the 24th Valencia on the extreme left—they'll have the farthest to go, but they're better foot-marchers. Cavalry battalions in the center, Sandoral infantry on the right, nearest the river. The 5th Descott and the 18th Komar will take the median and assault the camp's north gate. Colonel Menyez, you will have overall command of the left wing; Colonel Staenbridge, of the center; Major Gruder, of the right. I'll accompany the central command.

"Colonel Dinnalsyn, you'll split your guns into two Grand Batteries. One will accompany the 24th, one the Sandoral garrison battalions. Your objective will be to neutralize the enemy artillery in the corner bastions for the duration of the assault. One fast hard stonk, then shift fire to support, and when our banners are over the berm and palisade, cease fire and prepare to move up as directed. Understood?"

The artillery commander stroked his thin mustache with his thumb. "It can be done, *mi heneral.* But to be effective, I'll need time for ranging fire."

"I'll provide precise range data when we arrive," Raj said.

"That will be satisfactory, of course, *heneralissimo,*" Dinnalsyn said carefully, the crisp East Residence vowels sounding a little strained. From the glances, everyone knew what it meant: *it's bloody eerie.* "You have an excellent eye for it."

Raj continued: "Messers, your approaches will be by the following paths." His sword sketched them out, through the maze of badland cliffs, naming the battalions. "I hope I don't need to emphasize the absolute necessity of caution as you approach the edge of the badland zone and the low country directly north of the enemy camp. There's a company of the Rogor Slashers in place, guided by members of the Scout Company. They'll take out the Colonial watchposts immediately before you debouche into the plain, and there'll be very little time after that—the attack, and the usual rocket, will be your signal. Come out of the hills in column, deploy as you move, and hit the wall running. By that time, the artillery will have the bastions under fire. Nothing fancy, gentlemen; we go in with the bayonet and one round up the spout, climb the wall and sweep" —his sword moved from north to south— "the wogs out of their camp. Then we stop for the night."

He drew his watch and opened the cover. "Synchronize, please. It's 1900 at . . . *mark.*" There was a subdued clicking as stems were pressed home. "Two and a half hours to full dark. Colonel Dinnalsyn, move your guns out now. All battalions will be on their way by 19:30. I expect the artillery preparation to begin at 20:15 and the troops to go in at 20:30. It's only a kilometer and the Scouts have the paths clearly marked, so despite the night march that's plenty of time. Questions?"

There were only one or two, technical matters. The plan was simple—startlingly simple. *It's the* strategy *on this one that's complicated,* he thought.

"Then it's all settled bar the fighting. May the Spirit of Man be with us, Messers."

"It is," someone said softly. "The Sword of the Spirit of Man."

Embarrassed, Raj cleared his throat and nodded curtly. The Companions slapped fists in a pyramid of arms and moved away. Junior officers moved in to study the sand table for a few moments, then returned to their units.

Raj walked down the shoreline; it was hard here, rocks lacing the clay of the bank. The barges and rafts were beached as high as human muscle and dogs dragging at the ends of lariats could move them. They weren't planning to go any farther on the water. Many of the men were preparing escalade ladders: simple balks from the rafts, with crosspieces nailed along them, a spike at the top to hold the pole against the sloping surface of an earth berm, and cross-braces at the bottom to keep it from turning. Not very heavy—they hadn't far to go. One standard part of Civil Government training was carrying logs cross-country, units competing against each other—it taught teamwork on a very practical level.

The rest of the men were waiting, some double-timing or stretching under the direction of their platoon officers, getting out the kinks and stiffness of the long crowded voyage. Raj stopped now and then, calling a man by name or slapping a shoulder.

"Ensign Minatelli," he said to one very junior officer. The man's under-strength platoon was twisting their torsos with their rifles held over their heads.

"Sir," the young westerner said, bracing to attention. The men froze. He saluted with a snap.

"No names, no pack drill," Raj said easily. *Serious, but that's all to the good,* he thought appraisingly. Lower middle-class, not a social grouping you found many of in the Army and certainly not in the officer corps, but that was less of a disadvantage in the infantry.

"Ready for your first engagement at commissioned rank?" he said.

"Lot more to worry about, sir," the young man blurted. His sincerity was transparent.

Raj nodded. "The mental comfort level goes down as the rank goes up," he said. "If you take your work to heart. Carry on, son."

He walked on, to where detachments of the 5th were snapping the bridles of their dogs to a picket line. The cavalry troopers straightened, but they didn't come to attention; there was profound respect in their stance, but no formality.

"*Bwenya Dai,* dog-brothers," Raj said.

He smoothed a hand over the neck of one bitch-dog; it turned and snuffled at him, then licked its chops, satisfied at the scent of *Army* that marked ultimate pack-boundaries to a military dog.

"Nice beast," he said sincerely. Descotter farmbred, about a thousand pounds, lean and agile-looking but with powerful shoulders and chest. "Fifteen hands?"

"Ah, the best, that Pochita. is, ser," the corporal said. "Frum m'own kin's *ranchero*. Fifteen one, seven years old."

"Robbi M'Telgez," Raj said. "Southern edge of Smythe Parish, yeoman-tenants to Squire Fidalgo? Near Seven Skull Spring?"

"Yesser." M'Telgez visibly expanded a little. "'Tis true we're attackin' t' wog supply base, ser?"

Raj nodded. "A little stroll in the cool evening, and then we collect everything but Ali's underwear. The wogs may not like us helping ourselves, though."

The troopers grinned; catching the scent, the tethered dogs behind them showed their teeth in a distinctly similar expression.

"Carry on," he repeated.

Suzette was waiting beside Harbie and Horace. Seven thousand dogs would take up an intolerable amount of space in the strait confines of the badlands—that was why the operation was going in on foot—but he and his senior officers needed the extra mobility. Raj swung into the saddle and watched the last of the artillery moving out, teams disappearing into the canyon southward. Dust smoked up behind them, but not too much. Later in the summer it would have been a kilometer-high plume. Another reason to send the men in on foot and by widely separated paths.

"This is it, isn't it?" Suzette asked softly.

Raj nodded. "If it works, it's all over bar the shouting. If not . . ." He shrugged. "Well, we won't have to worry about that."

"And if it works, there's Barholm. Raj, he'll kill you the minute he doesn't need you any more."

Raj laughed, full and rich. "My sweet, at the moment that is the last thing on Bellevue I'm worrying about." *I'm not worrying about anything.* The operation was underway, and now all he had to do was deal with the unexpected; think on his feet and use his wits. He felt loose and easy, mind and body working together at maximum efficiency.

His face went blank. "Anyway, I'll have left some accomplishments behind, something that was worth doing."

Suzette touched his elbow; they'd reined a little aside from the bannermen and messengers. "Raj, speaking of things left behind . . . there's something you should know, just in case."

The boatman shivered. He was naked save for his loincloth and covered in soot mixed with tallow, the smell of the grease heavy about him. Ahead the little galley stroked its oars again, then came alongside. He could just see it in the growing dusk, the water lighter where the oars curled it into foam. Their careful stroke went *shush . . . shush . . .* through the night.

The Army officer lit the slowmatch and gave him a salute before vaulting over to the galley. It turned and stroked rapidly back upstream. He knelt on a burlap sack folded on the rough timbers of the raft and took the steering oar. It twisted in his hands, the familiar living buck of the Drangosh, the substance of all his days. He'd never steered a cargo like this before, though. The whole surface of the raft was covered with kegs of gunpowder, lumpy under the dark tarpaulin that covered them, outline broken by palm-fronds and branches. Iron hooks and spikes stood out all around the square vessel, anchored in the main balks.

The current was fast here in midstream, the banks just lines in the darkness to left and right. *Somebody* had to steer, though; otherwise the raft might swirl in towards the banks. He worked the oar carefully, never letting the end break free of the water. From a distance, in the dark, the raft would look like just another piece of river trash caught in the current. The fuse hissed.

There. Lights on the east bank, to his left. The wog camp. A scattering to his right: the ruins of Gurnyca. He bared his teeth. He'd had kin there, before the press-gang enlisted him in the Army. That was why he'd volunteered for this—though the thousand gold FedCreds and the land and the tax exemption for him and his family didn't hurt. But you had to live to enjoy those; revenge was a dish you could eat in advance.

And that Messer Raj. The priest is right. The Spirit *was* with him, you could see it in his eyes. For the Spirit, all men were the tools of Mankind.

A string of lights across the water: sentinel-lanterns along the wog pontoon bridge. Much bigger barges than the ones they'd used to build their own bridge up at Sandoral, with real prows and neat planking. The torches were oil-soaked bundles of rag on the ends of long sticks of ironwood, fastened to the railing of the roadway every fifteen meters or so. He crouched lower, tasting sour bile at the back of his mouth. There was a sheathed knife through the back of his loincloth, but that was for himself if he looked like being captured.

Closer, and he could see the spiked helmets and turbans of the soldiers pacing along the bridge. Cables swooped up out of the water to anchor the upstream prows of the pontoons, dark curves against dark water. Firelight glittered on patches of wave. He braced one foot against a timber, bare callused toes gripping, and threw the weight of back and shoulders against the tiller. The raft moved across the current, slowly, always slowly. His breath tried to sob out past tight-clenched teeth.

One of the wogs was singing, sounding like a man biting down on a cat's tail. It was hard dark outside the circles of firelight the torches cast, both moons down, only the arch of stars above. *Yes.* The raft was heading right between two pontoons. It might have gone right through without him aboard.

He waited until the shadow of the timbered deck above cut off the sky; there was reflected light enough from the torch on one of the pontoons. Then he raised a pole whose other end was set into the deck of the raft. The ironshod point sank deeply into the timber balk above as the weight of the raft and the force of the current drove it. Weight and current pushed the raft sideways, pivoting around the anchor driven deep into the hardwood above. The hooks along the side grated into the hull of the pontoon; he winced at the noise, but there was thick timber and three feet of earth on the roadway above. The raft heeled a little beneath him as they set fast and held against the long slow push of the water.

The boatman dove overside into the water and let the current take him out the south side of the pontoon bridge and a hundred meters downstream. Then he began to stroke in a fast overarm crawl, and the Starless Dark take secrecy. He had less than a minute to get out of killing range.

"Change off," Ensign Minatelli said.

The next platoon came up and took the escalade ladder off his men's shoulders. The shuttered bull's-eye lantern in his hand provided just enough light, although there were whispered curses and cries of pain in the tight confines of the dry wash.

"Let's get moving."

In a way it was fortunate that the wash was so narrow; there wasn't any way to get lost. He moved at a quick walk, stumbling occasionally over a clod or a rock. Men waited at junctions, directing the traffic along the proper path. A few minutes later he ran into the heels of the men ahead.

"*Halto!*" he hissed back.

Captain Pinya came down the line, identifying himself with a quick flick of his own lantern under his face. "We're there," he said. "Halt in place, prepare for action. Wait for the signal, then we go out in column, deploy into line on the move, and keep moving. There's a little more light out in the open."

I hope so.

He was starting to get some idea of how complicated it was to get hundreds of men moving in the same direction and have them arrive when you wanted them to. It was a lot more difficult than it looked when all you had to do was march when someone said, "By the left, forward."

All an ensign had to do in a field action was relay the orders, though. He was very glad of that.

"Fix bayonets. Load. Keep the muzzles *up*."

The last thing they needed was somebody getting stuck or shot because they fell over their feet. It was up to *him* to see that didn't happen.

Spirit.

✧   ✧   ✧

1018. Raj shut his watch with a snap.

Can't wait much longer. With their outposts gone, the enemy camp would be waking up *soon*. A last iron clank came from the artillery position to his left, about twenty meters away; it was dark enough that he could only see vague traces of movement there. The gunners moved with exaggerated care, setting the fuses behind a screen of blankets that would conceal the brief flashes of light from the enemy. They'd be firing blind, essentially, except for the directions he'd given—Center had given—although the wogs were displaying a pleasant abundance of lamps and watchfires.

Another messenger trotted up.

"Major Gruder reports right wing in position, ser." He handed over a note.

Raj flicked a match between thumb and forefinger. *This herd of handless cows is ready to stampede,* he read. Kaltin was *not* happy at having five battalions of second-rate garrison infantry under his direction besides the 7th.

"Tsk."

Kaltin wouldn't expect to get the best out of a force of Descotter cavalry with that attitude; why did he think infantry would respond any better? A good tactician and very loyal, but there were some jobs you just wouldn't give him. Raj grinned mirthlessly. The chances were he wouldn't be giving anyone any jobs, after this.

He turned to look to the right, toward the river. The tiny dots of the torches along the pontoon bridge glittered like stars in the darkness. *I would have left it farther south,* he thought. Better roads here, and what was left of Gurnyca gave a secure anchorage for the western end, but putting a point-failure source closer to your enemy was a terrible risk. *Ali's doing. He tends to arrogance.* He began a gesture to the messenger beside him; there wasn't any more time.

Smaller torches were running along the center section of the pontoon bridge. He pulled the binoculars from their case on Horace's saddlebow and focused them. Men leaned over the edge of the roadway, looking at the water below and pointing.

Raj turned his head aside. Even looking away, the flash of the explosion was bright; it lit the earthen walls of the Colonial fort the way a flash of lightning might, but for much longer. When he looked back a huge section of the pontoon bridge was *gone*, gone as if a vast mouth had bitten it away. There was a crater in the water, foaming as the river rushed back to fill the hole the blast had momentarily forced into it. Pieces of burning, shattered timber were describing parabolas through the night for thousands of meters all around. The sound hit like a giant rumbling thud, felt on the skin of the face and in the chest cavity as well as through the ears.

An alarm siren began to wail in the fort. More men were running out of it, heading through the west gate and onto the pontoon bridge, or what was left of it—large sections on either side of the gap had torn away their anchoring cables and were beginning to drift southward with the current. That threw more and more stress on the undamaged sections, cable and timber creaking and yielding as the two unconnected segments bent back. He could hear the gunshot cracks of materials yielding as they were pushed past their breaking strain. Parts of it were on fire, too; the sections above water would be tinder-dry, in this climate.

The officer in command of the base was probably an engineering specialist. His first thought would be to save the bridge. As if to confirm the thought, a fire engine pulled by six hitch of dogs thundered out onto the pontoon, dropped a hose overside and began spurting steam-driven water at the fires. Men dropped overside with ropes, swimming out for the anchor points. Others set up winches on the decking.

Raj chopped his hand downward. An aide put his cigarette to the touchpaper of a signal rocket and stepped back. The paper sizzled and the little rocket went skyward with a *woosh*, popping into a blue starburst high overhead.

POUMPF. POUMPF. POUMPF. POUMPF. Over and over again.

Tongues of fire shot into the blackness. Fifty-five guns, massed in two grand batteries of twenty-eight and twenty-seven pieces. Warm pillows of air slapped at his face from the nearby position. The night filled with the whirring ripple of shell fire, and seconds later the snapping *crack* of bursting charges and the red firefly wink over the bastions at each corner of the fortress walls. At three rounds a minute the shellbursts came at more than one per second over each target, an endless ripple of fire. The second stonk contained a proportion of contact-fused shells. The guns were firing at maximum elevation and nearly maximum range, their shells dropping down out of the sky at high angles. Dirt fountained up, and then a mammoth secondary explosion from the eastern bastion.

Somebody left his ready reserve ammunition exposed, he thought. He could imagine the scene in the redoubts, men running half-dressed from their bombproofs into the storm of razor-edged, high-velocity metal as they tried to crew their pieces.

"Dinnalsyn's on time and target," Raj said to himself, gathering the reins. *"Hadelande."*

He clapped heels to Horace's side and swung into a loping gallop down the slope. The flags crackled behind him, harness creaked, a bugle clanked rhythmically against the webbing buckles on a signaler's chest. Rock and dust spurted up under the dogs' paws, with a scent of bruised native scrub like bergamot. Trumpets sounded ahead of him—no point in keeping quiet after this—as the battalions poured over the ridgeline and down the last slope toward the flat fields. The routes he'd picked left them widely spaced, to minimize collisions in the dark, and the flaming chaos at each end of the north face of the Colonial base would help with the alignment.

The dense columns of men flowed forward onto the open ground, double-timing in battalion columns. Starlight glittered on a forest of bayonet points, sheened on the silver Starbursts at the top of the flagstaffs of their colors. He leaned back slightly, and Horace shifted to a swinging trot; they were coming up on the 5th Descott's position. The men gave a short roaring cheer as his flag went by to swing into position near the battalion commander's, a harsh male undertone to the crash and flicker of the guns.

He looked at his watch. 1040 hours. *Nearly on time. Amazing.* A memory prickled at him; nothing he'd ever experienced, but one of the holographic scenarios from Earth's long history of war that Center showed him. Not Hannibal this time, but someone else, and the battle had also been against Arabs . . .

lieutenant-general garnet wolseley, Center said. **tel el-kebir. twenty-five hundred years ago.** A pause. **the similarities are disquieting.**

Why? Raj thought. *This fellow Wolseley won, didn't he?* A night march and an attack on earthwork fortifications, as he remembered.

i was programmed to believe that a progressive improvement of human capacities is a priority, Center said. **the fact that two such similar engagements have occurred at this distance in time might support a cyclical rather than linear explanation of human history.**

Some things never change.

that, raj whitehall, is precisely the problem—and what we are attempting to change.

The 5th's buglers blew a six-note call and repeated it. Raj turned in the saddle to watch; the fires on the pontoon bridge were out of control, and the easternmost Colonial bastion was a column of flame, giving enough light to turn the night to dusk. The solid column of troops suddenly opened, like a man's outstretched hand when he flared his fingers. Each of the four companies of the 5th turned at an angle to the axis of advance and double-timed outward, following the pennant of the company commander. Thirty seconds later the bugle sounded again, and the company columns spread likewise into platoons, and the platoons flared out like opening fans. In less than four minutes what had been a dense column of men was a double line, rippling as the veterans dressed their ranks on the move with unconscious skill.

This was what the endless parade-ground drill was for: the movements had to be unconscious. So instinctive that they could be done exhausted, or under killing fire—or here, in darkness so bad you could barely see another man at twice arm's length. A line of men couldn't advance at speed for long, not on anything but absolutely flat table-top terrain. A column could maneuver, but it was a hideously vulnerable target with no offensive capacity to speak of.

Gerrin Staenbridge reined in beside him. "After that march, I'm never going to make a joke about the blind leading the blind again, *mi heneral.* If it hadn't been impossible to get lost, we would have."

There was strain in his voice. The possibilities for confusion were enough to turn a man's hair gray . . . which reminded Raj of the silver dusting he saw in his own every time he shaved.

The splatguns had been bouncing along behind the infantry. Now they trotted forward, drawing ahead. One hundred meters, two, three, then the teams wheeled. The crews leapt down and spun the elevating screws to maximum.

"About now," Raj said.

The cannonade lifted for an instant, and starshells burst over the ramparts of the fort. Raj stood in the stirrups and looked right and left, halfway between dread and hope under the wavering blue-white light. *All honor and glory to the Spirit of Man of the Stars,* he thought sincerely. No major units seemed to be missing, as far as he could see—although the right flank was mostly hidden, and that was the one he was most worried about. A long, wavering double line of men stretched across the plain, with gaps of several hundred meters between battalions. Several of the battalions *were* severely out of alignment with their target, marching at angles that would have tangled them with their neighbors eventually. As he watched they started to correct.

"Signaler," he said. The man dropped out of the saddle and set two rockets. They hissed aloft and burst.

Staenbridge drew his sword. "Battalion—"

"Company—" Manifold, down the line.

"Charge!"

The trumpets sounded and kept up their shrilling, a long brass screaming in antiphonal chorus as all the signalers caught up the note. A long swelling shout rose from one end of the field to the other. Flags slanted forward as the whole formation broke into a steady uniform trot.

Braaaaap. The splatguns fired, shot arching down at extreme range to spray the parapet. They kept firing over helmets as the troopers swept by. A pom-pom opened up from the wall ahead, and the flicker of muzzle flashes showed there were *some* wogs on the parapet, at least. The little quick-firer's shells went overhead with a nasty *whack-whack-whack* as it emptied its clip, and burst on the soil behind. Raj drew his revolver, tossed it to his left hand and drew his sword, letting the reins fall to Horace's neck. The dog stepped up the pace to a slow canter, keeping level with the men. The berm ahead loomed up with shocking speed, and the skeletal shapes of the watchtowers on either side. Company A of the 5th kept pace with them on either side, their boots crunching on the gravel of the roadway that ran into the gate.

A carbide searchlight flickered alight from one tower, stabbing into his eyes with hurting brilliance. Seconds later it disintegrated in a shower of fragments as five or six splatguns turned their attention to it. The observation platform at the top of the wooden tower came apart in a shower of splinters and began to burn. The trumpets shrilled on, and the men started to run.

They reached the edge of the ditch. Fire stabbed down at them and some tumbled into it, to lie still or shrieking on the spiked timbers there. More slid down into the ditch on their backsides, clambered carefully through the obstacles and the mud, and began climbing the steep slope on the other side. They scrambled in the heavy clay, chopping their rifle butts into the dirt. Others brought up the escalade ladders, setting their triangle-braced bases at the edge of the ditch and letting them topple forward. The spikes at the upper end hammered into the dirt and men ran up the cross-bars, climbing one-handed with their rifles in the other.

"Not much fire!" Raj said exultantly. *We caught them with their pantaloons down, and now it's too late!* Surprise was the best force multiplier there was, and it was working in his favor.

Staenbridge nodded. He turned to Bartin Foley and laid a hand on his shoulder. "Now."

The younger man grinned and leaned out of the saddle, extending his hook. One of his platoon commanders dropped the loop of a leather satchel over it. Then he lit a length of fuse-match that extended from under the buckled cover.

"Ha!"

Foley clapped his heels into his dog's flanks, heading for the timber gate that barred the northern entrance to the Colonial fort. Men were fighting hand-to-hand on the wall to either side, shooting and stabbing and swinging clubbed rifles; there had to have been Colonials on duty at the gate, at least, if not all around the walls. Bodies tumbled down the steep slope of the berm, dead or wounded. Troopers in Civil Government uniform shot through the stubby planks of the palisade at the top, or joined to pull the wood aside, or boosted their comrades over the pointed tops. Probably the towers on either side of the gate had held swivel guns as well as searchlights, but they were both blazing torches now, burning hard enough to make the heat noticeable at a hundred meters.

Foley covered the distance to the gate in a few seconds. A mounted man drew attention, even in the melee above him. Bullets kicked the gravel roadbed around him; once he swayed in the saddle and Staenbridge stiffened beside Raj. The satchel arched through the air and thumped into the dirt at the base of the gate, its momentum wedging it under the palm-log timbers where they swung at ankle height above the roadway. At the same instant he pulled the dog's head around; the beast whirled so quickly that it reared almost upright on its hind legs, with Foley hanging on like a jockey. It landed facing the way it had come, and running. The rider's display of skill would have been worthy of attention in itself, in any other context.

"Damned good man," Raj said, easing back the hammer of his revolver with the thumb of his right hand. Horace tensed under him.

". . . Five, six," Staenbridge said. "Yes, he is, and I wish to the Starless Dark he'd stop *volunteering* for this sort of shit, the hand's enough. Seven, eight—"

Barton Foley had covered three-quarters of the distance back to their position when the satchel charge blew. There were twenty-five kilos of powder in it; the gates disappeared from sight, and chunks of wood flew past them. Foley's dog yelped and leaped forward so quickly that he had to slug the reins back with brutal force to stop it. A splinter a double handspan long stuck out of one haunch; the animal kept trying to turn and reach the wound with its tongue.

Two of Foley's troopers grabbed the bridle while he dismounted; one of them threw a neckerchief over the dog's eyes while the other pulled the splinter out with a single swift yank. The dog's howl of agony was loud even by comparison with the noises of battle.

"Go!" Staenbridge barked. "Go, go, *go*."

The dust billowed away from the gate, showing a shattered ruin that sagged back out of the way. Bartin Foley was first through again, his riot gun in one hand; at his shouted direction a dozen men threw their shoulders against the splintered wreckage and walked it clear. Raj heeled Horace through a dozen paces, then drew him up with the pressure of his knees.

The interior of the camp was a checkerboard of stores in huge pyramids under tarpaulins, interspersed with tents. Some of the tents were on fire, and there was also light from iron baskets of burning greaseweed at the intersections. His head whipped left and right. To the left the Civil Government troops were already over the wall and down into the roadway that circled just inside it. The inner face of the berm was sloped dirt, or broad steps cut into the clay and faced with palm logs. Men poured down in, rallied around unit flags on the flat, moved off. There was a thick scattering of dead Arabs on the roadway, a few on the inner slope, more living ones running like blazes southward. To his right, toward the river, the fighting was still on the parapet itself. In a few places Civil Government banners waved from the parapet.

"All right," he said. *Just what I expected.* That section had had fewest of his veterans, and most of the Sandoral garrison troops. "Gerrin, let's collect some men and go help out. *Waymanos!*"

The issue of the day was no longer in doubt. Now he'd make sure the butcher's bill wasn't any higher than it had to be.

CHAPTER FIFTEEN

Breakfast was astonishing. *Well, we did just overrun a supply dump,* Raj thought, looking over the collection of delicacies.

He spooned up more potted shrimp. Peydro Belagez was eating them mixed with candied dates, which was something only a Borderer would do; Gerrin watched him with the horrified fascination of a gourmet, or a priest witnessing blasphemy. The commanders were seated at a long table in the huge pavilion tent that had been the base HQ. The Colonial engineers, left with time on their hands, had gone a little berserk. There were even *baths*, complete with kerosene-fired water heaters, enough for several hundred men at a time.

The morning air was fresh and hot, still a little smoky with the fires they'd spent half the night putting out. A bugle sounded outside, and a pair of mounted troopers trotted by with a long string of dogs on a leading rein: more of the force's mounts from the site where they'd landed. The barges and rafts were mostly here by now too, grounded on the riverbank or against the stub of the pontoon bridge that still extended halfway across. On the tall flagpole outside the HQ tent the Starburst banner snapped in the breeze.

The commander of the Rogor Slashers went on:

"And they still haven't stopped running, *heneralissimo.* They've split up into small parties and none of them show fight." Belagez's dark leathery face showed a combination of exhaustion and satisfaction. "Your instructions?"

"Ignore them," Raj said. "They weren't a problem in here, and they're not going to be one out there, either."

He swallowed another mouthful of excellent-quality *kave*—the Colony sat astride the trade-route from Azania and kept the best for itself—and looked at Suzette. She had peeled an orange and then set it aside untouched, looking a little pale. *Damnation. Think about that later.*

"Casualties?"

"Less than two hundred," Staenbridge said, sounding slightly surprised. "That's not counting walking wounded fit for duty. We only had twenty dead."

"Most of the live ones will pull through," Suzette added. "There are plenty of medical supplies here, and some excellent Colonial doctors, besides our own. Working under guard, of course."

"Prisoners?"

Kerpatik thumbed through his lists. "Over two thousand, *heneralissimo*. That is, two thousand military personnel. There were substantial numbers of camp followers here as well. The families of the soldiers have mostly fled. The, ah, commercial elements—" he rubbed thumb and the first two fingers of his hand together, "—they care little about the coinage as long as the metal is good."

Raj nodded. Where you had a military base, you got knocking-shops. He'd be willing to bet there was alcohol for sale too, Koranic prohibitions or not.

"Jorg, issue *Guardia* armbands to some of your footsoldiers and get that under tight control. We're still in the field, even if we've captured all the comforts of home. Let's not let the troops relax just yet."

"What about the prisoners?"

"Strip them down to their loincloths and let them go; tell them to start walking south. Now, we captured a good many documents here, including the daily logistics summaries."

Several men exclaimed in delight. That meant they would know the Colonial army's situation in detail, right down to the names of the units and their muster strength.

"Evidently they've been having problems getting the supplies from the railhead to the siege lines outside Sandoral—plenty here, but they're short of draft oxen and fodder over on the west bank."

Dinnalsyn nodded. "They were trying to use locomotive engines to rig up a couple of spare pontoons as steam tugboats, to pull raftloads up to Sandoral," he said. "I had a look; it would have worked, more or less. Whoever was in charge knew his business."

Raj nodded acknowledgment. "In any case, the Colonials have virtually nothing in the way of reserve with their field army. They were living from day to day on what their convoys brought in, once the countryside was laid waste. Now, Messers, here's what we'll do. Jorg, you're in charge here. How many dogs did we capture?"

Muzzaf Kerpatik looked up from a mass of papers. "Over twenty-five hundred, not counting gun teams, sir," he said.

"Good. Jorg, I'm leaving you all the infantry. Mount half of them—the best half—on the captured dogs. You'll also have, hmmm, Poplanich's Own and the 21st Novy Haifa for stiffening. And half the field guns. Move them north in parties of a couple of hundred; keep in continuous contact. Your objective is to prevent Tewfik from making any lodgment on the east bank. Shouldn't be difficult; there isn't much in the way of boats over there, and it would take weeks to put enough material together for another bridge. Which they couldn't build in the face of our artillery, anyway—but keep a sharp lookout; we don't want to get as overconfident as the previous tenants."

"Patrol the vicinity?"

"Vigorously. The infantry in good spirits?"

"Any better and they'd want to march on Al Kebir, *mi heneral.* Their tails are up."

"Deservedly so. Now, I'll take the rest of the cavalry, and the guns, over to the west bank. There are probably still intact supply trains on the road north, and I want to sweep those up immediately."

He rose, picking up his sword belt from the back of the chair. "I want to be on the move in no more than five hours. Tewfik is crazy like a ferenec, and Ali is just plain crazy; let's not give them time to think up any way out of their predicament. *Waymanos.*"

"That will not work, Ali my brother," Tewfik said.

His voice was dangerously calm, and he left out the honorifics. Ali turned his head slowly, the great ruby that held the clasp of his turban winking in the stray beams of light that came through ventilation slits in the ceiling of the pavilion high above.

The nobles and officers sitting on cushions around the carpet looked at Tewfik as well, mostly with the same expression they might have used if a man kicked a carnosauroid in the snout.

"Dog will not eat dog," Tewfik went on. "This has been proven many times, as any fool of a soldier would know. Rather," he corrected himself, "most dogs will not. Nine in ten. So we will lose all our cavalry at once, and cannot preserve a portion of our mobility by sacrificing the rest."

Ali's face went a mottled color. It had been a very long time since anyone had dared to call him a fool to his face, even by implication. Even his brother.

"Go!" he said, pointing with a trembling hand. "You are dismissed from the *durbar.* Return when you learn manners!"

Tewfik rose and bowed deeply, hand going to brow and lips and chest; the other clenched on the plain, brass-wired hilt of his scimitar.

His officers fell in about him. That brought another round of silent glances around the council carpet. It was also unheard-of for men to leave the Settler's presence without word. And Ali looked suddenly thoughtful, conscious of the gaps. The nobles remained, and the heads of the religious orders . . .

In the harsh sun outside, Tewfik halted, beyond earshot of the mamluks who stood like ebony statues around the Settler's tent.

"How long?" he said, to an elderly officer with a green-dyed beard.

"There is no reserve. None. The camp is on quarter-rations, but we have fifty thousand men, as many dogs, and twenty thousand camp followers here. There was no food to be had in Sandoral, none at all. I have set men to fashioning nets, and we may gain a little fish by trolling the river; but the *kaphar* hold the fort you planted on the eastern bank opposite the city, and the guns there command much of the water surface. There will be hunger by sundown, starvation by tomorrow's night. Our dogs will be too weak to carry men in three days, and dying in six. By then the men will be dying as well."

Tewfik's hand withdrew the scimitar a handspan, then rammed it home again. "If we lose this army, our people will perish," he said. "And we cannot maintain discipline, even, if we cannot feed the troops."

He looked around. "Ibrahim, put the camp on one-quarter rations— and the camp followers are to receive nothing. Confiscate *all* private supplies of food. Hussein, mount ten thousand men and be ready to ride within the hour."

"Glad to be out of the ruins," Staenbridge said, looking back at the walls of Gurnyca.

Raj nodded. The faint stink of the piles of heads still clung to the inside of his nose, an oily thing like overripe bananas. Almost as bad had been the rats and the scavenging sauroids, rabbit-sized scuttling things all spidery limbs and teeth. One had gone past him with a desiccated arm in its mouth, still wearing the lace-cuffed sleeve of a lady's day-dress.

"That sort of thing has to stop," he said quietly.

"I don't think the wogs will be invading us again in the near future," the other man said with a predatory smile.

Raj shook his head. "I mean it's got to *stop*. We did pretty much the same to the country around Ain el-Hilwa. Look at this!"

He gestured at the territory around them. A few weeks before it had been among the richest land in the Civil Government. Now the fields lay waste, empty except for the ragged scraps of sheep and cattle that the scavengers had left. Burnt stumps marked the remains of orchards, tall date palms and spreading citrus lying amid drifting ash. The adobe of the roofless peasant huts was already crumbling; the fired brick and stone of the burnt-out manors would last only a little longer. Weirs and sluice-gates and the windmills that watered the higher land were blackened wreckage as well. The long column of Civil Government troops rode through silence, amid a hot wind laden with sand. The sand would reclaim everything to the river's edge, in time.

"There are enough barbarians to fight, without wrecking civilization," Raj said. "*That's* why Ali has to be stopped. Barholm wants to unite the planet, even if it's only so he can rule it himself. Ali's a sicklefoot and he destroys for the love of it."

Staenbridge glanced around instinctively, with the gesture anyone in East Residence—or in the officer corps—learned to use when a too frank opinion of the Governor was voiced. Raj nodded silently. Staenbridge had a family to protect.

Raj's lips tightened. Suzette should be in no danger even if Barholm killed her husband; her family was old and well-connected. A child, though . . .

"Well, this will simplify *our* logistics," Bartin Foley said happily.

The wagons stood abandoned but not empty in the middle of the road, their trek-chains lying limp like dead snakes. From the sign, the teams had been driven on ahead with the dogs of the escort, but no attempt had been made to damage the cargoes.

"Which is fortunate," he murmured, taking off his helmet.

It was surprising; even now he had to remind himself not to scratch his head with his left . . . well, left hook. He juggled the bowl-shaped steel headpiece and ran a hand through sweat-damp black curls. His scalp felt cooler for an instant, then hot again as the noon sun struck it. He heeled his dog and rode slowly down the line of wagons. Half the loads were ammunition, loads for heavy siege guns. *Very* fortunate that the teamsters had been struck by blind panic. The other half was wheat biscuit and bundles of dried *advocati*.

"Ser."

A plume of dust was coming up the road from the south; the banner of the 5th and Messer Raj's personal flag at its head. He kneed his mount over to the side of the road, smiling to himself. Suzette wasn't along this time, and he suspected why. He knew the signs. Fatima had borne her first in Sandoral, during the winter Raj spent preparing to meet Jamal's invasion. The whole process was rather disturbing, like a good many things female, but the end product was delightful.

It was also pleasant not to be facing destruction at the hands of an army that outnumbered them seven to one.

The command group pulled up, the battalion fanning out into the fields on either side. "Drag it all down to the river?" Gerrin said.

Foley shook his head. "It's about half ammunition. If we push everything together and set a fuse . . ."

Troopers came in by squads and pulled out bales of *advocati* to bait their dogs, filling their own haversacks with Colonial hard tack and strips of dried mutton. It was a little past noon and intensely hot, the land and sky turned white in the blaze of the sun.

"Ser." A much smaller plume of dust this time, approaching from the north.

The officers corked their canteens and waited with a stolid patience that ignored the discomfort. Their dogs twitched ears and tails against the omnipresent Drangosh Valley flies. Antin M'lewis pulled up at the head of ten of his Scouts.

"Ser," he said, with a casual wave that approximated a salute.

"'Bout a thousand wogs comin', all cavalry, six guns. Five klicks off an' closin' fast."

Raj nodded, wiping sweat and dust from his face with his neck-erchief. "We'll give them a reception," he said. To a messenger: "My compliments to Majors Bellamy and Gruder, and would they close up quickly, please." He looked around at the terrain. "This should do; Gerrin, set up along this crestline."

"Guns to the left?" Staenbridge asked, pointing to the snags of a citrus orchard that ran down the gentle slope east of the road.

"By all means."

"I presume we don't intend to stay here long."

"No," Raj said. "The last thing we want is a general engagement; we'll just show them they have to stay bunched up and slow them down."

He turned to Foley. "Barton, how many wagon trains does this make?"

"Altogether? Including the ones wrecked when we were coming downstream?" At Raj's nod he continued: "Twenty-seven; four hundred twenty-two wagons of all sizes. Mostly these standard models," he concluded, waving a hand at the ones in the road.

"That means they shouldn't have recovered more than twenty or thirty tons of supplies altogether," he said. Softly: "Most excellent."

The messengers went out; on either side the 5th's troopers fanned out, sending their dogs back and unlimbering their entrenching tools for hasty heaped-earth *sangars* to their front. A few minutes later Ludwig Bellamy and Kaltin Gruder trotted up the roadway with their banners fluttering in the hot wind, the dust clouds of their commands behind them.

"*Mi heneral,*" Bellamy said, his beard-stubble golden against the brown tan of his face. "Dispatches from Colonel Menyez."

Raj took them and broke the seal; the wax was as soft as butter. "Ah. The Colonials are breaking camp outside Sandoral. I think friend Ali has just realized how badly his testicles are caught in the mangler."

The commanders grinned like a group of carnosauroids contemplating a dying sheep.

"This is their vanguard, then," Raj said, looking north. "All right. We'll punch them back, then move southward—they'll be substantially slower, but I don't want to take any chances with Tewfik. Messenger: to Colonel Menyez. I want enough barges to take us off held in constant readiness. We can always duck back across the river if they lunge."

"We'll have to keep a very close eye on them," Staenbridge said thoughtfully.

Raj tapped his chin with one thumb. "Constant patrols," he agreed. "I don't think they'll want to wear down their dogs with skirmishing, hungry as they are."

The carnivore grins widened. Gruder began to laugh; after a moment, the others joined in.

Center drew a graph across Raj's vision, of consumption balanced against maximum possible reserves. At the back of his consciousness there was a trace of feeling, a satisfaction colder and more complete than a human mind could feel.

"Hold your fire!" Raj snapped.

He blinked into the setting sun; four days in the saddle had left his eyes red-rimmed and sore, the Drangosh Valley was hell for dust. He wiped his sleeve across his face and brought up his binoculars. Around him on the hillock the platoon of the 5th lowered their rifles, and the crew of the splatgun looked up from their weapon. Horace stood under the shade of the carob tree and panted, washcloth-sized tongue hanging down, and drooping ears almost covering his eyes.

"Easy target, ser," the gunner said, hopefully.

Raj raised his binoculars. The main Colonial army was several kilometers away; this encampment was notably more ragged than the last. Hardly an encampment at all, with no baggage train; the animals had all been eaten, to judge from the cracked bones left in their campfires. Most of their cavalry were walking and leading their dogs behind them. Some were carrying the saddles as well.

It was the patrol riding towards his men on the hilltop that interested him now. There were two banners at its head, hanging limp in the hot still air. He waited patiently; a gust of breeze flapped them out. One was pure white; the other, black with a Seal of Solomon in red.

"Tewfik," Raj whispered. The sweat down his spine turned clammy.

"Ensign," he said. "We're staying for a moment; they're coming under a truce flag. Get something white and wave it on a stick. Water the dogs, but keep a careful look-out. And have someone set out a blanket, with a piece of hard-tack and some salt."

They were out of extreme field gun range of the Colonial camp, but you never knew.

"Sir," the Ensign said, relaying the orders.

A detail trotted downslope to the well in the courtyard of a burned-out steading. A trooper unstrapped the rolled blanket from behind his saddle, spread it on the scraggly twistgrass beneath the carob tree, and set out a canteen, two cups and a piece of Colonial flat biscuit with a small twist of gray salt on it.

The men were looking at Raj curiously. "What does it mean, sir?" the young officer asked.

"I think," Raj said slowly, "it means the war is over. Escort our guest to me."

Raj saw Tewfik's eye widen in surprise as he recognized the Civil Government commander. The Colonial was much as Raj remembered him from the parley just before the first battle of Sandoral five years ago, perhaps a little grayer. Looking a little gaunt from five days on quarter-rations, but still stocky and strong. Like a scarred bull in a pasture, confronting a younger rival and twitching his horns. Raj knew that Tewfik would be seeing far greater changes in him.

"*Salaam aleikoum,*" the Arab said, bowing slightly.

"*Aleikoum es-salaam,*" Raj replied in accentless Arabic. Center had given him that, and practice made it come smoothly. "And upon you, peace, Tewfik ibn'Jamal."

"Shall it be peace, then?"

"If the Spirit wills. Come, let us talk."

Raj gestured, and the troopers retreated down the slope, out of immediate earshot and with their backs to the supreme commanders. The two men walked into the shade of the carob. Tewfik's eye caught the bread and salt; also the fact that they hadn't yet been offered to him. There was wary respect on his face as he turned to face his enemy and let the saddlebags he carried over one shoulder drop to the ground.

Carefully, carefully, Raj told himself. *Take no chances with this man.*

indeed, Center said. A brief vision flashed before Raj's eyes: the same meeting, but with the relative positions reversed. **if my physical centrum had been located in al kebir, rather than east residence . . .**

I'd be the one trying to salvage something from the wreck, Raj acknowledged.

"I will not waste words," Tewfik said abruptly, into the growing silence. "You have won this campaign. Without even fighting a major battle. My compliments, young *kaphar*; it is a feat for the manuals and the historians to chew over."

"More than the campaign," Raj said quietly. "The war. And I would betray my ruler and my State, if I did not use this advantage to ensure the Colony is no longer a threat to the Civil Government. We have fought you every generation for nearly a thousand years; it's irrelevant who was at fault in any given war. It must cease."

Tewfik nodded, his face still cat-calm. "Yet it is said that *Heneralissimo* Whitehall fights also for the cause of civilization on Bellevue," he said. "We of the House of Islam brought man to this world. We built its first cities. We preserved much of what learning survived the Fall, and we are the other half of civilized life on this world. Would you see our cities burn and the books with them, while the howling peoples camp in the ruins?"

Raj inclined his head. "You admit that the Colony is ruined if your army is destroyed?"

"That is as God wills; but too many of our high nobles are with us, our best commanders and the leadership needed to maintain the unity of our state. And our best troops; we left nothing but garrison forces on the frontiers. If they do not return, there will be civil war— fourscore separate civil wars; instead of one Settler, we will have a hundred *malik al'taifas*, petty kings ruling factions. They will not be able to maintain the irrigation canals, nor guard the frontiers against the Skinners and the Zanj."

"Or us," Raj pointed out.

Tewfik shook his head. "Conquering a hundred splinter realms would be impossible. You would have to garrison them heavily and there would be constant revolt; our people will not tolerate direct rule by unbelievers, not without such punishment as would destroy what you tried to govern."

"What do you propose?"

The Arab nobleman took a deep breath. "I cannot rule," he said, touching his eye. "And Ali . . . he is my brother, but he is a disaster for all Muslims. One way or another, sooner or later, he would have ruined the Colony. Already he has killed many of our best men—and anyone else who was there at the wrong time.

"What I propose is this: half our army to be disarmed and sent to East Residence. I suggest that you use them to garrison the Southern and Western Territories; there they will be hostages against the Colony's good behavior. I will take the other half back with me to Al Kebir, and there rule as Vice-Governor in Barholm Clerett's name. My daughter Chaba will go to East Residence and wed Governor Barholm."

He shrugged, and for the first time smiled slightly. "I have no sons, and I fear I have been too indulgent with her—even allowing her to be taught to read. Perhaps it will be better for her thus."

Well, Raj thought, slightly dazed. *That's emphatic enough.* Center's sensor-grid came down over Tewfik's face, tracing blood flow, temperature, pupil-dilation.

subject tewfik is sincere, the computer-angel said. **probability 82% ±7.**

Raj was slightly startled. Usually the percentage was much higher, one way or another.

subject tewfik has an unusual degree of control over autonomic body functions. in your vernacular, a poker face.

"A moment," Raj said.

He turned and looked out over the dusty plain of the Drangosh. Then he turned back.

"That sounds acceptable, in outline," he said. "We'll have to settle a few details. Release of all Civil Government prisoners in the Colony, for instance; and an annual tribute sufficient to pay the twenty-five thousand men you'll be giving us. Customs, tariffs, that sort of thing the bureaucrats can settle."

Tewfik nodded, hesitated, then stroked his beard. "My offer, of course, would apply to any *other* Governor as well," he hinted. "From all reports, Governor Barholm is somewhat preferable to my brother Ali . . . but that is not a strong recommendation."

Meaning, take the Chair yourself and rule the world, Raj thought.

interpretation of subtext correct, probability 98% ± 1, Center clarified.

"How do I know this isn't a ploy to save Ali and half your army?" Raj said. "You could be planning to write the other half off. It'd still be a larger force than I have in the field, and campaigning down to the Drangosh delta would be a nightmare, particularly with this area too devastated to use as a base."

Tewfik smiled grimly and opened the saddlebag he'd brought. His curly-toed boot hooked it over to lie at Raj's feet. A head rolled out; fairly fresh, although the flies were already crawling around the hacked stump of the neck and the staring eyes. Raj did not need the ruby-clasped turban that rolled from the shaven skull to identify it.

"That for Ali," Tewfik said, and kicked the head to one side. "I should have done that years ago."

Raj raised his brows slightly. *I shouldn't be surprised if he's . . . decisive,* he decided. He gestured to the blanket. They sat down across from each other cross-legged, and shared the bread and salt. Raj laid the sword between them and Tewfik touched his hand to the hilt and blade.

"There shall be peace," Raj said. "I accept . . . in Governor Barholm's name."

"Wa sha' a-l-lah," Tewfik said, the formula full of a tired sincerity. He shrugged and spat on the head. "May God will it."

CHAPTER SIXTEEN

"All off!"

Raj swung down off the train. The East Residence station was crowded, full of the heat and smoke and steam of a busy summer's day. It felt humid after the Drangosh Valley; he rested his eyes on the hints of green higher up the hill and the fleecy clouds scattered across the sky. It was after 1900, near sunset, with Miniluna and Maxiluna both up, huge translucent globes hanging in a purpling sky.

"Move it, soldier!" the conductor said.

Raj smiled wryly and hopped down, ignoring the wooden steps the Central Rail slave was putting by the passenger car. He had a bandage over half his face, and he was dressed in common soldier's clothing—as a Descotter cavalry sergeant, which was probably what he'd have been if he hadn't been born to a noble family. The uniform brought a few cheers and careful claps on the back as he walked out through the station, a garrison bag slung over one shoulder.

That *was* unusual. Questions flew at him:

"Is it true *Heneralissimo* Whitehall cut off Ali's head with his own hand?"

"Are they going to march the prisoners through the streets?"

He smiled lopsidedly and pointed to his bandage; somebody thrust a goatskin of wine into his hand, and a free ticket to the bullfights. He dropped both of them off at the porticoed entrance to the train station—another of Barholm's construction projects—and plunged into the streets. They were thick with people, even though it was still normal working hours. Municipal flunkies were hanging ribbons and streamers from the standards of the gaslights, and a great cheer went up as an ox-wagon piled with huge wine casks halted at a corner.

The full treatment, he thought wryly. He nodded as the crowd began to chant his name when the wine cask was unloaded at the corner. *Barholm's not going to ignore that sort of thing.* It was bad

628

enough that he'd been popular with the troops. Having the capital city mob on his side, no matter how he'd put down the Victory riots six years ago, would be the final nail in the Governor's coffin. *I wonder if they know they're condemning me to death?* he wondered.

Probably not. They'd been very frightened, and the euphoria of relief would be all the stronger for it.

Well, at least the troops won't have any problems getting a drink and a lay when they get in. They deserved that.

He was close enough to hear two of the men dipping their cups into the head of the broached wine cask. They wore the knee breeches, full-sleeved shirts, and leather aprons of prosperous artisans; their shoes had good pewter buckles.

"To Messer Raj and the damnation of all wogs," one said, drinking. "Ah, not bad."

"Looks like Barholm pulled it off again," the other replied. "This'll keep the Chair under his fundament until the day he dies."

"That might be thirty years."

"Thirty more years of Barholm. Spirit. Ah, his wine's good, anyway, and we deserve it—our taxes paid for it. To Messer Raj, Mihwel."

"To the Sword of the Spirit of Man—we won't see his like again, worse luck."

Raj ducked into the tiled entrance of a public bathhouse. *Where . . .*

Center strobed an indicator above one door. Not surprising that a bathhouse had a connection to the catacombs; all this section of the city was underlain by the Ancient tunnels.

"Raj!"

Thom Poplanich stirred to life in the mirrored sphere that was Center's physical being.

He gripped his friend's shoulders. "You did it!" His eyes noted the fresh creases, and the leathery tan of the Drangosh Valley's sun and sand-laden wind. "You did it!"

Raj returned the *embrahzo*.

"I did my duty," he said quietly. He shook his head, as if the magnitude of it was only now striking him. "I've reunited Earth—"

bellevue.

"—Bellevue under Holy Federation and the Spirit of Man of the Stars."

"The Fall is over," Thom whispered, awed. "After a thousand years, it's over."

the next cycle has begun, Center clarified. **this is only a beginning, but the direction of maximum probability has been reversed. there is no longer a strong drive to maximum entropy here on bellevue; and from bellevue, the human universe may be reclaimed in time. fifteen thousand years of barbarism have been reduced to a maximum of another five centuries. beyond**

that, stochastic analysis is no longer adequate. my projections indicate that human capacities will have increased beyond my ability to analyze.

Raj laughed and ran a hand through his gray-shot curls. "I feel like a man who's been running down stairs and didn't notice that the staircase ended," he said. "The troops and the Colonials are on their way back; it'll take a while, but the first trains should arrive in hours. I came to say goodbye, before . . ."

Thom's smile died. "Before what?" he asked sharply.

Raj looked up in surprise at the tone of command in the other man's voice. "Before I report to the Governor," he said.

"Who no longer needs you. Who fears you," Thom said.

Raj shrugged. "I've done my duty to the Spirit of Man. I'm not going to flinch at the end. Barholm can't kill me deader than a Colonial bullet or a Brigadero's broadsword might have. It's not a safe profession, soldiering."

Thom turned, a terrible anger on his face. "There's no need for that! There's no need for that now—and even if there was, a ruler who treats a faithful servant that way doesn't deserve to rule, doesn't deserve to *exist*. Hasn't he done enough? More than any other man could have done?"

The shout rang in the strait confines of the sphere, then sank away as if the material had changed to absorb it.

raj whitehall has one further duty to the plan.

Raj put a comforting hand on Thom's shoulder. "I know. I said I was willing to die."

not that.

Both men started.

for six years, i have been training your friend here to rule as i trained you to fight. now it is time to put him on the throne of the reunited planet. you should find that easy, in comparison to the things you have already accomplished in my service.

The mirrored sphere flashed and vanished. They were disembodied viewpoints watching a huge crowd surge through the gardens of the Gubernatorial Palace, crying out and eddying around the iron order of the troops who guarded it. Raj recognized the shoulder-flashes of the 5th Descott and the Rogor Slashers, of Cruisers and Brigaderos units . . . and Colonials, still in their crimson djellabas but carrying Armory rifles.

The great ebony doors with their hammered silver Starbursts swung open. Barholm Clerett came through; bandaged and bruised, his hands bound before him. Gerrin Staenbridge walked beside him with drawn pistol, Bartin Foley on the other side, and a file of Descotters with fixed bayonets on either side. They hustled the blank-faced Barholm into a closed carriage at the foot of the marble stairs. Mounted troopers of the 1st Cruisers with drawn swords fell in around it, and the driver touched the white greyhounds of the team into action. The crowd parted reluctantly; a few rocks and lumps of dogshit flew at the carriage.

"To the frying post with the tyrant Barholm!"

"Death to Barholm the tax-eater!"

"Dig up Barholm's bones!"

The clamor might have turned to riot, but trumpeters blew a ceremonial fanfare from the balcony above. Tall windows swung open, and Raj Whitehall walked out and halted, his hands clasped behind his back.

Silence fell gradually, although the noise of the crowd was like distant surf or the rustling of leaves in dense forest.

Raj heard his own voice; the superb acoustics of the semicircular frontage of the Palace carried it out over the heads of the crowd.

"Citizens of Holy Federation! The tyrant Barholm is de-Chaired!"

Massed cheering broke over him like thunder, and cries hailing him governor. He raised his hand again.

"I am the Sword of the Spirit of Man, but not the Spirit's viceregent on Earth. Citizens, I give you your Governor. Governor Poplanich, grandson of Governor Poplanich, legitimate heir to the Chair."

In the slow, hieratic pace that the regalia imposed, Thom Poplanich paced out to stand beside his General. The sunlight blazed on metallized robes, on the Stylus and Keyboard in his hands.

"My people—" he began.

observe:

The sphere blinked. Raj saw himself standing under the great dome of the Cathedron that Barholm had built. A wedding was being held, a man and a woman standing in shimmering robes before the Patriarchal Arch-Sysup of East Residence, their hands entwined and bound with the sacred Cable. The man was Thom Poplanich; the woman was dark and round-faced, plain, with intelligent black eyes that sparkled with excitement. Raj saw himself step forward to give the groomsman's responses. It was obviously a great occasion of state; besides the nobles and clerics, his Companions were there, and Suzette . . .

Tewfik ibn'Jamal stood on the other side of the couple, in the place reserved for the father of the bride. His eye met the image-Raj's for an instant, and winked.

observe:

Chancellor Tzetzas stood and contemptuously turned his face to the pockmarked brick wall. Behind him the officer of the firing squad raised his sword. The rifles leveled and vomited smoke . . .

observe:

Raj stood in a testing room in the Armory, examining a rifle. He was older, his hair mostly gray. The weapon in his hands was one the younger self did not recognize; chunky and short, with a box-magazine protruding below the stock and a cocking-lever at the side. He raised it and fired at the target downrange. The rifle fired again

and again, spitting spent brass to the right, without any motion but pulling the trigger. And there was no smoke from the barrel . . .
   observe:
   A crowd of gaping peons stood at the edge of a wheatfield—somewhere in the Central Provinces, from the flat terrain and broad treeless horizons. Behind them were the mud hovels they dwelt in; in front of them a huge clanking machine snorted and backed, then surged out into the ripe grain. It moved slowly, a whirring contraption like a skeletal cylinder of boards bending down the heads of the stalks. Beside it went an ox-wagon, and threshed grain poured out of a spout into it as the machine chewed its way into the wheat. As Raj watched, it reaped as much land as a dozen peons could do in a day; from the sun, scarcely an hour had passed.
   observe:
   Sullen, shaven-headed Skinner nomads surrendered their huge sauroid-killing rifles to an officer in Civil Government uniform. A huge engine on linked treads of steel stood behind the officer, quivering with mechanical life; the twin trails of its passage stretched off into the distance, and weapons bristled from its armored hull. Overhead a flying machine circled, with stiff wings like a soaring pterosauroid and a buzzing propeller at the rear.
   observe:
   An older Raj stood in the Cathedron once more. Suzette was with him, older as well, but smiling. The groom walked to his place beneath the dome; for a moment Raj thought it was Thom, but then he saw the differences, the darker complexion and the beak nose. *Thom's son,* he realized.
   The image of a Raj twenty years older stepped forward, the bride's fingers resting on his arm. The young woman's green eyes glowed.
   observe:
   Bartin Foley as an old man, in a nobleman's formal civil clothes. He stood in the presentation room of the Palace, and bowed his head as an official Raj didn't recognize placed a gold-chain medallion over his head. Beside him on the table rested a book. On the cover, embossed letters read: *Raj Whitehall and His Times.*
   observe:
   He was looking down from the roof of a great shed. The dust motes in the air shook with the force of the energies below. Incomprehensible machines crawled by on a conveyor-belt. Men and women in overalls swarmed about them, fastening on parts with tools that hummed and screeched and whirred and sent showers of sparks across the concrete floor.
   A siren whooped. The noise ended as if cut off with a knife, and the workers downed tools and turned to troop out of the huge building.
   observe:
   A crowd gathered around a plinth in East Residence. They were just familiar enough to be disturbing, men with their hair in pigtails,

women in skirts scandalously short, to their knees. A poster read: *Elections to the Consultative Senate to be held.* Beneath: *Vote Reform! The Anti-Peonage Act needs your support!*

observe:

A train streaked by. Raj *thought* it was a train. It floated above the tracks with no visible support, and the locomotive was shaped more like a rifle bullet or an artillery shell than anything he recognized. The hum of its passage lingered in the air long after it had passed the horizon.

observe:

An avenue in East Residence, with a view down to the harbor. Raj could recognize a few of the buildings: the Cathedron, the Palace. Most of the rest had changed, in styles totally foreign. Before him was a mausoleum. The viewpoint swooped closer. The walls around the base were sculpted in bas-relief, and they showed his troops. Marching, making camp, charging with leveled bayonets. The central column held high-relief bronzes; here he recognized faces, Gerrin, Bartin, Kaltin— all his Companions, and Suzette. Their clasped hands ringed the broad pillar.

Atop it was a statue. A rider, on a great black hound. He was armed, but his outflung hand was empty, pointing to the sky. Below in gold letters was set:

RAJ WHITEHALL. THE CONQUEROR OF PEACE.

Beyond, from the bay where East Residence's harbor lay, something huge was lifting toward the heavens on pillars of pale fire.

Pigeons rose in a massed flutter of wings about the statue as the thunder of the starship's drive rolled across the plaza.

THE END